EAST OF THE SUN AND
WEST OF FORT SMITH

William Sanders

ISBN-13: 978-1-934648-66-7
ISBN-10: 1-934648-66-3

Trade Paperback Edition

September 15, 2008

A Publication of
Norilana Books
P. O. Box 2188
Winnetka, CA 91396
www.norilana.com

Printed in the United States of America

East of the Sun and West of Fort Smith

Norilana Books
Science Fiction

www.norilana.com

Other Books by William Sanders

(fiction)
Journey to Fusang
The Wild Blue and the Gray
The Next Victim
A Death On 66
Blood Autumn
The Ballad of Billy Badass and the Rose of Turkestan
Smoke
J.

(collections)
Are We Having Fun Yet?
Is It Now Yet?

(history)
Conquest: Hernando de Soto and the Indians, 1539-1543

East of the Sun and West of Fort Smith

WILLIAM SANDERS

To the Legends

CONTENTS

by William Sanders

INTRODUCTION
by Rick Bowes

This generously sized, beautifully designed book contains those stories the author wishes to have preserved under his name. When I was contacted about doing this assignment I thought the reading would be a formality since I'd followed Sanders's short fiction career almost from the start. In fact once I began I found myself reading, or in most cases rereading, all the stories. And I got a bit resentful when anything took me away from them.

In his own introduction William Sanders cites Kipling and Hemingway as being among his influences. Like theirs, his prose is clear and direct, his meaning unambiguous. You will never ask what it is that just happened nor will you doubt that what you read could have happened.

He reminds me of them most in those near-future stories in which he handles people in situations of danger and describes their balancing of duty and conscience. In "When This World Is All on Fire" it's a reservation policeman in a time of Global Warming, drought and desperation. In "Angel Kills" it's the executive officer of a detail of small planes guarding airliners against attacks by creatures that resemble winged angels. In "Amba" it's a hunter escorting rich clients on tiger shoots in the deteriorating ecology of the Russian/Manchurian border. This last story in fact pays homage to Hemingway's classic "One Trip

Across" and is impressive in the way Sanders never copies Hemingway's prose and is in no way playing out of his league.

Not that the author can't and doesn't mimic literary styles when it suits his purposes. "Billy Mitchell's Overt Act," Sanders's Alternate History take on the renegade U.S. Army aviator's life and on a very different Battle of Pearl Harbor, is largely a montage of invented quotes by witnesses and commentators—everyone from Hemingway himself to Woody Guthrie and Harry Truman. It's pitch-perfect and a tour de force.

Alternate History if it isn't done elegantly is a tiresome and mechanical thing—I absolutely no longer care what happened after the South won the Civil War. But this sub-genre is one of this author's specialties and he never misses. In "Dirty Little Cowards" Jessie James, from what we see of him, seems fussy and domestic. The stone cold killer is the man hired by the company which transports rich nerds back in time to commit famous murders; the man who is along to makes sure Mr. Howard gets good and dead. "Empire" is a marvelous romp that postulates a Napoleonic New Orleans that has attracted every reprobate from Davy Crockett to the Marquis de Sade. "Sitka" features Vladimir Lenin being Lenin and Jack London in all his magnetism and idiocy conspiring in Russian Alaska. The last of these stories is "Not Fade Away," a bleak and moving portrait of a Douglas Macarthur (a man for whom I otherwise have no sympathy whatsoever) who did not escape the catastrophe he engineered in the Philippines, and his search for redemption.

Sanders's best-known work is "The Undiscovered." All the attention paid to it has caused the author some distress. I know what it's like to wonder why this story is the chosen one instead of others that seem as good and as worthy of praise. In fact, "The Undiscovered" with its young, unknown William Shakespeare exiled to the New World and the bemused Cherokee narrator who becomes his captor and his friend is wonderful. Sanders is part Cherokee and he knows language. He uses both these resources to great effect in an unforgettable production of Hamlet by and for a native audience.

The Native Americans in this and such other stories as "Elvis Bearpaw's Luck," "Going after Old Man Alabama,"

"Tenbears and the Bruja," funny, magic, touchy, horny, intensely human gentlemen and ladies—are one of the strengths of this collection. In "Smoke" an elderly Cherokee medicine man in the late 18th Century United States solves a murder with and without the use of magic. The life and law of the tribe is beautifully evoked and the story takes on a layer of tragedy if the reader understands that within the lifespan of the children in the village this whole society will be uprooted and sent on the Trail of Tears.

"Words and Music" features a night-long session of Native American gospel music. Sanders speaks of his own childhood connection to gospel music—it's how his parents met—and that personal involvement shows. I feel a similar autobiographical tinge in "Dry Bones" with its 1950's rural Southern setting and its young narrator on the periphery of the investigation of a mysterious skeleton and the equally alien world of adult sex.

There's humor here. "Looking for Rhonda Honda" features shenanigans that make Bill Clinton seem pretty tame. "Going to See the Beast" raises the question of what exactly is so bad about being among The Left Behind. There's also sex and booze and drugs and loud music. This is a very human book. I won't say it's got everything. But it's got lots of stuff and that stuff is very fine indeed.

INTRODUCTION
by Willam Sanders

Of all the things I've had occasion to write for publication, I think these introductions may be the hardest. I just can't seem to get a handle on what I'm supposed to say, let alone how to say it.

And indeed you could make out a good case that it shouldn't be necessary; that the stories ought to stand (or not) on their own. The reader—the ordinary reader, anyway, as distinguished from the critical biographer—shouldn't need to know anything about the author or what gave him the idea for the story or how he had to rewrite it because his dog ate the first draft or whatever. After all, very little is known about the man who wrote as "B. Traven", and even that little is still the subject of controversy; but it is still possible to read his work with great enjoyment, and many generations have done so.

It's funny how things have worked out. Ever since somewhere in my early teens, I wanted to write; I wasn't sure just *what* I wanted to write. My preferences and ambitions were as unstable as any teenager's, but the basic bone-deep desire to write something and get it into print with my name on it never wavered.

(For a good many years I assumed I'd have to do something else too, since it didn't occur to me that it was possible to make a living from writing; I knew that there were a few best-selling authors who were doing all right for themselves, but for the most part I think I had an idea that writing for publication was just something people did for the glory of it or because they had something to say. I had some of the weirdest damn ideas as a kid.)

And even though I got sidetracked for a while, I never entirely abandoned the original dream. Even the years I wasted trying to make it in the music business, all the times I climbed aboard a bus for another town or walked down the shoulder of a highway lugging my guitar case, there was always at least one ratty manuscript, or the notes for one, somewhere in my duffle bag.

Paternity finally settled me down, as it has a way of doing, and made me get serious about a lot of things, including writing. Right after my daughter was born I acquired an old typewriter and started bringing home stacks of books from the public library, filled with new determination; and later that year, when we moved into the first of a series of cheap rent houses, one of the first things I did was create myself an "office" in the extra bedroom.

Over the next few years there were a lot of evenings when I came home from this or that construction or factory job, tired as three dogs and a cat, and it took just about all I had left to go roll another sheet into that ancient Royal upright, let alone apply my work-stiffened fingers to the keys; but somehow I stayed with it—motivated, it's true, less by any artistic muse than by the memory of the day's labors, and the prospect of tomorrow's, and a grim determination not to spend the rest of my life like this.

True, I wasn't very good at it in the beginning; in fact I was quite bad, and I owe a great debt to the editors who rejected my early efforts, even if it was usually for the wrong reasons. I don't even like to think of the environmental implications of all that paper I wasted. . . .

But in time I did start getting some things published, and eventually got enough going for me to be able to turn to writing full time—sports and outdoor writing at first and for a good many years, not exactly what I'd originally had in mind but at least by God it was *writing* and I was making a living of sorts at it—and finally, in the penultimate decade of a savage and tragic century, I tried my hand again at writing fiction and this time managed to get a number of novels published, with covers bearing my name and numbers on almost every page.

By the time my life hit the fifty-year point I was, indeed and indisputably, a Nauthor.

Now you can take that as the inspiring story of a man who pursued a lifelong dream until he finally attained it; or you can see it as the pathetic tale of a natural-born jackoff who finally found something he could do, after a lifetime of inability to hold a real job. (Even getting fired from an army during a war, which isn't easy.) My own view tends more to the latter, but call it as you like.

But—and here's where I've been going with this *apologia pro vita scabiosa mea*—all this time, all the different stuff I wrote or tried writing, I never even gave serious consideration to short stories.

And I'm damned if I know why. I've thought about this question a lot, and I still don't have an answer.

Certainly it wasn't from any lack of respect for the form. Very much the contrary; I had been a devoted reader and admirer of the short story since I was a teenager—and even before, for that matter; I seem to recall a Kipling addiction beginning at twelve, and I used to love to read the Ray Bradbury stories in the old *Saturday Evening Post*. I had long held in reverence such masters as Ambrose Bierce and Somerset Maugham and Ring Lardner and Dorothy Parker and John O'Hara, and very nearly worshiped Ernest Hemingway as a god.

Come to think of it, maybe that was the problem; maybe I was *too* much in awe. Maybe I was intimidated; maybe the great short fiction I'd read had left me with a feeling that here was something so demanding I couldn't possibly do it. That might well be it, or a big piece of it; I remember on occasion people would ask me why I didn't write short stories, and I'd reply, "Oh, I couldn't do that, I wouldn't even know how."

And indeed back in '93, when the late Roger Zelazny phoned me and asked me to contribute a story to an anthology he was editing, that was my initial reaction: "Come on, Roger, I don't do short stories, I write novels, you know that, I wouldn't even know how—"

He urged. I yielded. What followed is the first story in this volume; and what followed from that makes up the rest of the contents.

Thus it came to pass that, after a score of years of writing for publication—and a hell of a lot more, before that, of trying to—I finally found out what I was good at.

Not that I hadn't been good at anything before that; I'd written a number of very damned good novels (for, to be sure, a number of *very* damned bad publishers, but never mind that) and I went on to write several more. But the short story proved to be what I was best at, or at least the form in which I was most successful and got the most attention. (I notice that my Wikipedia page describes me as a writer "primarily of short fiction.")

And if that seems somewhat unfair to my other efforts, well, life, as we have so often been told, isn't fair.

Actually it's kind of swarthy.

This is not a Complete Collected Works Of; that's something usually reserved for after the author has assumed ambient temperature. It's true I've largely retired from fiction writing, along with a lot of other things; but it's still too early to flatly and irrevocably rule out the possibility that I might commit another story or two, some of these days. I'm not yet ready to declare that from where the Sun now stands I will write no more forever.

It comes close to being a complete collection of my short fiction to date; but even that needs qualifying. I have not included a couple of stories that were published, in earlier years, in minor genre magazines; they simply weren't very good, and their failure helped convince me that I couldn't do short stories.

Similarly, I have left out a few things which I wrote for non-genre magazines—and one execrable horror anthology—

which might perhaps be considered stories, but which were really no more than extended jokes. None would be of any interest now, except to a literary biographer of William Sanders, of which there are none.

(I have also omitted a story I did for a shared-worlds anthology based on Steve Stirling's "Draka" novels. It requires a considerable familiarity with the series, and in any case I was not altogether comfortable with the whole shared-world concept; it seems to me that the story is not entirely mine, but partly Steve's.)

All these stories are as they appeared in print, except that in a few cases I have reversed unwelcome editorial changes.

I considered various ways in which this collection could be organized: grouped according to genre or subgenre (e.g. fantasy, science fiction, alternative history) or perhaps subject matter (time travel, American Indian themes, etc.) But in the end I settled for a simple chronological arrangement, according to publication date—even though this is not necessarily the order in which they were written.

There is one exception: of the first two stories, "Elvis Bearpaw's Luck" was published a year after "Going After Old Man Alabama." However, "Elvis Bearpaw's Luck" occupies a special place for me, not only because it was the first successful short story I ever wrote, but because Roger personally asked me to write it; and so I put it first.

So you wanted an introduction. All right, then—

Reader, Book. Book, Reader. Can I get either of you a drink?

Written October 1993
First published December 1995

Elvis Bearpaw's Luck

Grandfather Ninekiller said, "A man always has the right to try to change his luck."

He said that right after I told him how my cousin Marvin Badwater had suddenly dumped Madonna Hummingbird, after both families had all but officially agreed on the match, and brought home a Comanche girl whose name nobody could even pronounce. Grandfather never had been one for that sort of gossip, but it was two years since he'd died and naturally he was interested in any news I might bring him when I came to put tobacco on his grave.

"The right to try to change his luck," he said again, in a kind of distant satisfied way, as if he liked the sound of what he had said. That's one thing about ancestors: they can be awfully repetitious. I guess they've got a lot of time on their hands in the spirit world, with nothing much to do but study up these wise-sounding little one-liners.

Anyway I said, "I don't know about that, *eduda*. What about what happened to Elvis Bearpaw?"

"I said a man's got the right to *try*," Grandfather said, not a bit bothered by my disrespectful interruption. There was a time when he'd have taken my head off, but being dead seems to have mellowed him some. "Whether he succeeds or not, now, that's another patch of pokeweed."

He laughed, an old man's spidery-dry cackle. "And then, too, it's not always easy to know whether you're changing it upwards or down. As in the case of the said Elvis Bearpaw . . . remember that, do you, *chooch*?"

"How could I forget?" I said, surprised.

"Hey," Grandfather said, "you were just a kid."

I was, too, but I'd have gotten mad as a wet owl if anybody had said so at the time. I was all of twelve years old that spring, and I saw myself as for all valid purposes a full-grown Cherokee warrior—hadn't the great Harley Davidson Oosahwe killed those three Osage slave-raiders when he was only thirteen? Warrior hell, I figured I was practically Council material, barring a few petty technicalities.

I might or might not have heard, in the days leading up to Game time, that Elvis Bearpaw was to be the Deer Clan's player that year. If I did, it wasn't something I paid much attention to. For one thing, being of the *Anijisqua*—Bird Clan—I had no personal interest in the matter; and for another, my mind was on a different aspect of the approaching Game days. This was the last year I was going to be eligible for the boys' blowgun contest; next year I'd be in the young men's class, and, unless Redbird Christie stepped on a rattlesnake in the next twelve months, getting my brains beat out like everybody else. So I was determined to win this year, and I was practicing my ass off every spare moment.

But for all my puckering and puffing, I wasn't exactly unaware of the goings-on around me. That would have been pretty damn difficult to say the least; back then, Game time still meant something, things were happening. Not like now. . . .

Well, maybe I shouldn't say that. Maybe everything just seems larger and more exciting when you're a kid; or maybe a man's memory likes to improve on reality. But it does seem to me that the Game time isn't what it used to be. It's almost as if people are merely going through the motions. Is it just me?

* * *

"Is it just me," I said to Grandfather Ninekiller, "or has Game time gone downhill in the last few years? Of course I'm not talking about the Game itself," I added hastily. You don't want to seem to disparage sacred matters when you're talking with an ancestor. "I mean, that's still the center of the whole year, always has been, always will be——"

"Wasn't always," Grandfather interrupted. "Back in the old days, in the Yuasa times, it wasn't at all like it is now. You know that, *chooch*."

"Well, yes." I knew, all right; he'd told me often enough, along with the other stories about the history of the People. Though there's always been a sort of not-quite-real quality to those old tales, for me at least; I've never been sure how much of that Yuasa business to take seriously. They even say there was a time when the People didn't have the Game at all, and who can imagine that?

"Anyway," I went on, "I meant the whole affair—the dances, the contests, the feeds and the giveaways—all the stuff that goes on when the People get together for the Game. I can't help feeling like there used to be a lot more to it, you know? But then I've noticed a lot of things seem to sort of shrink as you get older."

Grandfather snorted. "Tell me about it, *chooch*," he said bitterly. "You don't know the half of it yet."

Whatever . . . and be all that as it may, I recall that Game season as possibly the best of my lifetime. The sky was clear and the sun bright every day, with no sign of the storms and drizzly spells that so often come with the spring in the Cherokee hill country. Even the wind was at least reasonably warm—though of course it never stopped blowing, this being, after all, Oklahoma.

The weather was so fine, in fact, that some of the elders came to confer with Grandfather Ninekiller about whether it was really necessary to set out the broken glass and the ax heads to turn aside possible tornadoes. He told them probably not, but they went ahead and did it all the same; they said tradition was tradition and you couldn't be too careful about tornadoes, but I figured it was mainly because they'd already made the trip over to the ruins of Old Tahlequah to get the glass.

The tornadoes never showed up, but the people sure did. Oh, my, yes, the people, the People. . . .

They came from all directions, all day every day and sometimes at night, too. They began coming as much as half a moon before the Game days began, hoping to get good spots to camp—or, if they had the right connections, houseguest privileges with Cherokee families—but it wasn't long before all the regular campgrounds were full and you began finding people making camp in the damnedest places. Like this family of Pawnees my father found sleeping amid the broken walls of the old Park Hill post office.

They came from the Five Nations and the Seven Allied Tribes, but they also came from other tribes that had their Games at other times of the year. It was widely known that it was worth the journey just to enjoy Cherokee hospitality and sample the entertainment and do some wagon-tailgate trading.

Mostly they came from the Plains tribes to the west: Comanches and Kiowas and Apaches and Caddos and a few Cheyennes and Arapahos, all riding splendid horses and wearing beaded finery and the mysterious emblems of the peyote church. But there were also Quapaws and Otoes and Kaws and Poncas and lots of others. Osages, too, five of the big bastards, riding in a wagon made from the body of an old Cadillac car, come down to see how the enemy lived and do a little scouting, their lives safe during the Game-time truce.

There was even a delegation from the Washita Nation, of the far-off Arkansas hills, decked out in really weird outfits— fringed vests and pants, goofy-looking high-topped moccasins, quartz crystals big as your penis hanging around their necks— and spouting loony crap about "previous lives" and "channeling" to anybody they could corner. General opinion was that there wasn't a single drop of the real People's blood among the lot of them, and looking at them I could believe it, but nobody really objected all that much. If nothing else they were good for a laugh.

And after all, though nobody talks much about it, the truth is that most of the People have more white blood than they like to admit.

"It's not only because we took in so many of the surviving whites, after things went to hell for them," Grandfather Ninekiller said, the only time I ever raised the subject with him. "Clear back in Yuasa times, there were lots of mixed-bloods. Toward the end they outnumbered the full-bloods in a lot of tribes. Cherokees damn near screwed ourselves white, in fact, before it was over. How do you think your Grandmother Badwater got that red hair?"

"What about you, *eduda*?" I asked.

"Oh, I'm full-blood Cherokee," he said immediately. "And so were both of my parents. But my grandmother on my father's side, now, she was part white."

"Elvis Bearpaw is playing for the Deer Clan."

That was my uncle Kennedy Badwater, speaking to Grandfather Ninekiller. It was the day before the beginning of the Game period, and that was the first I can actually recall hearing about the honor that had fallen upon Elvis Bearpaw.

Grandfather said, "Well, he's always been an ambitious young man. This could be the big breakthrough for him."

They both laughed, and I joined in, in a quiet sort of way, from where I sat on the hard-packed ground next to Grandfather's seat. I wasn't, as I've said, all that interested in the subject, but there wasn't much else to do but listen in on the old men's conversation while I waited for Grandfather to need my assistance.

He'd been blind for three years by that time, and I'd lived with him the whole while, brought him the food that my mother cooked for him, filled and lit his pipe, helped him find various things around his cabin—not very often; he had a memory like a wolf trap—and generally served as his eyes and an extra set of hands. I'd helped him with certain items when he made medicine, too; and I'd led him, or rather accompanied him, around the village and to and from the various ceremonies and official functions where his duties took him. I'd sat at his feet at more Council meetings than I could have added up, hearing speech after speech on questions of war and peace and tribal politics, getting myself an unmatchable education but bored silly by it all at the time. . . .

"Word is he went to see Old Man Alabama as soon as they gave him the news," my uncle said. "Wonder what he did that for."

Old Man Alabama was a famous medicine man—a lot of people said witch—who lived on an island down on Lake Tenkiller, a little way above the old dam. He claimed to be the last living member of the Alabama tribe. His power was said to be tremendous and most people were afraid to even talk about him.

"Huh," Grandfather grunted. "Wonder why anybody would go to see that old nutcase. Old Man Alabama's the kind who give mad sorcerers a bad name."

I took a hardwood dart from the cane-joint quiver at my waist and held it up and sighted along it, checking for straightness. Not that there was any chance of finding anything wrong, as many times as I'd inspected those darts in the last few days, but it was something to do. My blowgun lay across my lap and I could have taken a few practice shots at some handy target while the old men talked, but it would have been a little impolite and I was trying to make a good impression on my uncle, who always gave me some sort of present at Game time.

"Looking for an angle," my uncle said.

"You know the old Cherokee saying," Grandfather said. "'Watch out what you look for. You might find it.'"

"Is that an old Cherokee saying?" my uncle said, grinning.

"Must be," Grandfather said, straight-faced. "I said it, and I'm an old Cherokee."

The following morning, out at the great field, they had the opening ceremony. As the ball of the sun cleared the horizon, the Master of the Fire, old Gogisgi Wildcat, lit the sacred fire.

Smoke rose against the brightening sky and Grandfather Ninekiller raised his voice in a song so ancient that even he didn't know what half the words meant; and when he finished, to a shouted chorus of "*Wado!*" from the assembled Cherokee elders, the Game days had at last begun.

Grandfather and I watched the start of the cross-country foot race, and the first heats of the shorter races—all right, I watched and gave Grandfather a running description—and then drifted over to take in the opening innings of the women's softball series. After that we walked slowly back across the fields to the outskirts of the town, where women tended fires and steam rose from big pots and the air was fairly edible with the smells of food. People called out invitations to come sample this or that—*kenuche*, corn soup, chili—and Grandfather generally tried to oblige; I couldn't see where he put it all in that skinny old frame. I didn't dare load up, myself, what with the blowgun competition coming up in the afternoon; but I did allow myself to be tempted by some remarkably fine wild grape dumplings, or maybe by the pretty Paint Clan girl who offered them to me. I was starting to take an interest in that girl business, those days.

I might as well have gone ahead and stuffed myself, for all the difference it made. That was how I felt, anyway, after a sudden puff of wind made me miss the swinging target completely in the final round of the blowgun shoot and I wound up losing out to Duane Kingfisher from up near Rocky Ford. Now, looking back, second place doesn't seem so bad—especially when I remember that the Osages killed Duane four years later, when he went on that damn fool horse-stealing raid—but at the time all I could see was that I'd lost. I felt as if I'd been booted in the stomach.

I was still feeling pretty rotten that night at the stomp dance. I don't even think I'd have gone if I hadn't had to accompany Grandfather Ninekiller. Sitting beside him under the Bird Clan arbor, watching the dancers circling the fire and listening to the singing and the *shaka-shaka-shaka* of the turtle shell rattles on the women's legs, I felt none of the usual joy, only a dull mean dog-kicking anger—at the wind, at Duane Kingfisher, mostly at myself.

After a while my Uncle Kennedy appeared from out of the darkness and sat down beside me. "*'Siyo, chooch*," he said to me, after exchanging greetings with Grandfather.

I said, "*'Siyo, eduji*," in a voice about as cheerful and friendly as an open grave. But he didn't appear to notice.

"Damn," he said, watching the dancers, "there's Elvis Bearpaw leading, big as you please."

Now he mentioned it, I saw that Elvis Bearpaw was in fact leading this song, circling the fire at the head of the spiral line of dancers, calling out the old words in a strong high voice. His face shone in the firelight as he crouched and turned and waved his hands. He was a husky, good-looking young guy, supposed to be something of a devil with the women. I don't guess I'd ever even traded greetings with him; his family and mine moved in different circles. Watching him now, though, I had to admit that he could sure as hell sing and dance.

"Don't think I ever saw him lead before," Uncle Kennedy said. "How about that?"

On the other side of me Grandfather made a noise that was part snort and part grunt. He wasn't a big admirer of the Bearpaws, whom he considered pushy assholes who'd lucked into more wealth and power than they knew what to do with.

"Saw you in the blowgun shoot today, *chooch*," my uncle remarked. "Tough luck there. But hell, you still came in second. Better than I ever did."

He was taking something from his belt, from up under the tail of his ribbon shirt. "Here," he said. "Didn't figure to give you this till later on, but you look like you could use some cheering up."

It was a knife, a fine big one with a deer horn handle and a wide businesslike blade; a man's knife, not a kid's whittler like the one I'd been carrying, and somebody had done some first-class work putting a glass-smooth finish on that lovely steel. . . . I said, "*Wado, eduji*," but my voice didn't come out entirely right.

"Got some good stiff saddle leather at home," my uncle said. "Make you a sheath for that thing, you bring it by sometime. Boy," he added admiringly. "Look at old Elvis go."

Out by the fire Elvis Bearpaw was getting down and winding up, his body rocking from side to side. There was something strange in his face, I thought, or maybe that was just a trick of the firelight. He called out a phrase and the other men responded: "*Ho-na-wi-ye, ho-na-wi-ye.*" And *shaka-shaka-shaka* went the turtle shells.

The next few days were a regular whirlwind of feasting and dancing and singing and sports, sports, sports: all the things needed to make a twelve-year-old boy decide that when he dies he wants to go some place where it's like this all the time.

I went to everything I could, with or without Grandfather, who was having to make a lot of heavy medicine in preparation for the approaching Game. I played stickball with the other Cherokee boys, of course, and even scored a couple of goals, though in the end the Choctaws beat us by one. I watched Uncle Kennedy win the rifle shoot and then saw him lose everything he'd won, betting on a horse race between the Seminoles and the Kickapoos. I went to the cornstalk shoot— going to have to try that myself next year, now I was big enough to pull a serious bow—and the tomahawk throw, the horseshoe matches and the wild-cow-roping contest, even the canoe race down on the river. And the bicycle race, the very last year they ever had it; it was getting impossible to find parts to keep those old machines rolling, and the leather-rope tires they had to use kept coming off in the turns and causing mass crashes. What was the name of that Wichita kid who won? I forget.

And every night at the stomp dance grounds there was Elvis Bearpaw out by the fire, singing and dancing his ass off, always with that funny strained expression on his face. Uncle Kennedy said he looked like he thought something might be gaining on him.

There was no stomp dance the night before Game day, naturally; too many of the dance leaders and other important persons would be spending the night taking medicine and making smoke and otherwise purifying themselves, getting ready for their parts in the Game.

That included Grandfather Ninekiller, who had to do some things so secret and dangerous that I wasn't even allowed to be in the cabin while he did them. I helped him lay out a few medicine items, made sure there was plenty of firewood in the box, and got the hell out without having to be told twice. That sort of business always scared me half to death. Still does.

I was supposed to be staying at my parents' cabin that night, but I didn't really want to go, not any sooner than I could help anyway. I'd never gotten along with them worth a damn; that might have been why they'd been so happy to send me off to live with the old man.

I stood for a moment thinking about it, and then I turned the other way and walked away from the town, off across the moon-white fields, following the distant *boom-boom* of a big Plains drum. Some of our Western visitors were having one of their powwow dances that night. I wasn't all that fond of that damn howling racket the Plains People call singing, but it would beat sitting around all evening listening to questions about the old man's health and complaints about my failure to visit more often and stories about how smart my younger brothers were.

I stayed at the powwow till pretty late, having more fun than I'd expected—all right, that Kiowa music has a good beat, you can dance to it—and hanging out with some of my buddies who'd sneaked off from their own families. Along about midnight I met a Creek girl named Hillary Screechowl and after a certain amount of persuasive bullshit on my part she took a little walk with me off into the woods. Where nothing really major took place, but we did get far enough to clear up a few questions I'd been wondering about lately.

It was really late, maybe halfway between midnight and daybreak, when I finally left the powwow area and headed back toward town. The moon had almost gone down but the stars were big and white, and I had no trouble finding my way across the darkened fields. The town itself was invisible against the blackness of the tree line, but a good many fires still burned there.

I took a shortcut through a narrow stand of trees and found myself near the Game grounds. For no particular reason—

still in no hurry to get to my parents' place, I guess—I changed course and walked along next to the south border of the grounds. I'd never before seen the place on the night before a Game, with everything laid out in readiness and nobody around. It was an interesting sight, but a little on the spooky side.

The long tables and benches shone faintly in the starlight, their wood scrubbed white over the years by generations of laboring women and wagonloads of wood ash soap. Everything was already in place for the players, of course, as was the ceremonial equipment up on the big packed-earth platform at the eastern end of the grounds. It had all been smoked and doctored late the previous day, in a ceremony closed to everyone except the chief medicine men of the twelve participating tribes, and covered with sheets of white cloth that would have paid for a whole herd of horses at any trade meet in Oklahoma.

All the people had gone home now, except for a couple of guards who were supposed to be keeping an eye on things. I wondered why they hadn't challenged me already. Sitting on their butts somewhere nearby, no doubt, having a smoke or even asleep.

I felt a surge of righteous twelve-year-old indignation at the thought. Not that there was any serious risk of intruders, let alone thieves—even Osage raiders wouldn't dare cross that sacred line—but still, when you had the honor of standing guard over the grounds, on the night before a Game at that. . . .

Then I saw Elvis Bearpaw coming out of the woods.

I didn't recognize him at first; he was no more than a vague shadow, half a bow shot away. For a moment I thought it was one of the guards, but then the starlight fell on his face and I recognized him. Without quite knowing why, I stepped back into the deep shadow beneath the trees, watching.

He was moving fast, almost at a run, and he was crouched down low like a bear dancer. He crossed the white lime medicine line without so much as an instant's hesitation and dived in between the nearest rows of playing tables. The sacrilege was so enormous that the breath went out of me and my vision went blurry, and when I could see and breathe again Elvis Bearpaw had disappeared.

I don't know why I didn't call out for the guards; the idea never even occurred to me. Instead I stood there for what felt like a long time, scanning the rows of tables and the open ground all around trying to figure out where he'd gone and what he was up to.

And I'd almost decided that I'd lost him, that he'd left the grounds as sneakily as he'd come, but then I finally thought to watch the Cherokee players' table, up in the middle of the front row and directly in front of the big platform. Sure enough, I was just in time to spot him when he popped up.

He didn't pop very high. All I could see was the top half of his head, silhouetted against the whiteness of the tabletop, and his hands as they reached up and then vanished beneath the white cloth.

By now my heart was trying to bang a hole in my chest and the blood was roaring in my ears like a buffalo stampede. I watched in paralyzed horror, waiting for lightning to strike or the earth to open or whatever was going to happen. Yet nothing did, even though now I saw that Elvis Bearpaw was doing something so unspeakably blasphemous that my mind couldn't take it in. A moment later he ducked back out of sight, and then after almost no time he appeared again from among the tables, running flat out back the way he'd come, into the shelter of the trees. He didn't make a sound the whole time.

It took a little while before I could move. At last I got my feet unstuck and began walking again, toward the town and my parents' cabin. When I got there the place was dark and I let myself in as quietly as I could, but my mother was waiting for me and she woke my father up and they both gave me a good deal of shit. Under the circumstances I hardly noticed.

Early next morning I went back to Grandfather's cabin. I hadn't slept much even after my parents finally let me go to bed. My feet felt like somebody else's and the light hurt my eyes.

"Damn, *chooch,*" Grandfather said, "what's happened to you? You sound like you were rode hard and put up wet."

So I told him about Elvis Bearpaw and what I'd seen him do. I'd been planning to tell him anyway; I just hadn't been sure when.

"*Doyuka?*" he said when I was finished. "You're sure?"

"No," I answered honestly. "I mean, I know I saw him and I know he went onto the grounds and in among the tables, and he did something. Whether he did what I thought I saw him do—well, the light was bad and I wasn't very close. And," I added, "I don't really want to believe it."

"Huh." His lined old face was as unreadable as ever, but there was something a little strange in the way he stood. His hands made a quick restless motion. "You tell anybody else?" he asked.

"No."

"Good." He turned his blind eyes toward me and gave me a toothless smile. "You always did have sense, *chooch*. Too bad certain other people don't have as much."

I said, "What are you going to do, *eduda?*"

He looked surprised. "Do? Why, you know perfectly well what I'm fixing to do, *chooch*. Right up there on that stage, in front of the whole world."

"I mean about Elvis Bearpaw," I said, a little impatiently. "Will you tell the Chief and the other elders? Will they stop the Game, or—" I flapped my hands. "Or what?"

"Oh, no, no. Can't do that, *chooch*. Too late now," he said. "No telling what might happen. All we can do is let things go on, the way they're supposed to. Afterward—" He shrugged. "Come on. Time we got ourselves out to the grounds."

We began walking in that direction. We weren't the only ones. People were pouring out of the town and the campgrounds like swarming bees, all of them heading toward the Game grounds. They all recognized Grandfather Ninekiller, though, and gave us plenty of respectful space so that despite the crowds around us we were able to talk freely.

"Anyway," Grandfather said as we passed the council house, "you forget my position. Once the sun's come up on Game day, I'm not allowed to talk to anybody, even the Chief, about the Game or the players. If I try to tell your story, I'll be in the shit nearly as deep as you-know-who. Shouldn't even be talking with you about it, strictly speaking." He rested his hand on my shoulder. "But what the hell."

It seemed pretty strange to be picking at fine points of Game protocol, after Elvis Bearpaw had practically pissed on everything and everybody. But I didn't say so.

Grandfather's hand tightened on my shoulder. "Don't worry too much about it, *chooch*," he said in a softer voice. "These things have a way of working themselves out."

At the Game grounds we waited outside the medicine line until Grandfather's two young assistants came and led him away toward the big platform. I watched them help him up the steps, and felt thankful that I wasn't allowed to go with him. Once inside the line, nobody was allowed to leave, or eat food, or drink anything but water, until the Game was ended.

By this time the surrounding area was covered with people, from the medicine line—or rather a little way back; most people had enough sense to leave a couple of bowstring lengths' worth of safe space—clear back to the edge of the woods. And into the woods, too; there were kids of all sizes, and quite a few grown men, sitting perched up in the trees like a flock of huge weird birds.

Most of the people sat on the ground, or on whatever seats they'd brought along; it was considered ill-mannered to stand, since that could block somebody's view. For the most part they sat in bunches of family and friends, and nearly every group had a couple of big baskets of food and water, because the no-eating rule didn't apply to the people watching from outside the line, and there was no reason to pass up the chance to make a little picnic of the occasion. There was a lot of laughing and talking and passing food and water gourds around; in fact the noise was pretty intense if you let yourself notice it.

Uncle Kennedy and his bunch had saved me a place, down near the southeast corner of the grounds, close enough to hear and see everything. I sat down, accepted a roasted turkey leg from Aunt Diana, wiggled my skinny young rump into a reasonably comfortable fit with the ground, and had myself a good long look around.

There was plenty to see, for sure. Out on the playing field, the players were already standing at their places behind the long tables, facing the platform and, roughly, the still-rising sun. Front and center, naturally, was the table of the Host Nation, manned by the seven players who represented the seven clans of the Cherokee nation. Elvis Bearpaw was right in there, standing straight as a bowstring. I couldn't make out any particular expression on his face, but then all the players were looking very straight-faced and serious, in accordance with the Game manners.

On their left stood the Seminole players, in their bright patchwork jackets, while on the other side of the Cherokees were the players from the Creek clans. Directly behind were the tables of the Choctaws and the Chickasaws.

Behind the tables of the Five Nations were those of the Seven Allied Tribes: Shawnee, Delaware, Sac and Fox, Potawatomie, Kickapoo, Ottawa, and Miami. I didn't know anything about their clan arrangements or how they chose their players, though no doubt they used some form of blind lot drawing like everybody else.

Each table was flanked by a pair of senior warriors, dressed all in black and carrying long hardwood clubs. The Deacons—I've never known why they were called that—would be watching the players constantly all through the game, for even the smallest violation of the rules.

Up on the big platform, looking out over the playing tables, sat the chiefs and senior medicine men and other leading persons of the twelve tribes. Our Chief, for example, was accompanied by the Clan Mothers of the seven clans. There was also the Crier of the Game, fat old Jack Birdshooter, and, down at the south end of the stage, Grandfather Ninekiller and his assistants.

Now that was how it was done when I was a boy. Later on a lot of things got changed. I can't say whether the changes were for good or bad. I only know I liked the old days.

When the sun was high over the fields, the Crier stepped to the front of the stage and called for attention. The Chief of the Cherokee Nation was about to speak.

Come to think of it, that's one thing I wasn't too sorry to see dropped from the ceremonies—that long-winded speech, or rather recitation, that the Chief always used to deliver to start things off. Not that the speech itself was so bad, but when you had to hear the damn thing every year, word-for-word the same every time. . . .

"Long ago there were only the People."

Marilyn Blackfox was a pretty good Chief in her day, but she never had much of a speaking voice. But it didn't matter, since the Crier immediately repeated everything she said in English, in a voice that carried like the bellow of a bull alligator. That was out of courtesy to the people of the other tribes, but it was also handy for the large number of Cherokees who couldn't understand their own language—not, at any rate, the pure old-style Cherokee that Chief Marilyn was speaking.

That didn't matter either, seeing that most of us had heard the speech so many times we could have recited it from memory in either language. I leaned back on my elbows and let my mind wander, while she droned on and on about how the People tried to treat the whites right, when they first showed up, only to learn too late that this was the most treacherous bunch of humans the Creator ever let live. And about the massacres and the hunger and the diseases and the forced marches and the rest of it: old stuff, though no doubt it was all true.

"But even in the days when it seemed the People would vanish from the world," Chief Marilyn went on, "our wise elders were given a prophecy—"

Well, here came the bullshit part. According to Grandfather, who should know, the prophecy was that fire would come from the sky and destroy the whites, leaving only the People.

Which, as everybody surely knows, wasn't how it happened. Oh, there was fire enough, when the whites and the black people began fighting each other—I've seen the blackened ruins of the cities, and the pictures in the old books—until the whole Yuasa nation was at war within itself.

But what finally finished the whites was that mysterious sickness that rushed across the land like a flash flood, striking both the whites, and the black people, too, even faster than their diseases had once wiped out the People.

The legend is that the Creator sent the sickness to punish the whites and free the People. But Grandfather once told me a story he'd heard from this own grandfather: the whites, or certain of their crazier medicine men, created that sickness on purpose, meaning to use it against the black people. Only somebody screwed up and it wound up taking the whites, too.

Some parts of the story are pretty hard to believe, like the business about people breeding little invisible disease bugs the way you'd breed horses. But I think there must be something to it, all the same. Because, after all, there are still a fair number of whites left; but have you ever met anyone who's ever seen a black person in the flesh?

Nobody knows why the People—and the ones with similar blood, like the Meskins—were the only ones the sickness didn't affect. Maybe the Creator has a peculiar sense of humor.

"And so at last the People reclaimed their lands." Chief Marilyn was raising her voice now as she got close to the end. "And life was hard for many generations, and they found that they had forgotten many of the old ways. But they still remembered one thing above all from their traditions, the one great gift from the Creator that had held their grandmothers and grandfathers together through the evil times of the past; and they knew that the Game could save them, too, if they remained faithful. And so it was, and so it is today, and so it always will be."

She stretched out both arms as far as they would go. In a high clear shout she spoke the words everybody had been waiting for:

"Let the Game begin!"

"Players," the Crier roared, "take your seats!"

Out on the field, the assembled players of the Five Nations and the Seven Tribes did so, all together and with as little noise as possible. They *better*; the hard-faced Deacons were already fingering their clubs, and even simple clumsiness could be good for a rap alongside the head. I mean, those guys loved their work.

While the players bowed their heads and studied the polished hardwood boards in front of them, one of Grandfather's assistants began beating on a handheld water drum, the high-pitched *ping-ping-ping* sounding very loud in the hush that had settled over the whole area. The other assistant led Grandfather—who was perfectly capable of managing by himself, but the routine was meant to remind everyone that he was truly blind—to the wooden table at the front of the stage. With one hand the assistant raised the lid of the big honeysuckle vine basket that took up the whole top of the table, while with the other he guided Grandfather's hand toward the opening.

Grandfather reached into the basket. The drummer stopped drumming. You could have heard a butterfly fart.

Grandfather stood there a moment, groping around inside the basket, and then he pulled his hand back out and held up a little wooden ball, smaller than a child's fist, painted white. You couldn't really see it at any distance, but everybody there knew what it was. There was a soft rustling sound that ran across the field, as the people all drew their breaths.

Without turning, Grandfather passed the little ball to Jesse Tiger, the Seminoles' elder medicine man, who stood beside him. And Jesse Tiger, having looked at the ball, passed it on to the Creek medicine man on his left; and so the little ball went down the line of waiting medicine men, till all twelve had examined it. At the end of the line, the Ottawa elder—I didn't know his name—handed it to Jack Birdshooter, the Crier. Who took a single careful look at the ball and shouted, in a voice that would have cracked obsidian:

"*AY, THIRTY-TWO!*"

There was another soft windy sound as several hundred People let out their breaths. Everybody was craning and staring, now, watching the players. None appeared to have moved.

The drummer was already pinging away again. Grandfather had his hand and most of his forearm down into the huge basket this time, and he didn't fool around before pulling out the second ball. The ball went down the line as before and the Crier took it and looked and blared:

"*OH, SEVENTEEN!*" And, after a pause, "*ONE-SEVEN!*" just to make sure some idiot didn't mistake the call for seventy.

Still no action on the field. The players' heads were all bent as if praying. Which, of course, most if not all of them were. I wondered what was going through Elvis Bearpaw's mind.

There went the drummer again, *ping-ping-ping.* There went Grandfather's hand, in and out, and there went the third little ball down the line of dark-spotted old hands. And there went Jack Birdshooter:

"*ENN, SIX!*"

A number that low, this early? That was a lucky sign. And sure enough, over toward the other side of the field, the Deacons were watching one of the Shawnee players as he reached out and carefully placed a polished black stone marker on one of the squares of the walnut board in front of him.

There was a muffled cheer from the watching crowd. Even the dignitaries up on the stage permitted themselves a soft chorus of pleased grunts. This Game was off to an unusually good start.

My uncle said, "Want some more of that turkey, *chooch?*"

"Here," my aunt said, handing me a big buckskin-covered cushion. "Might as well get comfortable. It's liable to be a long day."

Up on the stage the drummer was at it again.

It was a warm day for spring, and there was no shade out on the open ground around the playing field. My eyes were sore from my nearly sleepless night, so I kept them closed a good deal. Aunt Di claimed I fell asleep for a little while there, but I was just resting my eyes and thinking.

I lost track of the progress of the Game soon enough; it wasn't long before all the players had at least a few markers on their boards, and nobody could have keep an eye on all of them. That, after all, was part of what the Deacons were there for.

As best I could see from where I sat, Elvis Bearpaw had a good many markers down, though nothing all that unusual. His face, when he raised his head to listen for a call, was still giving nothing away.

The morning turned to afternoon and the sun began her descent toward the western rim of the sky. The shadow of the sun pole, in front of the platform, grew longer and longer. There was a big brush-covered roof above the stage, to shade the dignitaries, but it was no longer doing them any good. Most of them were squinting and shading their eyes with their hands. Grandfather Ninekiller, of course, didn't have that problem. He kept reaching into the basket and pulling out the little balls, all the while staring straight and blind-eyed toward that hard white afternoon sun. From time to time he would pause while his assistants put the lid back on the great basket and lifted it between them, on its carrying poles, and gave it a good shaking, rocking it from side to side to mix up the balls. By now I figured it must be a good deal lighter. I wondered if this Game would go on long enough for the basket to have to be refilled. That was something I'd never seen, but I knew it occasionally happened.

This one was starting to look like one of the long Games, too. Already a couple of the senior Deacons were checking the supply of ready-to-light torches in the cane racks beside the platform, in case the play went on into the night.

"*BEE, TWENTY-TWO!*" shouted the Crier. And down at the end of the front row, not far from where I sat, one of the Seminole players reached up and put another marker on his board.

The sun was going down in a big bloody show off beyond the trees, and the torches were already being lit and placed in their holders, when it finally happened.

By then I was so tired I was barely listening, and so I missed the call; and to this day I couldn't tell you what ball it was. I was sitting there next to Uncle Kennedy, munching honeycake and trying to stay awake, and my ears picked up the

Crier's voice as he boomed out yet another string of meaningless sounds, but all my mind noticed was that he seemed to be getting a little hoarse.

But then my uncle made a sudden surprised grunt. "*Ni*," he said sharply, and I sat up and looked, while all around us people began doing the same, and a low excited murmur passed through the crowd.

Down on the field, Elvis Bearpaw had gotten to his feet. The two nearest Deacons were already striding toward him, their clubs swinging, ready to punish this outrageous behavior, but Elvis wasn't looking at them. He was staring down at his board as if it had turned into a live water moccasin.

The Deacons paused and looked at the board too. One of them said something, though his voice didn't carry to where I sat.

All the people in the crowd began getting to their feet. Somehow they did it in almost-complete silence. There wasn't even the cry of a baby.

Other Deacons were converging on the spot, now, and after a moment one of them left the growing bunch of black-clad figures and trotted over to the stage. Again I couldn't hear what was said, but all the people on the stage obviously did. Their faces told us onlookers that our guess had been right.

The group of Deacons split and stepped back, except for the original pair, who were now standing on either side of Elvis Bearpaw. One of them jabbed him in the side with the end of his club.

Elvis Bearpaw's mouth opened. A strange croaking sound came out, but it wasn't what you'd call human speech.

The Deacon poked him again, harder. Elvis straightened up and faced the stage and seemed to shake himself. "Bingo," he said, so softly I barely heard him. Then, much louder, "*Bingo!*"

Everybody breathed in and held it and then breathed out, all together.

Old Jack Birdshooter had been doing this too long to forget his lines now. "Deacons," he cried formally, "do we have a Bingo?"

The Deacon on Elvis Bearpaw's right raised his club, saluting the stage. "Yes," he shouted, "we do have a Bingo."

And, needless to say, that was when the crowd went absolutely bat-shit crazy, as always, jumping up and down and waving their arms in the air, yelling and hooting and yipping till it was a wonder the leaves didn't fall off the trees, while the Deacons led Elvis Bearpaw slowly toward the platform. His face, in the dying red light, was something to see.

A long, long time afterward, Grandfather Ninekiller told me the inside story. That was after he had gone on to the spirit world, where he learned all sorts of interesting things.

"What happened," Grandfather said, "Elvis Bearpaw did go to see Old Man Alabama, just like we heard. Wanted some kind of charm or medicine for the Game. Old Man Alabama told him no way. Fixing the Game, that was too much even for a crazy old witch."

"How'd you learn all this?" I asked, a little skeptically. Grandfather hadn't been dead very long at the time, and I was still getting used to talking with him in his new form.

"Old Man Alabama told me," Grandfather said. "Hell, he died a couple of years ago. He's been here longer than me."

"Oh."

"Anyway," Grandfather went on, "Elvis Bearpaw went on and on, offered all kinds of stuff for payment. Finally Old Man Alabama said he could do one thing for him and that was all. He could tell him where the Bingo was going to fall."

"*Doyuka*?"

"Would I shit you? And you and I know what the silly bastard went and did."

"I was right, then," I said. "About what he was up to that night. He switched his game board with his neighbor's. With what's-his-name, that guy from the Wolf Clan."

"*Uh-uh*. Only he didn't understand how that kind of a prophecy works," Grandfather said. "Old Man Alabama told him where the Bingo was going to fall, and that was where it fell. Like I told you that morning," he added, "these things have a way of working themselves out."

* * *

But as I say, that was a lot of years later. That night, I could only guess and wonder, while they brought Elvis Bearpaw up onto the stage and the medicine men and then the chiefs came by one at a time to shake his hand, and Chief Marilyn with her own hands tied the winner's red cloth around his head. She was a short woman and she had to stand on tiptoe, but she managed. Then they did the rest of it.

He screamed a lot while they were doing it to him. They all do, naturally, but I don't think I've ever heard a Game winner scream as loud and as long as Elvis Bearpaw did. Some Seneca kids I talked with next day said they heard him clear over at their camp, on the far side of the ball field. Well, they do say that that's the sign of a good strong sacrifice.

And you know, they must be right, because it rained like a son of a bitch that year.

As noted in the introduction, "Elvis Bearpaw's Luck" was written at the personal invitation of Roger Zelazny for an anthology of gambling stories. He said he'd like something on "Native American themes." I got the impression he had in mind the gaming traditions of certain tribes, but I didn't know anything about that. Around Tahlequah, Oklahoma, at that time, there was only one game that mattered. (There was a joke people told: "How do you get a whole room full of Cherokees to say shit at the same time? Yell out 'Bingo!'")

Of course that was back before the great Indian-casino boom. I suppose the story is now somewhat dated.

This is an example, though, of the problems of categorization. It takes place in a post-catastrophe future, so it could be considered science fiction; but on the other hand there are supernatural elements, so it could also be classed as fantasy.

Personally I don't see anything all that fantastic about dead Cherokees being able to talk to the living. After all, they manage to vote in every tribal election.

Written November 1993
First published December 1994

Going After Old Man Alabama

Charlie Badwater was the most powerful medicine man in all the eastern Oklahoma hill country. Or the biggest witch, depending on which person you listened to; among Cherokees the distinction tends to be a little hazy.

Either way, when Thomas Cornstalk finally decided that something had to be done about Old Man Alabama, he didn't need to think twice before getting in his old Dodge pickup truck and driving over to Charlie Badwater's place. Thomas Cornstalk was no slouch of a medicine man himself, but in a situation like this you went to the man with the power.

Charlie Badwater lived by himself in a one-room log cabin at the end of a really bad dirt road, up near the head of Butcherknife Hollow. There was nobody in sight when Thomas Cornstalk drove up, but as he got down from the pickup cab a big gray owl fluttered down from the surrounding woods and disappeared into the deep shadows behind the cabin. A moment later the cabin door opened and Charlie Badwater stepped out into the sunlight. " *'Siyo, Tami, dohiju?*" he called.

Thomas Cornstalk half-raised a hand in casual greeting. He and Charlie Badwater went back a long way. " *'Siyo, Jali. Gado haduhne?* Catching any mice?" he added dryly.

Charlie Badwater chuckled deep in his chest without moving his lips. "Hey," he said, "remember old Moses Otter?" And they both chuckled together, remembering.

Moses Otter had been a mean old man with a permanent case of professional jealousy, especially toward anybody who might have enough power to make him look bad. Since Moses Otter had never in his life been more than a second-rate witch, this included a lot of people.

One of his nastier tricks had been to turn himself into an owl—he could do that all right, but then who can't?—and fly over the woods until he spotted a clearing where a possible rival was growing medicine tobacco. Now of course serious tobacco has to be grown absolutely unseen by anyone except the person who will be using it, so this had meant a great deal of frustration and ruined medicine all over the area. Quite a few people had tried to witch Moses Otter and put a stop to this crap, but his protective medicine had always worked.

Charlie Badwater, then a youthful and inexperienced unknown, had gone to Moses Otter's place and told him in front of several witnesses that if he enjoyed being a bird he could have a hell of a good time from now on. And had turned him on the spot into the mangiest, scabbiest turkey buzzard ever seen in Oklahoma; and Moses Otter, after a certain amount of flopping around trying to change himself back, had flown away, never to be seen again except perhaps as an unidentifiable member of a gang of roadkill-pickers down on the Interstate.

That, Thomas Cornstalk recalled, had been the point at which everybody had realized that Charlie Badwater was somebody special. Maybe they hadn't fully grasped just how great he would one day become, but the word had definitely gone out that Charlie Badwater was somebody you didn't want to screw around with.

Now, still chuckling, Charlie Badwater tilted his head in the direction of his cabin. "*Kawi jaduli*"? Got a pot just made."

They went inside the cabin and Thomas Cornstalk sat down at the little pineboard table while Charlie Badwater poured a couple of cups of hell-black coffee from a blue and white speckled metal pot. "Ought to be ready to walk by now," Charlie Badwater said. "Been on the stove a long time."

"Good coffee," Thomas Cornstalk affirmed, tasting. "Damn near eat it with a fork."

They sat at the table, drinking coffee and smoking hand-rolled cigarettes, not talking for the moment: a couple of fifty-some-odd-year-old full-bloods, similarly dressed in work shirts and Wal-Mart jeans and cheap nylon running shoes made in Singapore. Charlie Badwater had the classic lean, deep-chested, no-ass build of the mountain Cherokee, while Thomas Cornstalk was one of those heavyset, round-faced types who may or may not have some Choctaw blood from way back in old times. Their faces, however, were similarly weathered, the hands callused and scarred from years of manual labor. Charlie Badwater was missing the end joint of his left index finger. There were only three people who knew how he had lost it and two of them were dead and nobody had the nerve to ask the third one. Let alone Charlie.

They talked a little, finally, about this and that: routine inquiries about the health of relatives, remarks about the weather, the usual pleasantries that a couple of properly raised Cherokee men will exchange before getting down to the real point of a conversation. But Thomas Cornstalk, usually the politest of men, was worried enough to hold the small talk to the bare minimum required by decency.

"*Gusdi nusdi*," he said finally. "Something's the matter. I'm not sure what," he added, in response to the inquiry in Charlie Badwater's eyes. "It's Old Man Alabama."

"That old weirdo?" Charlie Badwater wrinkled his nose very slightly, as if smelling something bad. "What's he up to these days? Still nutty as a *kenuche* ball, I guess?"

"Who knows? That's what I came to talk with you about," Thomas Cornstalk said. "He's up to something, all right, and I think it's trouble."

Old Man Alabama was a seriously strange old witch—in his case there was no question at all about the definition—who lived on top of a mountain over in Adair County, not far from the

Arkansas line. He wasn't Cherokee; he claimed to be the last surviving descendant of the Alabama tribe, and he often gibbered and babbled in a language he claimed was the lost Alabama tongue. It could have been; Thomas Cornstalk couldn't recognize a word of it, and he spoke sixteen Indian languages as well as English and Spanish—that was his special medicine, the ability to speak in different tongues; he could also talk with animals. On the other hand it might just as easily have been a lot of meaningless blather, which was what Thomas Cornstalk and a good many other people suspected.

There was also the inconvenient fact that there were still some Alabamas living on a reservation down in Texas, big as you please; but it had been along time since anybody had pointed this out in Old Man Alabama's hearing. Not after what had happened to the last bigmouth to bring the subject up.

Whatever he was—Thomas Cornstalk had long suspected he was some kind of Creek or Seminole or maybe Yuchi, run off by his own people—Old Man Alabama was as crazy as the Devil and twice as nasty. That much was certain.

He was skinny and tall and he had long arms that he waved wildly about while talking, or for no apparent reason at all. Everything about him was long: long matted hair falling past his shoulders, long beaky nose, long bony fingers ending in creepy-looking nails. He walked with a strange angling gait, one shoulder higher than the other, and he spat constantly, tuff tuff tuff, so you could follow him down a dirt road on a dry day by the little brown spots in the dust.

It was widely believed that he had a long tongue like a moth's, that he kept curled up in his mouth and only stretched out at night during unspeakable acts. That was another story people weren't eager to investigate first hand.

He also stank. Not the way a regular man smelled bad, even a very dirty regular man—though Old Man Alabama was sure as hell dirty enough—but a horrible, eye-watering stench that reminded you of things like rotten cucumbers and dead skunks on the highway in hot weather. That alone would have been reason enough for people to give him a wide berth, even if they hadn't been afraid of him.

And oh, yes, people were afraid of him. Mothers hid their pregnant daughters indoors when they saw him walking by the house, afraid that even a single direct look from those hooded reptilian eyes might cause monstrous deformities to the unborn.

Most people, in face, avoided talking about him at all; it was well known that witches knew when they were being talked about, and the last thing people wanted was to draw the displeased attention of a witch as powerful and unpredictable as Old Man Alabama. It was a measure of the power of both Charlie Badwater and Thomas Cornstalk that they were willing to talk freely about him. Even so, Thomas Cornstalk would have been just as comfortable if Charlie Badwater hadn't spoken quite so disrespectfully about the old man.

"All I know," Thomas Cornstalk said, "he's been cooking up some kind of almighty powerful medicine up on that mountain of his. I go over that way pretty often, you know, got some relatives that call me up every time one of their kids gets a runny nose . . . anyway, sometimes you can hear these sounds, up where your ear can't quite get ahold of them, like those dog whistles, huh? And people see strange lights up on the mountain at night, and sometimes in the daytime the air looks sort of shimmery above the mountaintop, the way it does over a hot stove. Lots of smoke too, that's another thing. I got a smell or two when the wind was right and I don't know what the old man's burning up there but it's nothing I'd want in *my* medicine bag."

He paused, sipping his coffee, his eyes wandering about the interior of the cabin. Lots of medicine men live surrounded by all sorts of junk, their houses littered and smelly, walls and ceiling hung with bundles of dried herbs and feathers and skins and bones and other parts of birds and animals. Charlie Badwater's cabin, however, was as neat as a white doctor's office, everything stowed carefully away out of sight.

"I went up to see him, finally," Thomas Cornstalk said. "Or tried to, but he was either gone or hiding. I couldn't get close to the cabin. He's got the place circled—you know? You get to about ten or fifteen steps from the cabin and it starts to be harder and harder to walk, like you're stepping in molasses, till finally you can't go any farther. By then the cabin looks all runny, too, like it's melting. I had my pipe with me, and some good tobacco, and I tried every *igawesdi* I know for getting past a protective spell. Whatever Old Man Alabama has around that cabin, it's no ordinary medicine."

"Huh." Charlie Badwater was beginning to look interested. "See anything? I mean anything to suggest what's going on."

"Not a thing." Thomas Cornstalk pulled his shoulder blades together for a second. "Place made my skin crawl so bad, I got out pretty quick. Went home and smoked myself nearly black. Burned enough cedar for a Christmas-tree lot before I felt clean again."

"Huh," Charlie Badwater said again. He sat for a minute or so in silence, staring out through the open cabin door, though there was nothing out there but a stretch of dusty yard and the woods beyond.

"All right," he said at last, and got to his feet. "We better go pay Old Man Alabama a visit."

Thomas Cornstalk stood up too. "You want to go right now?" he said, a little surprised.

"Sure. You got something else you have to do?"

"No," Thomas Cornstalk admitted, after a moment's hesitation. He wasn't really ready for this, he thought, but maybe it was better to get on with it. The longer they waited, the better the chance that Old Man Alabama would find out they were coming, and do something unusually bad to try and stop them.

Charlie Badwater started toward the door. Thomas Cornstalk said, "You're not taking any stuff along? You know, medicine?"

Charlie Badwater patted his jeans pockets. "Got my pipe and some tobacco on me. I don't expect I'll need anything else."

Going out the door, following Charlie Badwater across the yard, Thomas Cornstalk shook his head in admiring wonder. That Charlie, he thought. Probably arm-wrestle the Devil left-handed, if he got a chance. Probably win, too.

* * *

They rode back down the dirt road in Thomas Cornstalk's old pickup truck. Charlie Badwater didn't own any kind of car or truck. He didn't have a telephone or electricity in his cabin, either. It was some mysterious but necessary part of his personal medicine.

The dirt track came out of the woods, after a mile or so of dust and rocks and sun-hardened ruts, and joined up with a winding gravel road that dipped down across the summer-dry bed of Butcherknife Creek and then climbed up the side of Turkeyfoot Ridge. On the far side of the ridge, the gravel turned into potholed county blacktop. Several miles farther along, they came out onto the Stilwell road. "Damn, Charlie," Thomas Cornstalk said, hanging a left, "you think you could manage to live further back in the woods?"

"Not without coming out on the other side," Charlie Badwater said.

The road up beside of Old Man Alabama's mountain was even worst than the one to Charlie Badwater's place. "I was here just this morning," Thomas Cornstalk said, fighting the wheel, "and I swear this mule track is in worse shape than it was then. And look at that," he exclaimed, and stepped on the brake pedal. "I know that wasn't there before—"

A big uprooted white oak tree was lying across the road. The road was littered with snapped-off limbs and still-green leaves. The two men in the pickup truck looked at each other. There hadn't been so much as a stiff breeze all day.

"Get out and walk, then," Charlie Badwater said after a minute. "We can use the exercise, I guess."

They got out and walked on up the road, climbing over the fallen tree. A little way beyond, the biggest rattlesnake Thomas Cornstalk had ever seen was lying in the road, looking at them. It coiled up and rattled its tail and showed its fangs but Charlie Badwater merely said, *"Ayuh jaduji,"* and the huge snake uncoiled and slid quietly off into the woods while Charlie and Thomas walked past.

"I always wondered," Thomas Cornstalk said as they trudged up the steep mountainside. "You suppose a rattlesnake really believes you're his uncle, when you say that?"

"Who knows? It doesn't matter how things work, Thomas. It just matters that they do work." Charlie Badwater grinned. "Talked to this professor from Northeastern State once, showed up at a stomp dance down at Redbird. He said Cherokees are pragmatists."

"What's that mean?"

"Beats me. I told him most of the ones I know are Baptists, with a few Methodists and of course there's a lot of people getting into those holy-roller outfits—" Charlie Badwater stopped suddenly in the middle of the road. "Huh," he grunted softly, as if to himself. Thomas Cornstalk couldn't remember ever seeing him look so surprised.

They had rounded the last bend in the road and had come in sight of Old Man Alabama's cabin. Except the cabin itself was barely in sight of all, in any normal sense. The whole clearing where the cabin stood was walled off by a kind of curtain of yellowish light, through which the outlines of the cabin showed only vaguely and irregularly. The sky looked somehow darker directly above the clearing, and all the surrounding trees seemed to have taken on strange and disturbing shapes. There was a high-pitched whining sound in the air, like the singing of a million huge mosquitoes.

"You were right, Thomas," Charlie Badwater said after a moment. "The old turd's gotten hold of something heavy. Who'd have thought it?"

"It wasn't like this when I was here this morning," Thomas Cornstalk said, looking around him and feeling very uneasy. "Not so extreme, like."

"Better have a look, then." Charlie Badwater took out a buckskin pouch and a short-stemmed pipe. Facing toward the sun, he poured a little tobacco from the pouch into his palm and began to sing, a strange-sounding song that Thomas Cornstalk had never heard before. Four times he sang the song through, pausing at the end of each repetition to blow softly on the tobacco. Then he stuffed the tobacco into the bowl of the pipe. It was an ordinary cheap briar pipe, the kind they sell off cardboard wall displays in country gas stations. In Cherokee medicine there is no particular reverence or importance placed on the pipe itself; the tobacco carries all the power, and then only if properly doctored with the right *igawesdi* words. Charlie Badwater could, if he had preferred, have simply rolled the tobacco into a cigarette and used that.

He lit the pipe with a plastic butane lighter and walked toward the cabin, puffing. Thomas Cornstalk followed, rather reluctantly. He didn't like this, but he would have followed Charlie Badwater to hell. Which, of course, might very well be where they were about to go.

Charlie Badwater pointed the stem of the pipe at the shimmering wall of light that blocked their way. Four times he blew smoke at the barrier, long dense streams of bluish white smoke that curled and eddied back strangely as they hit the bright curtain. On the fourth puff there was a sharp cracking sound and suddenly the curtain was gone and the humming stopped and there was only a weed-grown clearing and a tumble-down gray board shack badly in need of a new roof. Somewhere nearby a bird began singing, as if relieved.

"*Asuh*," Thomas Cornstalk murmured in admiration.

"Make me think, I'll teach you that one some time," Charlie Badwater said, "It's not hard, once you learn the song . . . well, let's have a look around."

They walked slowly toward the cabin. There wasn't much to see. The yard was littered with an amazing assortment of junk—broken crockery and rusting pots and pans, chicken feathers and unidentifiable bones, bottles and cans, a wrecked chair with stuffing coming out of the cushions—but none of it suggested anything except that you wouldn't want Old Man Alabama living next door. A big pile of turtle shells lay on the sagging front porch. There was a rattlesnake skin nailed above the door.

"No smoke," Charlie Badwater said, studying the chimney. "Reckon he's gone? Well, one way to find out."

He stepped up onto the porch, and turned to look back at Thomas Cornstalk, who hadn't moved. "Coming?"

"You go," Thomas Cornstalk said. "I'll wait out here for you. If it's all the same to you." He wouldn't have gone inside that cabin for a million dollars and a lifetime ticket to the Super Bowl. "Need to work on my tan," he added.

Charlie Badwater chuckled and disappeared through the cabin door. There was no sound of voices or anything else from within, so Thomas Cornstalk figured he must have been right about Old Man Alabama being gone. That didn't make such sense; why would the old maniac have put up such a fancy protective spell if he wasn't going to be inside? Come to think of it, how could he have laid on that barrier from the outside? As far as Thomas Cornstalk knew, a spell like that had to be worked from inside the protective circle. But nothing about this made any sense. . . .

Charlie Badwater's laugh came through the open cabin door. "You're not going to believe this," he called. "I don't believe it myself."

"What did you find?" Thomas Cornstalk said as Charlie came back out.

"About what you'd expect, mostly. A whole bunch of weird stuff piled every which way and hanging from the ceiling, all of it dirty as a pigpen and stinking so bad you can hardly breathe in there. Nothing unusual—considering who and what lives here—except these."

He held up a stack of books. Thomas Cornstalk stared. "Books?" he said in amazement. "What's Old Man Alabama doing with books? I know for a fact he can't read."

"Who knows? Maybe got them to wipe his ass with. Ran out of pine cones or whatever he uses." Charlie Badwater sat down on the edge of the porch and began flipping through the books. "Looks like he stole them from the school over at Rocky Mountain. Old bastard's a sneak thief on top of everything else."

"What kind of books are they? The kind with pictures of women? Maybe he's been out in the woods by himself too long."

"No, look, this is a history book. And this one has a bunch of pictures of old-time sailing ships, like in the pirate movies. Now why in the world—"

Charlie Badwater sat staring at the books for a couple of minutes, and then he tossed them aside and stood up. "I'm going to look around some more," he said.

Thomas Cornstalk followed him as he walked around the cabin. The area in back of the cabin looked much the same as the front yard, but then both men saw the blackened spot where a small fire had been burning. Large rocks had been placed in a circle around the fire place, and some of the rocks were marked with strange symbols or patterns. A tiny wisp of smoke, no greater than that from a cigarette, curled up from the ashes.

Charlie Badwater walked over the held his hand above the ashes, not quite touching the remains of the fire. Then he crouched way down and began studying the ground closely, slowly examining the entire area within the circle of stones and working his way back toward where Thomas Cornstalk stood silently watching. This was one of Charlie Badwater's most famous specialties: reading sign. People said he could track a catfish across a lake.

"He came out here," he said at last, "barefoot as usual, and he walked straight to that spot by the fire and walked around it—at least four times, it's pretty confused there—and then, well. . . ."

"What? Where'd he go?"

"Far as I can tell, he just flew away. Or disappeared or something. He didn't walk back out of that circle of rocks, anyway. And whatever he did, it wasn't long ago that he did it. Those ashes are still warm."

A small dry voice said, "Looking for the old man?"

Thomas Cornstalk turned around. A great big blue jay was sitting on the collapsing eaves of Old Man Alabama's shack.

"Because," the jay said, speaking in that sarcastic way jays have, "I don't think you're going to find him. Not anytime soon, anyway. He left sort of drastic."

"Did you see what happened?" Thomas Cornstalk asked the jay.

Charlie Badwater had turned around too by now. He was looking from Thomas Cornstalk to the say and back again. There was an odd look on his face; he seemed almost wistful. For all his power, all the fantastic things he could do, he had never been granted the ability to talk with animals—which is not something you can learn; you have the gift or you don't—and there are few things that can make a person feel quite as shut out as watching somebody like Thomas Cornstalk having a conversation with bird or beast.

"Hey," the jay said, "I got trapped in here when the old son of a bitch put that whatever-the-hell around the cabin. Tried to fly out, hit something like a wall in the air, damn near broke my beak. Thought I was going to starve to death in here, till you guys showed up. Tell your buddy thanks for turning the damn thing off."

"Ask him where Old Man Alabama went," Charlie Badwater said.

"I saw the whole thing," the jay said, not waiting for the translation. Thomas Cornstalk noticed that; he had suspected for some time that blue jays could understand Cherokee, even if they pretended not to. "Old guy walked out there mumbling to himself, stomped around the fire a little, made a lot of that racket that you humans call singing—hey, no offense, but even a boat-tailed grackle can sing better than that—and then all of a sudden he threw a bunch of stuff on the fire. There was a big puff of smoke and when it cleared away he was just as gone as you please."

"I knew it," Charlie Badwater said, when this had been interpreted for him. He squatted down by the fire and began picking up handfuls of ashes and blackened twigs and dirt, running the material through his fingers and sniffing it like a dog and occasionally putting a pinch in his mouth to taste it.

"Ah," he said finally. "All right, I know what he used. Don't understand why—there are some combinations in there that shouldn't work at all, by any of the rules I know—but like I said, what works is what works."

He stood up and looked at the jay. "Ask him if he can remember the song."

"Sure," the jay said. "No problem. Not sure I can sing it, of course—"

"I'll be right back," Charlie Badwater said, heading for the cabin. A minute later Thomas Cornstalk heard him rummaging around inside. The jay said, "Was it something I said?"

In a little while Charlie Badwater came back, his arms full of buckskin bags and brown paper sacks. "Lucky for us he had plenty of everything," he said, and squatted down on the ground and took off his old black hat and turned it upside down on his knees and began taking things out of the bags: mostly dried leaves and weeds and roots, but other items too, not all of them easily identifiable. At one point Thomas Cornstalk was nearly certain he recognized a couple of human finger bones.

"All right," Charlie Badwater said, setting the hat carefully next to the dead fire and straightening up. "Now how does that song go?"

That part wasn't easy. The jay had a great deal of trouble forming some of the sounds; a crow would have been better at this, or maybe a mockingbird. The words weren't in any language Thomas Cornstalk had ever heard, and Charlie Badwater said he'd never heard a song remotely like this one.

At last, after many false starts and failed tries, Charlie Badwater got all the way through the song and the jay said, "That's it. He's got it perfect. No accounting for tastes, I guess."

Charlie Badwater was already piling up sticks from the pile of wood beside the ring of stones. He got out his lighter and in a few minutes the fire was crackling and flickering away. "*Ehena*," he said over his shoulder. "Ready when you are."

"You want me in on this?"

"Of course. Let's go, Thomas. *Nula.*"

Thomas Cornstalk wasn't at all happy about this, but he walked across the circle to stand beside Charlie Badwater, who had picked up his hat and was holding it in front of him in both hands.

"This I've got to see," the jay commented from its perch on the roof. It had moved up to the ridgepole, probably for a better view. "You guys are crazier than the old man."

Charlie Badwater circled the fire four times, counterclockwise, like a stomp dancer, with Thomas Cornstalk pacing nervously behind him. After the fourth orbit he stopped, facing the sun, and began singing the song the jay had taught him. It sounded different now, somehow. The hair was standing up on Thomas Cornstalk's neck and arms.

Suddenly Charlie Badwater emptied the hat's contents onto the fire. There was a series of sharp fizzing and sputtering noises, and a big cloud of dense gray smoke surged up and surrounded both men. It was so thick that Thomas Cornstalk couldn't see an inch in front of his face; it was like having his head under very muddy water, or being covered with a heavy gray blanket.

Other things were happening, too. The ground underfoot was beginning to shift and become soft; it felt like quicksand, yet he wasn't sinking into it. His skin prickled all over, not painfully but pretty unpleasantly, and he felt a little sick to his stomach.

The grayness got darker and darker, while the ground fell away completely, until Thomas Cornstalk felt himself to be floating through a great black nothingness. For some reason he was no longer frightened; he simply assumed that he had died and this was what it was like when you went to the spirit world. *"Ni, Jali,"* he called out.

"Ayuh ahni, Tami." The voice sounded close by, but strange, as if Charlie Badwater had fallen down a well.

"Gado nidagal'stani? What's going to happen?"

"Nigal'stisguh," came the cheerful reply. "Whatever . . ."

Thomas Cornstalk had no idea how long the darkness and the floating sensation lasted. His sense of time, the whole idea of time itself, had vanished in that first billow of smoke. But then suddenly the darkness turned to dazzling light and there was something solid under his feet again. Caught by surprise, he swayed and staggered and fell heavily forward, barely getting his arms up in time to protect his face.

He lay half-stunned for a moment, getting the breath back into his lungs and the sight back to his eyes. There was hard smooth planking against his hands; it felt like his own cabin floor, in fact, and at first he thought he must somehow be back home. Maybe the whole thing was a dream and he'd just fallen out of bed . . . but he rolled over and saw bright blue sky above him, crisscrossed by a lot of ropes and long poles. He sat up and saw that he was on the deck of a ship.

It was a ship such as he had only seen in books and movies: the old-fashioned kind, made of wood, with masts and sails instead of an engine. Off beyond the railing, blue water stretched unbroken to the horizon.

Beside him, Charlie Badwater's voice said, "Well, I have to admit this wasn't what I expected."

Thomas Cornstalk turned his head in time to see Charlie Badwater getting to his feet. That seemed like a good idea, so he did it too. The deck was tilted to one side and the whole ship was rolling and pitching, gently but distinctly, with the motion of the sea. Thomas Cornstalk's stomach began to feel a trifle queasy. He hadn't been aboard a ship since his long-ago hitch in the marines, but he remembered about seasickness. He closed his eyes for a second and forced his stomach to settle down. This was no time to lose control of any part of himself.

He said, "Where the hell are we, Charlie?"

From behind them came a harsh cackle. "Where? Wrong question."

The words were in English. The voice was dry and high-pitched, with an old man's quaver. Both men said, "Oh, shit," and turned around almost in unison.

Old Man Alabama was standing on the raised deck at the stern of the ship, looking down at them. His arms were folded and his long hair streamed and fluttered in the wind. His mouth was pulled back at the corners in the closest thing to a smile Thomas Cornstalk had ever seen on his face.

"Not *where*," he went on, and cackled. "You ought to ask, *when* are we? Of course there's some *where* in it too—"

The horrible smile disappeared all at once. "Say," Old Man Alabama said in a different voice, "how did you two get here, anyway?"

"Same way you did," Charlie Badwater said, also in English. "It wasn't very hard."

"You're a liar." Old Man Alabama spat hard on the deck. "It took me years to learn the secret. How could you two stupid Cherokees—"

"A little bird told us," Thomas Cornstalk interrupted. He knew it was too easy but he couldn't resist.

"I used the same routine you did," Charlie Badwater said, "only I put in a following-and-finding *igawesdi*. You ought to have known you couldn't lose me, old man. What are you up to, anyway?"

Old Man Alabama unfolded his long arms and waved them aimlessly about. It made him look remarkably like a spider monkey Thomas Cornstalk had seen in the Tulsa zoo.

"Crazy Old Man Alabama," he screeched. "I know what you all said about me behind my back—"

"Hey," Charlie Badwater said, "I said it to your face too. Plenty of times."

"Loony old witch," Old Man Alabama went on, ignoring him. "Up there on his mountain, doing nickel-and-dime hexes and love charms, comes into town every now and then and scares the little kids, couldn't witch his way out of a wet paper sack. Yeah, well, look what the crazy old man went and did."

He stopped and shook himself all over. "I did it, too," he said. His voice had suddenly gone softer; it was hard to understand the words. "Nobody else ever even tried it, but I did it. Me."

He stared down at them for a minute, evidently waiting for them to ask him what exactly he'd done. When they didn't, he threw his hands way up over his head again and put his head back and screamed, "*Time!* I found out how to fly through time! Look around you, damn it—they don't have ships like this in the year we come from. Don't you know what you're looking at, here?"

Thomas Cornstalk was already glancing up and down the empty decks, up into the rigging and . . . empty decks? "What the hell," he said. "What happened to the people? The sailors and all?"

"Right," Charlie Badwater said. "You didn't sail this thing out here by yourself. Hell, you can't even paddle a canoe. I've seen you try."

Old Man Alabama let off another of his demented laughs. "There," he said, gesturing out over the rail. "There they are, boys. Fine crew they make now, huh?"

Thomas Cornstalk looked where the old man was pointing, but he couldn't see anything but the open sea and sky and a bunch of seagulls squawking and flapping around above the ship's wake. Then he got it. "Aw, hell," he said. "You didn't."

"Should have been here a little while ago," Old Man Alabama chortled, "when they were still learning how to fly. Two of them crashed into the water and a shark got them. Hee hee."

"But why?" Charlie Badwater said. "I mean, the part about traveling into the past, okay, I hate to admit it but I'm impressed. But then fooling around with this kind of childishness, turning a lot of poor damn sailors into sea birds? I know you hate white people, but—"

"Hah! Not just any bunch of sailors," Old Man Alabama said triumphantly. "Not just any white people, either. This is where it all started, you dumb blanket-asses! And I'm the one who went back and fixed it!"

He began to sing, a dreadful weird keening that rose and fell over a four-tone scale, without recognizable words. Charlie Badwater and Thomas Cornstalk looked at each other and then back at the old man. Thomas Cornstalk said, "You mean this ship—"

"Yes! It's old *Columbus's* ship! Now the white bastards won't come at all!" Old Man Alabama's face was almost glowing. "And it was me, me, me that stopped them! Poor cracked Old Man Alabama, turns out to be the greatest Indian in history, that's all—"

"Uh, excuse me," Thomas Cornstalk said, "but if this is Columbus's ship, where are the other two?"

"Other two what?" Old Man Alabama asked irritably.

"Other two ships, you old fool," Charlie Badwater said. "Columbus had three ships."

"That's right," Thomas Cornstalk agreed. "I remember from school."

Old Man Alabama was looking severely pissed off. "Are you sure? Damn it, I want to a lot of trouble to make sure I got the right one. Gave this white kid from Tahlequah a set of bear claws and a charm to make his girlfriend put out—little bastard drove a hard bargain—for finding me the picture in that book. Told me what year it was and everything. I'm telling you, this is it." Old Man Alabama stomped his bare feet on the deck. "Columbus's ship. The *Mayflower*."

"You ignorant sack of possum poop," Charlie Badwater said. "You don't know squat, do you? Columbus's ship was named the *Santa Maria*. The *Mayflower* was a totally different bunch of *yonegs*. Came ashore up in Maine or somewhere like that."

"These schoolkids nowadays, they're liable to tell you anything," Thomas Cornstalk remarked. "Half of them can't read any better than you do. My sister's girl is going with a white boy, I swear he don't know any more than the average fencepost."

Old Man Alabama was fairly having a fit now. "No," he howled, flailing the air with his long skinny arms. "No, no, it's a lie—"

Charlie Badwater sighed and shook his head. "I bet this isn't even the *Mayflower*," he said to Thomas Cornstalk. "Let's have a look around."

They walked up and down the deserted main deck, looking. There didn't seem to be anything to tell them the name of the ship.

"I think they put the name on the stern," Thomas Cornstalk said. "You know, the hind end of the ship. They did when I was in the Corps, anyway."

They climbed a ladder and crossed the quarterdeck, paying no attention to Old Man Alabama, who was now lying on the deck beating the planks with his fists. "Hang on to my belt or something, will you?" Thomas Cornstalk requested. "I don't swim all that good."

With Charlie Badwater holding him by the belt, he hung over the railing and looked at the name painted in big letters across the ship's stern. It was hard to make out at that angle, and upside down besides, but finally he figured it out. "*Mary Celeste*," he called back over his shoulder. "That's the name. The *Mary Celeste.*"

Charlie Badwater looked at Old Man Alabama. "*Mayflower*. Columbus. My Native American ass," he said disgustedly. "I should have let those white guys hang him, back last year."

Thomas Cornstalk straightened up and leaned back against the rail. "Well," he said, "what do we do now?"

Charlie Badwater shrugged. "Go back where we came from. When we came from."

"Can you do it?"

"Anything this old lunatic can do, I can figure out how to undo."

Thomas Cornstalk nodded, feeling much relieved. "Do we take him along?"

"We better. No telling what the consequences might be if we left him." Charlie Badwater stared at the writhing body on the deck at his feet. "You know the worst part? It was a hell of a great idea he had. Too bad it had to occur to an idiot."

"*Nasgiduh nusdi*," Thomas Cornstalk said. "That's how it is."

He looked along the empty decks once again. "You think anybody's ever going to find this boat? Come along in another ship, see this one floating out here in the middle of the ocean, nobody on board . . . man," he said, "that's going to make some people wonder."

"People need to wonder now and then," Charlie Badwater said. "It's good for their circulation."

He grinned at Thomas Cornstalk. "Come on," he said. "Let's peel this old fool off the deck and go home."

* * *

There really was an Old Man Alabama, back in the last days of the old Creek Nation; he was much feared as a sorcerer. My friend and informally-adopted grandfather, the late Louis "Littlecoon" Oliver, saw him several times as a boy

"Going After Old Man Alabama" was written right on the heels of "Elvis Bearpaw's Luck", Roger having also told me about another anthology that someone was putting together. So now I'd done a couple of stories, and found out they weren't nearly as hard to write as I'd thought; in fact I seemed to have a certain flair for the form. GAOMA even got some critical praise: "Quel humor devastateur!" exclaimed a French reviewer. How about that?

And yet I didn't do another one for almost two years.

Sometimes it takes me a while to get it.

Written July 1995
First published March 1996

The Undiscovered

So the white men are back! And trying once again to build themselves a town, without so much as asking anyone's permission. I wonder how long they will stay this time. It sounds as if these have no more sense than the ones who came before.

They certainly pick the strangest places to settle. Last time it was that island, where anyone could have told them the weather is bad and the land is no good for corn. Now they have invaded Powhatan's country, and from what you say, they seem to have angered him already. Of course that has never been hard to do.

Oh, yes, we hear about these matters up in the hills. Not many of us actually visit the coastal country—I don't suppose there are ten people in this town, counting myself, who have even seen the sea—but you know how these stories travel. We have heard all about your neighbor Powhatan, and you eastern people are welcome to him. Was there ever a chief so hungry for power? Not in my memory, and I have lived a long time.

But we were speaking of the white men. As you say, they are a strange people indeed. For all their amazing weapons and other possessions, they seem to be ignorant of the simplest things. I think a half-grown boy would know more about how to survive. Or how to behave toward other people in their own country.

And yet they are not the fools they appear. Not all of them, at least. The only one I ever knew was a remarkably wise man in many ways.

Do not make that gesture at me. I tell you that there was a white man who lived right here in our town, for more than ten winters, and I came to know him well.

I remember the day they brought him in. I was sitting in front of my house, working on a fish spear, when I heard the shouting from the direction of the town gate. Bigkiller and his party, I guessed, returning from their raid on the Tuscaroras. People were running toward the gate, pouring out of the houses, everyone eager for a look.

I stayed where I was. I could tell by the sound that the raid had been successful—no women were screaming, so none of our people had been killed or seriously hurt—and I didn't feel like spending the rest of the day listening to Bigkiller bragging about his latest exploits.

But a young boy came up and said, "They need you, Uncle. Prisoners."

So I put my spear aside and got up and followed him, wondering once again why no one around this place could be bothered to learn to speak Tuscarora. After all, it is not so different from our tongue, not nearly as hard as Catawba or Maskogi or Shawano. Or your own language, which as you see I still speak poorly.

The captives were standing just inside the gate, guarded by a couple of Bigkiller's clan brothers, who were holding war clubs and looking fierce, as well as pleased with themselves. There was a big crowd of people by now and I had to push my way through before I could see the prisoners. There were a couple of scared-looking Tuscarora women—one young and pretty, the other almost my age and ugly as an alligator—and a small boy with his fist stuck in his mouth. Not much, I thought, to show for all this noise and fuss.

Then I saw the white man.

Do you know, it didn't occur to me at first that that was what he was. After all, white men were very rare creatures in those days, even more so than now. Hardly anyone had actually seen one, and quite a few people refused to believe they existed at all.

Besides, he wasn't really white—not the kind of fish-belly white that I'd always imagined, when people talked about white men—at least where it showed. His face was a strange reddish color, like a boiled crawfish, with little bits of skin peeling from his nose. His arms and legs, where they stuck out from under the single buckskin garment he wore, were so dirty and covered with bruises that it was hard to tell what color the skin was. Of course that was true of all of the captives; Bigkiller and his warriors had not been gentle.

His hair was dark brown rather than black, which I thought was unusual for a Tuscarora, though you do see Leni Lenapes and a few Shawanos with lighter hair. It was pretty thin above his forehead, and the scalp beneath showed through, a nasty bright pink. I looked at that and at the red peeling skin of his face, and thought: well done, Bigkiller, you've brought home a sick man. Some lowland skin disease, and what a job it's going to be purifying everything after he dies. . . .

That was when he turned and looked at me with those blue eyes. Yes, blue. I don't blame you; I didn't believe that story either, until I saw for myself. The white men have eyes the color of a sunny sky. I tell you, it is a weird thing to see when you're not ready for it.

Bigkiller came through the crowd, looking at me and laughing. "Look what we caught, Uncle," he said, and pointed with his spear. "A white man!"

"I knew that," I said, a little crossly. I hated it when he called me "Uncle." I hated it when anyone did it, except children—I was not yet that old—but I hated it worse when it came from Bigkiller. Even if he was my nephew.

"He was with the Tuscaroras," one of the warriors, Muskrat by name, told me. "These two women had him carrying firewood—"

"Never mind that." Bigkiller gave Muskrat a bad look. No need to tell the whole town that this brave raid deep into

Tuscarora country had amounted to nothing more than the ambush and kidnapping of a small wood-gathering party.

To me Bigkiller said, "Well, Uncle, you're the one who knows all tongues. Can you talk with this whiteskin?"

I stepped closer and studied the stranger, who looked back at me with those impossible eyes. He seemed unafraid, but who could read expressions on such an unnatural face?

"Who are you and where do you come from?" I asked in Tuscarora.

He smiled and shook his head, not speaking. The woman beside him, the older one, spoke up suddenly. "He doesn't know our language," she said. "Only a few words, and then you have to talk slow and loud, and kick him a little."

"Nobody in our town could talk with him," the younger woman added. "Our chief speaks a little of your language, and one family has a Catawba slave, and he couldn't understand them either."

By now the crowd was getting noisy, everyone pushing and jostling, trying to get a look at the white man. Everyone was talking, too, saying the silliest things. Old Otter, the elder medicine man, wanted to cut the white man to see what color his blood was. An old woman asked Muskrat to strip him naked and find out if he was white all over, though I guessed she was really more interested in learning what his male parts looked like.

The young Tuscarora woman said, "Are they going to kill him?"

"I don't know," I told her. "Maybe."

"They shouldn't," she said. "He's a good slave. He's a hard worker, and he can really sing and dance."

I translated this, and to my surprise Muskrat said, "It is true that he is stronger than he looks. He put up a good fight, with no weapon but a stick of firewood. Why do you think I'm holding this club left-handed?" He held up his right arm, which was swollen and dark below the elbow. "He almost broke my arm."

"He did show spirit," Bigkiller agreed. "He could have run away, but he stayed and fought to protect the women. That was well done for a slave."

I looked at the white man again. He didn't look all that impressive, being no more than medium size and pretty thin, but I could see there were real muscles under that strange skin.

"He can do tricks, too," the young Tuscarora woman added. "He walks on his hands, and—"

The older woman grunted loudly. "He's bad luck, that's what he is. We've had nothing but trouble since he came. Look at us now."

I passed all this along to Bigkiller. "I don't know," he said. "I was going to kill him, but maybe I should keep him as a slave. After all, what other war chief among the People has a white slave?"

A woman's voice said, "What's going on here?"

I didn't turn around. I didn't have to. There was no one in our town who would not have known that voice. Suddenly everyone got very quiet.

My sister Tsigeyu came through the crowd, everyone moving quickly out of her way, and stopped in front of the white man. She looked him up and down and he looked back at her, still smiling, as if pleased to meet her. That showed real courage. Naturally he had no way of knowing that she was the Clan Mother of the Wolf Clan—which, if you don't know, means she was by far the most powerful person in our town—but just the sight of her would have made most people uneasy. Tsigeyu was a big woman, not fat but big like a big man, with a face like a limestone cliff. And eyes that went right through you and made your bones go cold. She died a couple of years ago, but at the time I am telling about she was still in the prime of life, and such gray hairs as she had she wore like eagle feathers.

She said, "For me? Why, thank you, Bigkiller."

Bigkiller opened his mouth and shut it. Tsigeyu was the only living creature he feared. He had more reason than most, since she was his mother.

Muskrat muttered something about having the right to kill the prisoner for having injured him.

Tsigeyu looked at Muskrat. Muskrat got a few fingers shorter, or that was how it looked. But after a moment she said, "It is true you are the nearest thing to a wounded warrior among this brave little war party." She gestured at the young Tuscarora woman. "So I think you should get to keep this girl, here."

Muskrat looked a good deal happier.

"The rest of you can decide among yourselves who gets the other woman, and the boy." Tsigeyu turned to me. "My brother, I want you to take charge of this white man for now. Try to teach him to speak properly. You can do it if anyone can."

KNOWE ALL ENGLISH AND OTHER CHRISTIAN MEN:

That I an Englishman and Subjeckt of Her Maiestie Queene *Elizabeth*, did by Misadventure come to this country of *Virginnia* in the Yeere of Our Lord 1591: and after greate Hardshipp arriued amongst these *Indians*. Who haue done me no Harme, but rather shew'd me most exelent Kindnesse, sans the which I were like to haue dyed in this Wildernesse. Wherefore, good Frend, I coniure you, that you offer these poore Sauages no Offence, nor do them Iniurie: but rather vse them generously and iustly, as they haue me.

Look at this. Did you ever see the like? He made these marks himself on this deerskin, using a sharpened turkey feather and some black paint that he cooked up from burned wood and oak galls. And he told me to keep it safe, and that if other white men came this way I should show it to them, and it would tell them his story.

Yes, I suppose it must be like a wampum belt, in a way. Or those little pictures and secret marks that the wise elders of the Leni Lenapes use to record their tribe's history. So clearly he was some sort of *didahnvwisgi*, a medicine man, even though he did not look old enough to have received such an important teaching.

He was always making these little marks, scratching away on whatever he could get—skins, mostly, or mulberry bark. People thought he was crazy, and I let them, because if they had known the truth not even Tsigeyu could have saved him from being killed for a witch.

But all that came later, during the winter, after he had begun to learn our language and I his. On that first day I was only interested in getting him away from that crowd before there was more trouble. I could see that Otter was working himself up to make one of his speeches, and if nothing else that meant there was a danger of being talked to death.

Inside my house I gave the stranger a gourd of water. When he had eased his thirst I pointed to myself. "Mouse," I said, very slowly and carefully. *"Tsis-de-tsi."*

He was quick. *"Tsisdetsi,"* he repeated. He got the tones wrong, but it was close enough for a beginning.

I held my hands up under my chin like paws, and pulled my upper lip back to show my front teeth, and crossed my eyes. I waggled one hand behind me to represent a long tail. *"Tsisdetsi",* I said again.

He laughed out loud. *"Tsisdetsi,"* he said. *"Mus!"*

He raised his hand and stroked his face for a moment, as if thinking of something. Then without warning he turned and grabbed my best war spear off the wall. My bowels went loose, but he made no move to attack me. Instead he began shaking the weapon above his head with one hand, slapping himself on the chest with the other. *"Tsagspa,"* he cried. *"Tsagspa."*

Crazy as a dog on a hot day, I thought at first. They must have hit him too hard. Then I realized what was happening, and felt almost dizzy. It is no small honor when any man tells you his secret war name—but a stranger, and a prisoner!

"Digatsisdi atelvhvsgo'i," I said, when I could finally speak. "Shakes Spear!"

> I am him that was call'd William *Shakspere,* of *Stratford-vpon-Auon,* late of *London*: a Player, of Lord *Strange* his Company, and thereby hangs a Tale.

Look there, where I am pointing. That is his name! He showed me that, and he even offered to teach me how to make the marks for my own. Naturally I refused—think what an enemy could do with something like that!

When I pointed this out, he laughed and said I might be right. For, he said, many a man of his sort had had bad luck with other people making use of his name.

> It hapt that our Company was in *Portsmouth*, hauing beene there engaug'd: but then were forbid to play, the Mayor and Corporation of that towne being of the *Puritann* perswasion. For which cause we were left altogether bankrupt: so that some of our Players did pawne their Cloathing for monny to return Home.

Perhaps someone had cursed him, since he sometimes said that he had never meant to leave his own country. It was the fault of the Puritans, he said. He did not explain what this meant, but once he mentioned that his wife and her family were Puritans. So obviously this is simply the name of his wife's clan. Poor fellow, no wonder he left home. The same thing happened to an uncle of mine. When your wife's clan decides to get rid of you, you don't have a chance.

> But I, being made foolish by strong Drinke, did conceive to hyde my selfe on a Ship bownd for *London*. Which did seeme a good Idea at the Time: but when I enquyr'd of some sea-faring men, they shewed me (in rogue Jest, or else mayhap I misconstrew'd their Reply, for I was in sooth most outragiosly drunk) the *Moonlight*, which lay at the Docke. And so by night I stole aboord, and hid my selfe vnder a Boate: wherevpon the Wine did rush to my heade, and I fell asleepe, and wak'd not till the Morrow: to

finde the Ship at sea and vnder Sayle, and the morning Sun at her backe.

Naturally it was a long time before we could understand each other well enough to discuss such things. Not as long as you might think, though. To begin with, I discovered that in fact he had picked up quite a bit of Tuscarora—pretending, like any smart captive, to understand less than he did. Besides that, he was a fast learner. You know that languages are my special medicine—I have heard them say that Mouse can talk to a stone, and get it to talk back—but Spearshaker was gifted too. By the time of the first snow, we could get along fairly well, in a mixture of his language and mine. And when words failed, he could express almost any idea, even tell a story, just by the movements of his hands and body and the expression of his face. That in itself was worth seeing.

> When I was discouer'd the Master was most wroth, and commanded that I be put to the hardest Labours, and giuen onely the poorest leauings for food. So it went hard for me on that Voyage: but the Saylors learn'd that I could sing diuers Songs, and new Ballads from *London,* and then I was vsed better. Anon the Captaine, Mr. Edward *Spicer,* ask'd whether I had any skill in Armes. To which I reply'd, that a Player must needs be a Master of Fence, and of all other Artes martiall, forasmuch as we are wont to play Battles, Duelles, Murthers &c. And the Captaine said, that soone I should haue Opportunity to proue my selfe against true Aduersaries and not in play, for we sayl'd for the *Spanish Maine.*

All this time, you understand, there was a great deal of talk concerning the white man. Most of the people came to like him, for he was a friendly fellow and a willing worker. And the Tuscarora girl was certainly right about his singing and dancing.

Even Bigkiller had to laugh when Spearshaker went leaping and capering around the fire, and when he walked on his hands and clapped his feet together several women wet themselves—or so I heard. His songs were strange to the ear, but enjoyable. I remember one we all liked:

> *"Wid-a-he*
> *An-a-ho*
> *An-a-he-na-ni-no!"*

But not everyone was happy about his presence among us. Many of the young men were angry that the women liked him so well, and now and then took him aside to prove it. And old Otter told everyone who would listen that once, long ago, a great band of white men had come up from the south, from the Timucua country, and destroyed the finest towns of the Maskogis, taking many away for slaves and killing the others. And this was true, because when the People moved south they found much of that country empty and ruined.

Spearshaker said that those people were of another tribe, with which his own nation was at war. But not everyone believed him, and Otter kept insisting that white men were simply too dangerous to have around. I began to fear for Spearshaker's life.

> At length we came vnto the *Indies*, being there joyn'd by the *Hopewell* and otherShips whose names I knowe not. And we attack'd the Spanish Convoy, and took the Galleon *Buen Jesus*, a rich Pryze: and so it came to pass that Will *Shakspeare*, Actor, did for his greate folly turn Pyrat vpon the salt Sea.

Then, early next spring, the Catawbas came.

This was no mere raid. They came in force and they hit us fast and hard, killing or capturing many of the people working in the fields before they could reach the town palisade. They rushed out of the woods and swarmed over the palisade like ants; and before we knew it we were fighting for our lives in front of our own houses.

That was when Spearshaker astonished us all. Without hesitating, he grabbed a long pole from the meat-drying racks and went after the nearest Catawba with it, jabbing him hard in the guts with the end, exactly as you would use a spear, and then clubbing him over the head. Then he picked up the Catawba's bow and began shooting.

My friend, I have lived long and seen much, but I never was more surprised than that morning. This pale, helpless creature, who could not chip an arrowhead or build a proper fire or even take five steps off a trail without getting lost—he cut those Catawbas down like rotten cornstalks! He shot one man off the palisade, right over there, from clear down by the council house. I do not think he wasted a single shot. And when he was out of arrows, he picked up a war club from a fallen warrior and joined the rest of us in fighting off the remaining attackers.

Afterward, he seemed not to think he had done anything remarkable. He said that all the men of his land know stick-fighting and archery, which they learn as boys. "I could have done better," he said, "with a long bow, and some proper arrows, from my own country." And he looked sad, as he always did when he spoke of his home.

From that day there was no more talk against Spearshaker. Not long after, Tsigeyu announced that she was adopting him. Since this also made him Bigkiller's brother, he was safe from anyone in our town. It also made me his uncle, but he was kind enough never to call me *edutsi*. We were friends.

> Next we turn'd north for *Virginnia*, Capt. *Spicer* hauing a Commission from Sir Walter *Ralegh* to calle vpon the English that dwelt at *Roanoke*, to discouer their condition. The Gales were cruel all along that Coast, and we were oft in grave Peril: but after much trauail we reached *Hatarask*, where the Captaine sent a party in small Boates, to search out the passage betweene the Islands.

> And whilst we were thus employ'd, a sudden
> greate Wind arose and scattered the Boates, many
> being o'erturned and the Mariners drown'd. But
> the Boate I was in was carry'd many Leagues
> westward, beyond sight of our Fellowes: so we
> were cast vpon the Shore of the Maine, and
> sought shelter in the Mouthe of a Riuer. Anon,
> going ashore, we were attack'd by Sauages: and
> all the men were slaine, save onely my selfe.

Poor fellow, he was still a long way from home, and small
chance of ever seeing his own people again. At least he was
better off than he had been with the Tuscaroras. Let alone those
people on the coast, if they had caught him. Remember the
whites who tried to build a town on that island north of
Wococon, and how Powhatan had them all killed?

> Yet hauing alone escap'd, and making my way
> for some dayes along the Riuer, I was surprized
> by *Indians* of another Nation: who did giue me
> hard vsage, as a Slaue, for well-nigh a Yeere.
> Vntil I was taken from them by these mine
> present sauage Hostes: amongst which, for my
> Sinnes, I am like to liue out my mortall dayes.

I used to have a big pile of these talking skins of his. Not that I
ever expected to have a chance to show them to anyone who
could understand them—I can't believe the white men will ever
come up into the hill country; they seem to have all they can do
just to survive on the coast—but I kept them to remember
Spearshaker by.

But the bugs and the mice got into them, and the bark
sheets went moldy in the wet season, and now I have only this
little bundle. And, as you see, some of these are no more than
bits and pieces. Like this worm-eaten scrap:

as concerning these *Indians* (for so men call
them: but if this be the Lande of *India* I am an
Hebrewe *Iewe*) they are in their owne Tongue
clept *Anni-yawia*. Which is, being interpreted, the
True or Principall People. By other Tribes they
are named *Chelokee:* but the meaning of this
word my frend Mouse knoweth not, neyther
whence deriued. They

I think one reason he spent so much time on his talking marks
was that he was afraid he might forget his own language. I have
seen this happen, with captives. That Tuscarora woman who was
with him still lives here, and by now she can barely speak ten
words of Tuscarora. Though Muskrat will tell you that she
speaks our language entirely too well—but that is another story.

Spearshaker did teach me quite a lot of his own
language—a very difficult one, unlike any I ever encountered—
and I tried to speak it with him from time to time, but it can't
have been the same as talking with a man of his own kind. What
does it sound like? Ah, I remember so little now. Let me see. . .
"*Holt dai tong, dow hor-son nabe!*" That means, "Shut up, you
fool!"

He told me many stories about his native land and its
marvels. Some I knew to be true, having heard of them from the
coast folk: the great floating houses that spread their wings like
birds to catch the wind, and the magic weapons that make
thunder and lightning. Others were harder to believe, such as his
tales about the woman chief of his tribe. Not a clan mother, but a
real war chief, like Bigkiller or even Powhatan, and so powerful
that any man—even an elder or a leading warrior—can lose his
life merely for speaking against her.

He also claimed that the town he came from was so big
that it held more people than all of the People's towns put
together. That is of course a lie, but you can't blame a man for
bragging on his own tribe.

But nothing, I think, was as strange as the *plei.*

Forgive me for using a word you do not know. But as far as I know there is no word in your language for what I am talking about. Nor in ours, and this is because the thing it means has never existed among our peoples. I think the Creator must have given this idea only to the whites, perhaps to compensate them for their poor sense of direction and that skin that burns in the sun.

It all began one evening, at the beginning of his second winter with us, when I came in from a council meeting and found him sitting by the fire, scratching away on a big sheet of mulberry bark. Just to be polite I said, *"Gado hadvhne?* What are you doing?"

Without looking up he said in his own language, *"Raiting a plei."*

Now I knew what the first part meant; *rai-ting* is what the whites call it when they make those talking marks. But I had never heard the last word before, and I asked what it meant.

Spearshaker laid his turkey feather aside and sat up and looked at me. "Ah, Mouse," he said, "how can I make you understand? This will be hard even for you."

I sat down on the other side of the fire. "Try," I said.

O what a fond and Moone-struck fool am I! Hath the aire of *Virginnia* addl'd my braine? Or did an Enemy smite me on the heade, and I knewe it not? For here in this wilde country, where e'en the Artes of letters are altogether unknowne, I haue begun the writing of a Play. And sure it is I shall neuer see it acted, neyther shall any other man: wherefore 'tis Lunacy indeede. Yet me thinkes if I do it not, I am the more certain to go mad: for I find my selfe growing more like vnto these *Indians*, and I feare I may forget what manner of man I was. Therefore the Play's the thing, whereby Ile saue my Minde by intentionall folly: forsooth, there's Method in my Madnesse.

Well, he was right. He talked far into the night, and the more he talked the less I understood. I asked more questions than a rattlesnake has scales, and the answers only left me more confused. It was a long time before I began to see it.

Didn't you, as a child, pretend you were a warrior or a chief or maybe a medicine man, and make up stories and adventures for yourself? And your sisters had dolls that they gave names to, and talked to, and so on?

Or . . . let me try this another way. Don't your people have dances, like our Bear Dance, in which a man imitates some sort of animal? And don't your warriors sometimes dance around the fire acting out their own deeds, showing how they killed men or sneaked up on an enemy town—and maybe making it a little better than it really happened? Yes, it is the same with us.

Now this *plei* thing is a little like those dances, and a little like the pretending of children. A group of people dress up in fancy clothes and pretend to be other people, and pretend to do various things, and in this way they tell a story.

Yes, grown men. Yes, right up in front of everybody.

But understand, this isn't a dance. Well, there is some singing and dancing, but mostly they just talk. And gesture, and make faces, and now and then pretend to kill each other. They do a lot of that last. I guess it is something like a war dance at that.

You'd be surprised what can be done in this way. A man like Spearshaker, who really knows how—*ak-ta* is what they are called—can make you see almost anything. He could imitate a man's expression and voice and way of moving—or a woman's—so well you'd swear he had turned into that person. He could make you think he was Bigkiller, standing right there in front of you, grunting and growling and waving his war club. He could do Blackfox's funny walk; or Locust wiggling his eyebrows, or Tsigeyu crossing her arms and staring at somebody she didn't like. He could even be Muskrat and his Tuscarora woman arguing, changing back and forth and doing both voices, till I laughed so hard my ribs hurt.

Now understand this. These *akta* people don't just make up their words and actions as they go along, as children or dancers do. No, the whole story is already known to them, and each *akta* has words that must be said, and things that must be done, at exactly the right times. You may be sure this takes a good memory. They have as much to remember as the Master of the Green Corn Dance.

And so, to help them, one man puts the whole thing down in those little marks. Obviously this is a very important job, and Spearshaker said that it was only in recent times, two or three winters before leaving his native land, that he himself had been accounted worthy of this honor. Well, I had known he was a *didahnvwisgi*, but I hadn't realized he was of such high rank.

> I first purpos'd to compose some pretty conceited
> Comedy, like vnto my *Loue's Labour's Lost*: but
> alas, me seemes my Wit hath dry'd vp from
> Misfortune. Then I bethought my selfe of the Play
> of the Prince of *Denmark*, by Thomas *Kyd*: which
> I had been employ'd in reuising for our Company
> not long ere we departed *London*, and had oft said
> to Richard *Burbage*, that I trow I could write a
> Better. And so I haue commenced, and praye God
> I may compleat, my owne Tragedie of Prince
> *Hamlet.*

I asked what sort of stories his people told in this curious manner. That is something that always interests me—you can learn a lot about any tribe from their stories. Like the ones the Maskogis tell about Rabbit, or our own tale about the Thunder Boys, or—you know.

I don't know what I was thinking. By then I should have known that white people do *everything* differently from everyone else in the world.

First he started to tell me about a dream somebody had on a summer night. That sounded good, but then it turned out to be about the Little People! Naturally I stopped him fast, and I told him that we do not talk about . . . *them*. I felt sorry for the poor man who dreamed about them, but there was no helping him now.

Then Spearshaker told me a couple of stories about famous chiefs of his own tribe. I couldn't really follow this very well, partly because I knew so little about white laws and customs, but also because a lot of their chiefs seemed to have the same name. I never did understand whether there were two different chiefs named *Ritsad,* or just one with a very strange nature.

The oddest thing, though, was that none of these stories seemed to have any *point*. They didn't tell you why the moon changes its face, or how the People were created, or where the mountains came from, or where the raccoon got his tail, or anything. They were just . . . *stories*. Like old women's gossip.

Maybe I missed something.

~~To liue, or not to liue, there lyes the~~

~~To liue, or dye? Shall I~~

~~To dye, or~~

~~To be, or what? It~~

He certainly worked hard at his task. More often than not, I could hear him grinding his teeth and muttering to himself as he sat hunched over his marks. And now and then he would jump up and throw the sheet to the ground and run outside in the snow and the night wind, and I would hear him shouting in his own language. At least I took it to be his language, though the words were not among those I knew. Part of his medicine, no doubt, so I said nothing.

God's Teethe! Haue I beene so long in this Wildernesse, that I haue forgot all Skill?   I that could bombast out a lyne of blank Uerse as readily as a Fishe doth swimm, now fumble for

Wordes like a Drunkard who cannot finde his
owne Cod-peece with both Handes.

I'm telling you, it was a *long* winter.

> For who would thus endure the Paines of time:
> To-morrow and to-morrow and to-morrow,
> That waite in patient and most grim Array,
> Each arm'd with Speares and Arrowes of Misfortune,
> Like *Indians* ambuscaded in the Forest?
> But that the dread of something after Death,
> That vndiscouered country, from whose Shores
> No Traueller returnes, puzzels the Will,
> And makes vs rather beare that which we knowe
> Than wantonly embarke for the Vnknowne.

One evening, soon after the snows began to melt, I noticed that
Spearshaker was not at his usual nightly work. He was just
sitting there staring into the fire, not even looking at his skins
and bark sheets, which were stacked beside him. The turkey
feathers and black paint were nowhere in sight.

I said, "Is something wrong?" and then it came to me.
"Finished?"

He let out a long sigh. "Yes," he said. *"Mo ful ai,"* he
added, which was something he often said, though I never quite
got what it meant.

It was easy to see he was feeling bad. So I said; "Tell me
the story."

He didn't want to, but finally he told it to me. He got
pretty worked up as he went along, sometimes jumping up to act
out an exciting part, till I thought he was going to wreck my
house. Now and then he picked up a skin or mulberry-bark sheet
and spoke the words, so I could hear the sound. I had thought I
was learning his language pretty well, but I couldn't understand
one word in ten.

But the story itself was clear enough. There were parts I didn't follow but on the whole it was the best he'd ever told me. At the end I said, "Good story."

He tilted his head to one side, like a bird. "Truly?"

"*Doyu*," I said. I meant it, too.

He sighed again and picked up his pile of *raiting*. "I am a fool," he said.

I saw that he was about to throw the whole thing into the fire, so I went over and took it from him. "This is a good thing," I told him. "Be proud."

"Why?" He shrugged his shoulders. "Who will ever see it? Only the bugs and the worms. And the mice," he added, giving me his little smile.

I stood there, trying to think of something to make him feel better. Ninekiller's oldest daughter had been making eyes at Spearshaker lately and I wondered if I should go get her. Then I looked down at what I was holding in my hands and it came to me.

"My friend," I said, "I've got an idea. Why don't we put on your *plei* right here?"

And now is Lunacy compownded vpon Lunacy, *Bedlam* pyled on *Bedlam*: for I am embark'd on an Enterprize, the like of which this Globe hath neuer seene. Yet Ile undertake this Foolery, and flynch not: mayhap it will please these People, who are become my onely Frends. They shall haue of Will his best will.

It sounded simple when I heard myself say it. Doing it was another matter. First, there were people to be spoken with.

We *Aniyvwiya* like to keep everything loose and easy. Our chiefs have far less authority than yours, and even the power of the clan mothers has its limits. Our laws are few, and everyone knows what they are, so things tend to go along without much trouble.

But there were no rules for what we wanted to do, because it had never been done before. Besides, we were going to need the help of many people. So it seemed better to go carefully—but I admit I had no idea that our little proposal would create such a stir. In the end there was a regular meeting at the council house to talk it over.

Naturally it was Otter who made the biggest fuss. "This is white men's medicine," he shouted. "Do you want the People to become as weak and useless as the whites?"

"If it will make all our warriors shoot as straight as Spearshaker," Bigkiller told him, "then it might be worth it."

Otter waved his skinny old arms. He was so angry by now that his face was whiter than Spearshaker's. "Then answer this," he said. "How is it that this dance—"

"It's not a dance," I said. Usually I would not interrupt an elder in council, but if you waited for Otter to finish you might be there all night.

"Whatever you call it," he said, "it's close enough to a dance to be Bird Clan business, right? And you, Mouse, are Wolf Clan—as is your white friend, by adoption. So you have no right to do this thing."

Old Dotsuya spoke up. She was the Bird Clan Mother, and the oldest person present. Maybe the oldest in town, now I think of it.

"The Bird Clan has no objection," she said. "Mouse and Spearshaker have our permission to put on their *plei*. Which I, for one, would like to see. Nothing ever happens around this town."

Tsigeyu spoke next. *"Howa,"* she said. "I agree. This sounds interesting."

Of course Otter wasn't willing to let it go so easily; he made quite a speech, going all the way back to the origins of the People and predicting every kind of calamity if this sacrilege was permitted. It didn't do him much good, though. No one liked Otter, who had gotten both meaner and longer-winded with age, and who had never been a very good *didahnvwisgi* anyway. Besides, half the people in the council house were asleep long before he was done.

After the council gave its approval there was no trouble getting people to help. Rather we had more help than we needed. For days there was a crowd hanging around my house, wanting to be part of the *plei*. Bigkiller said if he could get that many people to join a war party, he could take care of the Catawbas for good.

And everyone wanted to be an *akta*. We were going to have to turn some people away, and we would have to be careful how we did it, or there would be trouble. I asked Spearshaker how many *aktas* we needed. "How many men, that is," I added, as he began counting on his fingers. "The women are a different problem."

He stopped counting and stared at me as if I were wearing owl feathers. Then he told me something so shocking you will hardly believe it. In his country, the women in a *plei* are actually *men wearing women's clothes!*

I told him quick enough that the People don't go in for that sort of thing—whatever they may get up to in certain other tribes—and he'd better not even talk about it around here. Do you know, he got so upset that it took me the rest of the day to talk him out of calling the whole thing off. . . .

> Women! Mercifull *Jesu*! Women, on a Stage, acting in a Play! I shall feele like an Whore-Master!

Men or women, it was hard to know which people to choose. None of them had ever done anything like this before, so there was no way to know whether they would be any good or not. Spearshaker asked me questions about each person, in white language so no one would be offended: Is he quick to learn? Does he dance or sing well? Can he work with other people, and do as he is told? And he had them stand on one side of the stickball field, while he stood on the other, and made them speak their names and clans, to learn how well their voices carried.

I had thought age would come into it, since the *plei* included both older and younger people. But it turned out that

Spearshaker knew an art of painting a man's face, and putting white in his hair, till he might be mistaken for his own grandfather.

No doubt he could have done the same with women, but that wasn't necessary. There were only two women's parts in this story, and we gave the younger woman's part to Ninekiller's daughter Cricket—who would have hung upside-down in a tree like a possum if it would please Spearshaker—and the older to a cousin of mine, about my age, who had lost her husband to the Shawanos and wanted something to do.

For those who could not be *aktas*, there was plenty of other work. A big platform had to be built, with space cleared around it, and log benches for the people who would watch. There were torches to be prepared, since we would be doing it at night, and special clothes to be made, as well as things like fake spears so no one would get hurt. Locust and Blackfox were particularly good workers; Spearshaker said it was as if they had been born for this. They even told him that if he still wanted to follow the custom of his own tribe, with men dressed as women, they would be willing to take those parts. Well, I always had wondered about those two.

But Spearshaker was working harder than anyone else. Besides being in charge of all the other preparations, he had to remake his whole *plei* to suit our needs. No doubt he had made a fine *plei* for white men, but for us, as it was, it would never do.

> Many a Play haue I reuis'd and amended: cut short or long at the Company's desyre, or alter'd this or that Speeche to please a Player: e'en carued the very Guttes out of a scene on command of the Office of the Reuels, for some imagin'd Sedition or vnseemely Speeche. But now must I out-do all I euer did before, in the making of my *Hamlet* into a thing comprehensible to the *Anni-yawia*. Scarce is there a line which doth not haue to be rewrit: yea, and much ta'en out intire: as, the Play within the Play, which *Mouse* saith, that none here will

vnderstande. And the Scene must be moued from *Denmark* to *Virginnia*, and *Elsinore Castle* transformed into an *Indian* towne. For marry, it were Alchemy enow that I should transmute vnletter'd Sauages into tragick Actors: but to make royal *Danskers* of swart-fac'd *Indians* were beyond all Reason.

(Speak'st thou now of Reason, Will Shakespere? Is't not ouer-late for that?)

You should have seen us teaching the *aktas* their parts. First Spearshaker would look at the marks and say the words in his language. Then he would explain to me any parts I hadn't understood—which was most of it, usually—and then I would translate the whole thing for the *akta* in our language. Or as close as I could get; there are some things you cannot really interpret. By now Spearshaker was fluent enough to help me.

Then the *akta* would try to say the words back to us, almost always getting it all wrong and having to start again. And later on all the people in the *plei* had to get together and speak their parts in order, and do all the things they would do in the *plei,* and that was like a bad dream. Not only did they forget their words; they bumped into each other and stepped on each other's feet, and got carried away in the fight parts and nearly killed each other. And Spearshaker would jump up and down and pull his hair—which had already begun to fall out, for some reason—and sometimes weep, and when he had settled down we would try again.

Verily, my lot is harder than that of the *Iewes* of *Moses.* For Scripture saith, that *Pharo* did command that they make Brickes without Strawe, wherefore their trauail was greate: but now I must make my Brickes, euen without Mudd.

Let me tell you the story of Spearshaker's *plei.*

Once there was a great war chief who was killed by his own brother. Not in a fight, but secretly, by poison. The brother took over as chief, and also took his dead brother's woman, who didn't object.

But the dead man had a son, a young warrior named Amaledi. One night the dead chief appeared to Amaledi and told him the whole story. And, of course, demanded that he do something about it.

Poor Amaledi was in a bad fix. Obviously he mustn't go against his mother's wishes, and kill her new man without her permission. On the other hand, no one wants to anger a ghost—and this one was plenty angry already.

So Amaledi couldn't decide what to do. To make things worse, the bad brother had guessed that Amaledi knew something. He and this really nasty, windy old man named Quolonisi—sounds like Otter—began trying to get rid of Amaledi.

To protect himself Amaledi became a Crazy, doing and saying everything backward, or in ways that made no sense. This made his medicine strong enough to protect him from his uncle and Quolonisi, at least for a time.

Quolonisi had a daughter, Tsigalili, who wanted Amaledi for her man. But she didn't want to live with a Crazy—who does?—and she kept coming around and crying and begging him to quit. At the same time his mother was giving him a hard time for being disrespectful toward her new man. And all the while the ghost kept showing up and yelling at Amaledi for taking so long. It got so bad Amaledi thought about killing himself, but then he realized that he would go to the spirit world, where his father would *never* leave him alone.

So Amaledi thought of a plan. There was a big dance one night to honor the new chief, and some visiting singers from another town were going to take part. Amaledi took their lead singer aside and got him to change the song, telling him the new words had been given to him in a dream. And that night, with the dancers going around the fire and the women shaking the turtle shells and the whole town watching, the visiting leader sang:

"Now he pours it,
Now he is pouring the poison,
See, there are two brothers,
See, now there is one."

That was when it all blew up like a hot rock in a fire. The bad chief jumped up and ran away from the dance grounds, afraid he had just been witched. Amaledi had a big argument with his mother and told her what he thought of the way she was acting. Then he killed Quolonisi. He said it was an accident but I think he was just tired of listening to the old fool.

Tsigalili couldn't stand any more. She jumped into a waterfall and killed herself. There was a fine funeral.

Now Amaledi was determined to kill his uncle. The uncle was just as determined to kill Amaledi, but he was too big a coward to do it himself. So he got Quolonisi's son Panther to call Amaledi out for a fight.

Panther was a good fighter and he was hot to kill Amaledi, because of his father and his sister. But the chief wasn't taking any chances. He put some poison on Panther's spear. He also had a gourd of water, with poison in it, in case nothing else worked.

So Amaledi and Panther painted their faces red and took their spears and faced each other, right in front of the chief's house. Amaledi was just as good as Panther, but finally he got nicked on the arm. Before the poison could act, they got into some hand-to-hand wrestling, and the spears got mixed up. Now Panther took a couple of hits. Yes, with the poisoned spear.

Meanwhile Amaledi's mother got thirsty and went over and took a drink, before anyone could stop her, from the poisoned gourd. Pretty soon she fell down. Amaledi and Panther stopped fighting and rushed over, but she was already dead.

By now they were both feeling the poison themselves. Panther fell down and died. So did Amaledi, but before he went down he got his uncle with the poisoned spear. So in the end everyone died.

You do?

Well, I suppose you had to be there.

And so 'tis afoote: to-morrow night we are to
perform. Thank God *Burbage* cannot be there to
witnesse it: for it were a Question which should
come first, that he dye of Laughter, or I of Shame.

It was a warm and pleasant night. Everyone was there, even
Otter. By the time it was dark all the seats were full and many
people were standing, or sitting on the ground.

The platform had only been finished a few days before—
with Bigkiller complaining about the waste of timber and labor,
that could have gone into strengthening the town's defenses—
and it looked very fine. Locust and Blackfox had hung some
reed mats on poles to represent the walls of houses, and also to
give us a place to wait out of sight before going on. To keep the
crowd from getting restless, Spearshaker had asked Dotsuya to
have some Bird Clan men sing and dance while we were lighting
the torches and making other last preparations.

Then it was time to begin.

What? Oh, no, I was not an *akta*. By now I knew the
words to the whole *plei*, from having translated and repeated
them so many times. So I stood behind a reed screen and called
out the words, in a voice too low for the crowd to hear, when
anyone forgot what came next.

Spearshaker, yes. He was the ghost. He had put some
paint on his face that made it even whiter, and he did something
with his voice that made the hair stand up on your neck.

But in fact everyone did very well, much better than I
had expected. The only bad moment came when Amaledi—that
was Tsigeyu's son Hummingbird—shouted, *"Na! Dili, dili!"*—
"There! A skunk, a skunk!"—and slammed his war club into the
wall of the "chief's house," forgetting it was really just a reed
mat. And Beartrack, who was being Quolonisi, took such a blow
to the head that he was out for the rest of the *plei*. But it didn't
matter, since he had no more words to speak, and he made a very
good dead man for Amaledi to drag out.

And the people loved it, all of it. How they laughed and laughed! I never heard so many laugh so hard for so long. At the end, when Amaledi fell dead between his mother and Panther and the platform was covered with corpses, there was so much howling and hooting you would have taken it for a hurricane. I looked out through the mats and saw Tsigeyu and Bigkiller holding on to each other to keep from falling off the bench. Warriors were wiping tears from their eyes and women were clutching themselves between the legs and old Dotsuya was lying on the ground kicking her feet like a baby.

I turned to Spearshaker, who was standing beside me. "See," I said. "And you were afraid they wouldn't understand it!"

After that everything got confused for a while. Locust and Blackfox rushed up and dragged Spearshaker away, and the next time I saw him he was down in front of the platform with Tsigeyu embracing him and Bigkiller slapping him on the back. I couldn't see his face, which was hidden by Tsigeyu's very large front.

By then people were making a fuss over all of us. Even me. A Paint Clan woman, not bad-looking for her age, took me away, for some attention. She was limber and had a lot of energy, so it was late by the time I finally got home.

Spearshaker was there, sitting by the fire. He didn't look up when I came in. His face was so pale I thought at first he was still wearing his ghost paint.

I said, "*Gusdi nusdi?* Is something wrong?"

"They laughed," he said. He didn't sound happy about it.

"They laughed," I agreed. "They laughed as they have never laughed before, every one of them. Except for Otter, and no one has *ever* seen him laugh."

I sat down beside him. "You did something fine tonight, Spearshaker. You made the People happy. They have a hard life, and you made them laugh."

He made a snorting sound. "Yes. They laughed to see us making fools of ourselves. Perhaps that is good."

"No, no." I saw it now. "Is that what you think? That they laughed because we did the *plei* so badly?"

I put my hand on his shoulder and turned him to face me. "My friend, no one there tonight ever saw a *plei* before, except for you. How would they know if it was bad? It was certainly the best *plei* they ever saw."

He blinked slowly, like a turtle. I saw his eyes were red. "Believe me, Spearshaker," I told him, "they were laughing because it was such a funny story. And that was your doing."

His expression was very strange indeed. "They thought it comical?"

"Well, who wouldn't? All those crazy people up there, killing each other—and themselves—and then that part at the end, where *everyone* gets killed!" I had to stop and laugh, myself, remembering. "I tell you," I said when I had my breath back, "even though I knew the whole thing by memory, I nearly lost control of myself a few times there."

I got up. "Come, Spearshaker. You need to go to sleep. You have been working too hard."

But he only put his head down in his hands and made some odd sounds in his throat, and muttered some words I did not know. And so I left him there and went to bed.

If I live until the mountains fall, I will never understand white men.

> If I liue vntil our *Saviour's* returne, I shall neuer vnderstande *Indians*. Warre they count as Sport, and bloody Murther an occasion of Merriment: 'tis because they hold Life itselfe but lightly, and think Death no greate matter neyther: and so that which we call Tragick, they take for Comedie. And though I be damned for't, I cannot sweare that they haue not the Right of it.

Whatever happened that night, it changed something in Spearshaker. He lived with us for many more years, but never again did he make a *plei* for us.

That was sad, for we had all enjoyed the Amaledi story so much, and were hoping for more. And many people tried to get Spearshaker to change his mind—Tsigeyu actually begged him; I think it was the only time in her life she ever begged anyone for anything—but it did no good. He would not even talk about it.

And at last we realized that his medicine had gone, and we left him in peace. It is a terrible thing for a *didahnvwisgi* when his power leaves him. Perhaps his ancestors' spirits were somehow offended by our *plei*. I hope not, since it was my idea.

That summer Ninekiller's daughter Cricket became Spearshaker's wife. I gave them my house, and moved in with the Paint Clan woman. I visited my friend often, and we talked of many things, but of one thing we never spoke.

Cricket told me he still made his talking marks, from time to time. If he ever tried to make another *plei,* though, he never told anyone.

I believe it was five winters ago—it was not more— when Cricket came in one day and found him dead. It was a strange thing, for he had not been sick, and was still a fairly young man. As far as anyone knew there was nothing wrong with him, except that his hair had fallen out.

I think his spirit simply decided to go back to his native land.

Cricket grieved for a long time. She still has not taken another husband. Did you happen to see a small boy with pale skin and brown hair, as you came through our town? That is their son Wili.

Look what Cricket gave me. This is the turkey feather that was in Spearshaker's hand when she found him that day. And this is the piece of mulberry bark that was lying beside him. I will always wonder what it says.

> We are such stuff as Dreames are made on: and
> our little Life
>
> Is rounded in a sle

* * *

This is the one everybody made such a fuss about. It won the Sidewise Award for Alternate (sic) History and was shortlisted for the Nebula, the Hugo, and the Sturgeon. It has been anthologized again and again and people still mention it to me. In fact there are times when I wish I'd never written it; but then I remember those reprint-royalty checks that still come in each year.

A few historic notes:

Elizabethan spelling was fabulously irregular; the same person might spell the same word in various ways on a single page. Shakespeare's own spelling is known only from the Quarto and Folio printing of the plays, and the published poetry; and no one knows how close the published texts are to Shakespeare's original in wording, let alone spelling. All we have in his own hand is his signature, and this indicates that he spelled his own name differently almost every time he wrote it.

I have followed the spelling of the Folio for the most part, but felt free to use my own judgment and even whim, since that was what the original speller did.

I have, however, regularized spelling and punctuation to some extent, and modernized spelling and usage in some instances, so that the text would be readable. I assume the readers of this story are reasonably well-educated, but it seems unfair to expect them to be Elizabethan scholars.

Cherokee pronunciation is difficult to render in Roman letters. Even the syllabary system of writing, invented in the nineteenth century by Sequoyah, does not entirely succeed, as there is no way to indicate the tones and glottal stops. I have followed, more or less, the standard system of transliteration, in which "v" is used for the nasal grunting vowel that has no English equivalent.

It hardly matters, since we do not know how sixteenth-century Cherokees pronounced the language. The sounds have changed considerably in the century and a half since the forced march to Oklahoma; what they were like four hundred years ago is highly conjectural. So is the location of the various tribes of

Virginia and the Carolinas during this period; and, of course, so is their culture. (The Cherokee may not then have been the warlike tribe they later became—though, given the national penchant for names incorporating the verb "to kill", this is unlikely.) The Catawbas were a very old and hated enemy.

Edward Spicer's voyage to America to learn the fate of the Roanoke Colony—or rather his detour to Virginia after a successful privateering operation—did happen, including the bad weather and the loss of a couple of boats, though there is no record that any boat reached the mainland. The disappearance of the Roanoke colonists is a famous event. It is only conjecture—though based on considerable evidence, and accepted by many historians—that Powhatan had the colonists murdered, after they had taken sanctuary with a minor coastal tribe. Disney fantasies to the contrary, Powhatan was not a nice man.

I have accepted, for the sake of the story, the view of many scholars that Shakespeare first got the concept of Hamlet *in the process of revising Thomas Kyd's earlier play on the same subject. Thus he might well have had the general idea in his head as early as 1591—assuming as most do, that by this time he was employed with a regular theatrical company—even though the historic* Hamlet *is generally agreed to have been written considerably later.*

As to those who argue that William Shakespeare was not actually the author of Hamlet, *but that the plays were written by Francis Bacon or the Earl of Southampton or Elvis Presley, one can only reply:* Hah! *And again,* Hah!

Written February 1996
First published July 1997

Words And Music

Jimmy Hominy was fifty-four years old and had been a *didahnvwisgi*—what the whites called a shaman or medicine man; a lot of Cherokees said *adanvsgi*, wizard, and some said plainly *'sgili,* witch, though not to his face—for most of his adult life. He had also done a hitch in Nam, played guitar for Buck Owens on two national tours, and been married to a Kiowa woman, so all in all he figured he'd been around and not much could surprise him. But when the preacher from Limestone showed up at Jimmy's trailer out of Stick Ross Mountain Road and said his church house was being witched, Jimmy's chin dropped so far it nearly hit his chest.

"*Doyu?*" he said, rubbing a big callused hand over a face the color and texture of an old saddle. "Somebody's witching a church?"

"So they say," the preacher said. "You hadn't heard?"

"Hey," Jimmy Hominy said, "I stay clear of that end of the county. You go listening to those Indians down around Limestone, you're liable to hear anything."

He grinned at the preacher. "But then that's your job, right? Got to love all God's children. Even the ones he probably wishes he'd drowned, like the Sparrowhawk brothers. Better you than me, *chooch.*"

The preacher didn't return the grin. He was a bony-faced man somewhere in his forties, with a big nose and dark brown eyes. His thin straight black hair was combed forward in a failed effort to hide a hairline in full retreat, the inheritance of a white grandfather. He had on a really bad black suit.

His name was Eli Blackbird, but Jimmy Hominy usually thought of him simply as the preacher, because he was the only preacher Jimmy knew personally. Oh, every now and then some local Bible wrangler would come calling with the missionary light in his eyes—it would be a big coup to talk a notorious character like Jimmy Hominy into taking the Jesus road—but they didn't stay long enough to get acquainted.

But this one never got on Jimmy's case about following the old ways, or accused him of worshipping the Devil, and Jimmy had finally decided he was all right. Now here he was sitting at Jimmy's kitchen table with a story about the Sparrowhawk boys witching his church, and Jimmy didn't know what to think.

The preacher let out a long sigh and began fumbling in the pockets of his suit jacket. "I admit the Sparrowhawks aren't easy to love—"

He pulled out a black briar pipe and a plastic pouch and began cramming tobacco into the bowl, spilling a little blizzard of Prince Albert flakes in the process. Jimmy didn't say anything about it. The place was already in a mess anyway. Had been for a couple of years, ever since his wife died.

Jimmy said, "Yeah, Luther and Bobby Sparrowhawk been nothing but bullies and sneak thieves since they were kids. And yet their mama was a real fine lady."

The preacher nodded. "Oh, yes. Old Annie Sparrowhawk." He was fishing around in his pockets again. Jimmy pushed a box of wooden matches across the table. "Thanks . . . as a matter of fact, that's where the trouble began. Annie left that property to the church when she died, and her sons have been trying to get it back ever since."

He struck a match and applied it to his pipe. "Which," he said, puffing, "they can't do. Annie paid a lawyer to draw up a will, legal and airtight."

"What do they want with it? That rocky old land around Limestone's not worth anything. So damn poor the whites never even bothered to steal it."

"It is now," the preacher told him through a cloud of bluish smoke. "Word is some developer from Tulsa has plans for the area."

Jimmy thought about it. While he thought he held out his hand. "Uh, you think you could spare—"

The preacher handed over the tobacco pouch. Jimmy got his own pipe from his shirt pocket and loaded it and lit up. The preacher didn't notice that Jimmy didn't bother to use a match. Or if he did notice he pretended not to.

"Surprised they don't just burn you out," Jimmy said at last.

"They've made threats. But they're both on probation for assault as it is. Any rough stuff, they go to the pen. The sheriff already warned them."

"So now they're trying to witch you out. Wonder who they got to do it."

The preacher looked disappointed. He must have been hoping Jimmy would know who was doing the witching, or could find out. Probably thought people like Jimmy stayed in touch some way, like those white kids Jimmy's grandson was always talking with on his computer.

Jimmy said, "Could be they're trying to do it themselves. That's crazy, but then they're crazy."

"It's possible," the preacher agreed. "They do have a reputation for dabbling in, uh, the occult. And yet they both got religion last year. Bobby married a white girl from one of those holy-roller churches and now he and Luther are in there at every revival, shouting and speaking in tongues, even handling snakes."

"The snakes got my sympathy," Jimmy said sincerely.

He knew what the preacher was getting at. The boondocks holiness outfits were even stricter than other Indian churches when it came to "heathen" ways; some would kick you out just for going to stomp dances, let alone anything heavy.

But there was nothing so unusual about Cherokees trying to work both sides of that particular street. Almost all the people who came to Jimmy seeking cures for illness or protection against witchcraft or interpretations of dreams—he didn't do love charms—were solid members of Bible churches that officially condemned such things as the Devil's work. It was just something people didn't talk about.

Jimmy said, "I didn't think you preachers believed in these superstitions."

This time the preacher did grin. "That's the white half of me. The Indian half—" He spread his hands. "It doesn't really matter what I think. If the people believe the place is being witched, they'll stay away. You know that. Last Sunday we had half the usual turnout."

"So you thought if they heard you were bringing in your own *didahnvwisgi*—" Jimmy had to laugh. "Boy," he said, "now I've heard everything. The church asking a medicine man for help."

If the preacher minded being redassed he didn't let it show. He said, "Actually, I came to invite you to an all-night gospel singing. We're having one this Friday night."

Jimmy quit laughing. The preacher had hit one of his weak spots. He might be a long way outside the church, but he dearly loved Cherokee gospel music. Both his parents had been noted singers on the Oklahoma gospel scene; his older brother Clyde had sung with them, before running off to become a honky-tonk musician. Some of Jimmy's earliest memories were of all-night singings, and falling asleep in the back of the family pickup to the sound of gospel music coming through the trees.

He said, "Real old-fashioned Indian gospel? Not that fancy new crap, sounds like they're planning to go to Heaven in an elevator?"

The preacher nodded. "Should be a lot of good singers there."

"I thought you said people were staying away."

"They won't if they know you're going to be there."

Jimmy didn't know what to say to that.

"And," the preacher added, "the women are baking pies."

Jimmy groaned softly. Pie was his other weakness. "You got me," he said. "What time do you want me there?"

The preacher stood up. "Come by the house about seven." He was obviously trying hard not to look too pleased with himself. "We may as well go together."

"*Howa*," Jimmy agreed, getting up too. "You can tell them I'll be there."

Friday evening at almost exactly seven Jimmy Hominy stopped his old Mercury in front of Eli Blackbird's house near the tiny crossroads community of Limestone. The preacher came to the door as Jimmy stepped up on the porch. " *'Siyo, Jimi.*"

" *'Siyo, chooch.*" Jimmy nodded in the direction of the Mercury. "Let's take my car." He didn't want to ride in the preacher's little Japanese car, which was cramped and uncomfortable for a man his size and had screwy door latches besides.

"Sure." The preacher followed Jimmy out to the road and bent to open the Mercury's door. The dome light came on and he stopped, staring at the oversized guitar case lying in the back seat. "Bringing that thing?" he said. "Going to play, are you?"

"Could be," Jimmy said, going around to his side. "You never know."

The church was a small low concrete block building with no steeple or other identifying features except a four-by-eight plywood sign that read LIMESTONE INDEPENDENT INDIAN CHURCH. The words were repeated underneath in the curling black letters of the Cherokee alphabet.

Right now the building was dark except for a single bulb burning above the front door. The big grassy clearing beside the church, however, was lit by several floodlights rigged on poles or in the trees. A flatbed truck had been parked at the edge of the woods to serve as a stage, and two men were crouched on its bed doing something to a set of amplifiers, while a tall kid in a Seminole jacket fooled with the tuning knobs of an electric bass. Teenage boys were setting out rows of folding chairs. Other people stood or moved about the area, mostly near the long wooden tables where women served food on paper plates.

"I thought we'd have the singing outdoors," the preacher remarked as they got out of the Mercury. The dusty parking area was already half full of pickup trucks and heavy old cars. "Looks like a nice night for it."

It did. The sky was clear and full of fat white stars; a light warm breeze was coming through the woods, bringing various pleasant smells. It also carried the scent of blackberry pie from the tables. Jimmy's nose began to twitch.

"Well," the preacher said, "I better get up there." He gestured in the direction of the flatbed truck, where one of the men was now adjusting a floor-stand microphone. A brief horrible squeal came from the speakers. "Almost time."

When the preacher was gone Jimmy stood still for a moment, getting the feel of the scene. So far he couldn't detect anything wrong; at least the hair on his arms wasn't standing up, or his fingers tingling, or any of the other warning signs. If this place had been witched, it had been done very badly.

Or else, of course, it had been done very well.

He began to walk, staying in the shadows and avoiding people, making himself ignore the pie smell. As he neared the darkened church he started to pick up a certain vague sourness, like a single out-of-tune string. More curious than worried—whatever it was, it didn't feel dangerous—he moved closer.

He found it easily, under the front steps of the church: a little buckskin bundle, tied with rawhide. Dry things crunched and crackled as he rolled it in his hand. He didn't untie it; he knew pretty much what it contained. He walked back to his car and tossed the little bundle onto the front seat. Later, maybe, he would tie the bundle to a rock and drop it into a moving stream, and then whoever had made it would come down with severe chills for a week or so.

If this was the worst the Sparrowhawks could do, the preacher was worrying about nothing. Still, he was here now and he might as well do the job right.

He dug in his pockets and got out his short-stemmed pipe and the little bag of prepared tobacco, while up on the improvised stage Eli Blackbird commenced speaking into the microphone, welcoming the people who were now starting to drift over and take seats. The men behind him quit messing with the amps and began opening cases and getting out guitars.

Jimmy packed the tobacco carefully into the pipe, making sure not to spill a single flake. He did not sing or speak over the tobacco; there was no need. He had doctored the tobacco that morning, down by the banks of the little creek that ran behind his place, holding it up to the rising sun and stirring it with his forefinger, singing the appropriate *igawesdi* words, four times over. Now the tobacco was programmed, needing only to be burned to release its power.

He lit the tobacco and began walking, puffing. The preacher was now leading the crowd in "Amazing Grace":

> *"U-ne-hla-nv-hi U-we-ji*
> *I-ga-gu-yv-he-i—"*

Blowing smoke, Jimmy Hominy circled the church grounds counterclockwise, taking in the building and the singing area and even the two outhouses. The preacher began a prayer in Cherokee: *"Agidoda, galvladi ehi, galvquodiyu gesesdi dejado'a'i—"* He was still at it when Jimmy started around for the second time.

He circled the grounds four times, following carefully in his own tracks. He was aware of people looking at him—mostly sideways or behind his back—but nobody spoke to him, and the few people in his path suddenly found reasons to go stand somewhere else when they saw him coming.

At the end he knocked the ash out of the pipe and stood leaning on the Mercury's fender, listening to the music. The first group of the evening, the Gospel Travelers from Adair County, were hammering down hard on "I Will Not Live Always":

> *"U-tli-na-qua-du-li-hv ga-lv-la-di jo-sv-i,*
> *Ga-lo-ne-dv Ji-sa, u-wo-du-hi-yu,*
> *Da-ni-no-gi-sdi-sgv-i."*

Jimmy decided it was time to check out that blackberry pie.

It had been a good season for blackberries and two different women had just set out fresh pies as Jimmy came up to the table. Naturally he had to have a piece of each, so as not to hurt anybody's feelings. He was finishing the second piece when a voice behind him said, "'Siyo, Jimi. Jiyosihas'?"

Jimmy jumped and turned around. Idabel Grasshopper stood there, holding a big steaming pot. She said, "Want to try some of my chili, big boy?"

Jimmy had never considered that Idabel Grasshopper might show up. A lifelong member of Hogshooter Indian Baptist Church, she was a long way from home. But maybe she'd heard he was coming. Damn that preacher.

He said, "I think maybe your chili's too hot for me."

Idabel Grasshopper giggled and Jimmy made a note to kick himself in the ass, next time he felt limber enough, for encouraging her. As far back as he could remember, her two big goals in life had been to get Jimmy Hominy into the church and into her bed—preferably, but not necessarily, in that order. Change of life hadn't helped; in the last few years she'd just gotten holier and hornier. She'd also picked up about forty pounds and a Don Ameche mustache.

"And here you are at a gospel singing," she said. "Praise the Lord!"

"I just came to listen to the music," Jimmy mumbled. Damn that preacher.

"The music," she said severely, "doesn't mean a thing without the spirit. Now in Philippians two-ten it says—"

But Jimmy was no longer even pretending to listen. Over the top of her Brillo-pad perm, he had spotted the Sparrowhawk brothers coming across the parking area.

He hadn't seen either of them in years but they hadn't improved any in the ugly department. Luther, the older brother, seemed to have a few more facial scars, but otherwise there wasn't much difference between them; just a couple of lumpy, overgrown Indians, nearly as big as Jimmy, with hooky noses and eyes set way too close together.

All of a sudden, right at the edge of the grass, they stopped so hard they practically bounced.

Jimmy Hominy watched, ignoring Idabel, as they looked at each other and then tried again to cross the medicine line he had laid down. It was like watching a pair of big stupid birds flying into a plate-glass window.

Finally, looking pissed off, they turned and stomped back across the parking lot and got into a big pickup truck. A minute later they blasted out of the church grounds, throwing gravel. The crash of bad gear changes drifted back on the breeze as their lights disappeared up the road.

The preacher was standing over by the edge of the trees, smoking his pipe. "Did you see that?" he said as Jimmy came up. "Whatever you did, thanks—"

"Never mind that," Jimmy told him. "I'm going to kill you. That hooting sound you hear is the owl calling your name."

The preacher laughed softly. "Idabel's still after you?"

"'Big boy,'" Jimmy said, shuddering. "Nobody's called me that since Saigon."

Up on stage the Kingfisher Family were getting down with "Orphan Child:"

> *"Ja-ga-wi-yu-hi hna-quu ta-ti-hnu-ga di-je-na-sv*
> *Ju-no-ye-ni-quu de-hi-ni-yv-se-sdi ni-go-hi-lv."*

"Come on," the preacher said. "Let's get some coffee. Going to be a long night."

The night did take its time passing. Singers took their turns on stage, alone or by duets and trios and quartets, and most were at least reasonably good. Even the ones that weren't came off sounding fairly decent, thanks to the backup. Homer Ninekiller and Dwight Badwater had been playing at gospel singings for twenty or thirty years, Homer with his old Les Paul Gibson electric and Dwight with his even older Martin D-28 Dreadnought flattop, and they were good enough to fill in the holes for the most raggedy-assed group. The kid on bass wasn't in their class but he was okay, keeping up a steady boom-boom and not trying to show off.

The audience applauded and occasionally shouted *amen* or *praise the Lord* and now and then wandered off to the tables for pie and coffee. Little kids ran here and there chasing lightning bugs or just grab-assing around, till at last the night got too long for them and they fell asleep in their mothers' laps or in the back seats of cars.

Jimmy got himself a folding chair and found a place under a big oak tree where he could keep an eye on everything. He still wasn't convinced it was over with the Sparrowhawks. It had been too easy and those two were known for their blind-mule stubbornness. But the hours rolled by and there was no further sign of them. When Jimmy's watch showed midnight he felt sure this would be the time something would happen, but nothing did.

The preacher appeared out of the shadows. "Having a good time, Jimmy? I am, now I don't have to worry about the Sparrowhawks."

Jimmy grunted. It was now well after twelve by his watch and he was starting to think nothing was going to happen after all, but he still wasn't ready to admit it.

On stage the musicians were into an instrumental break while the next singing group was called. Homer Ninekiller was doing amazing things to "He Will Set Your Fields On Fire" and Dwight Badwater and the kid in the Seminole jacket were loping right along with him. *"Asv,"* the preacher said as they finished.

"Picked that one and sent it home naked," Jimmy agreed. "Who's on next?"

"The Disciples."

"Shit."

"Please," the preacher said reprovingly. "This *is* the Lord's service."

"Sorry," Jimmy said. "But I bet that's pretty much the Lord's opinion too."

The Disciples consisted of a loudmouthed preacher named Mason Littlebird, his incredibly fat wife, and their bigknockered teenage daughter. None of them could sing worth a damn and Mason Littlebird had a habit of preaching windy sermons, "witnessing" he called it, between songs. Watching Mavis Littlebird clambering up the ladder to the stage—the truck was already tilted over on its shocks from her mother's weight— Jimmy decided this was a good time to take care of some increasingly urgent business.

"See you," he told the preacher. "Got to visit the BIA office."

There was somebody already inside the outhouse when Jimmy got there. He shrugged and stepped off into the trees. Fine Indian he'd be if he couldn't even take a pee in the woods.

He gave a post-oak a good soaking down, hearing Mason Littlebird' s voice blaring through the trees. "And I used to be a sinner, a-men, I drank and gambled, praise the Lord, yes and I sinned with women, thank you Jesus—" Zipping up, he walked back out of the woods and managed to get himself a foam cup of black coffee without being spotted by Idabel Grasshopper, who was gazing toward the stage with a look of holy joy. Maybe, Jimmy thought hopefully, she's getting the hots for Mason instead of me. Amen, praise the Lord, *and* thank you Jesus if she does.

He was finishing his coffee when it all began to happen.

The Disciples were into a long depressing song about sinners going to Hell—the words in English, of course, none of them spoke Cherokee even though Mason claimed to be a full-blood—when all at once there was a Godawful racket from the speakers and then silence except for the voices of the Disciples, trailing off uncertainly as they turned to stare.

Homer Ninekiller and the bass player bent over the silent amplifiers. From the look on their faces Jimmy guessed the breakdown was a major one. He could smell the kind of smoke you got when electric things died.

He felt no serious concern. This sort of thing was always happening at these affairs; the cheap amplifier systems, that were all most Indians could afford, broke down all the time. And, as far as he was concerned, this time was as good as any. Anything that shut the Littlebirds up was okay with him.

Dwight Badwater, though, was speaking to the Disciples, who were still staring at the dead speakers. After a minute they turned back around, while Dwight went into a flatpicking introduction, and began again to sing. Their voices were thin and weak without amplification, but they tried, while Dwight Badwater's big flattop boomed behind them. There was a burst of applause.

Then, with a sickening cracking sound, the bridge tore clear off Dwight Badwater's guitar. It happened too fast to see; one second Dwight was sitting there playing big mellow acoustic chords and the next he was grabbing his right wrist, bloody where the lashing strings had cut it, and looking down in disbelief at the splintered top of that beautiful old Martin.

Jimmy Hominy felt as if he'd been kicked in the stomach. Yet something made him turn his head, just at that moment, and when he did he forgot all about old friends and ruined guitars.

Half a dozen men in white suits were coming across the parking area. Behind them, two more men were getting out of a big white van that practically glowed in the dim light. It was too far and too dark to make out faces or details, except for the man in the lead, but that was okay because he was the only one Jimmy was really looking at.

Not that he was anything special to look at; he was just an average-sized man—maybe a little on the short and slender side—in a fancy white suit. But Jimmy Hominy took one look at him, checked his watch again, and shook his head in disgust. "Son of a bitch," he muttered. "Forgot about Daylight Saving Time."

The stranger crossed the parking ground with a quick sure step that was almost a swagger. When he came to the edge of the grassy area he stopped. The others coming up behind him stopped too.

He stood for a moment studying the ground at his feet. Then his head came up and turned, slowly, until he was looking straight in Jimmy Hominy's direction; and he smiled, a wide flash of very white teeth, and stepped forward again. Along the ground on either side of him was a bright blue flash, too fast and too small to see unless you were looking for it, where the medicine line had been.

Jimmy Hominy felt something with cold feet walking up his backbone. As far as he knew there was only one person in all Creation who could do that. Well, okay, two, but he was fairly certain this wasn't the other one.

The other suits followed their leader through the break in the medicine circle, walking single file, none of them looking down or around. Behind them, shuffling along with hunched shoulders, came Luther and Bobby Sparrowhawk.

Jimmy started to move, to head the strangers off—to tell the truth he didn't know what the hell he meant to do—but Idabel Grasshopper came up beside him and grabbed his arm. "There you are," she said in the way of somebody finding a missing possession. "Look, who's that? Don't they look handsome."

The strangers were standing beside the stage now, while the leader spoke to Eli Blackbird, who nodded and then climbed up on the truck, raising his hands for attention. "Good news," the preacher shouted over the growing noise of the crowd. "We've got a new group here, and they've brought their own equipment. Soon as they get set up, we'll go on with the singing."

The white suits were already trooping back to their van. With amazing speed and efficiency they began carrying things from the van—speakers, amplifiers, cased instruments—and setting them up on stage. Meanwhile the Sparrowhawk brothers took seats on the front row and sat there side by side like a couple of mean toads, staring straight ahead and not speaking to anybody.

"See, Jimmy?" Idabel Grasshopper sighed. "Just when everything was going wrong, the Lord sent us help. That's how it is, if you have faith—"

By the time Jimmy got loose the strangers were all set up and standing ready on stage. The preacher stepped up to one of the shiny new microphones they had brought. "All right." His voice boomed out through the big speakers and rumbled off through the woods. "Let's all give a big welcome to—" He checked a piece of paper in his hand. "Brother Seth Abadon, and a group called Maranatha!"

The crowd applauded and amen'd. The preacher got off the stage, the strangers took a step forward—all together and on the same foot, like a half-time drill team—and the music began:

> *"Oh people, get ready,*
> *Oh people, get ready,*
> *Oh people, get ready,*
> *He's coming to take you away."*

Jimmy Hominy had worked his way up to the front now, and he put his hand to his back pocket, to the little pouch of extra-special tobacco he had brought along in case things got rough. But then, remembering how the stranger had broken that power circle without so much as a song or a word, he changed his mind. That tobacco was strong enough to knock seven witches on their asses at a range of seven miles, on the far side of seven mountains, with one good puff; but he had a feeling that using it against this well-dressed joker would be like trying to stop a buffalo with a blowgun.

So he let his hand fall empty to his side, and went over and stood under the big tree again, where he could study the men in the white suits. He'd never seen anything like them.

And yet there was nothing weird or shocking in their appearance. In fact the peculiar thing about them was that there *wasn't* anything peculiar about any of them. Even the most ordinary-looking people had various little details—a crooked nose, a big chin, a mole—that marked them as who they were; even white people, who did tend to look pretty much alike to Jimmy Hominy, had their own faces if you really looked. But these gents, except for their leader, might have come off some kind of assembly line. They were so exactly the same size and build that they could have swapped their snazzy Western-cut white suits around at random and all ended up with just as neat a fit; and Jimmy wouldn't have been a bit surprised to find out they were able to switch arms and legs and heads as well.

That was speaking of the five regular members of Maranatha. The leader—Seth Abadon, if that was his name; Jimmy figured he was also known by many other names—was something else. And that was screwy, too, because he didn't look all that different from the others, in any way you could put your finger on. He was a little shorter and more lightly built, and his suit fit him just a little better, but that was all . . . but he stood out on that stage like a timber wolf in a pack of stray mutts. Something in the way he stood, in the way he held his head; whatever it was, nobody in the world would have needed more than a single glance to know which of the strangers was The Man.

At Jimmy's side the preacher said, "Isn't it great? A real professional group showing up at a little country singing like this, we really lucked out tonight."

Jimmy snorted. "What's a bunch of *yonegs* doing here?"

"You think they're white?" The preacher sounded surprised. "They look Indian to me."

Actually you couldn't tell. The strangers' faces seemed to shift somehow in the yellowish light; it was like looking through a car windshield in a rainstorm, or trying to read with a pair of those cheap glasses off the rack at Family Dollar Store. They wouldn't come into focus; they looked sort of Indian, and then they looked sort of white, and now and then Jimmy caught flickering glimpses of other things he didn't even want to identify.

"Anyway," the preacher said, "who cares? Just listen to that music!"

Jimmy was listening; it wasn't exactly something you could ignore. Whoever these people were, they had brought some serious equipment: gleaming high-tech-looking amplifiers with lots of knobs and switches and colored lights, black studio-grade microphones, and great big speakers like the ones at the rock concert Jimmy had once attended with his grandson. One, standing right behind Brother Seth Abadon up by the truck cab, was easily the biggest speaker Jimmy had ever seen; the damn thing looked to be bigger than his trailer's front door.

The music surged and rolled from the speakers, not blasting nosebleed-loud like at the rock concert, but in a soft pulsing flood that soaked right through your skin and blended with your breathing and your heartbeat. There was no rejecting it; it got to you, like it or not, and Jimmy kept catching himself tapping a foot or nodding his head with the rhythm. Though why this was so he couldn't understand; it certainly wasn't the words of the song, which were simple-headed to the point of childishness:

> *"People, have you heard the call,*
> *Going out to one and all?*
> *Listen and you'll know it's true—*
> *He is coming after you."*

—they sang, in intricate high-rising harmonies, so tight it was impossible to tell who was singing which part. They had fine voices, too, clear and strong and dead true, never the faintest sourness or roughness to mar that amazing flow. If anything they were too perfect; the effect was that of drinking distilled water— so pure there was no flavor, nothing really there.

But the singing was only a part, and maybe the lesser part, of Maranatha's sound. The vocals rode along atop an elaborate structure of complex chords and driving runs laid down by the instruments: two rhythm guitars, bass, keyboard— the kind that hung around the player's neck rather than standing on legs—a sort of tambourine, and Brother Seth Abadon himself on lead guitar. None of the instruments were of any familiar make; the shapes, in fact, were a little disturbing if you looked closely.

The rhythm guitars chonged and whopped, the bass thudded, the keyboard wheeped and tootled, the tambourine jingle-jangled, and Brother Seth's white solid-body guitar threaded in and out with graceful ease; and over it all sang the voices of Maranatha:

> *"Oh brother, get ready,*
> *Oh sister, get ready,*

Oh children, get ready,
He's come to take you away."

"Who's taking who where?" Jimmy wondered under his breath. To the preacher he said, "Where are these guys from, anyway?"

There was no answer. Jimmy turned and saw that the preacher was staring wide-eyed and slack-faced in the direction of the stage. His head was nodding, his shoulders moved rhythmically, and he shifted his weight from foot to foot in time with the music. He didn't respond when Jimmy spoke his name; he didn't even appear to notice when Jimmy jabbed an elbow into his short ribs.

"The hell," Jimmy said, out loud and not caring who heard him.

Doing some staring of his own, he looked out over the crowd. Sure enough, all the faces he could see were looking toward the stage with the same glazed-and-dazed expression, and a lot of people had begun to sway from side to side in their seats or where they stood. More were standing now, he noticed, than had been before. As he watched, others rose slowly to their feet.

The music swelled and rose, and there was something new, a hungry triumphant note such as you might hear in the voices of a dog pack about to tree a coon. Jimmy turned back around and saw Brother Seth Abadon was looking at him.

—*Who are you?*

The words sounded in Jimmy's mind, not his ears. On stage, Brother Seth's mouth had not stopped singing, or smiling, but Jimmy had no doubt who had spoken. He wasn't particularly startled; he had known several old medicine men who could do that trick of talking to you inside your head.

He said, "I'm that tall Indian you always hear about things being ass-high to. Who wants to know?"

Still singing and smiling, still playing his white guitar, Brother Seth tipped his head to one side.

—*Interesting*, said the voice in Jimmy's head. *I didn't expect to find one of your kind here.*

Down front, where he had been standing ever since the amplifier breakdown, Mason Littlebird took an unsteady step toward the stage.

—*This is not your place*, the voice said. *This does not concern you. Go away.*

"Up yours," Jimmy said, and folded his arms.

Brother Seth shrugged. —*Then stay out of the way. I won't answer for your safety.*

The white guitar's neck swung down past horizontal as Brother Seth began a long riff, up through the scale and slipping in and out of the minors. Dense chords crashed from the speakers as the others followed, modulating to a higher key.

Jimmy saw that something strange was happening to the front of the huge speaker that stood behind Brother Seth. The black rectangular surface no longer looked solid; it looked more like a hole, an opening into some place of absolute darkness.

> *"Come to take you away, come to take you away,*
> *Come along, come along, he's come to take you away—"*

Jimmy felt a rush of dizziness, and something tugging him forward. He shut his eyes and clutched at the little leather bag, no bigger than his thumb, that hung around his neck. Almost immediately he felt the four things inside begin to move against his palm, and a moment later the dizzy feeling fell away. He opened his eyes and looked up at the smiling face of Brother Seth Abadon.

"All right, you son of a bitch," Jimmy Hominy said. "*All right.*"

Both the Mercury's rear doors were jammed shut and he had to crawl in and reach over the back of the front seat to get the oversized guitar case out of the back. He dragged it out of the car and laid it carefully on the fender and undid the snaps and lifted the lid, saying certain words in a language older than Cherokee.

Inside the case was a guitar that was like no other guitar in the world.

For one thing, there was the sheer outrageous size of it. Back in the Fifties, when Jimmy's brother Clyde had first begun to play roadhouse gigs with it, people said that that crazy Indian Clyde Hominy had built himself a guitar as big as a doghouse bass. That was a little bit of an exaggeration, but it was at least as big as one of those Mexican walking basses, that mariachi players call *guitarron.*

For another thing, the body wasn't wood, but steel. In fact it looked a little like a giant version of the old steel-bodied National, that the black bluesmen used to favor so highly. And then there was that neck, wide as Route 66, and that extra string. . . .

But those were merely the things anybody could see at a glance. What made the big guitar truly unique was known to no living man but Jimmy Hominy: the steel of its body had been cut *from the car Hank Williams was riding in when he died.*

Oh, there was a car somewhere in Tennessee that was supposed to be the Hank Williams death car, but it was a fake. Clyde Hominy had been home from Korea only a couple of months when they broadcast the news that Hank was dead, and he had taken off immediately eastward, hopping freights and riding boxcars in the freezing January nights, till he got to Oak Hill, West Virginia. He had stolen the big white Cadillac right out of the county impound yard, where it was waiting for the legalities to be settled, and had driven it all the way back to Oklahoma without once being stopped or spotted, protected by the special medicine given him by a great-uncle who had in his day been the top horse thief in the Indian Territory.

He had hidden the car in the woods, unsure what to do with it, until one night Hank had appeared to him in a dream and told him. Then he had boosted a welding rig from a bridge construction site, and cut and welded the huge box and its resonator from the heavy steel of the Cadillac's doors and fenders, carving the neck from wood from a lightning-struck walnut tree that stood in a hundred-year-old Indian graveyard near Lost City; and when he was done he had run the remains of the car off a cliff above the deepest hole in the Arkansas River, and had taken the guitar and hit the road.

Nobody but Clyde had ever been allowed to play it—that hadn't been hard to enforce, since few men even cared to try and lift it—until that night in '58 when Clyde, gunned down on a Tulsa street by a drunken and Indian-hating white cop, had passed the guitar and its secret on to his little brother as he lay dying in the hospital.

Jimmy stood for a minute looking down at the guitar, running his fingers over a roughly welded seam; Clyde had been after sound, not looks. Then he picked the guitar up, slung the buffalo-hide strap over his neck and shoulder, fitted the slide—not the usual glass bottleneck, but a four-inch section of twelve-gauge barrel cut from a sawed-off shotgun that had once belonged to Pretty Boy Floyd, and never mind *that* story—to his ring finger, stuck his pipe between his teeth and lit it, and headed back toward the stage.

When he got there he saw right away that there was no time left to screw around. Half the people were on their feet now and all of them were swaying in unison from side to side, their faces absolutely blank and their eyes huge. Mason Littlebird was at the foot of the metal ladder that went up to the stage, and a long line of men and women had formed behind him—Jimmy saw Idabel Grasshopper in there, and Eli Blackbird, and the Sparrowhawk brothers—all moving with the same strange slow step, as if wading in knee-deep water. The music had grown higher and the beat stronger, and the blackness within the enormous speaker was now lit by a faint red glow.

Jimmy shoved Mason Littlebird aside and went up the ladder fast, no hands. As his feet hit the truck bed he slammed a horny thumb across the strings of Clyde's guitar, making an ugly dissonant crash. He slashed out a wailing slide chord like a jail full of busted whores, walked down through the basses with first and second finger, and screamed back up on the high strings with the slide clear on top of the box. It was as crude and violent as an attack with a broken bottle.

And as effective. The wild riff cut through Maranatha's slick sound—it shouldn't have been able to do that, not even this guitar, not against amplified instruments, but a lot of impossible things were going down tonight—and disrupted the seamless harmony, wrenched the progression just the least bit off track, tangled itself around the pretty melody and turned it into something slightly but definitely nasty. Down front, Mason Littlebird paused with one foot on the ladder, and the people behind him stopped their slow-motion march. The rest of the audience continued their rhythmic swaying, but the motion had become a little uneven.

Brother Seth kept playing. He kept smiling, too, as he turned to look at Jimmy Hominy, but it wasn't the same smile as before.

—*So? You challenge me?*

"You got it," Jimmy said without taking the pipe from his mouth.

—*You have no idea what you're doing. Look!*

The nearest microphone turned suddenly into a giant rattlesnake, standing on its tail. It rushed at Jimmy, striking at his face, yellow venom dripping from long curving fangs.

And Jimmy laughed, thinking maybe this was going to work after all. Brother Seth Abadon might be—well, who he was—but obviously he didn't know everything. He didn't even know what half the Indians present could have told him: that *inada* was Jimmy Hominy's personal power animal and spirit guide. Jimmy said a couple of words and the rattlesnake slithered up his arm and wrapped itself companionably around his neck and went to sleep. He blew a long stream of smoke that condensed itself into a great monster of a rattlesnake, twice the size of the first, that reared up in front of Brother Seth.

"Mine's longer than yours," Jimmy pointed out.

Brother Seth looked from one rattlesnake to the other.

—*Interesting.* He made a gesture with his little finger and both snakes vanished. *Very well, then*—

He nodded to the other suits. Immediately Maranatha began laying down a quick-stepping two-four rhythm: no tune, just a steady repetition of a single major chord by rhythm guitars and keyboard, while the bass looped again and again through the same three-notes-and-rest phrase. It was a monotonous but compelling sound, holding the ear like the drone of a bagpipe.

Jimmy glanced out over the crowd and saw that the swaying had stopped. Everything, in fact, had stopped; people sat or stood in place, even those in obviously uncomfortable or off-balance positions—half out of their seats, or about to step off on one foot—and nobody, nothing, moved. They could have been a collection of window dummies.

—*Forget them*. The voice had an impatient edge. *They will keep, for as long as this takes.*

Without warning Brother Seth took off on a long spectacular guitar solo, picking out shower after shower of high brilliant notes, then dropping down to the bass strings to turn the showers into thunderstorms, and back up to the little frets for a display of lightning. It was a fantastic performance; and when it seemed the elaborate structure couldn't carry any more, Brother Seth spun a dazzling ribbon of sixteenth notes to wrap it all up like a Christmas package.

Whereupon Jimmy Hominy proceeded to play the whole thing back to him, note for note, but adding all sorts of extra little ornamental figures and grace notes, playing it all with just the first two fingers of his left hand. At the end, just for prickishness, he tacked on the opening bars of the theme from *Gilligan's Island.*

"Not bad," he said. "Know any more like that? I could sure use the practice."

And that was how it went for a long time, while the stars wheeled overhead and a small-hours ground mist crept out of the woods and wetted the grass. Brother Seth would build something marvelous, only to have Jimmy Hominy knock it to pieces and then kick the pieces off the stage. Very soon there was no smile at all on Brother Seth's face and what there was instead was not a good thing to see.

He played a moaning dirgelike blues, so mournful and lonesome and crying-about-your-mama sad that several owls in the trees nearby committed suicide by diving headfirst into the ground. Jimmy shut that down by interrupting with mocking puppy whines and hound-dog howls that he made with the slide. Brother Seth switched to a weird hypnotic modal number, like those ragas from India you heard in the Sixties. Jimmy picked up the basic line and turned it into a toe-tapping stinky-finger rag, ending up with a deliberately corny *dew-dew-dewdy-yew-dew* straight off *Hee Haw*.

All this time the audience remained frozen where they were, as they were, with never a twitch or blink. Jimmy wondered if they were all right, and whether they could see or hear what was going on. But he didn't wonder much, because the battle with Brother Seth was taking everything he had and it was starting to look as if even that might not be enough.

The sound from the speakers changed suddenly to a vicious shriek, hard-edged and merciless as a straight razor, as Brother Seth began a series of string-bending riffs evil enough to make the nastiest heavy-metal player sound like Lawrence Welk. Things without shapes appeared in the air and hung there gibbering at Jimmy Hominy. Flames broke out around him and the guitar in his hand started to smoke. The strings burned his fingers.

Well, he hadn't really expected a fair fight from Brother Seth Abadon. He took care of the immediate problems by puffing at his pipe—it was still burning, hadn't gone out all this while even though he hadn't had a chance to reload it; there were only two other men alive who knew that trick—and calling up a little rain to cool things down. He noticed Brother Seth didn't get wet.

But making rain took energy he didn't have to spare. The truth was, Jimmy Hominy was getting tired. His arms and shoulders ached, his hands were cramping, and his back hurt from the weight of the heavy guitar. Worse, his head was going numb; he was running out of ideas. He could still keep in there awhile longer, but he felt very doubtful about the final outcome.

At his side, a voice he hadn't heard in over forty years said, "In trouble, *chooch?"*

Clyde was standing there, grinning at him, a wispy, shadowy Clyde—Jimmy could see right through him—even more wasted-looking than when he was alive. Jimmy said, *"Din'dahnvtli!* What, uh, how—"

"No time." Clyde's voice was thin and scratchy, barely audible through the racket Brother Seth was making. "Here."

Clyde's hand came out and touched the guitar's tuning knobs. Jimmy couldn't see how such an insubstantial figure could hope to move material objects, but Clyde still had power over that guitar. *Whang boing chong*, he retuned the top three strings to a strange straight sixth, like nothing Jimmy had ever heard before. "Try it now."

It took Jimmy only a few seconds to get the hang of the new tuning and an idea of its possibilities. By then Clyde was looking even more washed-out.

"So that's what you do with that seventh string," Jimmy said. "I never did know."

"I'd of told you," Clyde said, "but I was sort of leaky at the time. Listen, you got to quit counterpunching and go after him. Way you're going at this, he's wearing you down. Before long you'll start to lose it." Clyde shook his head. "You don't want to know what happens then, *chooch*. Get him now, while you still got a chance."

He started to drift away. His feet didn't quite touch the stage. Jimmy said, "Don't go, Clyde. Stay with me."

"Can't, *chooch*. I'm already gonna catch hell for this." He glanced at Brother Seth, who was watching him with a bad expression. "And I do mean catch hell. . . ."

He drifted over to the enormous black speaker. There he stopped and looked back. "Oh, yeah. He can't play augmented chords. They make him crazy."

"How do you know so much about him?"

"Shit, *chooch*." Clyde's laugh had been spooky enough in life and it hadn't been improved by death. "Who do you think taught him to play?"

He stepped into the black rectangle and vanished. Just like that.

—*Your brother. I should have known.* Brother Seth was looking at Jimmy in a new way. *You know, I could use a man like you. You'd be worth an infinite number of—* He flicked a contemptuous look down at the Sparrowhawk brothers, still rigid like everybody else. *I would make it worth your while.*

"Full benefit package?" Jimmy said dryly.

—Among other things, you could talk with your brother whenever you wished.

"Yeah," Jimmy said, "but if I went to work for you he wouldn't talk to me."

More words sounded inside his head, but Jimmy Hominy was no longer listening. He was playing guitar.

He had no name for what he was playing. He had never played anything like it before, even in his imagination; and he knew as he played that he would never be able to do it again. It was a thing only of that moment, as one-time and singular as a snowflake or a murder.

It began with a few bars of almost aimless riffing up and down the frets, exploring the new tuning, staking out scales. It burst suddenly into a chopped-and-lowered version of "Blackberry Rag"—that was for Clyde, it had been his signature tune—and then slid sideways into a wailing "Third Stone From the Sun." That turned somehow into a peyote-ceremony song learned from a brother-in-law who was in the Native American Church; while he was visiting six-tone country, Jimmy threw in part of a tune the locals used to sing in Vietnam. He came back nearer home with a sobbing ay-ay-ay-ay *ranchera* heard one night on the radio, floating up from Mexico, and then stepped off into a quick "Billy In The Low Ground", using the slide to make the big guitar sound like a dobro. That gave way to something that sounded vaguely Cajun and could have been, Jimmy having briefly driven a truck out of Bossier City, but might have been French Canadian since he had also spent a long-ago summer playing at a club in Montreal and trying to get into a certain Mohawk waitress's pants.

Needless to say, he put in lots of augmented chords.

There was Django and Blind Lemon and Charlie in there, and Les and Merle and Jimi and some of every other crazy bastard who ever picked up a guitar. And, of course, there was plenty of Clyde Hominy. Now and then Jimmy had the feeling it was the guitar that was playing him.

But there was much more going on than a mere blending of odds and ends. Out of the wild mixture something else was growing, stretching itself and gradually taking over; call it music or medicine or magic, there was now a new thing which had never been before.

And Brother Seth Abadon, who had been trying to get in with an occasional frustrated lick of his own, suddenly gestured Maranatha to silence, and unslung his own guitar and let it dangle by the neck from his left hand, and stood there listening, unmoving as the audience, while Jimmy finished. Because— Jimmy understood it somehow, looking at him—for all his abilities and powers and attributes, creation just wasn't a part of what he was about. His talents lay in the other direction.

At the end, when Jimmy had wound up with a fast finger-picking run, Brother Seth smiled once again. —*Well. You seem to have made your point.*

He nodded toward the still-frozen crowd. —*Not, of course, that it matters. This pathetic handful of aboriginal relics? Less than a trifle, in the great game.*

The smile widened. —*And I'll get most of them anyway, in the end.*

"You went to a lot of trouble," Jimmy said, "for a trifle."

Brother Seth shrugged. —*I thought this would be amusing. As it has been, though in unexpected ways, thanks to you. One does require one's diversions.*

"You got some damn mean ways of getting your laughs."

—*I?* Brother Seth's eyebrows rose. *What about my worthy opponent, whom these fools adore? He grows bored and mountains fall, seas rise, stars explode. Whole worlds and their inhabitants vanish, usually in painful ways. And you think* me *cruel?*

"Wouldn't surprise me that's so," Jimmy said. "But then I never took much stock in either of you."

—*Interesting.* Brother Seth seemed to use that word a lot. *You refuse to serve me. Yet neither do you serve my adversary.*

"Guess I'm just not servant material."

—*Ah, yes.* Brother Seth shook his head. For just a second he looked tired. *I said much the same, a very long time ago. . . .*

He fell silent, looking off past Jimmy at nothing in particular. Jimmy realized the sky in the east was getting light.

—*Still.* Brother Seth waved a hand at the crowd. *I had a deal.*

"Not with me you didn't. Not with them, either."

—*And yet one hates to leave empty-handed.*

"Take what's yours," Jimmy said. "No problem."

Brother Seth crooked a finger. Down in front of the stage the Sparrowhawk brothers began moving, walking stiffly and clumsily—actually it wasn't all that different from their usual gait—back to the rear of the truck. They climbed the metal ladder and crossed the stage, not looking at anything or anybody. As Jimmy watched, Luther Sparrowhawk stepped into the front of the huge black speaker and was gone. A moment later Bobby Sparrowhawk followed.

—*And so much for that.*

Brother Seth snapped his fingers and Maranatha began packing away their instruments and clearing their equipment off the stage, moving with the same brisk efficiency as before. In hardly any time they had loaded everything back into the white van and were climbing aboard. The white van pulled out of the parking area, making no sound whatever, and disappeared down the road in the direction of Fort Gibson.

At that exact moment the bright disk of the sun cracked the eastern horizon. Immediately the crowd in front of the stage began to move and mill about, heads turning this way and that, arms stretching. There was a low murmuring and a few voices raised in vague surprise, nothing more. A baby started crying.

Jimmy got off the stage before anybody could notice him up there. As he reached the ground Idabel Grasshopper came up and clutched his arm. "Jimmy! Where'd you get to?" She looked up at the empty stage. "What happened to those nice men? I was just enjoying their music so much—"

Suddenly, on the front row, old Nettie Blackfox—nobody knew how old, over ninety for sure, and blind as a rock for the last twenty—stood up and began to sing:

> *"Ga-do de-jv-ya-dv-hne-li Ji-sa?*
> *O-ga-je-li ja-gv-wi-yu-hi—"*

Others joined in, rising to their feet if they weren't already standing, raising their voices in the old hymn that had come all the way from the eastern homeland, that the people had sung on the Trail of Tears while a third of the Cherokees in the world died:

> *"O-ga-hli-ga-hli yv-ha-quu-ye-no*
> *Jo-gi-la-wi-sdv-ne-di-yi."*

Jimmy found himself singing too, coming in on bass, while Idabel's voice beside him went for the highs; one thing you had to give Idabel, she could sure as hell sing:

> *"O-ga-je-li-ga . . .*
> > *(o-ga-je-li-ga)*
> *ja-gv-wi-yu-hi . . .*
> > *(ja-gv-wi-yu-hi)*
> *Ja-le-li-ga-no . . .*
> > *(ja-je-li-ga-no)*
> *ja-gv-wi-yu-hi . . .*
> > *(ja-gv-wi-yu-hi)"*

—while the sun continued to climb above the trees and somewhere a redbird began warming up for a song of his own.

After the singing ended Eli Blackbird climbed up onto the truck long enough for a quick closing prayer, saying the words almost mechanically, occasionally pausing and. shaking his head. After the amen he climbed slowly back down and made his way through the crowd to the parking lot, where Jimmy Hominy was already standing beside the Mercury, putting the big seven-string guitar back in its case.

"Boy," the preacher said, "I think I must have dozed off there for a while. I didn't even notice when our guests left. Wish I'd thanked them for coming."

He watched as Jimmy snapped the case shut. "I hate to admit it," he added, "but I missed your part, too. Sorry." He looked Jimmy up and down. "From the look of you, you've been playing to beat the Devil."

Jimmy closed his eyes. "Don't say that, *chooch,* " he said softly. "Don't say that. . . ."

I grew up around gospel music. In fact it's why I'm here, since that was how my parents met: my mother was playing piano for my father's quartet.

Indian gospel singing is a little-known world, outside certain parts of Oklahoma; and a disappearing one, what with the ongoing loss of the languages and the corrupting influence of white-dominated churches. The singings still take place, but the songs are liable to be modern ones and sung in English.

This story is based on real events; I was there, at the preacher's invitation. (There was some concern that things might get physical. It was the only time I ever wore a gun to church, and I didn't like it.) However, neither the Kingfishers nor the Gospel Travelers—very real groups, of great ability— were present at that particular singing. I hope they will forgive me for including them in this fictional account.

The other stuff might have happened too, for all I know. I had to leave early.

Written December 1995
First published August 1998

Billy Mitchell's Overt Act

I believe, therefore, that should Japan decide upon the reduction or seizure of the Hawaiian Islands the following procedure would be adopted. . . . Attack to be made on Ford Island at 7:30 A.M. Group to move in column of flights in V. Each ship will drop projectiles on the targets;
          —Brig. Gen. William Mitchell, Report of Inspection of U.S. Possessions in the Pacific, *Oct. 24, 1924*

GENERAL MITCHELL IN NEAR FATAL AEROPLANE CRASH

General William "Billy" Mitchell is reported in critical condition following a crash at Fort Sam Houston, Texas, on Monday. According to unofficial sources, the General's engine failed upon takeoff from a new flying field which he was inspecting. Details of his injuries have not yet been released.

General Mitchell had been assigned to Fort Sam Houston in March, after his dismissal as Assistant Chief of the Air Service. The removal was generally seen as a response by the present Administration to the General's public criticisms of its policies on national defense, particularly aviation.

The General has gained wide public notice with his controversial writings and statements on air power, including the

claim that aeroplanes can sink warships, which he demonstrated in 1921 in tests off the Virginia coast.
—Kansas City *Star,* Tuesday, Sept. 1, 1925

Well, the Army finally found a way to fix Billy Mitchell—they let him fly one of their airplanes. The Germans couldn't bring him down but the U.S. brass and Calvin Coolidge did it. These worn-out old kites that the boys have to use, why, it's a scandal. Black Jack Pershing had better ships down on the border in '17, chasing Pancho Villa—and not catching him.
—Will Rogers, syndicated column, Sept. 4, 1925

At first I felt as if my whole world had crashed with him. We had been married only a couple of years, and I had just had our first child. It all seemed too much to bear.

But now, looking back, I know that crash was a blessing. By that time Billy was really out of control, just spoiling for a big fight with his bosses. Pretty soon, they'd have given it to him—and they'd have won.

They would have forced him out of the service, and that would have killed him. Billy wouldn't admit it, but the army was his whole life. He might have lived another dozen years or so, but he'd have been dying of a broken heart all the while.
—Elizabeth Mitchell, letter to Burke Davis, quoted in *Billy Mitchell*

Near summer's end I received word that my old friend Billy Mitchell had been seriously hurt in a crash in Texas. Naturally I went to visit him as soon as my duties permitted.

I found him bearing his physical suffering with Spartan fortitude. Much worse, for him, was the frustration of helplessness. He talked wildly of calling reporters to his bedside to denounce what he regarded as the negligence and incompetence of his superiors, and of writing yet more inflammatory books and articles. I saw that he was still bent on the same foolhardy course, which could only end in a court-martial and the ruination of his military career.

I reminded him sharply that his first duty was to our country, which could ill afford to lose an officer of genius at a critical time in her history. I pointed out that publicity-seeking tactics were beneath a general officer's dignity. And I told him that for a military man to directly challenge lawful authority— even that of the President—as he was doing, could never be tolerated in a democracy such as ours.

My words must have taken effect, for from that time forward he began to moderate his tone, and to cultivate self-discipline and diplomacy. Thus was General Mitchell preserved for his unique destiny. Little did I suspect the part I had played in history.

—General Douglas MacArthur, *Reminiscences*

MacArthur claimed to have been responsible for Billy Mitchell's "conversion." Well, MacArthur always did give himself fall credit, that was his way. My own view is that Billy just thought things over and came to his own conclusions, because that was *his* way.

He had plenty of time to think. Smashed up as he was, there wasn't much else he could do. He told me once that the nights were the worst. The pain kept him awake, and he wouldn't take any drugs no matter how bad it got. You can call that guts or just Billy Mitchell being contrary as usual.

—Capt. Eddie Rickenbacker, *Between Wars*

Since my body was out of action, I decided to use the time to improve my mind. I began to study the history, language, and culture of Japan, believing as I did that Americans would one day have to deal with this astute, aggressive race.

In my reading I came across the term *gaishin-shotan*. Literally, this translates "to sleep on firewood and lick gall." To the Japanese, however, it means the acceptance of hardship and ignominy in order to take a future revenge, as in their tale of the forty-seven samurai who deliberately subject themselves to disgrace in a secret plan to vindicate their honor.

For the next decade and a half I slept many nights on firewood, and I cultivated a connoisseur's taste for gall. . . .

—Brig. Gen. William Mitchell, unpublished memoirs

When he returned to duty in the fall of 1927, he seemed a different man. No one was sure how seriously to take the metamorphosis. After all, this was General Billy Mitchell.

Even that was not strictly true. When he was removed as Assistant chief of the Air Service, he also forfeited the "temporary" star he had worn since 1918. At the time of the crash, technically, he was a colonel. The press, however, always called him "General Mitchell", to the chagrin of certain persons. But then those persons would always go livid at the mention of Billy Mitchell, in whatever context. He had stepped on too many toes; not everyone was willing to forgive and forget.

So he spent the next fifteen years at a series of obscure posts where nothing had happened since the Indian Wars, at jobs a competent sergeant could have handled, under senile or alcoholic commanders who knew nothing about aviation but did know that powerful figures in Washington would be grateful to the man who found a way to tie the can to Colonel Mitchell.

And through it all, through all the frustrations and petty humiliations that only a peacetime army can inflict on a man, he kept his head down and his mouth shut and soldiered on, till at last even the diehard Mitchell-haters had to admit that he had indeed changed.

They were wrong, of course. Billy Mitchell had never for a minute stopped being Billy Mitchell. He was merely borrowing a technique from the only navy people he had any use for—the submariners. He was running silent and submerged.

—Ladislas Farago, *The Ordeal of Billy Mitchell*

When we heard who our new wing commander would be, we all went a little nuts. To an army aviator of my generation, Billy Mitchell was close to God Almighty. We all knew the story, how he'd gone to the wall for aviation back in the Twenties, and the price he'd paid. And now he was going to command the Eighteenth! They'd even given him back his brigadier's star.

Then I thought about it and I said, "Oh, Lord! Whose bright idea was this?"

You see, the Hawaiian Department in the spring of '41 was a very strange, unreal little world, very insulated and pleased with itself. The Germans were far away and the Japs were known to be too backward to be a serious threat, so there was very little attempt at real soldiering. Having a smart-looking turnout of the guard, or a solid lineup of jockstrappers— everybody was absolutely obsessed with sports—was much more important than trivial details like teaching men to load and fire their rifles.

Sending a man like Billy Mitchell to a place like that was like hiring Jack the Ripper to play the piano in a whore house.

—Col. George Stamps, in *The 18th Bombardment Wing: An Oral History*

The decision to assign General Mitchell to Hawaii was my own. General Marshall approved it. Contrary to certain published reports, President Roosevelt was not involved.

We were faced with a growing threat of war in the Pacific. The Hawaiian Islands were obviously of vital strategic importance. it seemed to me that a recognized expert on air power would be more usefully employed there than running an artillery observation training school in Georgia, which was what he was doing at the time.

In the military we speak of the principle of calculated risk. In sending General Mitchell to command the 18th Bombardment Wing, I took such a risk. I accept full responsibility for the consequences.

—Gen. Henry H. Arnold, statement to the Joint Congressional Committee on the North Pacific Incident

The Flying Fortress at that time was the glamor ship of the Air Corps and there still weren't that many in service. The guys who flew them thought we were pretty hot stuff.

Mitchell knocked that out of us in a hurry. He worked us like a bunch of cadets. We trained as we had never trained before, doing things they had never taught us at flight school. In fact he had us doing things that would have gotten us busted down to permanent latrine orderlies anywhere else in the Air Corps.

The big thing then was high-level precision bombing. We had been taught that our function was to fly high above the enemy in a ladylike manner and drop our bombs, using the fancy new Norden bombsight which was supposed to let you put a bomb into a pickle barrel from 20,000 feet.

The Old Man said there was a time and a place for that and then there was a time to get down and get dirty. "Come in low," he would say, "get on top of the enemy before he knows you're coming, and stuff the bomb load up his backside."

One fool tried to argue that a low level attack made you a bigger target. The Old Man drilled him with that fifty-caliber stare of his and said, "Any man who goes to war thinking of himself as a target should have stayed home and knitted socks for the Red Cross. The point is to kill the bastards before they can make you *any* kind of target."

There was a rumor that Roosevelt had sent him to the Islands in the hope that his presence would deter Japan from starting trouble in the Pacific. I don't know whether he scared the Japs any but he sure as hell scared us.

—Lt. Col. Mark Rucker, "Billy's Boys", *Wings*, Feb. 1971

HONOLULU—Hawaii is one of the world's last proud bastions of peacetime complacency., Europe may be vibrating under Wehrmacht boots, London and Changking may be smoking from the latest air raids, the panzers may be driving across Russia slowed only by bad roads; but' people here regard these things the way the residents of an exclusive neighborhood regard the news of a gang shootout down on the docks. Every weekend the battleships tie up in pairs at their moorings in Pearl Harbor, while the sailors go on liberty and the officers attend important social functions. And the grass at Schofield Barracks is said to be the most neatly-trimmed grass in the U.S. Army.

Certainly no one believes war will ever come to the Islands. The only potential enemy in the Pacific is Japan and Japan is not taken seriously. The local view of the Japanese is wholly contemptuous and will astonish anyone who has seen, as I did in China, the professional abilities of the Japanese military.

One exception to the whimsical atmosphere can be found at Hickam Field, where General Billy Mitchell has a bunch of big Flying Fortress bombers. I had a chance to watch them work over the old battleship *Utah,* which is used as a target ship. They came in low and fast and they planted their practice bombs with the precision of top banderilleros. They were as good as anyone the Germans had in Spain and that is saying a good deal.

I was told that General Mitchell personally flew the lead plane. Clearly he is not one of those generals who die in bed.
                    —Ernest Hemingway, "Fishing Off Diamond Head",
          Esquire, July 1941

```
To:       Commanding General, Dept. of Hawaii
From:     Commander, 18th Bombardment Wing
Subject:  Reconnaissance
```

1. Current international developments suggest the possibility of armed hostilities between the United States and the Empire of Japan at some point in the near future. In the event of such hostilities, the Hawaiian Islands would be a prime target for an enemy attack using carrier-borne aircraft.

2. The history of the Japanese Empire indicates that such an attack would not necessarily be preceded by a formal declaration of war.

3. Surprise being essential in such an operation, the attacking force would most likely approach from the north or northwest, this part of the Pacific Ocean being virtually empty of naval and merchant shipping.

4. In keeping with the principle of surprise, the attack would probably be launched at dawn, perhaps on a Saturday or Sunday.

5. The period through mid-December will be the time of maximum risk. After this the seas of the North Pacific are usually too rough for carrier operations.

6. It is therefore recommended that a schedule of reconnaissance flights be instituted immediately,

using all available aircraft and concentrating on
the north and northwest sectors. Cooperation with
navy air units will be essential.

7. Aircraft should carry full defensive armament.
If detected by an approaching carrier force, it is
likely they will be attacked.

William Mitchell
Brig Gen USAAF

Of course everybody thought he was crazy. The navy fliers had a joke that Billy Mitchell had put in too many hours at high altitude without his oxygen mask. General Short would probably have thought that was a good one, except I don't think he knew what an oxygen mask was.

Short was the commanding general of the Hawaiian Department. He was an old infantryman with so little grasp of aviation that he wanted to take away our ground crews and train them as infantry. Still, Mitchell was obviously keeping his people hard at work, and Short was old-school enough to approve of that.

So Short let Mitchell have a fairly free hand in training his people. He listened to Mitchell's frequent warnings and predictions, though, with the amused indulgence you might give an otherwise gifted friend who happens to belong to some extremely weird religious cult. And he made it plain that there would be no nonsense about long-range recon flights, searching the northern seas for, as he put it, "imaginary Japanese bogeymen."

—Maj. Gen. Richard Shilling, *Pacific Command*

5 November 1941

To: Commander in Chief, Combined Fleet,
         Isoroku Yamamoto
Via: Chief of Naval General Staff,
         Osami Nagano
By Imperial Order:

1. The Empire has resolved on war measures in early
December, expecting to be forced to go to war with
the United States, Britain, and the Netherlands for
self-preservation and self-defense

2. The Commander in Chief, Combined Fleet, will
execute the necessary operational preparations.

3. Detailed instructions will be given by the Chief
of the Naval General Staff.

SENATOR TRUMAN: General Short, tell the committee your
opinion of General Mitchell prior to December nineteen forty-
one.
GENERAL SHORT: I considered him an outstanding and
dedicated officer. Some of his ideas struck me as rather fanciful,
but on the whole I regarded him as an asset to my command.
TRUMAN: Would you say there was friction between the two of
you?
SHORT: Not at all. He did have a tendency to push a bit beyond
appropriate limits, to try and bypass chains of command. But I
put that down to a commendable zeal.
TRUMAN: What about the matter of reconnaissance patrols?
Was that an example of, as you put it, fanciful ideas?
SHORT: More an example of his impatience with proper
procedures. General Mitchell was preoccupied with the idea of
an air attack on Hawaii. He wanted to conduct aerial patrols over
the waters surrounding the Islands, particularly to the north. As I
explained to him—more than once—offshore patrolling was the
navy's responsibility.
TRUMAN: Was the navy in fact flying patrols to the north?
SHORT: I assumed they were. Later I learned otherwise.
TRUMAN: General, are you familiar with the old army saying,
"When you assume . . . ?"
SHORT: I beg your pardon?
TRUMAN: Never mind. Weren't you aware of the international
situation? Did you in fact take any measures at all to protect
your command in case of trouble with Japan?
SHORT: Certainly. I instituted a major anti-sabotage program.
TRUMAN: Sabotage? You were worried about sabotage?
SHORT: Hawaii had—has—a large Japanese population.
TRUMAN: Were there ever any cases of sabotage by these
people?

SHORT: None. Obviously my security measures were effective.

TRUMAN: So you authorized no patrol flights by General Mitchell? And you had no knowledge that he was making them on his own?

SHORT: None whatever. Naturally I knew his aircraft were going off on long flights every day, but according to him these were merely training operations, meant to give the crews experience in long-range over-water navigation. It was only later that I learned that he and his officers had been falsifying their reports and flight logs. Since the beginning of November they had been flying regular patrols over the northwest sector to a radius of as much as eight hundred miles.

TRUMAN: And this was in violation of your orders.

SHORT: Direct and flagrant violation, sir. I was appalled.

—Hearings of the Joint Congressional Committee
on the North Pacific Incident, March 3, 1947

Captain Mark Rucker was just about ready to call it a day. It was getting late and he was a long way from home.

He was, in fact, about 800 miles northwest of Oahu. That was much farther out than the book said he should be; but Rucker's boss had spent his life rewriting the book.

Brigadier General Billy Mitchell had come a long way since the stormy days of the 1920s, but he was still a man obsessed. He was by no means alone in believing war with Japan to be imminent, but he thought he knew exactly where and how it would begin. Any morning now, a Japanese carrier force would come pounding down out of the North Pacific and launch a surprise strike against the U.S. bases in Hawaii. If history was any guide, they wouldn't bother to declare war first.

He had even worked out the route they would take: across the emptiest part of the sea, between the 40th and 45th parallels, out of range of patrol planes from Midway and the Aleutians. East of the International Date Line, they would swing southeast and make directly for Hawaii.

He was so sure he was right that, once again, he was laying his military neck on the line. For over a month, under various pretexts and subterfuges, his B-17 pilots of the 18th

Bombardment Wing had been flying regular patrols over the northwest sector. There were too few planes for proper coverage, but Mitchell felt anything was better than simply sitting blind, waiting for the enemy to attack.

He hadn't been entirely dishonest, though, in writing the flights up as long-distance training missions. In the course of these patrols, his airmen had developed a whole bag of tricks for extending the B-17's range. Captain Rucker wasn't seriously worried about getting home. He had been farther out than this, many times.

All the same, Rucker was relieved to see that he was reaching the end of his ten-degree patrolling arc. Time to head for the barn . . . but then his copilot, Lieutenant Ray Agostini, began shouting and pointing off to the north. A moment later Rucker saw it too, a great gray blur against the darkening sea.

My God, he thought. We've got somebody's whole navy up here.

—Walter Lord, *Day of Battle*

Admiral Yamaguchi argued that we should maintain air patrols while en route to Hawaii. I opposed this on grounds of security. Should a scout plane encounter an enemy or neutral vessel, the ship might radio news of the sighting, thus warning the Americans of the presence of a carrier-force in the North Pacific.

Admiral Nagumo agreed. No planes would be launched until the morning of the attack. However, each carrier would keep six fighters in readiness during the daylight hours.

Late on the afternoon of 5 December, the cruiser *Abukuma* signalled that her lookouts had spotted an airplane off to the south. No one else could see anything in that direction, the sky being quite cloudy. Admiral Nagumo ordered the *Akagi* to launch her ready fighters. The six Zeroes searched the area but found nothing and had to return in the gathering dusk. Meanwhile our radiomen reported no transmissions anywhere in the vicinity.

After some discussion it was decided that the alarm had been false. We would proceed as planned. But the incident

obviously had worried Admiral Nagumo. Later that evening I
saw him on the bridge, staring unhappily at the southern sky.
      —Capt. Minoru Genda, *I Flew For The Emperor*

Captain Rucker was already climbing through the clouds,
heading for home, by the time the Zeroes took off. He never
even realized they were after him. But he had something else to
worry about: the B-17's radio, which had been acting up for
hours, was now refusing to transmit at at all. He would have to
wait till he got back to Hawaii to make his report.

    At 2215 the B-17's wheels finally touched down at
Hickam Field. Rucker's long day, however, was far from over.
General Mitchell was waiting at the control tower, as he often
did—there was a rumor that the "Old Man" hadn't slept since
1925—and when he heard Rucker's report he fairly exploded.
Within minutes, the unfortunate pilot was hustled into Mitchell's
car for a wild high-speed run up to Fort Shafter.

    Mitchell's ballistic driving style was legendary, and
Rucker found the ride even more terrifying than his recent brush
with the Japanese. But nothing was as scary as the experience
that followed. Less than an hour later the young captain, still in
his sweaty flight suit and needing a shave, found himself in a
room fall of generals and admirals and lesser brass, all of them
firing questions at Rucker and arguing among themselves.

    Under their grilling, Rucker had to admit that he hadn't
gotten a very good look at the mystery ships. He was sure that he
had seen at least three carriers and a couple of battleships, with
various other unidentified vessels; he believed they were
heading southeast.

    Admiral Kimmel was frankly skeptical. So was Admiral
Bellinger, the navy air commander. Army fliers were notoriously
imaginative when it came to ship sightings. If Rucker had seen
anything at all, it was probably a Russian freighter. For that
matter, Japanese fishing fleets often turned up in those waters,
raising questions as to what they were up to.

    General Short appeared confused; he was an elderly man
and he had been awakened from a sound sleep. He seemed less
interested in what Rucker had seen than in what the airman had

been doing up there in the first place. That Mitchell had been running a regular system of unauthorized reconnaissance flights, deliberately contravening Short's orders, was far more upsetting than any ship movements. As he later testified, only the lateness of the hour and the uncertainty of the situation stopped him from placing Mitchell under arrest.

General Martin, commander of the Hawaiian Air Force and nominally Mitchell's immediate superior, was no help; by now he was a very sick man, suffering from ulcers—not surprising in a man caught between Short and Mitchell. He took almost no part in the discussion.

Some time after Midnight a consensus was reached. At dawn Bellinger's big PBY patrol seaplanes would go check the northwest sector in a proper manner. Just in case they found something, the fleet would go on alert. There was no point bothering Washington until more was known.

As the meeting broke up, Rucker overheard an exchange between a couple of naval officers:

"Well, it's finally going to happen."

"War, you mean?"

"No, no. I mean Billy Mitchell's court-martial. I can't believe it's taken this long."

—Gordon Prange, *Resort to Arms*

It was never clear just how the thing was managed. Later accounts and recollections were contradictory and vague. Pilots remembered being awakened in the middle of the night and given a hurried, rather cryptic briefing; air and ground crewmen had the usual enlisted man's memories of working frantically and being shouted at. The one thing everybody recalled was an atmosphere of great urgency and secrecy. Whatever was happening, it was big.

No one questioned for a moment the legitimacy of what they were doing. Even instructions to load the B-17s with live bombs went unchallenged. The armorers were draftees, with a few career NCOS; none were in the habit of questioning direct orders from generals.

As for the pilots, they testified later that it never occurred to them that General Mitchell might be acting without authority. Off the record, most agreed that it would have made little difference. They would, they said, have followed the Old Man to bomb Hell with water balloons.

(Mark Rucker, the only one who knew the truth, was lost in the sleep of the utterly exhausted. Mitchell had ordered him to "go get some rest" and he had been only too glad to oblige.)

The men labored on through the night, swarming over the hulking olive-green bombers by the glare of floodlights, filling the long-range tanks with high-octane aviation fuel, hoisting the ugly fat bombs into the yawning bays, passing up belts of gleaming .50-caliber ammunition. Meanwhile the rest of the Hawaiian command, from General Short to the soldiers at Schofield Barracks, slumbered unawares.

At four in the morning the first B-17 rolled down the floodlit runway and climbed away, its exhausts flaring blue-white against the night sky. It was Rucker's plane; but it hardly needs saying that this time Billy Mitchell was at the controls.

—Martin Caidin, *The Glory Birds*

Just before sunrise a radio message was received from Admiral Yamamoto relating the wish of the Emperor that the Combined Fleet should destroy all enemy forces. Officers and men listened joyfully to the reading of the Imperial Rescript. We were filled with firm resolve to justify His Majesty's trust and set his mind at ease by doing our utmost duty in the attack on Pearl Harbor.

After this the fleet began final refueling operation. This was hard and tricky business and very dangerous. Close attention was required to prevent collisions. Also, we were deeply unsafe from attack. Normally our carriers steamed in double column, first the *Akagi* and *Kaga*, then the *Soryu* and *Hiryu*, last the *Shokaku* and *Zuikaku*. Thus all ships could give good mutual protection fire. But during the refueling all ships sailed over a wide surface making room for the tankers to come amongst us. All maneuver was impossible including turning the carriers into the wind to launch planes.

I was standing on the flight deck of the Shokaku watching the refueling with Lt. Watanabe. The sky was very cloudy and the wind brisk but the sea was not very rough. Lt. Watanabe said, "This is a sign that Heaven favors our mission."

Just at that time the cruiser Chikuma began firing her guns rapidly toward the south. I looked forward and saw twelve large airplanes emerge through the clouds, flying directly towards us in a graceful and resolute manner.

"On the other hand," Lt. Watanabe said, "I could be wrong."

—Lt. Cdr. Kazuo Sakamoto, *Zero Pilot*

It was eight-thirty when we found the Japanese. We had been in the air for four and a half hours—not to mention being up most of the night before that—and we were feeling, shall we say, a bit tuckered. But when we broke through the clouds and saw what was waiting for us, everyone became remarkably *alert.*

I mean, I hadn't realized the Japanese even *owned* so many carriers. All those lovely great wooden flight decks down there below us—I had the *strangest* thought that they could have made the most marvelous dance floor, right on top of the Pacific Ocean.

However, there was no time for that sort of thing. The ships were already opening fire and big dirty puffs of smoke appeared all about us, unreasonably close and making the most *ghastly* noise. I reached for the bomb release, while up in the cockpit Major Stamps announced: "Okay, guys, stick your heads between your legs and kiss your asses goodbye. Here we go."

—Capt. Basil Crispos, unpublished manuscript

Mitchell's B-17s had arrived at the worst possible time. Slowed to a nine-knot crawl for refueling, their usual tight defensive formation in disarray, Nagumo's ships were wide open.

The Japanese gunners put up a withering storm of AA fire, all the same. Flak chopped the port wing clean off Lt. Jack Devlin's Fortress, sending it spinning into the sea. Capt. Roy Earle's bomber simply vanished in a great blinding explosion.

By now everyone was being hit. Great holes appeared in wings and fuselages; controls went mushy as flying surfaces shredded away. Fires broke out and engines began to smoke. Yet the ten remaining planes roared on; as would be proved again and again over the next few years, the B-17 was an almighty hard airplane to shoot down.

The human body was less durable. Already the Fortresses were becoming flying abattoirs where wounded men screamed in pain and rage and copilots wrestled the controls from dead pilots.

Then they were over the target.

—Edward Jablonski, *Flying Fortress*

Watching from *Akagi's* bridge, Captain Genda was professionally impressed. The big bombers were faster than they looked and their pilots obviously knew their business. Brave men, too, to attack at such a low altitude; Genda felt an impulse to salute.

A stick of bombs exploded off *Akagi's* port bow. *Kaga* and *Soryu* vanished for a moment behind towering columns of water, only to reappear a moment later, untouched. It seemed the Combined Fleet might escape harm after all.

Then a B-17 roared close overhead, through a wall of fire from *Akagi's* guns. Genda looked up and saw a number of black objects dropping out of the bomber's belly, like a sow giving birth to a litter of pigs. A second later *Akagi's* flight deck erupted in flame and smoke and Genda was knocked off his feet. As he hit the deck Admiral Nagumo landed on top of him.

At about the same time *Soryu* took a bomb through her flight deck, starting fires on the hangar deck below. *Zuikaku*, turning sharply to dodge the bombs, plowed into the tanker *Shinkoku Maru*, tearing a huge hole in the tanker's side and crumpling the brand-new carrier's bow. The destroyer *Akigumo* took a stick of bombs amidships that broke her in two.

Then the bombers were gone, climbing sharply away into the clouds. All, that is, but one.

On *Akagi's* shattered bridge, supporting a dazed Nagumo, Genda watched in amazement as a single Fortress came circling back, trailing smoke. Every ship in the fleet was firing at it, even the mortally wounded *Akagi*, but it bored through the flak in a shallow dive, heading straight for *Kaga.* Genda realized suddenly what the American was doing.

—John Toland, *Rising Sun*

Our plane was the last one in the formation and we were still hauling ass out of there, Lt. Martinez pouring on the gas, trying to get up into the clouds before those Zeroes could take off. I was manning the port waist gun, watching to see if anything was after us. So I saw the whole thing.

You could see the Old Man's plane was hit bad. Smoke was trailing out behind and it looked like part of his port wing was gone. There was no way to know about the crew, of course, but I think they must have all been dead by then. There's just no other way the Old Man would have done what he did.

He hit that Jap carrier square in the middle of her flight deck, right next to the bridge island. For a second you could see the tail of his plane sticking up there like part of a big dead bird. Then there was this huge explosion, like nothing I'd ever seen before. It must have been like the end of the world for those poor damn Japs.

I felt like I ought to say a prayer or something. But I just wasn't up to it. I had a piece of shrapnel through my leg and it was really starting to hurt like a son of a bitch.

—M/Sgt. Darrell Hatfield, interviewed by Quentin Reynolds,
They Called It North Pacific

The President had called a meeting in the oval office at 3 P.M. to discuss the deteriorating situation in the Pacific. He was just telling us how he still hoped to avoid war with Japan—at least until Hitler was defeated—but that if war did come, he wanted the Japanese to commit the first overt act. Then a naval officer came in with a message from Hawaii.

"My God," the President said upon hearing the news. "This is terrible. I was afraid of something like this."

Secretary Knox said, "Mr. President, they were clearly on their way to attack Pearl Harbor. There's just no other explanation. Surely that justified a pre-emptive strike."

The President shook his head. "Frank," he said, "you know that and I know that, but I've got to sell this to the American people. And they've all grown up on cowboy movies. They still think the good guy never draws first."

Secretary Hull said, "What will you do now, sir?"

"Ask Congress to declare war," the President said. "There's no choice now. We're committed."

He turned to me. "Find out if Mitchell is still alive, Henry. I'd like to have the crazy bastard shot, but I suppose I'm going to have to give him the Medal of Honor. He's started the war and he may as well be its first hero."

—Secretary of War Henry Stimson, private diaries

By midmorning *Kaga* had sunk and *Akagi* was a blazing hulk. *Soryu* was still seaworthy but unable to fly off planes, and *Zuikaku*, her bow damaged, was having trouble keeping up. But Nagumo, now flying his flag in *Shokaku*, refused even to consider turning back. He had never believed they would take the Americans by surprise; he had always expected to have to fight his way in. His losses so far had been heavy, but not unacceptable.

The Combined Fleet pushed onward, shadowed at a discreet distance by Bellinger's seaplanes but otherwise unmolested. The tankers had been left behind and the warships were now making almost thirty knots. Now some pilots begged to be allowed to launch an attack; their planes lacked the range for a round trip, but they were ready to make a one-way suicide raid. Nagumo vetoed the idea. He had lost too many planes and pilots already.

In Hawaii, despite great and general confusion about what had happened, it was realized that there was now no choice but to finish what Mitchell had began. A message went out to Admiral Newton, just outbound for Midway with *Lexington* and a stout escort force: forget Midway, turn north,, find the Japanese and attack when in range.

Only eight B-17s had made it back, none in remotely flyable condition. Hickam Field still had a dozen new A-20 attack bombers and thirty obsolete B-18s. Late in the afternoon, when a PBY reported the carrier group only 500 miles from Oahu, the decision was made to strike with what was at hand.

The A-20s were very fast, too quick even for the nimble Zeroes; they hit and ran without loss. But their small bomb loads were inadequate against warships, and their pilots were green; they damaged a couple of destroyers, nothing more.

The B-18s arrived an hour later. They had no business there at all. Essentially little more than modified DC-3 transports, they could barely make 120 mph. They carried only two machine guns and no armor. They were slaughtered. None survived; none even got near the target.

But the massacre left the Zeroes low on ammunition. They began landing to reload, while Nagumo watched the sky. Soon it would be dark and he would have all night to run toward Hawaii, to get in range for a dawn attack.

That was when *Lexington's* planes appeared overhead. One of the fastest carriers in the world, "Lady Lex" had been powering northeast all day with a bone in her teeth. Now her scout bombers fell out of the clouds in near-vertical dives against Nagumo's carriers. *Hiryu* was ripped apart, then the lame *Zuikaku,* while bombs again mauled *Soryu.* In the twilight, *Shokaku's* pilots tailed the victorious SBDs back to *Lexington* and put two torpedoes into her, but she managed to limp into Pearl Harbor next day.

That morning, when he had read the Imperial Rescript to his officers, Nagumo had commanded the biggest carrier force ever assembled. Now, a short December day later, he was down to two carriers, one a helpless cripple. And there was no telling what other American forces might be out there.

It was time to quit. As darkness fell, the remains of the Pearl Harbor attack force turned and headed back toward Japan. Meanwhile Kimmel's battleships, which had finally sortied from Pearl Harbor, waddled slowly northward, striving doggedly to reach the scene of the fight that had, like history, already left them behind.

—Fletcher Pratt, *Battles That Changed History*

On Saturday, December 6—a day which will live in infamy—air and naval forces of the Empire of Japan attempted to launch an attack against American forces in Hawaii.

Fortunately, the approaching force was detected and destroyed by American military and naval aircraft. A great airman, General Mitchell, gave his life in the battle, as did many other brave men.

I ask that Congress declare that since the unprovoked and dastardly attempt by Japan on Saturday, December 6, a state of war has existed between the United States and the Japanese Empire.

—President Franklin D. Roosevelt to Congress, Dec. 8, 1941

Billy Mitchell died as he had lived, an outrageous and incorrigible spirit; a loose cannon on the deck of history, and an annoying problem for those who argue, as is now fashionable, that individuals cannot affect the course of great events. Since the day in 1914 when Gavrilo Princip gunned down the Archduke Ferdinand in Sarajevo, no single act by a single man has had such enormous consequences.

Unquestionably, Mitchell had handed Japan a calamitous defeat. A priceless asset, the finest carrier force in the world, had virtually ceased to exist even before the war was properly begun. Even worse was the loss of so many expert pilots and seamen, who could never be replaced in time to meet the American counterattack.

And the ambitious plan of conquest had been thrown fatally off schedule. Everything—the landings in Malaya and Luzon, even the delivery of the formal declaration of war—had been timed to the projected December 7 attack on Pearl Harbor. Like the Germans they admired so much, the Japanese militarists were good at devising highly complex schemes of war; unlike their allies, however, they seemed unable to think on their feet, to react quickly and improvise when things failed to go as planned. The Japanese blitz, which was supposed to conquer all of Southeast Asia in three months, never quite recovered its balance.

On the debit side, the quick victory had made the Americans dangerously overconfident. The image of the Japanese as myopic, buck-toothed buffoons had been reinforced; all that was needed was to "slap the little yellow bastards down" and teach them not to trifle with their racial superiors. Reality would come soon enough, during the bloody campaign to relieve the Philippines—where the U.S. Navy would lose more ships than had been present at Pearl Harbor that morning—and the shock and disillusionment would do much to turn the American public against the war.

But all that was in the future. For now, America had a hero.

—William Manchester, *Pacific Crucible*

There was smoke on the water, there was fire upon the sea,
When General Billy Mitchell flew against the enemy —
"Smoke on the Water," copyright 1942 by Woody Guthrie

A hero! Why would anyone call that son of a bitch a hero? The only thing I can say for him, he had the decency to get killed.

So he stopped a Japanese attack on Pearl Harbor. Look, our people in Hawaii weren't helpless, you know. They had radar, so they'd have spotted the Japs coming and been ready for them. And then after beating off the attack we could still have gone after their carriers and sunk them. We'd have kicked their asses, you better believe it.

And if the Japs had fired the first shots, then the American people would have gotten together behind the President, and we'd have stayed in there and won the war properly.

As it was, thanks to Mr. Hero Billy Mitchell, we never did have a unified war effort against Japan, the way we did against Hitler. The isolationists ran around calling the President a warmonger, claiming Mitchell had secret orders from the White House, all that crap. Of course the Republicans were glad to have an excuse to oppose the President on any question, while the liberals were never comfortable about going to war to protect white colonialism in Asia. And John Q. Public, poor bastard, just didn't want to fight any wars anywhere if it could be avoided.

So the war in the Pacific dragged on indecisively, year after year, and the opposition grew—my God, we even had people marching against the war, right in front of the White House! Young punks were writing "Hell, no, I won't go!" on draft-office walls, enough-to make you puke. Till finally it got so bad the President just gave up and announced he wouldn't run again in '44.

I always thought it was a mercy that FDR died right after the election. At least he didn't have to watch Dewey making that half-assed peace with Tokyo—and we wouldn't even have gotten that, only Hitler was finished and Stalin's troops were massing on the Chinese border and the Japs realized they'd get—a better deal with us than they would from Moscow.

And FDR didn't live to see the Communists overrun Asia, even obscure places like Korea and Indochina, and the U.S. not doing a goddamn thing about it because by that time the public was so sour on the Far East that it was political suicide even to talk about getting involved in anything west of Hawaii. Thousands of American boys died relieving the Philippines, after that prancing tinhorn MacArthur managed to get himself trapped there—listen, don't get me started on MacArthur—and ten years later when the Hukbalahaps marched into Manila and proclaimed the People's Republic of the Philippines, you had senior congressmen telling the press that the U.S. had no vital interests in the region! Why, that shifty-eyed little weasel Richard Nixon stood up in the House and said there was nothing in Southeast Asia worth the loss of a single American life!

That, by God, was Mitchell's legacy. He was just a goddamn cowboy.
   —Senator Harry S. Truman, interviewed by Merle Miller, 1961

They must have made a mighty noise, those twelve B-17s, as they swept northward across the island of Oahu in the darkest hours of Saturday morning. Surely some of the men at Schofield Barracks heard them—men in all-night crap games, or standing guard, or down in the latrine putting an extra shine on a pair of boots against the morning's inspection. Most of us, though, were sound asleep.

Maybe we did hear, at some level. Maybe the roar of those forty-eight Wright Cyclone engines vibrated its way down to where we lay in our bunks, into our sleeping consciousness, so that we stirred briefly before returning to the lonely dreams of soldiers.

Whether we heard or not, it is certain that none of us had any idea at all that our world was about to be altered forever, in ways we could never imagine or understand.

> —James Jones, "The Day It Happened,"
> *Saturday Evening Post,* December 9, 1961

I wrote this story for the first of Harry Turtledove's Alternate Generals *series. At the time I was quite proud of it; I'd put in a lot of research work, getting the realtime information right, and I thought I'd done a pretty good job doing the various voices.*

But as it turned out, the story attracted almost no attention outside of the specialized world of alternative-history fans. Eventually it was made known to me that most people didn't know who Billy Mitchell was. Aaghh. The times in which we live. . . .

Two of the quotations are authentic historical ones. You figure out which.

Written June 1996
First published September 1998

Ninekiller and the *Neterw*

Jesse Ninekiller was five thousand feet above the Egyptian desert when his grandfather spoke to him. He was startled but not absolutely astonished, even though his grandfather had been dead for almost thirty years. This wasn't the first time this had happened.

The first time had been way back in '72, near Cu Chi, where a brand-new Warrant Officer Ninekiller had been about to put a not-so-new Bell HU-1 into its descent toward a seemingly quiet landing zone. He had just begun to apply downward pressure on the collective pitch stick when the voice had sounded in his ear, cutting clear through the engine racket and the heavy *wop-wop-wop* of the rotor:

"*Jagasesdesdi, sgilisi!* You don't want to go down there right now."

Actually it was only later, thinking back, that Jesse recalled the words and put them together. It was a few seconds before he even realized it had been grandfather's voice. At the moment it was simply the shock of hearing a voice inside his helmet speaking Oklahoma Cherokee that froze his hands on the controls. But that was enough; by the time he got unstuck and resumed the descent, the other three Hueys in the flight were already dropping rapidly earthward, leaving Jesse well above and behind, clumsy with embarrassment and manhandling the

Huey like a first-week trainee as he struggled to catch up. Badly shaken, too; he didn't think he'd been in Nam long enough to be hearing voices. . . .

Then the tree line at the edge of the LZ exploded with gunfire and the first two Hueys went up in great balls of orange flame and the third flopped sideways into the ground like a huge dying hummingbird, and only Jesse, still out of range of the worst of the metal, was able to haul his ship clear. And all the way back to base the copilot kept asking, "How did you know, man? How did you *know?*"

That was the first time, and the only time for a good many years; and eventually Jesse convinced himself it had all been his imagination. But then there came a day when Jesse, now flying for an offshore oil outfit out of east Texas, got into a lively afternooner with a red-headed woman at her home on the outskirts of Corpus Christi; and finally she got up and headed for the bathroom, and Jesse, after enjoying the sight of her naked white bottom disappearing across the hall, decided what he needed now was a little nap.

And had just dropped off into pleasantly exhausted sleep when the voice woke him, sharp and urgent: "Wake up, *chooch!* Grab your things and get out of there, *nula!*"

He sat up, blinking and confused. He was still blinking when he heard the car pull into the driveway; but he got a lot less confused, became highly alert in fact, when the redhead called from the bathroom, "That'll be my husband. Don't worry, he's cool."

Not buying that for a second, Jesse was already out of bed and snatching up his scattered clothes. He sprinted ballocky-bare-assed down the hall and out the back door and across the scrubby lawn, while an angry shout behind him, followed by a metallic *clack-clack* and then an unreasonably loud bang, indicated that the husband wasn't being even a little bit cool. There were more bangs and something popped past Jesse's head as he made it to his car, and after he got back to his own place he discovered a couple of neat holes, say about forty-five-hundredths of an inch in diameter, in the Camaro's right rear fender.

In the years that followed there were other incidents, not quite so wild but just as intense. Like the time Grandfather's voice woke him in the middle of the night in time to escape from a burning hotel in Bangkok, or when it stopped him from going into a Beirut cafe a couple of minutes before a Hezbollah bomb blew the place to rubble. So even though Grandfather's little visitations never got to be very frequent, when they did happen Jesse tended to pay attention.

As in the present instance, which bore an uneasy similarity to the first. The helicopter now was a Hughes 500D, smaller than the old Huey and a hell of a lot less work to drive, and Egypt definitely didn't look a bit like Nam, but it was still close enough to make the hairs on Jesse's neck come smartly to attention when that scratchy old voice in his ear (his left ear, for some reason it was always the left one) said, *"Ni, sgilisi!* This thing's about to quit on you."

Jesse's eyes dropped instantly to the row of warning lights at the top of the instrument panel, then to the dial gauges below. Transmission oil pressure and temperature, fuel level, battery temperature, engine and rotor rpm, turbine outlet temperature, engine oil pressure and temperature—there really were a hell of a lot of things that could go wrong with a helicopter, when you thought about it—everything seemed normal, all the little red and amber squares dark, all the needles where they were supposed to be. Overhead, the five-bladed rotor fluttered steadily, and there was no funny feedback from the controls.

Beside him, in the right seat, the man who called himself Bradley and who was supposed to be some kind of archaeologist said, "Something the matter?"

Jesse shrugged. Grandfather's voice said, "Screw him. Listen. Make about a quarter turn to the right. See that big brown rock outcrop, off yonder to the north, looks sort of like a fist? Take a line on that."

Jesse didn't hesitate, even though the lights and needles still swore there was nothing wrong. He pressed gently on the cyclic stick and toed the right tail-rotor pedal to bring the nose around. As the Hughes wheeled to the right the man called Bradley said sharply, "What do you think you're doing? No course changes till I say—"

Just like that, just as Jesse neutralized the controls to steady the Hughes on its new course, the engine stopped. There was no preliminary loss of power or change of sound; one second the Allison turbine was howling away back there and the next it wasn't. Just in case nobody had noticed, the red engine-out light began blinking, while the warning horn at the top of the instrument console burst into a pulsating, irritating hoot.

Immediately Jesse shoved the collective all the way down, letting the main rotor go into autorotation. Under his breath he said, "Damn, *eduda*, how come you always cut it so close?"

"What? What the hell?" Bradley sounded more pissed off than seriously scared. "What's happening, Ninekiller?"

Jesse didn't bother answering. He was watching the airspeed needle and easing back on the cyclic, slowing the Hughes to its optimum speed for maximum power-off gliding range. When the needle settled to eighty knots and the upper tach showed a safe 410 rotor rpm he exhaled, not loudly, and glanced at Bradley.

"Hey," he said, and pointed one-fingered at the radio without taking his hand off the cyclic grip. "Call it in?"

"Negative." Bradley didn't hesitate. "No distress calls. Maintain radio silence."

Right, Jesse thought. And that flight plan we filed was bogus as a tribal election, too. Archaeologist my Native American ass.

But there was no time to waste thinking about spooky passengers. Jesse studied the desert floor, which was rising to meet them at a distressing rate. It looked pretty much like the rest of Egypt, which seemed to consist of miles and miles and *miles* of simple doodly-squat, covered with rocks and grayish-yellow sand. At least this part didn't have those big ripply dunes, which might look neat but would certainly make a forced landing almost unbearably fascinating.

"Get set," he told Bradley. "This might be a little rough."

For a minute there it seemed the warning had been unnecessary. Jesse made a school-perfect landing, flaring out at seventy-five feet with smooth aft pressure on the cyclic, leveling off at about twenty and bringing the collective back up to cushion the final descent. As the skids touched down he thought: *damn*, I'm good.

Then the left skid sank into a pocket of amazingly soft sand and the Hughes tilted irresistibly, not all the way onto its side but far enough for the still-moving rotor blades to beat themselves to death against the ground; and things did get a little rough.

When the lurching and slamming and banging finally stopped Bradley said, "Great landing, Ninekiller." He began undoing his safety harness. "Oh, well, any landing you can walk away from is a good one. Isn't that what you pilots say?"

Jesse, already out of his own harness and busy flipping switches off—there was no reason to do that now, but fixed habits were what kept you alive—thought of a couple of things one pilot would like to say. But he kept his mouth shut and waited while Bradley got the right door open, his own being jammed against the ground. They clambered out and stood for a moment looking at the Hughes and then at their surroundings.

"Walk away is what we get to do, I guess," Bradley observed. He took off his mesh-back cap and rubbed his head, which was bald except for a couple of patches around the ears. Maybe to compensate, he wore a bristly mustache that, combined with a snubby nose and big tombstone teeth, made him look a little like Teddy Roosevelt. His skin was reddish-pink and looked as if it would burn easily. Jesse wondered how long he was going to last in the desert sun.

He climbed back into the Hughes—Jesse started to warn him about the risk of fire but figured what the hell—and rummaged around in back, emerging a few minutes later with a green nylon duffel bag, which he slung over his shoulder. "Well," he said, jumping down, "guess we better look at the map."

Grandfather's voice said, "Keep going the way you were. Few miles on, over that rise where the rock sticks out, there's water."

Jesse said, "*Wado, eduda,*" and then, as Bradley looked strangely at him, "Come on. This way."

Bradley snorted. "Long way from home, aren't you, to be pulling that Indian crap? I mean, it's not like you're an Arab." But then, when Jesse started walking away without looking back, "Oh, Christ, why not? Lead on, Tonto."

Grandfather's few miles turned out to be very long ones, and, despite the apparent flatness of the desert, uphill all the way. The ground was hard as concrete and littered with sharp rocks. Stretches of yielding sand slowed their feet and filled their shoes. It was almost three hours before they reached the stony crest of the rise and saw the place.

Or *a* place; it didn't look at all as Jesse had expected. Somehow he had pictured a movie-set oasis, a little island of green in the middle of this sandy nowhere, with palm trees and a pool of cool clear water. Maybe even some friendly Arabs, tents and camels and accommodating belly dancers . . . okay, he didn't really expect that last part, but surely there ought to be something besides more God-damned rocks and sand. Which, at first, was all he could see.

Bradley, however, let out a dry-lipped whistle. "How did you know, Ninekiller? Hate to admit it, but I'm impressed."

He started down the slope toward what had looked like a lot of crumbling rock formations and sand hillocks, but which Jesse now realized had too many straight lines and right angles to be natural. Ruined buildings, buried by sand?

Jesse said, "Does this do us a lot of good? Looks like nobody lives here any more."

"Yeah, but there's only one reason anybody would live out here."

"Water?"

"Got to be." Brad nodded. "This is a funny desert. Almost no rain at all, but the limestone bedrock holds water like a sponge. Quite a few wells scattered around, some of them pretty old."

"Maybe this one went dry," Jesse suggested. They were getting in among the ruins now, though it was hard to tell where they began. "Maybe that's why the people left."

"Could be. But hey, it's the best shot we've got." Bradley glanced back and grinned. "Right, guy?"

He stepped over what had to be the remains of a wall—not much, now, but a long low heap of loose stone blocks, worn almost round by sand and wind. The whole place appeared to be in about the same condition; Jesse saw nothing more substantial than a few knee-high fragments of standing masonry, and most of the ruins consisted merely of low humps in the sand that vaguely suggested the outlines of small buildings. These ruins were certainly, well, *ruined*.

But Bradley seemed fascinated; he continued to grin as they picked their way toward the center of the village or whatever it had been, and to look about him. Now he stopped and bent down. "Son of a bitch," he said, very softly, and whistled again, this time on a higher note. "Look at this, Ninekiller."

Jesse saw a big block of stone half buried in the sand at Bradley's feet. Looking more closely, he saw that the upturned surface was covered with faint, almost worn-away shapes and figures cut into the stone.

"Hieroglyphics," Bradley said. "My God, this place is Egyptian."

Egyptian, Jesse thought, well, of *course* it's Egyptian, you white asshole, this is *Egypt*. No, wait. "You mean ancient Egypt? Like with the pyramids?"

Bradley chuckled. "I doubt if these ruins are contemporaneous with the pyramids, guy. Though it's not impossible." He straightened up and gazed around at the ruins. "But yes, basically, those Egyptians. I'd hate to have to guess how old this site is. Anywhere from two to four thousand years, maybe more."

"Holy shit," Jesse said, genuinely awed. "What were they doing out here? I thought they hung out back along the Nile."

"Right. But there was a considerable trade with the Libyans for a long time. They had regular caravan routes across the desert. If there was a first-class well here, it would have been worth maintaining a small outpost to guard the place from marauding desert tribes."

He flashed the big front teeth again. "Kind of like Fort Apache, huh? Probably a detachment of Nubian mercenaries under Egyptian command, with a force of slaves for labor and housekeeping. They often sent prisoners of war to places like this. And, usually, worked them to death."

He took off his cap and wiped his sweaty scalp. "But we're going to be mummies ourselves if we don't find some water. Let's look around."

The well turned out to be square in the center of the ruined village, a round black hole fifteen feet or so across and so deep Jesse couldn't see if there was water at the bottom or not. Hell's own job, he thought, sinking a shaft like that in limestone bedrock, with hand tools and in this heat. He kicked a loose stone into the well and was rewarded with a deep muffled splash.

"All *right*," Bradley said. "I've got a roll of nylon cord in my bag, and a plastic bottle we can lower, so at least we're okay for water."

Jesse was studying the ground. "Somebody's been here. Not too long ago."

"Oh, shit," Bradley said crankily, "are you going to start with that Indian routine again?" Then he said, *"Hah!"*

Next to the well, lying there in plain sight, was a cigarette butt.

"Should have known," Bradley said after a moment. "No doubt the nomadic tribes and caravan guides know about this place. Good thing, in fact, because the well would have filled up with sand long ago if people hadn't kept it cleaned out."

"Bunch of tracks there." Jesse pointed. "These desert Arabs, do they go in for wearing combat boots?"

"Could be." Bradley was starting to sound unhappy. "We better check this out, though."

It didn't take an expert tracker to follow the trail away from the well and through the ruined village. There had been a good deal of booted traffic to and from the well, and the boot wearers had been pretty messy, leaving more butts and other assorted litter along the way. "Hasn't been long," Bradley said. "Tracks disappear fast in all this sand and wind. You're right, Ninekiller." He stopped, looking uneasily around. By now they were at the western edge of the ruins, where the ground began to turn upward in a long rock-strewn slope. "Somebody's been here recently."

A few yards away, Jesse said, "Somebody's still here."

On the ground, in the sliver of black shade next to a low bit of crumbling wall, lay a man. He was dressed in desert-camo military fatigues, without insignia. A tan Arab headcloth had been pulled down to cover his face. He wasn't moving and Jesse was pretty sure he wasn't going to.

"Jesus," Bradley said.

The dead man wasn't a pleasant sight. There had been little decomposition in the dry desert air, but the right leg was black and enormously swollen. The camo pants had been slashed clear up to the hip and what looked like a bootlace had been tied just above the knee. It hadn't helped.

"Snakebite," Bradley declared. "Sand viper, maybe. Or even a cobra."

"More tracks over here," Jesse reported. "Somebody was with him. Somebody didn't stick around."

The footprints climbed a little way up the slope and then ended. In their place was a very clear set of tire tracks—a Jeep, Jesse figured, or possibly a Land Rover—leading off across the slope and disappearing out into the desert. The driver had thrown a lot of gravel when he left. Lost his nerve, Jesse guessed. Found himself out here in the empty with no company but a dead man and at least one poisonous snake, and hauled ass.

A large camouflage net, lying loose on the ground beside the tire tracks as if tossed there in a hurry, raised interesting questions. Jesse was about to remark on this when he realized that Bradley was no longer standing beside him, but had moved on up the slope and was now looking at something else, something hidden by a pile of rocks and masonry fragments. "Come look," he called.

Jesse scrambled up to join him and saw another hole, this one about the size and proportions of an ordinary doorway. A rectangular shaft, very straight-sided and neatly cut, led downward into the ground at about a forty-five-degree angle. Some kind of mine? Then he remembered this was Egypt, and then he remembered that movie. "A tomb?" he asked Bradley. "Like where they put those mummies?"

"Might be." Bradley was scrabbling around in his duffel bag, looking excited. "It just might be—ah." He pulled out a big flashlight, the kind cops carry. "Watch your step, guy," he said, stepping into the hole. "You don't want to be the next snakebite fatality."

Bradley seemed to assume Jesse was coming along. That wasn't a very sound assumption; screwing around with any kind of grave was very high on the list of things Indians didn't do.

And yet, without knowing why, he climbed over the heap of scree and rubble and stepped down into the shaft after Bradley.

Bradley was standing halfway down the stone steps that formed the floor of the shaft. He was shining his flashlight here and there on the walls, which were covered with colored pictures. The paint was faded and flaking, but it was easy to make out lively scenes of people eating and paddling boats and playing musical instruments—some naked dancing girls in one panel, complete with very candid little black triangles where their legs joined—as well as other activities Jesse couldn't identify. Animals, too, cats and baboons, crocodiles and hippos and snakes; and, in among the pictures, lines of hieroglyphic writing.

There were also some extremely weird figures, human bodies with bird or animal heads. "What are they," Jesse asked, pointing, "spirits?"

"Gods," Bradley said. "*Neterw*, they were called. The one with the jackal head, for example, is Anubis, god of burials and the dead."

"This one's got a boner."

"Oh, yes. Ithyphallic figures weren't unusual." Bradley headed down the steps, swinging his flashlight. "But we can look at the art later. Let's see what we've got down here."

The shaft leveled off into a narrow passageway. The walls here were covered with murals too, but Bradley barely spared them a glance as he strode down the corridor. "Ah," he said as the hall suddenly opened into a larger and very dark space. "Now this is—oh, my God."

Behind him, Jesse couldn't see at first what Bradley was ohing his God about. He looked over Bradley's shoulder into a low-ceilinged chamber, about the size of a cheap motel room. The flashlight beam showed more paintings on the walls and ceiling. It also showed a stack of wooden boxes against the back wall.

Bradley crossed the room fast and began yanking at one of the boxes. The lid came off and thudded to the stone floor. "Shit," Bradley cried, shining his light into the box. He reached in and hauled out what Jesse instantly recognized as an AK-47 assault rifle. Kalashnikov's products tend to make an indelible impression on anyone who has ever been shot at with them.

Bradley leaned the rifle against the wall and opened another box. This time it was a grenade he held up. "Bastards," he said, almost in a whisper.

Another corridor led off to the rear. Bradley charged down it, cursing to himself, and Jesse hurried after him, disinclined to wait alone in the dark.

The corridor was a short one, ending in another room about the size of the first. It contained an even bigger stack of boxes and crates, piled to the ceiling. Some wore red *danger-explosives* markings in Arabic and English. There were also a number of plastic jerricans full of gasoline. No wonder they went outside to do their smoking, Jesse thought. What the hell was this all about?

Bradley ripped off the top of a cardboard box. "Great," he said sourly, and pulled out a small oblong packet. "U.S. Army field rations. Good old Meals, Ready to Eat. Possibly the most lethal item down here. Wonder where they got them?"

He flashed the light around the room. The chamber was fancier than the other one. Somebody had even painted fake columns along the walls.

"Bastards," he said again. "A priceless treasure of art and knowledge, and they used it for a God-damned terrorist supply dump."

"What do you suppose they did with the mummy?" Jesse asked, thinking about those stories about the mummy's curse. And that snake-bit guy lying outside.

"Oh, that was probably disposed of centuries ago, along with any portable valuables. Tomb robbing is a very ancient tradition in this country." Bradley made a disgusted sound in his throat. "Here." He tossed the MRE packet to Jesse and fished out another. "We better do lunch. We've got a burial detail waiting for us, and I don't think we'll have much appetite afterwards."

They buried the dead man in a shallow grave, using a couple of shovels that they found in the outer chamber of the tomb, piling rocks on top. "Rest in peace," Bradley said. "You poor evil little son of a bitch." He wiped his forehead with his hand. The heat was incredible. "Let's get out of this sun," he said. "Back to the tomb."

Back in the outer chamber, he tossed his shovel into a corner and sat down on a crate. He took off his cap and hoisted the water bottle and poured the contents over his head. "Needed that," he said. "I'll go get a refill in a minute."

"Don't bother," Jesse told him. "There's a big plastic jug of water over here, nearly full." He was poking around in a clutter of odds and ends by the front wall. "You can save your flashlight, too." He picked up a big battery lantern and switched it on.

"Sons of bitches made themselves at home, didn't they?" Bradley clicked his flashlight off. "Ninekiller, I'm about to commit a major breach of security. But the situation's pretty unusual, and there's no way to keep you out of it, so you'd better know the score."

He leaned back against the wall, his head resting just beneath a painting of an archer taking aim from a horse-drawn chariot. "Does the name Nolan mean anything to you?"

"Isn't he the American . . . renegade, I guess you'd say, supposed to be working for the Libyans? Running some kind of commando operation?" Jesse sat down on the floor next to the entrance. "I heard a few rumors, nothing solid. They say he's hiring pilots."

"Yes. Quite a few Americans are working for Khaddafi now," Bradley said, "fliers mostly, young soldier-of-fortune types gone bad. But Nolan is an entirely different, higher-level breed of turncoat. It's not easy to impress people in this part of the world when it comes to terrorism, sabotage, and assassination, but Nolan is right up there with the best native talent. The Colonel values his services very highly."

A circuit closed in Jesse's head. "So that's what this business is all about. Archaeology hell, you were hunting Nolan."

"A preliminary reconnaissance," Bradley said. "Word was he had something going on in this area. You wouldn't have been involved in any real action."

"Nice to know this was such a safe job," Jesse said dryly. "Why not just let the Egyptians do it?" Another realization hit him. "That's right, I remember what I heard. Nolan's a rogue CIA officer, isn't he? You guys want him out of the way without any international embarrassment."

"That, of course, I couldn't tell you," Bradley said calmly. "Your need to know extends only to the immediate situation."

He picked up one of the AK-47s from the open box. "Sooner or later, somebody is going to show up here. Too much to hope that it'll be Nolan himself, but at least it'll be somebody from his outfit. If the odds aren't too bad, and we make the right moves, we'll have a handle on Nolan and a ride out of here." He hefted the AK-47. "Know how to use one of these?"

"The hell," Jesse said angrily. "I'm a pilot, not a gunfighter. Do your own bushwhacking. You're the one who works for the CIA."

"Oh? Who do you think owns Mideast Air Charter and Transfer Services?" Bradley paused, letting that sink in. "You're a pilot? Okay, I'm an archaeologist. No shit," he said, and glanced around the tomb chamber. "Got my degree from the University of Pennsylvania, did my field work over at Wadi Gharbi. That's where they recruited me . . . and there was a time when I'd have given a leg and a nut to find something like this. Well, as it turns out, I've made myself a valuable discovery of a different kind."

He looked at Jesse. The Teddy Roosevelt grin didn't even try to make it to his eyes. "But you're welcome to sit on your ass and play conscientious objector while I take the bastards on alone. Then if they kill me you can tell them all about what an innocent bystander you are. I'm sure they'll believe you."

"Son of a bitch."

"So I've been told." He got up and walked over and held out the AK-47. "Take it, Ninekiller. It's the only way either of us is going to get out of this place alive. Or even dead."

Bradley insisted they maintain a constant watch, taking turns up at the crest of the rise, hunkering in the inadequate shade of the fist-shaped rock outcrop and staring out over the empty desert. "Have to, guy," he said. "Can't risk getting caught down in that tomb when the bad guys arrive."

When the sun finally went down, in the usual excessively spectacular style of tropical sunsets, Jesse assumed they'd drop the sentry-duty nonsense for the night. Bradley, however, was unyielding. "Remember who these people are," he pointed out, "and what they're up to. Moving by night would make good sense."

He thumbed his watch, turning on the little face light. It was getting really dark now. "I'll go below and catch a few Z's, let you take the evening watch. You wake me up at midnight and I'll take over for the graveyard shift. That okay with you, guy?"

Jesse didn't argue. He hardly ever turned in before midnight anyway. Besides, he didn't mind spending a few hours away from Bradley and the God-damned tomb. Both were starting to get on his nerves.

Alone, he slung the AK-47 over his shoulder and walked up the slope, taking his time and enjoying the cool breeze. It wasn't so bad now the sun was down. The stars were huge and white and a fat half-moon was climbing into the black sky. In the silvery soft light the desert looked almost pretty.

A dry voice in his left ear said, " '*Siyo, chooch.*"

Jesse groaned. " '*Siyo, eduda.* What's about to happen now?"

There was a dusty chuckle. "Don't worry, *chooch.* No warnings this time. Turn around—and keep your hands off that war gun."

Jesse turned. And found himself face to face with Wile E. Coyote.

That was who it looked like at first, anyway: the same long pointy muzzle, the same big bat ears and goofy little eyes. But that was just the head; from the neck down, Jesse saw now, the body was that of a man about his own size.

Jesse said, "Uh."

Grandfather's voice said, "This is Anpu. Anpu, my grandson Jesse."

"Hi," Coyote said.

That's it, Jesse thought dazedly. Too much time out in the sun today, God *damn* that Bradley. Talking coyotes—no, hell, no coyotes in Egypt, must be a jackal. Sure looks like a coyote, though. Then memory kicked in and Jesse said, "Anubis. You're Anubis."

"Anpu." The jackal ears twitched. "The Greeks screwed the name up."

"Anpu wants you to meet some friends of his," Grandfather said.

"This way," Anpu said. "The way you were going, actually."

He walked past Jesse and headed up the slope, not looking back. Grandfather's voice said, "Don't just stand there, *chooch.* Follow him."

"I don't know, *eduda,*" Jesse said as he started after the jackal-headed figure. "This is getting too weird. How did you get hooked up with this character?"

"He's the god of the dead, in these parts. And, in case you've forgotten," Grandfather pointed out, "I'm dead."

Anpu was standing at the base of the fist-shaped rock outcrop. "Here," he said, pointing.

Jesse saw nothing but a big cleft in the rock, black in the moonlight. He'd seen it dozens of times during the day. "So?" he said, a little irritably.

Anpu stepped into the cleft and disappeared, feet first. His head popped back out long enough to say, "Watch your step. It's pretty tricky."

Jesse bent and stuck his arm down into the crack. His fingers found an oval shaft, just big enough for a man's body, angling steeply down into the rock. It was so well camouflaged that even now he knew it was there, he couldn't really see it.

"It's all right, *chooch*," Grandfather said. "Go on."

Jesse stuck a cautious foot into the hole. There were notches cut into the wall of the shaft for footholds, but they weren't very deep. Gritting his teeth, he let himself down into the darkness.

He couldn't tell how far down the shaft went, but the absolute blackness and the scariness of the climb made it feel endless. The rock seemed to press in on him from all sides; he gasped for breath, and might have quit except that going back up would be just as bad. The tunnel bent to one side and then there was nothing under his feet. He probed with one toe, lost his grip, and plummeted helplessly out of the shaft and into open space. Off balance, he hit cross-footed and fell on his ass onto very hard flat stone.

He opened his eyes—he didn't know when he'd closed them—and saw immediately that he was in another tomb. Or another underground chamber, anyway, complete with art work on the walls and ceiling. This one was filled with a soft, slightly yellowish light; he couldn't see the source.

Anpu was standing over him, reaching down a hand. "Are you all right?" the jackal-headed god asked anxiously. "I should have warned you about that last bit. Sorry."

Jesse took the hand and pulled himself to his feet. Suddenly a tall, beautiful woman in a flowing white dress came rushing up, shoving Anpu out of the way and putting her arms around Jesse's neck. "Oh, poor man," she cried, pulling Jesse's head down and pressing his face against her bosom. It was one hell of a bosom. "Did you hurt yourself? Do you want to lie down?"

"This is Hathor," Anpu said. His voice sounded muffled; Jesse's ears were wonderfully obstructed for the moment.

"Goddess of love and motherhood," Grandfather's voice said. "Get loose, *chooch*, there's others to meet. Later for the hot stuff."

Jesse managed to mumble something reassuring and Hathor reluctantly let him go. As she stepped back he realized she had horns. Not just little ones, either, like the ones on the Devil in the old pictures. These were big, curving horns like a buffalo's, white as ivory and tipped with little gold balls.

A deeper voice said, "Nasty bit of work, that access tunnel. We don't like it either. But the main entrance shaft is sealed, and buried by sand as well."

The speaker was another animal-faced figure, this one with the head of a shaggy gray baboon atop a short, skinny human body. He looked a little like Jesse's high school principal. "I am Thoth," he added.

"God of wisdom and knowledge," Grandfather explained in Jesse's left ear.

"And this," Anpu said, waving a hand at a fourth individual, "is Sobek."

Jesse would just as soon have missed meeting Sobek. From the shoulders down he looked like a normal man—though built like a pro wrestler—but above that grinned the head of a crocodile. The long jaws opened, revealing rows of sharp teeth, and a voice like rusty iron said, "Yo."

"I still don't get what he does," Grandfather admitted. "Got a feeling I don't want to know."

"Sorry we can't offer refreshments," Anpu apologized. "We didn't come prepared for social occasions."

"Excuse me," Jesse said, "but where did you all learn English?"

"Your grandfather taught us," Thoth replied. "This afternoon, in fact."

"That fast?" Talk about quick studies.

"Of course," Thoth said stiffly. "Simple brain-scan. I mean, we *are* gods."

"Yeah," Grandfather's voice said, "but I tried first to teach them Cherokee and they couldn't get it worth a damn."

Jesse looked around the chamber. It was larger than the ones the Arabs had been using, and finer. The ceiling was cut in an arching vault shape, and the pictures on the wall had been carved in low relief as well as painted. "Nice place," he said politely. "Somebody loot this one too? I don't see any mummies."

"As a matter of fact," Thoth said, "this tomb was never used. It was built for the last commander of this outpost, a nobleman named Neferhotep—"

"He screwed up bad back in Thebes," Sobek croaked, "and Pharaoh sent him to this shit-hole."

"—who was killed," Thoth went on, glaring at Sobek, "in a clash with Libyan raiders. His body was never recovered. Soon afterward the outpost was abandoned."

"So what are you, uh, gods doing here now?" Jesse was trying not to stare at Hathor. That gown was so thin you could see right through it, and she wasn't wearing a damn thing underneath. For that matter none of the neterw had exactly overdressed; the others wore only short skirts and assorted jewelry.

"A mistake," Anpu said. "Strange business. You see, the dead man, the one you buried today, happened to be a very distant but direct descendant of the Pharaoh Ramses the Great. Though of course it's unlikely he knew it."

"The death of one of royal blood," Thoth said, "so near an unused tomb, somehow resulted in a false reading in the House of the Dead."

"Osiris stepped on his dick," Sobek growled. "Old Green-Face is losing it."

"Even Osiris," Anpu protested, "could hardly have predicted such an improbable coincidence."

"Oh, I don't know." Thoth looked thoughtful. "Perhaps not such a farfetched chance as it might seem—"

He produced a polished wooden box, bound in gold, about the size and shape of an attaché case. Sitting cross-legged on the floor, he flipped a jeweled catch and the box opened into two sections. The lower half, which rested flat on his lap, contained a long ebony panel with rows of carved ivory pegs. The upper section was entirely filled by a smooth rectangle of some dark crystalline stone. Thoth tapped his fingertips over the pegs and a row of hieroglyphics appeared on the surface of the crystal, glowing with a faint greenish light.

"Let's see," Thoth mused. "Ramses the Second lived thirty-two centuries ago. He had over one hundred known offspring by his various wives. Now assuming an average number of progeny—"

"At any rate," Hathor sighed, "the four of us were sent, and here we are." She gave Jesse a smile that would have given the Sphinx an erection. "Well, perhaps things could be worse."

"—and a conservative estimate of three point five generations per century—" Thoth's fingers were dancing on the pegs. The crystal was covered with hieroglyphics.

"But," Jesse said, "if it was all a mistake, why are you still here?"

"—allowing a reasonable factor for infertility and infant mortality—"

Anpu shrugged. "Come on. I'll show you."

He led the way to an arched doorway at the rear of the chamber. Hathor and Sobek followed behind Jesse. As they left the room Thoth was staring at the crystal and scratching his head with one finger. "That can't be right," he muttered.

"At the rear of this tomb," Anpu explained as they made their way down a long hallway, "is what you might call a portal. Every burial center in Egypt has at least one. It's—" He stopped and looked back at Jesse. "I can't really explain it to you. It's a place where we can pass back and forth between this world and ours. Mortals can't even see it, let alone penetrate it."

"Except when they die," Hathor added, "and we come and get them."

"Which hasn't happened for a long time," Anpu said, nodding. "It's been almost two thousand of your years since anyone was interred with the necessary procedures. We were really disappointed to find out this was a false alarm. We had hoped the people were returning to the old ways."

He turned and started walking again. Only a few paces along the corridor, he stopped again. "There," he said. "You see the problem."

A huge slab of stone, apparently fallen from the ceiling, totally blocked the passageway. It was as big as a U-Haul trailer.

"It happened just after we arrived," Anpu said. "Evidently, when the other man drove away, the vibration caused the fall. Of course it must have been badly cracked already."

"And now you can't get back? To—wherever you came from?"

Anpu shook his head. "The nearest other portals are off in the Nile valley. I'm not sure we could make the journey." He looked at the great stone slab and his ears drooped a little. "But we may have to try."

"Never," Hathor declared. "That sun, that wind. My skin. No."

Jesse noticed a strange, impractical-looking contrivance lying on the floor, an assemblage of improvised ropes and levers. He recognized a couple of machine-gun barrels, and twisted-together rifle slings. He said, "What's this?"

"Something Anpu invented," Sobek grunted. "He calls it an *akh-me*. Doesn't work for shit."

"It seemed worth a try." Anpu kicked dispiritedly at the device. He looked at Jesse. "Can you help us? Your grandfather says you know about machinery."

Jesse studied the barrier. "I don't know. It's not in my usual line—" He felt Hathor's eyes upon him. "Maybe," he said. "I'll think about it. Let me sleep on it."

They went back up the corridor. As they entered the burial chamber Thoth looked up. "It's right here, I tell you." He touched a fingertip to the glowing crystal. "There's no arguing with the numbers. Everyone in the world is a descendant of Ramses the Second."

At midnight Jesse walked back down to the other tomb to wake Bradley. Anpu walked with him, for no apparent reason but sociability. Halfway down the slope they met Bradley coming the other way, lugging his rifle. "Hey, guy," he said cheerfully. "Get some sleep, now. I'll wake you at daybreak."

He went on up toward the big rock. Anpu chuckled. "Your friend can't see me. Not if I don't want him to, anyway."

"He's not my friend," Jesse said, more emphatically than he meant to.

Anpu looked curiously around as they entered the tomb. "I haven't really taken the time to look at the other tombs around here," he remarked as Jesse switched on the battery lantern. "This one isn't bad, actually."

Jesse leaned his AK-47 against the wall by the door. "Other tombs?"

"Oh, yes. Quite a few nearby—all sealed and hidden, of course. You'd never find them if you didn't know where to look."

He leaned forward, examining a hieroglyphic inscription on the wall. Jesse said, "What's that say, anyway?"

Anpu tilted his head to one side. "A free translation," he said after a moment, "might be: 'There once was a goddess named Isis, whose breasts were of different sizes. One was dainty and small, almost no breast at all, but the other was huge and won prizes.'"

"Get out of here."

"All right," Anpu said. "Have a pleasant night, Jesse."

When he was gone Jesse looked around briefly and then picked up the battery lantern and went down the corridor to the rear chamber. The air felt cooler there and the floor was cleaner. He took a gray military blanket from a stack in one corner and made himself a pallet on the floor, rolling up another blanket for a pillow. Lying down and switching off the lantern, he wondered if he would be able to sleep in this place, but he did, almost immediately, and without dreams.

When he awoke—he didn't know how long he had been asleep; later, though, he thought it couldn't have been long—it was with the distinct feeling that he was no longer alone in the burial chamber. That might have been because somebody was trying to take his clothes off.

He said, "Wha," and fumbled for the battery lantern and switched it on.

Hathor was crouching over him, tugging at the waistband of his pants. "You must help me," she said urgently. "I don't understand these strange garments."

Jesse blinked and shook his head. "Well, that is, ah—"

"Don't worry, *chooch*," said the voice in his left ear. "She's not out to steal your soul or anything like that. She just wants to get laid. It's been a long time since she did it with anybody who wasn't at least a couple thousand years old."

Hathor was now yanking his shoes off. Jesse skinned his sweaty T-shirt up over his head and reached to undo his belt buckle. Grandfather's voice said, "I'll leave you two alone now."

As Jesse got rid of his briefs—wishing he'd worn a better pair—Hathor rose to her feet and undid a clasp at her shoulder, letting the white gown fall away, leaving her naked except for wide gold bracelets on her wrists. "I shall give you love," she announced. "I shall serve you a feast of divine pleasure."

Throbbingly ithyphallic, Jesse watched as she put a foot on either side of him. The horns, he decided, weren't so bad once you got over the first shock of seeing them. In fact they were kind of sexy.

She knelt, straddling him. "Yes," she said, bending forward, mashing those astonishing breasts against his chest, "impale me with the burning spear of your desire." Clasping with arms and thighs, she rolled onto her back, pulling him on top of her, heels spurring him. "Oh, fill my loins with your mighty obelisk," she cried, "come into me with the Nile of your passion. Do me like a hot baboon, big boy!"

Well, Jesse thought, you always did like horny women with big ones. . . .

He awoke again to disturbing dreams of Vietnam; sounds of gunfire and rotors rattled in his ears. The room was still dark but his watch showed almost eight o'clock. Hastily he dressed, pausing as he felt the bracelet on his right wrist. Hathor's; she must have put it there as he slept. Memories of the night came rushing back, and he stood for a moment grinning foolishly to himself.

Then he heard it again, faint but unmistakable: a rapid snapping, like popcorn in a microwave.

He jerked his shoes on, not bothering with socks, and ran down the corridor to the front chamber. He was halfway across the room, going for the gun he had left there, when a man appeared in the doorway: no more than a vague dark shape in the poor light that came down the entrance corridor, but Jesse knew immediately that it wasn't Bradley. He saw a dull glint that had to be a gun barrel.

Without hesitation he threw his hands in the air as high as they would go. "Don't shoot!" he yelled, wishing he knew how to say it in Arabic. "See? No gun. *Salaam aleykum*," he added somewhat desperately. "Friendly Indian. Okay?"

The gun swung his way and his insides went loose. But either the man got the idea or, more likely, he realized it wasn't a good idea to fire shots inside a room full of munitions. A harsh voice hawked up several syllables in what sounded like Arabic, and then, in a loud shout, "No-lan! No-lan!"

An answering shout came from outside. The man jerked his weapon and said, "*Yalla.* You come. Quick."

He backed slowly up the corridor, keeping Jesse covered. Jesse followed, hands still in the air, sphincter clenched. The sunlight blinded him as he reached the foot of the stone steps and he stumbled, and was yelled at. At the top of the steps the gunman said, "Stop."

Jesse stopped, blinking against the glare, trying to focus on the three backlit figures standing before him. A big booming voice, American by accent and cadence, said, "Well, what have we got here? Speak English, fella?"

Jesse thought about replying in Cherokee, just to confuse matters, but he didn't think that would do any good. He nodded. "Sure."

He could see all right, now. The man who had found him stood four or five feet away, a dark, skinny little bastard dressed in desert camo, like the snakebite victim they had buried yesterday. A face that was mostly nose and bad teeth stared unpleasantly at Jesse from the shade of a sand-tan headcloth. To his left stood another who was virtually his twin in build, ugliness, and attitude. Both men held AK-47s, pointed at Jesse's belt buckle.

It was the third man, the one who had just spoken, who got and held Jesse's attention. He wore the same unmarked camo-and-headcloth outfit as the others, but if he was an Arab Jesse was Princess Leia. He was taller than Jesse, six feet at least, with broad shoulders and a big beefy face. A rifle dangled casually from his right hand.

"Nolan," Jesse said without thinking.

The big man fixed him with bright blue eyes. "Do we know each other?"

"Everybody's heard of you." Shovel a little, never hurts. "All the pilots around this part of the world, anyway."

"Pilots? Ah." Nolan nodded. "You'll be the one who piled up that Hughes, down yonder beyond the ridge."

Before Jesse could reply a fourth man came down the slope, feet sliding in the loose rocks and sand. "Hey, Nolan," he began, and then stopped, seeing Jesse. "What the hell?" he said. "Who's this?"

"One of your professional colleagues," Nolan told him. "Apparently he was flying that Hughes."

The new arrival was about Jesse's height and rather slight of build, with small sharp pretty-boy features. He wore light-blue coveralls and a baseball cap. His hands were empty but a shoulder-holstered pistol bulged beneath his left armpit.

"No shit?" The accent was Southern. "How'd you do that, man?"

"Engine failure," Jesse said.

Looking past the Southerner, Jesse saw that there was another helicopter sitting on the ground on the far side of the rise. He could just see the tail and part of the main rotor. It looked like a French Alouette but he wasn't sure.

What he couldn't see, anywhere, was Bradley. That might be good. Probably it wasn't.

Nolan said, "Well, I wish you'd had it somewhere else. That wreck is liable to draw all sorts of attention. Can't believe it hasn't been spotted already." He gave Jesse a speculative look. "Just what were you doing around here, anyway?"

Jesse shrugged. "Flying this guy around." Play it dumb, that shouldn't be too much of a reach. "He said he was an archaeologist."

The pilot, if that was what he was, laughed. Nolan grimaced. "Maybe he should have been. He wasn't worth a damn at what he was trying to do."

"Is he all right?" Jesse asked innocently.

"Not so you'd notice," the pilot said. "In fact he's pretty damn dead."

"He tried to ambush us," Nolan told Jesse. "It was a stupid business. The odds were impossible and he didn't have a clue what he was doing."

Jesse felt sick. He hadn't liked Bradley but still . . . why hadn't the damn fool called him when he saw the helicopter coming? Maybe he had. Maybe he hadn't realized how little Jesse could hear, down in that tomb. Or maybe he'd just decided he was John Wayne.

One of the gunmen said something in Arabic. Nolan said, "He wants to know if you buried the man who was here."

Jesse nodded. "We didn't kill him. Looked like a snake got him."

"We know," Nolan said. "It's why we're here. That worthless punk who was with him took off and tried to make the border, only he happened to run into some of our people. They interrogated him and sent a message. I came at first light."

He jerked his head at the Arab who had spoken. "Gamal only wanted to thank you for burying his cousin. Don't be misled. He'll kill you just as quickly if you make a mistake."

"So," the pilot said, "what now?"

"Shut the place down," Nolan said. "We've got to assume it's been compromised. Why else would a CIA agent be sniffing around?" He rubbed his chin and sighed. "God, what a mess. . . . I'll take Gamal and Zaal and set some charges."

"Going to blow it all?"

"Yes. Damn shame, after all the effort and risk that went into bringing all that material here. But it's not as if there weren't plenty where it came from." He looked at Jesse. "You better keep an eye on this joker till we're done."

The pilot nodded and reached for his pistol. "Gonna take him back with us?"

"Oh, sure," Nolan said. "Major Hamid can ask him some questions—"

Suddenly the man called Gamal let out a high excited screech and grabbed Jesse's right arm. "*Shoof, shoof,*" he cried. "No-lan, *shoof!*"

The other Arab joined in, shouting and squawking, pushing for a better look. Nolan barked something short and pungent and both men fell silent. Then everybody stood and stared at the gold band on Jesse's wrist.

Nolan took the arm away from Gamal and bent his head, studying the bracelet closely. "Where did you get this?" he asked softly.

Jesse said, "Well, there was this old Egyptian lady—"

Nolan sighed again, straightened, and hit Jesse hard in the stomach with his fist. Jesse doubled up and fell to his knees, retching and fighting for air. "Now," Nolan said patiently, "stop being silly and tell me where you got that bracelet. Did you find it around here?"

Unable to speak, Jesse nodded. The pilot said, "What's going on, Nolan?"

"Look at it," Nolan said. "That gold, that workmanship. You've never seen anything like it outside the museum in Cairo."

"Old, huh?" The pilot whistled, like Bradley. "Worth money?"

"Worth a great deal, even by itself. If there's more around here—"

"God damn," the pilot said. "All right, bud. Where'd you find it?"

Still on his knees, clutching his midriff and trying to breathe, Jesse looked past the two renegades and up the slope. A dark prick-eared head had popped up out of the hole in the fist-shaped rock. Silhouetted against the bright sky, Anpu looked even more like that cartoon coyote.

"If Gamal and Zaal have to get it out of you," Nolan said, "you won't like it."

Anpu wiggled his ears. A skinny arm came up and waved. Anpu pointed with exaggerated motions at the backs of Nolan and his men. Then he jabbed his finger downwards, toward the rock. He grinned and disappeared.

Jesse raised a hand. "Okay," he said weakly. "Let me up. I'll show you."

He got to his feet and started up the slope. "Be careful," Nolan warned, falling in behind him. "This better not be a trick."

Up by the rock outcrop Jesse stopped. The pilot said, "Shit, there ain't anything here."

"Over here." Jesse showed them the hole. Nolan bent down and felt around with one hand. His eyebrows went up. "It goes down to this tomb," Jesse said. "Lots of interesting stuff down there."

"I'll be damned." Nolan's voice was almost a whisper. "Ray, have you got a flashlight?"

"Sure." The pilot unclipped a small black cylinder from his belt and passed it over. "Not real big, but she's brighter than she looks."

"Come on, then." Nolan handed his AK-47 to the man called Zaal. He stepped into the shaft and began working his way downward. When he had vanished from sight the pilot, looking very dubious, climbed down after him.

That left Jesse and the two Arabs, who were still eyeing him and fingering their weapons. He stood still and didn't eye back. Inside his head he was trying to replay the climb down the shaft. By now they should be about halfway down. Now Nolan would have reached the bend in the tunnel. Big as he was, he'd have a tight time of it. Now he should be almost there. Now—

The scream that came up the shaft was like nothing Jesse had ever heard. Or ever wanted to hear again, but almost immediately there was another one just like it.

Both Arabs made exclamations of surprise. Zaal ran over, still clutching his own AK-47 and Nolan's, and stared down the shaft. Gamal simply stood there with his mouth open and his eyes huge.

That was about as good as it was likely to get. Jesse put his hands together in a double fist and clubbed Gamal as hard as he could on the side of the neck. The AK-47 came loose easily as Gamal's fingers went limp. Jesse turned and put a long burst into Zaal, who seemed to have gotten confused to find himself holding two rifles. He swung the AK-47 back and shot Gamal in the chest a couple of times, just in case he hadn't hit him hard enough. Then he went and looked down the tunnel, keeping the gun ready but not expecting to have to use it.

Sure enough, Anpu stuck his head out of the hole. "Are you all right?" he asked. "Well," he said, seeing the two bodies, "not bad. Your grandfather said you could take care of yourself."

Some muffled nightmare sounds floated up the shaft. Anpu cocked his head and winced. "That Sobek," he murmured. "Good at what he does, but so *crude.* . . ."

He looked at Jesse and cleared his throat. "I realize this isn't a good time," he said apologetically, "but about that matter we discussed—"

"I'll see what I can do," Jesse said. "Looks like I owe you."

A couple of hours later, standing by the rock outcrop, Jesse said, "Now you're certain this is going to work?"

"Hey, *chooch.*" Grandfather sounded hurt. "Don't question an elder about his medicine. Have I ever let you down?"

Jesse snorted. "Where were you this morning?"

"You mean why didn't I wake you up, so you could run out and get yourself killed along with that white fool? He didn't have a chance," Grandfather said, "and you wouldn't have either. Be glad you were in the back room, where you couldn't hear till it was too late."

Jesse nodded reluctantly. "I guess you're right," he said. "Let's do it."

He looked around one more time. The *neterw* were standing there, as they had been for an hour or so, watching him with expressions of polite patience. Hathor raised a hand and wiggled white fingers and smiled. Sobek fingered something out of his back teeth and belched. None of them spoke.

Jesse picked up the little black box from between his feet, being careful not to foul the two wires that ran down into the tunnel. "Fire in the hole," he called, and thumbed the red button.

The noise was much less than he expected, just a dull quick *boomp*. The ground jumped slightly underfoot. That was all.

Anpu was already moving past him, sliding feet-first into the shaft, ignoring the smoke and fumes pouring out of the hole. "You'd better stay here," he said to Jesse. "It might be hard for you to breathe down there."

He dropped out of sight. Grandfather said, "Like I say, this is my medicine. Ought to be, after three years in the Seabees and eight in that mine in Colorado. Not to mention the Southern Pacific—"

A high-pitched yipping came up the tunnel. Anpu sounded happy.

"One thing I know," Grandfather finished, "is how to shoot rock."

"Then why didn't you just tell them how to do it?" Jesse wanted to know. "Why bring me in?"

"Trust those four with explosives? I may be dead but I'm not stupid. The thing about gods," Grandfather said, "they got a lot of power, but when you get right down to it they're not very smart. I remember once—"

Anpu's head and shoulders emerged from the hole. He was grinning widely. His tongue hung out on one side.

"It worked," he said cheerfully. "It was perfect. Shattered the rock into small fragments without damaging anything else. As soon as we can clear away the rubble—nothing Sobek can't handle—we can reach the portal and be on our way."

He went back down the shaft. Thoth was right behind him, then Sobek. Hathor paused and touched Jesse's cheek. "Call me," she said, and stepped gracefully into the hole.

"How about that," Grandfather said. "It worked."

"For God's sake," Jesse said, "you weren't sure? I thought you said—"

"Listen," Grandfather said defensively, "it's been a long time. And that funny plastic explosive those A-rabs had, I never used anything like that before."

Jesse shook his head. He walked around the rock outcrop and started down the side of the ridge, toward Nolan's helicopter. An Alouette, all right. He'd never even ridden in one. This was going to be interesting.

Grandfather said, "Can you drive that thing, chooch?"

"Sure," Jesse said dryly. "It's my medicine."

It took three tries to get the Alouette started and off the ground. Lifting clear at last, struggling with the unfamiliar controls, Jesse heard: "You got it, *chooch*? I'm cutting out now."

"You're staying here, *eduda?*" The Alouette kept trying to swing to the left. Maybe it wanted to go home to Libya.

"Going back to the spirit world," Grandfather said. "That portal of theirs is a lot easier than the regular route."

Jesse got the Alouette steadied at last, heading northward, and let out his breath. What next? Try to make the coast, ditch the Alouette in a salt marsh, walk to the coastal highway and try to hitch a ride to the nearest town.

He had a little cash, and if he could get to Alexandria he knew people who would be good for a no-questions one-way trip out of this country. If things got tight that gold bracelet ought to buy a lot of co-operation. It wasn't going to be easy, but the alternative was to land at some airfield, tell his story to the authorities, and spend the next lengthy piece of his life in an Egyptian prison.

"Take care, *sgilisi*," Grandfather said. "I'll be around."

Like that, he was gone. Jesse almost felt him leave.

After a minute Jesse sighed and settled back in the seat. Feeding in more throttle, pressing cautiously against the cyclic, he watched the airspeed needle climb. Below him, the Alouette's shadow flitted across the sand and the rocks, hurrying over Egypt.

"Ninekiller and the Neterw" was written for the Roger Zelazny memorial anthology Lord of the Fantastic. *(Originally titled* Friends of Roger, *and I was disappointed when Avon changed it.) We were asked to write something showing Roger's influence; that was a no-brainer for me, since he had not only gotten me into writing short stories in the first place but had suggested, and shown in some of his own work (e.g.* Eye of Cat*), the possibilities of American Indian themes in speculative fiction. He had also been the one to demonstrate what could be done with ancient myths in SF, though I hadn't as yet tried anything of the sort in my own work.*

I have already indicated that Roger was an old and valued friend; we went back a lot of years, to a mid-sixties establishment in Baltimore where I was playing guitar and allegedly singing—but the story is a long and convoluted one and I have told it elsewhere. Enough to say that his death came as a brutal blow to me, and to a lot of other people, many of whom had never met him.

This is, of course, another somewhat dated story, in view of later developments in the Middle East. In particular the ineffable Col. Khaddafi has publicly renounced any involvement in terrorism and subversion against his neighbors; and one can hardly doubt the word of so distinguished a gentleman, can one?

Written September 1996
First published June 1999

Dirty Little Cowards

The client said, "Should I go on down there and, uh, get undressed?"

"You might want to wait," Allison told him. "They're not quite ready yet."

"All right," the client said. "Whatever you say."

"It's just that, you might have noticed, it's pretty cool in here," Allison said. "Have to keep it that way. The equipment, you know."

"Yes." The client nodded. "It *is* a little chilly."

Actually there was a visible sheen of sweat on his face, but that almost certainly had nothing to do with the temperature.

"They'll let us know when it's time," Allison assured him. "Won't be long now."

At the other end of the main control console, the man named Burns silently damned Allison for a mealymouthed fool. It wasn't going to hurt this overprivileged jackoff to stand around the tank room naked and shivering for a few extra minutes. Now he'd be hanging out in here, asking questions and generally being a pain in the ass, for that much longer. Trust Allison, though, to suck up to the clients.

"I have to admit I'm a little nervous," the client admitted in a voice that suggested in fact he was a lot nervous. He rubbed his hands together and then shoved them deep into the pockets of his expensive-looking gray suit.

He was a medium-sized man, a little on the short side; Burns, remembering the TV and netzine shots of a decade or so ago, had thought he'd be bigger. But then the pictures hadn't been very clear, or given much time, the news people no doubt figuring that the public wasn't interested in yet another incomprehensible financial scandal. Considering how he'd gotten away with it, they must have been right.

He looked no older than thirty-five or forty, though Burns knew he had to be well past that bracket. His thick dark wavy hair showed no gray, and his wide evenly-tanned face was without lines or wrinkles. That didn't mean anything, though. Nowadays people wore the faces and bodies they could afford.

And it went without saying that this one could afford plenty; otherwise he wouldn't be here. There were very few people in the country who could pay for a private timetap, even the ordinary passive—and legal—variety. As for the kind of specialized service Mr. Tedesco offered his clients. . . .

The door from the hallway slid open and a stocky dark-faced man, dressed in white coveralls, stepped into the control room. "Devereaux," Allison greeted him. "I believe you've met—"

"Yeah." Devereaux nodded perfunctorily in the client's direction without really looking at him. "They in yet?" he asked Burns.

Burns shook his head. "Should be any minute."

Almost immediately the speaker on the wall said, "Control, this is Projection. We have a tap."

"Ah," Allison said. "Here we go."

He touched a couple of keys. One of the two big viewscreens mounted above the console came to blurry black and gray life, quickly resolving into a view of a good-sized room, rather plainly appointed, where a number of people were seating themselves at a long table.

"St. Joseph, Missouri. Monday morning, April third, eighteen eighty-two. Like to take a look?" Allison asked.

The client moved eagerly to stand beside Allison, watching the screen, where the picture was now panning from right to left, giving glimpses of a couple of young boys and then a middle-aged woman in a high-collared dress, before settling on a gaunt bearded man who sat at the head of the table. "My God," the client said, "it's him, isn't it?"

The bearded man's lips moved. The picture blurred again, cleared briefly in a close-up of a blue-patterned plate on a plain white surface, and then suddenly went black. Allison said, "Shit!" and Devereaux said, "What the hell?"

The client bent forward, staring at the darkened screen. "What's wrong?" His voice had gone up almost an octave.

Burns was studying the bank of instruments next to the screen. "Let's have the sound," he told Allison.

Allison touched another key and a high nasal voice filled the room: "—we give thanks for the food with which you have blessed us—"

"It would appear," Burns said dryly, "that our man has merely bowed his head and closed his eyes."

"—in Jesus' name, amen." The screen lit up again and the voice added, "Zee, would you pass the biscuits, please?"

"Praying," Allison said. "I'll be damned. Guy kills people, holds up banks and trains, but he says prayers at the breakfast table righteous as you please. How about that?"

The client was still staring at the screen, which now showed food being loaded onto a plate. He said, "Could you show *him* again?"

Devereaux snorted. Burns said, "This isn't a TV show. What you see on that screen is what the host sees, nothing more or less. We have no control over what he chooses to look at."

"Not until we have an active tap," Allison added.

"Oh. Right. Sorry." The client flushed slightly. "Mr. Tedesco explained all that. I don't know what I was thinking."

The bearded man was on screen again, seeming to look directly at them. He had deep-set eyes and a keen, rather disturbing gaze. "More gravy?" he asked.

Another voice, male and deeper, replied from somewhere outside the host's field of vision: "Thanks, Jesse, don't mind if we do. Do we, Bob?"

Burns pushed himself back from the console and swung around in his chair. "Better get on down there," he advised the client.

"Yes." The client, however, made no move to leave. "Uh, does anyone ever, well—" He cleared his throat. "You know. Not make it back."

Burns sighed. "There's no question of 'making it back,'" he said patiently. "Remember, you're not actually going anywhere. You'll be right down the hall, in the tank, the whole time. I'm sure Mr. Tedesco went over this with you."

"Well, sure." The client made a fidgety face. "I know I don't go anywhere *physically*. But my mind, my identity, is going to be off in the past, well over a century before I was born—"

"We don't really know that," Allison interjected. "It may be a telepathic link of some sort. Nobody really knows how it works."

"Whatever." The client waved an impatient hand. "I'm going to be inside the host's head, right? I'm going to be taking over Robert Ford's mind and body, for a little time. I'll *be* him."

"What you're asking," Burns said, "is what if the host gets killed while you're still on tap."

The client nodded. Burns said, "Then the answer is, we don't know. It's never happened, here or anywhere else. And we go to great lengths to make sure it doesn't happen. That's why we'll be monitoring vital signs, ready to yank you out if anything goes wrong." He indicated Devereaux with a tilt of his head. "That's also why you'll have backup along."

"Anyway," Allison put in, "there's nothing to worry about in this case. Nothing's going to happen to your host, because history records that nothing did. Not on this particular day."

That, Burns thought, was a neat bit of reassuring rubber-science bullshit. Maybe the past was nailed down and maybe it wasn't; there were people ready to argue either way—but so far nobody had been crazy enough to take a pry-bar to history in order to find out. In fact that was the best single reason for protecting the client at all costs: lose the poor bastard back there, and you might somehow lose yourself and your whole world as well.

The client continued to stand there, looking unhappy. "I tell you what," Burns said, thinking screw this. "If you don't want to do it, it's not too late to cancel. Just say the word."

He gestured at the screen. "Or we can do a regular passive tap, if you like. Instead of going into the tank, you can go to the VR room and put on the helmet, and we'll jack you through to Projection. You'll get almost the same trip—see everything the host sees, hear everything he hears, experience almost all his sensations. No risk at all," Burns said, keeping his voice absolutely neutral. "Elderly history professors and wimpy little graduate students do it all the time. It's even legal."

He folded his arms and stared at the client. "Of course, you'll only be an observer, along for the ride. At the end, you still won't know what it's really like to do it. Will you?"

For a moment Burns thought he'd blown it, pushed too hard. The client's face went red and then pale. But then he said, "You're right." His head moved in a jerky nod. "Not much point in doing it, really, if there's no risk."

He turned toward the door. Halfway there he paused and looked once more at the bearded man on the viewscreen. "You know," he said, "I've always felt a certain kinship with him."

When the door closed behind the client Burns said, "Sure. He made his pile ripping off banks, too."

Devereaux was laughing soundlessly, his shoulders shaking. Allison let out his breath with a soft whistling sound. "Burns, you crazy son of a bitch. One of these days you'll give a client too much shit and he'll walk. Then you'll be doing some walking of your own, while Mr. Tedesco makes sure you never work in timetaps again. What then?"

He gave Burns a mean little grin. "You won't like unemployment. They work your ass off in those compulsory labor camps."

Devereaux came across the room and studied the big screen, where the bearded man was now ladling something onto his plate. "So that's Jesse James," he mused. "Bad-looking mother. You know, I never pictured him with a beard."

"He may have grown it as a disguise," Burns said. "He was doing that sort of thing at the time. Calling himself Thomas Howard, and the like."

"You've got to quit letting the clients get to you," Allison said to Burns. "I know they can drive you crazy. Like this one Mr. Tedesco told me about, wanted to do Jack the Ripper. Mr. Tedesco said he must have talked for an hour, going over it again and again, explaining all the different reasons it couldn't be done—starting with the basic impossibility of tapping a host who's never been identified—"

"They still don't know who old Jack was, huh?" Devereaux asked.

Allison shook his head. "Besides, there are no really accurate time-and-place coordinates for any of his murders. Anyway," he said, "at the end, all this silly asshole said was, 'All right, how much is it going to cost me?'"

Burns was watching one of the secondary monitor screens, which showed a not very clear view of the tank room. The client was standing beside one of the tanks, unbuttoning his shirt. A coverall-clad attendant stood by, holding the suit jacket, waiting for the rest. "Looks like he's going through with it," Burns remarked.

"Sure. The money he's put down for this little adventure, he's not going to back out now. Mr. Tedesco doesn't give refunds."

Allison shook his head again, more slowly. "Why do they do it?" he said, surprising Burns. "Guys like this—" He jerked a thumb at the monitor, where the client could now be seen peeling off his underwear. "They've got the brains to make the big scores, money to do anything they want. Wouldn't you think they could find something smarter to do?"

"It's the rush," Burns said. "The rush they hope they'll get from doing something clear off the normal scale. They're already at the top of whatever they do professionally, so there's not much of the old rush left there. And they've already tried just about everything else they ever wondered about."

"You ask me," Devereaux said, "they're trying to prove how long their dicks are."

"That too," Burns agreed.

The tank-room monitor screen now showed a nude figure struggling into a shiny one-piece suit, aided by a couple of attendants.

"Well," Allison said, "it's their money. If it was me, though, I sure as hell wouldn't waste it playing cowboys. If I could afford to spring for a private timetap, I'd tap Jack Kennedy while he was screwing Marilyn Monroe."

Burns winced. Even Allison ought to know better—

"Control," the speaker called, "this is Projection. We have acquired backup tap. Repeat, we have backup tap."

The second big viewscreen lit up, displaying a picture almost identical to the first, except that the viewpoint appeared to be a meter to the right and a little lower. Devereaux said, "Okay, time to do it," and headed for the door.

When he was gone Burns said, "Damn it, Allison, don't *ever* mention Kennedy in front of Devereaux."

"Because of Dallas? For God's sake," Allison said irritably, "I'm getting so tired of that shit. Whatever he did in Dallas—"

"What Devereaux did in Dallas," Burns said in a hard flat voice, "was what had to be done. The client flipped out, the hit was falling apart, maybe the whole world was about to come unwrapped, who knows? All right, things got messy, there were some tracks that didn't get cleaned up. I'm telling you, Devereaux did what had to be done. You weren't there. You weren't even here."

He picked up his headset and slipped it on, shutting out any reply. After a moment Allison shrugged and put on his own headset, switching off the speaker. He could speak to Burns now, via the headset's built-in microphone, but he made no attempt to do so.

There was no time left for conversation anyway. Down in the tank room the attendants were fitting the bulbous black helmet over the client's head, while over by the second tank Devereaux was suiting up unassisted. Burns watched the monitor as both men, now indistinguishably suited and helmeted, climbed into their tanks and were sealed in.

Now the attendants busied themselves at the control panels on the wall. There was a quick loud beep in the headset and the instrument panel between the main viewscreens began to come alive with flickering digital readouts. Burns studied the display for a couple of minutes and then keyed his microphone. "Control to Projection," he said. "Okay to activate backup."

He watched Devereaux's display carefully—you always sent the backup man through first, just in case there was something nasty and unprecedented waiting back down the line; if anything ever did go wrong, it was understood that the backup man was more expendable than the client—until the voice in the headset said, "Projection to Control. Backup tap now active."

Burns waited. After a moment the view on the right screen dropped suddenly to the tablecloth, and a quick barking cough sounded in the headset. Jesse James's voice said, "You all right, Charlie?"

"Backup confirms control," Burns said into the mike. "Send in the client."

He expected the readouts to go momentarily crazy—they usually did on insertion—but the bounce, when it came, wasn't as big as he'd anticipated. No doubt this particular host was almost as shit-scared as the client. Looking at Jesse James's restless wary eyes, Burns couldn't blame either of them. He had to wait several long seconds before the client remembered to raise his hand—or rather the host's—and scratch his nose, in the prearranged signal confirming he had control of the host's body.

"I swear," Jesse James commented, "you two been as jumpy as a couple of old cats this morning. Didn't you get enough sleep?"

The James family appeared to be almost done with breakfast. Country people, brought up to the rhythms of farm life, they wouldn't be inclined to dawdle over the morning table, never mind that the head of the household was now in a line of work with more flexible hours. Allison said, "Looks like we cut this one pretty close." He glanced up at the twin clock readouts—nowtime and taptime—and then at Burns. "Should have started sooner."

Burns didn't reply. Maybe Allison was right, but it didn't matter now. Besides, given the duration limits on an active tap—the record so far was a little under an hour, but nobody was going to risk taking a client anywhere near maximum—you always had to shave the timing on the thin side. There would be unimaginable hell to pay if a client found himself being jerked out of tap just before the big moment.

At the head of the table Jesse James rose to his feet. "Mighty good breakfast, Zee," he said to the woman. "Bob, Charlie, let's go into the front room. We need to talk some business."

The client's readout numbers danced frantically, pulse and blood pressure climbing almost to danger levels, as the three men went into the next room. At least the client didn't seem to be having any trouble controlling the host body. It helped that he and Robert Ford were close in height and build. Devereaux's display hardly flickered.

The front room evidently served a dual function of living room and spare bedroom; there were several chairs and the usual pictures and ornaments of a nineteenth-century parlor, but a small bed or cot stood against one wall. It was a close, stuffy place, and as Jesse closed the door behind them he said, "Sure is hot, ain't it?"

He shrugged out of his jacket, revealing a pair of holstered revolvers hanging from a wide leather belt. "Now about that bank in Platte City," he began, and turned to hang the jacket over the back of a chair. "Frank thinks we ought to ride over there tomorrow and—"

He paused, staring at the far wall of the room, where was hung a large framed print of a black race horse. "Damn," he said, "that picture's all dusty. Hold on."

Picking up a large feather duster from a corner shelf, he started to cross the room. Then he stopped, peering out the windows at the dusty street outside. There was no one in sight, but he said uneasily, "Somebody could see me from out there, couldn't they? I'm trying to lay low these days, since the governor put out that reward on me."

He began unbuckling his gunbelt. "Better not give them anything to talk about," he said. "Don't need folks around here wondering what kind of man wears his guns inside his own house."

He laid the gunbelt carefully on the bed, leaving the pistols in their holsters, and turned back to recover the feather duster. "This'll just take a minute," he said apologetically. "I'm awful fond of that picture. Had me a horse like that, no law could catch me."

But the picture hung too high on the wall, and after a couple of ineffective dabs with the duster he pulled up a chair and climbed onto it, standing with his back to the room, flicking the duster through fussy little arcs. "Looks crooked," he muttered.

The client stood rooted in place; he hadn't moved since entering the room. Christ, Burns thought, don't freeze, you dumb son of a bitch, you've been through this a dozen times on the VR simulator, you know exactly what to do—

The view on the client's screen tilted slightly for a second, while his display registered a small sharp pain spike. Burns guessed Devereaux had kicked him. A moment later he began to move, appearing at the edge of Devereaux's field of view, taking slow weird sleepwalker steps. He did have his gun in his hand, though; that was something.

Up on his chair, Jesse James had tucked his duster under one arm and was now fiddling with the picture, evidently trying to make it hang properly. "Say," he said without looking around, "does this look straight to you?"

A couple of meters behind him, the client was raising Robert Ford's heavy revolver, holding it out at arm's length as if on a target range. His face was absolutely white. Beside the screen, the digital display seemed on the verge of meltdown.

"Uh oh," Allison said softly.

The big .45 came into view at the bottom of the client's screen. It was wobbling like a leaf in a windstorm. The hammer was already all the way back; a wonder the idiot hadn't shot himself in the foot. As the client struggled to steady the crude sights on the man on the chair, Burns felt a chilly sinking sensation.

"He's losing it," Allison said. "He's going to blow it."

Up on his chair Jesse James said, "Didn't you boys hear me? I said, does this look straight to you? I can't tell from up here."

Any moment, Burns realized, the outlaw was going to turn around, and then it would all go to hell. "Shoot," he whispered uselessly. "God damn it, shoot."

"What in the hell?" Jesse's head began to turn. "What's wrong with you two this morning?"

"That's it," Allison said.

There was a big loud *boom* in the headset. Jesse James stopped moving. The duster fell to the floor. His feet took a couple of aimless little half-steps and then he toppled off the chair and crashed to the floor and lay still.

"Back of the head," Allison observed. "Right behind the ear. Damn, I wish I could shoot like Devereaux."

The client was still holding the unfired revolver out in front of him. His mouth hung open; his eyes were huge. He seemed not to notice as Devereaux carefully but quickly took the gun from his hand. "Did I do it?" he asked in a high childish voice. "I did it, didn't I?"

"You did it." Devereaux was now pushing the butt of Charles Ford's still-smoking Colt into the client's unresisting hand. "Now we've got to get out of here."

"I did it," the client said wonderingly. "I did it. I shot Jesse James."

From the next room came the sounds of cries and running feet. Burns hit the microphone key. "Control to Projection," he said. "Extract client and backup, and terminate taps."

Projection came back in less than a minute: "Client and backup recovered." Both viewscreens went blank and Projection added, "Taps terminated. All systems clear."

Burns started to remove his headset, remembered, and keyed the tank room. "Hey," he said, and on the monitor screen the attendants turned to look toward the camera. "Take Devereaux out of there," he told them, "and give him time to get away before the client comes out."

He pulled off the headset and tossed it on top of the console. Allison was already punching keys and flipping switches, shutting down the various systems, and Burns joined in. "Jesus," Allison said, "what a mess that was."

Burns shrugged. "It's over. Another day's work."

"And one we'll never have to do again. That's one good thing about this job, isn't it? They're all one-time operations. You never have to repeat, because it's impossible."

He stood up and stretched. "Of course that little fact is also going to put us both out of work one of these days. We've sure used up a lot of the big hits," he said. "Unless somebody finds a way to extend the range farther back."

"They will," Burns said. "After all, ten years ago the maximum range for a tap was twenty-four hours. It was just a curiosity."

"I hope you're right. Even another fifty years would bring in a bunch of good ones. Mr. Tedesco says he gets approached all the time, guys wanting to reserve the Lincoln hit."

Allison laughed. "Could get pretty strange, though, if they stretch it back too far. What if some day we have to do Julius Caesar? Can Devereaux speak Latin?"

Burns turned off the last switch, checked the console once more, and stood up. "I'm out of here," he announced.

"Not waiting for the client?" Allison asked as they walked toward the door. "First Devereaux, now you. He's going to be very disappointed."

"I'm sure you'll console him."

"Hey," Allison said, "somebody's damn well got to do it. Right now he's still in shock—he sort of believes he did the hit, but he doesn't really have a handle on it. Somebody has to do some stroking, settle him down, make sure he leaves here absolutely convinced that he killed Jesse James. Otherwise maybe his rich buddies hear him voice a certain dissatisfaction with Mr. Tedesco's services, and that won't do at all."

"Uh huh," Burns said, pushing open the door. "But that's not the only reason, is it?"

"Hell, no," Allison said calmly. "It's a chance to do some cultivating and bonding. What's wrong with that? The client may be an asshole, but he's an asshole with money and power. I don't plan to do this shit for the rest of my life."

Out in the corridor Burns said, "Well, don't stay up too late drinking with the client and telling him what a hero he is. We've got another job coming up next week, and we need to start working on the program tomorrow."

"So soon?" Allison groaned. "I was hoping to get a little time off. What's this one?"

"New York," Burns said, locking the control-room door. "Guy named Malcolm X."

"Really?" Allison's forehead furrowed. "I thought we already did him. Last month, wasn't it?"

"You're thinking of the other one," Burns told him. "In Memphis."

"Oh, yeah. Say," Allison said, "did you remember to turn off the lights?"

This one was written backwards, as you might say: I had a title in my head and eventually wrote a story to go with it.

Written August 1996
First published August 1999

Jennifer, Just Before Midnight

It was just before midnight when Graham saw the woman at the bar. Or rather that was when he noticed her; she had, he realized, been standing there for some time, and his eyes must have picked up her presence repeatedly, but only as another figure in the human swirl around him. She was young and pretty, but that was true of most of the women in the room, and, as far as Graham had noticed, of those attending the convention in general. The con scene had definitely undergone major evolution in that regard in the last decade or two. Either that, Graham reflected sourly, or the advancing middle years had affected his perceptions. That sounded eminently plausible.

Be that as it might, the hotel bar had been lined all evening with bright-faced, trim-haunched young women—you weren't supposed to call them "girls" any more, though if some of the ones drinking here tonight were twenty-one he was H.P. Lovecraft—flashing perfect teeth and displaying, from beneath severely abbreviated ensembles, a great deal of smooth, uniformly tanned skin. Graham had admired them in a vague distant way, as he might have admired the lines of a fast sports car without feeling any real desire to drive it. They seemed almost an alien species; their reality barely touched his.

This one, however, was looking straight at him.

There was no doubt about it. She had turned clear around, to stand with her back to the bar, and her gaze was full on Graham. It was hard to read her expression from across the dim and smoky room, but he thought she was smiling.

And here she came now, pushing off from the bar with her elbows, moving gracefully through the crowd, holding her drink carefully in front of her with both hands. As she passed, men turned their heads to look—one large young fellow in a Klingon costume spilled beer on his lap, watching the motion of her hips, and got a blistering look from the little redhead beside him—and, the con scene having evolved in more than one respect, so did quite a few women.

But Graham's primary reaction was to groan silently, and then to raise his drink and down a large and hasty swallow of bourbon. Not now, he thought and wanted to scream, Christ, not now of all times, I *knew* I shouldn't have come to this stupid thing—

"I don't even want to go to the stupid thing," he had said, Wednesday morning. "I hate conventions."

"You used to love them," Margaret reminded him. "You know you did, Keith. We had some good times at the cons."

"That was a different scene. Nowadays—" He shook his head, a little angrily, a lot tiredly. He hadn't had much sleep the night before. Or any other night, for longer than he could recall.

"It's not the way it used to be," he told Margaret. "Now, most of the cons you go to, it's wall-to-wall Trekkies and role-players and costume freaks. And New Agers, and grown men and women whose lives peaked the first time they saw *The Rocky Horror Picture Show*—"

"Oh, come on. The cons always did attract oddballs and misfits. That was half the fun, wasn't it? And," she added, "I'll not mention how a certain elongated young Nebula nominee was dressed the first time a certain promising young illustrator laid eyes on him."

"Sure." Graham had to grin briefly at the memory. "But no matter how silly we got, there was always the basic premise that this was about certain types of written fiction, and the people who wrote it and read it. Nowadays, half the guests at the average con don't read at all and don't see why they should."

He stopped, wondering why he was ranting like this. He sat down in the uncomfortable chair beside Margaret's bed and took her hand in both of his, feeling the bones through the frighteningly thin covering of flesh. "I'm sorry," he said. "But really, I don't want to go."

"But it's something you need to do," she insisted. "You already promised the committee—"

"They'll understand. They know about you. I already explained that I might not be able to make it."

"Bullshit," she said distinctly. "There's no reason whatever that you can't go. Either I'll be all right or I won't, and if I'm not there won't be anything you or anyone else can do about it."

She raised her head an inch or so from the pillow. "God damn it, Keith, I'm not going to let you waste any more of your life haunting my bedside. You know what they said—it could happen any time, or I could still be lying here this time next year. You're fifty-four years old. You don't have that kind of time to throw away."

Her head fell back; she breathed deeply for a moment, looking up at the ceiling with pain-widened eyes. Those eyes, Graham thought with a bottomless sorrow, those wonderful violet eyes. Nothing else remained of the Margaret of years past; her face was now no more than a pallid mask of lined and taut-drawn skin, and beneath the kerchief on her head was only bare scalp where that dense red-brown mane would never grow again. The wasted shape beneath the stiff white hospital sheet was a cruel caricature of the magnificent body Graham remembered.

"I've got this damned hideous *thing* inside me, and it's killing me." Her voice was very weak but her words came out crisply clear. "I'm not going to let it kill you too. Or let you use it as an excuse for refusing to live."

She turned her head on the pillow, looking at Graham. "Besides, you need this professionally. You haven't had a book out in two years, only half a dozen stories and nothing at all since last winter—you've all but quit, haven't you? And I suppose that's natural, it can't have been easy for you to write or even think while you had to deal with what's been happening to me . . . but you've got to get back to work, and soon. The longer you wait, the harder it'll be."

She glanced about the hospital room. "And you do need to take care of business. The insurance isn't going to cover all of this." Her lips pulled back in a crooked smile. "Not to mention what those ghoulish bastards are going to charge for hauling my ashes."

He squeezed his eyes shut. "I wish you wouldn't say things like that."

"Why not?" she said. "You may write fantasy, but it's reality time now. You better learn to deal with it."

She reached across with her free hand and patted his forearm. "Go to the convention, Keith. It'll do you good. Consider it a refresher course in having a life," she said. "God knows you need it."

Graham blinked; his hand jerked slightly, almost spilling his drink. He looked up at the girl—the woman—from the bar, who was now standing on the far side of his table, one hand resting on the back of the other chair.

"Hello," she said.

Not, "Hi," Graham noticed, but a genuine hello; give her a point there, anyway. He saw now that she was even prettier than she had looked from across the room: long legs, slender waist, fine-boned features that came very close to qualifying as authentically beautiful—even despite her efforts to spoil them with over-the-top makeup; her lipstick could have stopped traffic in a Seattle fog. Thick taffy-blond hair hung to her bare tanned shoulders. Quite a lot of her was bare, in fact; the little denim skirt barely reached below her crotch, while the skimpy matching top exposed many square inches of flat smooth belly and served to advertise, rather than seriously conceal, a really impressive chest.

She said, "You're Keith Graham, aren't you? I recognized you from the dust-jacket photos. Mind if I sit down?"

A reader? Have to be reasonably nice, then; as Margaret always liked to point out, the readers were the ones who paid the rent and kept you from having to get a real job. This one might look like a reject from a Dallas Cowboy Cheerleaders tryout, but what the hell. At least she wasn't decked out in fake medieval costume, and she didn't appear to be packing any quartz crystals.

Hastily, a bit clumsily, he got to his feet, pushing back his own chair and rising to his full rangy six feet three—Big Stoop, Margaret had named him on their first night together, after a character in the old *Terry and the Pirates* comic strip— and reaching for the other chair, before he remembered you weren't supposed to do that any more either. But the blonde didn't object; in fact she seemed to take the old-fashioned courtesy for granted, and she stepped back and stood waiting while he pulled the chair out for her. "Thanks," she said, sitting down and setting her drink on the table. "I hope I'm not bothering you. It's just that you look as if you could use some company. And I've really enjoyed your work."

Graham sighed. "Actually," he said, resuming his seat, "I'm afraid I'm not going to be much company to anyone. You see—"

"Oh, I know," she said quickly. "About your wife. I'm sorry."

Graham frowned. There had been nothing in any of the publications about Margaret's condition; she had insisted on that.

He said, "How did you know?"

She shrugged. "I heard from—somebody I know on the committee. Never mind," she said. "I don't imagine you want to talk about it. I just wanted you to know that I understand."

Graham was filled with a sudden terrible anger. No you don't, he shouted inside his head, you understand nothing. How can you understand what it means to love and live with someone for a quarter of a century, until you become almost components of a single whole, and you find yourselves answering each other's questions before they are asked? And then to see her body, that you know so well you could find her blind in a crowd of thousands by her private scent alone, turn into a death trap for her splendid brave spirit; and to stand helplessly while one door of hope after another slams shut in her face . . . how, you flawless nitwit, could you possibly understand?

"I'm sorry," she said then. "I shouldn't have said it that way. Of course I can't understand what it's like for you." She picked up her drink and turned it in her hands without tasting it. "I don't suppose anyone ever really knows what anything is like for anyone else."

Astonished, Graham could only stare at her.

She extended a hand across the table. "I'm Jennifer."

Graham took the hand, which was pleasantly soft and cool.

"Jennifer," he repeated stupidly. Thinking, oh my God.

"They're all Jennifers. Even the ones who aren't named Jennifer."

Thus Margaret, three years ago—was it?—at the last convention they had attended together. A colleague of long acquaintance, and approximately their age, had just disappeared into an elevator with an edible-looking young fan in buttock-high cutoffs and a Star Wars T-shirt; and Margaret had remarked that old Roy seemed to have found himself a Jennifer.

"You didn't know?" she said to Graham. "All women do, at least in our age bracket. You get a bunch of middle-aged women sitting around dishing, somebody asks what's happening with so-and-so, somebody else says, 'Oh, you hadn't heard? Her husband's got a Jennifer.'"

"A kind of code?" Graham asked, interested. "Like in a certain type of joke the gay guys are always named Bruce?"

"Something like that. Only it's not a joke, at least not to the woman whose husband has gone Jennifer-crazy. Never mind booze, gambling, even drugs—there's nothing in the known cosmos that can make a middle-aged man throw all judgment to the winds, trash his own life and those of everyone around him, like a willing barely legal girl."

She looked about the crowded convention floor, which, now Graham noticed, seemed fairly alive with Jennifer material. "I can understand it," she said. "They *are* lovely. And I imagine they can do a lot for an older man's ego. We menopausal women have no sense, you know. Just when we need to hang on to the men we've got, when our chances of replacing them are in freefall, we miss no chance to bust your asses. Then we wonder why you run off with the Jennifers."

"I don't," Graham pointed out.

"No," Margaret said, laughing, "you don't, do you? I may have the only truly monogamous man left on the North American landmass. But that's just because I keep you too tired to get up to any extramural antics. Come on, Big Stoop." She pulled him toward the elevators. "You're starting to look a little too fresh and rested. We'd better do something about that before a Jennifer gets you."

Graham downed the rest of his bourbon in a single shaky sallow. About to signal to the waitress, he looked at Jennifer. "Anything you want?"

She raised her drink, a horrible-looking blue concoction, and took a tiny sip. "Ooh," she said, making a face. "Yes, something besides this thing. In fact I think I'd like to have what you're having."

"Are you sure?" Graham asked dubiously. "It's straight bourbon on the rocks."

"Sounds perfect. Please."

Graham caught the waitress's eye, pointed to his empty glass, and held up two fingers. The waitress nodded and hurried off through the crowd. Jennifer was looking at her drink. "Looks like some kind of toilet bowl cleaner, doesn't it?" she said. "Tastes like it, too."

"What is it?"

"A blue kamikaze, they call it. I don't know what's in it. Somebody bought it for me." She pushed the drink away. "I wonder who thinks up these weird drinks."

Bored bartenders, according to Margaret. "Bored bartenders," Graham said.

"I believe it. You know," Jennifer said, "I remember that story of yours about the invisible bartender—"

The waitress reappeared with two bourbons. Graham signed for them and stood up. Much as he hated to interrupt—no one had mentioned that story in a long time, and it was one of his favorites—certain pressures had become critical. He said, "Excuse me," and headed for the rear hallway.

The men's room was deserted when he got there, surprising considering the crowd in the bar. But then, as he was finishing up, a familiar nasal bray said, "Well, well. How's it, Keith my man? Getting any?"

Graham zipped and turned. Lenny Devlin grinned at him from the doorway, flashing slightly yellow teeth beneath a graying mustache. "Saw you there," Devlin said, coming in and heading for the urinals, while Graham washed his hands. "Got yourself something young, huh?"

He hunched his stubby frame closer to the target area, leaned an elbow against the wall, and looked over his shoulder at Graham. "So Straight Arrow Graham finally joins the dirty old men's club. About time, too. Haven't I told you all these years, the cons are where the young pussy is? Never did understand you guys who brought your wives along."

Graham suppressed a desire to upend the little bastard—a degenerate Munchkin, Margaret had called him—and shove his head into the toilet. He said, "Let it go, Lenny. I'm not in the mood."

"No? Then let me have a crack at her." Devlin's guffaw filled the confined space. "I tell you, Keith, the biggest breakthrough of my life—next to getting the Hugo—was finding out that the young ones aren't just hotter-looking, they're actually easier to nail. They're still open, you should pardon the expression, to a little adventure. Like a one-nighter with a noted author." He turned around, yanking at his zipper. "After they hit legal drinking age, they start looking for commitments and relationships. Fuck which."

There was no use trying to respond; the little man's ego was impenetrable even to direct insult. Graham dried his hands and left, hearing behind him Devlin's moist laugh and a shout of, "Once more into the breach, Sir Keith! Give her one for me!"

Re-entering the bar, he looked toward his table, half expecting it to be empty. But Jennifer was still sitting there, hands folded on the table, waiting, evidently, for him. To his faint disgust he found he was very glad to see her; and he hurried back across the room, trying to ignore the stirrings of an old excitement.

Some time later, Jennifer set her empty glass on the table and said, "Enough. It's getting late."

Graham was amazed to see that it was going on one o'clock. Time, the old wheezer had it, flew when you were having fun; and he had to admit that he was having something very close to a good time.

Jennifer had turned out to be remarkably good company, and not merely for the obvious reasons. For all her bimbo-Barbie appearance, she clearly had a first-class mind; she actually spoke English, too, and so far she had not once said "totally" or spiked her sentences with meaningless interjections of "like."

She also possessed a near-encyclopedic knowledge of Graham's published work. Being in this respect no different from any other author, he took this as a sign of outstanding intellect and taste.

With real regret, then, he said, "Calling it a night?"

"Oh, no." She pushed her chair back and stood up, smoothing the little denim skirt over her golden thighs. "I want to dance. Come on."

There was no dance floor as such, but there was a small, more or less clear area near the back wall where a few couples were moving minimally about to recorded music. Graham said, "I don't think—"

"I don't want you to think." Jennifer grasped his hand firmly and tugged. "I just want you to dance with me."

Reluctantly, he got up and followed her. The music was loud and fast and he wondered what he was supposed to do; but then as they reached the dance area the record ended and a slow tune came on, Billy Joel's "An Innocent Man." Jennifer turned to face him and he took her hand and put his right arm lightly about her waist. The top of her head was barely level with his chin.

"I haven't done this in a long time," he confessed, moving his feet tentatively, trying to find the step.

"It's like riding a bicycle," she said. "Some things you never lose."

"I've heard that expression all my life," Graham told her. "But you know, last summer I tried to ride a bicycle and nearly killed myself."

She moved closer and rested her face against his shoulder. His hand at her waist registered the rhythmic sway of her hips. "You're doing just fine," she assured him.

Her perfume was a little on the heavy side but he inhaled it greedily. "You smell good," he said after a couple of minutes.

"You feel good," she replied, and emphasized her words with a quick light thrust of her pelvis against him. Then, as his body involuntarily responded, "Oh, my. . . ." She looked up at him, eyes widening slightly. "My, *my*. I think I'm impressed."

Graham felt the blood darken his face. He stopped—the song was almost over anyway—and stepped back, still holding her hand. "I'm too old to play games," he said more harshly than he had intended. "What's happening?"

She tilted her head and smiled. "What's happening?" she repeated. "Not much of anything, that I can see. Not at the moment."

Her hand tightened suddenly on his. "What I think is *about* to happen, though," she said in a lower voice, "I think we're about to go up to your room and more or less screw our brains out. Is that all right with you?"

Graham opened his mouth, closed it, and opened it again. The second time he heard himself say, "Why not?"

But up in the room, sitting still fully dressed on the edge of the bed, he said, "I'm sorry, Jennifer. I really don't think this is a good idea."

She paused in the middle of the room, barefoot, one hand on the single button of her denim top. "Feeling guilty?" she asked quietly. "Because of your wife?"

He nodded. She came over and stood before him. "Listen," she said, "you've got to stop thinking that way. How long has it been, now?"

"You mean since—" He had to think. "A couple of years, I guess. Closer to three, really."

"Then don't you think your wife would understand? Don't you think she knows you have needs?"

"That's what she said," Graham admitted. "The last time I saw her before leaving for this convention, she said something like that. Said I should go ahead and find someone to take care of my needs."

Actually Margaret's words had been, "Get out there, Big Stoop, and find yourself a Jennifer." But there was no way Graham was going to repeat that, let alone explain it, to this one or anyone else.

"Then," Jennifer said, "for God's sake show her some respect and quit second-guessing her. You don't have the right." She made a little gesture at her body. "Do it with me, do it with somebody else, do it with your right hand or not at all, but don't lay your own failure of nerve at her feet. She doesn't need it right now."

Graham thought it over. "Yes," he said finally, and nodded. "You're right. Thanks."

He toed off his shoes without untying them and began unbuttoning his shirt. Jennifer took a couple of backward steps, still facing him, and undid the top and let it slide off her shoulders. She did something at her waist and the skirt dropped to the floor, leaving her standing in tiny, almost transparent powder-blue panties and a lacy little matching bra.

Graham's hands seemed suddenly to belong to someone else.

Her eyes on Graham's face, Jennifer popped the catch between her breasts and slipped out of the bra. There had been no engineering trickery at work; everything stayed high and firm and full. Her nipples were unusually large and bright pink.

She hooked her thumbs into the waistband of her panties and eased them down over her flanks. The blond hair proved to be original; a fine flaxen spray decorated her pubic mound. Her skin fairly glowed in the light from the bedside lamp.

"Well?" she said, and put her hands on her hips. "If you're too old to play games, you must be old enough to undress yourself."

Hurriedly he got to his feet, shucking out of the shirt and reaching for his belt buckle. Jennifer moved past him and stretched herself luxuriously on the bed. "All right," she said approvingly, watching, as he got out of his pants.

Naked, he stopped beside the bed. "Ah—just remember, it *has* been a long time."

She laughed, making everything bounce and ripple. "The way it looks from here," she said pointedly, "it's definitely been long enough."

She held out her arms and opened her thighs. "Come on, now. Time to get back on that bike and start pedaling."

Heart hammering, he mounted her. At the first warm sliding contact she clutched at him and shuddered. "See," she whispered, "you haven't lost it. Haven't lost a thing—"

The rest of the night was a scented blur of couplings and uncouplings, of humpings and pumpings and ridings and bestridings, all over the big bed and then at various locations around the room and even once in the shower. Jennifer was an agile and imaginative partner with, it developed, no inhibitions whatever as to techniques, positions, or orifices. She was also able, somehow, to cause Graham to tap into unsuspected reserves of stamina, so that he found himself doing things he had not dreamed of for decades.

Gray light was beginning to filter through the window curtains when Graham finally fell asleep, feeling Jennifer's breath on his neck and the soft flattening of her breasts against his back. From the rhythm of her breathing he thought she was still awake, and he wanted to speak to her, but the thought got away from him and he slipped away into the darkness.

When he awoke the room was brightly lit and Jennifer was no longer beside him. He sat up, after a confused moment, and looked around, just as she came padding naked out of the bathroom.

"Oh, wow," she said. "I didn't want to, like, wake you up."

He blinked as she crossed the room and began picking up her clothing. "Man," she said, "I must have been, like, totally shitfaced, you know?" She glanced at him and grinned. "Because, like, I don't remember *anything*."

She bent, stepped into the powder-blue panties, and hiked them up over her hips. Her movements were entirely unselfconscious; she might have been tying a shoe or brushing her hair.

"I mean, like, don't get me wrong," she added quickly. "I'm sure you're a cool dude and we had a good time and all." She grinned again, and this time she did look a little embarrassed. "It sure *feels* like we had an awesome time, know what I'm saying? But it's just, like, totally *gone*. Those fucking blue kamikazes, I guess."

She hooked the bra over her shoulders and fitted her breasts into the cups. "Don't be, like, offended or anything," she said, "but I don't even remember who you are."

His mouth felt very dry. "For God's sake, Jennifer—"

She giggled. "Jennifer? Hey, dude, sounds like you got pretty wasted yourself. My name's not Jennifer," she said, hooking the bra's catch. "I'm Stephanie. Guess you can't remember either."

She pulled the skirt on. 'Hey," she said, "are you, like, on TV or anything?" She zipped, buttoned, and made a small tugging adjustment. "That's right," she said, "they're having some kind of, like, Star Trek convention or something, aren't they? At, like, the hotel? I think I heard about that." She shrugged into the top. "Are you, like, into that? I don't know anything about it. I just went there for a drink because they're not too careful about checking ID."

Wonderful, Graham thought. An underage psycho with multiple personalities. If only I can get her out of here before she turns into Greta the Axe Murderer.

She bent again and picked up her shoes, looked at them, and made a dismissive face. "Well," she said to Graham "like I say, it must have been pretty decent. Sorry I can't remember. But hey, have a good one, okay?"

Picking up her purse, carrying the shoes in her other hand, she opened the door. "Shit," Graham heard her mutter, "what fucking time is it, anyway?"

The door closed behind her. Graham lay back and, after a moment, laughed softly to himself. It wasn't a very humorous laugh.

That was when the bedside phone rang. He cursed, rolled over, and grabbed up the receiver. "Yes?" he said.

A small timid voice said, "Mr. Graham? This is the front desk. I'm afraid there's been some kind of mistake." Graham heard apologetic throat-clearing sounds. "Apparently there was a phone call for you last night, but for some reason you were never paged. We're very sorry—"

"Never mind," Graham said quickly. "Where was the call from? Is there a message?"

"Yes, in fact, you're to call St. Andrew's Hospital at—"

"I know where it is," Graham interrupted. "You've got the number there, don't you? Go ahead and ring me through."

A few minutes later Graham was listening to another faceless voice, this one a woman's, cool and efficient-sounding but softened by an obvious sympathy. "Mr. Graham," it said, "I'm afraid Margaret passed away last night, just before midnight."

He bent forward until his face almost touched his knees. His mouth opened without making any sound. For an instant it felt as if all his skin had been stripped away.

"For what it may be worth," the voice added after a moment, "it was very peaceful. It happened in her sleep and she never woke up. The nurses say she actually appeared to be smiling."

Graham sat up as the voice talked on. He hardly heard, let alone paid attention to the words. The telephone receiver hung all but forgotten in his hand as he stared across the room, at the bright-red lipstick message printed on the mirror:

SO LONG,
BIG STOOP
IT WAS GOOD FOR ME
WAS IT GOOD FOR YOU?

"Jennifer" came out of a time of great pain and stress, for myself and others, which I still am not at liberty to talk about. I wrote it on a summer night when I was sitting at a bar near my home, watching the pretty young college girls and talking occasionally with the waitress. Suddenly the story was there, and I walked home and wrote it all at one sitting and then went back to the bar, where I showed it to the waitress. She was impressed, though not impressed enough to get me anywhere.

Written September 1998
First published October 1999
First published in English September 2000

Creatures

Alison Sinclair hated Clea Hardesty and so of course she always went to her parties.

The reasons for her hatred were old and had never been really clear even in the beginning, but the reasons no longer mattered, only the hatred. Clea's all too frequent triumphs were Alison's crushing disasters, sometimes sending her to bed for days; Clea's unreasonably rare reverses were Alison's intense delights.

(That time at the formal dinner, when Clea had unthinkingly addressed the President's wife by his mistress's name—Alison still got excited enough, thinking about it, to play with herself, even though it had been a couple of years ago.)

That was the chief and overriding reason for always going to Clea's parties: the chance that something just might go wrong, some hostess-humiliating incident or faux pas, and just Alison's luck it would happen at the one she missed. That was a thought not to be endured.

Riding the elevator up to Clea's place, Alison's husband said, "I don't know why we have to go to this thing. You can't stand Clea and I can't stand her parties."

"You can't stand parties, period," Alison said, not quite accurately but close enough for routine marital harassing fire. "If it were up to you we'd never go out at all."

"She's not going to have any animals there, is she?" he said. "I hate animals."

Alison clenched her teeth and took a deep breath through her nose. "If you say anything like that at the party," she got out after a moment, "within anyone's hearing, I will personally push you off the terrace. And I think it's a fifty-two-floor drop. Even if they can repair you afterwards—which I doubt, you're the one who keeps reminding me nobody's *really* immortal—it's going to hurt like hell when you hit the street."

He shrugged. "Oh, all right. I don't actually hate them," he said. "As long as they're in zoos or something, or out running around wherever they live. I just don't want any damn hairy beasts close to me. What was that thing last time?"

"A tiger cub. There are less than a thousand tigers left in the world, outside of zoos."

"Well," Dolan said feelingly, "if I could have caught the little bastard after it pissed on my shoes, there would have been one less."

Alison turned her head to look at him, but he was gazing straight ahead, at the gleaming surface of the elevator doors, his face without any recognizable expression. This present marriage, she told herself, wasn't working out at all. Dolan hadn't been a bad husband, in the time they'd been together—how long now? hard to keep track, so many years, so many men (and women, but never mind that) sometimes she wondered what it was going to be like after a couple of centuries or so—but he didn't have a clue about the things that mattered. Or else he simply didn't care. Either way, it wasn't working.

For now, however, there was still the party to be gotten through. Dolan would just have to be watched; she'd have to stay close to him all evening, and that meant she wouldn't be able to circulate properly but there was no help for that. Failure to mingle might look bad and even be remarked on, but compared to the appalling possibilities if Dolan made one of his awful remarks—

"Clea," she said in her frostiest voice, "is concerned about endangered species. So is everyone who'll be there, except for you."

"Clea," he said, still not looking at her, "is concerned about staying up with the trends. Right now endangered animals are in, so she's developed an interspecies conscience. If the next craze is for big-game hunting, Clea and the rest of you will be fighting to be the first to fly up to Alaska and gun down the last surviving musk ox."

"You son of a bitch," Alison said.

"So I understand," he said cheerfully. "But I really don't remember her all that well."

Wanting to kick him, Alison nevertheless wondered if he hadn't put his finger on something important. Where, after all, did you draw the line between trendiness and simple lack of originality? Maybe, she thought, Clea wasn't quite on the cutting edge any more . . . but the brief surge of hope collapsed almost instantly; Clea was always on the cutting edge, she was one of those who defined that edge.

"Shut up, Dolan," Alison said as the elevator came to a stop. "Just shut up."

The party was not a large one, no more than twenty or thirty people. That was about usual for one of Clea's parties; and just right, too, Alison thought with hating admiration. More bodies, and Clea's famous penthouse would have begun to feel a little small; fewer guests, on the other hand, might give the impression of social slippage. Damn, the detestable bitch was good.

She stood for a moment looking about, surveying the room, running a quick tactical analysis of the scene and its possibilities; but then a tall male figure materialized in front of her, blocking most of her view. "Well, well," Zack Chernoff said, grinning down at her and Dolan. "If it isn't my favorite couple. The prestigious team of Loomis and Sinclair, here at last."

"Zack." Dolan shook the tall man's outstretched hand. "If it isn't us, then what?"

"Why, then, it's someone else who got a couple of really good knockoff morph jobs." The tall man embraced Alison and briefly nibbled the air next to her earlobe. "My, Alison, you're looking distinctly edible tonight." He dropped his voice. "You'll be happy to know you haven't missed anything. Clea still hasn't unveiled her surprise of the evening. But she's disappeared somewhere," he added, glancing around, "so it probably won't be long now."

"If it's got big teeth," Dolan announced, "or an unreasonable number of extremities, or tries to have sex with my leg, I'm out of here." He shuddered theatrically. "Well, I'm for the bar. Alison, shall I get you your usual?"

"Please," she said.

As Dolan moved away through the crowd, Zack said, "Nice lad. Just doesn't housebreak very well, does he?" He gave Alison a look that very nearly qualified as a leer. "Let me know when you're ready to try the mature type."

"Dream on, dreamer," she told him, more or less automatically. "Don't you wish."

In truth the thought of coupling up with Zack wasn't at all an unattractive one; he was actually quite a gorgeous man. Of course they all were, now everyone (or at least practically everyone, everyone who counted anyway) could have the face and body he or she wanted, but still there were differences; just as with clothing and hairstyles, not every morph look worked for its wearer—but Zack's worked very well indeed.

Which it shouldn't have, at least by conventional thinking. Most people went for the youthful look—some of the women present tonight appeared to be barely past puberty; at least that was the impression they seemed to be trying for—but Zack, with typical perversity, had chosen to let a little bit of age show. Nothing major, just a few very tiny lines at the corners of his eyes, the skin of face and hands not quite leathery but definitely on the weathered side; just enough to make his point. . . .

And a pretty pointless point it was, in Alison's private opinion. True, Zack was a bit older than Dolan or herself, might well be the oldest guest at the party; but with human life expectancy now measured in hundreds and probably thousands of years (maybe even more, people like Zack and Dolan kept saying it wasn't forever but they didn't *know*, did they?) it was ridiculous to make a fuss over a few mere decades. Yet Zack insisted on playing the elder, for no better reason than some basic compulsion to be different.

That was why, despite his undeniable attractions (those bright blue eyes in that tanned craggy face! those big knuckly hands!), Alison had never been seriously tempted to try it with Zack. He was just too much of a wild card. Dolan might be a handful to manage, but Zack would be impossible.

"Ah, well, you don't know what you're missing," Zack said mock-sadly, when it became obvious she wasn't going to reply. "The older the violin, and all that."

"Give it a rest," Alison said impatiently, trying to see past him. Who was that making all the noise over by the north windows? "You're not that much older than me anyway. Forty or fifty years, big deal."

"Thirty-eight," he said, wincing, "please, don't twist the knife. But oh, dear child, *what* years they were. When I was born the Process didn't even exist, outside of a couple of experimental laboratories. I spent my formative years, and quite a few of my adult ones, knowing—like everyone else in the world—that some day, all too soon, I was going to grow ugly and feeble and eventually die."

He shook his head, his face serious now. "Your generation were Processed in early childhood, before you were old enough even to understand what you were being saved from. Trust me, it makes a difference in one's perspective. And now," he added, "we have another generation, as different from yours as yours from mine. Perhaps more so—"

Alison wasn't really listening, she'd heard all that stuff before from Zack and others his age and anyway the noise from the far side of the room was getting worse; Alison craned her neck, trying to see, and Zack at last noticed and stepped aside. "Well, well," he murmured. "Speak of the rough beast . . . why in God's name did Clea have to invite *that?*"

Quite a few guests had gathered over by the north windows, but through a gap in the group Allison could clearly see the center of attention: a short, hairless man, waving his arms and talking very loudly.

"It's just shit," he cried to someone Alison couldn't make out. "You know it's shit. Don't pretend you don't."

"Here we are." Dolan reappeared at her side, holding a couple of glasses. "Alison?" And, as she took her drink from him, "Looks as if Troy's getting into full cry."

"I was just talking to Alison," Zack said, "about differences in generational viewpoints. The ones like Troy, who were Processed before birth—they frighten me, don't they frighten you? They make me feel as old and endangered as one of those damned whales Clea's always nattering about."

"I mean," the short man was saying, not quite but almost shouting, "all those old plays and books and operas and all that, maybe they meant something back when they were written, but who *cares* now? Nobody lives that way any more, do we?"

"I don't know," Dolan said thoughtfully. "I think Troy Wagner would have been a monster no matter when he was born. Too bad they didn't impose the Moratorium just a little sooner. As I understand it, Troy was one of the very last batch."

"Maybe they've decided to move it back retroactively," Zack said hopefully. "Maybe that's what he's doing here. Maybe he's tonight's endangered species. At midnight an Authority squad will show up and take him out on the terrace and shoot him."

"Don't we all wish," Dolan said. "I'd never complain about Clea's parties again."

Zack said to Alison, "Say, speaking of endangered beasties, I heard something today that'll interest you. Seems they've spotted a couple of blue whales, somewhere down in the Antarctic."

"Really?" Dolan raised his eyebrows. "Alive and well, eh?"

"Apparently so. Of course they've got all sorts of air and surface craft shadowing them, at a discreet distance." Zack sighed. "Good luck to the poor things. Mock Clea as we will, the animals do have a thin time of it nowadays, what with people spreading out all over the planet—the Moratorium *did* come much too late, you know, and far too many loopholes even now—"

Well, Alison thought, at least she could stop worrying about Dolan embarrassing her. No matter what horrible social clunker he managed to drop—and if he and Zack got into one of their usual conversations, the possibilities were bottomless— nobody was going to notice. Not with Troy Wagner here.

"Of *course* I don't understand it," Troy was saying vehemently as Alison worked her way across the room. "Neither do any of you. You just pretend to, because it makes you feel like such smart bastards."

Zack had been being rhetorical; even he wasn't that out of it. He knew perfectly well why Clea had invited Troy Wagner. Obnoxious as the man could be, Troy was beyond question the social catch of the season, the party guest most in demand, and getting him had been yet another (Alison ground her teeth briefly) major coup for Clea.

It wasn't that Troy Wagner was enormously rich; he was that, certainly, but then so was everyone else present, so was practically everyone in the world if you thought about it, the whole concept of wealth no longer had any real meaning though some dinosaurs like her parents insisted on acting as if it did . . . and it definitely wasn't his personality, though there were those who pretended to find him amusing. No, Troy Wagner was someone who counted because he was someone who counted, that was all, that was how it worked.

("But what does he *do?*" Dolan had asked, more than once; and there you had it, Dolan's hopeless inability ever to get it. As if anybody *did* anything, any more—but it was a waste of time trying to explain that to Dolan.)

"I'll tell you one good thing they had back then, though," Troy continued, not quite so loudly. "Servants. Yes," he said, as some of the other guests made sounds of surprise, "I mean live, human servants. Bots are all right, but they can be so *stupid*, and they don't really *care*, do they? I'd just like to be able to come in and have a real living set of human hands to help me off with my things and mix me a decent drink—I swear that bot bartender I've got must have been given the circuits from a pesticide mixer—and at least *pretend* to give a shit."

He gulped at his drink. "And besides," he snickered, "you could fuck them if you wanted."

Alison was close enough now to see the details of the elaborate abstract holotat pattern that covered his bare scalp, its colors constantly changing. Troy had been one of the first to go for the hairless look, as he would undoubtedly be one of the first to dump it when it became too popular.

She'd never before seen Troy Wagner at such close range; she hadn't realized how short he was. That was one thing that still hadn't yielded to modern technology: nobody had yet found a way to morph bone length. Maybe that was why he was so noisy.

"Friend of mine has a collection of antique erotica," he went on. "This one pic, fellow bends the maid over the piano and buggers her standing up. Try doing that with a domestic bot."

He was, Alison thought, utterly loathsome. She wondered how she could get him for her own next party. Of course then it would look as if she were playing copycat or catch-up to Clea, but there was no avoiding that, there never was, God damn it.

"Might have had a bit of a recruitment problem, Troy." That was Ron, Clea's silly-ass husband; his voice carried the forced jocularity of someone going along with a gag he didn't really understand. "Don't suppose anyone would be keen on waiting on *you* hand and foot, would they?"

"Probably not," Troy agreed cheerfully. "I say they should have brought back slavery. Be nice to have a few slaves about the place. I could whip them when I got bored."

Ron said something Alison didn't catch. Troy waved a multiringed hand, flashing gilded mandarin-length nails. "Who said anything about Processing them? Mortal slaves, immortal masters, it's positively classical. Too late now, too bad."

There was a chorus of slightly uncertain laughter, or rather tittering. At Alison's elbow a woman muttered, "Where did Clea get this one? He's *insane*."

Clea? Alison realized suddenly that Clea still hadn't put in an appearance. Vanished from her own party, with Troy Wagner on a roll? What was the woman up to now?

And then, just like that, there she was, standing in the rear hallway door, clapping her hands, calling out in that wonderful clear carrying voice: "Everyone! Everyone, please!" and Alison, turned with all the others, feeling the prickly rush of blood to her face, waiting for it.

Clea looked stunning; that went without saying. Her thick long hair, raven-black tonight, was piled on top of her head in a swirling coiffure that somehow managed to look elaborate and casual all at once. She wore a dress of some shimmery dark-blue material, really just a high-waisted skirt with cross-straps that came up around her neck but left her splendid high breasts bare; a delicate silver chain—Alison had seen it up close, knew it consisted of a string of tiny silver porpoises—swung from one nipple ring to the other. Fashionable, even a bit creative, but nothing too daring; that was Clea, all right.

Beside her stood a tall gray-haired woman in a simple white dress. Alison had never seen her before.

"Everyone," Clea said again, though by now they were all silent and listening, even Troy Wagner, "I want to welcome you all and thank you for coming to my little affair."

"She say something about an affair?" Zack's voice said in Alison's ear.

She glanced around; Zack and Dolan had come up on either side of her, unnoticed. "There you are," Dolan said, grinning.

She made a furious gesture for silence. Clea was saying, "—sure you all came here expecting to see rare and endangered wildlife, such as we had last time."

"Be still my beating heart," Dolan muttered.

"But tonight—" Clea blinded everyone briefly with a smile. "Tonight, something a little different."

She half-turned and gestured to indicate the gray-haired woman. "Everyone, this is Grace."

What the hell?

"Please make her welcome," Clea added as the woman stepped hesitantly forward. And then, waving her hands, "All right, let the party resume!"

"No animals?" Dolan's voice held both relief and incredulity. "Is there a God after all?"

Alison barely heard him; her mind had gone momentarily blank. What was Clea—

Gray hair?

"Oh, you're kidding," Dolan said, not bothering to lower his voice. "Tell me it's not true."

Gray hair?

"I don't believe it either," Zack responded. "Incredible."

A woman nearby was asking someone, "But how did she get that look? Is her hair frosted, or—"

"How?" another woman replied. "Never mind how, *why?* Don't tell me this is the new fashion. If it is I refuse to do it."

The gray-haired woman was moving forward now, very slowly, looking about her in an uncertain and almost frightened way. Alison stared; everyone stared at the short gray hair— really a silver that was almost white—and the network of lines that radiated over the woman's face.

"Holy shit," a man's voice said then, much too loudly. "A mortal!"

For a moment Alison was sure Clea had finally blown it, gone too far; even in a sophisticated crowd like this there were limits, there was such a thing as bad taste. Hope surged wildly within her, stopping her breath . . . but then there was a general excited murmur and the guests began moving to surround the gray-haired woman, smiling and chattering, and blackness rose within Alison Sinclair as she realized that Clea Hardesty had done it again.

"Really remarkable," Ron was saying to someone over by the bar. "She was part of a group they found last month, on some island off the coast of Georgia. A dozen or so, I think, quite a little community. Of course the Authority's got the place sealed off, at least for now—priceless study opportunity, everyone says, invaluable scientific resource—but you know Clea, always knows the right people, always gets what she wants."

Alison was staring at the woman in dull fascination, vague childhood memories struggling just beneath the limits of conscious recall. She had seen the old pictures, like everyone else, but. . . . She felt an impulse to push forward and put her hand to the wrinkled face, touch the silvery-white hair.

Some of the guests were already doing so. The woman recoiled slightly, pulling back from their inquisitive hands, but then she relaxed. "Touch me if thee wants," she said in a high soft voice. "Thee may as well have thy fun."

"Grace is a Quaker," Clea explained brightly. "A member of a religious group. They don't believe in the Process, or morphing, or—well, you get the idea."

Religious? That was something of a rarity in itself; hardly anyone bothered with religion any more. Why worry about the Hereafter if you didn't have to go at all?

Beside Alison Zack said, "And I'd forgotten." His voice was very strange. "How could I have forgotten?"

Alison looked at him. His eyes were strangely shiny and there were wet-looking streaks down his cheeks. "She's beautiful," he whispered.

Alison wondered what briefly was wrong with him. But it didn't matter, all that mattered was finding a way to even the score. She couldn't let Clea get away with this; whatever it took, whatever it cost, she had to strike back. But how?

"We don't condemn thee," Grace was saying to the people nearest her, "for wanting to prolong thy lives. We do not judge. But for ourselves, we believe that life is to be lived rightly and justly, and then ended with dignity, making way for another generation of souls."

That got a moment's silence; people looked at each other and there were some shrugs and raised eyebrows, but no one offered any spoken comment or reply.

"We break no laws," the woman added. "We only asked to be left in peace, to live and die according to our own consciences. Apparently thy Authority will not grant even this."

Dolan said, "Well, this is an interesting change, anyway. You suppose Clea's found a new wave to ride? Vanishing wildlife getting to be passé?"

"No." Zack seemed to have trouble speaking; he cleared his throat. "No," he said again, "Clea's still on the same theme— maybe not technically, certainly not scientifically, but—"

He shook his head. "By any terms that mean anything, Grace there represents a rare and endangered species just as much as that pair of blues down in the Antarctic."

The whales, Alison thought, that was it. That was it. That would do it.

"Because she's mortal?" Dolan asked.

"Because," Zack said, "she's human."

Have to make a cruise party of it, of course. Fly all the guests down to the Antarctic, have a ship waiting, all fixed up with a bar and a band and all—

"That's a hell of a thing to say," Dolan said angrily.

Troy Wagner's voice blared across the room, cutting through the talk and the background noise: "Oh, bullshit! I don't believe a fucking word of it."

"Prosecution rests," Zack said.

"I mean, come *on*," Troy protested. "There aren't any mortals left, are there? I thought they got rid of them all."

Everyone was looking uncomfortable; there were several coughs and the sounds of shuffling feet. This was something you simply didn't talk about in company. Trust Troy to be outrageous, but even for him this was over the line.

"Hey," he said defensively, "don't get me wrong. It was just something that had to be done. And I'm fucking glad somebody had the sense and the balls to do it."

He gestured with his drink, spilling a little of it. His face was flushed.

"All those people," he said, "no way in hell to Process them all—too many even in this country, let alone the rest of the world, all those grubby little places where they never did anything but blow each other up and pop out babies like hot rolls and expect *us* to feed them, like we were really going to fix them up to live forever? Hah."

He snorted noisily. "And the unwashed hordes sure as shit weren't going to just go on living their short squalid lives while their betters got immortality and the rest of the package. They'd have made trouble and we'd have had to do something about them sooner or later anyway, so why not right away? Besides," he said, "even here, there wasn't any real *need* for so many people, was there? Not with bots and nanos doing all the work."

He paused to drain the glass in his hand. "Christ, somebody get me another of these . . . so I say," he said, "a fucking good thing they did what they did, back then. I just wish they'd saved a few for domestic help."

Alison heard the braying voice without really registering the words; she was still thinking about the whale-watching party. Of course there would be difficulties, the Authority would undoubtedly issue a ban on private vessels or aircraft getting anywhere near the blues, but that wouldn't be hard to get around, not with Dolan's influence and connections. And Zack knew people too, he'd help, she might have to fuck him in return but that wouldn't exactly be a hardship. . . .

Troy Wagner was pushing his way through the crowd, pausing at the bar to appropriate a drink the bot bartender had been fixing for someone else. "Out of the way," he growled. "I gotta see this."

The other guests stepped back as he stopped in front of the gray-haired woman, weaving slightly. "Hi," he said. "You for real, honey?"

He reached out and ran his hand over her short gray hair, ruffling it, and then suddenly pinched her cheek between thumb and forefinger. "Well, fuck," he said, "looks like you must be. Everything's real, and nobody'd get a morph job like that, even for a gag." He grinned at her. "Want a job? I need a maid."

Grace reached up and pushed his hand away. "Thee is drunk," she said quietly.

"Yeah," Troy agreed, still grinning. "And *thee* is *old*, and pretty soon *thee* is going to be *dead*. But I can get *sober* if I want to."

Clea said something to him in a low voice. Troy said, "Oh, hey, it's all right. Ol' Gracie and I are just getting acquainted, right?" He waved his glass. "Somebody get her a drink."

"I do not drink," the woman said.

"No shit?" Troy looked appalled. "Damn, that's *sick*. Dope, then?"

Ron appeared beside Clea, smiling fixedly at Troy. "Lighten up, Troy," he said with desperate heartiness. "You know, Grace here was born just about the same time as you."

"No! That right, Gracie?" Troy did an exaggerated double-take. "You mean this is how I'd look by now, with no morphing and no Process? Christ, somebody remind me to find those scientists and kiss their butts."

His grin suddenly vanished. "It's true, isn't it, Gracie? You wouldn't be bullshitting us, would you?"

A helicopter, Alison thought. For spotting the whales, and maybe for taking guests for a closer look. Or maybe a good big motorboat would be better. Have to get some advice.

"What I mean," Troy said in a very different voice, "I don't suppose maybe you might be just a little bit *younger* than you claim? Like—" He shoved his face close to hers, while she pulled back in obvious fear. "Like, say, maybe you were born just a little bit *after* the Moratorium?"

There was a general intake of breath. Someone said softly, "Good God."

The woman's face was going gray as her hair. She sagged sidewise, leaning on a chair for support with one hand, scrabbling at her chest with the other. She seemed to be having trouble breathing; her mouth opened and she gasped audibly.

"Uh huh," Troy said smugly. "What I thought. She's a fucking illegal."

The woman was trying to sit down, clutching the chair back, struggling for balance. Ron made an uncertain move toward her, reaching out with ineffectual hands, but too late. A moment later she slid to the floor, rolled over on her back, made a curious sound in her throat, and lay still. Her eyes stared vacantly at the ceiling.

"Now what?" Troy asked loudly. "What're you up to, Gracie?"

"No," Zack said. He began shoving his way through the crowd that was now clustering around the fallen woman. "Let me through, God damn it—"

He dropped to one knee beside her and took her wrist, then put his fingers to the side of her throat. After a moment he raised his head and looked around with wide shocked eyes. "She's dead," he said.

They all stared at him. Even Troy Wagner seemed unable to speak.

Finally Clea said, "Ah, you mean—"

"Dead," Zack repeated. "Deceased. No longer living. I'm sure," he said with vicious sarcasm, "you're all familiar with the concept. In theory, at least."

He bent over the woman and used his fingertips to close her eyes. "Heart attack would be my guess, but what do I know?"

His hand moved up and stroked the gray hair. For a moment Alison thought he was going to say something else; but then he got to his feet with an abrupt motion and headed toward the front hall, while people scattered from his path. A minute or so later they heard the elevator doors open and close.

Troy Wagner said, "Oh, she is not, either." He took a couple of quick steps forward and suddenly kicked the woman sharply in the ribs. "Get up," he screamed. "Come on, get the fuck up from there—"

He drew back his foot for another kick; but then Clea came up beside him and took him by the arm and said, "All right, Troy, stop it, that's enough," and very firmly led him away, down the back hallway.

No one else moved or spoke. They all stood looking down at the woman on the floor, their faces blank with wonder.

After a long time someone said softly, "Wow."

"Never saw anyone die before," Ron mused. "Never saw anyone dead, for that matter."

Trust Ron to say the obvious. "For God's sake, Ron," a woman said impatiently, "who has?"

And that was it; who had? Oh, people still died, or rather were killed; the Process could only do so much. Aircraft crashed, earthquakes flattened whole buildings with their occupants; people still did stupid things or were just in the wrong place at the wrong time. People occasionally killed other people, too, despite the Authority's best efforts, and were executed for it in turn. And now and then, for whatever private reasons, someone stepped out of a high window, or opened a vein or two with a sharp implement, opting out of immortality. . . .

It happened all the time; everyone knew that. It was, after all, the one thing that made the Moratorium workable. But it was something that happened to other people, in other places. It wasn't quite real.

Someone said, "I guess this means someone somewhere gets to have a baby."

Dolan shook his head. "Not if she was an illegal. They won't count her."

There was another long silence, broken only by small sounds of movement as the guests closed in for a better look. Finally a woman said, "Uh, is that all? I mean, she's not going to, you know, *do* anything else . . . ?"

"I don't think so," a man told her. "I think that's pretty much it."

"Boy," someone else said, "Vivian's going to be sorry she missed this."

Well, Alison thought, looking out the big north windows, at the lights of the city that stretched on and on toward the ends of the world: well, the poor stupid whales could swim on in peace and quiet after all. There was no point in bothering them, now. Whales or elephants or hippogriffs, it wouldn't make any difference. Nothing, *nothing* would ever top this.

It was true that Alison Sinclair hated Clea Hardesty more than anyone else alive.

* * *

Odd bit of history here; "Creatures" was originally written for an anthology on the theme of endangered species. The editor didn't like it, and for a while it seemed neither did anybody else—I've never understood why, I think it's one of my better stories. Then one day I was contacted by a fellow in Warsaw, looking for original material to translate; and so it came about that this story was first published in Polish. It was a curious sensation, seeing a story of mine in print for the first time and not being able to read a word of it or even pronounce the title.

Written January 1999
First published June 2000

Smoke

Standing on the bank of the little stream, facing the sun that was just beginning to rise over the nearest ridge, the old man named Smoke poured tobacco into his palm, cautiously shaking the little buckskin bag until it was empty and tucking it into a fold of his fringed hunting coat. He raised both hands to face level, so that the rays of the rising sun shone full on the small mound of dark Cherokee leaf.

Now he stuck the forefinger of his free hand into the little pile of tobacco and began stirring with a gentle circular motion. As he stirred, he raised his dry old voice in an *igawesdi* medicine song, chanting the secret words that were not Cherokee but a much older language, no longer spoken by any living people.

At the end of the song he paused and blew very lightly on the tobacco; then he raised it to the sun again and began the *igawesdi* once more. Four times in all he sang the song, always stirring, always keeping the tobacco in the sunlight; four times he blew on the acrid crumbled leaves.

Done, he got out the little bag and carefully refilled it, making sure not to spill so much as a flake of the tobacco. It was good strong tobacco; he had grown it himself, in a secret mountainside clearing, protected by a charm to keep hunters and others away, since of course serious tobacco had to be grown absolutely unseen by anyone but the one who would be using it.

Now, however, it was "doctored" tobacco, "remade" for a particular purpose, and needing only to be smoked in order to release its power. And so it was to be treated with respect; it would have been very bad to drop any.

Stowing the buckskin pouch in the bigger medicine bag that hung at his hip, he turned and started down the narrow trail that ran alongside the fast-running little creek. But he had taken only a few steps when he heard the high young voice from somewhere downstream: *"Ni, edutsi!"*

He stopped, his dark lined face registering anger. Then his expression cleared and he smiled very slightly. *"Ni,"* he called back.

A moment later the spring-green bushes parted and a half-grown boy appeared. *"Osiyo, Inoli,"* Smoke said. "What do you mean, coming up here and hollering when I'm making medicine? You know better than that."

The boy called Badger said, "I heard you singing, Uncle. I waited till you were through."

"How did you know I was done?" Smoke asked, trying to sound angry but not doing it very well. Badger was his only sister's daughter's boy and his favorite of all his younger relations.

"You taught me that *igawesdi,*" Badger said. "For finding lost things, right? Did you lose something?"

"Never mind that." In fact Smoke had lost a treasured ear ornament the other night at a stomp dance and was hoping to use the tobacco to help him find it, but he wasn't going to admit that to the boy. "Anyway," he added. "you shouldn't trail your elders and sneak up on them like that."

Badger tossed his shaggy black hair back. It was a warm day and he wore only a buckskin breechclout and pointed-toe moccasins.

He said, "Nine Killer wants you. Something bad has happened."

"Doyu? Then let's go." Nine Killer was the town headman. Not that that gave him any right to issue orders to Smoke or anyone else—a Cherokee headman's power was very limited, a matter of personal prestige rather than any vested

authority. But Nine Killer was a good smart headman, and respectful of custom; he wouldn't have sent for the town's senior medicine man without good reason. "What's the matter?" Smoke asked as Badger led the way back down the trail.

"Otter's dead," the boy said over his shoulder. "Somebody killed him."

"*Eee,*" Smoke said, surprised. "Who did it?"

Badger stepped over a fallen log and looked back. "Nobody knows," he said. "That's why Nine Killer wants you."

"Big Head found him," Badger told Smoke. "He was going fishing this morning and when he went down to the river there was Otter, lying on that sandbar below the bluff, with a knife stuck in him."

By now they were passing through the town, which had come unusually alive this morning, though nobody much seemed to be doing any useful work; people talked excitedly in little groups, while others were walking in the direction of the river. News of Otter's death must have spread like a brush fire in a dry summer.

The town was a fairly typical Overhill Cherokee community of the time: a loose collection of houses strung out along the river, between the high-water mark and the cultivated fields beyond. Most of the houses were solid log cabins, chinked with mud and roofed with pine bark, though a few families still lived in the old-style wattle-walled homes.

In Smoke's youth the town had been a closer place, the houses clustered tightly together around the big central council house, and surrounded by a high palisade for protection against attack. But the raiding days were all but over, now; most of the traditional enemy tribes—such as the distant but dreaded Iroquois Nations to the north—were paying a brutal price for having helped the English King in his recently-ended war with the white colonists, and were having all they could do just to survive, never mind bothering anybody else.

As was true for the Cherokees as well, of course; the final peace with the Americans had cost the Principal People much of their best lands, and yet still the pressure continued from the insatiable white settlers . . . but at least the days of blood were more or less at an end. Now the People could live in peace while they tried to adjust to the enormous changes in their world.

Only now something had happened that might destroy that peace. Smoke pulled his hunting coat closer about him; warm as the day was, he felt suddenly a little cold.

There was a considerable crowd down by the riverbank when Smoke and Badger arrived. They all stood well back, though, up in the shadow of the trees, above the still-fresh marks of the last spring flood.

The little sandbar lay white and clean in the sunlight, sloping gently down to the water's edge. It would have been quite a pretty little scene, if it hadn't been for the dead man lying on his back on the sand, a few bowstrings' length back from the water's edge. Even from the high-water line, Smoke could see the knife handle protruding from the body.

Nine Killer stood beside the corpse, along with the man named Big Head. Both of them were looking very serious. So was everybody in sight, come to that. Except for the dead man, who didn't look any particular way but dead.

"Stay back there," Nine Killer called as Badger pushed through the crowd. Then he recognized Smoke. "*Osiyo, Gog'sgi,*" he said then, relief in his voice. "Come see."

Smoke walked slowly down the bar, watching the ground, keeping well clear of the lines of tracks that already marked the sand. "*Osiyo,*" he greeted Nine Killer and Big Head, and looked down at the body. "*Osiyo,* Otter, you drunken fool," he muttered. "What did you get yourself into this time?"

"I found him," Big Head said. His voice was a little unsteady. "He was just lying here like this."

"Anybody else around?" Smoke asked.

"No," Big Head said. His head wasn't particularly big; the name came from a dream he had had. "Didn't see anybody at all, all the way to the river."

"I made everybody stay clear," Nine Killer said to Smoke, "until you could get here. Figured we didn't need a lot of people tracking around, messing up the sign."

Smoke gave a quick nod of approval, without looking at Nine Killer. He was studying the body at his feet. Otter lay with his arms flung out to either side, his eyes open, staring up blankly at the sky; a thin, long-limbed young man dressed in badly fitting trousers of dark blue broadcloth, such as the traders sold, but no shirt. His hair was chopped off at neck length, in the style some of the young men now favored.

The knife had gone in just below his breastbone; the angle of the handle showed that the killer had given an upward thrust, to be sure of getting the heart. The sand beneath and around the body was soaked with blood; the flies were already swarming, paying little attention to Big Head's attempts to shoo them away.

"This is bad," Nine Killer said in a low voice.

Smoke looked up sharply, switching his attention momentarily from Otter to the headman. Nine Killer was an imposing figure, tall and powerfully built; no longer the young warrior who had killed nine Catawbas in a single battle, he was still a man in the prime of life, and age had only added dignity to his bearing. Standing there now, wearing only a breechclout and a blanket thrown over his shoulders—Smoke guessed he had come quickly when he heard about Otter, not waiting to dress properly—he could not have been mistaken for anything but a leading man.

But just now he looked worried; there were lines about his eyes besides the ones the years had put there.

"A very bad thing," he said, and shook his head. "There could be big trouble."

Smoke knew exactly what Nine Killer meant; he had been thinking along the same lines, all the way down the hill with Badger. The situation had all sorts of ugly possibilities.

Murder was not unknown among the Cherokees, but it was far from common. Killing an enemy was an honored act— probably half the men in the town had names incorporating the verb "to kill"—but among themselves the Principal People were expected to keep their violent impulses firmly in check.

The penalty for transgression was simple and, except in very unusual cases, without appeal: the victim's clan kin would take blood vengeance, a life for a life. It was not merely their right but their absolute duty.

If possible, the avenging clan would kill the slayer; but if this proved impracticable, any member of the killer's clan could be taken instead. Either way, the execution would be a privileged act; no counter-retaliation would take place. There would be no long-running blood feud.

Still, as Nine Killer said, there could be much trouble before this affair was settled. Tensions always ran high in the wake of a killing, and the sacred harmony of the community would be endangered. Nine Killer was right to be worried.

"Otter was Wolf Clan," he said to Smoke. "They'll be demanding blood. And right now we don't even know who did it. Is there any way you can tell?"

Smoke looked at the headman for a moment. "A finding medicine for the truth?"

"Something like that."

"Huh. Maybe." Smoke kept his face straight. "Maybe we won't need it. Let's try using our own eyes, first, and our good sense. Sometimes that's all the medicine you need."

He studied the ground for a moment. "Look at the tracks," he said. "What do they tell you?"

The other two men glanced briefly at the lines of footprints in the crumbling sand. That was all it took; they were, after all, Cherokees.

"One set of tracks," Big Head said. "Came out here, walked back."

"A lot deeper coming out than going back," Nine Killer added. His forehead wrinkled itself up like a folded blanket. "Somebody killed Otter and then carried him out here? That's crazy."

"Crazier than that. Look at all the blood," Smoke said. "All of it right here, not a drop anywhere else. Otter was carried here while he was still alive. Then the other man stabbed him."

Big Head and Nine Killer stared at him. "*Eee*," Big Head said finally. "Why would anybody do that?"

"And *how?*" Nine Killer asked. "Otter wouldn't just let himself be carried around, like a baby, and then lie there and let somebody stick a knife in him." He looked down at the body again. "Maybe he was tied?" he said doubtfully.

"*Unh-tla,*" Smoke said, and pointed. "No marks on his arms or legs. Besides, tied or not, he'd have struggled. And the sand under him isn't disturbed at all."

A voice said, "I can tell you that part."

All three men turned, as a short, stocky young man came through the crowd and stepped out onto the sand. He was dressed in ragged, rather dirty white-style shirt and trousers. His face was a bad color and he moved slowly, as if in pain.

"Yellow Bird," Nine Killer said. "What can you tell us?"

Yellow Bird started toward them, stumbling a little, walking right across the line of footprints. Nine Killer started to speak but Smoke said quietly, "It's all right. The tracks have told us all they're going to."

"Otter was drunk," Yellow Bird said as he came near. His voice was thick and dry. "We got drunk last night, Otter and me, out at Fenn's place."

The three older men looked at one another. Jack Fenn was a half-breed, the son of a white trader—killed, some years ago, by a Creek raiding party—and a Deer Clan woman. He lived just outside of town, in a big house his father had built, like a white man's home; there he sold the usual trade goods— powder, beads, cloth, metal pots, knives, whatever the People wanted—in exchange for furs and deerskins.

All of which was fine, but he also sold whiskey and rum; he even kept a room where people could buy the stuff by the drink. Fenn's place had been the scene of many fights and other troubles, and the liquor he sold had caused endless problems among the people of the town. There had been talk of running him off; but he was still one of the People—even if he didn't act like it—and under the protection of the powerful Deer Clan.

"We got drunk," Yellow Bird repeated. His eyes were red and his face looked swollen. "We got a jug and we came back this way and we sat down under a tree, up by the river trail, and drank some more, and finally we went to sleep on the ground. Anybody could have picked Otter up and carried him off," Yellow Bird said. "The shape he was in, he wouldn't have known it."

Nine Killer was looking disgusted. "And you didn't see or hear anything?"

"I was as drunk as he was," Yellow Bird confessed. "Whoever did it, they could have done the same to me if they wanted."

He looked down at the body. "Can I see that knife?"

Smoke said, "Sure," and bent down and pulled the knife from Otter's body, feeling the back edge of the blade grate slightly on bone. The handle was covered with sticky drying blood and he didn't like the thought that he was getting it on his hand, but then he'd have to smoke himself clean after this anyway.

The knife was an ordinary butcher knife, of the kind sold by traders throughout the First Nations, with a wide curving blade and a plain wooden handle. The edge had been resharpened in the usual way, so that the bevel was all on one side, for skinning—or for scalping, which after all was basically a skinning job.

There was nothing unusual about it except the rawhide wrapping around the handle. But Yellow Bird said, "That's Otter's own knife. I remember when he put that rawhide on, after he dropped it on some rocks and broke a piece off the handle."

"Huh." Smoke looked at the knife a moment longer and then turned and spun the bloody weapon out across the river, where it skipped a couple of times before disappearing beneath the cool green water. Nobody objected.

"Could it have been an enemy raid?" Big Head mused. "No, they'd have scalped him. White men, maybe?"

"No white men could have come through here without our knowing it," Smoke told him. "Anyway, those tracks were made by pointed-toe moccasins. No, it wasn't an outsider. Whoever did it is right here in this town."

Turning back to Yellow Bird, he said, "Did anything happen out at Fenn's place? A fight, maybe?"

Yellow Bird rubbed his eyes with both hands, like a sleepy child. "There was something," he mumbled. "Some trouble between Otter and Fenn. I don't remember much, though. It's all like a fog inside my head."

"What's inside your head," Nine Killer said angrily, "is that buzzard piss you got from Jack Fenn. If you—"

He stopped suddenly, looking back up the sandbar. "Panther Shooter," he said in a different voice. "I was wondering when he would show up."

A big, heavyset man was walking down the bar toward them with slow deliberate steps. His upper body was wrapped in a red trade blanket, though his muscular legs were bare. His head was down as he studied the footprints in the sand. There would be no need to explain their meaning to him; as the town's most successful hunter, Panther Shooter could read sign as well as any man alive.

He was also Otter's mother's eldest brother, and the leading warrior of the Wolf Clan. Now, Smoke thought, the trouble begins.

Sure enough, Panther Shooter's first words to Nine Killer were, "Who did this?"

"We don't know yet," the headman said.

"He was drunk," Yellow Bird put in stupidly.

Panther Shooter gave the younger man a look that would have withered a whole cornfield. "With you, I guess? Drinking Fenn's whiskey again?" He spat on the sand. "No matter," he said, speaking to Nine Killer again. "He was a worthless fool, but he was the Wolf Clan' worthless fool. We will do the right thing. We will cover Otter's bones with blood."

"Yes," Smoke told him, "but whose blood? That's what we're trying to find out."

Nine Killer began walking back up the sandbar, toward the still-growing crowd of onlookers. The other men followed close behind.

"Listen," he cried. "We want to know what happened here. Does anybody know anything about it?"

From the back of the crowd a strong deep voice said, "I can tell you a little."

The crowd parted, with a certain amount of jostling, and a lean, handsome-faced young man came striding through. He wore the old-fashioned buckskin breechclout and leggings. That was no surprise; Little Dog was one of the conservative faction among the People, opposed to the growing tendency to adopt white ways, and he made a point of dressing in traditional style.

"I was at Fenn's place last night," he said. "I saw what happened there."

"You?" Nine Killer said. "At Fenn's? Why?"

Little Dog looked away. "My sister," he said, and everyone sighed in understanding. Little Dog's sister Walela had been Otter's wife; still was, strictly speaking, but just barely, because a couple of moons ago she had taken up with Jack Fenn.

Cherokee marriages tended to be pretty loose and short-lived; there was no penalty for adultery, and either spouse could call it quits at any time, for any reason or none. Walela, however, had been particularly shameless, ever since she first tasted whiskey, first lying with any man who would get her a drink, then going right to the source. Nowadays it was common knowledge she spent more nights at Fenn's than at home.

"I went to Fenn's to see if she was all right," Little Dog said, "and to try to get her to stop shaming the family. She wouldn't listen. She was already pretty drunk herself."

"And Otter was there?" Smoke asked.

"No. He came in just as I was about to leave. Yellow Bird was with him," Little Dog said. "They were drunk too. Otter wanted Walela to come home with him. She said no and he grabbed her arm and started to pull her toward the door. Fenn told him to stop it and he let go Walela's arm and pulled out his knife."

Several people sucked in their breaths and exchanged looks. Nine Killer said, "He went after Fenn with a knife?"

"Not really. He just waved it around, made a lot of talk, said he was going to kill Fenn, you know how he was when he was drinking." Little Dog's voice was level and without expression but his face showed profound contempt. "Then he picked up a jug of whiskey and said he was taking that in payment for Walela lying with Fenn." His voice did waver a little, now. "He said," Little Dog added with obvious difficulty, "that Fenn had to pay for riding his mare."

Little Dog paused; you could see him pulling himself together. "And then," he went on, "when Otter and Yellow Bird were going out the door, Fenn said, 'Some day somebody's going to take that knife away from you and kill you with it.'"

He looked past Nine Killer and Smoke, at the body lying on the sandbar. "And it looks like somebody did."

"Fenn." Panther Shooter's voice was low and harsh, like the growl of an angry bear. "That's who did it. Good. I was afraid it would be somebody I wouldn't enjoy killing."

"Wait, wait," Smoke protested. "We don't know that yet."

"Good enough for me," Panther Shooter said impatiently. "Otter threatened Fenn. Fenn followed him and killed him when he was too drunk to fight back. Everybody knows what a coward Fenn is."

A murmur ran through the crowd, getting louder. But Smoke said again, "Wait," and held up both hands. "This is wrong. It's not fitting to be arguing like this in the presence of the dead."

"Smoke is right," Nine Killer said decisively. "We'll talk this out in the proper way, tonight in the council house."

He looked at Panther Shooter. "You will wait until then before you do anything?"

Panther Shooter didn't look happy about it, but after a moment he took a deep breath and let it out. "All right. Tonight."

"I didn't do it," Jack Fenn insisted. "I didn't kill him."

Evening, now, and everybody was gathered in the council house, each clan sitting together in its section around the big seven-sided building: elders in front, everyone else to the rear. Nine Killer sat on his bench in the center and, for this occasion, Smoke sat to his right.

Jack Fenn stood in front of the Deer Clan's section, facing Nine Killer and Smoke. "Why would I kill him?" he asked. "To get his wife? I already had her. Because he insulted me? I pay no attention to the barking of a scabby dog."

He was a short, wiry man, about thirty summers of age, dressed in white-style clothing—ruffled white shirt and dark trousers—though his feet were shod in center-seam Cherokee moccasins, and copper ornaments dangled from his earlobes. His hair was a dark reddish-brown rather than the glossy black of a fullblood; his skin was on the light side, too, and his features were small like those of a white man. But his eyes were the dark brown eyes of the People, and just now they showed desperation and fear. As well they might; here and now, he was safe—it was absolutely forbidden to bring weapons into the council house, or to commit any sort of violence in its sacred space—but if the decision went against him, he was a dead man as soon as he walked out the door.

Panther Shooter said, "Otter told you he was going to kill you. You saw a chance and killed him first."

Sitting to the rear, among the women of the Paint Clan, Otter's wife Walela spoke up. "He didn't do it," she said. She had once been a pretty woman but drink had aged her badly. "He was with me all night."

Panther Shooter snorted loudly. "You would say black was white for this half-*yoneg*," he said scornfully. "Besides, you were probably too drunk yourself to know anything."

Nine Killer said sharply, "None of that kind of talk inside the council house. Panther Shooter, you know better than that."

He looked at Jack Fenn. "Little Dog says you talked about killing Otter with his own knife."

"That's right," Yellow Bird put in. He looked a little better than he had that morning but not much. "I remember now," he said.

Fenn swung around to face Yellow Bird. "And how do we know *you* didn't kill him?"

"Me?" Yellow Bird looked shocked. "He was my friend."

Smoke cleared his throat. "Whiskey has led more than one man to kill a friend," he said pointedly. "But Yellow Bird was very drunk. And those footprints were not made by a staggering man."

"Locust, then," Fenn said, and gestured toward a broad-shouldered young man who sat in the middle of the Blue Clan's section. "He could have done it. He and Otter were enemies, ever since that business with the horse."

Everyone fell silent for a moment, considering this. It was true that there was bad blood between Otter and the man named Locust. A favorite horse of Locust's had disappeared one night, and had later turned up in the possession of a white settler, who refused to give the horse up. The white man hadn't known the name of the Cherokee who had sold the horse to him, but his description had sounded a lot like Otter; and Otter had vanished the same night as the horse, and had returned to town many days later, dressed in fancy new clothes—somewhat the worse for wear—and showing signs of having been on a long drunk.

Locust had accused Otter to his face of stealing the horse and selling it to the white man; and Otter had laughed, and told Locust a man shouldn't have a horse if he couldn't hold onto it. And Locust had said that the same thing ought to apply to wives, and the two men had scuffled in the town street before being separated by Nine Killer and others.

Locust rose to his feet in the middle of the Blue Clan's section. "It's true I hated Otter," he said calmly. "And I say right now that his death is no loss. But," he raised his voice over the general muttering, "I didn't kill him last night. If I had wanted to kill him I would have done it in the open, for everybody to see, and then admitted it like a man."

He sat back down. There was an uncertain pause. Fenn's eyes were those of a trapped animal, flickering now here, now there. He seemed about to speak.

But then Black Fox stood up beside Jack Fenn. A husky middle-aged fullblood, he was the brother of Fenn's dead mother and therefore Fenn's closest clan kin.

"I speak for the Deer Clan," he said. "We are not satisfied that our brother, here, is guilty of killing Otter. We have heard no one say they saw him do it. We have heard only a lot of guessing, like the gossip of old women."

He looked straight at Panther Shooter. "We do not accept our brother's guilt. If his life is taken, or that of any other of the *Ani-awi*, we will take a life in turn."

Before Panther Shooter could reply, old Drowning Bear, of the Blue Clan, said, "We say the same, with regard to our brother Locust."

It was a bad moment. All about the big council house people were looking this way and that, and their faces, in the flickering light of the torches and the central fire, were not good to see. Violence and blood were in the air, held in check only by the sanctity of the council house.

But Nine Killer had risen from his split-log seat. "*Hesdi!*" he shouted. "Stop this!"

And, when quiet had been more or less restored, "People, this will not do. This is not right."

He turned slowly, looking at all of them in turn. "In all my life," he said, "I have never heard of such a thing, that one of the Principal People should kill another in secret. Or that any man should fail to step forward and accept the consequences of his acts. I think it must always have been unknown among us, because there is no tradition to guide us in this matter."

He reached out a hand and touched Smoke on the shoulder. "And so I am asking my old friend Smoke to help us. Perhaps his medicine can reveal the truth."

Smoke remained seated—enough people, he thought irritably, were popping up and down tonight, like so many ground squirrels—but he inclined his head. "I will try," he said.

Panther Shooter was talking in low tones with some of the other Wolf Clan men. After a moment he turned back to face Nine Killer. "All right," he said. "We can't do anything for the next three days and nights anyway. We have to bury our brother."

He folded his arms and looked at Smoke. "You have that long, then. In three days, if you can tell us the name of the killer, we will be in your debt. If not—" He glanced at Jack Fenn, then at Locust. "Then we will do as we see fit. *Nasgi nusdi,*" he finished. "That's how it is."

* * *

Walking away from the council house, Nine Killer said, "Can you do it?"

"I'll try," Smoke said again.

"Good. I hope you succeed." Nine Killer's voice was heavy with worry. "Otherwise something very bad is going to happen . . . Fenn!" He fairly spat the name. "I could kill him myself."

"You think he did it?" Smoke asked mildly.

"Probably. I don't care," Nine Killer admitted. "Whoever actually did it, it was caused by that evil stuff he sells. I'd be glad to see the Wolf Clan rid us of Fenn," he added. "But then the Deer Clan will take a life in return, and then we'll have a blood feud that will destroy this town. Unless Black Fox and his brothers can be convinced that Fenn is really blood-guilty."

He gave Smoke a sidelong look. "So if you should find some way . . . you know what I'm saying."

"You want me to make false medicine?"

"Did I say that?"

The two men grinned at each other in the darkness. Smoke laid a hand on Nine Killer's arm. "Don't worry," he said gently. "Truth is a funny thing. It comes out in the strangest ways. I have some ideas."

Three nights later, Smoke stood in the center of the council house and said, "I guess you're all wondering why I called you all together here."

There was a chorus of chuckles, especially from the older men. Everybody in the council house—and it was packed tonight; people were standing up or sitting on the floor and a few young boys even sat in the rafters overhead—knew exactly why they were there. The old medicine man's sarcasm was what was needed, though, to ease the tension in the air.

Everybody was dressed in their best tonight, as befitted such a serious occasion. Most of the elders wore trade-blanket robes and fancy turbans with egret or eagle feathers. Shiny silver gorgets swung at the men's throats, and elaborate ornaments dangled from their stretched earlobes. The women too were decked out in their best dresses and even the children had been cleaned up a bit.

Smoke still wore his old fringed hunting coat, but he had put on his best turban and a couple of white egret feathers, and his good moccasins. He thought he looked pretty good.

He gestured to the boy named Badger, who stood behind him, next to a big honeysuckle-vine basket with a tight-fitting lid. Badger picked up the basket, looking a little nervous, and held it up at waist level.

Smoke said, "Jack Fenn, come here. Locust too. *Ehena.*"

Jack Fenn rose from his seat and came forward. His face was almost green, but he held himself straight and he moved with a steady pace. Locust joined him with an air of almost bored calm; he might have been on a visit to an unusually dull bunch of relatives.

"Now," Smoke said, "we're going to settle this—"

With his left hand he removed the lid from the basket. Reaching inside with his right, moving very fast for an old man, he pulled out the biggest rattlesnake anyone there had ever seen.

"*Inada,* here," he said, over the sudden chorus of gasps and exclamations and the buzz of the snake's rattles, "is going to help us. I doctored him with a special medicine I learned from my grandfather."

Nobody was listening all that closely; they were all looking at the snake. It lay lazily across Smoke's hands—which were not gripping it, only supporting it—its big flat head slightly raised, seeming to look this way and that. Its tongue flicked in and out, in and out, almost too fast to see. Its dangling tail vibrated gently, sending out a low-pitched whir. It didn't give the impression of being angry, but how could you tell with a snake?

"Locust," Snake said, "come lay your hand on this snake, and tell us whether you are guilty of Otter's death. Tell the truth, and you have nothing to fear. But if you lie," he warned as Locust stepped forward, "he'll bite you. The medicine will tell him."

Locust shrugged. "And should I be afraid?" He reached out and laid a hand on the rattlesnake's body, midway between Smoke's hands. "I tell you, I did not kill Otter."

"Good," Smoke said approvingly. "Spoken like an honorable man. Go sit down."

He turned to Fenn. "And now—?"

Jack Fenn was staring at the snake. His face had gone whiter than ever, like the belly of a fish; his eyes were huge. "No," he said. "No." He said it first in English, then in Cherokee.

Behind Smoke, sitting on his bench, Nine Killer said, "You have to do it, Fenn. Or else we'll know why."

Fenn licked his lips with a long tongue. "No," he said once more, his voice gone hoarse.

His hand dived suddenly into the front of his broadcloth jacket and came out clutching a pistol. "Nobody touches me," he said, swinging the weapon from side to side, while everybody sat stunned by the incredible sacrilege. "Stay away."

He began backing toward the doorway. Behind him, a couple of men got to their feet, ready to jump him, but Smoke waved to them to sit down. "Let him go," he commanded. "No violence in the council house."

At the door Fenn called, "Don't come after me. I'll kill anybody who gets on my trail."

A moment later he was gone. Immediately the Wolf Clan men began getting to their feet, their faces furious; but Smoke cried, "*Hesdi!*" and they all stopped moving.

"You can go after him later, if you want," he told them. "Right now, we are not finished with this medicine. Sit down."

And, as they reluctantly re-seated themselves, he said, "Little Dog, come here."

"What?" Little Dog stood up, but he looked confused, and he made no move to come forward. "Why?"

"Yes," Panther Shooter said, "what does Little Dog have to do with this? We know now that Fenn killed Otter."

"Do we? Or do we only know," Smoke said, his voice rising, "what everyone here already knew—that Jack Fenn is afraid of snakes?"

That got a moment's quiet. "It's so," a man said, somewhere over among the Hair Clan. "When he was a boy even the girls used to scare him with little green grass snakes."

"Little Dog," Smoke said, "you said something, that morning when we were looking at Otter's body. You told us Fenn had said somebody was going to kill Otter with his own knife, and then you said somebody had done it."

"I said that," Little Dog assented. "What of it?"

"But," Smoke said, "the knife was already gone. I threw it in the river myself. *So how did you know it was Otter's knife?*"

Everybody was staring at Little Dog now. They had even forgotten the rattlesnake.

"I," Little Dog said, and stopped. "I must have seen it—"

"You couldn't have seen it from where you were," Nine Killer spoke up. "Not well enough to recognize it. And you were too far away to hear Yellow Bird telling us whose knife it was. So how *did* you know?"

Little Dog's eyes were very strange. His mouth opened and then closed without any sound coming out.

"But you can settle these questions," Smoke said in a reassuring voice. "Just come up here and lay your hand on *inada*, same way Locust did. If you didn't do it. . . ."

Little Dog looked at the snake, which looked back at him. He started to take a step forward. Then he stopped.

"No," he said. His voice was almost steady. "No, I'd rather have a clean death. Put the snake away, old man. It's true. I killed Otter."

He turned to face the Wolf Clan men. "I stayed at Fenn's place a little while, after Otter and Yellow Bird left, trying to talk Walela into coming with me. When I left, I took the trail by the river."

He glanced over at Yellow Bird. "I saw those two drunken fools lying asleep under a tree, and I thought of what Otter had done to my sister, how he had been the first one to give her the whiskey that ruined her. And I picked him up and carried him down to the river and stabbed him with his own knife."

The council house was absolutely silent now. Even the rattlesnake had quit buzzing.

"I was going to throw him into the river," Little Dog added, "but then I remembered the fight, and I thought maybe Fenn would be blamed. Then he would be killed too, and then maybe Walela would become an honorable woman again."

He came forward, then, but not toward Smoke; he walked over and stood facing Panther Shooter. "I have some things I need to do," he said, "to make sure my family is all right. Will you give me until the next full moon?"

Panther Shooter didn't hesitate. "Yes."

"Then I'll be waiting for you. Down by the river, on the same sandbar, I think that's the best place, don't you?"

He turned and walked toward the door, not looking to either side. There was no need for further assurances. In all the long history of the Principal People, no man had ever failed to keep an appointment of that kind.

"Uncle," Badger said on the way home, "will you teach me that medicine some time? What you did with the snake?"

Smoke laughed softly. "Oh, yes, the snake. Hold on."

He stopped, looked both ways up and down the trail, and took the basket from Badger's hands. He took off the lid and tipped the rattlesnake gently out onto the ground. It made no move to coil or strike; it only lay there a moment and then slithered off into the brush, without so much as a rattle.

"I can teach you," Smoke said, "how to make a snake stupid with tobacco and some other herbs, till you can handle him without getting bit. And I can teach you how to milk his poison, so even if he does bite you it won't hurt. That's all the medicine I did tonight."

Badger said, "But you knew already that Little Dog was the one. So why did you go through all the rest of it?"

"It was a chance to get rid of Jack Fenn," Smoke said. "A worthless fellow, and a danger to the People with that whiskey of his. I remembered he was afraid of snakes. I figured he'd run, and he did. He won't be back."

He sighed. "And as for Little Dog, the snakes are in his own head. I think he's got some wrong feelings for his sister. That always makes a man crazy."

He reached out a hand and ruffled the boy's hair. "Come on. Let's see what your mama can give us to eat."

I suppose this is the odd story out, in this collection; it isn't speculative fiction in any possible sense, and doesn't pretend to be. It was written for a collection of historical mystery stories, third in a popular collection.

I'd never written a mystery short story before—though I'd written several mystery novels; in fact over half of my published novels were mystery and suspense rather than SF— but I thought this one turned out rather well.

Written May 1999
First published October 2000

Looking For Rhonda Honda

The minute she clanked into the office I knew she was trouble.

Okay, she didn't clank, not really; body armor hasn't clanked since before I was born. But people like her always seem as if they *ought* to clank, or at least jingle a little. Maybe it's the attitude they all seem to wear with it.

She said, "You're Johnny Noir?"

I sat back in the creaking old swivel chair and looked at her. That wasn't hard work at all. She had pale skin and nice small features, maybe a little on the sharp side. Short-cropped reddish-brown hair showed beneath her squared-off black beret. She was a little on the short side, but what there was of her, under that snug-tailored black one-piece suit, looked pretty good. Of course it was hard to tell, with so much of her upper body concealed by that damned bulky vest.

Which was silly, since nobody really needs to wear that kind of heavy protective gear any more—you can buy a vest off the rack, now, capable of stopping anything short of an antitank projectile, and light and thin enough that your own tailor couldn't spot it—but then that wouldn't send the message: *My job is so important, people try to kill me to stop me from doing it.*

I couldn't guess her age. Who can, nowadays? She looked somewhere in her middle twenties, but for all I knew she was old enough to be my grandmother. For all I knew she could *be* my grandmother; the old dear had been talking lately about getting a new morph job.

I said, "Yes. And you're not, are you?"

She ignored that. So much for dry humor; it wasn't my best subject at detective school. She was looking around the office with an expression that might have indicated either scorn or routine professional paranoia. I couldn't really tell, with those wraparound mirror shades hiding her eyes.

She finished her inspection and looked at me again. "My name is immaterial," she said in a dry flat voice. "You can call me Margo."

She didn't offer her hand. I had a feeling that wasn't all she wasn't going to offer. I said, "Well, Ms. Immaterial—uh, Margo—what can I do for you?"

"We need you to find somebody," she said.

"We?" I looked past her but I didn't see anybody else.

Her mouth pulled tight at the corners. "I . . . represent the interested persons," she said reluctantly. "Please don't ask questions. You'll be told everything you need to know."

She took a quick step forward and leaned across my desk. For a second I thought she was warming to the Noir charm after all, but she was merely reaching for the battered old phone. She picked it up, jabbed quickly at the buttons, and handed it to me. I held it up to my ear just as a familiar voice said, "Noir?"

"Chief." I caught myself sitting up a little straighter.

"Listen closely, Noir." The Chief's voice was high and hoarse, with an edge like a cheap steak knife. About the same as usual, in other words. "Somebody is going to tell you what she wants you to do. Do it."

I said carefully, "I see."

"The hell you do. You got no idea at *all*—Christ, *I* don't know how far up this comes from. The person in your office right now? She's not really there. Anything she says to you, you never heard. Whatever you wind up doing for the people she works for, it never happened. Am I getting through, Noir?"

I said, "Is this an order?"

There was a moment of silence, broken only by the Chief's wheezy breath. "Of course not, stupid," he said finally. "How can I order you to do something that's never going to happen, for people who don't exist? Especially when I'm not even talking to you right now."

He hung up. "Yes, *sir*," I said to the dead phone.

Margo was undoing the front of her bulletproof. Hope sprang to life again, but she was just getting something out of an inside pocket. "Here," she said.

She reached across my desk again, this time holding a disk which she popped into the ancient computer with a gesture that sneered. She tapped a few keys, her fingers moving faster than I could follow, and the page I'd been working on disappeared, to be replaced by a head-and-shoulders portrait of a blond-haired woman.

"This," Margo said, "is the person we want you to find."

The face that looked back at me was pretty, maybe even beautiful if you liked that tanned-SouCal-goddess look. There was a time when I would have said she was in her late teens or early twenties. Now, I wouldn't even bother trying to guess.

"She have a name?" I queried.

"Immaterial," Margo said immediately.

"Related, are you?"

Margo grimaced. "I know, but I'm serious. Her birth name really *is* immaterial, because she's not using it now."

She reached out and touched the keys again, and the picture changed to a full-length shot of what appeared to be the same woman, standing next to a purple-and-black motorcycle. She was dressed in elaborate protective gear: full snug-fitting leathers, high-topped racing boots, lace-on plastic knee and elbow guards, even a shiny perforated breastplate, all of it neatly color-coordinated to match the bike. Other figures, similarly dressed, stood around in the background, or sat on other bikes.

Jesus, I thought. A roadgrrl.

"According to our information," Margo went on, "she is now known as Rhonda Honda."

Marvelous. Now it was beginning to add up. You get these cases all the time: somebody's darling daughter runs off to join a roadgrrl gang, and the distressed family wants her back. Or now and then it's somebody's darling wife; that happens too.

Damn unusual, though, for somebody like me to catch a case like this. Not if the people concerned could afford anything better. . . . I said, "You know, you'd do better to take this to one of the big private agencies, like Herod Foxxe or Gabriel Mallet—they've got the staff and the facilities, I'm just a—"

"No." She was shaking her head. "We've already tried that. It's been six months now since she disappeared, and it took a private agency most of that time to find out the little we know now. You're familiar with the Peter Pick Agency?"

I nodded, repressing a couple of adjectives and a noun that came to mind. Margo said, "Their man was able to determine that she'd joined up with these bikers—"

"Roadgrrls."

"Roadgirls?" She did a kind of double take. "I'm not—"

"Roadgrrls." I pronounced it carefully for her, trying not to grin. She probably didn't know it, but she'd given her age away with that one word. Nice clean morph job, but this babe had to be at least as old as me.

"Bikers," I told her, "are a lot of overage punks who hang around cheap bars and pool halls—or nursing homes, now—and trade lies about how tough they were in the old days. Roadkids are a whole different breed."

"Yes." She nodded vigorously. "You know about these things, Noir. You worked undercover among the outlaw clubs for almost a year, when you were with the state police. Still got your own bike, don't you?" Christ, somebody knew *way* too much about me. "You can get close to these people, talk their language. That's why we picked you."

She gestured at the photo on the screen. "That was taken by the Peter Pick op just before he lost her. Supposed to be a good man, but he let her slip away. Somewhere near Salinas, as I recall. His report's on that disk."

I studied the picture. "Just what did you have in mind, if I do find her? If you want strongarm stuff, go back to Peter Pick."

"No, no." She scaled a white card across the desk at me. It bore a hand-printed phone number. "Just call that number when you find her. Any time, day or night. We'll take it from there."

As I stowed the card in my wallet she said, "Noir—this really is important. More important than you can imagine."

"I'll give it my best."

"Of course you will." This time she actually smiled. "After all, you're a Public Investigator."

At home, that evening, I put dinner in the microwave and fired up my computer—an old Micromac, still better than what I had at work—and checked my messages. The only new one was from my ex-wife, asking why the current alimony payment was late, and threatening various actions, including coming down and unscrewing my head, if it got any later.

I groaned and hit the reply button. *Dear Blanche,* I typed, knowing that would piss her off. Or "him", I'm supposed to say, but screw it, gendermorph be damned, I'll start going along with that the day she/he quits grabbing half my pay. . . . *As you undoubtedly know,* I wrote, *the city is broke right now. I haven't been paid for a month. You'll get yours if and when I get mine.*

I sent it off and turned off the mail, not wanting to read the reply. For God's sake, I wouldn't mind so much, but Blanche, or rather Mad Marvin, makes more from a single pro wrestling match than I make in a month.

The microwave dinged. I got my dinner out and brought it back to the little desk, balancing the hot box on my lap and eating it while reading the online news. Not that I really gave a damn, but it was a distraction from the tasteless soysteak.

Not much of the news was new. The President was still undergoing treatment for undisclosed medical problems; the First Lady had issued another statement promising he'd be back on the job any day. I wondered why anybody gave a damn. After all, the Presidency had been an almost wholly ceremonial office for over a decade. But the public took a keen interest in the First Family and their problems; like the old British royal family, they had prestige—and money, and therefore power—all out of proportion to their legal status.

Here at home, the mayor and the city council continued to argue over whose idea it had been to invest the entire municipal treasury in Indian government bonds, two weeks before the Pakistanis nuked New Delhi into an ashtray. An Alaskan nationalist militia, a militant Kwakiutl splinter faction, and an animal-rights group had all claimed credit for last week's sinking of a Japanese fishing vessel with no survivors. The Dow-Jones showed Blood-Crip stock up and Mafia down.

Dinner finished, I poured myself a shot of bourbon for dessert, dug out Margo's disk, and pulled up the Pick op's report.

It was a very neat, professional report. Unfortunately it didn't really contain much information. The subject had definitely been identified as the person now known as Rhonda Honda. She was now riding with, and probably a member of, a motorcycle gang known as the Devil Dolls. That was all, though the Pick guy tried to pad it out to make it sound more substantial.

I punched up the full-length photo again and sat back and looked at it, remembering Margo saying "bikers." She'd better not make that mistake around any real bikers, or roadkids either, or she might find herself needing that bulletproof for real. That's one thing the two groups do have in common, besides motorcycles and attitude: they hate each other, enough to get severely physical with outsiders who confuse them.

Actually the difference is mainly one of styles and generations. Your classic biker is a traditionalist: raggedy-assed denim, heavy boots, wind-in-the-armpits vests covered with faded patches, with the rawhide-faced old mamas favoring fringed leather bras and lots of body piercings.

Roadgrrls, on the other hand, go in for the armored look: bright-colored high-tech protective gear, the kind of thing you might see on a dirt-bike racer or a hockey player. Their male counterparts prefer snug-fitting racing leathers and everybody wears spaceman-looking full-face helmets.

Even more important, while any real biker would walk before he'd ride any bike but a Harley—preferably one made before the Xiang-BMW takeover—no roadkid would be caught dead on anything that slow and old-fashioned. Their tastes run to hot Japanese and European sportbikes, preferably customized beyond recognition. This one appeared to have herself a new Honda Kamikaze.

The bourbon glass was empty. I poured myself another one. "Here's looking for you, kid," I said to the picture on the screen.

Mike Donne said, "You know, Noir, I wonder about you sometimes."

We were sitting in his office at the Gabriel Mallet Agency. It was a lot bigger than mine; it was nearly as big as my apartment. He had on a light gray suit that had to have cost as much as I made in a month. I didn't care about the office, but I did envy him that suit. The last good suit I had, a nice Italian silk job, got ruined a year or so back by some paint-spraying animal-rights activists protesting the exploitation of silkworms.

I wouldn't have minded a morph job like his, either. He looked younger than he had when we were on the force together, a decade and a half ago. Any morph work I could afford would probably leave me looking worse than ever. Go to some cut-rate clinic, get some alcoholic doctor who switches my dick with my nose, no thanks.

Donne said, "When are you going to give it up, Noir? You're too good a detective to spend the rest of your life in a cheesy little office and a crappy old apartment."

I said, "I'm a public cop, Mike. It's what I do."

He made a disgusted face. "It's what nobody does any more, and you damn well know it. I'm not even talking about anything new—as long as we both been alive, anybody who really wanted something guarded went to a private security outfit, or if they wanted somebody caught they hired a bounty hunter. Hell, they had private contractors running jails, clear back last century. We're just seeing the logical development of trends."

He snorted. "Haven't you been paying attention to what's going on? The city's broke, the state's in receivership, and the United States is a geographical expression. The President is a figurehead and lately he doesn't even bother showing up to make speeches and wave at parades. Face it, Noir, the public sector has had it. Why should cops be exempt?"

Donne shook his head. "It's the twenty-twenties, Noir. It's the day of the corporation. Forget the old days," he added angrily. "I was there too, remember? But it's *over.*"

He sounded really pissed off. Probably I made him uncomfortable. Most of the corporate ops despise public detectives, regarding us as low-rent losers or worse; Donne was one of the few who'd even talk to me.

"All the same," he went on, "you're right, this business with the missing babe smells funny. I'll check into it. Kid down in the basement, owes me a couple of favors, he can hack into anything."

"Thanks," I said, getting up.

"No sweat. Call me this evening at home, I'll let you know if I've turned up anything. Be careful," he said as I started for the door. "These people sound like bad news."

"There's some other kind?" I said. "Like you say, this is the twenties."

"Devil Dolls," Crazy Norm said, "yeah, sure, new club. They split off from Hell's Belles last year."

He glanced furtively over his shoulder as he spoke. It was midafternoon and the bar was half empty, nobody close enough to overhear us, but Crazy Norm had to have his little drama.

"I've done business with them," he added. Crazy Norm was one of the biggest hot-bike-parts dealers on the Coast. "Don't really know much about them, though. Why?"

I pulled out the photo of Rhonda Honda, which I had printed out last night. "Sorry," he said after a glance. "Never seen her with the Dolls or anywhere else."

Up at the bar one of the customers groaned. The television set at the end of the bar was showing a talking-head of the First Lady. "Our next guest," she was saying, "is the well-known—"

"Loudmouthed bitch," another customer said. "Hey, Ray, shut her off."

There was a chorus of agreement. The bartender reached over and the voice ceased. The picture, though, remained, and as the camera pulled back to a waist-up shot there were appreciative murmurs and whistles. The First Lady's talk show might be unpopular with this crowd, but her latest morph job had been spectacularly successful, and she was visibly not wearing a bra.

"What you oughta do," Crazy Norm said, "try Coyote Bay. Big rally and swap meet this weekend, all the clubs will be there. Better watch your ass if you do go," he added. "One wrong move around those roadgrrls, you could wind up getting a free gendermorph job, know what I'm saying?"

I thanked him for his concern and stood up to go. As I left the guys at the bar were still trading remarks about the First Lady's new knockers.

I called Donne as soon as I got home. "Noir," he said, sounding relieved. "Glad you called. Listen, I—"

He paused. "Huh," he said after a moment. "Thought I heard something . . . anyway," he continued, "it was no sweat getting into Peter Pick's files. Turns out we've been hacking their confidential records, and all the other major agencies', for years. Been a very valuable resource."

"I can imagine."

"Yeah. But what you can't imagine is what I turned up today. Your little friend in the bulletproof? You'll never guess who she works for." His voice dropped. "Two words. Fur—"

Modern silencers are very efficient; with a good one, properly fitted, there is no sound at all. What can't be silenced, however, is the sound a bullet makes hitting human flesh and bone. It's not loud, but it's very distinctive. Even over a telephone.

Donne stopped speaking. Then he said again, in a very weak voice, "*Fur—*"

A clatter in my ear said he'd dropped the phone. There was a heavy thud, as of something heavy hitting the floor. Something about the size and weight of a medium-sized private detective.

The phone clicked off. A moment later I was standing there listening to a dial tone.

The sun was going down out over the Pacific when I pulled into the storage park where I kept the bike.

I was keeping it in a rented lockup partly because things like motorcycles tend to walk away where I live, and partly to keep my ex from grabbing it for back alimony. I swung the metal door open and stepped inside. The big black Suzuki looked like a space ship in the dim light. Reddish sunlight winked off chrome.

Everything looked okay. It should; I'd spent enough money and sweat keeping it that way. The Suzuki GSX1300 Hayabusa was the fastest street bike made during the last century, and there weren't many left. It was easily the most valuable thing I owned.

I pushed it out onto the concrete drive and climbed aboard. I'd already changed into my old black racing leathers, back at the house. I stuck the key in the ignition and pulled full choke and thumbed the button. The starter whined and then the engine burst into full heavy-metal song. A little while later I was sitting at an Interstate Corporation tollbooth, counting out money under the supercilious single eye of the robot attendant.

I didn't try to get very far that night. All I wanted right now was to get clear of the city. Whoever had hit Mike Donne might or might not be looking for me, but I wasn't hanging around to find out. Or waiting till the body was found and the Mallet people cranked up their we-avenge-our-own machinery. They'd want to ask me some questions, and they wouldn't be nice about it, especially if they didn't like the answers. My badge wouldn't mean a thing, either; the giant conglomerate that owned the Mallet Agency could buy and sell the city, PD and all, out of petty cash.

And I didn't even have a gun. The Department's insurance company had made us stop carrying them.

Up beyond Obispo I got off the payslab and found a cheap motel. I didn't get much sleep. Mostly I lay there in the dark muttering, *"Fur?"*

Coyote Bay might once have been an actual functioning town; now it was nothing but a collection of dilapidated buildings, most of them empty and boarded up, strung along the ruined old coastal highway, between rusting railroad tracks and a narrow strip of beach.

But by the time I pulled in off the tollroad, around noon the next day, Coyote Bay had become quite a bustling place. Roadkids were everywhere, riding slowly up and down the sand-blown street, sitting on parked bikes, or just wandering about on foot. The air reverberated with the crackling blare of high-revving engines and non-stock exhausts.

Here and there, dubious-looking characters sat or stood next to folding tables or parked pickup trucks, displaying various odds and ends—motorcycle parts and accessories, weapons, drugs, even lingerie, most of it either illegal or, almost certainly, hot—for sale or trade.

I stopped the Suzuki in front of an abandoned motel and stood for a few minutes studying the crowd. It was a warm day, and lots of the guys had peeled off their leathers and were walking around in T-shirts and shorts. The roadgrrls, though, weren't about to lose their cherished look for anything so trivial as comfort; their bright-colored outfits definitely added something to the scene.

It was quite a gathering; I recognized clubs from all up and down the Coast: Vampires, Roadkill, Black Widows—you don't want to hear about *their* admission requirements—even a big contingent of Road Goths in their distinctive outfits, faces painted white and bits of tattered black lace trailing from beneath flat-black armor. A couple of shaven-headed young grrls strolled past, holding hands and leading a Dalmatian puppy on a leash; the spiky lettering on their breastplates read VENICE BYKEDYKES.

Finding the Devil Dolls was simple enough. From the minute I put the sidestand down, the old Suzuki began collecting a fascinated little crowd; as I'd hoped, riding in on a classic bike was enough to get me at least temporary acceptance, even though a blind man could have spotted me for an outsider. I sat there and answered technical questions for a few minutes, while jocks and grrls gathered around and goggled; then I asked my question.

"The Dolls?" A husky roadjock in skin-tight pink leathers stepped from the crowd, everybody moving hurriedly out of his way; the Oscar Wilde Motor Corps are easily the most dangerous gang in the state and their members get the kind of total respect the old Angels used to. "Sure, they're here. Camping down at the south end of the beach. What do you want with *them?*" His plucked eyebrows went up about an inch. "No accounting for *tastes,* I suppose. . . ."

"Camping" was an overstatement; the Dolls, like most of the other groups present, had merely picked themselves an area and occupied it. A couple of plastic tarps had been set up as sunshades, and a few sleeping bags and blanket rolls lay scattered about on the sand. Roughly in the middle of the area were the blackened remains of a big driftwood fire. That was just about it.

I stopped the Suzuki at the edge of the weed-cracked concrete parking lot that bordered on the beach. Down here, the sand had piled up into a line of low dunes dotted with scrubby bushes.

A few yards away, a line of shiny parked sportbikes gleamed in the sun. I gave them a brief scan, but there were at least a dozen or so that might have been the one in the photo; evidently purple and black were the Devil Dolls' club colors.

Out on the beach and among the dunes, roadgrrls wandered about, drinking beer and passing joints and talking, or lay stretched out on blankets in the sun. Here, on their own staked-out turf, several of them had felt secure enough to shed their silly plastic protective gear in favor of cutoff shorts and T-shirts, or bikinis—with or without tops—or, in a couple of cases, nothing at all.

Believe it or not, though, that wasn't what got my attention.

Nearby, a grrl stood leaning against the half-demolished metal guardrail that separated the parking lot from the beach. Her back was to me and I couldn't see her face, but everything else set off recognition signals: long blond hair, purple-and-black armor—

Maybe this was going to be easier than I'd expected.

I shut off the engine and said, "Excuse me," and she turned to face me and so much for *that*. Nose too big, mouth too wide, eyebrows too heavy; not even close.

I said, "Sorry, my mistake. I was looking for Rhonda Honda."

"Nah, man." Flat drawn-out *a*'s, Boston girl a long way from home. "My name's Vonda. That's Rhonda Honda ovah yondah."

I started to ask her to say that again. Then I was afraid she would. Shaking my own head, feeling a desire to hit it sharply a couple of times, I looked where Vonda was pointing.

And sure enough, there she was, the grrl from the picture. I wondered why I hadn't spotted her before. She stood out like a racing greyhound in a pack of mutts, and not just because she was a good six inches taller than the rest. Easily half of the other roadgrrls on the beach had that same leggy-blonde look, but it was as if somebody had been practicing and then finally got it right.

She was walking along between a couple of other Dolls, a redhead and another blonde, and swigging at a can of beer. I watched her for a moment, trying to decide on my next move. Truthfully, I hadn't thought things out beyond this point.

As it turned out she was the one who saved me from overloading my brain any farther. Suddenly she glanced my way and her face broke into a blinding smile. "Oh, hey," she cried, "check it out!" And came running across the sand toward me, shoulder guards clacking, while the others turned to stare.

It wasn't, of course, my smoldering good looks that had pushed her button; her eyes were fixed on the Suzuki. "Wow," she breathed as she stopped beside the front wheel, and hunkered down for a better look at the engine. "It's beautiful—"

The other Dolls were moving in now, bunching up in a semicircle behind her, looking at the bike and then, with considerably less admiration, at me. "Who's this asshole?" somebody asked, not bothering to lower her voice.

The one named Vonda said, "He was askin' about Rhonda."

It was a nasty moment. I could feel them all tensing, practically crouching to spring. Various sharp shiny implements began to appear, amid a clicking and clattering of flick blades and butterfly handles. My insides felt very loose. For all the superficial fun-in-the-sun look of the scene, this was a bad spot for anybody—particularly male—who didn't belong. These were no Girl Scouts; they weren't into sitting around the campfire singing old songs and roasting weinies—but one wrong step and they'd be roasting mine.

I said to Rhonda, "Can we go somewhere and talk?"

A big, seriously mean-looking brunette said, "No way, man. What the fuck you think—"

Rhonda was getting up. "It's all right, Donna." She tilted her head toward the nearby road. "Want to go for a ride? I'd like to see what that thing will do."

A few minutes later we were roaring off down the old coastal highway, Rhonda in the lead. Right away it was clear she knew what she was doing. She laid the purple-and-black bike over till her knees almost scraped the crumbling concrete, and she blasted out of the turns like a rocket. Keeping up with her took all my concentration; the road had become a very narrow place and the horizon kept tilting at unreasonable angles.

Not that we were going flat-out by any means; like every other public road in the state, this one was too gnarled and potholed for real balls-to-the-wall riding. But we were going damn fast, all the same, engines shrieking like buggered banshees; and then as she led the way into a long blind turn I picked up a change in the note of her exhaust, and her shoulders hunched as if bracing for something. Without pausing to think about it I downshifted fast and rolled off throttle and clamped down hard on the brakes.

Rhonda's Honda was already sliding to a smoking, fishtailing stop. The Suzuki's greater weight took me on past her and for a sickening moment I thought it was all over but then the brakes took hold and the big bike stopped dead.

Just beyond the front tire, the pavement ended in a jagged break, clear across the roadway. Thirty or forty feet away, the other half of the earthquake-shattered bridge hung over a deep rocky gorge. I could have spat over the handlebars into the gap.

Rhonda Honda pulled off her helmet and grinned at me. She tossed her head, making that long blonde hair flare and bounce for a moment. "All *right*," she said.

I stared at her, momentarily speechless. Had she just tried to kill me? Or was this merely her idea of a good laugh? Her face gave nothing away; her smile was innocent as an upper-middle-class baby's.

She said, "So why were you looking for me?"

I returned her grin, trying to look much cooler than I felt. "There was a guy asking around about you," I told her. "Down in the city, a couple weeks ago."

"And you thought you'd get a reward for finding me?" The smile went away very fast.

"Nah." I shrugged. "He didn't say anything about a reward. But he had this picture and, well, you looked cute, okay? I just wanted to meet you."

It sounded phony as hell to me, and I only tried it because I couldn't think of anything else. But after a second her face cleared and she said, "Why, that's sweet. I'm flattered."

She laughed. "Only I'm afraid you had a long ride for nothing. See, I've got . . . a girlfriend, you know? Donna. You kind of met her, back there."

"Oh." I managed to look disappointed. "Sorry."

"That's all right." She started her engine. "Come on. I'll ride back with you."

* * *

I spent the rest of the day skulking about Coyote Bay, trying to figure out what to do now. I still had the number Margo had given me, but I wasn't ready to call in yet. Not until I had some answers, and right now I wasn't even sure what the questions were.

As the setting sun began to turn the ocean red, I wandered over to where a couple of locals had set up an outdoor grill and were serving greasy soyburgers at extortionate prices. I bought one, handing a fifty across the counter and getting a dirty look and a handful of small bills back. I walked away, munching on the burger and counting my change. I wouldn't have been surprised to find I'd been shorted, but it was all there.

I fanned the bills out, idly, and looked at them, thinking how little they bought compared to when I was younger. Now, I wondered why they even bothered printing anything smaller than fives. Even the new Richard Nixon three-dollar notes were barely worth carrying. Dead Presidents, it seemed, weren't what they used to be. Just like live ones—

I stopped, feeling the world miss a shift.

"No," I said out loud.

"You see," I told Rhonda Honda, "this old friend of mine died yesterday."

We were down at end of the beach, in between a couple of dunes. It was dark now. Behind me, on the other side of the dune, I could hear occasional shouts and laughter: the Devil Dolls, settling in for the evening's partying.

They hadn't been happy to see me again; the one called Donna had made some very detailed threats, in fact, before Rhonda got her pacified. I hoped she stayed that way. Things were intense enough as it was.

Rhonda turned to face me. She'd shed most of her roadgrrl outfit now, all but her shoulder and shin guards, with shorts and a bikini top. Her flawless skin shone silver in the starlight.

"Yeah. He died trying to tell me something. *Fur*," I said, turning the helmet in my hands. "That was what I heard. Didn't make any sense. A shipment of hot furs? Animal-rights terrorists? What?"

I wished now I hadn't waited till dark. I'd have liked a better look at her facial expression.

"But he wasn't saying *fur*, was he? I didn't get it till just a little while ago . . . *First Family*," I said, "that's what he was trying to say, wasn't it? That's who's looking for Rhonda Honda, and doing everything necessary—including killing people—to make sure the whole thing stays secret."

She took a step backward. Even in the deep shadow between the dunes I could see the whites of her eyes.

"So I ask myself, what's the story? Runaway First Family offspring? We haven't seen the President's daughter in the news lately, have we? But then we haven't had a White House sex scandal in a long time, either. Another young intern who couldn't resist the Presidential charm? Maybe even carrying a little addition of her own to the Family—"

From the darkness Margo's voice said, "You ask too many questions, Noir. I warned you about that."

She came walking around the dune, stepping carefully in the loose sand. In that black outfit she was almost invisible, but the starlight was enough to pick up the flash of her teeth. And the gun in her hand.

"Margo." Rhonda Honda's voice carried tones of an old familiarity. "I should have known he was one of yours."

"Mine?" Margo laughed shortly. "Just temporary help, that's all." She looked at me. "Bad help, too. You were supposed to call in when you found her. Not take her for starlight walks and pour out your pathetic heart."

She gave a contemptuous snort. "Of course we weren't stupid enough to depend on your following orders. Your Chief warned us you weren't a team player." Her left hand came up, holding a small shiny object between thumb and fingertips. "So I put this little tracker on your bike. That's not much of a lock on that storage shed, Noir."

Rhonda Honda said, "I'm not going with you. You can't make me."

"Sure you are." Margo's voice was almost warm. "And sure I can. Don't be silly."

She tossed the beeper aside and made a quick gesture. Half a dozen bulky, dark-suited forms materialized from back of the dune.

"I've brought some help," Margo told Rhonda, "in case they're needed. But I hope you're not going to be difficult. It's over, you know that. And if you make a fuss," she added, "call for help or anything silly like that, you'll just cause a lot of your new friends to get hurt."

One of the men behind her said, "Want me to go get the car?"

Margo shook her head. "Too conspicuous, with all these damned motorbikes around. No, we'll all just go for a nice quiet little walk."

"Bring this guy along too?"

"Oh, yes." Margo gave me a bright smile. "Noir's a loose end. A *talkative* loose end. Can't have that."

"You can't do this," Rhonda Honda protested.

"Oh, stop snivelling," Margo said impatiently. "We can do anything we want, you of all people know that. Now then—"

That was when Donna came charging out of the dark, knees and elbows, plastic armor clattering, screaming like a whole ward full of madwomen. God knows how long she'd been there, or what she was doing there in the first place. Maybe she'd followed Rhonda and me out of jealous suspicion.

Margo half-turned, the pistol coming up in her hand. I threw the helmet at her, a clumsy underhanded pitch that missed by a foot but was still good enough to throw her aim off; the gun muzzle flashed—no sound—and then Donna hit her like a first-string offensive blocking back taking out a dangerous tackle. You could have heard the impact a block away.

The pistol flew from Margo's hand as she went down, and I fielded it in time to snap a shot at the nearest man in black, who was hauling out some sort of machine pistol. He went down and I threw a couple more slugs at his buddies, who were scattering out among the dunes. Something popped past my ear, though I didn't hear any bang. These people must have gotten a quantity deal on silencers.

By now there was plenty of racket coming from behind me; the Devil Dolls had finally realized something was going on. There were high-pitched shouts and curses and a man's voice cried, "Oh, *shit*, look out—" On the ground at my feet, Margo and Donna were rolling over and over, grappling and punching. Neither of them seemed to be doing much damage; they were both too well armored for serious catfighting.

I emptied the pistol in the general direction of the bad guys, threw it away, and grabbed Rhonda Honda by the wrist. "Come on," I told her. "Time to get out of here."

We ran around the dune and almost collided with a trio of Devil Dolls going the other way; one had a length of chain, one carried what looked like a machete, and the third—who appeared to be entirely naked—was brandishing a big chunk of driftwood. They paid us no mind; they were in a hurry to get in on the fun.

The Suzuki still stood where I'd left it. I mounted up and hit the button, hearing Rhonda's Honda come alive behind me.

A mile or so east of Coyote Bay I pulled over and cut the engine. She eased to a stop beside me and we looked at each other. "Well," she said. "Thanks, whoever you are."

She glanced up the road, in the direction of the payslab. "Riding south?"

I nodded. She said, "Then I guess this is where we—"

I said, "I'm not playing the sap for you, Mr. President."

For a second she went absolutely rigid. Then she sort of sagged, all over. "God," she said in a totally different voice. "You knew?"

"I just figured it out. Too much heavy action for a simple First Family runaway or another Presidential bedroom scandal. Who'd go to all that trouble—let alone kill—to keep the lid on something that ordinary?"

I looked her up and down. "Nice morph job. Only six months?"

She shrugged. "I always was a quick healer."

"You've got to go back," I said. "Back to Washington, back to the job and the Family. I won't give you any speeches about how it's your duty. It's just the only way you'll be safe."

"I'm not letting them change me back," she said flatly. "No matter what."

"Who said you had to? I'm no student of history," I said, "but even I could list a lot of antics your predecessors got up to, every bit as outrageous as this, and the public loved it. And they'll love this."

I looked her over again. "Of course you're going to have to lose the ensemble, and the rest of the roadgrrl bit. I mean, there are limits. How'd you get into that, anyway?"

"I figured it was the last place anybody would look for me. And I rode bikes a lot when I was younger, only quit because they said it was bad for my image . . . what about the First Lady?"

"What about her? She can discover she's always liked girls—that'll work, everybody likes lesbian celebrities. If she can't handle it you can dump her. She's not very popular, you know."

"That's true. The last poll showed she was hurting my ratings." Rhonda rubbed her face thoughtfully. "You really think I can get away with it?"

"Getting away with it," I said, "is the American way."

I never saw her again. At least not in person; like everybody else I watched her coming-out press conference, and I followed the news long enough to satisfy myself that I'd been right. The public ate it up; the Presidential ratings hit an all-time high. And when the First Lady revealed that she had always preferred to lead when she danced, her own popularity went up too.

Me? I went back to L.A., back to the job and the life. I thought I might catch some trouble, but nobody bothered me. Nobody even said anything to me about the whole business. After all, none of it had ever happened.

You can sweep anything under the rug if you've got a big enough broom.

A couple of weeks later my ex showed up and tried to kill me. But that's another story.

"Rhonda Honda" was another special-invitation story, this one for one of Esther Friesner's "Chicks In Armor" series. "Anything you want to write," Esther said. "Just as long as it's got women wearing some kind of armor." I said I'd give it a shot and headed back toward the office, and halfway there the first line popped into my head and the rest of it pretty much wrote itself.

At the time I was unaware of Garrison Keilor's "Guy Noir" character. If I'd known I might have given my man a different name. And then again I might not.

Written November 2000
First published October 2001

When This World Is All On Fire

"Squatters," Jimmy Lonekiller said as he swung the jeep off the narrow old blacktop onto the narrower and older gravel side road. "I can't believe we got squatters again."

Sitting beside him, bracing himself against the bumping and bouncing, Sergeant Davis Blackbear said, "Better get used to it. We kick this bunch out, there'll be more."

Jimmy Lonekiller nodded. "Guess that's right," he said. "They're not gonna give up, are they?"

He was a husky, dark-skinned young man, and tall for a Cherokee; among the women of the reservation he was generally considered something of a hunk. His khaki uniform was neat and crisply pressed, despite the oppressive heat. Davis Blackbear, feeling his own shirt wilting and sticking to his skin, wondered how he did it. Maybe fullbloods didn't sweat as much. Or maybe it was something to do with being young.

Davis said, "Would you? Give up, I mean, if you were in their shoes?"

Jimmy didn't reply for a moment, being busy fighting the wheel as the jeep slammed over a series of potholes. They were on a really bad stretch now, the road narrowed to a single-lane dirt snaketrack; the overhanging trees on either side, heavy with dust-greyed festoons of kudzu vine, shut out the sun without doing anything much about the heat. This was an out-of-the-way part of the reservation; Davis had had to check the map at the tribal police headquarters to make sure he knew how to get here.

The road began to climb, now, up the side of a steep hill. The jeep slowed to not much better than walking speed; the locally-distilled alcohol might burn cooler and cleaner than gasoline but it had no power at all. Jimmy Lonekiller spoke then: "Don't guess I would, you put it that way. Got to go somewhere, poor bastards."

They were speaking English; Davis was Oklahoma Cherokee, having moved to the North Carolina reservation only a dozen years ago, when he married a Qualla Band woman. He could understand the Eastern dialect fairly well by now, enough for cop purposes anyway, but he still wasn't up to a real conversation.

"Still," Jimmy went on, "you got to admit it's a hell of a thing. Twenty-first century, better than five hundred years after Columbus, and here we are again with white people trying to settle on our land. What little bit we've got left," he said, glancing around at the dusty woods. "There's gotta be somewhere else they can go."

"Except," Davis said, "somebody's already there too."

"Probably so," Jimmy admitted. "Seems like they're running out of places for people to be."

He steered the jeep around a rutted hairpin bend, while Davis turned the last phrase over in his mind, enjoying the simple precision of it: running out of places for people to be, that was the exact and very well-put truth. Half of Louisiana and more than half of Florida under water now, the rest of the coastline inundated, Miami and Mobile and Savannah and most of Houston, and, despite great and expensive efforts, New Orleans too.

And lots more land, farther inland, that might as well be submerged for all the good it did anybody: all that once-rich farm country in southern Georgia and Alabama and Mississippi, too hot and dry now to grow anything, harrowed by tornadoes and dust storms, while raging fires destroyed the last remnants of the pine forests and the cypress groves of the dried-up swamplands. Not to mention the quake, last year, shattering

Memphis and eastern Arkansas, demolishing the levees and turning the Mississippi loose on what was left of the Delta country. Seemed everybody either had way too much water or not enough.

He'd heard a black preacher, on the radio, declare that it was all God's judgment on the South because of slavery and racism. But that was bullshit; plenty of other parts of the country were getting it just as bad. Like Manhattan, or San Francisco— and he didn't even want to think about what it must be like in places like Arizona. And Africa, oh, Jesus. Nobody in the world wanted to think about Africa now.

The road leveled out at the top of the hill and he pointed. "Pull over there. I want to do a quick scout before we drive up."

Jimmy stopped the jeep and Davis climbed out and stood in the middle of the dirt road. "Well," Jimmy said, getting out too, "I wish somebody else would get the job of running them off now and then." He gave Davis a mocking look. "It's what I get, letting myself get partnered with an old 'breed. Everybody knows why Ridge always puts you in charge of the evictions."

Davis didn't rise to the bait; he knew what Jimmy was getting at. It was something of a standing joke among the reservation police that Davis always got any jobs that involved dealing with white people. Captain Ridge claimed it was because of his years of experience on the Tulsa PD, but Jimmy and others claimed it was really because he was quarter-blood and didn't look all that Indian and therefore might make whites less nervous.

In his own estimation he didn't look particularly Indian or white or anything else, just an average-size man with a big bony face and too many wrinkles and dark brown hair that was now getting heavily streaked with gray. He doubted that his appearance inspired much confidence in people of any race.

The dust cloud was beginning to settle over the road behind them. A black-and-white van appeared, moving slowly, and pulled to a stop behind the jeep. Corporal Roy Smoke stuck his head out the window and said, "Here?"

"For now," Davis told him. "I'm going to go have a look, scope out the scene before we move in. You guys wait here." He turned. "Jimmy, you come with me."

The heat was brutal as they walked down the road, even in the shady patches. At the bottom of the hill, though, Davis led the way off the road and up a dry creek bed, and back in the woods it was a little cooler. Away from the road, there wasn't enough sunlight for the kudzu vines to take over, and beneath the trees the light was pleasantly soft and green. Still too damn dry, Davis thought, feeling leaves and twigs crunching under his boot soles. Another good reason to get this eviction done quickly; squatters tended to be careless with fire. The last bad woods fire on the reservation, a couple of months ago, had been started by a squatter family trying to cook a stolen hog.

They left the creek bed and walked through the woods, heading roughly eastward. "Hell," Jimmy murmured, "I know where this is now. They're on the old Birdshooter place, huh? Shit, nobody's lived there for years. Too rocky to grow anything, no water since the creek went dry."

Davis motioned for silence. Moving more slowly now, trying to step quietly though it wasn't easy in the dry underbrush, they worked their way to the crest of a low ridge. Through the trees Davis could see a cleared area beyond. Motioning to Jimmy to wait, he moved up to the edge of the woods and paused in the shadow of a half-grown oak, and that was when he heard the singing.

At first he didn't even recognize it as singing; the sound was so high and clear and true that he took it for some sort of instrument. But after a second he realized it was a human voice, though a voice like none he'd ever heard. He couldn't make out the words, but the sound alone was enough to make the hair stand up on his arms and neck, and the air suddenly felt cooler under the trees.

It took Davis a moment to get unstuck; he blinked rapidly and took a deep breath. Then, very cautiously, he peered around the trunk of the oak.

The clearing wasn't very big; wasn't very clear, either, any more, having been taken over by brush and weeds. In the middle stood the ruins of a small frame house, its windows smashed and its roof fallen in.

Near the wrecked house sat a green pickup truck, its bed covered with a boxy, homemade-looking camper shell— plywood, it looked like from where Davis stood, and painted a dull uneven gray. The truck's own finish was badly faded and scabbed with rust; the near front fender was crumpled. Davis couldn't see any license plates.

A kind of lean-to had been erected at the rear of the truck, a sagging blue plastic tarp with guy-ropes tied to trees and bushes. As Davis watched, a lean, long-faced man in bib overalls and a red baseball cap came out from under the tarp and stood looking about.

Then the red-haired girl came around the front of the truck, still singing, the words clear now:

> *"Oh, when this world is all on fire*
> *Where you gonna go?*
> *Where you gonna go?"*

She was, Davis guessed, maybe twelve or thirteen, though he couldn't really tell at this distance. Not much of her, anyway; he didn't figure she'd go over eighty pounds or so. Her light blue dress was short and sleeveless, revealing thin pale arms and legs. All in all it didn't seem possible for all that sound to be coming from such a wispy little girl; and yet there was no doubt about it, he could see her mouth moving:

> *"Oh, when this world is all on fire*
> (she sang again)
> *Where you gonna go?"*

The tune was a simple one, an old-fashioned modal-sounding melody line, slow and without a pronounced rhythm. It didn't matter; nothing mattered but that voice. It soared through the still mountain air like a whippoorwill calling beside a running stream. Davis felt his throat go very tight.

> *"Run to the mountains to hide your face*
> *Never find no hiding place*
> *Oh, when this world is all on fire*
> *Where you gonna go?"*

The man in the baseball cap put his hands on his hips. "Eva May!" he shouted.

The girl stopped singing and turned. Her red hair hung down her back almost to her waist. "Yes, Daddy?" she called.

"Quit the damn fooling around," the man yelled. His voice was rough, with the practiced anger of the permanently angry man. "Go help your brother with the fire."

Fire? Davis spotted it then, a thin trace of bluish-white smoke rising from somewhere on the far side of the parked truck. "Shit!" he said soundlessly, and turned and began picking his way back down the brushy slope.

"What's happening?" Jimmy Lonekiller said as Davis reappeared. "What was that music? Sounded like—"

"Quiet," Davis said. "Come on. We need to hurry."

"Go," Davis said to Jimmy as they turned off the road and up the brush-choked track through the trees. "No use trying to sneak up. They've heard us coming by now."

Sure enough, the squatters were already standing in the middle of the clearing, watching, as the jeep bumped to a stop in front of them. The man in the red baseball cap stood in the middle, his face dark with anger. Beside him stood a washed-out-looking blond woman in a faded flower-print dress and, next to her, a tall teenage boy wearing ragged jeans and no shirt. The boy's hair had been cropped down almost flush with his scalp.

The woman was holding a small baby to her chest. Great, Davis thought with a flash of anger, just what a bunch of homeless drifters needed. Running out of places for people to be, but not out of people, hell, no. . . .

The red-haired girl was standing off to one side, arms folded. Close up, Davis revised his estimate of her age; she had to be in her middle to late teens at least. There didn't appear to be much of a body under that thin blue dress, but it was definitely not that of a child. Her face, as she watched the two men get out of the jeep, was calm and without expression.

The van came rocking and swaying up the trail and stopped behind the jeep. Davis waited while Roy Smoke and the other four men got out—quite a force to evict one raggedy-ass family, but Captain Ridge believed in being careful—and then he walked over to the waiting squatters and said, "Morning. Where you folks from?"

The man in the red baseball cap spat on the ground, not taking his eyes off Davis. "Go to hell, Indian."

Oh oh. Going to be like that, was it? Davis said formally, "Sir, you're on Cherokee reservation land. Camping isn't allowed except by permit and in designated areas. I'll have to ask you to move out."

The woman said, "Oh, why can't you leave us alone? We're not hurting anybody. You people have all this land, why won't you share it?"

We tried that, lady, Davis thought, and look where it got us. Aloud he said, "Ma'am, the laws are made by the government of the Cherokee nation. I just enforce them."

"Nation!" The man snorted. "Bunch of woods niggers, hogging good land while white people starve. You got no right."

"I'm not here to argue about it," Davis said. "I'm just here to tell you you've got to move on."

The boy spoke up suddenly. "You planning to make us?"

Davis looked at him. Seventeen or eighteen, he guessed, punk-mean around the eyes and that Johnny Pissoff stance that they seemed to develop at that age; ropy muscles showing under bare white skin, forearms rippling visibly as he clenched both fists.

"Yes," Davis told him. "If necessary, we'll move you."

To the father—he assumed—he added, "I'm hoping you won't make it necessary. If you like, we'll give you a hand—"

He didn't get to finish. That was when the boy came at him, fists up, head hunched down between his shoulders, screaming as he charged: "*Redskin motherfu—*"

Davis shifted his weight, caught the wild swing in a cross-arm block, grasped the kid's wrist and elbow and pivoted, all in one smooth motion. The boy yelped in pain as he hit the ground, and then grunted as Jimmy Lonekiller landed on top of him, handcuffs ready.

The man in the red cap had taken a step forward, but he stopped as Roy Smoke moved in front of him and tapped him gently on the chest with his nightstick. "No," Roy said, "you don't want to do that. Stand still, now."

Davis said, "Wait up, Jimmy," and then to the man in the red cap, "All right, there's two ways we can do this. We can take this boy to Cherokee town and charge him with assaulting an officer, and he can spend the next couple of months helping us fix the roads. Probably do him a world of good."

"No," the woman cried. The baby in her arms was wailing now, a thin weak piping against her chest, but she made no move to quiet it. "Please, no."

"Or," Davis went on, "you can move out of here, right now, without any more trouble, and I'll let you take him with you."

The girl, he noticed, hadn't moved the whole time, just stood there watching with no particular expression on her face, except that there might be a tiny trace of a smile on her lips as she looked at the boy on the ground.

"No," the woman said again. "Vernon, no, you can't let them take Ricky—"

"All right," the man said. "We'll go, Indian. Let him up. He won't give you no more trouble. Ricky, behave yourself or I'll whup your ass."

Davis nodded to Jimmy Lonekiller, who released the kid. "Understand this," Davis said, "we don't give second warnings. If you're found on Cherokee land again, you'll be arrested, your vehicle will be impounded, and you might do a little time."

The boy was getting to his feet, rubbing his arm. The woman started to move toward him but the man said, "He's all right, damn it. Get busy packing up." He turned his head and scowled at the girl. "You too, Eva May."

Davis watched as the squatters began taking down the tarp. The girl's long red hair fairly glowed in the midday sun; he felt a crazy impulse to go over and touch it. He wished she'd sing some more, but he didn't imagine she felt like singing now.

He said, "Roy, have somebody kill that fire. Make sure it's dead and buried. This place is a woods fire waiting to happen."

Davis lived in a not very big trailer on the outskirts of Cherokee town. Once he had had a regular house, but after his wife had taken off, a few years ago, with that white lawyer from Gatlinburg, he'd moved out and let a young married couple have the place.

The trailer's air conditioning was just about shot, worn out from the constant unequal battle with the heat, but after the sun went down it wasn't too bad except on the hottest summer nights. Davis took off his uniform and hung it up and stretched out on the bed while darkness fell outside and the owls began calling in the trees. Sweating, waiting for the temperature to drop, he closed his eyes and heard again in his mind, over the rattle of the laboring air conditioner:

> *"Oh, when this world is all on fire*
> *Where you gonna go?*
> *Where you gonna go?"*

It was the following week when he saw the girl again.

He was driving through Waynesville, taking one of the force's antique computers for repairs, when he saw her crossing the street up ahead. Even at half a block's distance he was sure it was the same girl; there couldn't be another head of hair like that in these mountains. She was even wearing what looked like the same blue dress.

But he was caught in slow traffic, and she disappeared around the corner before he could get any closer. Sighing, making a face at himself for acting like a fool, he drove on. By the time he got to the computer shop he had convinced himself it had all been his imagination.

He dropped off the computer and headed back through town, taking it easy and keeping a wary eye on the traffic, wondering as always how so many people still managed to drive, despite fuel shortages and sky-high prices; and all the new restrictions, not that anybody paid them any mind, the government having all it could do just keeping the country more or less together.

An ancient minivan, a mattress roped to its roof, made a sudden left turn from the opposite lane. Davis hit the brakes, cursing—a fenderbender in a tribal patrol car, that would really make the day—and that was when he saw the red-haired girl coming up the sidewalk on the other side of the street.

Some asshole behind him was honking; Davis put the car in motion again, going slow, looking for a parking place. There was a spot up near the next corner and he turned into it and got out and locked up the cruiser, all without stopping to think what he thought he was doing or why he was doing it.

He crossed the street and looked along the sidewalk, but he couldn't see the girl anywhere. He began walking back the way she'd been going, looking this way and that. The street was mostly lined with an assortment of small stores—leftovers, probably, from the days when Waynesville had been a busy tourist resort, before tourism became a meaningless concept—and he peered in through a few shop windows, without any luck.

He walked a couple of blocks that way and then decided she couldn't have gotten any farther in that little time. He turned and went back, and stopped at the corner and looked up and down the cross street, wondering if she could have gone that way. Fine Indian you are, he thought, one skinny little white girl with hair like a brush fire and you keep losing her.

Standing there, he became aware of a growing small commotion across the street, noises coming from the open door of the shop on the corner: voices raised, a sound of scuffling. A woman shouted, "No you don't—"

He ran across the street, dodging an oncoming BMW, and into the shop. It was an automatic cop reaction, unconnected to his search; but then immediately he saw the girl, struggling in the grip of a large steely-haired woman in a long black dress. "Stop fighting me," the woman was saying in a high strident voice. "Give me that, young lady. I'm calling the police—"

Davis said, "What's going on here?"

The woman looked around. "Oh," she said, looking pleased, not letting go the girl's arm. "I'm glad to see you, officer. I've got a little shoplifter for you."

The girl was looking at Davis too. If she recognized him she gave no sign. Her face was flushed, no doubt from the struggle, but still as expressionless as ever.

"What did she take?" Davis asked.

"This." The woman reached up and pried the girl's right hand open, revealing something shiny. "See, she's still holding it!"

Davis stepped forward and took the object from the girl's hand: a cheap-looking little pendant, silver or more likely silver-plated, in the shape of a running dog, with a flimsy neck chain attached.

"I want her arrested," the woman said. "I'll be glad to press charges. I'm tired of these people, coming around here ruining this town, stealing everyone blind."

Davis said, "I'm sorry, ma'am, I don't have any jurisdiction here. You'll need to call the local police."

She blinked, doing a kind of ladylike double-take, looking at Davis's uniform. "Oh. Excuse me, I thought—" She managed to stop before actually saying, "I thought you were a real policeman." It was there on her face, though.

Davis looked again at the pendant, turning it over in his hand, finding the little white price tag stuck on the back of the running dog: $34.95. A ripoff even in the present wildly-inflated money; but after a moment he reached for his wallet and said, "Ma'am, how about if I just pay you for it?"

The woman started to speak and then stopped, her eyes locking on the wallet in his hand. Not doing much business these days, he guessed; who had money to waste on junk like this?

While she hesitated, Davis pulled out two twenties and laid them on the nearby counter top. "With a little extra to pay for your trouble," he added.

That did it. She let go the girl's arm and scooped up the money with the speed of a professional gambler. "All right," she said, "but get her out of here!"

The girl stood still, staring at Davis. The woman said, "I mean it! Right now!"

Davis tilted his head in the direction of the door. The girl nodded and started to move, not particularly fast. Davis followed her, hearing the woman's voice behind him: "And if you ever come back—"

Out on the sidewalk, Davis said, "I'm parked down this way."

She looked at him. "You arresting me?"

Her speaking voice—he realized suddenly that this was the first time he'd heard it—was surprisingly ordinary; soft and high, rather pleasant, but nothing to suggest what it could do in song. There was no fear in it, or in her face; she might have been asking what time it was.

Davis shook his head. "Like I told that woman, I don't have any authority here."

"So you can't make me go with you."

"No." he said. "But I'd say you need to get clear of this area pretty fast. She's liable to change her mind and call the law after all."

"Guess that's right. Okay." She fell in beside him, sticking her hands in the pockets of the blue dress. He noticed her feet were barely covered by a pair of old tennis shoes, so ragged they were practically sandals. "Never rode in a police car before."

As they came up to the parked cruiser he stopped and held out his hand. "Here. You might as well have this."

She took the pendant and held it up in front of her face, looking at it, swinging it from side to side. After a moment she slipped the chain over her head and tucked the pendant down the front of her dress. "Better hide it," she said. "Ricky sees it, he'll steal it for sure."

He said, "Not much of a thing to get arrested for."

She shrugged. "I like dogs. We had a dog, back home in Georgia, before we had to move. Daddy wouldn't let me take him along."

"Still," he said, "you could have gone to jail."

She shrugged, a slight movement of her small shoulders. "So? Wouldn't be no worse than how I got to live now."

"Yes it would," he told her. "You've got no idea what it's like in those forced-labor camps. How old are you?"

"Seventeen," she said. "Well, next month."

"Then you're an adult, as far's the law's concerned. Better watch it from now on." He opened the right door. "Get in."

She climbed into the car and he closed the door and went around. As he slid in under the wheel she said, "Okay, I know what comes next. Where do you want to go?"

"What?" Davis looked at her, momentarily baffled. "Well, I was just going to take you home. Wherever your family—"

"Oh, come on." Her voice held an edge of scorn now. "You didn't get me out of there for nothing. You want something, just like everybody always does, and I know what it is because there ain't nothing else I got. Well, all right," she said. "I don't guess I mind. So where do you want to go to do it?"

For a moment Davis was literally speechless. The idea simply hadn't occurred to him; he hadn't thought of her in that way at all. It surprised him, now he considered it. After all, she was a pretty young girl—you could have said beautiful, in a way—and he had been living alone for a long time. Yet so it was; he felt no stirrings of that kind toward this girl, not even now with her close up and practically offering herself.

When he could speak he said, "No, no. Not that. Believe me."

"Really?" She looked very skeptical. "Then what *do* you want?"

"Right now," he said, "I want to buy you a pair of shoes."

* * *

An hour or so later, coming out of the discount shoe store out by the highway, she said, "I know what this is all about. You feel bad because you run us off, back last week."

"No." Davis's voice held maybe a little bit more certainty than he felt, but he added, "Just doing my job. Anyway, you couldn't have stayed there. No water, nothing to eat, how would you live?"

"You still didn't have no right to run us off."

"Sure I did. It's our land," he said. "All we've got left."

She opened her mouth and he said, "Look, we're not going to talk about it, all right?"

They walked in silence the rest of the way across the parking lot. She kept looking down at her feet, admiring the new shoes. They weren't much, really, just basic white no-name sport shoes, but he supposed they looked pretty fine to her. At that they hadn't been all that cheap. In fact between the shoes and the pendant he'd managed to go through a couple day's pay. Not that he was likely to get paid any time soon; the tribe had been broke for a long time.

As he started the car she said, "You sure you don't want to, you know, do it?"

He looked at her and she turned sidewise in the seat, moving her thin pale legs slightly apart, shifting her narrow hips. "Hey," she said, "somebody's gotta be the first. Might as well be you."

Her mouth quirked. "If it ain't you it'll prob'ly be Ricky. He sure keeps trying."

With some difficulty Davis said, "Turn around, please, and do up your safety belt."

"All right." She giggled softly. "Just don't know what it is you want from me, that's all."

He didn't respond until they were out of the parking lot and rolling down the road, back into Waynesville. Then he said, "Would you sing for me?"

"What?" Her voice registered real surprise. "Sing? You mean right now, right here in the car?"

"Yes," Davis said. "Please."

"Well, I be damn." She brushed back her hair and studied him for a minute. "You mean it, don't you? All right . . . what you want me to sing? If I know it."

"That song you were singing that morning up on the reservation," he said. "Just before we arrived."

She thought about it. "Oh," she said. "You mean—"

She tilted her head back and out it came, like a flood of clear spring water:

> *"Oh, when this world is all on fire*
> *Where you gonna go?"*

"Yes," Davis said very softly. "That's it. Sing it. Please."

Her family was staying in a refugee camp on the other side of town; a great hideous sprawl of cars and trucks and buses and campers and trailers of all makes and ages and states of repair, bright nylon tents and crude plastic-tarp shelters and pathetic, soggy arrangements of cardboard boxes, spread out over a once-beautiful valley.

"You better just drop me off here," the girl said as he turned off the road.

"That's okay," Davis said. "Which way do I go?"

At her reluctant direction, he steered slowly down a narrow muddy lane between parked vehicles and outlandish shelters, stopping now and then as children darted across in front of the car. People came out and stared as the big police cruiser rolled past. Somebody threw something unidentifiable, that bounced off the windshield leaving a yellowish smear. By now Davis was pretty sure this hadn't been a good idea.

But the girl said, "Up there," and there it was, the old truck with the homemade camper bed and the blue plastic awning rigged out behind, just like before. He stopped the car and got out and went around to open the passenger door.

The air was thick with wood smoke and the exhausts of worn-out engines, and the pervasive reek of human waste. The ground underfoot was soggy with mud and spilled motor oil and

God knew what else. Davis looked around at the squalid scene, remembering what this area used to look like, only a few years ago. Now, it looked like the sort of thing they used to show on the news, in countries you'd never heard of. The refugee camps in Kosovo, during his long-ago army days, hadn't been this bad.

Beyond, up on the mountainsides, sunlight glinted on the windows of expensive houses. A lot of locals had thought it was wonderful, back when the rich people first started buying up land and building homes up in the mountain country, getting away from the heat and the flooding. They hadn't been as happy about the second invasion, a year or so later, by people bringing nothing but their desperation. . . .

Davis shook his head and opened the door. Even the depressing scene couldn't really get him down, right now. It had been an amazing experience, almost religious, driving along with that voice filling the dusty interior of the old cruiser; he felt light and loose, as if coming off a marijuana high. He found himself smiling—

A voice behind him said, "What the hell?" and then, "Eva May!"

He turned and saw the man standing there beside the truck, still wearing the red cap and the angry face. "Hello," he said, trying to look friendly or at least inoffensive. "Just giving your daughter a lift from town. Don't worry, she's not in any trouble—"

"Hell she's not," the man said, looking past Davis. "Eva May, git your ass out of that thing! What you doing riding around with this God-damn woods nigger?"

The girl swung her feet out of the car. Davis started to give her a hand but decided that might be a bad move right now. She got out and stepped past Davis. "It's all right, Daddy," she said. "He didn't do nothing bad. Look, he bought me some new shoes!"

"No shit." The man looked down at her feet, at the new shoes standing out white and clean against the muddy ground. "New shoes, huh? Git 'em off."

She stopped. "But Daddy—"

His hand came up fast; it made an audible crack against the side of her face. As she stumbled backward against the side of the truck he said, "God damn it, I *said* take them shoes off."

He spun about to face Davis. "You don't like that, Indian? Maybe you wanta do something about it?"

Davis did, in fact, want very much to beat this worthless *yoneg* within half an inch of his life. But he forced himself to stand still and keep his hands down at his sides. Start a punch-out in here, and almost certainly he'd wind up taking on half the men in the camp. Or using the gun on his belt, which would bring down a whole new kind of disaster.

Even then he might have gone for it, but he knew that anything he did to the man would later be taken out on Eva May. It was a pattern all too familiar to any cop.

She had one shoe off now and was jerking at the other, standing on one foot, leaning against the trailer, sobbing. She got it off and the man jerked it out of her hand. "Here." He half-turned and threw the shoe, hard, off somewhere beyond the old school bus that was parked across the lane. He bent down and picked up the other shoe and hurled it in the opposite direction.

"Ain't no damn Indian buying *nothing* for my kid," he said. "Or going anywhere *near* her. You understand that, Chief?"

From inside the camper came the sound of a baby crying. A woman's voice said, "Vernon? What's going on, Vernon?"

"Now," the man said, "you git out of here, woods nigger."

The blood was singing in Davis's ears and there was a taste in his mouth like old pennies. Still he managed to check himself, and to keep his voice steady as he said, "Sir, whatever you think of me, your daughter has a great gift. She should have the opportunity—"

"Listen close, Indian." The man's voice was low, now, and very intense. "You shut your mouth and you git back in that car and you drive outta here, right damn *now*, or else I'm on find out if you got the guts to use that gun. Plenty white men around here, be glad to help stomp your dirty red ass."

Davis glanced at Eva May, who was still leaning against the truck, weeping and holding the side of her face. Her bare white feet were already spotted with mud.

And then, because there was nothing else to do, he got back in the car and drove away. He didn't look back. There was nothing there he wanted to see; nothing he wouldn't already be seeing for a long time to come.

"Blackbear," Captain Ridge said, next morning. "I don't believe this."

He was seated at his desk in his office, looking up at Davis. His big dark face was not that of a happy man.

"I got a call just now," he said, "from the sheriff's office over in Waynesville. Seems a reservation officer, man about your size and wearing sergeant's stripes, picked up a teenage girl on the street. Made her get into a patrol car, tried to get her to have sex, even bought her presents to entice her. When she refused he took her back to the refugee camp and made threats against her family."

Davis said, "Captain—"

"No," Captain Ridge said, and slapped a hand down on his desk top. "No, Blackbear, I don't want to hear it. See, you're about to tell me it's a lot of bullshit, and I *know* it's a lot of bullshit, and it doesn't make a damn bit of difference. You listen to me, Blackbear. Whoever those people are, you stay away from them. You stay out of Waynesville, till I tell you different. On duty or off, I don't care."

He leaned back in his chair. "Because if you show up there again, you're going to be arrested—the sheriff just warned me—and there won't be a thing I can do about it. And you know what kind of chance you'll have in court over there. They like us even less than they do the squatters."

Davis said, "All right. I wasn't planning on it anyway."

But of course he went back. Later, he thought that the only surprising thing was that he waited as long as he did.

He went on Sunday morning. It was an off-duty day and he drove his own car; that, plus the nondescript civilian clothes he wore, ought to cut down the chances of his being recognized. He stopped at an all-hours one-stop in Maggie Valley and bought a pair of cheap sunglasses and a butt-ugly blue mesh-back cap with an emblem of a jumping fish on the front. Pulling the cap down low, checking himself out in the old Dodge's mirror, he decided he looked like a damn fool, but as camouflage it ought to help.

But when he got to the refugee camp he found it had all been for nothing. The truck was gone and so was Eva May's family; an elderly couple in a Buick were already setting up camp in the spot. No, they said, they didn't know anything; the place had been empty when they got here, just a little while ago.

Davis made a few cautious inquiries, without finding out much more. The woman in the school bus across the lane said she'd heard them leaving a little before daylight. She had no idea where they'd gone and doubted if anyone else did.

"People come and go," she said. "There's no keeping track. And they weren't what you'd call friendly neighbors."

Well, Davis thought as he drove back to the reservation, so much for that. He felt sad and empty inside, and disgusted with himself for feeling that way. Good thing the bars and liquor stores weren't open on Sunday; he could easily go on a serious drunk right now.

He was coming over the mountains east of Cherokee when he saw the smoke.

It was the worst fire of the decade. And could have been much worse; if the wind had shifted just right, it might have taken out the whole reservation. As it was, it was three days before the fire front crossed the reservation border and became somebody else's problem.

For Davis Blackbear it was a very long three days. Afterward, he estimated that he might have gotten three or four hours of sleep the whole time. None of the tribal police got any real time off, the whole time; it was one job after another, evacuating people from the fire's path, setting up roadblocks, keeping traffic unsnarled and, in the rare times there was nothing else to do, joining the brutally overworked firefighting crews. By now almost every able-bodied man in the tribe was helping fight the blaze; or else already out of action, being treated for burns or smoke inhalation or heat stroke.

At last the fire ate its way over the reservation boundary and into the national parkland beyond; and a few hours later, as Wednesday's sun slid down over the mountains, Davis Blackbear returned to his trailer and fell across the bed, without bothering to remove his sweaty uniform or even to kick off his ruined shoes. And lay like a dead man through the rest of the day and all through the night, until the next morning's light came in the trailer's windows; and then he got up and undressed and went back to bed and slept some more.

A little before noon he woke again, and knew before he opened his eyes what he was going to do.

Captain Ridge had told him to take the day off and rest up; but Ridge wasn't around when Davis came by the station, and nobody paid any attention when Davis left his car and drove off in one of the jeeps. Or stopped him when he drove past the roadblocks that were still in place around the fire zone; everybody was too exhausted to ask unnecessary questions.

It was a little disorienting, driving across the still-smoking land; the destruction had been so complete that nothing was recognizable. He almost missed a couple of turns before he found the place he was looking for.

A big green pickup truck was parked beside the road, bearing the insignia of the U.S. Forest Service. A big stocky white man in a green uniform stood beside it, watching as Davis drove up and parked the jeep and got out. "Afternoon," he said.

He stuck out a hand as Davis walked across the road. "Bob Lindblad," he said as Davis shook his hand. "Fire inspector. They sent me down to have a look, seeing as it's on federal land now."

He looked around and shook his head. "Hell of a thing," he said, and wiped his forehead with the back of his hand.

It certainly was a strange-looking scene. On the northeast side of the road there was nothing but ruin, an ash-covered desolation studded with charred tree stumps, stretching up the hillside and over the ridge and out of sight. The other side of the road, however, appeared untouched; except for a thin coating of powdery ash on the bushes and the kudzu vines, it looked exactly as it had when Davis had come this way a couple of weeks ago.

The Forest Service man said, "Anybody live around here?"

"Not close, no. Used to be a family named Birdshooter, lived up that way, but they moved out a long time ago."

Lindblad nodded. "I saw some house foundations."

Davis said, "This was where it started?"

"Where it *was* started," Lindblad said. "Yes."

"Somebody set it?"

"No question about it." Lindblad waved a big hand. "Sign all over the place. They set it at half a dozen points along this road. The wind was at their backs, out of the southwest— that's why the other side of the road didn't take—so they weren't in any danger. Bastards," he added.

Davis said, "Find anything to show who did it?"

Lindblad shook his head. "Been too much traffic up and down this road, last few days, to make any sense of the tracks. I'm still looking, though."

"All right if I look around too?" Davis asked.

"Sure. Just holler," Lindblad said, "if you find anything. I'll be somewhere close by."

He walked off up the hill, his shoes kicking up little white puffs of ash. Davis watched him a minute and then started to walk along the road, looking at the chewed-up surface. The Forest Service guy was right, he thought, no way in hell could anybody sort out all these tracks and ruts. Over on the unburned downhill side, somebody had almost gone into the ditch—

Davis almost missed it. A single step left or right, or the sun at a different angle, and he'd never have seen the tiny shininess at the bottom of the brush-choked ditch. He bent down and groped, pushing aside a clod of roadway dirt, and felt something tangle around his fingers. He tugged gently and it came free. He straightened up and held up his hand in front of his face.

The sun glinted off the little silver dog as it swung from side to side at the end of the broken chain.

Up on the hillside Lindblad called, "Find anything?"

Davis turned and looked. Lindblad was poking around near the ruins of the old house, nearly hidden by a couple of black tree stubs. His back was to the road.

"No," Davis yelled back, walking across the road. "Not a thing."

He drew back his arm and hurled the pendant high out over the black-and-gray waste. It flashed for an instant against the sky before vanishing, falling somewhere on the burned earth.

By the turn of the century I had become seriously concerned about global warming. (Yeah—what took me so long? Me and practically everybody else?) I felt I ought to write something about it. This was the result.

As it happened, though, the story came out in the fall of '01, a time when people had other things on their minds. But then I don't suppose it made any difference. By then the US had come under the control of a bunch of reactionary pongids who didn't even believe there was such a thing as global warming; and the events of that fall were to hand them a lock on the power—which was crazy and stupid, but by then people had gone crazy and most of them were already stupid—and so the climate continued to go to shit along with practically everything else.

Even without these apocalyptic events, though, it would have been fatuous to expect a single story in a specialized magazine to make any difference. But you do what you can. I suppose it's the same impulse that makes people throw their hands over their heads when a building falls on them.

Written November 1997
First published October 2001

He Did The Flatline Boogie And He Boogied On Down The Line

The dude is sitting at this table way in the back of this little bar. The light is bad and at first I'm not even sure he's the right one, but then he looks up and waves a couple of fingers at me. When I get back to his table he sticks out a hand and says, "Hi. You're the guy they call Dead Henry?"

I don't do anything about the hand. I just look at him and say, "I hear you've been looking for me.

"Right," he says, "sit down. Want a drink?"

I shake my head. "I don't do booze," I tell him, and he makes this little face like that's what he expected and picks up his glass, while I slide into the seat across from him. Man, I don't see how anybody can drink that shit. I mean, look how it fucked up my parents.

While he sucks on his drink I check him out. He doesn't look like a cop, not that that means anything since the ones you have to worry about never do, but I'm not really sweating that anyway. The Feds don't give a major shit about street dealers like me, not enough to send an undercover man looking for me, and the local cops already know where to find me. And do, every month at collection time.

"An old dude, really wasted looking." That was what the street kids said, when they told me this guy nobody had seen before was asking around about where he could find Dead Henry the main neck man. Looking him over now, I figure they had him pretty well nailed. Oh, he's not like *old* old, but he's getting up there. Maybe somewhere in his forties, maybe even a little more, I can't really tell after they get double my age.

The punks were sure as hell right about the wasted part. The dude is taller than me, six feet at least, but I bet I've got twenty pounds on him. His hands are all big and bony like a Halloween skeleton, and you can see the shape of his skull under the skin of his face, which is a very bad kind of greenish white. His eyes are big and dark with lots of red around the edges and humongous bags underneath. His hair and his shirt collar, which meet in back, are the same dirty gray, and he needs a shave.

All in all he looks more or less like most of my customers, except for being so much older. But I keep getting the feeling I've seen him before, and it's eating at me. Remembering faces is very important in my business.

He puts down his glass and says, "They tell me you're the main Necrodone connection around here."

Well, he doesn't fuck around, does he? "Maybe," I say. "How much did you have in mind?"

I mean, it's not like you never get these old freaks coming around wanting to try the new stuff. It's not real often they want neck, though. Most of your dopers in that age bracket go for the various uppers and downers, or coke or crack if you can get it, and now and then some grandpa type asks if you've got acid. And of course they all smoke weed—though mostly they grow their own nowadays, or know somebody who does, so it's not worth a serious dealer's trouble handling that bulky shit—but you hardly ever see a Necrodone user over thirty or so. Maybe they figure they're getting close enough to the real thing, you know what I'm saying?

So I guess this one is probably some small-town dealer in the city to make a buy, not big enough to do business with a main connection, and I am trying to think where I can put together a quantity batch of neck. But he is giving me a funny look and now he says, "Oh, I get it. No, I'm not looking to score," and hearing his voice again makes the light finally kick on in my head and I know who he is.

"Shit," I say, feeling my face go all stupid-looking. "You're Jerry Duane Austin."

He leans back in his seat and smiles, not a feelgood smile but more like the bottom half of his face is cracking open. "Son of a bitch," he says after a minute. "Didn't think anybody under forty ever heard of me. What, your daddy used to play my CD's?"

My old man's idea of music was the sound of his hand upside my head or Mom's, but I don't want to go there right now. "Old guy I used to know," I say instead, "taught me guitar, he made me listen to everything you ever recorded. Said you were the best since Stevie Ray."

"Huh," he says, and rubs his face with one hand. "Son of a bitch," he says again.

Jerry Duane Austin was, no shit, the best blues guitar man to come out of the late Nineties, just about the only one from those days that I could ever stand to listen to. I nearly wore my fingers down to the knuckles trying to copy some of his riffs—looking at the size of his hands now, I can see why I never even got close—and the first half a dozen pieces I learned to play were songs he wrote. I still have all his stuff in my collection, some of it so old it's even on tape. That's going back to around the time I was born, nearly.

"Never mind that," he says, doing a little brushing-away number with his fingers, which I notice are shaking. "Listen," he says, "I'm looking for a girl."

My face goes all hot and prickly. "Wrong man, dude," I say, feeling like punching him and maybe about to do it. "I *deal*, okay? I'm not a fucking pimp."

"No, no." He's shaking his head and waving both hands. "I mean there's a particular girl I'm trying to find. Or woman, I guess I ought to say, but she's so young. . . ."

He puts his head down in his hands like he's praying. Maybe he is. While he gets it together I look around the place. I've never been in here before, even though I must have passed right by the door about a million times while working the street.

I stay out of bars, partly because I don't drink but also because there's no action for me in a place where half of my regular customers aren't even old enough to get in. This one is dark and dirty, lots of cigarette smoke which I really hate, and all the customers are older guys wearing work clothes or cheap suits. The juke box is playing some whiny-ass ancient thing, the Eagles I think—my mom used to listen to them—and you can smell the toilet clear across the room.

"Sorry," Jerry Duane says, sitting up straight and reaching for his drink again. "Like I was saying, I'm looking for this girl. I thought you might be able to help."

"She's a neck-head?" I figure I already know the answer.

"Last I heard." His voice is very tight, like he wants to scream but isn't letting himself do it. "At least some people I know ran into her a few weeks back, here in the city, and they said from the way she talked she was getting heavily into the Necrodone scene."

I wonder if he knows what a standard number that is around here. They show up all the time along the street, daddies and uncles and brothers and sometimes even the numbnuts hometown boyfriends, looking for the dear sweet little angel who disappeared in the big bad city. Now and then they even hire some jackoff PI who takes their money, comes around and asks a few questions just to make it look like he's doing something, and finally tells them the facts of life that they could have got for free from any cop.

Everybody on the street has picked up walking change off dudes like this, giving them bullshit information that never does them any good because, face it, nobody gets found in the city unless they want to and if the poor silly little bitch wanted to talk to them she'd have used the fucking phone or the public email down at the bus station. Usually she's doing just fine turning tricks or dealing street dope—or both—and the last thing she wants to see is anybody or anything from the past. Why do they think she left in the first place?

Any minute, I think, this one is going to pull out a picture and show it to me. And, sure enough, he does.

"Her name's Jane Ann," he says, passing it across the table. "Recognize her?"

The photo is a small Polaroid holo, shot from too close up with too much flash, so the girl in it looks like an albino. Long curly blond hair, kind of a round face, big soft-looking lips done in that purple lipstick they were all wearing last year. Goofy little grin, please-don't-hit-me eyes. I say, "No."

This is of course bullshit. Sure I recognize her, how could I *not* recognize her when I see her every day, been seeing her every day for fucking years, on the street or riding the bus or the subway, lying on beds in neck houses or getting into cars with uptown tricks, every so often being loaded into an ambulance or spread out inside a chalk outline on some bloody piece of sidewalk. Fuck knows how many of her there are, or where they all come from.

But the look on Jerry Duane Austin's face tells me he is not ready to hear any of this. Whoever this Jane Ann was, he thinks she's the only one there's ever been. And that's sad, man, but because he's who *he* is—or was—I keep what I'm thinking to myself.

Anyway, I told him straight enough: I don't recognize this particular one.

I say, "What's she, your daughter?"

He looks down into his drink and makes a little dry hacking sound tht I guess is as close to a laugh as he can do right now. "Well," he says, "when you think about it, I *am* old enough—"

He takes the picture back. "It was August of last year," he says, "and I was playing this gig in San Antone." Looking at my face, he does that weird laugh again. "Oh, sure, I'm still working. Haven't recorded anything in years, no major tours, but I still get plenty of appearances. My agent's trying to set up a comeback, says people are ready for my sound again."

Right now I wonder if this dude could play with himself with both hands. I mean, anybody can see he's got himself seriously fucked up. Seeing how he's looking at that stupid Polaroid, I have a pretty good idea why.

"She showed up backstage," he says in this soft voice, "don't know how she got in but they don't check ID very close in small clubs like that. And yeah, we had your basic all-night fun and games, just like you're thinking, just like I'd done more nights in more towns than you could add up on that fancy computer sticking out of your shirt pocket. Hell, it's not like I didn't get my share in my day, not to mention being married three times—one of them even got a book and a TV movie out of how bad she said I treated her—so you wouldn't think I'd lose it, would you, over some underage Texas groupie?"

He lets out this sigh. "Only," he says, "it turned into something else. . . ."

"And now she's taken off?" I ask him.

"We were together almost a year," he says, so low I can barely hear him over the bar noise. "She lived with me, went on tour with me, we did it all. She made me feel so God-damned *good*, you know? She never made me feel old."

He puts the holo back in his pocket, very carefully. "She disappeared a couple of months ago," he says, "just like that, no fights, no big scenes, no warnings, one day she just wasn't there any more."

"She a doper?" I ask, and he shrugs his shoulders.

"She did a little," he tells me, "like everybody else on the music scene. If that's her problem then I guess I'm to blame, because I was the one got her started. But she wasn't doing anything heavy, didn't have a habit."

His mouth twists to one side. "All I can think of, her father died this spring and she got real bent about it. Went on this big trip about death, talked on and on about it, read books, saw priests and suchlike, real morbid. Maybe, I don't know, I didn't give her enough support or something. Maybe," he says, "that's why she got interested in Necrodone, huh? Wanted to see what it's like?"

Could be. People do neck for lots of different reasons. There's even a half-assed church that uses it, claims near-death is a sacred experience, though I think most of the people who join are just lookin for an excuse to dope without feeling like dopers. The way they keep getting busted, the law must figure the same way.

Me, I've never done neck for anything but straight laughs. I mean, I like the feeling of being on the edge—and man, there's just *no* edge like the edge of that old dude's sickle, know what I'm saying?

Jerry Duane says, "I'll pay you to help me look for her. I've got plenty of bread, because they used that song of mine in that movie. Find Jane Ann for me, you can name your price."

"No," I say without having to stop and think, because I have already seen this coming. "No, I don't want your money. I'll help you look for her, no charge" He opens his mouth but I keep on: "If we do find her, though, I want your axe."

"My axe?" he says, surprised like. "You mean the guitar I use on stage?"

"The one you used to play," I say, "that old Les Paul Gibson, that you used in the first couple of videos. You still got it?"

"Yeah, sure. It's pretty old, may need some work, I haven't played it in years," he says, "but you find Jane Ann, sure, it's yours. Why not?"

"Come on, then," I say, getting up. "May as well get started."

"Where are we going?" he wants to know.

"Up front," I tell him, "we're going to see my partner."

Fat Slim looks at the holo and says exactly what I already knew he was going to say. "Don't recognize her," he says to Jerry Duane, "but that doesn't mean a thing. These kids come through here all the time, and there's no way I could remember their faces even if I had any reason to."

We are standing on the front steps of the neck house, which is an old two-story brownstone that probably used to be somebody's home they couldn't afford. It is the middle of the afternoon but the sky is cloudy and everything along the street looks dark and gray. Through the open door behind Fat Slim I can hear the steady *eeeeeeee* of the eek boxes. Sounds like business is good today.

Fat Slim hands the picture back to Jerry Duane. "I don't really look at them," he explains, "except just enough to size them up, spot the obvious flipouts and trouble freaks or the ones who look like they might not be able to handle it physically, like they're having trouble breathing or something. Your babe didn't have anything like that wrong with her, did she?"

Jerry Duane shakes his head. "Then," Fat Slim says, "she could be in there right now and I wouldn't necessarily know it. I don't think she is, but—" He jerks his thumb toward the doorway. "Want to go in and have a look?"

Jerry Duane looks at me. "Go ahead," I say. We have this basic rule in the partnership: I deal the shit on the street and keep the supply coming, and Fat Slim runs the neck house. We don't second-guess each other. He wants to let Jerry Duane in, it's cool with me.

The light inside is strong, brighter than outside in fact, and I get out my shades and put them on. Most neck houses are pretty dim—I've been in some where you had to practically feel your way around—but Fat Slim likes to be able to see what he's doing. The other places, he'll tell you, it doesn't matter since they don't *know* what they're doing, but Fat Slim was a Navy med tech for thirteen years before they busted him out and he runs the place like a regular clinic. Costs a bit more, but we've never yet lost a customer, which is why we stay in business and the cops are reasonable to deal with. I mean, you lose just one of these freaks and there's going to be all kind of shit come down, I don't care who you think you paid off, know what I'm saying?

The people who had the place before us knocked out a lot of walls—I think they had a dance school—so the downstairs is mostly one big room. We've got eighteen beds in there, could have more but Fat Slim says he can't do a proper job on more than that, and then there are the private rooms upstairs for the customers with serious money. Real beds, too, not mattresses on the floor like in the cheap neck houses. You can get them for nearly nothing at Goodwill and this way Fat Slim and his helpers don't hurt their backs bending over to help the customers.

Right now, because it's early, only about half of the beds are in use, plus one more customer is on his way out the back door. "Check it out," Fat Slim tells Jerry Duane. "Who knows, maybe you'll get lucky."

I follow Jerry Duane as he walks slowly along the aisle between the two rows of beds. The customers are all flatted out, lying there on their backs with their eyes hidden by the little cloth sleep masks—that's another class touch we provide—and their faces pale and slack. Beside each bed the eek box is showing a green line straight as an E string and singing its one-note song.

Jerry Duane says almost in a whisper, "They look . . . *dead.*"

"They are," I remind him. "That's, like, the point, you know?"

"Yeah, but—" Jerry Duane licks his lips. Damn, he's got a long tongue. Must have been fun for Jane Ann. "I mean," he said, "they look *really* dead."

"And as my esteemed partner just told you," Fat Slim says, "that's exactly what they are. Really, clinically fucking dead. Just not permanently."

He waves a big black hand at the bodies on the beds. "Oh, the correct term is supposed to be 'near-death' or 'para-terminal'—you read the literature, there's even a few precious assholes like to say 'thanatomimetic', for Christ sake." Fat Slim reads a lot, even real books, not just net stuff. "But I guaran-fucking-tee you, every one of these fools is deader than shit, by any reasonable medical definition. Look at the EKGs. Flat as piss on a plate."

Jerry Duane is looking at the customers, one by one. Only four of them are women and it is easy to see by his face that none of them is Jane Ann.

"Interesting shit, Necrodone," Fat Slim says. "Developed accidentally, like most of the major head drugs. Way I heard it, this guy was working on an antidote for nerve gas, something that wouldn't have the side effects of atropine. Came up with this stuff, thought at first he'd really blown it big, had himself a new poison instead. Only then his lab animals started coming back to life after an hour or so." He grins, showing us his steel teeth. "Wonder how they got any human test subjects, to start."

"Hell, that's never hard," I tell him. "Any kind of shit you want to mix up, I can walk down the street and say, 'Here, try this,' and there's plenty of assholes ready to—"

All of a sudden there is a loud *woop-woop-woop* coming from beside the bed down at the far end. Fat Slim says, "Fuck," and takes off very fast. Jerry Duane says, "What?"

"Overtime alarm," I explain. "See, a neck trip's only supposed to last about an hour, then the stuff wears off and your heart starts pumping again and you're okay." And nobody in the world knows, even after all the studies, why you're not a total vegetable from going that long with no blood to your brain, but then there are plenty of things nobody understands about Necrodone. "Only now and then somebody gets stuck, and needs a little help getting back."

Fat Slim has shut off the alarm and is loading the big syringe. Jerry Duane watches, face getting greener than ever, as he shoves the spike into the stiff's arm and thumbs the plunger down.

"Actually," I say, "that one probably wasn't in any danger. Most people can go a bit over an hour with no problems—last I heard, the record's up past an hour and a half—but we always wake them up after an hour, if they're still under. Fat Slim likes to leave a safety margin."

The line on the customer's eek box has begun to kink and bounce and the *eeeeeee* has changed to a steady *eek, eek, eek*. Fat Slim slaps the customer gently on both cheeks and pulls off his eye mask. "Welcome back," he says, "and thank you for flying with us. Come on, now, kid, sit up."

When the customer is sitting on the edge of the bed, shaking his head, Fat Slim comes back down the aisle toward us. "God," Jerry Duane says, "I hate to think of Jane Ann in a place like this."

"You better hope she *did* go to a place like this," Fat Slim growls. "And there aren't many. Most of the cheap neck houses, they just shoot the poor bastards up and give them a place to flop. Here, we charge more but we take care of our stiffs. We even provide EKG monitoring, which nobody else does."

A certain street gang ripped off the eek boxes from a hospital warehouse, looking for dope, and sold them to us for practically free because they didn't know what they were. I don't really understand what good they do, but they look cool and impress the shit out of the university kids—who have way more money than the street punks, and don't mind paying it out for some extra protection.

"The worst, though," Fat Slim goes on, "is doing neck alone. I can't believe how many idiots do that, nobody around to time them and bring them back if they get in trouble." He holds up the works he has just used. "Never know when you may need the old resurrection cocktail."

He's got that right. I'd guess more than half of the neck users around here shoot up alone—or with somebody else who's necked out too, which comes to the same thing—and now and then they get found permanently flatlined, usually when somebody notices the smell.

It's kind of depressing sometimes, dealing to these street punks and knowing what they're going to do, but hey, business is business. I don't see how I'm supposed to be responsible for what some geek does with what I sell him. They piss and moan that they don't have the money to use a good safe neck house like ours, but fuck that. Let them get off their lazy butts and make something of themselves, like I did. This is America, man.

Fat Slim shitcans the used spike, being very careful not to nick himself. Jerry Duane says, "What's that, that you gave that boy?"

"Private formula," Fat Slim tells him, "mostly Lidocaine, little meth, some other odds and ends. Maybe I ought to patent it, huh?"

That afternoon we hit all the regular neck houses, even a couple that almost nobody knows about. Jane Ann isn't at any of them and nobody recognizes her face from the photo. We walk back along the street, stopping now and then while I show the holo to people I know.

Jerry Duane is pretty quiet. He has seen a lot of very bad sights in the last couple of hours. The lowest class of neck houses are not fun scenes. It was even starting to get to me, toward the end. That last one, with all those wasted stiffs lying there on those moldy mattresses and the smell so bad you could hardly breathe, Jesus! Some people have no standards at all.

But now, as we are passing the bar where I met him, he speaks up. "Listen," he says. "I want to try it."

"Try what?" I say, and then I get it. I should have expected it. "Neck? You want to try a neck trip?"

He nods. "I want to find out what it's like. Maybe it'll help me understand what's happened to Jane Ann. And maybe it'll be easier for us to talk, when I do find her, if I've done it too."

I look at him for a minute or two. It is getting late and the lights are coming on along the street, but even in the dim light I can see that his eyes have kind of a desperate expression. This is a dude who is ready to try anything because he doesn't feel like hc has anything left to lose.

Well, I think, why not? I don't see how it's going to help him, but I don't see how it can hurt, either.

"All right," I say. "Let's go back to the house."

A little while later, filling a throwaway works, Fat Slim says, "Okay, the thing you want to do is just relax and go with it. You're going to feel a little scared when it first starts to hit you, but don't let yourself panic. If you start to freak, I'll have to bring you out."

Lying on the bed, one sleeve rolled up, Jerry Duane says, "Okay." His voice is kind of scratchy, like his throat is dry. "I'm cool with it," he says.

Fat Slim looks at me and shakes his head and grins. We are in one of the upstairs rooms, just the three of us. Jerry Duane is already hooked up to the eek box and it is eeking away, faster than it would be doing if he was quite as cool with it as he says.

Seeing me rolling up my own sleeve, Fat Slim says, "You going to neck out too? Little early for you, isn't it?"

I stretch out on the other bed, next to Jerry Duane. "Thought I'd better go along," I say. "First time, he might want some company." I look at Jerry Duane. "If that's all right with you."

"You can do that?" he asks. "Go with me? How's that possible?"

"Just another unexplained phenomenon," Fat Slim says, loading up a second disposable, "in the wonderful fucking world of Necrodone. Most of the best scientific minds agree that it's *not* possible, that it's only doper folklore based on the occasional shared hallucination, but you'll see. Not everyone can do it, but Dead Henry here is one of the best."

"How about you?" Jerry Duane asks him, and Fat Slim gives a big loud snort.

"The hell, man," he says, "I don't do this shit." Which is true. Fat Slim doesn't even smoke weed, or drink anything but beer. "Hey," he says to Jerry Duane, "do you want some doper doing this to you?"

While Fat Slim is hooking up my eek box I reach across the space between the two beds. "Take my hand," I tell Jerry Duane. "It helps if we hold hands to start with. Don't ask me why."

He gives me a funny look. "Christ," I say, "just take it, what do you think, I'm not queer or anything." Actually I am but that is none of his business. "And pull the mask down so it covers your eyes. They tend to open when you go under and you'll go damn near blind from staring at the light, if you don't use the mask."

I pull down my own with my free hand and take a couple of deep breaths. Jerry Duane's hand is sweaty and cold. I hear him say, "Shit!" and figure Fat Slim has stuck him. A couple of minutes later I feel the sting of the spike in my own arm. Like the nurse always tells you, it doesn't hurt a bit.

Fat Slim is right about trying not to panic. All the same, I'll tell you something a lot of neck-heads won't admit: *everybody* freaks, at least a little, when the Necrodone starts to hit. I don't care how many times you've been there and done it, you can't help having at least a second or two of blind shitless fear, as the messages start coming in from all over your body: *hey, asshole, you're dying!*

Then the dark comes down, and it's darker than any other dark you ever saw, it's like you can't even remember what light looks like, and there's no feeling in your hands and feet and then in your arms and legs and then no feeling anywhere, and the last thing you hear is the *eeeeee* of the eek box registering flatline and it's the loudest thing in the world but then it's gone too, everything's gone, *you're* gone, you're just . . . *not*, any more, you never were.

And then—it's probably less than a second later in real time, nobody knows because nobody's ever figured out a way to measure neck-trip time—you fall up.

That's the only way I can describe it: you fall straight up, right out of your body, till you're hanging there like in some kind of magic act, above the bed. You can see again, now, you can even look down and check out your own stiff if you want to, though I hardly ever do that any more. I mean, I don't need neck to look at myself, that's why they make mirrors, right? But a lot of people, specially first-timers, get real hung up on that part. I can feel Jerry Duane beside me and I know that's what he's doing right now.

Understand, that's the only way I can pick him up. I can't see him or hear him—even if he could talk, which he can't, because there are no words beyond flatline, you don't even know what words are or what they're for—and I don't know his name any more because that's a word too, I don't know mine either. But I can feel he's there, and I know he can feel me too.

And now comes the light.

I guess everybody has heard about the light, it's something they all talk about, and out of all the stupid shit that has been written and told about the neck experience, this is the one thing you can absolutely believe. Nobody has ever really told it the way it is—and don't even get me started on how they tried to show it in that fucking movie—but I don't think anybody can, because there's no words that cover it. Like I say, it happens in a place where words don't mean anything.

There's this incredible white light, you never knew anything could be so clean and white, coming down from somewhere above and filling the room till you can't see anything but the light. And you start falling up again, faster and faster, falling up into the light, it's getting brighter all the time, if you looked at a light like that while you were in your body I think it would blind you for life but this doesn't hurt at all, it feels good. It's like the light is cleaning away all the bullshit and the hangups and you're, like, *free*, you know what I'm saying?

Falling up into the light, I can still feel this somebody beside me, only now we're both becoming part of the light, sort of dissolving in it, like meth crystals in a speed-freak's spoon.

You know how during a really great come, there's a moment when everything goes away and it's like you're everywhere and nowhere at the same time? That's the closest thing I can think of, but this is a million times more intense and it goes on and on.

Some people say they see these patterns in the light, and now and then somebody even claims he saw a face, but I've never seen anything like that. I guess it has something to do with how your head happens to be wired up, or maybe what you're expecting. Like I keep saying, there's a lot about neck that nobody understands.

But some people also hear music, and now for the first time ever, even though I must have done a couple hundred neck trips or more, I start to hear it too. It's not like any music I ever heard before, maybe a little like somebody on a really fantastic keyboard setup but with more texture, maybe somewhere between a sitar and a pipe organ, here I am again with no words for what I'm trying to tell about.

And the tune, I swear, is Jerry Duane Austin's great single from '99, the one that goes:

> *"Death come walking*
> *No use talking*
> *Death come riding*
> *No use hiding*
> *There ain't nowhere*

Nowhere he can't find
And that Hanging Man
Hanging Man stays on my mind."

Only of course there are no lyrics, just the tune over and over, with chords and harmony lines that I don't think you could write down on any kind of staff or play on any instrument ever made. There was a time years ago, when I still wanted to be a musician, that I thought Jerry Duane Austin was God. Maybe this is how his music would sound if he was.

And the music is part of the light and I'm, we're, part of it, oh, fuck this. Words words words, listen, it's all bullshit. If you've been there and done it you already know what it's like and if you haven't then all the words in all the languages in the world can't tell you about it.

All this time the clock is running, down in the live world—I don't know why but I always think of it as "down"—and Fat Slim is laying out the spikes and the resurrection cocktail just in case, and the one-hour mark is coming up on the timer, but there's not even the idea of time there in the light.

But of course, since this is after all just a neck trip and not something like a heart attack or a bullet through the head, finally there comes a point where the light starts to fade and I'm falling back down out of the light and into the big black hole, and I hate it and try to fight it but the pull is too strong and next thing I know a couple of big hands are shaking me by the shoulders and Fat Slim's voice is saying, "All right, partner, you're back. How are things in scenic Croak City?"

I pull up the mask and see that Jerry Duane is already sitting on the edge of his bed, watching me. So he beat me down. That's not unusual with first-timers. Most of them don't even last half an hour.

"Far out," he says, which I haven't heard anybody say since my grandpa died.

I sit up and begin kicking my feet and slapping my hands together, getting the blood flowing again. That's one of the downsides of doing neck, your feet and hands sort of go to sleep and it hurts like a son of a bitch when the circulation starts to come back. "You okay?" I ask Jerry Duane.

"I'm fine," he says. "Man, what a trip. Thought I'd been around some, but I never been anywhere like that."

I get to my feet and stomp around a little, feeling the blood tingling in my toes. Jerry Duane says, "Uh, look—what you did, going with me? I mean, thanks, I could feel you there and all, it made everything a lot less scary. Only—" He hunches his shoulders, like he's about to try to pick up something heavy. "Man, does anybody ever, you know, *meet* somebody . . . over there?"

I know what he's asking. There's been a lot of argument about it, among the neck-heads and the researchers too. "Tough question," I tell him. "I wish I knew the answer. It's never happened to me, or to anybody I knew well enough to be sure they weren't hosing me, but you do hear stories. People who claim they had some kind of encounter with somebody else who happened to be necked out somewhere else at the same time, or even somebody they knew who was no-shit dead."

Since I know damn well where he's trying to go with this, I go on: "One thing for sure, it's extremely rare—if it happens at all—and it's not anything anybody knows how to control. There's no way, that anybody's come up with so far, to actually go looking for somebody over the line."

"Whatever claims some weasels make," Fat Slim puts in, "to separate the stupid from their money. Spirits of the dead contacted while you wait, and all that. Neck's done wonders to revive certain very old scams."

Jerry Duane stands up and starts to move toward the door. "What do I owe you guys?" he asks.

"On the house," I say before Fat Slim can speak. "We're, like, honored."

He reaches in his pocket and at first I think he is going to insist on paying, but then I see he is getting out that picture of Jane Ann. "You better keep this," he says, "in case you need it to help you find her. I've got plenty more." He takes out a pen and writes something on the back. "Call this number if you learn anything. Anything at all."

When he is gone I say, "Christ, he's really jammed up over this girl," and Fat Slim does another of his snorts.

"Yeah," he says. "Poor bastard."

"I can't imagine," I say, "needing anybody like that."

"I know," Fat Slim says. "Which poor bastard did you think I meant?"

It takes me till the middle of next week to find Jane Ann. And I know what I said, but a lot of things get more possible when you know who to ask and can pay for the answers. Especially if, like me, you can pay with something people want even more than money.

The room is on the top floor of a scabby old apartment building down near the park. Nobody answers when I knock. After I decide nobody is going to, I get out a couple of special little tools and have a talk with the piece-of-shit lock, and less than a minute later the door opens.

The first breath I take, I start to wish I'd left it closed.

But I step back into the hallway, which luckily is still deserted, and fill my lungs—one interesting side effect of being a neck user, you get so you can hold your breath for a long time—and go in. It takes only one quick glance around the little room to find her.

I'd just as soon not tell you what she looks like. Later, I hear they figure she's been lying there at least two weeks, maybe more. They say it's hard to be sure because neck does funny things to the decomp process. All I know, she looks like hell and smells worse.

She doesn't look much like the picture any more, that's for sure. But I can still tell who she is. Or was.

Naturally I get my ass out of there as fast as I can move it, with the rest of me following along very close. I make a couple of calls, one to the cops and one to Jerry Duane's answering machine, from a pay phone at the Port Authority. Then I get on the train—flying leaves too many tracks—and take a long vacation up in Toronto, where I have friends and business acquaintances who do not go in for asking questions or giving out answers.

I mean, you can't be too careful. Even if nobody saw me going into her place or coming out—and you can't ever assume that—I have been asking about this babe and even showing her picture all over this end of town. And I have a record of dope busts, even if they never got a conviction, and this is a dope death.

Which, nowadays, is all they need to pull me in on suspicion, like maybe I was the one who sold her the shit she went out on. As long as some cop's prepared to swear that there's a reasonable probability of a drug angle, they can keep me just about as long as they like, never mind charges or hearings, all legal as hell according to the U.S. Supreme fucking Court—dope being a clear and present danger, and all that.

And even if they never do charge me with anything, they can take everything I've got, right down to my spare pair of jock shorts, and keep it unless I can prove I didn't buy it with dope profits. I've got most of my money stashed in a lot of blind-bogus bank accounts and I don't think they could find them all, but with all the electronic shit they've got now, they can fix it so I don't dare go near a nickel of it. Not to mention if I can't show a legit means of support they can stick me in a labor camp—pardon me all to hell, Work Education Center—for six to a year of compulsory rehab, and they'll do it, too.

So it is no time to be taking chances, and I stay up north for the rest of the summer, which is too hot to spend in the city anyway. But I may be worrying about nothing, because from the stories in the U.S. newspapers at the stand down near where I'm staying, Jane Ann's case is not exactly getting the high-profile treatment. Just another tragic teenage drug death, is how they're playing it, which is fine with me.

I am still in Toronto when I hear about Jerry Duane.

NINETIES POP STAR DEAD IN DRUG OVERDOSE.

That's what one of the headlines says, and it is pretty typical. About the only thing they get right is the dead part.

A lot later, after I finally come home, Fat Slim gives me the story.

"I got the details," he tells me, "from the good Detective Sergeant Carmody, when he came around for the monthly donation to the Carmody Children's Education Fund. Which, by the way, has now undergone a definite increase, indexed the Sergeant says to overall inflation rates, so now you're back you might want to put in a little overtime to help make up the deficit. Like there's this whorehouse up in the District, they want to set up a supply line, have the stuff on hand for certain well-off customers who want to try the necrophilia thing without actually. . . ."

"Yeah," I say. "Takes all kinds."

"Well," he says, "you might go up there and have a talk with the management. Like I say, we're developing a cash flow problem."

He sits down on the nearest bed. As it happens we are in the upstairs room where Jerry Duane and I took our neck trip. The masks are still lying on the pillows. I think about taking Jerry Duane's, sort of like to remember him by, but that would be a little too weird even for me.

"There's no doubt about it," Fat Slim says. "It was deliberate. He had enough Necrodone in him to kill a water buffalo. And he had all these pictures of Jane Ann, even clippings from the stories when she died, lined up on the bed beside him. He'd fixed himself up, too, shaved and cleaned up and put on one of his stage suits. Dude was going out in style."

"He leave a note?"

"According to Carmody, there was a sheet of hotel stationery with the words HOLD ON, BABY, I'M COMING. Which," Fat Slim says with one of his snorts, "mysteriously disappeared later, and there is no reference to it in any of the reports or the news stories."

"Why the broom job?"

"Carmody didn't know, just that word came down that this was to be treated as an accidental overdose and no mention of the S-word. Rumor has it that his agent and the recording-company executives figured this was the best way to play it, in terms of the big re-release package that's already in the works. Puts him in the tradition of Janis and Jimi and Elvis and the others, you know? Only writers get to commit suicide. Anyway," Fat Slim says, "I don't suppose much pull had to be exerted to get the right ruling. After all, it's not as if anybody gave a shit."

"So he thought he could go after her," I say, thinking out loud. "Like if he went out the same way, maybe he'd hook up with her in the next world."

"Or the neck world," Fat Slim says, and we both laugh. I mean, I feel bad the dude did it, but Jesus *Christ,* what a dumb idea. Fucking Texans, I swear.

About a month later I hear once again that somebody is asking around on the street, looking for me. I wonder if maybe I came back from Canada too soon, but when I go to check it out I meet this very straight-looking young dude in a really neat suit, who hands me a card that says he is from some law firm. "Mr., ah, Henry," he says. "I have something for you."

He takes me to where his car is parked and opens the trunk and there inside, no shit and swear to God, is a cream-finish Les Paul Gibson guitar with a leather strap that says JERRY DUANE AUSTIN.

"Just before his, ah, demise," the suit says, "Mr. Austin added a codicil to his will, leaving this instrument to you. I must say it's taken some doing to find you."

He hands me an envelope. "This was to be given to you as well," he says. "It has not been opened."

Inside the envelope is a sheet of paper with some writing in pen and ink. It is not easy to read but I finally make it out:

Dead Henry my man—

If you are reading this it means I am now music history. Don't let it bum you out, little bro. This is the first time this century that I know what I'm doing. I promised you this axe if you found Jane Ann, and you found her. Not the way I had in mind, but a deal is a deal. Anyway, it's not like

I've got any use for it any more. Enjoyed our little trip together. See you, maybe—

The signature is just a big tangly scrawl but I know what it says. Probably some autograph freak would pay good money for it but fuck that. I wad it up and throw it on the sidewalk and pick up the Gibson and start walking, while the suit stands there looking at me like he's wondering where I stash my horns and tail.

And, no matter what bullshit you may have heard or read, that's the true story of what happened to Jerry Duane Austin. But you didn't hear it from me.

I think about him sometimes, specially evenings when I sit around playing that old Gibson and trying to get the changes right on "Hanging Man Blues" or whatever. As a musician he's still my number one hero, but man, he was one weird mother.

Do I think he found Jane Ann and they're together now, somewhere inside the big light? Oh, hell, no.

Look, man. Whatever games your head plays when it thinks it's time to go, there's nothing out there. Dead is dead, and everybody does it alone.

Know what I'm saying?

This was another one that started as a title. I had a surprising lot of trouble finding anyone to publish it. Usually they said it was too "dark", which told me I must have something pretty good.

Written August 1995
First published June 2002

The Scuttling
Or, Down By The Sea With Marvin And Pamela

The Bradshaws got back from their vacation late Friday evening and discovered right away that they were not alone.

Marvin Bradshaw was coming up the front walk, having gone across the road to pick up their accumulated mail from the neighbors, when he heard his wife scream. He ran up the stairs and into the house, cursing and wishing he had tried a little harder to get that pistol permit; but there were no intruders to be seen, only his wife standing white-faced and trembling in the kitchen, pointing in the direction of the sink. "Look," she said.

He looked, wondering what he was supposed to, see. Everything was as he remembered, but then he had never given much attention to the kitchen area, which after all wasn't his department. He said, "What?" and then he saw something small and dark moving rapidly along the sink's rim. Now he saw another one, slightly larger, going up the wall behind the faucets.

"Son of a bitch," Marvin Bradshaw said. "Cockroaches."

"I came in here to get a drink of water." Pamela Bradshaw's voice was almost a whisper, as if that one scream had used up all her volume reserves. "I turned on the light and

Marvin, they were *everywhere*. They went running in all directions." She shuddered. "I think one ran over my foot."

Marvin Bradshaw stepped toward the sink, but the cockroaches were too fast for him. The one on the sink dived off into space, hit the floor, and slipped into a barely visible crack beneath the baseboard. The one on the wall evaded Marvin's slapping hand and disappeared into the cupboard space above the sink. Marvin swore in frustration, but he felt a little relieved too; he hadn't really been eager to crush a cockroach with his bare hand.

"Cockroaches," he said. "Wonderful. Bust your ass for years, finally get out of the city, away from the dirt and the coloreds, into a two-hundred-grand house on one of the best pieces of ocean-front property on Long Island. And then you go away for a couple weeks, and when you get home you got cockroaches. Jesus."

He glared at his wife. "You know who's responsible, don't you? You had to go hire that God-damned Mexican maid."

"Inez is Guatemalan," Pamela protested. "And we don't know—"

"Mexican, Guatemalan, who gives a fuck?" Marvin had never seen the point of these picky-ass distinctions between people who said *sí* when they meant yes. Maybe you needed to know the difference between Japs and Chinamen and other slopes, since nowadays you had to do business with the yellow assholes; but spics were spics, whatever hell-hole country they came from.

"The fact remains," he said, "we never had cockroaches here, and then two months ago you hired her, and now we do. I'm telling you, you let those people in, you got roaches. Didn't I run that block of buildings in Spanish Harlem for your father, back before we got married? Cockroaches and Puerto Ricans, I saw enough of both. Don't tell *me*."

"I'll speak to her when she comes in tomorrow."

"No you won't." He took a sheet of folded paper from the stack of mail in his left hand. "That was what I was coming to tell you. Look what your precious Inez left us."

She took the paper and unfolded it. The message was printed in pencil, in large clumsy block capitals:

NO MAS. YOU NO PAY ME 5 WIKS NOW. GO LIV SISTER IN ARIZONA. PLES SEN MY MONY MARGARITA FLORES 72281 DEL MONTE TUCSON AZ 85707.

INEZ

Marvin took the note back and wadded it up and hurled it at the kitchen wastebasket, missing. "Comes in here, turns our home into a roach motel, runs out on us when our backs are turned, then she expects to get paid. Lots of luck, you fat wetback bitch."

Pamela sighed. "I'll miss her, all the same. You know, I was working with her, trying to help her remember her past lives. I believe she was a Mayan princess—"

Marvin groaned. "Christ sake," he said, "not now, all right?"

He hadn't had much fun over the last two weeks. He hadn't liked Miami, which had been swarming with small brown people, and where there had been nothing to do but swim— which in his book was something you did only to keep from drowning—or lie around getting a tan, if you were asshole enough to want to look colored. The flight home had been delayed again and again. All in all, this was no time to have to listen to Pamela and her New Age crap.

"Okay," he told her, "we'll go out, get something to eat. Monday I'll call an exterminator. Antonio's okay? I could go for seafood."

Driving away from the house, he considered that at least there was one good side to the situation: eating out would give him a chance to have some real food, rather than that organic slop that Pamela tended to put on the table. He suspected this was merely a cover for her basic incompetence in the kitchen; chopping up a lot of raw vegetables was as close to real cooking as she could manage.

"Marvin," Pamela said suddenly, "you said an exterminator. You mean someone who'll kill the cockroaches?"

He glanced at her, wondering what the hell now. "What, you're worried about chemicals, poisons, like that?"

"Well, that too." Pamela paused, frowning. Marvin realized he'd just handed her something else to be a pain in the ass about. "But what I was going to say," she went on, "isn't there some other way? Besides killing them?"

"Christ." Marvin ground his teeth. "You want to get rid of the roaches but you don't want the poor little things hurt? What's that, more Oriental mumbo-jumbo? The roaches might be somebody's reincarnated souls?"

"I wish you wouldn't be so negative about reincarnation," she said stiffly. "I suppose it's not part of the religion you were brought up in."

Actually Marvin Bradshaw's parents had never shown any interest in any religion at all, and he had followed their lead; churches were places you went for funerals and weddings, and then only if you couldn't get out of it. All he had against reincarnation was that it was believed in by people from India— such as the one who collected fat payments for sitting around in a sheet spouting this shit to Pamela and a bunch of other goofy middle-aged women—and Hindus, after all, were just another variety of little brown bastards who ought to go back where they came from. (Which, in the case of the said Baba Lal Mahavishnu, Marvin suspected would be somewhere in New Jersey; but that was another matter.)

"In any case," Pamela added, "it's not true that human beings can be reborn as insects. That's a Western misconception."

"Then—"

"Still and all, Marvin." Pamela bashed right on over him, an avalanche-grade unstoppable force. "Babaji says it's always best to avoid harming any living creature. The karma accumulates. All those roaches, there must be hundreds, even thousands—disgusting to our eyes, of course, but so many lives. I can't imagine the karmic consequences of killing them all."

"Then what do you want me to do about the fucking things? Ask them nicely to leave? Get them their own place? How about you go talk to them," he said, enraged beyond control. "That would make any self-respecting insect hit the road."

She didn't answer. From the tone of her silence Marvin figured one of them would be sleeping in the guest bedroom tonight. Well, that was another bonus.

Pamela kept up the silent treatment almost all the way through dinner. Marvin knew it was too good to last. Sure enough, as he was finishing up his lobster, she started in again. "My God," he said, "couldn't you wait till we're out of here? Talking about roaches, what are you, trying to make me sick?"

He leaned back and looked at the remains of his meal. He didn't really like lobster all that well; held just ordered this one to jerk Pamela's chain. Antonio's was one of those places with live lobsters in a big glass tank, so you could pick yours out and have them boil his ass alive. Marvin had enjoyed saying "boil his ass alive" and watching Pamela cringe. She hadn't been too horrified, he noticed, to clean her own plate. Probably thought all those clams and scallops had died naturally. Ocean roadkill, maybe, run over by a submarine.

He got up, tossing his napkin on the table, and headed for the men's room. As he was coming back the proprietor stepped not quite into his path. "Mr. Bradshaw," Antonio said. "I hope your dinner was satisfactory."

Marvin nodded and tried to smile. Antonio was small and dark and his black hair was a little too glossy; but he came from a Portuguese family that had been in the area for a couple of centuries at least, and he ran a hell of a good restaurant. Marvin thought that Antonio was okay for, well, an Antonio.

"No offense," Antonio said, glancing around and lowering his voice, "but I couldn't help overhearing your conversation just now."

"You and everybody else in the place," Marvin said. "Sorry if she upset your customers, talking about cockroaches. She's been kind of weird, last year or so. Think she's getting change of life."

"Oh, that's all right." Antonio made a quick no-problem gesture. "No, what I was going to say, you're not the only one with roaches. I've heard a lot of people complaining, the last couple of weeks. It's like they just moved into the area." He made a face. "In my business it's something you worry about."

Marvin thought it over. So it wasn't just his house. Must be the new people moving in, bringing the pests with them. The standards had really gone to hell around here since that housing-discrimination lawsuit.

"Point is," Antonio went on, "it won't be easy getting an exterminator any time soon. You'll do well to get one by the end of next week."

"Shit!" Marvin said, louder than he meant to. "Hey, Antonio, I can't live with those things in the house for a week. You must know some people, guy in your   line.   You   know anybody might be willing to make a special call? I'll make it worth their while."

Antonio shook his head. "Believe me, all the ones I know are already making 'special calls' and charging through the nose, too." He rubbed his chin. "Now there's one possibility, maybe . . ."

"Talk to me. Come on, Antonio. Help me out here."

"Well—one of my bus boys," Antonio said, "the one doing that table by the door, see? He's got this grandfather, supposed to be good at getting rid of roaches and rats and the like."

Marvin saw a short, chunky, very dark kid in a white apron. Coarse, badly-cut black hair. Huge cheekbones, heavy eyebrows, big nose. "What's he," Marvin said, "Mexican?" Thinking, *no way.*

Antonio laughed. "Actually, he's an Indian."

"From India?" No way in *hell*. "Doesn't look it."

"No, no. American Indian. Some small tribe I can't even pronounce, got a reservation upstate."

"Huh." Marvin stared, amazed. As far as he knew he had never seen an Indian in these parts before. That was one thing you had to say for Indians, compared to other kinds of colored people: they kept to themselves, lived out in the sticks on reservations, didn't come pushing themselves in where they weren't wanted.

"I don't really know much about it," Antonio admitted. "Some people I know in Amityville, the old man did a job for them and they were very pleased. But they didn't tell me a lot of details."

"Huh," Marvin said again. "A redskin exterminator. Now I've heard everything."

"He's not an exterminator, strictly speaking." Antonio gave Marvin an odd grin. "This is the part your wife's going to like. He doesn't kill anything. He just makes the pests go away."

Marvin turned his stare onto Antonio. "This is a gag, right? You're going to tell me he blows a horn or something and they follow him away, like the Pied fucking Piper? Hey, Antonio, do I look like I'm in the mood for comedy?"

"No, this is for real." Antonio's face was serious. "I'm not sure how he does it—what I heard, he sort of smokes them out. Indian secret, I guess."

"I'll be damned." For a moment Marvin considered the idea. Indians did know a lot of tricks, everybody knew that. "Nah. Thanks, but I'll wait till Monday and hit the yellow pages. Hell, I can stand anything for a few more days."

But later that night, about to go to bed—in the guest bedroom, sure enough—he felt a sudden thirst, and went down to the kitchen to get himself a beer; and when he turned on the light, there they were.

Pamela hadn't been exaggerating. The cockroaches were everywhere. They swarmed over the sink and the counter and the dishwasher, the refrigerator and the walls and the floor: little flat brown oblongs that began running, all at once, when the light came on, so that the whole room appeared to squirm sickeningly for a moment. In almost no time most of the roaches had vanished, but a few remained, high on the walls or in other inaccessible places. Through the glass doors of the china cupboard Marvin could see a couple of them perched on top of a stack of antique bone-china dishes.

Then he glanced up and saw that there was a large roach on the ceiling directly above his head. Its long feelers waved gently as if in greeting. It seemed to be looking at him, considering a drop.

"Jesus Christ!" Marvin shouted, and ran from the kitchen without stopping to turn off the light.

His hands were shaking as he picked up the phone. The restaurant was closed for the night, and when he dialed Antonio's home phone he had to listen to a lot of rings before Antonio picked it up.

"Listen," Marvin said over Antonio's sleepy protest, "you know that old Indian you were telling me about? How fast do you think you could get hold of him?"

Next morning when Marvin went nervously into the kitchen for his coffee, there were no roaches to be seen. He knew they were still there, hiding during the daylight hours; still, it wasn't so bad as long as he couldn't see them.

He poured himself a cup of black coffee and went out through the sliding glass doors to the sun deck. The sun was well up above the eastern horizon and the light hurt his eyes; he wished he'd brought a pair of shades. He sat down at the little table at the north end of the sun deck, keeping his back to the sun.

The Bradshaws' house was built at the edge of a rocky bluff, sixty or seventy feet above the ocean. If Marvin cared to look straight down, through the cracks between the planks of the sun deck, he could see the white sand of what Pamela liked to call "our beach." It wasn't much of a beach, just a narrow strip of sand that sloped steeply to the water. At high tide it was almost entirely submerged.

He tested his coffee cautiously. As he had expected, it was horrible. Have to start interviewing replacement help; Pamela's efforts in the kitchen were going to be almost as hard to live with as the cockroaches.

Cockroaches. He made a disgusted face, not just at the bitter coffee. He had really lost it last night. Now, sitting in the bright morning sunlight with the cool clean wind coming off the sea, he couldn't believe held gone into such a panic over a few bugs. Calling Antonio up in the middle of the night, for God's sake, begging him to bring in some crazy old Indian. Going to be embarrassing as hell, eating at Antonio's, after this.

Marvin raised the cup again and took a mouthful of coffee. God, it tasted bad. Even more gruesome than Pamela's usual coffee-making efforts, which was saying something. There even seemed to be something solid—

He jerked suddenly back from the table, dropping the cup, spilling coffee over himself and not noticing. He raised his hand to his mouth and spat onto his palm the soggy cadaver of a drowned cockroach.

Marvin leaped to his feet and dashed for the railing and energetically emptied his stomach in the direction of the Atlantic Ocean. When the retching and heaving at last subsided he hung there for several minutes, clutching the rail to keep from collapsing to the deck, breathing noisily through his mouth.

It was then that Pamela appeared in the kitchen doorway. "Marvin," she said, "a couple of men are out front in a pickup truck. They say you sent for them."

The kid from Antonio's was standing on the front porch, hands jammed into his ass pockets. With him was a little old man—no more than five feet tall, not much over a hundred pounds—with a face like a sun-dried apple. They both wore faded jeans and cheap-looking checkered work shirts. The old man had on a mesh-backed cap with a Dolphins emblem on the front and some kind of feather dangling from the crown. Behind them in the driveway sat an old pickup truck, its paint so faded and scabbed with rust that it was impossible to tell what color it had originally been.

The kid said, "Mr. Bradshaw? Mr. Coelho said you had a roach problem."

The old man said something in a language that sounded like nothing Marvin had ever heard. The kid said, "My grandfather needs to have a look around before he can tell you anything."

Marvin nodded weakly. He still felt dizzy and sick. "Sure," he said, and led the way back to the kitchen.

Pamela came and stood in the kitchen doorway beside Marvin. They watched as the old Indian walked slowly about the kitchen, bending down and studying the baseboards, running his fingers under the edge of the counter and sniffing them, peering behind the refrigerator. Suddenly he squatted down and opened the access doors and reached up into the dark space beneath the sink. A moment later he was standing up again, holding something small and wiggly between his thumb and forefinger. His wrinkled dark face didn't really change expression—it hadn't been wearing any recognizable expression to begin with—but there was something like satisfaction in his eyes.

He spoke again in that strange-sounding language. The kid said, "He needed to know what kind of roaches you had. He says no problem. This kind is easy."

The old man went out on the sun deck and flipped the cockroach over the rail. He came back and said something brief. "He says one hundred dollars," the kid translated.

For once Marvin was in no mood to argue. He could still taste that coffee-logged cockroach. "When can he start?"

"Right now," the kid said. "If that's okay."

The kid went back up the hall—Marvin thought he should have had Pamela go along to make sure he didn't steal anything, but it was too late now—while the old man continued to study the kitchen. A few minutes later the kid was back with a pair of nylon carry-on bags, which he set on the counter beside the sink. The old man nodded, grunted, unzipped one of the bags, and began rummaging inside.

While he was rummaging the kid said, "Any animals in the house? Dogs, cats?"

Pamela shook her head. Marvin said, "Hell, no." That was something he couldn't understand, people keeping dirty hairy animals in the house. Maybe a good guard dog, but even he belonged outside, behind a fence.

"It would be better," the kid said, "if you could go somewhere, like out of the house, till this is over."

"Yeah?" Marvin grinned. "You'd like that, wouldn't you?"

Pamela kicked his ankle. To the Indian kid she said, "Is this going to involve any toxic chemicals?"

"No, no, nothing like that." The kid gestured at the pile of stuff the old man was taking out of the bag. "See, we don't even use respirators. No, it's just, well, better if you're not here."

"Uh huh," Marvin said. "Forget it, Geronimo. Nice try."

The kid shrugged. "Okay." He turned and began unzipping the other bag.

By now the old man had laid out several bundles of what looked like dried weeds. Now he selected four of these and twisted them together to form a single long bundle. From the bag he took a roll of ordinary white twine and began wrapping the bundle tightly from end to end, compressing it into a solid cylinder about the size and shape of a rolled-up newspaper. He put the rest of the stuff back into the bag and spoke to the kid.

The kid had taken out a small drum, like a big tambourine without the metal jingles, and a long thin stick with one end wrapped in what looked like rawhide. He gave the drum a tap and got a single sharp *poong* that filled the kitchen and floated off down the hallway.

The old man produced a throwaway butane lighter, which he lit and applied to one end of the herb bundle. Marvin expected a quick flare-up, but the stuff showed some reluctance to ignite. The old man turned the bundle in his fingers, blowing gently, until at last the end of the bundle was a solid glowing red coal.

By now smoke was pouring from the bundle in thick white clouds, billowing up to the ceiling and then rolling down to fog the whole room. Marvin started to protest, but then he decided that the smell wasn't bad at all. He recognized cedar in there—for an instant he recalled the time he had been allowed to burn the family tree after Christmas because his father was too drunk—and something that might be sage, and other things he couldn't guess at.

Hell, he thought, you could probably market this shit for some serious bucks. The old ladies in particular would go big for a new house scent.

Now the old Indian was turning this way and that, waving the smoldering bundle, getting the smoke into all the corners of the room. The kid started beating his drum, *poong*

poong poong poong, and the old man commenced to sing. At least that was what he seemed to think he was doing, though for sure he was no Tony Bennett. It was a weird monotonous tune, maybe half a dozen notes repeated over and over, and the words didn't sound like words at all, just nonsense syllables such as a man might sing if he'd forgotten the lyrics.

Whatever it was, Marvin Bradshaw didn't like it a damn bit. He started to speak, to tell the old man to get on with the fumigating and never mind the musical production number. But the two Indians were already walking past him and up the hallway, trailing clouds of smoke and never missing a beat or a hey-ya. Marvin said, "Oh, fuck this," and turned to follow, to put a stop to this crap before it went any farther.

Pamela, however, moved to block the doorway. "Marvin," she said, very quietly but in a voice like a handful of razor blades.

He recognized the tone, and the look in her eyes. There were times when you could jerk Pamela around, and then there were times when simple survival required you to back off. There was no doubt which kind of time this was.

"All right," Marvin said crankily, "let me go after them anyway, keep an eye on them. God knows what the redskin sons of bitches are liable to walk off with . . . is that liquor cabinet locked?"

The drumming and singing and smoking went on for the rest of the morning. The old man insisted on doing every room in the house, upstairs and down, as well as the basement, attic, and garage.

At one point Marvin paused on the stairs, hearing his wife on the hall phone: "No, really, Theresa, I swear, a real Native American shaman, and he's doing a smoke ceremony right here in our house. It's so exciting . . . "

There was a lengthy pause. Lengthy for Pamela, anyway. "Oh," she said at last, "I used to feel guilty about them, too. I mean, all the terrible things that were done to them. But you know, Babaji explained that really, the Native Americans who have it so hard nowadays—poverty and alcoholism and so on—

they're the reincarnated spirits of white soldiers who killed Native people in earlier times, and that's how they're working off their karma."

Upstairs the kid was banging the drum and the old man was chanting and smoke was rolling back down the stairs, but Marvin stayed to listen a moment longer.

"I wish you'd been there," Pamela was saying. "Jessica told about giving some change to this poor homeless Negro she saw in the city, and Babaji said that giving was always good for one's own karma but after all, in a previous life, that man was probably a slave-ship captain."

There was a happy sigh. "It's just as Babaji says, Theresa. Once you understand how karma works, you realize that everything really *is* for the best."

Marvin snorted loudly and went on up the stairs. "Space," he mumbled, "the final fucking frontier."

A little before noon, having smoked up the garage until you could barely find the cars without feeling around, the old man stopped singing and held the smoke bundle up over his head. The kid quit drumming and said, "That's all."

"That's it?" Marvin folded his arms and stared at the kid. "And for this you expect me to cough up a hundred bucks?"

The old man was bent over, grinding the glowing end of the bundle against the floor to extinguish it. Without looking up he said something in Algonquin or whatever the hell language it was.

The kid said, "You don't have to pay now. We'll come back tomorrow. If you're not satisfied with the results by then, you don't have to pay at all."

Marvin started to tell him not to waste his time. But the old man turned and looked at Marvin with dark turtle eyes and Marvin heard himself say, "Okay. Sure. See you then."

When they were gone Marvin went back into the house and got out the key to the liquor cabinet. It wasn't often that he had a drink this early in the day but his nerves were just about shot.

The smoke had thinned a good deal inside the house, but the scent was still strong; he could even smell it out on the sun deck, where he took his drink. He leaned against the railing and looked out over the ocean, enjoying the salt breeze and the swishing mutter of small waves over the sand below. Saturday morning shot to hell, but at least it was over. Maybe there'd be a good game on TV in the afternoon, or a fight. Even a movie, as long as there weren't any Indians in it.

He became aware that his fingertips were tapping steadily on the railing, thumping out a medium-fast four-four beat that was, he realized then, the same rhythm the Indian kid had been beating on his drum.

"Jesus H. Christ," he said aloud. And downed his drink in one long shuddering gulp.

Pamela stayed on the phone for the rest of the afternoon, telling her big story to one cuckoo-clock friend after another. Since this kept her off Marvin's back, he figured the whole thing had almost been worth it.

He went into the kitchen and stuck a frozen dinner into the microwave. The smoke smell was still very pronounced, though the air looked clear and normal now. He took the cardboard tray out to the sun deck and ate his lunch, letting the sound of the ocean drown out the Indian music that kept running through his head.

Later, he tried without success to find a game on television. All the sports shows were taken up with silly crap like tennis. That would just about make it perfect, spend the afternoon watching a couple of bull dykes batting a stupid ball back and forth across a net. Finally he found a Bronson movie he hadn't seen before, and after that, over on PBS, Louis Rukeyser had some really interesting things to say about the stock market; and so Marvin made it through the afternoon, and most of the time he hardly noticed the smoke smell at all. And only a few times, maybe once or twice an hour, did he catch himself tapping a foot or finger to the beat of the Indian kid's drum.

When they went out to dinner that evening, Marvin drove clear to the next town up the coast, to a not particularly good and way to hell overpriced steak house, rather than eat at Antonio's. He was feeling particularly pissed off at Antonio, whom he suspected of setting the whole thing up as a practical joke. Ought to drown the grinning little greaseball, Marvin thought, in his own fucking lobster tank.

A little after eleven that night, Marvin was sitting in the living room, trying to read Rush Limbaugh's latest book, when Pamela called him from the head of the stairs.

He had the radio on, tuned to a New Jersey station that played country and western—which he hated, but he was trying to use one irritation against another; a bunch of Gomers singing through their noses might cancel out that God-damned Indian racket that wouldn't get out of his mind. Pamela had to call several times before he got up and came to the foot of the stairs. "What?"

"You'd better go out and have a look, Marvin," she said calmly. "There are people down on our beach."

"Oh, fuck." He'd always known it would happen sooner or later, but why did it have to happen now? "Get me my shotgun," he said, "and phone the cops."

Pamela didn't move. "Don't overreact, Marvin. I don't think there are more than two of them, and they don't seem to be doing anything. They're not even close to the house. Probably just walking along the beach in the moonlight."

"Sure." Marvin threw up his hands. "Right, I'll just go see if they'd like a complimentary bottle of *champagne*. Maybe a little violin music."

He went down the hallway and through the kitchen, muttering. Probably some gang of crack-head punks from the city, looking for white people to rob and rape and murder. Pamela wouldn't be so God-damned serene when they tied her up and took turns screwing her in the ass before they killed her. He hoped they'd let him watch.

The glass door slid silently open and Marvin stepped sockfooted out onto the deck. The tide was out and the sea was calm, and in the quiet he could definitely hear voices down on the beach.

He reached back through the door and flipped a switch. Suddenly the area beneath him was flooded with light, bright as day. One of the voices made a sound of surprise and Marvin grinned to himself. It hadn't cost much to have those big lights installed underneath the deck, and he'd known they'd come in handy some night like this.

He walked quickly across the deck and peered over the railing. It was almost painful to look down; the white sand reflected the light with dazzling intensity. He had no trouble, though, in seeing the two men standing on the beach, halfway between the house and the water. Or in recognizing the two brown faces that looked up at him.

"Hi, Mr. Bradshaw," the Indian kid called. "Hope we didn't disturb you."

The old man said something in Indian talk. The kid said, "My grandfather wants to apologize for coming around so late. But it was a busy night at the restaurant and Mr. Coelho wouldn't let me off any sooner."

"What the fuck," Marvin said, finally able to speak.

"You ought to come down here," the kid added. "You'll want to see this."

The logical thing to do at this point, of course, was to go back in the house and call the police and have these two arrested for trespassing. But then it would come out, how Marvin had gotten involved with the red bastards in the first place. The local cops didn't like Marvin, for various reasons, and would probably spread the story all over the area, how he had hired an Indian medicine man to get the cockroaches out of his home.

And if he simply shot the sons of bitches, he'd go to jail. There was no justice for a white man any more.

Marvin went back through the house. Pamela was still standing on the stairs. "It's those damn Indians," he told her as he passed. "If they scalp me you can call nine-one-one. No, you'll probably bring them in for tea and cookies."

He went out the front door and around the house and down the wooden stairway to the beach. The two Indians were still there. The old man was down in a funny crouch, while the kid was bent over with his hands on his knees. They seemed to be looking at something on the ground.

"Here, Mr. Bradshaw," the kid said without looking up. "Look at this."

Marvin walked toward them, feeling the sand crunch softly beneath his feet, realizing he had forgotten to put on any shoes. Socks full of sand, great. He came up between the old man and the kid and said, "All right, what's the," and then in a totally different voice, "Jesus God Almighty!"

He had never seen so many cockroaches in all his life.

The sand at his feet was almost hidden by a dark carpet of flat scuttling bodies. The light from the floodlamps glinted off their shiny brown backs and picked out a forest of waving antennae. Marvin leaped back and bumped into Pamela, who had followed him. "Look out, Marvin," she said crossly, and then she screamed and clutched at him.

The cockroaches, Marvin saw now, were not spreading out over the beach, or running in all directions in their usual way. They covered a narrow strip, maybe three feet wide, no more; and they were all moving together, a cockroach river that started somewhere in the shadow of the house and ran straight as Fifth Avenue across the sandy beach, to vanish into the darkness in the direction of the ocean. Marvin could hear a faint steady rustling, like wind through dry leaves.

"You wanted them out of your house," the kid said. "Well, there they go."

"How. . . ." Pamela's voice trailed off weakly.

"They're going home," the kid said. "Or trying to."

Marvin barely heard the words; he was watching the cockroaches, unable to pull his eyes away from the scurrying horde. He walked toward the house, studying the roaches, until he came up against the base of the bluff. Sure enough, the roaches were pouring straight down the rock face in a brown cataract that seemed to be coming from up under the foundation of the house.

"See," the kid was saying, "the kind of roaches you got, the little brown cockroaches like you see in houses in this part of the country—they're not native. Book says they're German cockroaches, some say they came over with those Hessian mercenaries the King hired to fight Washington's guys. I don't know about that, but anyway the white people brought them over from Europe."

Marvin turned and stared at the kid for a moment. Then he looked down at the cockroaches again. "Fucking foreigners," he muttered. "I should have known."

"Now down in Florida and around the Gulf," the kid added, "you get these really big tropical roaches, they came over from Africa on slave ships. Then there's a kind that comes from Asia, very hard to kill."

Pamela said, "And your grandfather's, ah, medicine—?"

"Makes them want to go back where they came from. Well, where their ancestors came from. Makes them *have* to. Look."

Marvin was tracking the cockroach stampede in the other direction now, out across the beach. The moon was up and full, and even beyond floodlight range it was easy to see the dark strip against the shiny damp low-tide sand.

At the water's edge the cockroaches did not hesitate. Steadily, without a single break in the flow, they scurried headlong into the sea. The calm water of the shallows was dotted with dark specks and clumps that had to be the bodies of hundreds, maybe thousands of roaches. Marvin found himself remembering something he'd heard, how you could line all the Chinamen up and march them into the ocean and they'd never stop coming because they bred so fast.

The old man spoke as Marvin came walking back across the sand. The kid said, "He says he'll leave it on the rest of the night, in case you got rats or mice."

"It works on them too?" Pamela asked.

"Sure." The kid nodded. "No extra charge."

"The hell," Marvin said, "you're going to claim you people didn't have rats or mice either, before Columbus?"

"Some kinds. Woods and field mice, water rats, sure. But your common house mouse, or your gray Norway rat, or those black rats you see in the city, they all came over on ships."

"I don't see any," Pamela observed.

"Oh, you wouldn't, not yet. The bigger the animal, the longer the medicine takes to work. Matter of body weight. You take a real big gray rat, he might not feel it for the rest of the night. Along about daybreak, though, he'll come down here and start trying to swim back to Norway or wherever."

The old man spoke again. "My grandfather says we'll come back tomorrow, so he can turn the medicine off. Can't leave it on too long. Things . . . happen."

At their feet the cockroaches streamed onward toward oblivion.

Marvin slept badly that night, tormented by a persistent dream in which he ran in terror across an endless empty plain beneath a dark sky. A band of Indians pursued him, whooping and waving tomahawks and beating drums, while ranks of man-sized cockroaches stood on their hind legs on either side, shouting at him in Spanish. Pamela appeared in front of him, naked. "It is your karma, Marvin!" she cried. He saw that she had long antennae growing from her head, and an extra set of arms where her breasts had been.

He sat up in bed, sweating and shaking. The smoke smell in the room was so strong he could hardly breathe. "Gah," he said aloud, and fought the tangled covers off him and got up, to stand on wobbly legs for a moment in the darkness.

On her side of the bed Pamela mumbled, "Marvin?" But she didn't turn over, and he knew she wasn't really awake.

He went downstairs, holding tight to the banister, and got a bottle of Johnny Walker from the liquor cabinet. In the darkened hallway he took a big drink, and then another, straight from the bottle. The first one almost came back up but the second felt a lot better.

He carried the bottle back upstairs, to the guest bedroom, where he cranked the windows wide open and turned on the big ceiling fan and stretched out on the bed. He could still smell the smoke, but another belt of Scotch helped that.

He lay there drinking for a long time, until finally the whiskey eased him off into a sodden sleep. He dreamed again, but this time there were no Indians or cockroaches; in fact it was a pleasant, restful dream, in which he found himself strolling across gently rolling pasture land. Big oak trees grew along the footpath where he walked, their branches heavy with spring-green leaves. Sheep grazed on a nearby hillside.

In the distance, at the crest of a high hill, rose the gray walls and battlements of an ancient-looking castle. A winding dirt road led up to the castle gate, and he saw now that a troop of soldiers in red coats were marching along it, headed in his direction. The *poong poong poong poong* of their drum carried across the fields to Marvin, and he could hear their voices raised in song:

> *hey ya hey yo hey ya*
> *yo hey ya hey na wey*
> *ah ho ha na yo*
> *ho ho ho ho*

He awoke again with the sun shining through the windows. He lay for a long time with a pillow over his face, knowing he wasn't going to enjoy getting up.

When he finally emerged from the guest bedroom, sweaty and unshaven, it was almost midday. Passing the main bathroom, he heard the shower running. Pamela would have been up for hours; she always got up ridiculously early, so she could do her silly meditation and yoga exercises on the deck as the sun came up.

Marvin was sitting in the living room drinking coffee when the doorbell rang. He lurched to his feet, said, "Shit!", and headed for the front door. Sunlight stabbed viciously at his eyes when he opened the door and he blinked against the pain. He opened his eyes again and saw the two Indians standing on his porch.

"Sorry if we're a little early," the kid said. "I have to be at work soon."

Marvin regarded them without warmth. "The fuck you want now?"

"Well, you know, Mr. Bradshaw. My grandfather did a job for you."

Marvin nodded. That was a mistake. When the agony in his head receded he said, "And now you want to get paid. Wait here a minute."

There was no way these two clowns could make a claim stick, but he didn't feel up to a nasty scene. His wallet was upstairs in the bedroom, but he knew Pamela kept a little cash in a vase on the mantlepiece, for paying delivery boys and the like. He dug out the roll and peeled off a twenty and went back to the front door. "There you are, Chief. Buy yourself a new feather."

The old man didn't touch the twenty. "One hundred dollars," he said. In English.

Marvin laughed sourly. "Dream on, Sitting Bull. I'm being a nice guy giving you anything, after you stank up my house. Take the twenty or forget it."

The old man jabbered at the kid. He didn't take his eyes off Marvin. The kid said, "You don't pay, he won't turn the medicine off."

"That's supposed to worry me? If I believed in this crap at all, I wouldn't want it 'turned off.' Leave it on, keep the roaches away forever."

"That's not how it works," the kid said. "It won't affect anything that wasn't in the house when the medicine was made."

Marvin thought of something. "Look, I tell you what I'll do. You give me some of that stuff you were burning yesterday, okay? And I'll write you out a check for a hundred bucks, right now."

After all, when you cut past the superstitious bullshit, there had to be something in that smoke that got rid of roaches better than anything on the market. Screwed up their brains, maybe, who knew? Take a sample to a lab, have it analyzed, there could be a multi-million-dollar product in there. It was worth gambling a hundred. Hell, he might not even stop payment on the check. Maybe.

But the old man shook his head and the kid said, "Sorry, Mr. Bradshaw. That's all secret. Anyway, it wouldn't work without the song."

Marvin's vision went even redder than it already was. "All right," he shouted, "get off my porch, get that rusty piece of shit out of my driveway, haul your red asses out of here." The kid opened his mouth. "You want trouble, Tonto? You got a license to run a pest-control business in this county? Go on, *move!"*

When the rattling blat of the old pickup's exhaust had died away, Marvin returned to the living room. Pamela was standing on the stairs in a white terry robe. Her hair was wet. She looked horribly cheerful.

"I thought I heard voices," she said. "Was it those Native Americans? I hope you paid them generously."

Marvin sank onto the couch. "I gave them what they had coming."

"I'm just disappointed I didn't get to see them again. Such an honor, having a real shaman in my house. Such an inspiring ceremony, too. Remember that lovely song he sang? I can still hear it in my mind, over and over, like a mantra. Isn't that wonderful?"

Singing happily to herself, *hey ya hey yo hey ya*, she trotted back up the stairs. And *poong poong poong poong* went the drum in Marvin's head.

He spent the rest of the day lying on the living room couch, mostly with his eyes closed, wishing he could sleep. He made no move toward the liquor supply. He would have loved a drink, but his stomach wouldn't have stood for it.

The hangover didn't get any better; at times it seemed the top of his skull must surely crack open like an overcooked egg. His whole body ached as if he'd fallen down a flight of stairs. Even the skin of his face felt too tight.

Worst of all, he was still hearing Indian music, louder and clearer and more insistent than ever. Up to now it had been no more than a nuisance, one of those maddening tricks the brain occasionally plays, like having the *Gilligan's Island* theme stuck in your mind all day. Now, it had become a relentless clamor that filled the inside of his head with the savage boom of the drum and the endless ululation of the old man's voice; and from time to time Marvin put his hands over his ears, though he knew it would do no good. He might even have screamed, but that would have hurt too much.

Pamela had vanished around noon; off to visit her crazy friends, Marvin thought dully, never mind her poor damn husband. But around four he tottered into the kitchen—not that he had any appetite, but maybe some food would settle his stomach—and happened to glance out through the glass doors, and there she was, down on the beach. She wore a long white dress and she appeared to be dancing, back and forth along the sand, just above the line of the incoming tide. Her hands were raised above her head, clapping. He couldn't hear the sound, but his eyes registered the rhythm: *clap clap clap clap*, in perfect synch with the drumming in his head and the boom of blood in his throbbing temples.

The sun went down at last. Marvin left the lights off, finding the darkness soothing. He wondered if Pamela was still down on the beach. "Pamela!" he called, and again; but there was no answer, and he decided he didn't give enough of a damn to go look for her.

But time went by and still no sign of her, and finally Marvin got to his feet and shuffled to the door. It wasn't safe, a white woman out alone on a beach at night. Besides, he needed some fresh air. The stink of smoke was so bad it seemed to stick to his skin; he itched all over.

He went slowly down the wooden steps to the little beach. The moon was up and full and the white sand fairly gleamed. He could see the whole beach, clear out to the silver line that marked the retreating edge of the sea.

He couldn't see Pamela anywhere.

He walked out across the sand, with no real idea what he expected to find. His feet seemed to move on their own, without consulting him, and he let them. His body no longer hurt; even his headache was gone. The drumming in his head was very loud now, a deafening POONG POONG POONG POONG, yet somehow it didn't bother him any more.

The damp sand below the high-tide mark held a line of small shoeless footprints, headed out toward the water. Marvin followed without haste or serious interest. He saw something ahead, whiter than the sand. When he got there he was not greatly surprised to recognize Pamela's dress.

The footprints ended at the water's edge. Marvin stood there for a while, looking out over the moonlit ocean. His eyes were focused on nothing nearer than the invisible horizon. His toes tapped out a crunchy rhythm on the wet sand.

He took a step forward.

Up at the top of the bluff, sitting on a big rock, the Indian kid from Antonio's said, "There he goes."

Beside him his grandfather grunted softly. "How long's it been?"

"Since she went in?" The kid checked his cheap digital watch. The little bulb was broken but the moonlight was plenty strong. "Hour and a half. About."

"Hm. Didn't think he was that much bigger than her."

"She had small bones."

"Uh huh." The old man grinned. "I saw you when she took off her dress. Thought you were going to fall off the bluff."

"She did have a good shape," the kid said. "For a woman her age."

They watched as Marvin Badwater walked steadily into the sea. By now the water was up to his waist, but he kept going.

"Guess he can't swim," the kid remarked.

"Wouldn't do him much good if he could. Come on, son. Time we were leaving."

As they walked back to the truck the kid said, "Will you teach me to make that medicine?"

"Some day. When you're ready."

"Does it have a name? You know, what we—you—did, back there. What do you call it?"

"A start."

The kid began laughing. A moment later the old man joined in with his dry wispy chuckle. They were still laughing as they drove away, up the coast road and toward the distant glow of the main highway.

Behind them the sea stretched away flat and shining in the moonlight, its surface broken only by the small dark spot that was the head and shoulders of Marvin Bradshaw, wading toward Europe.

This was another one that came back from a lot of editors. I always wondered whether it was because they didn't understand it or because they did.

Written December 1999
First published July 2002

Empire

"History," the Emperor often said, "is a lie agreed upon."

"And who'd know better?" Captain Houston said, when I quoted the line to him. "About history, and about lies. Having been responsible for such a hell of a lot of both, in his day."

He did not say it loudly, though; his usual alligator-bellow voice was for once a discreet murmur, though no one was nearby. Houston was a bold young man, even by the standards of his kind; but mocking the Emperor was a dangerous business, especially during that final year.

In any case I did not reply, and after a moment he chuckled and glanced at me. We were walking down the swept gravel walk toward the front driveway of the palace, the Emperor having told me to see Captain Houston to his carriage. Captain Houston had just returned from a secret mission deep in Spanish territory, and had found his way back from Florida to New Orleans through hundreds of miles of wilderness known only to his Indian friends, so presumably he was capable of finding his own way out; but the Emperor was always one for the courtesies.

"You ought to write a history-book yourself," Houston said, grinning. "The things you've seen and heard, it'd be worth reading."

"Slaves do not write histories," I pointed out.

"I heard somewhere that there were slaves who wrote books," Houston said. "Back in Roman times."

"This is not the Roman Empire," I answered, and bit off the irreverent addendum, "However much His Majesty likes to think so." I had no wish to match him for riskiness of wit; for myself I have always found bravery a vulgar quality, and those who possess it generally tiresome—though I did like Sam Houston, who had a keen sense of irony, no doubt acquired from living with the Cherokees.

"Well," he said, "there's my carriage, Albert," giving my name the English pronunciation rather than the proper one. "Good night."

Three days later the British arrived.

I was there when the Emperor got the word; in fact I was the one who brought it to him, though only in the sense of taking the sealed message from the dispatch rider—who was sweating, even though it was a December day and quite cool for New Orleans—and carrying it on a silver tray into the Emperor's private study. I did not, of course, know the contents, but I had my suspicions.

The Emperor read the message, smiled slightly, and tossed it onto his desk. "Well, Albert," he said, "the ball would seem about to begin. His Britannic Majesty's forces have put in their long-awaited appearance off our shores."

It was not, you understand, any great surprise. It was common knowledge, even in the streets of the city, that a large Royal Navy squadron, with a convoy of troop transports, had been working its ponderous way across the Gulf, shadowed at a discreet distance by Lafitte's people.

The Emperor got to his feet, slowly and clumsily, breathing loudly with the effort. I made no move to assist him; His Majesty's increasing corpulence and deteriorating health were among the many things one was required not to notice.

He walked over to the great windows that overlooked the palace grounds. "Ah, Albert," he said, his back to me. "Do you know, at times I wish myself back in France."

I said nothing, merely stood in respectful silence. I knew what was coming, having heard it so many times before.

"I have not seen France since the year 1793," he mused, his back to me. "Yet in some sense it will always be my second home. Strange; I have no such feelings, now, for Corsica."

He turned slightly, placing his face in profile. The morning light sharply silhouetted the famous features; the body might have grown corrupted, but that incredible head was still as beautiful as ever.

"Perhaps," he said wistfully, "I should have stayed. That was my intention, after all, when the traitor Paoli drove the Buonapartes from Corsica. I had no thought but to return to France and resume my military career. It was sheer chance that that American ship happened to be in the harbor, while I was seeking passage to Marseilles to rejoin the family, and that I fell to talking with the captain—and made a sudden impulsive decision, and the rest, as they say, is history."

He turned and smiled at me. "Who knows? Had I followed my original plan, surely I would by now be an officer of rank in the forces of the Republic. Not that that would be such an enviable fate, now," he added, "after the drubbing the British and their allies have given the Republic's armies. But perhaps I could have changed all that, eh? That fellow Wellington might have found General Buonaparte a harder adversary."

"As indeed he soon shall, sire," I murmured.

"What? Oh, yes, of course. Excellent, Albert!" He laughed. "Yes, it would seem the Duke and I are destined to do battle, in one possible world or another."

His mouth twisted. "If, if. If not for Paoli's treachery, I could have been the liberator of my homeland, and spent the rest of my days as ruler of Corsica. Treachery is a terrible thing, Albert, to be execrated above all other human sins."

I kept my mouth shut and my face blank, and tried to suppress the picture in my mind—of the late Colonel Burr, or rather his ghost, listening to that last little homily. The exquisite treachery by which the Emperor had disposed of his old partner would for sheer seamless detail have impressed a Borgia.

History, by the way, still seems silent on the question of just when and how the former Captain Buonaparte, now a newly commissioned lieutenant in the tiny United States army, chanced to meet then-Senator Burr. I have an impression it was at some sort of social function in New York, but I may be mistaken; at the time, after all, I was still a half-grown servant boy in a wealthy New Orleans household, being educated above my station by a capricious and indulgent owner. (Interestingly, it is possible that the Emperor and I were learning English at the same time.)

Whenever and wherever it happened, it was certainly one of the most fateful encounters of all time. I wonder if they recognized each other, in that first moment, as two of the same breed? Much as two sharks in the lightless depths of the ocean must apprehend their common species. . . .

"But then," the Emperor said with sudden joviality, "in that case who would now reign over the interior of North America? Perhaps your famous and talented relative Tecumseh, eh?"

"Tecumseh is Shawnee, sire," I said very diffidently. "My father's people were Choctaw." Not that it mattered; my mother having been quadroon, I was unequivocally "black" under the laws of the Empire.

"Albert, Albert." He laughed softly and gave me a fond look. "I tease you, but you know how highly I esteem you. See here." He adopted the manner of one who has just made an important decision. "You have been a good and faithful servant for many years. When this business with the English is concluded, I intend to free you."

I bowed my head, as if overcome. "Sire," I said most humbly.

He did this, on the average, two or three times a year. It meant nothing. As many men—and women—had learned, the Emperor was too great a man to be bound by a trivial thing like a promise. But one had to pretend.

The next day they had a big council in the palace war-room. Standing beside the door, awaiting requests for drinks or whatever else the military leaders of the Empire might require, I witnessed the whole thing.

"So," the Emperor said, looking down at the map that covered most of the great conference table, "our guests have arrived, and we must make ready to welcome them. The question is, where?"

"No sign of any landings yet," Colonel Crockett observed. "They're just sort of hanging around offshore. Last message I got from Sam, he said he could just make out their sails, out in Chandeleur Sound."

He scratched absently beneath his fringed buckskin jacket; a gross discourtesy in the royal presence, but the Emperor tolerated much from the eccentric and extremely able chief of scouting operations. Half the alligators in the swamps were in Crockett's pay and the other half his blood relatives—or so it was said.

General Jackson snorted loudly. "By the Eternal, I don't suppose your 'boys' could trouble themselves to give us a more detailed report?" He and Crockett hated each other; it was one of those deadly personal enmities at which the Tennesseeans excel. "At least an estimate of the enemy's numbers?"

"No need," the Emperor said mildly. "We have, after all, a full roster of the enemy's forces, and have had for some time."

This was true. The Emperor's secret agents were everywhere, on both sides of the Atlantic, and very good at their work. If he had wanted to look it up, he could probably have learned the name of the trooper who watered Wellington's horse.

The Emperor was studying the map. "I confess," he said, "I am having trouble envisioning how they plan to do this."

Even with my own utter lack of military knowledge, I could see the problem. New Orleans is an oddly situated port; below the city, the river runs a hundred miles or so before reaching the sea—but it does not flow through solid land, but down the middle of a strange narrow alluvial peninsula that sticks out far into the Gulf, a kind of penis of the continent. The whole shoreline is a perfect mess of lakes, bays, bayous, and cypress swamps, with hardly any firm ground. How the Duke of

Wellington proposed to get past all that was more than I could understand.

"Can he come straight up the river, do you think?" the Emperor suggested dubiously.

"It would be difficult." General Latour, the chief of engineers, gestured at the map. "The passage is not an easy one, after all. They would need local pilots—"

"Not impossible to get," Captain Lafitte put in. "Many of the people along the river and the coast are Spanish, and none too loyal to the Empire."

"But they would still have to get past our shore batteries," Latour went on. "Especially here, at Fort St. Philippe."

"Yes." The Emperor nodded. "But how else? Land on the shores of Lake Borgne, or the Ponchartrain?"

Lafitte stepped forward. "Not so simple as that, my Emperor. Lake Borgne is not deep enough for big ships. They could cross it in shallow-draft boats, if they have them, and work their way up the bayous, but it would be a difficult and risky business." He tapped the map with a fingertip. "And the Ponchartrain would be even harder."

He grinned. "Now me, I know half a dozen ways to get at this city through the bayous above Barataria Bay. But Wellington could never do it, not without my people to guide him."

Neatly done, I had to admit; a diplomatic reminder of the service the Barataria pirates had done the Emperor, by refusing British attempts to buy their aid, and later by doing sterling work in keeping track of the movements of Lord Nelson's ships.

Of course it could have been pointed out that Lafitte and his brigands were at least partly to blame for the whole situation, since the official *casus belli,* according to the British, lay in their constant and heavy depredations against British and Spanish shipping—under perfectly legal letters of marque from the government of Republican France—but that would have been specious; the British had long had designs on the Mississippi, control of which would make them once again masters in North America. Lafitte had merely supplied a handy pretext.

"By the great Jehovah!" General Jackson was given to such bombastic oaths; it was one of his many annoying traits. "I still can't believe they plan to attack New Orleans at all. This Wellington must be a fool. He could land at Mobile—a bunch of Creek squaws could overwhelm our defenses there—and march overland, raising the Indian tribes against us. The red devils would be glad enough to join them—"

"They would," Colonel Crockett assented grimly. "Thanks to the treatment they've had from people like you."

The two men exchanged glares. The Emperor said pointedly, "The savages are not our present problem. The Duke of Wellington is. And, General Jackson, I assure you he is no fool."

It was hardly a secret that he detested Jackson as an ill-bred lout—most civilized people did—and distrusted him for his arrogant ambition. But however troublesome and even dangerous Jackson might be, he was the one man who could control the fractious backwoodsmen who populated the interior of the Empire and made up much of its army. The Tennesseeans and Kentuckians and Indianans and the rest had been happy to break away from the United States—the fledgling republic east of the mountains had never meant much to them—and join in the "liberation" of the Spanish province of Louisiana; but their allegiances were personal rather than national, and the Emperor, for all his charm, had never captured their hearts as had Colonel Burr.

Now Burr was gone, and only Jackson still held their childish loyalties. And so the Emperor dared not eliminate him; and so Andrew Jackson, alone among the Emperor's original co-conspirators, remained obnoxiously alive. There was no doubt, though, that he was a competent officer in his way.

Now he gave Crockett a final withering look and turned back to the map. His neck, above the high gold-braided collar of his uniform coat, was even redder than usual. "So what do we do, then?" he asked, as always omitting even the most basic forms of respectful address.

The Emperor rubbed his face with one hand. "There is not a great deal we *can* do, until we have a clearer idea of the direction of the attack. We must not spread ourselves thin, trying to cover all the possible approaches. No," he said, "much as it goes against my instincts, for now we wait."

So we waited; everyone waited, while the life of the city underwent dramatic changes. Troops marched through the streets, volunteer units drilled in parks and fields, women made bandages against the anticipated carnage; and the warehouses along the river-front began to fill up with cotton and sugar, there being no way to ship anything out now that the Royal Navy waited at the river's mouth.

Then one of Crockett's men brought word that a force of warships had been seen on the river, working their way upstream. A few days later a message arrived from Fort St. Philippe that the place was under bombardment.

"Well, now we know," the Emperor said. "Wellington and Nelson have chosen the direct approach. I had expected something less obvious."

"Begging the Emperor's pardon," General Latour said, "but do we in fact know?"

"That's right," General Jackson agreed. "Could be a feint."

"Quite true. We will wait a bit longer before fully committing ourselves. However," the Emperor said, "we can make a beginning. Latour, I want the defensive works along the river strengthened—requisition slaves from the plantations hereabouts, you have my authority. Jackson, bring me a report on what artillery we have available. If they are coming up the river, we will need every gun we can lay hands on."

He glanced out the windows and sighed. "The greatest city on the North American continent," he said, "the beautiful, sophisticated capitol of a country of inexhaustible riches. Parks, opera houses, institutions of learning, fine homes . . . and," he slammed his fist suddenly down on the table, "not one God-damned cannon-foundry! No one can be bothered with manufacture here, they are all determined to get rich from cotton and sugar-cane. *Merde!* Right now I would trade half of this city for a few batteries of heavy field guns."

He fell silent. No one ventured to speak. Even Jackson for once had sense enough to keep quiet.

Certainly no one offered to point out that the Imperial army had at one time possessed a superb corps of artillery, with modern weapons purchased from France and brought in despite the British blockade—and had lost most of it, first in Mexico and then, two winters ago, in the dreadful retreat from Canada. Especially Canada. One definitely did not talk about Canada.

Really, there were so *many* things one did not talk about nowadays.

Over the next two weeks all eyes, so to speak, were turned south, as the British bombardment of Fort St. Philippe continued. Messages from the scene spoke of constant heavy fire from bomb-ships—whatever they might be—while a relief party, sent overland, was ambushed by British marines and all but wiped out.

The atmosphere in the city grew tense and strange, as news of these events trickled down to the populace. The most absurd rumors began to circulate, and here and there citizens were attacked—a couple fatally—on suspicion of being British spies.

Indeed the times seemed to bring out the demented. One day not long before Christmas, while I was in the city on a minor errand, I was suddenly accosted on the street by the Mad Marquis. "Hey, boy," he cried, and put his face close to mine. "Haven't seen you in a long time. Come," he said, hooking my arm in his, "walk a little with an old man. I have no one to talk with, these days."

I glanced nervously about; I had no wish to be seen in the company of the Marquis, who managed to cut a notorious figure even in hard-to-shock New Orleans.

He was not a native of Louisiana, but of France, where he had once been famous—or infamous—for his scandalous writings and equally scandalous personal life. He had been repeatedly imprisoned, first by the royal government and then by the revolutionaries; but then the family contrived to have him shipped off to America, where he could no longer embarrass them. The Emperor tolerated his presence—a favor to certain friends with influence in Paris; anything to maintain the all-important French alliance—on the condition that he refrain from publishing his outrageous writings within the Empire. (They were, however, widely though illegally circulated in the United States; former President Jefferson was said to be quite a devotee.)

He and I had met at a certain establishment, where he was a regular customer—too old for active participation, he still paid to watch whippings—and where I occasionally made a bit of pocket-money, without the Emperor's knowledge, playing the pianoforte. The proprietress had known my mother.

"Albert, Albert," he said now, "how does His Majesty? Well, one hopes?"

I said that His Majesty did quite well. "Good," he said. "I so admire the Emperor, you know. In a world of canting hypocrites, a man who knows how to take what he desires!"

He dug an elbow into my ribs. "The affair of Colonel Burr, for example. Magnificent! I am dazed with admiration!"

Again I looked about, this time in real fear. No one was anywhere near, but still I tried to pull away. His grip, however, was amazingly strong.

"Oh, not to worry," he added. "No one has been talking. Merely a cynical old man's speculation—but I see by your face that I was right. Ha! Never fear, the secret is safe with me."

He leered conspiratorially at me. "The public all believe the story they have so often been told, and why not? It is, after all, a masterpiece of fiction—I say this as an author in my own right—and the corroborative evidence! The incriminating letters in Spanish, the drawings of the defenses of New Orleans and Mobile, the bag of Spanish gold pieces, the final heart-rending note confessing all—my friend, if I were not such an experienced creator of imaginative tales I would believe it too."

By now I was fairly gibbering with horror, yet he kept his hold and continued: "But the crowning gem, ah! That the smoking pistol clutched in his lifeless hand should be the very weapon with which he had killed Monsieur Hamilton! Sheer poetry!"

I managed to wrench myself free, finally, and I am not ashamed to admit I took to my heels. I had not realized how dangerous the old maniac was. Or what a shrewd intelligence functioned within that deranged head.

(All the same, he was wrong about the pistol. In fact, as I once heard Colonel Burr tell the Emperor, it was Hamilton who furnished the weapons for the famous duel. That detail was not part of the original package, as it were; the story simply arose somehow—possibly from some journalist of the popular press— and was repeated until it became widely accepted. Mr. Irving even put it in his history-book.)

Reaching the corner, still at a run, I almost collided with a couple of buckskin-clad figures. A hand grabbed my jacket and pulled me to a stop, and I started to protest, but then I recognized the laughing faces of Colonel Crockett and Captain Houston. "Here, now," Houston said, "what's the hurry?"

"Been talking to the old Mar-kee?" Crockett asked, grinning. "Boy, he's a piss-cutter, ain't he?"

I was too breathless to speak. "Come on," Houston said. "We were just on our way to get us a drink."

They pulled me into a dark and dingy little tavern, where a few idlers sat talking and playing cards. A burly man in homespun clothing looked at me and said loudly, "No niggers allowed in here!"—and in less than a second found himself on his back on the floor, with Crockett's foot on his chest and Houston's knife at his throat.

"You got something to say," Crockett inquired gently, "about who we choose to drink with?"

A few minutes later we were seated in the rear of the room with a jug on the table before us. The people at the nearby tables had considerately moved away and given us our privacy. The one who had spoken first was nowhere to be seen.

"Drink up," Houston advised me. "You look like you could use it."

The raw corn whiskey was quite the worst drink I had ever tasted, but I managed to get a little down, and my nerves did settle a bit. Crockett and Houston applied themselves to the jug with gusto. "Damn good booze," Crockett said approvingly. "Here's to Andy Jackson, the son of a bitch."

"Better drink to crazy old King George," Houston suggested. "Could be we ought to get in practice."

"Is it that bad?" I asked.

"Half a dozen years ago," Crockett said, "I would have said we'll kick their asses back into the Gulf. Now—" He shrugged. "This army ain't what it used to be."

"Oh, shit," Houston said dolefully. "Here he goes again, playing the old soldier."

"Playing hell. I been in this from the start, son. I was toting a rifle under Old Hickorynuts back when we were just a bunch of raggedy-assed rebels, didn't know what we were getting into except that Burr made it sound good and his little French pard was the fightingest one human we'd ever saw. I was there when we marched into this town for the first time and kicked the Dons out, when you were still just a brat."

He paused to lubricate his throat. "And I was there when we fought Mister President Jefferson's pitiful little army—the ones that didn't run away or change sides—when the States tried to take Tennessee and Kentucky back. I was there when we took West Florida from the Dons, too. By then we had the best damn army, for its size, in the world. Hell, the Prussians used to send officers over here to study old Nap's methods. But then—"

He spat on the dirt floor. "Then we couldn't quit. Spent a year putting that fool Joseph on the throne of Mexico and another two years trying to keep him there—quit looking at me like that, Albert, I don't give a coon's ass whose brother he was, he was a God-damned fool and ending up in front of a 'dobe wall was no more than he deserved."

I grabbed the jug and took another drink. This time it went down almost easily.

"Used up a big piece of the army in Mexico," Crockett continued, "specially the cavalry. Lost Pike there, too, best damn officer we had, Jackson ain't a scratch on Zeb Pike's ass as a general. Then before we'd even started to recover—"

"Canada," Houston said. "He's going to tell about Canada."

"What for? Ever'body in the whole world knows what happened. Shit." He made a face. "Oh, it was gonna be so easy. All them Catholic Frenchmen in Canada were so eager to rise up agin the King and jine us. And France was gonna send ships and troops to invade up the St. Lawrence at the same time. Only," he said, "turned out the French Canucks didn't like us no better than they did the redcoats, and Nelson caught the invasion fleet leaving France and made fishbait of the poor bastards, and the weather turned against us—Jesus H. *Christ*, you wouldn't believe it could get that cold!"

"And Tecumseh picking that time," Houston said, "while you were all off up north, to set the tribes on the war path. I remember that."

"Yep. So we had to fight our way through the Indians just to get back home. What there was left of us," Crockett said bitterly.

Houston said, "But that was eighteen-twelve, Davy. They got the army built back up now, nearly to strength."

"They got a bunch of men carrying weepons. Takes more than that to make an army. Them white-trash boys jine up to get away from home, soljering looks easier than plowing and the uniform's good to impress the girls, but they never seen no real fighting. 'Cept now and then marching off with Andy Jackson to burn out some village of peaceful Creeks, sure as hell never faced British reg'lars. Neither have you, either of you."

"True," I said. "The Emperor never takes me on campaign." For which God, if He exists, be thanked on bended knee.

"It ain't like nothing you ever seen." Crockett shuddered. "The way they come on, all in step, not making a sound, it's *skeery* is what it is. And that was just Packenham's men in Canada, not even top regiments. Wellington's boys are supposed to be even better. Can we stop 'em? Damn if I know."

He fell silent, his face morose. Houston reached for the jug. "Don't pay Davy any mind," he said. "It'll be all right."

A few days later Fort St. Philippe fell.

* * *

"Never seen nothing like it," Colonel Crockett told the Emperor and the others, at the hastily-convened council that followed. "They bombarded that place steady, all night and all day and all the next night too. Must of throwed in every mortar shell in the Royal Navy. Then, the second morning they stopped shelling, and here come the marines out of the woods and rushed the fort. Didn't take long, there weren't no real defense left. Me and Sam watched the whole thing from across the river."

"Thank you for the report, Colonel." The Emperor's shoulders sagged. "This is terrible. The river is now open, almost all the way to the city. Latour, can we put in more batteries downstream? "

"No time, my Emperor. Moving and emplacing guns in that terrain—" General Latour shook his head. "Besides, we have concentrated all our available artillery at English Turn, on your Majesty's orders. We would have to take away—"

"No, no, you are right. We must not weaken the defenses there. Well." The Emperor sighed. "At least now there is no doubt where they will come."

"Beg the Emperor's pardon, I'm not so sure." Crockett was looking thoughtful. "They're on the river, all right, but not all of them. Not nigh as many ships as we seen when they first showed up. And no telling where the others are, now they got Lafitte's boys bottled up in the Barataria."

"Holding back a reserve," Jackson said, snorting. "Any fool can see that, by the Almighty!"

"Maybe," Crockett said. "Guess we'll know the answers soon enough."

But the British were slow in coming. Not an easy business, of course, working their way against that current and negotiating the tricky channel; apparently there were several groundings. Still, it did seem they were taking their time.

Christmas came, and was duly celebrated by the French and Spanish Catholics of the city, though ignored or scorned by the Protestant Americans. The Emperor attended mass at the great church, as usual concealing his personal agnosticism beneath a cloak of public piety.

All other days, he rode down to the site of the defensive works at the great river bend called English Turn. There was a fairly good road along the levee, so he went by carriage; and, for unclear reasons, I was required to go along. There was nothing much to see but a lot of earthworks along the river, and black and white men laboring alike to reinforce them with sand-bags, while others wrestled guns into position. I stood by and shivered in the chilly wind—it was a cold winter for New Orleans—while the Emperor bustled about, talking with officers and men, now and then personally supervising the placement of a cannon. The years seemed to drop from him at such times; he was in his element. For myself I was happier when we returned to the palace, where I could be in mine.

Thus it was that I was with the Emperor the day it all came down.

It was a dank and chilly morning, three days before year's end. A heavy gray fog had moved in off Lake Borgne during the previous evening, and now hung above the river and the eastern swamps, and the plantation fields between, as we rolled southward along the river road. Sitting up on the seat next to the driver, I wrapped a blanket about myself and cursed through my chattering teeth. What a ghastly day to go out, but the Emperor was quite insistent. Nelson's ships had been sighted on the river, the previous afternoon, only a few miles south of English Turn; clearly the time was almost at hand.

Suddenly a horseman appeared through the fog up ahead, riding hard toward us. Seeing us, he took off his hat and began waving it frantically up and down.

The driver and I looked at each other. I shrugged and, after a moment, the driver pulled the horses to a stop.

Almost immediately a window opened beneath us and the Emperor's voice came up to us, demanding to know why we were stopping. But by that time the rider was upon us; a slender handsome young man, dressed, I saw now, in the bright uniform of an ensign in the Louisiana Hussars.

"Please," he gasped, "sir—uh, y'r Majesty—"

"Never mind," the Emperor said impatiently. "What do you want, lad?"

The boy—he really was not much more—took a deep breath and gathered himself visibly. "I have to report, your Majesty," he said with strained formality, "that the enemy are attacking our position in strength."

The Emperor's head appeared through the carriage window. "What?" he cried, and then paused, hearing, now the horses' hooves were silent, the distant rattle and pop of musket fire from somewhere on down the river.

"But the guns," he said then, staring at the horseman. "I hear neither our artillery nor the ships' guns!"

The lad shook his head. "Not the ships, sir. They came in from the east—looks like they crossed Lake Borgne yesterday, in the fog, and moved up through the bayous, and then early this morning they came up out of the swamp and across the plantation fields—one of Colonel Crockett's scouts spotted them, but, uh, well, General Jackson didn't believe him at first—" He stopped, looking appalled at his own indiscretion. "Uh, that is to say—"

The Emperor said, "Name of God! They attacked from the landward side?"

"Yes, sir." The ensign nodded. "Where our defenses were weakest, and of course all the big guns are emplaced to cover the river—"

"The English," the Emperor said, "do they have artillery?"

"Don't know, your Majesty. Haven't brought them into play yet, if they do. Plenty of infantry, though. Must be a thousand, maybe two thousand, hard to tell in this fog. They just keep coming." The ensign's eyes were blinking rapidly. "General Jackson sent me to warn you—"

"Yes, yes." The carriage door opened; the Emperor began clambering down, not waiting for me to attend him. Before I could get down from the seat, he was already standing in the road, snapping his fingers at the young officer. "Your horse," he said. "Give me your horse."

"Sir? Your Majesty?" The ensign looked blank, but then he must have seen the Emperor's expression more clearly. "Yes, sir," he said hastily, and swung down. "Uh, shall I—"

"You shall get out of my way." The Emperor was already hauling himself into the saddle, clumsily and with obvious pain. "Driver, follow me. Let the ensign ride with you."

Swinging the horse about, digging his dress boot heels into its flanks, the Emperor disappeared at a gallop into the fog, toward the growing noise of battle. After a moment the driver raised his eyebrows and put the team in motion again, while the young ensign scrambled aboard and pulled himself up beside us.

Already we could see the flashes of gunfire through the mist ahead, and now louder explosions came rolling up the road to meet us: cannon getting into the action at last. I looked inquiringly at the young hussar, but he shook his head. "No idea," he said hoarsely. "No telling whose—"

Then there was a blast like all the thunder in the world, and another right on its heels, and his face went even paler. "Oh, my God," he whispered. "Warships firing broadsides. The bastards are hitting us from the river too."

It hardly required a formal military education to see the implications: the defenders caught between advancing British infantry in one direction and the fire of the ships' guns raking them from the other.

The ensign was climbing down now. "You better wait here," he called up to the driver.

The driver pulled the carriage to a stop, while the ensign dropped to the ground, just as the first soldiers appeared through the fog coming the other way. Infantry, wearing the blue uniforms of the Empire, and running very hard. . . .

Perched up on top of the carriage, I had a fine view of the rout. They ran past us on either side, hardly a man even seeming to notice us except as an obstacle; their eyes were enormous in their smoke-blackened faces and their mouths mostly hung open. A few clutched at bloody wounds.

Horsemen appeared now, most of them in flight as well, a few—officers, I supposed—evidently trying, without success, to stop the retreat. Horse and foot, the hurrying tide jammed the road and spread out over the open fields to our left, without order or discipline but with a splendid unity of direction: away from the British, toward the city and safety, while behind them the guns still bellowed and muskets and rifles cracked.

Our hussar ensign stood in the middle of the road, waving his sword, shouting at the fleeing men, ordering them to turn back, till he tripped—or was tripped—and went down and disappeared under all those running feet. I closed my eyes for a moment in revulsion.

When I opened them I saw that the driver was pointing. "Look," he said, and after a moment I saw them, the Emperor and General Jackson, charging their horses this way and that amid the hurrying throng, slowly being forced back along the road by weight of numbers. Jackson was slashing this way and that with his sword, without apparent effect; the Emperor, who rarely wore side-arms, was in any case having to use both hands to control the hussar's frightened horse.

And quite soon they went past us too, Jackson on the left—he turned and gave me a furious look as he passed, God knows why—and the Emperor on the right. The Emperor did not even glance our way. His face was terrible to see.

Finally they were all past, leaving us alone on the levee-top road, though off across the open ground a few stragglers still picked their way through the sugar-cane trash. And, a few minutes later, a fresh batch of men came out of the fog, moving less hurriedly and in a far more orderly manner. Even in the misty light, their red coats looked very fine.

The driver's nerve broke, then; without a word he scrambled down from the seat and took off up the road, after the departing Imperial troops. Left alone, I took the reins and quieted the restive horses, and a few minutes later found myself surrounded by grinning red-coated infantrymen. "Wot's the matter, then, Uncle?" one called up to me. "Run off and leave you, did they?"

Another cried, "Look, boys! Burn my arse if this ain't Boney's carriage! Look here, on the doors!"

They all gathered around, staring and chattering; then all fell silent as an elegantly-uniformed man came riding up on a horse. "You men!" he called. "Who gave the order to break formation?" Then, seeing the carriage, "Damme!"

He looked at me. "Emperor's driver, are you?"

"Merely a manservant," I told him. "Sir."

"Major Grigsby, 7th Fusiliers." He gave a mocking little half-salute. "Can you drive this thing, then, my man?"

"After a fashion."

"Then," he said, "be so good as to do so, until you reach a point where you can turn off this road, which you are now blocking, and which we need for the guns." He turned. "Sergeant, detail four men to escort this vehicle, and guard it against the light-fingered. The commander will enjoy this, I should think."

A beefy-faced man said, "Sir, what about the nigger?"

"Guard him, too. The commander may want to question him." He turned his horse. "The rest of you, back in formation and resume your advance. Keep the damned rascals on the run."

When they were gone one of my guards gave me a gap-toothed grin. "You 'eard the Major," he told me. "No tricks, now, and look smart. You're going to meet the Dook."

Sir Arthur Wellesley, First Duke of Wellington, was a tall, lean, imposing man with a long-nosed aristocratic face that would not have looked out of place on a Roman statue. By the time he got around to me it was late in the evening, and he must have put in a very long hard day indeed, yet he showed no signs of fatigue. Or much else; I had the impression of a man who, in Sam Houston's phrase, played his cards close to his vest.

Our interview was quite short; it did not take long for him to realize that I was merely a household servant, who knew nothing of the Emperor's military plans and had never overheard anything of possible value—or who, at any rate, was never going to admit otherwise.

"I have no idea," he said at last, "whether you are as stupid as you pretend, or very clever indeed. Some officers, in my position, would issue instructions to see if a sound whipping would improve your memory. But no fear." He allowed himself a very slight smile. "It hardly matters. The lines of battle, from this point forward, are inevitable."

He paced back and forth a bit, looking at me. It was dark outside and the interior of the tent was lit by a single candle.

"So," he said, "what shall I do with you? Strictly speaking, you are not a prisoner of war, since you are not a soldier or even a free man . . . would you like to be?"

He raised an eyebrow. "My orders are to free any slaves who wish to join our forces."

"I would like to be free," I told him. "I have, however, no wish to join your forces or any others."

"Ah. Want to be your own man, eh? A worthy ambition, by God." He actually chuckled, very softly and very briefly. "Well, for the moment, I think you had best remain with us. You have seen quite a lot, I'm sure, whilst waiting about."

That was true; I had had nothing to but watch, while men and guns came ashore from the transports and were formed up in order and sent marching northward along the river road. It had been an impressive sight, and not an encouraging one from the Imperial viewpoint.

"You might," Wellington added, "be tempted to run back to your master. I'm sure he'd be interested in what you could tell him. Better to keep you out of temptation's way."

And so I spent the next two days as a prisoner who was not quite a prisoner. The distinction was largely ignored by the soldiers, who made me do various menial tasks about the camp, and occasionally kicked me for no particular reason.

It was from the British side, then, that I watched the final Battle of New Orleans. Not being a soldier, I could make little sense of what I saw—not that I could see much anyway, from where I stood near a battery of unreasonably loud cannon.

But I could see that the outcome was not much in doubt. The British obviously had an overpowering superiority in artillery—the defenders having lost so many guns at English Turn, and the invaders having brought plenty of their own; a child could have seen the discrepancy at a glance, once the battle was joined. Wellington's gunners—joined by Nelson's seamen, who had brought heavy ships' cannon ashore to reinforce the army—turned a devastating storm of shot on the Imperial lines, answered only by weak and scattered fire. Even standing to the rear, I was deafened and well-nigh blinded by the steady and excruciating roar, and my bowels felt very loose; I cannot imagine what it must have been like for those who were its targets. I had had no idea that war was such a noisy and messy business. It looked so much neater in the paintings and engravings.

Then Wellington's infantry advanced in their implacable ranks, and after that I lost any real grasp of what was going on. I could see the battle only as a distant indistinct dark line—one that soon began to grow even more distant, moving first raggedly and slowly, then with much greater speed, to the north, in the direction of the city.

"Buggers are running again," one of my guards observed. "That's it, then. Be a jolly old time tonight in Noo Orleens."

At some point, late in the afternoon, my guards simply disappeared. Heading for the city, no doubt, not wanting to miss out on the looting and general sport.

After an irresolute pause, I set off in that direction myself, walking along the river road. No one paid me any mind; everyone was hurrying toward the city. Already plumes of smoke had begun to appear above the rooftops, indicating that this was going to be a long night.

Then suddenly there was a stir of activity up ahead and I saw the Duke of Wellington sitting on his horse by the roadside, taking reports from dispatch riders and conferring with some officers. I started to detour around the scene, only to be stopped short by Wellington's voice: "You there! The Emperor's servant!"

I turned and walked back and looked up at the Duke. "Well," he said, "your master has lost the hand. And, I believe, the game."

"Yes, sir," I said, blank-faced.

"He seems to have given us the slip," Wellington said. "Would you know anything about that? Ever hear anything to suggest what plans your Emperor might have made, for a contingency such as this?"

"No, sir. I do not believe," I said truthfully, "he ever seriously envisioned such an event."

"Ah, yes. Quite." A quick nod. "Well, well, no matter." To an officer at his side he added, "Boney's done for, no matter where he's gone. Now we hold New Orleans, the Empire can be strangled at our pleasure."

"And then," the officer said, "perhaps we shall see about the damned Yankees and their so-called United States of America."

"Very possibly." The Duke shook his head. "Please God, not until after I have relinquished command to some younger man. I grow tired. I wish to go home."

To me, then: "Go your way, then. You are free—at least insofar as His Britannic Majesty's forces are concerned. If you ever do see your master again, thank him for the carriage. I intend to ride in it, when I enter his city tomorrow."

"On New Year's Day," another officer murmured.

"Why, yes. So it will be," the Duke said, sounding surprised. "Do you know, I had forgotten."

It was dark by the time I made my way into the city. It was a dangerous time to walk the streets; British soldiers were everywhere, helping themselves to whatever struck their fancy— including any women so foolish, or adventurous, as to be caught out-of-doors. From every direction came the sounds of breaking glass, male shouts and female screams, and the odd gunshot.

A hand grabbed my arm and jerked me into the mouth of a dark alley; another hand clamped itself over my mouth. A familiar voice hissed in my ear, "Quiet, now, Albert!"

Released, I turned and said, "It's all right. There's no one nearby."

"Good," Houston said, and Crockett grunted agreement. "Where you been?"

"You wouldn't believe me," I said, "What happened? Today, I mean?"

"Just like I was afeared," Crockett said. "Our boys broke. Stood their ground pretty good at first, but then they seen them redcoats coming on and on, never missing a step, never making a sound, sun shining off them bayonets, it was too much."

"The Tennessee militia broke first," Houston added. "And then the Kentuckians, on the left. But then everybody was taking off. Nearly, anyway. The ones who didn't mostly got bayonetted or captured, I guess."

"Jackson's dead," Crockett said with a certain satisfaction. "Tried to stop the rout, started hitting out with that God-damned sword of his, and somebody shot him right out of his saddle."

I said, "They say the Emperor has disappeared."

"He commandeered the St. Louis steamboat," Houston told me. "Guess that's where he's bound."

"Will you be joining him?" I asked. "If you can escape from the city?"

"No." Crockett spat. "Had enough of soljering. Me and Sam figure to head out west. Trap furs or something."

"Want to come along?" Houston grinned. "See the wild frontier."

"Thank you," I said, "but I think not. I believe I know where I can find employment. Once order has been restored, Madame Letitia's establishment should find itself doing a great deal of business. I'm sure she will need a good pianoforte player."

"Then so long." Crockett slapped me on the back. "And good luck."

"To you as well," I said, meaning it; though I had full faith in their ability to survive and escape, if any men alive could do it. "*Bonne chance*," I added, as they moved away down the alley.

"Yeah," Houston's voice drifted back through the darkness; and then, with a sardonic chuckle: "*Vive l'Empereur. . . .*"

* * *

Written for the second Alternate Generals *antho, this was the one that got me my second Sidewise Award. Which struck me as rather funny, since it had been as much as anything else a kind of lampoon of the whole AH genre; but I didn't turn it down.*

Written October 1997
First published July 2002

Tenbears And The *Bruja*

He came riding across the flats in the late afternoon on a very dusty bay horse, heading for the little town or maybe village that hunkered at the foot of the big red mesa. There was no good reason for a town to be there but then there was no good reason for him to be where he was either.

He was a tall lean no-ass Indian in his middle thirties. He wore a black hat with a drooping eagle feather in back, and blue denim shirt and jeans bleached nearly white by the sun. His hair was done in braids that hung halfway down his chest. There was nothing particularly unusual about his appearance unless you counted the medium-sized rattlesnake curled familiarly about his left leg below the knee.

His name was Luke Tenbears. He had been in the desert for six days and he was starting to feel every minute of it. Right now even a pissant town like this one looked good to him.

It definitely wasn't much of a place. Riding slowly down the single street, the clop-clop of the bay's hooves echoing off the adobe house fronts on either side, he decided it just barely qualified as anywhere at all. The biggest structure in sight was a dilapidated old church with a Spanish-style bell tower, facing on a tiny plaza. On the other side of the plaza was a long low adobe building that he took to be something official, since the entrance was flanked by a wind-tattered Stars and Stripes and an even raggedier New Mexico state flag. That answered one question, anyway; he had been wondering if he might have wandered across the line into Mexico without knowing it.

An old Ford automobile sat parked in front of the long building. One of the front wheels was missing and the axle was supported by a stack of adobe blocks. Beside it, perched on its stand, was a shiny black Henderson motorcycle. Both the car and the motorcycle bore the white-lettered word POLICIA. There were no other motor vehicles in sight, but a pretty healthy-looking burro was loitering about near the church.

None of this interested Luke nearly as much as the fountain in the middle of the plaza. He got down, wincing as saddle-stiff muscles raised objections to the sudden movement, and led the bay over to the fountain. Taking off his hat, holding the eagle feather carefully out of the way, he got a hatful of water and held it out. The bay buried its muzzle in the hat crown and drained the water in a single grateful slurp. While Luke was getting the horse a refill a voice behind him said, "Hey, *Indio*."

He waited till the bay was drinking again before he turned around. A fat man with a drooping black mustache stood staring at him. "Yeah, you," the fat man said. Actually it came out more like *joo*; the accent was really intense.

Luke noticed the fat man wore a sagging cartridge belt—though with only a few cartridges in the loops—and a big holstered revolver. Pinned to the sweaty front of his khaki shirt was a large gold badge.

Walking slowly past Luke, he patted the bay's flank. "Nice horse," he said. "What's his name?"

"Doesn't have one," Luke told him, refilling the hat once again. This time he poured the contents over his head.

"No?" The fat man snorted. "Where you steal him?"

Luke wiped water from his eyes and didn't reply. After a moment the fat man said, "What you doing here, *Indio*? Looking for something else to steal?"

"Just passing through." Luke glanced up and down the street. "There anywhere in this town a man could get some eats? Couple of beers, maybe a bath?"

"Not if the man is an *Indio*." The fat man's lip curled. "If indeed an *Indio* can be called a—*chinga!*" His eyes went wide as dinner plates and he leaped backward a good three feet. "You got a rattlesnake on your leg!"

"Sure do," Luke agreed. "Not much gets by you, does it?"

The fat man was grabbing at his holstered pistol, while the snake's tail began a soft whirring buzz. Luke said, "Don't do that."

He didn't raise his voice when he said it, or make any particular moves, and he wasn't wearing a gun of his own; but the fat man stopped still as the statue of St. Bartholomew in front of the church behind him. After a second the chubby fingers fell away from the gun. "You better get out of here," the fat man said, his voice uneven. "Go on, now. No more trouble."

Luke stood and looked at him, thinking of several possible things to do next. While he was thinking a woman's voice called, "*Hola, Indio!* You hungry?"

She stood in the middle of the street on the far side of the plaza: long thick black hair, dark strong face, well-filled white blouse, big black skirt whipping in the dry breeze, bare feet set wide apart in the dust. Hands on hips and very damn splendid hips too from the look of them.

So far not all that remarkable, any number of women to answer that description in any number of towns like this on both sides of the border; but this one was taller than the local average, easily five and a half feet by Luke's slightly dazed estimate, and nothing willowy about her either. He was so busy thinking what a big fine woman she was that she had to call out again before he realized she was talking to him.

"Come on, *Indio*," she said, and gave the fat man a look that would have sliced the balls off a grizzly bear. "Never mind El Jefe. I'll take care of you."

The fat man sputtered, started to speak, and then suddenly turned and gave Luke a big grin. "Oh, yes," he said almost cheerfully. "You go with her, *Indio*. She'll take care of you all right." His grin got wider and his voice higher. "*Es una bruja, Indio*. You know what means *bruja*? Witch!"

He broke into a wet nasty laugh that stopped in a choking gobble when the woman made a curious little gesture at him. Luke put the wet hat on his head. "Right with you," he said to the woman, and reached for the bay's reins. "Okay if I bring my horse?"

"Sure," she said. "And your snake too. Just don't bring that pig beside you."

As they walked together down the street the woman said, "My name's Margarita. You want to tell me yours?" She gave him a quick flash of eye-hurting white teeth. "Or maybe you don't give out your name?"

"Luke Tenbears," he told her. "*Diez osos*," he added in translation.

"I know what it means." She tilted her head to one side. "What kind of Indian? Navajo?"

"Comanche."

"Huh. Long way from home." She glanced down. "Nice snake. Where'd you get him?"

The rattlesnake raised its flat spearpoint head and looked up at her. "I've got a name, you know," it said in a dry reedy voice.

"His name's Dwight," Luke told the woman.

Her eyebrows went way up. "*Dios!* A horse that doesn't have a name and a snake that does."

"Also," the rattlesnake said, lisping slightly, "I really really *hate* it when people talk about me right in front of me. As if I'm some complete *idiot* who can't understand. I mean, it's so *rude*."

"Dwight hasn't eaten for a spell," Luke explained. "He gets kind of snippy when he's hungry."

"Quit *apologizing* for me," Dwight said, and lapsed into sullen silence.

"Here," Margarita said. "This is my house."

She lived in a small brush-roofed adobe house, about like any other house in the little town. When Luke had unsaddled and fed the bay, she said, "Come inside," and led him into the cool dimly-lit space of the single room. To Dwight she said, "There's a big rat under the woodpile out back."

"Muchas gracias, señorita," Dwight murmured formally, and uncoiled himself from around Luke's leg and disappeared out the door, rattling softly to himself.

"So," Margarita said to Luke, "want to wash up first?"

"A bath would be fine," Luke said. "But I hate to put you to the trouble—"

"Forget it," she said, and bent to drag a big old iron tub out into the middle of the floor. "It's worth it just to piss El Jefe off. Now sit down and get comfortable, because this is going to take some time."

She was right about that; it was a hell of a job hauling water in from the nearby well and heating it on the little stove until the tub was full. Luke offered to help but she wouldn't permit it. "It's nothing," she said. "I do this all the time." Watching her, Luke realized that she was fantastically strong. Be damn, he thought, I may be in love. Or trouble. Or both. Assuming there's a difference.

He expected she would leave the room when he started to undress, but she leaned her back against the wall and folded her arms and looked straight at him. "Go ahead," she said. "I want to watch you."

He hesitated and then turned his back, while she laughed deep in her belly. When he took off his shirt he heard her suck in her breath. *"Ay,"* she said softly, and a moment later he felt her fingertips on his back, tracing the big deep scars. "What did this to you?"

"Shrapnel," he said. "You know, shell fragments."

"Ah. You were in the big war, in France? In the army?"

"Marines. Place called Belleau Wood."

He took off his boots and peeled down his jeans and padded over to the tub, feeling her watching him. As he climbed in she walked around to stand at the foot of the tub. "I embarrass you," she said, grinning. "Will this help?"

With a series of quick moves she shucked off the white blouse and then the big skirt. She wore nothing underneath. Her body looked hard and taut, her belly absolutely flat, but her breasts were big and high. Luke felt a shock run from the base of his spine clear to the top of his head.

"Hey," she said calmly, "we were going to end up naked together anyway. We both knew that, soon as we laid eyes on each other. Why be silly about it?"

She giggled, then, like a dirty little girl. "You like to look at my titties, huh?" Suddenly her big brown nipples vanished, to be replaced by a pair of long-lashed brown eyes that gazed warmly at Luke. "All right if they look back?"

Luke sat there in the tub for a second or two, trading stares with Margarita's knockers. Then he lifted his hands and made a series of quick passes in the air, and sang a short high-pitched phrase without recognizable words, up in the back of his throat.

Almost immediately his penis broke water like the bow of a surfacing U-boat. As Margarita clapped her hands and made admiring sounds, it continued to grow, on and on past the limits of normal erection and then those of possibility, two feet and now a yard and soon clear to the low ceiling, where it looped itself twice around a rafter and came shooting back down to circle the room, still lengthening itself, snaking here and there about the furniture and at last wrapping itself around Margarita half a dozen times, to end with the big red-brown knob right in front of her face, tapping her gently on the nose.

"Damn, I'm good," Luke said.

Margarita was laughing delightedly. "Damn, you sure are," she said, as Luke clicked his tongue twice and everything returned to more or less normal. "You some kind of medicine man?"

"My grandfather was," Luke explained. "He taught me a few things." Before they decided he was a witch and killed him, he added in his mind but didn't say.

"Boy." She shook her head, making her long black hair flare out like a crow's wings. "Come on, let's get you cleaned up and I'll fix something to eat. I got a feeling we're both going to need our strength."

* * *

When he was done with his bath she dried him with a big rough towel, reaching down at the end to give him a quick friendly tweak. But as he reached for her something else got his attention, maybe a sound from outside, and he stopped and said, "Wait," and went to the door, wrapping the towel around his waist.

A couple of ratty-looking men in straw hats were leading his horse away. One had a shotgun slung across his back and the other wore a holstered pistol. Luke said, "Hey," and then he saw El Jefe standing across the road, giving him a bad-toothed grin.

"Sorry, *Indio,*" the fat man called. "I think maybe this is a stolen horse. I got to impound him until you can prove where you got him." He put a hand on the butt of his revolver. "You got any problem with that?" he asked hopefully. "Want to maybe do something about it?"

When Luke didn't reply he laughed. "No? All right, go back to *la bruja.*" He made a complicated obscene gesture with his free hand. "She'll give you a ride!"

As darkness gathered outside, Margarita cooked and served a near-black *mole con puerco* with stacks of warm corn tortillas and all sorts of fascinating little side items. "Holy shit," Luke said reverently, tasting. "Now this is some real magic, all right."

Some time later, over a jug of authentically great mescal, she said, "I'm glad you came. I was going crazy. Man, I hate this town."

She looked out the door. "They hate me back, of course. *Bruja,* they say, and then spit. I get blamed for every cross-eyed baby that's born and every spell of bad weather. Nobody ever talks to me but El Jefe, and he only wants to fuck me. Well, and the priest mumbles at me in Latin when I go by. I'm not sure he doesn't want to fuck me too."

"Why don't you leave?" Luke asked, picking up the jug. "Go somewhere else. Santa Fe, maybe. Even California."

She snorted. "How? Walk away from here, across the desert? You been out there, man, you know what it's like. Even the coyotes carry canteens and box lunches. And nobody around here is going to give me a ride, that's for sure."

She gave him a sudden look. "Come to think of it, you're stuck here too, now El Jefe's got your horse. What you going to do about that?"

Luke shrugged. "Steal another one, I guess. That one wasn't much good anyway."

"Take me with you when you go," she begged. "Please."

Luke considered it, nodded. "Sure." He slugged at the mescal and set the jug carefully on the table before turning to her. "Hey," he said, "we can worry about all that later. Right now—"

He held out his arms and she came to him, snuggling fiercely against his chest. "Oh, yes," she said breathlessly, and that was when the roof caught fire.

There was no warning smell of smoke, no preliminary flickers and crackles; there was just a big loud rush of flame overhead, all at once, and blazing bits of brush starting to fall as Luke and Margarita jumped to their feet. This, Luke realized without even having to think about it, wasn't the, work of some stray spark; a fire like this had to have been set on purpose. And now he could hear, over the fast-growing roar of the flames, voices from outside. He couldn't make out the words but he had a pretty good idea they weren't friendly.

He grabbed up his boots and hat—luckily he'd put on his jeans and shirt for dinner—and reached for Margarita, who was slapping out a bit of burning roof that was trying to set fire to her skirt. But as they started out the door a gun went off and something small and nasty went *wheeow* off the adobe next to the entrance. "Shit!" Luke said, ducking back out of the doorway, yanking Margarita with him, hearing her cursing in Spanish. "Now what the hell—"

"Hey, *Indio!*" came El Jefe's unmistakable voice from outside. "Come on out! We let you go, okay? We just want *la bruja!*"

Luke was already reaching down the front of his shirt, pulling out the little buckskin bag that hung around his neck on a sweat-black thong. "Hang on a minute," he said to Margarita.

"A minute?" She glanced around with fear-wide eyes. "I don't think we *got* a minute, man—"

She was right about that; the little house was already full of smoke, so dense and pungent it was almost impossible to breathe, while overhead the blazing roof was clearly about to collapse as the flames ate through the cottonwood rafters. But Luke got the little bag open and shook some dark fine powder into the palm of his hand. "Here we go," he said, dipping a fingertip in the stuff. "Hold still."

Quickly he drew his finger across her forehead, leaving a single narrow line, and then put a dot on each cheek. His finger dipped again and he made the same marks on his own face, chanting softly as he did so in a language that was neither Spanish nor Comanche but much older than either. "All right," he said, and stepped toward the doorway. "Come on."

Margarita shivered. "Why not?" she said, and shrugged. "Better to get shot than burn up."

"No, it's okay." He took her hand and led her through the door. Nobody shot at them. "See?"

The house was surrounded by a lot of rough-looking people, mostly men but a few women too. Quite a few of them held guns or machetes, and several others carried torches. The burning house lit the scene almost as bright as day. El Jefe stood in front of the house, his pistol in his hand. Beside him was a tall, lean, long-faced man in a dark robe, holding a large wooden cross that he waved in the direction of the house. His lips were moving but Luke couldn't hear any words for the roar and crackle of the fire.

Luke began walking in the general direction of El Jefe and the priest. After a moment's hesitation Margarita fell in beside him. "Crazy," she muttered.

"Hey, *Indio,*" El Jefe shouted again. He was looking past Luke and Margarita, still looking at the flaming house. "Last chance. Why you want to burn with her?"

By now Luke was close enough to hear the priest mumbling rapidly in what he took to be Latin. His eyes were truly weird in the firelight, and his lips were loose and wet. He too was watching the house, ignoring Luke and Margarita even though they were now right in front of him.

"My God," Margarita said. "They can't see us?"

"Or hear us," Luke told her as they walked past El Jefe and the priest, close enough to brush elbows. "Comanche horse-stealing charm. Been in my family for seven generations. Not much of it left," he added. "I been saving it for an emergency."

They walked through the line of villagers, still undetected, and on up the empty street. Dwight slithered out from between a couple of darkened houses and wrapped himself around Luke's leg. "What a *ghastly* little town," he remarked. "I *told* you we should have gone to Taos."

The plaza was deserted and there were no lights showing in the long building; evidently all of El Jefe's men were down at the burning. Luke noticed the motorcycle still standing there, its chromework picking up the light from the rising moon. "That El Jefe's bike?" he asked.

Margarita nodded. "He got the town to pay for it, said it was for police work. But it's just his toy. You should see the fat fool trying to ride—" She stopped and turned to look at Luke. "Oh," she said. "Yes. I love it."

The Henderson rocked gently forward as Luke pushed at the handlebars. The stand folded up with a soft clunk as the tires took the weight and Luke began pushing the motorcycle across the moonlit plaza. Charm or no charm, he wasn't quite ready to actually fire the damn thing up right in front of the police station.

At the edge of town he stopped and bent to study the bike's layout. "You know what you're doing?" Margarita asked skeptically.

"Learned to ride one in the Corps," he said, fiddling with the gas cock and the choke, adjusting the spark advance. "Only that was a Harley and this is a Henderson—"

It took a good many kicks and he was starting to wish his grandfather had given him a medicine for starting balky engines, but then there came a sudden coughing roar and the Henderson began to vibrate under his hands. He dropped hit ass onto the saddle with a sigh of relief and Margarita climbed on behind him. "Get a good grip," he advised her. "This is about to get seriously bumpy."

The desert floor shone white in the Henderson's headlight as Luke gunned the heavy bike across the flat. Now and then there was a clump of cactus or brush to be dodged, and a couple of times the tires hit soft patches of sand and he almost lost it, but somehow he kept the motorcycle more or less upright and more or less on course. Behind him he could hear Margarita alternately laughing and cursing, her arms gripping his body tightly, her face pressed against his back.

Out in the empty land, beyond sight of the lights of the town—there was a faint reddish glow, if you knew where to look, that had to be the light from the burning house—he slid the Henderson to a sand-flying stop. "Here?" he asked.

"Yes," Margarita said, "please," so he held the bike steady while she got off and then he laid it carefully down, no use even trying to get the stand to hold in this soft sandy ground, and turned to see that she was already taking off her clothes. The moon was big and high and her skin shone in its light like Navajo silver.

"I imagine *you* two want to be *alone,*" Dwight observed, uncoiling from around Luke's leg. "Think I'll go see if I can find a nice gopher. I never *did* catch that tiresome rat."

"Hurry," Margarita said, stepping out of her skirt. "Holy Mary, that big hot thing jumping and shaking between my legs, I never felt anything like it in my life. I'm so wet, hurry please."

She began rubbing her bush with both hands, moaning excitedly, while Luke clawed at his own clothes. When he was naked she stretched out on the sand, beckoning to him. "Come on," she urged, raising her bottom and rolling her hips. "Get on top of me."

"No." Luke dropped to his knees beside her. "This way."

He flipped her over and she said, "Oh, yes, like animals, that's good," and arranged herself on hands and knees as he knelt behind her. Holding his almost painful erection in one hand, twisting the other in her hair and pulling her head back, he mounted her. As his penis slid into her she made a low guttural sound and then, *"Empuje!"* and her hips slammed back to meet his thrust. "Like animals," she said again. "Yes, wait, let me try something—"

Just like that, she was a mountain lioness, twisting and squalling beneath him, her tail curving and jerking to one side,

while he dug at the ground with his hind paws and his own tail
thrashed in time with the violent jabs of his short barbed penis.
The scent of her maddened him and he raised his own voice in a
long yowling wail and bit at her furry pelt—

—and with a wrenching *snap* they were a wild mare and
her stallion, lunging and bucking, whinnying their shared
brainless ecstasy. His big square teeth nipped her neck; his long
forelegs straddled her sweating flanks—

—and *snap* and they were a couple of rutting timber
wolves, and he clasped her sleek body with his strong front legs
and stabbed at her with his long chisel-pointed member and
howled over her bristling back—

—but *snap* again and once more they were just a man
and a woman fucking on the ground. "I can't hold it," Margarita
panted. *"Ayudame, querido*, help me—"

"Right," Luke said in her ear, clutching her hips, keeping
himself deep inside her, forming the words in his mind and
wondering if he could really pull this off. "Just a second—"

And then, for a time, the snakes and jackrabbits and
burrowing owls were treated to the sight of a pair of enormous
snow-white buffalo coupling in the moonlight. Their hooves tore
and pounded the earth; their bellowing could have been heard
halfway to Mexico. Nothing like it had been seen in these parts
since the last time the big ice came south. Even the tortoises
woke up and waddled out to watch.

Luke's mind had shut down altogether; his whole
consciousness was now a single raging red lust, radiating from
the two melon-sized balls that hung between his great driving
hind legs. His belly pressed hard against her shaggy rump as he
rammed his huge shaft deep into her mighty vault. Horns
tossing, she braced herself to take his incredible weight—later
she said it was like being fucked by a hairy mountain—and
blared her joy to the night.

At the moment of earth-shaking climax (that was no
corny metaphor; they *did* make it shake, causing at least one
minor rockslide on the side of the nearest mesa) he threw back
his head and joined his roar to hers. Seconds later, still pumping
into her, he felt the shift beginning and tried to fight it, but the

buffalo brain just wasn't up to the job. "Shit!" he cried as they collapsed together onto the sand, humans again and right now a couple of pretty damn tired ones.

"Ay, " Margarita sighed beneath him. "That was good."

Too spent to reply, Luke lay on top of her, still in her, still emptying himself. When the last spurting spasm subsided he pulled out and rolled off and stretched out beside her. "Wham, bam," he offered, "and thank *you*, ma'am."

He wanted very badly to put his arms around her and go to sleep right there and then. But it wouldn't do; they weren't all that far from the town yet, and come morning El Jefe would be furiously following their all too easily followed trail— motorcycle tracks being, in this year of 1922, not exactly common in the New Mexico desert.

"Well," Luke said and got to his feet. That hurt; everything hurt. It had been a long time since he had done a major shape change and he had forgotten how sore you felt afterward. "We better get our clothes back on and get out of here. You see my shirt anywhere?"

Dwight came slithering out from a patch of prickly pear. "My," he said. "Quite *impressive,* one must admit."

He yawned, showing his fangs. A good-sized bulge now showed about halfway between his head and tail. "A young prairie dog of *no* breeding," he murmured, "but with a certain naive charm . . . of course," he went on, "normally one wouldn't dream of actually *watching*. But that little exhibition you two put on was hardly, well, *intimate*. I don't know if you noticed, but toward the end the jackrabbits were applauding."

A few minutes later, straddling the Henderson again— Dwight muttering, "God, I *hate* this thing!"—Luke looked back over his shoulder at Margarita. "Wonder if there's enough gas to make it to the next town."

"Only one way to find out," she told him. "Let's go, *Indio*."

He twisted the throttle grip and off they went, bumping and banging over the moon-pale flat, laughing like maniacs. Behind them a long rooster-tail plume of dust hung white in the air for a little while before settling softly back to the desert floor.

* * *

This one brings back some memories . . . I needed money, as usual. I heard that a certain editor was taking submissions for an anthology of erotic fantasy. Not exactly my bag, but I was ready to try anything. I strained my skull for a couple of days till finally I came up with an idea, and sat up late that night—the deadline was only a few days off—writing it up.

Which at the time was not such a simple matter; by then I did have a computer that someone had given me, but it was an ancient Sanyo that didn't even have a printer—I had to set up my typewriter (also an antique) next to the monitor and copy the text out manually.

But I got the story finished, and just as the sky was starting to get lighter in the east I went to save it—and the damned old Sanyo ATE THE LAST HALF.

I think I got pretty weird at that point. But I couldn't afford to wig out; I really really *needed the money. So I drank a great deal of coffee and cranked myself up with sweet pastries— I didn't dare go to sleep, I knew I'd lose it—and succeeded in reconstructing the text from memory.*

The editor turned the story down. Said it didn't have enough of a plot. Plot? In an erotic fantasy? Nobody ever tells me anything. . . .

I said shit repeatedly and stuck the typescript away— there was no point in even trying to unload a story like that on any of the usual suspects—until, years later, I published it myself in my first story collection.

Written July 2001
First published August 2002

Duce

Ritter rested his forearm across the steering wheel of the stolen taxi and looked at his watch. "Not long now," he said.

In the back seat Gruhn looked up from the submachine gun in his lap long enough to say, "If he isn't late."

He snapped the magazine into place with a sharp click. "He does not seem," he said, "to be a punctual person."

Ritter laughed softly. "When I was attached to the embassy here, we had a joke that he had made the trains run on time but no one had been able to make him do the same."

Gruhn made a derisive snorting sound. Ritter turned and looked back over the seat back. "Well," he said, "after all, from his viewpoint it's not necessarily a bad thing. Makes it harder," he grinned at Gruhn, "for certain people."

Gruhn snorted again. "He's not concerned about security. Just look at the fool, riding around in that open car."

"You're right about that. Even those two carloads of bodyguards—he's been known to play childish games, having his driver speed up and slow down, just to confuse them. He simply doesn't take the danger seriously. You see," Ritter said, "he believes his people love him."

"Even though several of them have tried to kill him."

Ritter spread his hands. "He is very good at believing what he wants to believe and ignoring unwelcome facts. Like most people, only more so . . . but yes," he said, "if he had any sense he'd save that beautiful Astura for parades, and get himself something with armor and bullet-proof glass. Like the Führer."

He rubbed his chin, which itched from two days without a chance to shave. He hated the dirty feeling of a stubbly face, though it did add a convincing touch to his appearance, especially behind the wheel of a taxi in this town.

"But then," he said, "if he had any sense we wouldn't have to be here doing this job, would we?"

Gruhn growled a wordless assent, nodding. He leaned back in the seat and looked at the big wooden-stocked Beretta submachine gun lying across his thighs. "Clumsy Italian piece of shit," he muttered. "I could do this better with my MP44."

"A weapon which will not even exist for several more years," Ritter pointed out. "We're creating enough of a paradox being here in our own short-lived flesh, without leaving something like that lying around afterwards."

He jerked a thumb at the red-painted cylinders lying on the seat beside Gruhn. "Besides, the grenades are going to be your main weapon. And I know," he added quickly, "you'd rather have a couple of *Stielhandgranaten*, but the Breda is a perfectly good grenade and there are damned good reasons it won't do to leave anything pointing to the Reich. As you know."

Gruhn raised a finger and an eyebrow. "*Jawohl,*" he said dryly, "*Herr Sturmbannführer.*"

Ritter turned back around without saying anything more. Let it go. It was all nonsense anyway; Gruhn was an expert killer with any sort of weapons or for that matter none. Griping was just his way of dealing with the strain of waiting. Ritter couldn't really blame him; his own nerves were tight as the high strings on a piano.

Of course they were both on edge from fatigue; it had not been an easy couple of days. Almost immediately on arrival it had become obvious that the original plan was, for various reasons, utterly impossible. That wasn't catastrophic; it had been understood all along that they might have to improvise—all Skorzeny's men were trained to do that, to think on their feet and use whatever resources came to hand. But it hadn't been easy, all the same; it had taken time to study the possibilities and reconnoiter the area—Ritter knew the city streets fairly well, having been stationed here for two years before the war, but too much was at stake to trust to memory—and come up with a new plan.

And, in the meanwhile, to stay alive and at liberty in this city where there were no friends or allies and no safe places to go. Ritter spoke the language fluently, but not well enough to pass for a native, and Gruhn's heavily-accented Italian was worse. A couple of obvious foreigners checking into a hotel would almost certainly have drawn the attention of the very efficient secret police, who made a point of having informants in such places.

So they had spent the first night in a small public garden near the river, hiding under the bushes like American Indians in one of Karl May's books, taking turns sleeping. At least they could do that; they could sleep anywhere, after some of the places they had slept over the last few years.

Then last night they had hung out in a cheap and dimly-lit bar, keeping to themselves and speaking to no one, just a couple of unshaven men in rumpled dark suits with a battered leather bag on the floor between them, until it was time to go shopping—as Gruhn put it—for a car.

By the time they had finally got themselves a taxi, and then disposed of the driver's body, it was too late for worthwhile sleep, though Gruhn had napped a little in the back seat during the last hour before dawn. All in all it was no wonder they were snapping at each other like a couple of peevish old ladies.

Gruhn said, "All right, but I wish we had some help on this. You've got to admit our chances of success would be a lot better."

"True. And plenty of people in this city right now would gladly risk their lives to help us, if they knew what we intend.

But it's too risky," Ritter said. "These people inform on one another as enthusiastically as the Irish."

"*Scheisse,*" Gruhn said. "You think I meant Italians? What good would they be? I meant we need some more of our own people."

"Undoubtedly," Ritter agreed. "But it was not possible to send more. So said the good Doktor Niedermann, and who should know better the limits of his own machine?"

In fact, the old man had been frankly dubious about sending even two men. "It will tax the capacity of the projector to the limit," he said, shaking his head. "We will be lucky if it doesn't burn itself up on the first transmission, let alone sending a second. A third is not to be thought of."

And, looking even more worried: "Besides, the more men we send, the greater the paradox effect. As it is we may be about to bring the world to an end."

"The world is already about to end," Himmler told him. "The Russians are on the outskirts of Berlin. The Führer is virtually a prisoner in his own bunker. If there is a chance to save the Reich, it is worth any risk. If not, then the world is not worth preserving."

"Of course," Ritter said now, "we could go home and ask for help. Take the train up to Berlin, demand to see the Führer, lay it all out for him: '*Mein Führer,* we have come from five years in the future. Your friend and ally Benito Mussolini is about to have a very bad idea, which will lead him to do something very foolish. As a result, Germany will lose the war, the Red Army will overrun Berlin, and you yourself will either be killed or taken prisoner. Therefore we are here to assassinate Il Duce. Would you please lend us a few good men to make sure we get him? Yes, we were sure you would.'"

Gruhn was laughing, something he rarely did. "Yes, yes. I can picture this. Or perhaps," he said, "we could find ourselves and recruit ourselves to help. Since we now outrank ourselves—"

Ritter winced. "My God, Mannfried, don't make jokes about that. I don't even want to think about it."

Dr. Niedermann had been very emphatic: "If you succeed—"

"They will succeed," Himmler said sharply. "Have no doubt of that."

"If you succeed," Niedermann said again, not even looking at Himmler, "and if you survive, you may be tempted to try to make your way back to Germany. You must not, do you understand? The paradox effect, if you were to come in contact with your previous selves—"

"They know," Himmler said sharply. His face was slightly flushed; he was not accustomed to being ignored. Especially by elderly academics in shabby white jackets. "These men do not need you to tell them their duty. They understand the nature of the mission. They will do what is necessary." He looked at Ritter and Gruhn. "They are SS. They know how to die."

"So?" Dr. Niedermann didn't look particularly impressed. "No doubt they do. It is not, after all, an unusual skill. A great many people seem to be managing it these days."

Over by the door Skorzeny gave a massive rumbling chuckle.

Himmler's neck was fiery red by now, yet he said no more, only smiled a tight little smile. No doubt he was thinking of what awaited Dr. Niedermann once the transmission was done. There was no way the scientist could be allowed to live, not with the knowledge he carried in his head, not with the Russians practically on the doorstep.

"Well, then, gentlemen," Dr. Niedermann said, "who is to be first?"

"You realize," Gruhn said, "even now, if the Führer knew about this mission, our heads would roll. He still regards Mussolini as his friend."

Ritter turned around again and looked at him. "'Now'? I should think so, Gruhn. *Now,* why should the Führer be unhappy with Il Duce? *Now,* things are going rather well for Germany, and if the Italians have not been very useful allies—"

"All right, all right." Gruhn held up a hand. "He *will* remain loyal to Mussolini to the end. Skorzeny told me—will tell me? *Ficke!"* he cried impatiently. "There is no language for this. You know what I meant to say."

"Yes," Ritter said. "I know."

He turned back around and looked again at his watch and then reached for the starter. Better get the engine warmed up; it was a truism that Il Duce was often late but never early, but in this country all the rules had exceptions.

The starter motor whined and complained for a couple of seconds before the engine fired, shaking the cab briefly, and then settled down to a sluggish idle. "Roll down your windows," he told Gruhn, and began rolling down his own. "This thing probably has a leaky muffler. Carbon monoxide poisoning, just what we need now."

The old Fiat was a ridiculous car for a job like this, but it had the supreme virtue of inconspicuousness. A better, faster automobile, sitting on a side street just off Il Duce's morning route, might have drawn attention; but even the two policemen who had walked by, a few minutes ago, had given the parked taxi only a single uninterested glance.

Ritter could see them now, over on the far side of the little piazza, keeping an eye on the handful of people who stood waiting on the sidewalk. Out-of-towners, Ritter guessed, hoping for a look at the Great Man; he spotted a couple of small children clutching little flags and bouquets of flowers. On this side of the piazza, though, there was no one in sight except for a pair of hurrying figures, dressed in flowing black, coming up the street. A priest, he saw now, and a nun. Half the people in this country seemed to be in religious orders.

He said, "Any time now. Be ready."

"I am ready," Gruhn said a bit stiffly. "*You* be ready. Yours is the difficult part—"

A sudden sharp tapping sound made them both jump. Ritter jerked around and saw that the priest was rapping with his knuckles on the right front door. The nun stood beside him, holding a large basket.

"Signore," the priest said, "a little offering for the poor?"

"No." Ritter shook his head vigorously. "No."

"Please, signore." The priest gestured at the nun's basket. "To buy bread for the orphans?"

"No." Ritter wanted to scream but he kept his voice down. He shook his head again and made go-away motions. "*Se ne vada.*"

"How uncharitable," the priest said, and pulled out a large pistol and pointed it at Ritter, while the nun reached into her basket and produced a submachine gun of a make Ritter didn't recognize, with a long thick cylinder where the muzzle should be. "Keep still, my son," the priest told Ritter. "Hands on the wheel."

Gruhn said, "*Scheisse!*" and started to move. The nun raised her odd-looking weapon. There was no sound except the rapid clatter of the bolt, but Gruhn grunted sharply and slumped back onto the seat.

The priest was already yanking the door open and sliding in beside Ritter, keeping the pistol trained. Without taking his eyes off Ritter he said, "Is he dead?"

It took Ritter a second to realize that the last words had been in English.

The nun was getting into the back seat and closing the door. "I think so," she said, also in English. "Shall I make sure?"

"Not necessary." The priest's eyebrows went up suddenly. "*Scheisse*'?" he said. "Germans?"

Ritter nodded without thinking. The priest said, "How about that."

He was a big, broad-shouldered young man with dark curly hair and pale, rather delicate features. His hands were white and soft-looking, but he held the pistol in a solid competent grip, the muzzle dead steady. A .45 military automatic, Ritter saw, like the one he had taken off that American prisoner in the Ardennes before shooting him.

The priest, or whatever he was, said, "Speak English?"

"No."

"So? Ina, shoot him in the back of the head."

Ritter's shoulders hunched involuntarily. The priest laughed. "Ah, yes. Never mind, Ina. Good," he said. "My German is terrible."

Across the piazza, the people on the sidewalk were craning their necks and staring up the avenue. The policemen continued to watch them. Evidently no one had noticed anything.

"Well, well," the priest said. "German time travelers, here to assassinate Il Duce. But why? What's the point?"

"Go to hell."

"Oh, come now. The game's up. Satisfy my curiosity, where's the harm in that? Look here," the priest said, "let's do a swap. You tell me why you've come to kill Mussolini, and I'll tell you if your mission succeeded."

Ritter stared at him. "You too? I mean—from the future?"

"Of course. A somewhat more distant future than yours."

Ritter's disbelief must have shown on his face. The priest said, "Think about it. How else would we know about you, except that we got here the same way?"

And, after a pause to let Ritter consider it: "So tell me, have we got a deal? Don't you want to know what finally happened to your country?"

Why not? "Mussolini," Ritter said, "is about to destroy everything. In a few more days he will make the decision to invade Greece."

"Greece? Whatever for?"

Ritter shrugged. "No good reason. A childish attempt to impress the Führer, I think. Anyway, it will be a disaster. The Greeks will beat the Italians and throw them back, with the help of the British. The Führer," Ritter said, "will find it necessary to intervene, lest the British turn this into a new front on the southeastern flank of the Reich, within bombing range of the Rumanian oil fields.

"Next spring," Ritter said, "the Wehrmacht will come down through the Balkans and overrun Greece. Unfortunately the Yugoslavs choose this time to be impossible. The whole affair takes much longer than it should. The—" He paused, searching for the word. "The timetable is disrupted. The invasion of Russia has to be put off for a month. Winter arrives and catches us still out on the steppes, with Moscow not taken and the conquest not complete. It is a very, very bad winter."

"And?"

"And," Ritter said, "in time, because of this, we lose the war. When we . . . left, the Russian tanks were already in the suburbs of Berlin."

The priest's face was almost comical to see; his eyes stared and his mouth hung slightly open. "Incredible," he said after a moment. "And yet it must be true. Why else would the Third Reich make such a ridiculous use of their greatest scientific discovery? Why else would Mussolini matter so much?"

"It answers a lot of questions," the nun said. "Still pretty damned hard to believe, though."

"We're here," the priest pointed out. "What could be harder to believe than that?"

Ritter said, "Now you tell me your part. Did we succeed?"

"Oh, yes. Very much so." The priest gestured with his free hand in the direction of the main avenue. "In the time we come from, history records that on the morning of October 10, 1940, Benito Mussolini was assassinated on his way from his home to his offices at the Palazzo Venezia, by two men who suddenly drove past his bodyguards in a stolen taxi and threw grenades into the back of his car. The two assassins were immediately gunned down by Il Duce's bodyguards. They have never been identified."

The nun said, "That's what the history books say where *we* come from. In a very considerable part of the world you'll read that the great Mussolini was murdered by terrorists from the international Jewish-Bolshevik conspiracy."

It took Ritter a moment to analyze this. "We won?" he said dazedly.

"Oh, yes." Suddenly the man looked older; his shoulders sagged a little. "You won, all right. *How* you won. It took a few years, but after the defeat of Russia the outcome was never again in serious doubt."

"As of 1956," the woman said, "almost everything west of the Urals is ruled by the Reich or its allies. There are some Russian forces still at large in Siberia, but they do nothing but fight among themselves."

"I," Ritter said. "This, it—" His throat constricted; he struggled to speak. "England?" he asked.

"Still more or less free," the man said, "but neutralized. After half a dozen years of war, with no successes and the enemy still as strong as ever, the British people got tired of going hungry and doing without and seeing their men go off to get killed in Churchill's failed efforts. They turned the government out and the new PM let Berlin know he was ready to deal. They got pretty good terms, considering. Not even a German occupation, except for a couple of Luftwaffe bases. And a Gestapo liaison office in London, mostly to keep the press and the BBC in line."

He laughed suddenly. "What's funny, though," he said, "in view of what you just told us—you know the only country on the Continent that's kept its full independence? Greece. Seems Hitler rather admires them. Ancient warrior race, and all that."

"The Führer still lives?"

"Oh, yes. Alive and well, getting a little old but not perceptibly mellowing."

It was all too much to take in. Ritter said, "*Mein Gott.*"

"Your God, all right," the woman said. "Ours didn't come through for us so well. As usual."

The priest said something in a language Ritter didn't recognize, his voice sharp and angry. "Remember who you are," he added in English. "Even if you do look great in that super-*shikse* outfit."

A circuit closed in Ritter's mind. "*Juden?*"

"You were expecting maybe Ituri pygmies? Oh, I see, the outfits threw you off. Merely a useful disguise—after all, this *is* Rome. Religious types all over the place, many of them with foreign accents, nobody ever notices. Really, I'm surprised you didn't think of it.

Ritter was surprised too. It would have been perfect.

"Yes," the young man said, "I'm afraid your victory was a bit incomplete. You'll be disappointed to know that despite the best efforts of your countrymen and their friends, we haven't yet become extinct. Quite a few of us remain, especially in North America."

"Ah," Ritter said. "Americans."

"Geographically, yes. My colleague, behind you, is from Toronto. Her government would be most upset to know what she's doing. They've been at peace with the Reich for a long time now."

"Your government wouldn't be too happy either," the woman said.

"America is still neutral?" Ritter asked. "In, ah, your time?"

The young man made a disgusted snorting noise. He sounded almost like Gruhn. "The United States," he said, "is still officially at war with Germany, but only because nobody's been willing to take the political risk of signing a peace treaty. There hasn't been any major action for years. The Germans aren't up to mounting an invasion—Hitler never has had any enthusiasm for amphibious operations, you know that. And the Reich is just too damn big and powerful to screw around with, especially now with the Caspian oil fields and the Volga tank factories all at full production. Now and then somebody's ship gets torpedoed, or there's a spy trial, and the Führer and President MacArthur make a lot of chest-thumping speeches, but it's all bullshit."

Ritter was getting confused. "But you," he said, "I mean, you're here—"

"Oh, I get it. You thought we were on some kind of military mission? No, no," the man said. "Nothing like that. We represent . . . a consortium, you might say."

"Jews?"

Both of them laughed out loud. "That part really gets you, doesn't it?" the woman said.

"Actually," the man said, "the group we represent is fairly ecumenical in all senses of the word. But yes, I'm afraid there are a good many of us subhumans involved. Especially at the scientific end. You know," he said, "degenerate Jewish science and all that."

"Dr. Einstein did the original theoretical work," the woman added.

"Yes." The man's lips twitched downward. "Dr. Einstein hasn't been listened to very closely in official circles, since a little experiment based on his theories somehow turned most of the University of Chicago campus into a large smoking crater. Luckily there were others, in what you might call the private sector, who still appreciated the good Doctor's ideas."

Ritter had never heard of Einstein, but he didn't say so. He said, "Then you didn't use Dr. Niedermann's invention?"

"Niedermann? Can't say I've heard of him," the man said. "He was the one who made the breakthrough in your own time?"

"Yes."

"And you did say you were losing the war when you left. So I'm guessing this was a last-minute thing, developed under the pressure of desperation?"

Ritter nodded. "Well, there you are, then," the man said. "If Germany went on to win the war by conventional means—thanks to your own heroic efforts here today—then there wouldn't have been any particular need for bizarre research projects. Most likely your Dr. Niedermann would have been dismissed as a crank."

True enough, Ritter reflected. In fact Niedermann had been in serious trouble, as being politically unreliable, and had only been saved from arrest by Himmler's sudden obsession with bizarre scientific—and not so scientific—secret projects.

"The original idea," the woman said, "was to send a team back to kill Hitler. There was a lot of debate about that, Dr. Einstein didn't like the idea of deliberate assassination at all, but nobody could suggest a better use for the device. Then, while the equipment was being calibrated, some anomalies turned up in the field. Eventually it was determined that someone in the past had already made such a transit."

"Which," the man said dryly, "came as a considerable shock. Especially when the details became clear. Two men leaving northern Germany on April 28, 1945? And materializing in Rome on this particular day in 1940? No one could imagine what the connection might be, yet obviously it must be something of supreme importance to cause the Reich to play its last hole card."

He made a little gesture with his free hand. "And so here we are. It was a great gamble sending us—oh, you should have heard the arguments, white-haired scientists and distinguished scholars screaming at each other like drunk truck drivers, this came so close to never happening and frankly even when I stepped into the accelerator I was more than half convinced the whole thing was insane—but they were right. Here we are and here you are, about to change the world, about to save the fortunes of the Third Reich, the most important assassination since the Archduke Ferdinand."

Ritter only half heard the last words. "We won," he said again, almost whispering. "Will win."

"Absolutely. Only of course," the man said, "you won't, now. Because you aren't going to kill Mussolini after all, now we're here. One temporal rearrangement cancels another. Fascinating, huh?"

Ritter's peripheral vision registered movement. He looked past the young man's face, out through the open window of the cab and across the little piazza, where the group of onlookers had begun to move excitedly forward. One of the policemen stood at the curb, hands up, motioning them back. The other was staring up the street, shading his eyes with one hand.

The bogus priest raised his big pistol slightly. "Shall I kill you?" he said. His voice was casual; he might have been offering Ritter a smoke. "I don't suppose it matters, really. I'm sure you're on a suicide mission. They'd hardly risk letting you hang around back here afterwards, not with what you know—not to mention the paradox factor. If you've got a poison capsule or something that you want to use, go ahead. Or would you prefer I shoot you?"

"If you fire that thing," Ritter said, "you'll never get away."

"But I'll never get away anyway," the man said cheerfully. "Don't you get it? As soon as I kill you, that's it for your mission. The future changes back to what it was, and therefore I'm not here. Neither of us will be here."

He leaned back, smiling at Ritter. "You see, we're both the children of refugees from Nazi Europe. Ina's father got out of Spain a week before Franco knuckled under to Hitler and started shipping Spanish Jews off to the camps. He met her mother on the boat to New York. My parents were both born here in Italy, but they met in a refugee camp in Illinois. So," he said, "once your mission fails, we no longer exist. Because we never will."

"I wonder what it's going to feel like, winking out like that," the woman said. "If there's any feeling at all. It should be an interesting experience."

Down at the corner, another pair of *carabinieri* had appeared and were taking up station in the middle of the side street, ready to block any traffic from the avenue until Il Duce had passed.

The young man said, "It appears that the great one approaches. Okay, then—"

Suddenly there was a commotion in the back seat, a muffled cry from the woman and the rattle of the silenced machine pistol. The man beside Ritter started to turn, but then Gruhn came lunging across the seat back, grabbing the big .45 in both hands and forcing it downwards. "Go," he yelled to Ritter. His face was covered with blood. "I got the Jew bitch."

Ritter was already reaching for the gearshift. "Hurry," Gruhn said, struggling to hold the pistol down against the seat. "We can still—"

The young man hit Gruhn on the back of the neck with the edge of his free hand. Gruhn went limp, sagging across the seat back. Ritter had the car in gear and moving by now, accelerating hard down the narrow street. The two carabinieri turned and held up their hands and then, seeing the taxi wasn't stopping, started to unsling their weapons.

Beside him, the young man was having trouble getting his gun free from Gruhn's unconscious grasp. Ritter clenched his teeth and kept going, flooring the gas pedal, thinking there was no chance at all but you had to try. Maybe ram Mussolini's car—

The young man said, "What the hell," and let go the gun and reached over and gave the wheel a sharp yank. Caught by surprise, Ritter tried to straighten out again but it was too late. The taxi bucked violently as the front wheels banged up over the curb. The marble facade of an office building appeared over the hood.

Just before the impact Ritter heard the young man say, "Heil Hitler, motherfucker."

Benito Mussolini said, "Why have we stopped?"

It was the fourth time he had said it in the last few minutes. He was shifting restlessly, irritably, in the back seat of the big black Lancia Astura, looking this way and that.

In the front seat Ercole Boratto, his long-time chauffeur, said once again, "I don't know, Duce."

Mussolini craned his neck, trying to see past the car that blocked the street just ahead. A couple of his bodyguards stood beside it, weapons at the ready. The others had already fanned out and disappeared up the street. Another car like it sat a little way behind the Astura.

"I can't see a thing," Mussolini said peevishly.

Boratto turned and glanced back at him. "Duce, I really wish you'd get down until we know what's happening. With respect, you are very exposed."

"That would be a fine thing, wouldn't it? What an inspiring leader I'd be, groveling on the floor of my own car in fear of some imaginary assassins."

Boratto sighed and went back to watching the street, keeping his hand on the pistol on his lap.

"Aha," Mussolini said a few minutes later. The head of the bodyguard detachment had reappeared at last, walking back down the middle of the street. With him was an officer of the carabinieri. "Now," Mussolini said, "maybe we'll get some answers. Ercole, go find out what this nonsense is all about."

Boratto started to protest. Mussolini said gently, "Ercole, I gave you an order."

Looking very unhappy—Mussolini smothered a laugh—Boratto got out of the car, still holding his pistol, and walked up the street. Mussolini watched as he talked with the two men. By now more of the bodyguards were coming back.

When Boratto returned his face was a good deal clearer. "It seems to have been a false alarm, Duce," he reported, climbing back into the car. "An automobile wreck. A taxi crashed into a building."

"Oh, yes, our famous Roman taxis." Mussolini made a face. "The most dangerous machines known to man. Even our German friends have nothing so terrifying. I should send some of them to Africa to help Graziani. Was anyone injured?"

"There seem to be two bodies in the car, Duce," Boratto said. "The police are still trying to pry the doors open. It's pretty badly smashed."

"Probably drunk," Mussolini said contemptuously. "Alcohol is a terrible thing, Ercole. As you know, I never drink it. A pledge I made to my dear wife, many years ago."

"Yes, Duce."

"Consider, Ercole," Mussolini went on. "Who are the two most powerful leaders in the world today? Chancellor Hitler and myself, of course. And neither of us drinks."

He leaned back in the seat, watching the bodyguards piling into their car. "Well, at least the boys got a little exercise. So silly, Ercole. I know my destiny," he said. "I will never be killed by bullets."

He flapped a hand. "Drive on, Ercole. *Andiamo.*"

I got the idea for this story from something Hitler said toward the end of the war. I would like to make it clear that I am not in the habit of getting my ideas from the late Reichschancellor.

Written June 2002
First published May 2003

Dry Bones

It was a hot summer day and I was sitting under the big tree down by the road, where we caught the bus when school was in, when Wendell Haney came up the road on his bike and told me somebody had found a skeleton in a cave down in Moonshine Hollow.

"No lie," he said. "My cousin Wilma Jean lives in town and she came by the house just now and told Mama about it."

I put down the Plastic Man comic book I had been reading. "You mean a human skeleton?" I said, not really believing it.

Wendell made this kind of impatient face. "Well, of *course* a human one," he said. "What did you *think?*"

He was a skinny kid with a big head and pop eyes like a frog and when he was excited about something, like now, he was pretty funny-looking. He was only a year younger than me, but I'd just turned thirteen last month and a twelve-year-old looked like a little kid now.

He said, "Gee, Ray, don't you want to go see? Everybody's down there, the sheriff and all."

Sure enough, when I looked off up the blacktop I saw there was a lot of dust hanging over the far end of Tobe Nelson's pasture, where the dirt road ran down toward Moonshine

Hollow. Somebody in a pickup truck was just turning in off the road.

I stood up. "I'll go get my bike," I told him. "Go on, I'll catch up with you."

I went back to the house, hoping Mama hadn't seen me talking to Wendell. She didn't like for me to have anything to do with him because she said his family was trashy. They lived down a dirt road a little way up the valley from us, in an old house that looked about ready to fall down, with a couple of old cars up on blocks in the front yard. Everybody knew his daddy was a drunk.

Mama was back in the kitchen, though—I could hear her through the window, singing along with Johnny Ray on the radio—and I got my bicycle from behind the house and rode off before she could ask me where I was going and probably tell me not to.

I caught up with Wendell about a quarter of the way across Tobe Nelson's pasture. That wasn't hard to do, with that rusty old thing he had to ride. When I came even with him I slowed down and we rode the rest of the way together.

It was a long way across the field with no shade anywhere along the road. Really it wasn't much more than a cow path, all bumpy and rutty and dusty, and I worked up a good sweat pedaling along in the sun. On the far side of the pasture the ground turned downhill, sloping down toward the creek, and we could ease off and coast the rest of the way. Now I could see a lot of cars and trucks parked all along the creek bank where the road ended.

At the bottom of the hill I stopped and got off and put the kickstand down and stood for a minute looking around, while Wendell leaned his bike against a tree. A good many people, men and women both, were standing around in the shade of the willows and the big sycamores, talking and looking off across the creek in the direction of Moonshine Hollow.

Moonshine Hollow was a strange place. It was a little like what they call a box canyon out west, only not as big. I guess you could call it a ravine. Anyway it ran back into the side of the ridge for maybe half a mile or so and then ended in this big round hole of a place with high rock cliffs all around, and a couple of waterfalls when it was wet season.

I'd been up in the hollow a few times, like all the kids around there. It was kind of creepy and I didn't much like it. The trees on top of the bluffs blocked out the sun so the light was dim and gloomy even on a sunny day. The ground was steep and rocky and it was hard to walk.

It wasn't easy even getting there, most of the year. First you had to get across the creek, which ran strong and fast through this stretch, especially in the spring. It was only about thirty or forty feet across but you'd have had to be crazy to try to swim it when the water was high. And that was just about the only way in there, unless you wanted to take the road up over the ridge and work your way down the bluffs. A few people had done that, or said they had.

In a dry summer, like now, it was no big deal because you could just walk across without even getting your feet wet. Except that right now Deputy Pritchard was standing in the middle of the dry creek bed and not letting anyone cross.

"Sheriff's orders," he was saying as I moved up to where I could see. "Nobody goes in there till he comes back."

There was a little stir as somebody came pushing through the crowd. Beside me Wendell said softly, "Uh oh," and a second later I saw why.

Wendell's daddy was tall and lean, with black hair and dark skin—he beat a man up pretty bad once, I heard, for asking him if he was part Indian—and mean-looking eyes. He stopped on the edge of the creek bank and stared at Deputy Pritchard. "Sheriff's orders, huh?" he said. "Who's he think he is?"

Deputy Pritchard looked back at him. "Thinks he's the sheriff, I expect," he said. "Like he did the last couple of times he locked you up."

Everything got quiet for a minute. Then, farther down the bank, Tobe Nelson spoke up. "What's he doing," he said, "asking the skeleton to vote for him?"

He was a fat bald-headed man with a high voice like a woman, always grinning and laughing and making jokes.

Everybody laughed now, even Wendell's daddy, and things felt easier. I heard Wendell let his breath out.

Somebody said, "There they are now."

Sheriff Cowan was coming through the trees on the far side of the creek, pushing limbs and brush out of his way. There was somebody behind him and at first I couldn't see who it was but then I said, "Hey, it's Mr. Donovan!"

"Well, *sure*," Wendell said, like I'd said something dumb. "He was the one who *found* it."

Mr. Donovan taught science at the junior high school in town. Everybody liked him even though his tests were pretty hard. He was big and husky like a football player and the girls all talked about how handsome he was. The boys looked up to him because he'd been in the Marines and won the Silver Star on Okinawa. I guess half the men around there had been in the service during the war—that was what we still called it, "the war," even though the fighting in Korea had been going on for almost a year now—but he was the only one I knew who had a medal.

I always enjoyed his class because he made it interesting, showing us things like rocks and plants and even live animals. Sometimes he let me help when he did experiments. When he saw I liked science he helped me pick out some books in the school library. He offered to loan me some science fiction magazines he had, but I had to tell him no because there would have been big trouble if Daddy had caught me reading them.

Sheriff Cowan climbed down the far bank of the creek and walked over to stand next to Deputy Pritchard. His face was red and sweaty and his khaki uniform was all wrinkled and dusty. He looked up and down the line of people standing on the creek bank. "I don't know what you all heard," he said, "and I don't know what you thought you were going to see, but you're not going to see anything here today."

A couple of people started to speak and he raised his hand. "No, just listen. I've examined the site, and it's obvious the remains are too old to come under my jurisdiction." He tilted his head at Mr. Donovan, who had come up beside him. "Mr.

Donovan, here, thinks the bones might be thousands of years old. Even I don't go back that far."

After the laughter stopped he said, "He says this could be an important discovery. So he's going to get in touch with some people he knows at the university, and have them come take a look. Meanwhile, since the site is on county land—"

"Is not," Wendell's daddy said in a loud voice. "That's our land, on that side of the creek. My family's. Always has been."

"No it isn't," Sheriff Cowan said. "It *used* to be your family's land, but the taxes weren't paid and finally the county took over the property. And nobody ever wanted to buy it."

"I guess not," Tobe Nelson said. "Just a lot of rocks and brush, not even any decent timber."

"I don't care," Wendell's daddy said. "It was ours and they taken it. It ain't right."

"That's so," Sheriff Cowan said. "It's not right that you managed to throw away everything your daddy worked so hard for, while your brother was off getting killed for his country. Just like it's not right that your own family have to do without because you'd rather stay higher than a Georgia pine than do an honest day's work. And now, Floyd Haney, you just shut up while I talk."

Wendell's daddy looked madder than ever but he shut up. "All right, then," Sheriff Cowan said, "as I was saying, since it's county property, I'm closing it to the public till further notice. Tobe, I want you to lock that gate up at the main road, and don't let anybody cross your land to come down here without checking with me first. Or with Mr. Donovan."

A man said, "You mean we can't even go look?"

"Yep," the sheriff said. "You hard of hearing?"

Mr. Donovan spoke up. "Actually there's not much to see. Just a hand and a little bit of the wrist, sticking out from under a pile of rocks and dirt, and even that's partly buried. We're just assuming that there's a whole skeleton under there somewhere."

"Not that any of you could find that cave," Sheriff Cowan said, "even if I let you try. I'd have walked right past it if he hadn't been there to show me."

He started waving his hands, then, at the crowd, like somebody shooing a flock of chickens. "Go on, now. Everybody go home or back to the pool hall or something. Nothing to see down here."

People started moving, heading toward their cars, talking among themselves and glancing back in the direction of Moonshine Hollow. Wendell's daddy was walking our way and Wendell sort of scooched down behind me, but he went right past us and climbed into his old pickup truck and drove away, throwing gravel and dirt as he went up the hill. When he was gone we went over and got our bikes, without speaking or looking at each other. There was a lot I wanted to talk about but I could tell Wendell wasn't in the mood.

"Lot of foolishness," Daddy said that evening over supper when I told him the story. "Going to have a bunch of damn fool scientists, now, poking around and spouting off a bunch of crap."

Daddy didn't like scientists because they believed in evolution. He used to ask me if Mr. Donovan was teaching evolution at the school. He said he could get him fired if he was.

He said, "I'm not surprised, though. There's a good many caves and holes up in that hollow. That's why they call it Moonshine Hollow, you know, the bootleggers used to hide their whiskey there during Prohibition. Could be some bootlegger's bones," he said, "that hid in there running from the law. Or maybe a runaway nigger back in slave times. Probably not even an Indian at all."

"Mr. Donovan says the bones are a lot older than that," I said, and Mama gave me a warning look. She didn't like for me to argue with Daddy about anything. She said it wasn't my place.

Daddy said, "Oh, that's a crock. Damn scientists know everything, to hear them tell it. I heard one on the radio telling how far it is to the moon." He snorted. "Guess he'd been there and measured it off."

Mama said, "Who wants pie?"

Later on, Mr. Donovan told me how he happened to find the skeleton.

He was hiking up in the hollow, looking for things he might be able to use in class next year. He was working his way along the foot of a bluff, where there were a lot of great big boulders that had fallen down from above, when he saw a snake of a kind he didn't recognize. Before he could get a good look it slipped in behind a boulder that rested against the rock of the bluff.

So Mr. Donovan went up to the boulder, and after walking around it and pushing aside some brush he found a gap between it and the bluff. He got out his flashlight from his pack and shone it into the hole, still looking for the snake, and saw what looked like a dark opening in the face of the rock. Without stopping to think about it, he squeezed himself through the gap to have a closer look.

"One of the dumbest things I've ever done," he told me. "You never, *never* go into a place like that alone. Don't tell the school board, Raymond, but I'm a real idiot sometimes."

Behind the boulder, sure enough, a hole led back into the rock. The opening was so low he had to bend over double and then get down on his hands and knees and crawl—"getting stupider by the minute," he said—but then it opened up and he found himself in a small cave.

The floor was covered with loose rock that he guessed had fallen from the ceiling. He squatted down and picked up a few pieces and looked at them by the light of his flashlight, hoping for fossils, but they were just plain old rock.

Then he turned over a big flat slab and saw the hand bones.

"It took a few seconds to register," he said. "The light was bad and the bones were still half buried, just barely exposed. I started to poke at them, and then I realized what I was looking at and yanked my fingers back. Then I just sat there for a little while, as the implications sank in."

I said, "How'd you know they were so old?"

"I didn't," he admitted. "Archaeology isn't my field, after all. But they sure as hell *looked* old, and if there was any chance they were then they needed to be protected. So maybe I bluffed the sheriff a little. But that's our secret, right?"

Mr. Donovan didn't waste any time and neither did his friends from the university. They showed up next Saturday afternoon.

"I'm just an ignorant old country boy," Tobe Nelson said, talking to a bunch of people in front of the church after service let out the next morning. "When that schoolteacher said some scientists were coming, I was expecting old men in beards and white coats, you know?"

He shook his head, grinning. "Then here come this nice-looking young couple driving up in front of my house in a brand-new bright red Mercury, with a little house trailer hitched on behind. I took them for tourists that had lost their way, till they got out and came up and introduced theirselves and wanted to know if they could set up camp down by the creek."

Daddy said, "You let those fools onto your land?"

"Hey," Tobe Nelson said, "they asked me real nice, and they paid me some good money. The nice part would have been enough, but I sure didn't turn down the money either."

He laughed his high-pitched laugh. "But I tell you what, if I was young and I had me a car like that and a woman like that, you wouldn't see me spending my time digging up a bunch of old bones. I could think of a *lot* better things to do."

It stayed hot and dry. Wednesday afternoon I rode my bike down toward the little crossroads store to get myself a soda pop. On the way, though, I stopped by Tobe Nelson's pasture gate and got off and stood for a while leaning on the fence and looking off down the trail toward Moonshine Hollow. The gate wasn't locked now and I could have gone on in but I was pretty sure I wasn't supposed to.

Then I heard somebody pull up behind me, and when I turned around there was Mr. Donovan, sitting behind the wheel of the war surplus jeep he drove. "Hey, Raymond!" he called. "Be a buddy and open the gate for me, will you?"

I went over and undid the latch and swung the big gate open and held it back while he drove through, and then closed it and pushed until the latch snapped shut. "Thanks," Mr. Donovan said, stopping the jeep. "So what have you been doing with your summer, Raymond? Anything interesting?"

"Not really," I said. "Too hot to do very much."

"I heard that. Say," he said, "how would you like to meet a couple of real scientists?"

Would I? I said, "Sure," and he got out and picked up my bike and tossed it in the back of the jeep while I got in, and off we went. That was when he told me about how he found the cave, while we were bumping across Tobe Nelson's pasture.

Pretty soon we were rolling down the hill toward the creek. Even before we got to the bottom I saw the red car parked near the creek bank and, just beyond, a shiny bare-metal trailer.

Mr. Donovan stopped the jeep in the shade of a big tree and we got out and walked toward the trailer, which I saw now had a big canvas awning coming off one side, with a table and some chairs underneath. A man got up from the table and came toward us. "David," Mr. Donovan called. "Working hard, I see."

"To the verge of exhaustion," the man said, and turned his head and yelled back over his shoulder, "Maddy! Bob's here!"

The trailer door opened and a woman came out. "Oh, hi," she said, and then, looking at me, "And who's this?"

"This is Raymond," Mr. Donovan said, "one of my best students. Raymond, meet David and Madeleine Sloane."

The man stuck out his hand and I took it. The woman came trotting over from the trailer and put out her hand too. "So," she said, "you like science, Raymond?"

"Yes, ma'am," I said, and she threw her head back and laughed.

"'Ma'am,'" she said, "my God, you make me sound like your grandmother. Call me Maddy. Everybody does."

"Come sit down in the shade," the man said. "We're just taking a little break."

He was a medium-sized young man with blond crewcut hair and glasses. That was about all I noticed. He wasn't the one I was looking at.

The woman said, "Well, Raymond, would you like a Coke?"

She was the prettiest lady I'd ever seen outside of the movies. She was taller than me and I'd hit five feet five right before my birthday. She had light brown hair, cut off short at the nape of her neck, and dark blue eyes and nice white teeth.

She was wearing a red top thing with no sleeves, tied up so her stomach was showing, and shorts that I saw were blue jeans with the legs cut off. Whoever cut them off hadn't left much. Her legs were tanned and they just went on and on.

I said, "Yes, ma'am. Uh, Maddy."

"Bob? Anything for you?" He shook his head and she went back to the trailer.

We went over and sat down at the table under the awning. I noticed there was a noise coming from somewhere nearby, like a power lawnmower, but I couldn't see where it was coming from. "Generator," David Sloane said, seeing me looking around. "You know, for electricity."

"Quite a fancy setup you've got here," Mr. Donovan said.

"Oh, yes," David said. "All the civilized comforts money can buy." His face got a little funny when he said that last part. "What a good thing some of us have it," he added, so low I could barely hear him, and he looked off toward the trailer just as Maddy came back out carrying a bottle of Coke.

"Did you want a glass and ice?" she asked me. I shook my head. "Good," she said. "I had you figured for a bottle man." She dragged up a chair and sat down. "Bob Donovan, I'm going to strangle you, bringing company around when I'm looking like this." I saw now there were some dusty smudges on her arms and legs. "Just look at me," she said. "Like a field hand."

"Been grubbing away?" Mr. Donovan said, grinning. "How's it going?"

"Slowly," David said. "As it's supposed to."

"It's quite a process," Mr. Donovan said to me. "The earth's got to be removed very gradually, just a little bit at a time, so as not to damage whatever's underneath. And everything's got to be measured and recorded. Takes a lot of patience and steady hands."

"Actually," Maddy said, "we're still working through that pile of loose rock from the ceiling fall. And having to examine every bit of it too, in case—" She stopped and looked at David. "Show them the point, why don't you?"

David started to say something, but then he grunted and got up and headed for the trailer. "Wait till you see this," Maddy said. I sipped my Coke and tried not to stare at her. Around our part of the state you didn't see very many grown women in shorts, because most of the churches said it was a sin. My Uncle Miles, who was the pastor of the Baptist church where we belonged, even said they weren't supposed to wear their hair bobbed short.

Just about the only women you saw dressed the way Maddy Sloane was right now were the trashy ones who hung around the pool hall in town, or the honky-tonks out at the county line. But it was easy to see that this one wasn't trashy at all.

David came back carrying a little flat wooden box and set it down on the table in front of me. He opened it and pulled back some cotton and said, "There. Look what we found this morning."

I tried not to look disappointed. I'd seen Indian arrowheads before, who hadn't? People were always finding them along the creek banks, or turning them up plowing. A couple of the boys at school had regular collections.

Now I looked closer, though, this one didn't look like any arrowhead I'd seen. It was sure a beauty, made of some kind of shiny yellowish-brown stone with dark bands running through it, and really well made. It was pretty big, maybe three inches long, and it didn't have the usual notches on the sides, just one big notch at the bottom. There was a kind of groove going up the middle.

Mr. Donovan said, "I'll be damned. Clovis?"

"I'd bet on it," David said. "And I saw enough of them last year, on that dig in New Mexico."

I said, "Do you know what kind of Indians made this kind of arrowhead?"

"Not Indians. At least not the kind you're thinking about. More like their prehistoric ancestors."

"And it's a spearhead," Maddy said. "Bows and arrows hadn't been invented yet."

"Wow." I ran my finger over the smooth stone. "Old, huh?"

David nodded. "Just how old, well, there's still some pretty hot arguing going on. Well over ten thousand years, though."

"To give you an idea," Mr. Donovan said to me, "that thing was very likely made to hunt mammoths with."

"Wow," I said again. "But you don't really know if it goes with the skeleton, do you?"

They all looked at each other. "Damn," Maddy said. "You're right, Bob, this one's sharp."

"That's right," David told me. "No guarantee the skeleton's from the same time period. Not even safe to guess yet."

"Still nothing on that?" Mr. Donovan asked.

David shrugged. "It's damned old, all right. Just from a superficial examination of the exposed bones, I'm nearly sure there's some degree of fossilization. But so far there's nothing to date it." He sighed. "Best would be the new radiocarbon test, that Dr. Libby's been working on up at the University of Chicago. But half the archaeologists in the country are waiting in line for that. Could be a long time before we have an answer."

"But," Maddy said, "now you see why we're excited about this site. It could be really important."

David stood up and stretched. "And so we need to get back to work. Sorry."

He picked up the box and closed it carefully. I saw that there were some numbers marked on the lid. As he carried it back to the trailer Maddy said, "Raymond, it was great meeting you." She reached over and put her hand on my shoulder. "Come back and see us again some time, won't you?"

"Sure." My voice didn't come out quite right. "I will."

But as it turned out I didn't see the Sloanes again for quite a while. I rode down there several times over the next few days, but there was never any sign of them, just the trailer sitting there and the generator running. I guessed they were up at the cave, working, and I thought about going up the hollow and trying to find them but I didn't know the way.

By now everybody was talking about them. Especially about Maddy. "Parades around practically naked," my Aunt Ethel, who worked at the Ben Franklin five-and-dime store in town, said to Mama. "She was in the store yesterday. Looked like a you-know-what."

Uncle Miles even worked them into his sermon the next Sunday. "I'm reminded," he said, "of the old colored spiritual, 'Them bones, them bones, them dry bones, now hear the word of the Lord.' Some people need to quit worrying about a lot of dry bones and start hearing the word of the Lord."

Next morning I woke up with a head cold. It wasn't all that bad, but it was enough for Mama to keep me in bed for a couple of days and indoors for the rest of the week. I spent the time reading and listening to the radio and mostly being bored and wishing I could go see David and Maddy again.

Daddy came in from town one evening with a big grin on his face. "That schoolteacher of yours," he said to me, "I got to say one thing for him, he's no sissy."

"What happened?" I asked, and Daddy laughed.

"Damnedest thing," he said. "Floyd Haney came up to him in front of the diner, drunk as a skunk as usual, and started cussing him out—still going on about that land across the creek—and when the schoolteacher tried to walk past him Floyd took a swing at him. Next thing you know Floyd was flat on his ass. I saw the whole thing from across the street."

"Mr. Donovan hit him?"

"Fastest left I ever saw. Deputy Pritchard drove up while Floyd was still laying there, but the schoolteacher said he didn't want to press charges. Probably right," Daddy said. "It never does no good, locking Floyd's kind up. Some folks are just the way they are."

Finally I got to feeling better and Mama let me out of the house again. Naturally I took off right away for the creek.

Mr. Donovan's jeep was sitting there when I came down the hill, and as I stopped the bike I saw they were all three up by the trailer sitting under the awning. As I walked toward them I could hear Maddy talking, sounding angry.

"I don't believe this," she was saying. "The most important discovery of the century, and you're acting as if it's a bomb that's going to explode in your face."

"It is," David said. "Oh, sure, maybe not for you. Your tight little rich-bitch ass isn't the one on the line, is it? Nobody pays any attention to graduate students." His voice was getting louder. "I'm the poor son of a bitch with the ink still fresh on his doctorate. If I blow this I'll be lucky to get a job at City College of Rooster Poot, Arkansas."

They looked up and saw me, then, and they got all quiet and embarrassed-looking, the way grown people do when kids catch them quarreling. After a second Maddy said, "Why, hello, Raymond."

I said, "Maybe I ought to go?"

"No, no." Maddy waved her hands. "I bet you'd like a Coke, wouldn't you? Why don't you just go help yourself? The box is just inside the door, you can't miss it."

I went over to the trailer and climbed up the little steps and opened the door. Sure enough, there was a refrigerator, the littlest one I'd ever seen, just inside. I could see up into the front part of the trailer, which was mostly taken up by a bed that needed making. I got myself a Coke and went back out just as Mr. Donovan was saying, "Anyway, I hope these are all right."

I saw now that there was a big yellow envelope on the table and a couple of stacks of big glossy photographs. David was holding a picture up and looking at it from different angles. "Oh, yes," he said, "this is really first-class work. Thanks, Bob."

"Been a while since I've done any darkroom work," Mr. Donovan said. "Took a couple of hours just to dig out my old equipment and get it dusted off. Glad the prints turned out okay."

I walked over and looked at the photos while they talked. One of the ones on top was a close-up shot of a skull, half buried in the ground. Another one looked like a full-length view of the whole skeleton. I picked that one up for a closer look and then I saw something that didn't make any sense at all.

"Hey," I said. "He's wearing clothes!"

They all turned and stared at me. I said, "If the skeleton's as old as you said, wouldn't they have rotted away by now?"

"Oh, shit," David said, and reached over and snatched the picture out of my hand. "Bob, why'd you have to bring—"

"Shut up, David," Maddy said. "Raymond, come here."

I walked around the table and stood in front of her. She took both my hands in hers and looked right into my face. "Raymond," she said, "you wouldn't do anything to hurt us, would you?"

"No, ma'am," I said. My throat had tightened up till I could barely talk. "No, Maddy."

"And if you knew something that could cause trouble for us, you wouldn't tell? I don't mean anything bad or illegal," she said quickly. "Just something that could make a lot of trouble."

"No." I didn't know what she was talking about but I would have agreed with anything she said.

"Then come on," she said, standing up and picking up a big battery lantern that was sitting on the table. "There's something I want to show you."

David stood up too, fast. "You will like hell."

"Don't be stupid, David," Maddy said without looking at him. "And for once in your life try trusting someone."

"Raymond's a smart boy," Mr. Donovan said. "He'll cooperate, once he understands."

"Oh, all right," David said, throwing up his hands, "why not? Hell, let's hold a press conference. Call the White House, invite Truman for a look. Bring in the damn United *Nations*."

"Watch your step," Maddy said as we started across the dry creek bed.

It was a long hard walk up the hollow to the cave, and hot even in the deep shade under the trees. By the time we got there I was wishing I'd brought the rest of that Coke along.

About halfway up the hollow Maddy turned left and started up a steep slope, covered with big loose rocks, to the foot of the bluff. "Here," she said, and I saw what Sheriff Cowan had meant. If I hadn't known there was a cave there I'd never have guessed.

"It's a little rough getting through the brush," she said, "but we didn't want to advertise the location by clearing it away."

She walked around to the side of a gray boulder, big as a good-sized car, that rested against the face of the bluff. She switched on the battery lantern and pushed aside some bushes and disappeared behind the boulder.

"You know," Mr. Donovan said as we started after her, "I believe this must have been sealed off until recently. Look at all that loose rock and earth down below. There's been a slide, not too long ago. Maybe that last big rainstorm in May set it off."

"You could be right," David said. "There's hardly any animal sign in the cave."

I pushed through the brush and found myself in a narrow little space, dark except for the light that was coming from off to my right. "You'll have to get down and crawl a little way," Maddy called back. "It's not too bad."

It was as far as I was concerned. The light from up ahead helped, but it was still a scary place, and going through the tightest part I could feel the whole world pressing in on me. The air was cold, too, with a creepy dead smell. I wanted to yell but I choked it down because I didn't want Maddy to think I was a coward. Then the hole got bigger and the light got brighter and there I was in the cave.

"Sorry about the light," Maddy said as I straightened up. "We usually use carbide lamps, which are brighter. But they're a pain to get started and I don't feel like fooling with it."

It wasn't a fancy cave like the ones in the books, with stalactites and all. It was just a kind of room, about the size of a one-car garage. It looked even smaller because of all the stuff stacked and piled over by the walls—shovels and trowels, big round screen-wire dirt sifters, boxes and bags and a lot of things I didn't recognize.

In the middle of the floor a space had been marked off with wooden pegs and lengths of twine. Inside that the ground had been dug or scraped down for a foot or so, and in the dug-out space lay the skeleton.

It didn't look much like the ones in the Halloween decorations. It looked more like a bundle of loose sticks, till you got a good look. It lay on its left side with its knees drawn up part way, and its left arm flung out straight. The right hand was out of sight up near its chest.

And sure enough, it was wearing clothes, and they didn't look like Indian clothes to me. It was hard to be sure, but it looked more like some kind of one-piece outfit, like the coveralls my cousin Larry wore when he worked at the Texaco station in town. Maddy held the light up higher and now I saw it had on shoes, too. Or rather boots, with big heavy-looking soles. Actually I could only see one, because the left foot was still buried.

After a minute I said, "I don't get it."

David said, "Welcome to the club, kid."

"Don't feel bad," Maddy said. "Neither does anyone else."

David went around and squatted down by the hole and reached down and touched the right sleeve. "You asked a good question, back there," he said. "Fabric should have rotted away a long time ago, but just look at this stuff. Oh, it's deteriorated badly, it's brittle and flimsy, but it's still in a hell of a lot better condition than it should be. Than it *can* be."

"But then," I said, thinking I got it now, "it must not be as old as you thought. Must be, uh, modern."

David nodded. "That would be the logical conclusion. The condition of the bones, the partial fossilization, well, there might be some other explanation, chemicals in the soil or something. The Clovis point you saw could have been here long before this guy arrived. But there's just one other thing."

He moved a little to one side and motioned to me. "Come look at this."

I went over and hunkered down beside him, though I didn't really want to get any closer to that skeleton. He said, "Hold that light closer, Maddy. Look here, Raymond."

He was pointing at a big long rip in the material covering the right shoulder. He pushed the cloth aside with his fingertips. "See that?"

I saw it. I'd seen one like it a couple of weeks ago, lying on a bed of cotton in a little box on the table by the creek.

"And so," David said, "what we have here is a man in modern clothes with a ten-thousand-year-old Clovis point embedded in his shoulder. Which, of course, is flatly impossible."

"Modern is right," Maddy said. "I cut a tiny little piece from the cuff and studied it under the microscope, and it's not any natural fiber. In fact it's not exactly woven fiber at all, it's more—I don't know what the hell it is, that's the truth, I've never seen anything like it and textiles are a specialty of mine."

"The boots are synthetic too," David said. "And the fasteners are some kind of hard plastic."

I thought it over for a minute. "But that's—" I remembered, then, a story in a science fiction magazine I'd had, before Daddy took it away from me and told me he'd whip me if he ever caught me reading that crap again.

I said, "You think he was a time traveler."

"Did I say that?" David made a big show of looking around. "I didn't hear anybody say that, did you?"

"Now you see," Maddy said, "why we're having to keep this secret for now. David's got to be careful how he handles this, because a lot of people are sure to call it a fake. It could destroy his career."

There was something sticking out of the ground just behind the skeleton's lower back, a dark object about the size of a kid's book satchel. Or that was my guess, though you really couldn't see much of it. I said, "What's this?"

"Once again," David said, "I'm damned if I know. Looks like some kind of pack he was carrying, but what's in it I couldn't tell you. Maybe his lunch, maybe his spare socks, maybe something we wouldn't even recognize."

"Like," Maddy said, "whatever got him here. From wherever—whenever—he came from."

"I didn't hear that either," David said. "Anyway I haven't looked inside and I'm not going to. Not even going to dig it out so it *can* be opened. If and when it gets opened, it's going to be by somebody of absolutely impeccable professional standing, with a bunch of other respected paragons on hand for witnesses."

"Have you got anyone yet?" Mr. Donovan asked.

David shook his head. "Everybody's out on digs right now. Most of all I want Dr. Hoban of the University of Pennsylvania, but he's in Iraq for the rest of the summer."

"That old bastard," Maddy said. "You know damn well he'll steal all the credit for himself."

"I wish I had your optimism," David said. "More likely he'll denounce the whole thing as a fraud and me as a lunatic or worse."

"Of course," Mr. Donovan said, "if the government gets wind of this, and somebody thinks there might be something in that pack with possible military applications—"

"Oh, my God," David said. He put his hands up to his face. "I hadn't even thought of that. Marvelous."

I was looking at the skull. It wasn't "grinning", as they say. The jaws were open and it look like it was screaming in pain. I shivered. It really was cold in there.

I said, "It was the spear that killed him, wasn't it?"

"Looks that way," Maddy said. "Looks as if he dragged himself in here—maybe for shelter, maybe trying to hide—and simply bled to death. That's got to have been a terrible wound."

"Wonder what happened," Mr. Donovan said. "To cause them to kill him, I mean."

"Maybe he broke some local taboo," Maddy said. "We found a few small objects, that apparently fell out of his pockets—another point like that one you saw, a bone scraping tool, a kind of awl made from deer horn. Evidently he was doing some collecting. Maybe he picked up something he shouldn't."

"Or maybe they just killed him because he was a stranger." David looked down at the skeleton. "Poor bastard, you sure wound up a long way from home, didn't you?"

"How'd he get buried?" I asked.

"Flooding," Maddy said. "Silt and sand washing in. This cave's been flooded several times in the distant past."

"The floor of the hollow would have been a lot higher back then," Mr. Donovan added. "Say, that's another possible dating clue, isn't it?"

"Maybe." David shrugged. "When you get right down to it, the date doesn't really matter now. If this burial is even a hundred years old, we're looking at the impossible. Christ, *fifty*."

He stood up. "Come on. Raymond's seen enough. Probably wondering by now if we're crazy or he is."

By the time I got home it was nearly supper time. Daddy came in a little bit later, while I was sitting on the couch in the living room trying to think, and right away he said, "Raymond, you been hanging around with them college people, down at the creek? Don't lie to me," he added before I could answer. "Two different people said they saw you on your bicycle headed that way."

I said, "Tobe Nelson said it was all right, Daddy. I asked him and he said it was all right, long as I close the gate."

"That's *Mister* Nelson to you," Mama said from the doorway.

Daddy said, "I don't care if General MacArthur told you it was all right for you to go down there. I'm the one says what you can and can't do, and I'm telling you to stay away from them people. I don't want you having nothing to do with them and I don't want you going down there as long as they're there."

I said, "Why?"

"Because I say so," he said, starting to get red in the face, "and you're not so big I can't still whip your ass if you don't mind me." I started to speak and he said, "Or I can do it right now if you keep talking back."

So I didn't say any more. I wasn't really afraid of him— he hadn't laid a hand on me since I was six, he just liked to talk tough—but I knew he'd get all mad and stomp and holler around, and Mama would start crying, and I didn't feel like going through all that right now. I had enough on my mind.

I did stay away, though, for the next couple of days. I figured David and Maddy didn't need me coming around, with all they had to do and think about.

Wednesday I decided to go into town to the library and see if they had some books about archaeology. I told Mama where I was going and she said, "You're not going down to the creek, are you, to see those people? You know what your daddy said."

"Just to the library," I said. "Promise."

"You be careful, then," she said. "I don't really like you riding that thing down the road."

It was only a couple of miles into town but the weather was still hot, so by the time I got there I was pretty sweaty. Going by the Texaco station I slowed down, thinking about getting me a cold drink, and then I saw the red Mercury parked out front.

David Sloane came out of the side door as I pulled up. "Raymond," he said, raising a hand. He looked at my bike and said, "Hm. You get around pretty well on that bike, don't you? Wonder if you'd consider doing me a big favor."

He got out his wallet. "Five bucks," he said, "if you'll tell Maddy that I'm stuck in town with car trouble, and I'll probably be coming in pretty late."

I hesitated for a second. Daddy would be really mad if I went down there again. I was taking a big enough chance just standing here talking to David.

But I was too embarrassed to tell David about Daddy, and I really did want to see Maddy again. And if it came down to it I could say I was doing a Christian duty by helping someone. There wouldn't be much Daddy could say to that.

Besides, there was a lot I could do with five dollars. I said, "Sure," and took the five and stuck it in my pocket and off I went, back up the road, standing on the pedals to get up speed.

When I got down to the creek things looked funny, somehow, and then I realized it was because I was used to seeing the red car sitting there by the trailer. Mr. Donovan's jeep was there, though. Good, I thought, maybe he'd give me a ride back to town.

But I didn't see him or Maddy anywhere, so I figured they must be up at the cave. I leaned the bike on its stand and started toward the creek, but then I stopped and looked back at the trailer. I really was dry from riding in the hot sun, and I knew Maddy wouldn't mind if I got myself a nice cold Coke first.

The generator motor was rattling away as I walked toward the trailer. I went up the little metal steps and saw that the door wasn't quite shut. I pushed it open and started to go in, but then I caught something moving out of the corner of my eye and I turned my head and saw them on the bed.

Mr. Donovan was lying on top of Maddy. Her legs were sticking up in the air and they were both sort of thrashing around. Neither of them had any clothes on.

I stood there for a minute or so, standing on the top step with my head and shoulders inside the door, just staring with my mouth open. They didn't look around. I don't think they were noticing much just then.

Finally I got myself unstuck and jumped down off the steps and ran, up the creek bank, not really looking where I was going, just getting away from that trailer. I felt sick and angry and ashamed and yet kind of excited too. My skin felt hot and not just from the sun.

I mean, I knew about what they were doing. I was thirteen, after all. But it just didn't look at *all* like I'd imagined.

I got my bike and wobbled off up the road, nearly falling a couple of times. At the top of the hill I remembered David's message, and the five dollars. So now he was going to think I'd cheated him, but I couldn't help that. I wouldn't have gone back down there for all the money in the United States.

Saturday night I woke up in the middle of a dream about Maddy and the skeleton—I don't want to tell about it, it was pretty awful—and sat up in bed, listening, the way you do when you don't know what woke you. It seemed like I could hear the echo of a big loud boom, and then a rumbling sound dying away. In the next room Mama's voice said, "What was that?"

"Thunder," Daddy said. "Go back to sleep."

Next morning as we left for church, I saw a lot of dust hanging over the road across Tobe Nelson's pasture, and what looked like a police car heading toward the creek. The dust was still there when we came home, but I didn't see any more cars.

Late in the afternoon while we were sitting on the porch Sheriff Cowan came by. "Afternoon," he said to Daddy. "Wonder if I could ask your boy a couple of questions. Don't worry, he's not in any trouble," he added, smiling at Mama.

Daddy said, "Raymond, answer the sheriff's questions."

Sheriff Cowan sat down on the edge of the porch and looked up at me. "I understand you've been spending a lot of time down by the creek lately. Been friendly with those friends of Mr. Donovan's?"

"He was," Daddy said, not giving me a chance to answer. "That's over."

"That right?" Sheriff Cowan raised one eyebrow. "Well, then I'm probably wasting my time. You haven't been down there in the last couple of days?"

"No, sir," I said.

"Oh, well." He let out a big loud sigh. "So much for that. Sorry to bother you folks."

Daddy said, "Mind if I ask what this is about?"

Sheriff Cowan turned his head and looked off across the valley. "Night before last, somebody broke into Huckaby's Feed and Supply and stole half a case of dynamite. Last night they used it to blow up that cave."

I said, "*What?*" and Mama made little astonished noises. Daddy said, "Well, I'll be damned."

Sheriff Cowan nodded. "Yep, did a pretty thorough job, too. The whole bluff's all busted up and caved in, great big chunks of rock every which way."

He took off his hat and scratched his head. "Tell you the truth, I can't hardly believe somebody did that much damage with half a case of DuPont stump-blower. It's strange," he said. "Tobe Nelson claimed there were two explosions, too, a little one and then a big one, but nobody else heard it that way." He shrugged. "Maybe some kind of gas in the ground there? Who knows?"

Mama said, "My Lord. Who would do such a thing?"

"Oh," Sheriff Cowan said, "there's no doubt in my mind who did it. But I don't expect I'll ever prove it."

Daddy said, "Floyd Haney."

"Yep. Nobody else around here that crazy and mean," Sheriff Cowan said. "And he was sure nursing a grudge about that land."

He stood up and put his hat back on. "But like I say, I'll never prove it. I thought maybe Raymond might have seen or heard something, but I should have known that was too much to hope for."

He chuckled down deep in his throat. "You know the funny part? He had all that work and risk for nothing. Those two scientists already pulled out."

"They're gone?" I said, louder than I meant to.

"Yep," Sheriff Cowan said. "Drove right throught town, late yesterday afternoon, pulling that trailer. So they must have found out there wasn't anything important there after all. Probably just some old animal bones or something."

"Probably," Daddy said. "Bunch of foolishness."

And that's about all there is to tell. David and Maddy never came back, and nobody else ever tried to find that cave again. Not that it would have done them any good. I went up into Moonshine Hollow once, a long time later, and the whole place was smashed up so bad you couldn't even tell where you were.

Mr. Donovan left too, later on that summer. He went back into the Marines and I heard he got killed in Korea, but I don't really know.

Wendell's daddy got caught with a stolen truck, later on that year, and got sent off to the penitentiary, where everybody said he belonged. Sheriff Cowan never did charge him with blowing up the cave, but he didn't make any secret of believing he did it.

And maybe he was right, but I wasn't so sure. My cousin Larry was working the evening shift at the Texaco station when David and Maddy stopped for gas on their way out of town, and he said Maddy was crying and it looked like she'd been roughed up some. And Aunt Ethel mentioned to mama that David had been in the store on Saturday buying an alarm clock. But I never said anything to anybody.

People talked, for a while there, about that strange business in Moonshine Hollow. But it didn't last long. Everybody's mind was on the news from Korea, which was mostly bad, and then by next year all anybody wanted to talk about was the election. I guess by now I'm the only one who even remembers.

And sometimes I sure wish I didn't.

This is the one that got me my second Nebula nomination.

At the time I finished "Dry Bones" I felt sure that it was the best story I'd ever written. Now, I'm not so sure; "Words And Music" might top it, or "When This World Is All On Fire." The author is not the right one to be making these comparisons anyway.

One thing, though, I did know for certain: this was as good as I was ever going to get. That was a strange and difficult knowledge to deal with. It still is.

Written November 2002
First published February 2004

At Ten Wolf Lake

The wind was blowing down the lake from the west, not hard but enough to raise little waves that bounced the Beaver gently as I landed and taxied over to the company dock. Miles Tulugaq was standing on the end of the dock, next to the gas pump, holding a coil of rope. I sat there in the cockpit for a minute flipping off switches and going through the rest of the shutdown routine, and then I climbed out and stood on the port float and helped Miles with the mooring lines before climbing up the wooden ladder to join him.

"Everything OK?" he said, and I nodded and passed him the clipped-together paperwork. I raised my arms over my head and stretched, feeling the usual all-my-joints-but-one stiffness after sitting in that cockpit all morning and thinking as usual how one of these days I was going to find a company that flew something with a roomier cockpit and Alaskan Bush Charters could kiss my large hairy ass. "Boy," I said, "me for a hot tub and some beer."

"Sorry, Jack," Miles said, giving me a big wide Inuit grin. "Got another job lined up, I'm afraid. Levitt says tell you to grab something to eat and then get up to the office."

I groaned to myself. I'd been looking forward to a good rest. True, it was only the middle of the day, but the morning's flight had been a dynamite haul—a dozen cases of Du Pont for a mining outfit—and flying explosives always makes me nervous and leaves me wrung out afterwards.

But it was no good arguing about it. I already knew I was the only pilot available—we were running short-handed just then; Gomez was in the hospital in Anchorage after scattering pieces of a nearly-new Cessna all over a bay up the coast while trying to land in a fog. I said, "Not more dynamite?"

"Nah." Miles fell in beside me and we walked back along the dock. The weathered boards felt pleasantly rough under my soles.

"People, this time," he said. "Some kind of camping party, wants to go up to Ten Wolf Lake. That's all I know."

Well, at least they wouldn't explode. On the other hand dynamite doesn't get airsick. Or want to talk.

"How's the plane?" Miles asked. "Anything Manny needs to take a look at?"

"Everything's fine."

"Then you better go get yourself some lunch. Take your time," he said. "I've got to put the seats back in the plane, and stow their gear and top up the tanks."

He grinned at me again. "Let me know when you're ready to go meet the clients. I want to see this."

The clients were waiting in the office, standing bunched up over by the front windows looking out at the lake. There were four of them, two males and two females. They all appeared to be about the same age, definitely not young any more but not yet what you'd call middle-aged. They all wore expensive-looking outdoor clothing, complete with waffle-stomper boots and bulky down jackets. I didn't see how they stood it; as usual Levitt had the office way too warm.

"Here he is," he said as I came in. "Your pilot, ladies and gentlemen. Captain Moss."

They were staring like a tree full of owls; a couple of them had their mouths open. Behind me I heard Miles make a muffled snorting sound.

I gave Levitt a dirty look—that "Captain" business always gets on my nerves, which of course is why he does it— and said, "Just call me Jack. If you're all ready to go?"

One of the men, a pale pinch-faced character in a red baseball cap, burst into a big braying laugh. "Oh, shit," he said, shaking his head. "That's a good one."

He turned toward the desk. "But really," he said to Levitt, "when's the pilot going to be here?"

The woman standing beside him hit him on the shoulder with the back of her hand. "For God's sake, Roland," she said.

I said, "Sir," in my flattest voice, and when he looked back at me, "I assure you it's not a joke. I'm a fully qualified pilot—Mr. Levitt can show you a copy of my license if you'd like—and I'll be flying you to Ten Wolf Lake today. Unless of course you want to cancel?"

The other man was waving both hands like somebody leading a band. "No, no," he said. "That's, ah, it's—"

He sort of shook himself and took a couple of steps toward me. "Bob Harrison," he said, and stuck out his hand. "Delighted to meet you, Captain Moss. Ah, Jack."

I shook his hand and he said, "Don't mind Roland. He was just taken by surprise. As I'm afraid we all were."

"Yeah," Roland said. "Nobody told us the pilot would be a Bigfoo—"

The woman whacked him again, harder this time, and he said, "Uh, sorry, sorry. No offense. Just slipped out, you know?"

Bob Harrison said, "I'm afraid Roland's right, all the same. We had no idea you would be, um, a Hominid American."

He gave me a quick nervous smile. He was a short stocky guy with black hair and a ragged little mustache. He looked to be a few years older than the others.

"Not that that's a problem," he added quickly. "On the contrary, it's a real privilege. An honor," he said, starting to sound a little desperate.

He looked around. "Why don't I introduce everyone?" He put his arm around the skinny blond woman who stood beside him. "My wife Kate."

Kate gave me a shy smile. "Hi."

"And," gesturing toward the loudmouth and the woman who had been hitting him, "the Bradshaws, Roland and Edith."

I stood looking at them, not saying anything, for a count of four—never hurts to make them sweat a little—and then I said, "Pleased to meet you all. Shall we get going?"

I herded them out the door and got them moving in the direction of the dock, with Miles leading the way. Going across the parking area, the woman named Edith dropped back to walk beside me. "Hello," she said.

She didn't offer her hand, which was nice, and unusual for a human; I know they do it to be friendly but we really don't like it. I mean, we live among them now and mostly we get along but having to *touch* them. . . .

This one kept her hands in the pockets of her down jacket as she said, "I want to apologize for my husband. He's not really a bigot. Just an asshole with a big mouth."

I couldn't argue with that. I looked down at her with a bit more interest. She was short and built small, with dark hair cut short in back and shiny, alert-looking brown eyes. I think a human male would have considered her pretty, but what do I know?

She said, "You have to remember, none of us has ever even met a Hominid American before. I don't believe there are any in Philadelphia."

"Probably not. We're not much on cities."

"Still," she said, "he knew better than to say—what he said."

I stopped and looked down at my feet. "Size fourteen," I said. "That's pretty big, I guess. By your standards."

She laughed. "Yes, but that's no excuse for saying so."

We started walking again, catching up with the others. I said, "Well, it's not the worst thing we've been called. But it's true we don't much care for it."

"What do you call yourselves, then?"

I told her. "Oh, dear," she said. "I don't think I could pronounce that."

"No. Your throat muscles can't make some of our sounds. But," I said, "you don't have to bother with that fancy Hominid American business either. When we're speaking English we mostly say homin or just hom."

She didn't ask any more questions, but all the way to the dock I could feel her taking quick little looks at me. I could guess why; she was probably thinking I wasn't really all that big. At six feet three and a bit over three hundred pounds, I'm fairly typical for an adult male homin, and you can see humans that big or bigger on any decent pro football team.

And even though we've been out of the woods, as you might say, for a good many years now, most humans are still under the influence of those old stories, which made us out to be gigantic. They forget that the original reports mostly came from relatively short people—such as Miles's ancestors—and that footprints in snow or mud always erode out bigger than the feet that made them. And then too the fur probably makes us look bigger.

As for that overpowering stench we were supposed to have, Mama always said the humans were just smelling what they'd done when they saw us.

Out at the end of the dock I stood and waited while Miles helped the clients down the ladder and into the plane. I noticed Edith clutched at him pretty solidly, even though she didn't look the nervous type. Well, my nose had been picking up frustrated-female pheromones ever since I got near her. Maybe Roland's mouth was the only big thing he had.

When they were all on board I climbed down onto the float and cast off the mooring lines for Miles to haul in. I hoisted myself up into the cockpit and shut the door. Bob Harrison had taken the seat beside me, and I hadn't heard any argument about it; it was plain to see he was the leader of this little pack. "Well," he said, "off we go, eh?"

I buckled myself in and began the startup routine: select center tank, prop pitch lever all the way back, carb heat to cold, generator switch on.

"Where'd you learn to fly?" Bob Harrison asked. "In the armed forces?"

Mixture to three-quarters rich. "Federal minority job training program," I said. "We don't do military service." Open throttle about a quarter.

"Oh, yes," he said, "I heard that somewhere. You're nonviolent, then?"

I choked back a hoot; this one had obviously never been in a barroom full of hom construction workers on Saturday night. "No," I said, "just the uniform requirements. Same reason there are almost no hominid cops." I took my right foot off the rudder pedal and wiggled my toes at him. "We don't wear shoes."

Or even clothes if we can help it, I started to add but didn't. One reason I hate to fly human passengers is that I have to keep those damn company coveralls on the whole time. I was already starting to itch all over.

He said, "I see. So then—"

"Look," I said, "please don't be offended, but I need to concentrate just now, all right?"

I flipped the main battery switch and the instrument panel came alive. I reached down and turned on the boost pump and waited till the fuel pressure needle swung past five psi. The engine hadn't had time to cool down completely after the morning's flight but I gave the primer a couple of strokes anyway. Left and right magneto switches on.

I thumbed the starter switch up and held it while the old Pratt & Whitney turned over, groaning with reluctance at first. The prop blades whipped by in front of the battered red cowling, faster and faster, and then there was a cough and a rumble as the engine caught and I let go the starter switch and eased the throttle back a little. As soon as the oil pressure gauge registered 50 psi I shoved the prop pitch lever all the way forward and switched off the boost pump.

"Everybody buckled up?" I said, and heard a series of hasty clicks behind and beside me because, of course, they hadn't.

With a landplane this would have been time to check the magnetos and a couple of other things, but obviously a floatplane doesn't have brakes so any time you run the engine up you're going to go somewhere, and right now there wasn't enough water in front of the Beaver for anything like that. So I pushed the mixture lever to full rich and gave her a little gas and jockeyed her away from the dock and got her turned around into the wind, using the little rudders on the floats, and then I ran the P&W up to 1750 and did the mag check. The drop was shop-manual perfect, which was no surprise at all in an engine Manny had worked on. I cycled the prop pitch through full range and had a quick look over the instruments. Nothing was waving its arms at me. I said, "Here we go, then."

Flaps down to takeoff position. Quick silent prayer to the ancestors, then throttle to the wall. The old Beaver blared and bellowed and charged forward across the lake, the trees along the shoreline blurring as she picked up speed. I felt the little surge as the floats broke surface tension and began to plane. At 35 knots I hit the switch to retract the water rudders; there was enough pressure on the control surfaces now to hold her straight with the pedals. I watched the airspeed indicator and when it hit 65 I gave the stick a bit of back pressure to break her loose and then the wings took the weight and the Beaver quit being an overpowered motorboat and began to do what she was meant to do.

In the back seat Roland said, "Buddy, I apologize again. You are, no shit, a pilot and a hell of a slick one too."

I should have made some reply, I guess, but I was busy setting the flaps to climb and adjusting the trim for a climb rate of 500 feet per minute. I wouldn't have known what to say anyway. I'm just no good at talking with the higher products of evolution.

The day stayed clear and sunny so everybody had a fine view of the scenery on the way up to Ten Wolf Lake. It was the last week in May and everything was nice and green, though there were still some patches of snow up under the trees. They'd picked a pretty good time for their camping trip or whatever they were up to; another month and the weather would be warmer, but then the blackfly season would have started too.

About halfway there Bob Harrison said suddenly, "Ten Wolf Lake. Do you know how it got the name?"

I shook my head. "I'm sure there's a story, but I've never heard it. But then I'm not originally from this part of Alaska."

"Are there wolves around there, then?" Kate asked. She sounded a little nervous.

"Oh, sure." The Alaskan bush and she wants to know if there are wolves? What did she expect, hamsters? "Quite a few," I said. "You might see some while you're there. Don't worry, though, they don't go in for attacking people. They're really pretty shy."

Her husband said, "What do you people call the place? I mean, what's its Sasquatch name?"

I shrugged. "Beats me. I don't speak a word of Sasquatch."

He was looking confused again. I said, "Sasquatches live way down south of here, in the Cascades. Not in Alaska." Actually there probably are a few, the way everybody gets around nowadays—we get a good many Siberian Kaptars coming over looking for work, and I even know where there's an Australian Yowie tending bar in Sitka—but I've never met any.

Kate said, "So you're—?"

"Arulataq. That's the main tribe around these parts. With a good many Toonijuq, though they're mostly over in Canada."

"I'll be damned," Bob said. "And you can't understand each other's languages?"

I looked at him. "How's your Arabic?"

He thought that over. "All right," he said, "point taken."

"I speak Arulataq," I said, "and English and a little Russian, and a few odds and ends of Inuit and Tlingit. That's it."

In fact that wasn't quite true. My ex-wife was Windigo, and I picked up quite a bit of that before she got pissed off at me and went back to Quebec. Especially toward the end there, when I learned a good many new words, of a kind I hadn't even known she knew. But it wasn't something I wanted to talk about.

* * *

Ten Wolf Lake was surrounded by wooded mountains that broke the wind, so the water was flat and calm as I brought the Beaver in. It looked the same as the last time I'd been there; the cabin was still standing—something you can't always count on, with parties of hunters and fishermen getting drunk and setting fires—and the roof appeared to be reasonably intact. There was no dock but there was a spot in close to shore where the water was deep enough for the Beaver, and a little while later the clients were standing on the bank under the trees, surrounded by their piled-up possessions. At least they hadn't brought as much junk as most city campers.

Bob Harrison said, "I don't know if Mr. Levitt told you, but there's another couple coming to join us. They should be arriving in a few days."

The others were looking around them, at the cabin and the lake and the woods. The scent of excitement was very strong, along with a little bit of what might be fear. There was something else, too, something I couldn't identify, but it's always hard to be sure with humans.

I said, "You want me to come back and check on you, say in a week? Bring you any supplies?"

"No need." He pulled out a cell phone and held it up. "We'll just call if we need anything."

They all lined up and waved as I fired up the P&W again and ran the Beaver down to the far end of the lake and got her turned around. I didn't really need that much run—unloaded, a Beaver takes off like a buggered bat—but I wanted to make sure they couldn't see me as I peeled off those coveralls. It was a clumsy business getting them off in that little cockpit, but it was worth it. I opened the side window a little so the wind could ruffle through my fur as I took off.

It was getting pretty late in the day when I set the Beaver down again. I struggled back into the coveralls—you never knew who might be around, even out here in the boondocks—and taxied back up to the dock, where Miles was waiting. This time I saw he had Manny with him.

"So he returns," Manny said as I came up the ladder. "Hallo, tall, dark, and unsightly." It came out more like *und oonzitely*; five years in this country hadn't been nearly enough to shake Manny's Black Forest accent.

I said, "Mannfried, my vertically challenged bro. Stand on Miles so I can see you better."

We laughed and Manny reached up so we could slap hands. Miles said, "You two. I swear."

I looked down at Manny, wondering as always how someone only three feet tall could be related to me. But the scientists say it's definite; the DNA evidence proves Kobolds are hominids, and not even a separate species.

I never knew why Manny wound up in Alaska, but I was glad he had, because he was one hell of a mechanic. He could crawl right into the tightest parts of the plane, too.

Right now, though, I was just as happy he hadn't been around to meet bigmouth Roland. The last fool to call Manny a dwarf was now known around Fairbanks as One-Ear Willie.

I left them to finish putting the Beaver to bed for the night, and walked on up the dock and across the lot. The office was closed up and Levitt's car was gone so he must have shut down early today. That was fine with me. I got out my keys and got into my pickup truck. A couple of minutes later I was heading down the gravel road toward town.

I'd meant to go straight home, but about halfway there I got to feeling really hungry—I hadn't had much of a lunch, after all. Then I saw the little roadhouse off to the right of the road amid a grove of trees, and I pulled in and stopped without having to think about it.

I parked the truck and got out and stood for a minute looking the place over. The ancestors knew how many times I must have driven past it in the couple of years I'd been working for Alaskan Bush Charters, yet I'd never stopped and never really paid it any attention. It wasn't much to look at; just a small log building and a big sign with the magic words HOT

FOOD—COLD BEER. I didn't see any other vehicles in the lot. Maybe they were closed.

But I went up and tried the front door, and it opened, so I went inside. There were maybe half a dozen tables and a small bar or counter. I went over to the bar and started to sit down on one of the high stools and then a loud raspy voice said, "Hey! Hey, ape-shape! What do you think you're doing?"

A skinny, bald-headed man came around the end of the counter, looking seriously angry. "I guess you can't read?" he said, pointing.

I looked up and saw a big hand-lettered sign:

NO MONKYS
NO INDIANS
DOGS WELCOME

"Go on, God damn it." He came closer, making shooing motions with his hands. "Get out of here."

I didn't move; I was too surprised, really, to do or say anything.

He leaned on the counter and stared at me. "Listen here," he said in a lower, very intense voice. "The United States Supreme Court says you're people. Says you can vote and go to school and everything. I can't do anything about that, the white man's already lost control of this country anyway. But they say I got to serve a bunch of damn dirty apes in my own place of binness, and I'm not taking that kind of shit laying down."

He reached under the counter suddenly and came up with a gun. It was a huge shiny revolver, some kind of Magnum I thought. The kind people in the back country carried to stop bears.

"And don't even *think*," he said, pointing it at me, "about starting anything. I'll kill you before you can get within reach."

He'd do it, too; I could smell the hate and the fear coming off him so strong I could barely breathe. I got up slowly, keeping my hands in sight, and backed toward the door. "Go on," he yelled after me. "Run to the law if you want. I don't give a damn."

Out in the truck I sat for a couple of minutes, shaking from the reaction. I hadn't run into anything like this in years; I'd forgotten what it felt like.

Not that there weren't plenty of places that managed to avoid serving homs, or tried to; but usually they ran cute little tricks like the "no shoes, no service" gag, or claimed their tables were all booked up or something. They didn't just come out and say it in your face like this.

I'd thought that was all behind us, or nearly so. You still heard stories—Alaska always has gotten more than its share of diehards and crazies—but the incidents were getting increasingly rare. And they weren't quite real, because they always involved people you didn't know, in places you'd never been.

Now here was one practically in my back yard. He couldn't have been here very long, or I'd have heard about him. Must have just recently taken over the diner.

I wanted badly to go back in and take it, and him, apart; but then I'd wind up in trouble with the law, and Levitt would fire me and my life would generally go to hell and it wasn't worth it. Besides, the old shithead might shoot me—and he'd get away with it, too; he'd swear I attacked him and he had to fire in self-defense, and it would be his word against a dead hom's.

So I started the truck and drove on to town, making a note to pass the word to some people I knew in Hominid Rights Watch. They'd make a lot more trouble for him than I could. There was some satisfaction in the thought.

But just before reaching town I stopped the truck again on a deserted stretch of road and got out and ran over to the edge of the woods and stood for a long time pounding both fists against a big tree, till the pain finally made me stop; and then I got back in the truck and drove on home with the blood and bits of bark still sticking to the fur of my arms.

Next Thursday morning when I came to work Levitt was standing in the office doorway. "Jack," he called as I got out of the truck. "More passengers for you."

One look at the couple waiting in the office and I knew they had to be the ones Bob Harrison had told me about. They were about the same age group as the others, and they had that same look; I don't know how to describe it. The man was tall and bony, with nearly as much hair on his face as mine. The woman was squat and dark and working on a pretty decent mustache of her own.

They didn't act at all surprised to see me. I remembered Bob Harrison with his cell phone.

"Jerry and Doris King," the man said, shaking my hand. "We were supposed to come with Bob and the others, but we had a little family emergency at the last minute."

"That's OK," Levitt said from behind the desk. He peered at me over the tops of his thick Elvis Costello glasses. "Jack will be glad of the chance to see your friends again. He really hit it off with them."

I said a couple of rude words in Arulataq and Levitt snickered and said, "Well, you'd better get going. You've still got that load of drill bits to haul when you get back."

The Kings weren't as talkative as the others. On the way up to Ten Wolf Lake he asked me a couple of questions about the weather, nothing more. She just sat in back and didn't speak at all until we got to there.

But as I flew over the lake and started to bring the plane around she said suddenly, "Jerry, look!"

I glanced back but I couldn't see where she was pointing. Jerry was looking out his window and nodding, and I tried to see past him but he was blocking my view. Then he moved his head and I could see just a little bit. Just enough to catch a very brief glimpse of a couple of fast-moving shapes, indistinct as shadows, streaking along the edge of the cabin clearing and vanishing into the woods. They were gone so fast I might have wondered if I'd really seen anything at all, if I hadn't been too busy flying an airplane to give it any thought.

I got the Beaver turned into the wind and set her down on the lake, which was a bit bumpier than last time but still easy water. There was nobody in sight, and that surprised me; I'd expected they'd all come running when they heard the plane. Maybe, I thought, they'd gone hiking or something.

But then the cabin door opened and Bob Harrison came out. He waved as I nudged the Beaver up to the shore, and by the time I got the engine shut down and the doors open he was striding across the clearing towards us, buttoning his shirt awkwardly and stuffing it into his pants as he came.

Something moved back at the cabin and I saw Kate standing in the doorway, doing hasty things to her clothes. So we'd interrupted a little something? I laughed to myself and climbed out onto the port float to help the passengers disembark.

They went straight to Bob Harrison, with a little flurry of smiles and handshakes. Doris turned and started trotting across the clearing to meet Kate, who was on her way down from the cabin now. I got busy with a mooring line, tying the Beaver up to a handy stump. "Bob," I heard Jerry say. "You're looking good. Everybody all right? Where are Roland and Edith?"

"They went for a run," Bob said, and I paused, surprised; those two definitely hadn't struck me as the athletic type. Maybe the fresh air and the outdoor life had charged their batteries somehow.

It certainly seemed to have worked on Bob; as Jerry said, he was looking good. He stood straighter, he didn't wave his hands nervously when he talked, and his face looked firmer and more confident; his mustache even looked fuller and not so silly. When he came toward me there was a smooth spring in his step that hadn't been there before. "Jack," he said. "Good to see you again."

I managed to have my hands full of the Kings' gear in time to get out of the handshake routine, so instead he gave me a hand with the unloading. Doris and Kate were coming down to join us now; Kate ran ahead and gave Jerry a big hug. Now I noticed, she was looking good too. In fact I couldn't remember seeing a human woman move like that, except maybe in the Olympics on TV. Maybe there was something in the water here.

They smelled different, too. Or Bob did, anyway; I didn't get close enough to Kate to be sure. The sour nervous scent was gone, and the other one, the strange one, was much stronger than before. I still couldn't identify it, though something in the back of my head was trying to make a connection.

When everything was unloaded Bob said, "All right, I guess we'd better get you moved in," and then to me, "Have a safe flight back," and they all started picking things up and heading toward the cabin. Doris King gave me a look—I think she'd been expecting me to carry her stuff for her; dream on, lady—but then she hoisted her duffel bag and moved off after the others.

I waited till they had disappeared into the cabin and then I went over to the edge of the woods to take care of some pressing personal business. I hosed down a big cedar and reached for the coveralls' clumsy zip, and then I saw something lying on the ground, almost hidden by the underbrush.

It was part of the front leg of a half-grown deer. The hoof was still attached and intact, but the rest of it was mostly exposed bone with a few scraps of ragged, bloody skin. I didn't even have to bend down to see the tooth marks.

"There's something weird," I told Manny after I got back, "about that bunch up at Ten Wolf Lake."

"Hah." Manny snorted. "They're *all* weird, my large friend. Haven't you learned that yet?"

That was something I envied Manny; he wasn't the least bit intimidated or put off by humans. His people, after all, had been interacting with them for hundreds of years, while we were hiding in the woods. He told me once, with a perfectly straight face, that Himmler had tried to recruit a Kobold SS unit toward the end of the war. "As if we'd fight," he said, "for that bunch of losers who couldn't even get a swastika the right way round."

It wasn't quite noon yet, but I decided to go ahead and eat and then get on with the next job. I went out to get my lunch out of the truck and that was when I saw the blue pickup parked next to mine. There was a sticker on the back bumper with a drawing of a big hairy fist and the words FIRST BEINGS POWER. I sighed and went around to the driver's side and said, "Charley."

Charley Rockslide rolled down his window. He looked a little angry, but then he usually did. "Moss," he said in Arulataq. "And don't call me that skinface name. Just Rockslide, OK?"

"So what brings you here?" I said, and then I noticed the human sitting next to him. "Hello," I said in English.

The man grunted and raised a hand. He was pretty young, with long black hair; Indian, I was pretty sure, definitely not white and the wrong facial shape for Inuit.

"Jimmy Raven," Charley said. "Jimmy, my cousin Moss." That wasn't exactly right, but close enough; there aren't any words in English for some of the homin relationships.

"Speaking of skinfaces," I said in Arulataq, "what are you doing riding around with one? Considering the things I've heard you say about them?"

I knew the answer; I was just jerking his chain. Charley belonged to a radical hominid-power organization that went in for loud speeches and marches and demonstrations and anything else they could do to get on TV. There weren't very many of them, but they managed to get a lot of attention all the same. Most of the older homs regarded them as a lot of noisy assholes. Not that there wasn't a lot of truth in the things they said; it was just that they *were*.

And at first they'd been down on humans in general, calling them "slugs" and saying we should have wiped them out back before the Ice Age and so on; but lately they'd been getting tight with a local Indian-militant fringe group calling themselves War Party. Which was almost certainly where this one came in.

I said in English, "Pleased to meet you," and Jimmy Raven grunted again; he sure wasn't the talkative type. Or maybe Charley had been telling him things about me.

Charley said, "We'd like to engage your professional services."

He said it in English, not that there was any doubt who "we" included. I looked at him for a couple of seconds before deciding he was serious. "Charley," I said, "what are you up to?" Not that there was any doubt about that either. At least in general terms.

"We need some flying done," Charley said. "That's simple, isn't it? And you're one of us—"

"The hell I am."

"I mean you're a First Being." Charley and his gang wouldn't say "hominid"; they said it meant we were second-rate humans when in fact it was the skinfaces who were the degenerate branch of the family. They didn't say that last part any more, since they hooked up with War Party, but they still wouldn't use the word.

I said, "Number one, I doubt if you've got the money. You're not talking about calling a taxicab, you know."

"We've got the money," Jimmy Raven said, speaking up for the first time. "Don't worry about that."

They probably did at that. I knew how they got it, too. So did every hom in Alaska and half the humans. Even if nobody had been able to catch them at it yet.

"Then," I said, "you're talking to the wrong guy. Go in the office there and see Levitt. He's the one who books the flights."

Charley shifted himself around a little and rubbed his face. "Well," he said, still speaking English, "see, we'd really rather not do that." He lowered his voice, though there was nobody else nearby or even in sight. "We had in mind something kind of off the record, you know?"

"Charley," I said, "the plane doesn't belong to me. I can't just borrow it for personal purposes. Even if I wanted to."

Jimmy Raven said, "OK, what if we chartered it to go somewhere and then you went somewhere else instead?"

"Oh, sure. And then burn my license and take a job on a pipeline crew. You have any idea what they do to pilots who file bogus flight plans? They're really tough on that sort of thing nowadays, with all the terrorist stuff going on. You wouldn't believe the controls they've got."

"Everybody has to take risks and make sacrifices," Charley said, "in the cause of social justice."

He'd started talking like that about a year ago, after he went to that big international hominid conference in Seattle and got to hanging out with a bunch of Maoist yetis from Nepal. Before that he was just your basic loudmouthed punk.

"Oh, moose shit. Save that for the TV interviews, OK? Social justice my ass," I said. "You've got a shipment of dope you want brought in. Either that or some of those guns you fools are buying with the dope money."

I ran my hand over the shiny fender of the pickup truck. "Well, some of the money, anyway. You didn't buy this with your unemployment checks."

Charley's face was even uglier than usual. Shave him and he'd be a dead ringer for that old man at the roadhouse.

He said, "I should have known." He was speaking Arulataq again. "I should have known better than to ask you to do anything for your own kind. Too busy snuggling up to the skinfaces—"

"Like your friend here? Or those white college kids you sell that Sasquatch grass to?" I stepped back from the truck. "I think you're leaving now."

He opened his mouth and I said, "In fact I think you left about fifteen minutes ago. Didn't you?"

It was easy to see he wanted to take this farther—the fight smell was coming off him in a regular cloud—but I knew he wasn't going to try. I had the size and the reach on him and I've got, let's say, a certain reputation.

Jimmy Raven, I noticed, was sitting very still and quiet and keeping his hands on his knees. Smart Indian.

Charley said a really bad word in Arulataq and started the pickup and jammed it into reverse and backed out, and then he swung it around and tore out of the parking lot in a shower of gravel and the clash of a clumsy gear change. I watched till he was gone and then I unlocked my own truck and got my lunch bag and took it down to the dock.

Miles was there, loading the drilling bits into the Beaver. "Heard some commotion," he said. "What's happening?"

I sat down on a piling. "Just some crazy stuff," I said. "I swear everybody's gone crazy. Feel like I'm in one of those late-night horror movies."

He laughed and went back to what he was doing, and I opened the bag and reached in; and then all of a sudden I thought of something, and I started laughing and laughing, till Miles must have thought I'd lost my damn mind.

* * *

About a week later I came back from a flight to Kenai and found Levitt waiting on the dock. "Got another flight up to Ten Wolf Lake," he said. "They phoned in a big list of supplies they wanted. Miles is in town getting it now."

I followed him back to the office and handed him the paperwork from the morning's delivery. While he was filing it I went over and had a look at the big calendar on the wall by his desk.

"What are you doing?" he said, blinking at me.

"Nothing," I said. "Just checking something."

The Harrisons were standing on the shore of the lake as I came in. I didn't see any of the others.

It didn't take long to unload the supplies they'd ordered—there was quite a lot of it, but Miles had packed it with his usual efficiency—and after the last box was ashore I said, "Looks as if you're planning to be here awhile."

"Yes," Bob said. "Actually we don't know quite how long. There have been . . . some changes in our plans."

He was looking *really* good. They both were. Kate looked ten years younger.

He said, "Well. Thank you."

I said, "I almost told Levitt to get somebody else. But then I checked the calendar."

"Calendar?" He looked baffled. "I don't—"

"Quarter moon," I said. "I guessed I'd be safe."

They looked at each other and then at me and then at each other again and then Kate started laughing, very high in her throat. She put her hands up to her cheeks. "Oh, my God," she said in a whisper.

Bob said, "You know?"

"I figured it out."

He started laughing too, then, or rather chuckling in a kind of growly way. "Well," he said, "what the hell."

He turned and cupped his hands to his mouth and shouted, "All right, everybody! Come on out! He knows!"

There was a long pause. The only sound was the soft lapping of the waves against the Beaver's floats.

Then they started coming out of the woods, first Jerry and Doris King—both of them completely naked; at the time I barely noticed—and then the wolves, coming from all directions, more wolves than I'd ever seen in one place, stepping silently out of the shadows beneath the trees and stopping at the edge of the clearing, all of them staring straight in my direction.

I felt the hair rising all down my back. Not that I was surprised—I'd known they were there, been smelling them ever since I landed. But knowing wasn't the same as seeing; million-year-old voices in my head were screaming at me to run like hell.

A moment later Edith Bradshaw appeared, walking slowly along beside an enormous gray wolf. She didn't have any clothes on either. Her left hand rested on the wolf's back, just behind his shoulders. She was smiling.

"You know," Bob said, "it's really good that you're the first one to know. It's so appropriate."

Kate nodded. "You see, you inspired us. Your example."

I tried to say, "What?" but it came out as a shapeless dry-throat croak.

"We talked about it, after you'd gone," Bob said, "how you and your people had given up your long secrecy and taken your place in the so-called civilized world. How you had defied prejudice and demanded respect and dignity. Watching you fly that airplane, thinking of all that represented—well, as Kate says, it was an inspiration to us."

"So," Kate said, "we talked about it, and we made the decision. We're going to come out too."

"Uh," I managed to say. "You—?"

"Not just this group, of course," Bob said. "We'll have to go back, carry the message to others like us, so we can come out as a people. It's going to take time and organization and hard work. Which is why we're staying here a bit longer than we'd intended. We've got a lot of planning and discussing to do."

"And this is the perfect place for it," Edith said, coming up next to the Harrisons. The wolf sat down on his haunches beside her and she stroked his head. I realized suddenly that the unsatisfied-female scent was gone. In its place was one I remembered from a couple of years ago, before my marriage went to hell.

For no good reason I said, "Where's Roland?"

Edith tilted her head in the direction of a skinny, slightly mangy-looking wolf trotting across the clearing toward us. "He had a late night," she said.

"By the way," Bob said, "that full-moon business—it's just a legend. No idea how it got started."

Jerry King said, "We'd really appreciate it if you wouldn't say anything about this just yet."

Oh, well, actually I'm going to hold a press conference when I get back. . . . I said, "I wouldn't dream of it."

"So," Miles said as he tied the mooring lines, "how's everybody up at Ten Wolf Lake?"

"Miles," I said, "I think the minority situation around here just got even more complicated."

I got the idea for this one while playing with one of my collection of computer flight simulators. Hey, every boy needs a hobby.

Written June 2003
First published April 2004

Sitka

Late in the afternoon, a little before sundown, the fog moved in off the ocean and settled in over the islands and peninsulas of the coast. It wasn't much of a fog, by the standards of Russian America in late summer; just enough to mask the surface of the sea and soften the rough outlines of the land.

On the waterfront in the town of New Arkhangelsk, on the western side of the big island that the Russians called Baranof and the natives called Sitka, two men stood looking out over the harbor. "Perfect," one of them said. "If it'll stay like this."

The other man looked at him. "Perfect, Jack? How so?"

The first man flung out a hand. "Hell, just look. See how it's hanging low over the water?"

The other man turned back toward the harbor, following his gesture. He stood silently for a moment, seeing how the fog curled around the hulls of the anchored ships while leaving their upper works exposed. The nearest, a big deepwater steamer, was all but invisible down near the waterline, yet her masts and funnels showed clear and black against the hills beyond the harbor, and the flag of the Confederate States of America was clearly recognizable at her stern.

"Perfect," the man called Jack said again. "Just enough to hide a small boat, but not enough to hide a ship. Less chance of a mistake."

He was a powerfully-built young man with curly blond hair and a tanned, handsome face. His teeth flashed white in the fading light. "After all," he said, "we don't want to get the wrong one, do we, Vladimir?"

The man called Vladimir, whose last name was Ulyanov and who sometimes called himself Lenin, closed his eyes and shuddered slightly. "No, that would be very bad." His English was excellent but strongly accented. "Don't even joke about it."

"Don't worry," the younger man said. "We'll get her for you."

"Not for me. You know better than that."

"Yeah, all right. For the cause." Jack slapped him lightly on the upper arm, making him wince. "Hey, I'm a good socialist too. You know that."

"So you have assured me," Lenin said dryly. "Otherwise I might suspect—"

He stopped suddenly as a pair of long-bearded Orthodox monks walked past. Jack said, "What," and then, "Oh, hell, Vladimir, don't you ever relax? I bet they don't even speak English."

Lenin looked after the two black-robed figures and shook his head. "Two years away from the twentieth century," he murmured, "and still the largest country in the world is ruled by medieval superstition. . . ."

He turned to the younger man. "We shouldn't be standing here like this. It looks suspicious. And believe me," he said as Jack started to speak, "to the people we are dealing with, *everything* looks suspicious. Trust me on this."

He jerked his head in the direction of a nearby saloon. "Come," he said. "Let us have a drink, Comrade London."

As the two men started down the board sidewalk, a trio of dark-faced women suddenly appeared from the shadows and fell in alongside, smiling and laughing. One of them grabbed Jack's arm and said something in a language that was neither English nor Russian. "For God's sake," Jack said, and started to pull free. "Just what we need, a bunch of Siwash whores."

"Wait." Lenin held up a hand. "Let them join us for now. With them along, no one will wonder what we are doing here."

"Huh. Yeah, all right. Good idea." Jack looked at the three women. They weren't bad-looking in a shabby sort of way. The one holding his arm had red ribbons in her long black hair. He laughed. "Too bad I'm going to be kind of busy this evening. Give them a bath, they might be good for some fun."

Lenin's nose twitched slightly. "You're not serious."

"Hell, no. I may be down on my luck but I'm still a white man."

Lenin winced. "Jack, I've got to talk to you some time about your—"

The saloon door swung open and a couple of drunken Cossacks staggered out, leaning on the unpainted timber wall for support. When they were past Lenin led the way through the narrow doorway and into a long, low-ceilinged, poorly-lit room full of rough wooden tables and benches where men, and a few women, sat drinking and talking and playing cards. An old man sat on a tall stool near the door, playing a slow minor-key tune on an accordion. The air was dense with smoke from cheap *mahorka* tobacco.

"There," Lenin said. "In the back, by the wall, where we can watch the door."

He strode up to the bar, pushing past a group of sailors in the white summer uniform of the Imperial German navy, and came back a moment later carrying a bottle and a couple of glasses. "One minute," he said, setting the glasses down and pouring, while Jack dragged up a bench and sat down. "I've got an idea."

Stepping over to the next table, Lenin beckoned to the three women. They looked blank. "Come," he said, in Russian and then in English, and at last they giggled in unison and moved over to join him. "Here." He set the bottle in the center of the table, making exaggerated sit-down motions with his free hand. "*Saditye*'. You sit here," he said, speaking very slowly. He touched the bottle. "You can have this. *Ponimaitye?*"

As they seated themselves, with another flurry of giggles, Lenin came back and sat down across from Jack. "There," he said. "That's the only table in the place close enough for anyone to overhear us. Better to have it occupied by harmless idiots."

Jack snorted. "For God's sake, Vladimir!"

"Laugh if you like," Lenin said. "I don't take risks. Already I have been arrested—"

"Me too."

"Pardon me." Lenin's voice was very flat. "You have been arrested by stupid American policemen, who beat you and threw you in a cell for a few days and then made you leave town and forgot about you. You have been detained briefly, at a military outpost, for prospecting for gold without a permit. You have no idea what a Cheka interrogation is like. Or," he said, "what it is like to live under the eyes of a vigilant and well-organized secret police force and their network of informers."

He lifted his glass. "What is that American idiom? 'The walls have ears,' yes? In the Russian Empire they have both ears and eyes—and feet, to run and tell the men with the big boots what you say and do. Until you have been stepped on by those boots, you have no business to laugh at the caution of those who have."

At the next table the woman with the red ribbons in her hair said, "I'm looking at him and I still don't believe it."

She said it in a language that was not spoken anywhere in that world.

The woman beside her pushed back her own hair, which was done up in thick braids that hung down to the swell of her bosom under her trade-blanket coat. She said in the same language, "Well, he *was* one of the great figures of history, for better or worse."

"Not Lenin," the woman with the red ribbons said impatiently. "Jack London. He's gorgeous. The pictures didn't even come close."

Across the table, the third woman was doing something with one of the sea-shell ornaments that dangled from her ears.

She looked over at the men's table for a moment and then smiled and nodded without speaking.

"Hand me that bottle," the one with the red ribbons said. "I think I'm in love."

"Of course," Lenin said, "for me things did perhaps work out for the best. Siberia wasn't pleasant, but it gave me time to think, to organize my ideas. And then the authorities decided to send some of the Siberian exiles even farther away, to this remote American outpost of the empire, and in time this presented . . . possibilities."

Jack gave a meaningless grunt and reached for his own glass, staring off across the room. The German sailors were clustered around the accordion player, who was trying to accompany them on "Du, Du Liegst Mir Am Herzen." Some of the Russians were giving them dirty looks but they didn't seem to notice.

"That's right," Jack muttered. "Sing, have yourselves a good time. Get drunk, find some whores, get skinned in a rigged card game. Just for God's sake don't go back to the ship tonight."

The woman with the red ribbons said, "He looks a lot younger. Than Lenin, I mean."

"Only six years' difference in their ages," the woman with the braids said. "But you're right. Or rather Lenin looks older—"

"Sh." The other woman raised a finger, still fiddling with her seashell ear pendants. "Quiet. I've almost—there. There." She dropped her hands to her lap and sat back. "Locked on and recording."

"All right." the woman with the red ribbons said. She reached up and pushed back her hair with a casual-looking motion, her hand barely brushing the area of her own ear. A moment later the woman beside her did something similar.

"Oh," the one with the red ribbbons said. "Yes. Nice and clear. All this background noise, too, I'm impressed."

The one with the braids said, "Speaking of background noise, we need to generate some. We're being too quiet. We're supposed to be cheap whores drinking free vodka. Time to laugh it up again."

Lenin glanced over at the next table as the three women broke into another fit of noisy giggles. "They seem to be making inroads on that bottle," Lenin said. "If you want any more, you'd better go get it before they finish it off."

"They're welcome to it," Jack said. He looked at his own glass and grimaced. "Damn vodka tastes like something you'd rub on a horse. How the hell do you people stand it?"

"Practice."

"Yeah, well, better you than me. What I'd give for a taste of good old honest John Barleycorn."

"It's available," Lenin said. "Though probably not in a place like this. It's just very expensive, like everything else not made in Russia, thanks to the exorbitant import duties. Another blessing from our beloved official bureaucracy."

"Tell me about it," Jack said. "Came up here figuring to dig some gold, make a little something for myself instead of always being broke on my ass. Found out foreigners have to have a special permit to prospect or even to travel in the interior, no way to get it without paying off a bunch of crooks behind government desks. So I said the hell with it."

"And you were caught."

"Yep. Damn near went to jail, too, but by then I'd hit just enough pay dirt to be able to grease a certain Cossack officer. And here I am, broke on my ass again and a long way from home. I'm telling you, Vladimir," he said, "if you wanted somebody to blow up that bunch of greedy sons of bitches who run things here, I'd be your man and I wouldn't charge a nickel to do it."

He rubbed his face and sighed. "Instead I'm about to go blow the bottom out of a German battleship and kill a bunch of people who never did me any harm, all for the sake of the great workers' revolution. How about that?"

* * *

The three women exchanged looks. The one with the red ribbons said, "No." She squeezed her eyes shut. "*No.*"

"So it's true." The woman with the seashell ear pendants shook her head. "Incredible."

"Watch it," the one with the braids said, breaking into a broad sloppy smile. "Lenin's already nervous—see, he's looking around again. Act drunk, damn it."

"That's easy," the woman with the red ribbons said, reaching for the vodka bottle. "After hearing that, I *need* a drink."

"In fact," Lenin said, "you are doing it for the price of a ticket back to your own country. Not that I question your socialist convictions, but right now you would blow up your own mother—"

Jack's hand shot across the table and clamped down on Lenin's forearm. "Don't you ever speak to me about my mother," he said thickly. "You got that?"

Lenin sat very still. His face had gone pale and there were pain lines at the corners of his mouth. "Yes," he said in a carefully even voice. "Yes, I apologize."

"Okay, then." Jack let go and gulped at his drink. "Just watch it."

Lenin rubbed his forearm. After a moment he said, "Go easy on that vodka. You're going to need a clear head and steady hands tonight."

Jack gave a short harsh laugh. "Save your breath. Even I'm not fool enough to tie one on when I'm going to be handling dynamite in the dark. Make a mistake with that much giant, it'd be raining Jack London for a week. Mixed up with a couple of Aleut paddlers, too, they'd never get the pieces sorted out."

He sipped his drink again, more cautiously. "Not that it's all that tricky a job," he added. "Nothing to it, really. Come alongside the *Brandenburg,* just forward of her aft turret, so we're next to the powder magazine. Arm the mine, start the timer—neat piece of work there, your pal Iosif knows what he's doing—and ease the whole thing up against the hull till the magnets take hold, being careful not to let it clang. Take the forked stick and slide the mine down under the waterline, below the armor belt, and then tell the boys to high-tail it. Hell, anybody could do it."

He grinned crookedly. "When you get right down to it, you only need me to make sure we get the right ship. Those Aleuts are the best paddlers in the world, but they wouldn't know the *Brandenburg* from the *City of New Orleans*."

The woman with the braids said, "You know, I never believed it. I got into some pretty hot arguments, in fact. 'Ridiculous' was one of the milder words I used."

The one with the seashell ear pendants said, "Well, you were hardly alone. All the authorities agree that Jack London's involvement in the *Brandenburg* affair is merely a romantic legend, circulated by a few revisionist crackpots. I don't know any responsible scholar who takes it seriously."

She chuckled softly. "And oh, is the shit going to fly in certain circles when we get back! I can hardly wait."

"Not quite true," Lenin said. "I also need you to make sure that our aboriginal hirelings don't change their mind and run away home with their advance money. If they haven't already done so."

"Oh, they wouldn't do that. See," Jack said, "they think it's a Russian ship we're after."

Lenin's eyebrows went up. "You told them that?"

"Hell, I had to tell them something. So they'll be there. The way they hate Russians, they wouldn't pass up a chance like that. Christ," Jack said, "I know we did some rotten things to the Indians in the States, but compared to what your people did to those poor devils. . . ."

"Oh, yes. The exploitation of native peoples, here and in Asia, has been one of the worst crimes of the Tsarist state."

"Yeah, well," Jack said, "all I'm saying, the boys will do their job and I'll do mine. Quit worrying about it."

* * *

"Hey," the woman with the braids said. "Go easy on that stuff. You're going to make yourself sick."

"I'm already sick," the woman with the red ribbons said. "Just thinking about it, sitting here listening to them talk about it, seeing it about to happen, I'm as sick as I've ever been in my life. Aren't you?"

"Now what happens after that," Jack said, "whether things turn out the way you want, I can't guarantee. I'll sink the ship for you, but if it doesn't get you your war, don't come to me wanting a refund."

Lenin's lips twitched in what was very nearly a smile. "That," he said, "is perhaps the surest part of the entire business. Believe me, nothing is more predictable than the reaction of the Kaiser to the sinking of one of his precious warships in a Russian port."

"Really? I don't know as much as I should about things like that," Jack admitted. "Foreign rulers and all, I need to read up . . . but I can see how it would make him pretty mad. Mad enough to go to war, though?"

"Wilhelm will be furious," Lenin said. "But also secretly delighted. At last he will have a pretext for the war he has wanted for so long."

Jack frowned. "He's crazy?"

"Not mad, no. Merely a weakling—a cripple and, according to rumor, a homosexual—determined to prove his manhood by playing the great warrior."

"Ah." Jack nodded slowly. "A punk trying to pick a fight to show he's not a punk. Yeah, I know the kind. Saw a good many of them when I was riding the rails."

"Even so. Wilhelm has been looking for a fight ever since ascending the throne. Since no one has so far obliged him, he contents himself with playing the bully."

Lenin nodded in the direction of the German sailors, who were now roaring out "Ach, Du Lieber Augustin" in somewhat approximate harmony. "As for example this little 'good-will cruise,'" he said. "This series of visits to various ports by a *Hochseeflotte* battleship. Nothing but a crude show of force to impress the world."

"Showing everybody who's the boss?"

"Exactly. And therefore its destruction will be taken as a response to a challenge."

"Hm. Okay, you know more about it than I do." Jack shrugged. "Still seems pretty strange, though, starting a war hoping your own country will get whipped."

"I don't like it," Lenin said. "I am Russian, after all, and this isn't easy for me. But there is no better breeding ground for revolution than a major military defeat. Look at France."

"The Communards lost, didn't they?"

"True. They made mistakes, from which we have learned."

"If he says anything about omelettes and eggs," the woman with the red ribbons said through her teeth, "I'm going to go over there and beat his brains out with this bottle. Screw the mission and screw non-interference and screw temporal paradox. I don't care. I'll kill him."

Jack said, "You know, the joke's really going to be on you if Russia wins."

"Not much chance of that. Russia's armed forces are a joke, fit only to keep the Tatars in line and occasionally massacre a village of Jews. The officers are mostly incompetent buffoons, owing their rank to family connections rather than ability. The troops are badly trained, and their equipment is decades out of date. The German military, on the other hand, are very nearly as good as they think they are."

"Russia's a big country, though."

"Yes. A big country with too much territory to protect. A German offensive in the west, a Japanese attack in the east—it will be too much. You'll see."

"You're awfully sure the Japs are going to come into it."

"Comrade London," Lenin said softly, "where do you think our funds come from? Who do you think is paying for this business tonight?"

The three women stared at one another. "Now that," the one with the braids said after a moment, "is going to knock *everyone* on their butts."

"The Japs are bankrolling us?" Jack said incredulously. "For God's sake, why?"

"They have territorial ambitions in Asia. Russia has become an obstacle. A war in Europe would create opportunities."

"Damn." Jack looked unhappy. "I don't know if I like that part. Working for Orientals against white—all right, all right," he said quickly, seeing Lenin's expression. "I didn't say I wouldn't do it. All I want is to get back home. I don't really care if I have to go to work for the Devil."

He looked at Lenin over the rim of his glass. "If I haven't already. . . ."

"Oh, dear," the woman with the braids said. "He does have some unfortunate racial attitudes, doesn't he?"

"So did Ernest Hemingway," the one with the red ribbons said without looking up from the bottle. "And I thought we were going to have to peel you off him with a steam hose."

"The interesting question," Lenin said, "is whether the other European countries will become involved. The French may well decide that this is an opportunity to settle old scores with Germany. The others, who knows? This could turn into a general conflict, like nothing since Napoleon."

"What the hell. As long as the United States doesn't get involved," Jack said. "And that's not going to happen. We've just barely *got* an army, and they're still busy with the Indians. The Confederates, now, they just might be crazy enough to get in on it."

"If the war spreads, so much the better," Lenin said. "Because if it spreads, so will the revolution."

He took out a heavy silver pocket watch and snapped it open. "And now I think we should be going. It is still several hours, but we both have things we must do."

He started to push himself back from the table. Jack said, "Wait. Just one more thing."

Lenin sank back onto the bench. Jack said, "See, I've been thinking. Suppose somebody were to hire somebody to do something against the law. And maybe the man doing the hiring was the cautious type, and wanted to make sure the other bastard didn't get talkative afterwards. Maybe the law might catch him and beat the story out of him, maybe he might just get drunk and shoot his mouth off. I mean, you never know, do you?"

Jack's voice was casual, his expression bland; he might have been asking about a good place to eat.

"But when the job involves a bomb," he said, "then there's one sure way to make sure the man *never* talks, isn't there? With the little added bonus that you don't have to pay him. Not," he added quickly, "that I'm suggesting anything. I don't really think you'd do something like that. Not to a good old revolutionary comrade."

He leaned forward, staring into Lenin's eyes. "But just in case I'm wrong, you might be interested to know that a few things have been written down and left in safe hands, and if I don't make it back tonight there are some people who will be reading them with deep interest by this time tomorrow."

Lenin sat unmoving, returning the younger man's stare, for perhaps five seconds. Then he laughed out loud. "*Nu, molodyets!*" He slapped the table with his palm. "Congratulations, Comrade London. At last you are learning to think like a Russian."

"Looks like they're leaving," the woman with the braids said. "Do we follow them, or—"

The woman with the red ribbons said, "I can't stand this."

Suddenly she was on her feet, moving very fast, brushing past Lenin and grabbing Jack by the arms, pushing him back against the wall. "Listen," she said, speaking quickly but with great care, "listen, you mustn't do this. You're about to start the most terrible war in your world's history. Millions of people will die and nothing will come of it but suffering and destruction. Listen," she said again, her voice rising. "You have a great talent—"

Jack stood looking down at her, open-mouthed, as her voice grew higher and louder. "Damn!" he said finally. "Vladimir, did you ever hear the like? Sorry, honey." He reached up and pulled her hands away, not roughly. "Me no speak Tlingit, or whatever the hell that is."

He grinned and slapped her bottom. "Run along, now. Big white brothers got heap business."

And to Lenin, "Give her a few kopecks, would you, or she'll follow me like a hound pup. And then let's get out of here."

The woman with the red ribbons said, "But I *heard* myself speaking English!"

They were climbing slowly up a hillside above the town of New Arkhangelsk. It was dark now, but the stars gave a good deal of light and the fog didn't reach this high.

The woman with the shell ear pendants, walking in the lead, said without looking around, "That's how it works. Don't ask me why. Some quirk of the conditioning program."

"It was covered in training," the third woman said. "Don't tell me you forgot something that basic. But then as much vodka as you put away, it's a wonder you can remember where you left your own ass . . . you didn't take the anti-intoxicants, did you?"

"They make my skin itch."

"Gods." The woman with the braids raised her hands in a helpless flapping motion. "You're a menace, you know? One of these days we're going to stop covering for you."

"No we won't," the woman in the lead said. "We'll cover for her this time—going to be a job doctoring the recording, but

I can do it—and we'll keep on covering for her. For the same reason she's helped cover for us, when we lost it or just blew it. The same reason everyone covers for their partners. Because when you're out on the timelines there's no one else you can depend on and when you're back home there's no one else who really knows what it was like."

She stopped. "Hold on. It's getting a little tricky."

She took out a pair of oddly-shaped goggles and slipped them on. "All right," she said. "Stay close behind me. It shouldn't be much farther."

The Aleuts were waiting in the shadow of a clump of cedars as Jack came walking down the beach. *"Zdras'tye,"* one of them said, stepping out and raising a hand. "We ready. Go now?"

"Da. Go now." Jack's gold-field Russian was even worse than their pidgin. "Uh, *gdye baidarka?"*

"Von tam." The man gestured and Jack saw it now, a long low black shape pulled up on the shore.

"Harasho." Jack made a come-on gesture and the two men followed him down to the water's edge. His boots made soft crunching sounds in the damp sand. Theirs made none at all.

Together they lifted the big three-man sea kayak and eased it out until it floated free. Jack slid the heavy pack off his back, while the two Aleuts began the elaborate process of cleaning their feet and clothing, getting rid of any sand that might damage the boat's sealskin covering.

The forward paddler said cheerfully, "We go kill Russians, *da?"*

"Oh, yes," Jack said in English. "More than you know, you poor ignorant bastard. More than you'll ever know."

The woman with the red ribbons said, "I'm sorry. I let it get to me and I'm sorry." She turned her head to look at the other two. "It's just the stupid stinking *waste* of it all."

They were well up on the hillside now, sitting on the trunk of a fallen tree, facing out over the dark fog-blanketed harbor. It was the last hour before midnight.

The woman with the seashell ear pendants said, "It was a dreadful war, all right. One of the worst in all the lines—"

"Not that. All right, that too, but I meant him. Jack London," the woman with the red ribbons said. "You know what happens to him after this. He's going to ruin himself with drink and then shoot himself in another five years, and never write anything in a class with his best work from the other lines. And now we know why, don't we?"

"Guilt? Yes," the woman with the seashell ear pendants said. "Probably. But that's just it. He *is* going to do those things, just as he *is* going to sink the *Brandenburg* tonight, because he's already *done* them and there's nothing you can do about it."

She raised a hand and stroked the red-ribboned hair. "And that's what gets to you, isn't it? The inevitability. That's what gets to all of us. That's why we burn out so soon."

The woman with the braids said, "How many known timelines are there, now, that have been mapped back this far?"

"I don't know." The woman with the seashell ear pendants shrugged. "Well over a hundred, the last I heard."

"And so far not a single one where it didn't happen. One way or another, a huge and bloody world war always breaks out, invariably over something utterly stupid, some time within the same twenty-year bracket. Talk about inevitability."

"I know all that," the woman with the red ribbons said. "But this is the first time I've had to watch it happening. With someone I cared about getting destroyed by it."

She put an arm around the woman beside her and laid her head on her shoulder, making the seashell ear pendants clack softly. "How much longer?" she said.

"Not long. Any time now."

They sat looking out into the darkness, watching for the tall flame that would mark the end of yet another world.

"Sitka" grew out of an online group discussion on possible alternative-history themes, specifically other ways in which World War I or its equivalent might have broken out.

Depressingly but realistically, nobody suggested any ways in which the war might not have happened.

Written November 2003
First published February 2005

Angel Kills

I was there when Carmody got his twenty-second angel. I'd been there when he got some of the others, but I hadn't actually seen it happen, having been pretty busy myself at the time.

This time, though, I had the best seat in the house: I was flying Carmody's wing. That was pretty unusual, since as squadron exec I led my own flight; but there was a virus going around and we were running shorthanded, and then at the last minute Robinson's wife went into labor and I took his place so he could go to the hospital.

The angels showed up late in the patrol, going after a United 757 that was coming in to the south runway, and we intercepted and scattered them with no damage to either side. I didn't even get in a shot, being occupied covering Carmody. Orozco, coming up behind, said later that she'd taken a couple of shots and missed. That was all of us; as I say, we were shorthanded.

This bunch of angels weren't very aggressive; they started disappearing almost as soon as we showed up. The 757 touched down unharmed, except for tires smoking from a too-fast landing. So much for that, I thought, checking the clock and the fuel level as we swung out over the big freeway interchange and started a tight circle back toward Sky Harbor. We tried to avoid flying over downtown Phoenix if we could help it; the chainsaw racket of tuned-up Lycomings made the citizens nervous.

Then Carmody's voice came through the headphones: "Huey, two o'clock low!"

I looked but I didn't see anything. Balls, I would have said if it had been anybody else, but everybody knew about Carmody's freakish eyesight. I craned my neck to stare down past the cockpit coaming, and sure enough, there the bastard was, down low, flying east above Buckeye Road. What it was doing, why it hadn't vanished with the others, there was no point in trying to guess; trying to figure angels is a good way to go crazy.

Carmody was already rolling into a steeply descending pursuit curve, the little biplane dropping like a stooping falcon toward the flitting white shape below. I followed him down, looking around quickly in case it was a trap—not that anybody's ever heard of angels trying anything that tricky, but you never know—and a moment later I heard him call, "Alfa Two, clear me."

"Alfa One," I said, "you are clear."

The actual kill was no big deal. The angel was still flying straight and level—maybe there was something wrong with it, whatever that would mean in angel terms—and Carmody simply dropped down astern and fired. From my position I couldn't see the flash of Carmody's gun, but a red spot appeared on the angel's back, right between the wings, and then almost instantly there was a great big yellowish flash and the angel was gone.

Carmody was yelling at me again. "Alfa Two, can you confirm?"

"Affirmative," I said. You had to observe all the formalities with Carmody or he'd get his jock in a knot. "Destruction confirmed," I added for the record. They didn't like us to say "kill" on the radio; it upset some people.

There was a sudden scream in the earphones. "Control to Alfa One," a woman's voice said, sounding very excited. "Congratulations! You did it!"

That was when I realized what had just happened. I'd forgotten about Carmody's record. As of now, he was the top scorer in the United States and maybe the world. The Russians were claiming one of their guys had knocked down sixty or so, but if you believed that you'd believe anything.

Carmody's port wings lifted as he started to turn back toward home, while sounds of cheering came through the earphones; and I followed, thinking: well, now the bullshit starts to get deep.

It was two days later that Lewis showed up. Carmody was off to Washington to get his hand shaken by the President, leaving me in charge, so I got to meet the new man first.

He strode briskly into the office and came to attention in front of my desk. I let him stand there for a few seconds while I looked him up and down. Healthy-looking lad, solid shoulders under his crisp uniform blouse, wiry no-ass build. On the short side, but then if he hadn't been he wouldn't have gotten hired; a Pitts cockpit just isn't roomy enough for the big boys. You could have called him handsome, I suppose, if you liked that strong-jawed, clean-cut look. Kind of a three-quarter-size Li'l Abner.

I said, "Sit down, for God's sake."

"Yes, sir." He went over and sat in the nearest chair. I swear he managed to sit at attention.

I started to tell him to knock it off, but then I realized I wouldn't be doing him a favor. Carmody would love him, just as he was. We weren't really a military organization—technically we were a branch of the Transportation Security Administration, just like the guy who puts your baggage through the scanning machine—but Carmody thought we ought to be, and he could get very tiresome if you didn't go along with his little Dawn Patrol fantasy.

I said, "I've looked at your records. You did pretty well in training." In fact he'd been close to the top of his class; his scores were sure as hell better than mine had been. "So," I said, "I'm sure you can answer a simple question for me."

I reached into the top drawer and took out a mounted photo and held it up. "What is this?"

He glanced at the picture. "Sir," he said, "that is a Hostile Unidentified Entity. Popularly known as an angel."

"Uh huh." I laid the picture on the desk, face up. "Officially we're supposed to call them HUEs, because 'angel' offends the religious whackos who form such an important part of our revered President's base of support. And for official purposes we go along with it, and on the radio we call them Hueys because somebody might be listening. Unofficially, though, among ourselves, we call them angels, same as everybody else." Even our heroic leader, Lord Carmody Ye Penis-Headed.

"Yes, sir," Lewis said.

I wanted badly to tell him to quit calling me "sir", but I knew if I did he'd say, "Yes, sir," and then I'd have to kill him and that would look like hell on our efficiency report. I sighed and tapped the picture with my fingertips.

"Wrong answer, in any case," I told him. "You told me what this is *called.* I asked you what it *is.* And the correct answer is: nobody knows."

"Uh, yes sir. I mean, no sir." His smooth-shaven cheeks went faintly pink. "That is—"

"Nobody knows what they are," I said. "Nobody knows if they're alive, or some sort of non-living devices, or something else that we don't have any words for. Nobody knows if they're intelligent, or just programmed, or being directed from wherever they come from, not that anybody knows where that is either. Or even if where they come from is a 'where' in the sense of a location in our universe."

It was obvious he wanted to speak, but I raised a hand. "No, Lewis, just listen, all right? I'm aware they went over all this at the training school. And you took notes and learned the answers for the tests but deep down, like everybody else, you wondered if they were telling you the whole truth. Didn't you? Didn't you sort of figure that when you finally got out and joined an operational squadron, you'd find out the *real* story?"

I stood up and walked around the desk. "Well, I hate to disappoint you, but what they told you is pretty much the straight word. There aren't any secrets. At least none that anybody in the field knows. Maybe the government's got something more, but if they do they're not sharing it with us."

I hung my ass on the edge of the desk and looked down at him. "We still don't know what the angels are. They don't show up on radar, and they don't leave any heat signature except when they're using those cutting torches or energy-beam weapons or whatever the hell they are. Nobody's ever had a chance to study one, because they explode and vanish without a trace when you kill them. Try to capture them and they simply disappear, and you're lucky if they don't kill you first. A lot of good men died, Lewis, finding out how much we don't know. Made the supreme sacrifice to expand the boundaries of our ignorance."

I paused, but he didn't say anything, not even another yes-sir. He actually appeared to be thinking. Amazing.

"We think we know a few things about them," I said. "We think we know they never go after anything on the ground, but all we really know is that they haven't done it so far. We think we know a little about their performance envelope, but it's all just extrapolation from observation. There's no scientific basis, because by any of the known rules of aerodynamic science they can't fly at all. Those white wings don't have enough area even for gliding flight, let alone the kind of hairy-ass maneuvering these bastards do."

In fact there's a very persuasive theory that the "wings" aren't for flying at all; that they serve some other purpose that we can't even guess at. But no doubt Lewis knew about that too.

"But then," I added, "by any scientific rules, they can't exist. And nobody knows for sure if they do, as we understand physical existence."

I picked up the picture again and looked at it. It was a typical gun camera shot, grainy and fuzzy, but you could still see all the main details. An angel looks anything but angelic when you see its face up close. If you can call that a face; if that's even what it is. That nasty-looking V-shaped slit that looks like a mouth could just as well be its equivalent of an asshole.

"It's been a little over two years since they showed up, Lewis, and the state of our knowledge can be summed up in the words: jack shit. All we know for sure is that they like to cut airplanes open in midair and do horrible things to the people inside. And we don't even know why they do that—food, tissue specimens, hell, sacrifices, they could have a religion for all we can say—and it's possible we never will."

I tossed the picture onto the desk. "The other thing we know is that it's our job to stop them from doing it. Which gets us back to you and the reason you're here, so let's get you processed in and then we'll go see what you can do with a Pitts."

Lewis was already suited up and waiting for me outside the ready room door, helmet tucked under his arm, when I came out of the office a couple of hours later. He didn't quite come to attention when he saw me, but he pulled himself up even straighter as he said, "Ready, sir?"

"Right with you." I went into the ready room and got my helmet out of my locker—screw the coveralls, it was too damn hot and Carmody wasn't around to give me shit about regulations—and went back outside. Lewis was still standing there, gazing up at the sky to the west, where not much was happening. A 737 was climbing steeply over downtown Phoenix, too high now to identify the airline. Lower and closer, you could just make out the little shiny dots that had been its escort, wheeling back toward the airport, their job done now that it had enough speed and altitude to be safe. The buzz of their engines sounded toylike at this distance.

Lewis said, "Seems awfully quiet, sir."

Without looking at him I said, "Where are you from, Lewis?"

"Rawlins, Wyoming. That's in the western part—"

"I know where it is. Been very many angel attacks there?"

"No, sir. We're over six thousand feet."

And the angels can't, or at least don't, operate higher than about a mile. Which is why they show up around airports—since they can only get at the planes during takeoff or landing—and also why Denver finds itself a major international airline hub.

I said, "And you thought things would be livelier at a place like this, did you? Fighting off hordes of angels, day after day?"

"Well, not exactly—"

"Oh, I don't blame you. The way the news media go on, you could easily get the impression it's a regular combat zone over any major airport."

I nodded in the direction he'd been looking. "In fact, though, this is pretty typical. We'll go for two or three weeks, occasionally a month or more, without seeing an angel. Then all of a sudden there they are, and things get intense for a little while, and then they're gone and it's back to routine patrolling again."

He stood for a moment digesting this. "Yes, sir," he said finally. "I suppose I didn't realize . . . I mean, you hear about a new angel attack almost every day or two."

"Sure. *Somewhere* in the world, they materialize and try for a plane. But you'll find that usually that was the only attack reported that day, anywhere. Now and then there'll be two in a twenty-four-hour period, on a few rare occasions three or four, but I've never heard of more. And almost never twice in a row at the same location."

I turned to face him. "I hope you really like to fly around in circles, Lewis, because that's what you're going to be doing for most of your time here. Come on."

We walked over to the hangar area. The heat was coming up off the concrete apron with brutal force; it was like walking across the top of a stove.

The two planes were sitting at the front of the hangar with their noses sticking out like a couple of inquisitive puppies. They looked slightly comical, despite their black-and-white government-cop paint jobs: dinky little open-cockpit biplanes with spatted wheels, like something from the nineteen-thirties. They certainly didn't look like professional killers.

But then they'd never been designed for that; they'd always been strictly for sport, for competition aerobatics and air-show exhibitions. If you'd told Curtis Pitts, back in the forties, that his basic design would one day prove to be the perfect weapon in a specialized war, he'd have laughed in your face.

It's true, all the same. Only a little gymnast like the Pitts can mix it up with the darting, jinking, flitting angels. The military tried with their big proud jets, and lost too damn many of them before they finally admitted defeat and left the job to us.

Larabee came out the side door of the hangar. "Everything ready?" I said, and Larabee nodded.

"Didn't want to roll them out till you got here. Leave them sitting out in that sun even a few minutes, you'd get a blistered ass when you climbed in." Larabee grinned. "This the new man?"

"This is Lewis," I told her, and she gave him an up-and-down once-over and then looked at me and raised one eyebrow, just a little bit, still grinning. I stifled a laugh and made a follow-me gesture to Lewis and we walked on into the hangar.

I gave my plane a quick walk-around and then hoisted myself into the tiny cockpit—you don't so much climb aboard a Pitts as pull it on like a pair of pants—and sat for a moment, enjoying the slightly cooler air inside the hangar, before starting the primary check routine. I flipped the battery switch and watched the instruments come alive. Nothing seemed to be waving its arms at me. I glanced up at the light gun on its mount above the upper wing. The little red LED was on, showing the auxiliary battery fully charged; even though this wasn't a combat flight, we were supposed to be ready for action any time we left the ground.

The gun was the one wrong-looking thing about the Pitts, and even then it didn't look like a weapon. After all, it was just a glorified flashlight, totally harmless to humans or any other living thing except an angel.

Which is yet another of those questions without answers. Why should a beam of highly focused light, at a certain notch on the red spectrum—basically a modified laser—have such instant and terminal effects on any angel it hits? Nobody even has a credible theory on that one. They only discovered it by accident, while trying to develop a new aiming system; and thank God, if there is one, that they did, because so far it's the *only* way anybody's found to kill the bastards. An angel can take any number of direct hits from a cannon shells or rockets without even seeming to notice, but nail him with the light gun and he's gone.

And there are other advantages, like being able to shoot them off a plane under attack without harming the aircraft or the people inside. In fact the light gun represents one of the few positive developments in the war against our angelic visitors.

I looked over at Lewis. He gave me a thumbs-up signal. I switched off and jacked myself up out of the tiny cockpit and said, "Okay, Larabee, let's roll them out."

We climbed to six thousand and I led the way northward, past the ragged brown bulk of Piestewa Peak and the shiny sprawl of the wildly misnamed Paradise Valley. Somewhere down there, I remembered, there used to be a field for ultralight aircraft and gliders. Christ, had it only been a couple of years ago that people thought nothing of flying around at low altitudes, moving slower than a good motorcycle, with nothing worse to worry about than engine failures and bad weather? Even ordinary private flying was just a memory over large areas of the country, except for the few privileged bastards who could afford something like a Learjet. Last I heard, Cessna was laying off half their work force.

Finally we were over more or less empty desert. I thumbed the mike switch and said, "Okay, Lewis. Try and stay with me."

I opened the throttle and eased the nose down into a shallow dive, building a bit of speed, and then suddenly I yanked the Pitts up into a vertical climb, watching between my feet as the horizon came into view through the clear panel in the cockpit floor. I gave her a little rudder, keeping her perpendicular, while the airspeed needle swung rapidly counterclockwise. Just as the Pitts ran out of speed I kicked hard right rudder.

The world beyond the cockpit went momentarily crazy as the Pitts flipped sidewise into a stall turn and pinwheeled down the sky, the Lycoming screaming like an axe murderer. When the nose was pointing straight down I steadied her and then threw the stick over. Maricopa County rotated through 360 degrees as it rushed up toward me. I hauled back on the stick and pulled her out of the dive, somewhat lower than the authorities would have approved of, and kept going up into a loop. At the top of the loop I changed my mind, rolled upright, said why not and continued through a triple snap roll, and then leveled out and looked around for Lewis.

I couldn't see him anywhere. I started to get on the radio, to ask where he was, but then I had a horrible thought. I checked the mirror.

There he was, snuggling up behind me like a mad proctologist. I said, "Jesus!" involuntarily, and then, still with the mike off: "All right, pretty boy, let's dance."

I spent the next hour leading Lewis around the sky, trying to lose him. It was a very long hour.

I took him through Cuban eights and hammerhead stalls and outside snap rolls, boomerang turns and inverted loops and negative flick rolls, damn near everything in the book and a few things that aren't. An observer on the ground might have concluded that the pilot was having some sort of seizure. The only thing I left out was tailslides; the way Lewis kept coming up behind me, I was afraid I'd fall right into him.

And I couldn't shake him. Every time I paused and looked around, there he was. He had sense enough to back off and give me room when a maneuver called for it, but then here he'd come again. At the end, after a particularly violent series, I checked the mirror and he was following me inverted.

I sighed and flicked on the mike. "Right," I said. "Point made and taken. Let's go home."

Later that afternoon I locked the office and headed for the parking lot, pausing to watch the six o'clock patrol take off. Tsosie's Delta flight, back up to strength now; the virus seemed to have run its course. The blare of their engines rattled off the hangar fronts as they lifted off.

The demonstrators were waiting outside the gate beyond the security booth. Having our own parking lot and our own gate is one of the minor perks of the job, but then the religious gazoonies found out about it and they'd been picketing ever since. They yelled incomprehensibly as I drove past, and a couple of them waved signs: SLAY NOT GODS ANNOINTED. WOE UNTO THEM THAT RESIST THE LORD'S JUDGEMENTS. An old lady wore a sandwich-board placard that warned bluntly HELL AWAITS YOU.

At least they'd quit trying to block the gate, after several confrontations with the law. They weren't giving up, though. According to them the angels were just that: heavenly spirits sent by God to punish humanity for being wicked. For us to try and stop them was blasphemous; to kill them was a sin even worse than oral sex.

Not that all the religious knuckle-walkers felt this way. On the contrary, the majority held to a counter-theory that the angels were in reality Satanic beings, come to torment the world, their appearance merely a trick by Lucifer—a fallen angel himself—to shake people's faith. *They* thought we were wonderful; they'd come down to the gate and wave flags and Bibles at us and sing hymns and pray loudly for us. Often the two groups would get into a singing and yelling competition, each trying to drown the other out; and a couple of times they fell to beating the shit out of each other in front of God and the CNN cameras.

And yet they just might have been onto something, in an assbackwards sort of way. At least some knowledgeable people had suggested that the old Biblical and medieval stories of angels with flaming swords might represent some earlier visitation.

Anyway, their ideas weren't any screwier than some of the other explanations you could hear. Like the story, widely believed in many parts of the world and among the looser-headed types in this country, that the angels were escapees from a secret CIA program. Somebody even made a movie about it.

I was living out in Glendale at the time, in a moderately crappy little duplex on a street with a silly name. At the front door I paused to empty the mailbox. As usual there was nothing but junk mail: subscription offers, solicitations for charity, a letter from my ex-wife's lawyer. I went inside and back to the kitchen, where I threw the lot into the trash bin.

I got a frozen pasta dinner out of the freezer and stuck it in the microwave and waited till the beeper beeped. I opened the box again and issued myself a beer and carried everything back into the living room and sat down in the big chair and reached for the remote and switched on the TV and almost immediately said, "Oh, Christ."

The angels had gotten another airliner. Worse, it had crashed into a populous suburb of Melbourne, destroying homes and starting fires over a large area.

"The fires seem to be under control now," an Australian-accented voiceover was saying, while the camera panned over a row of burning houses and then steadied on a group of men in fire-fighting outfits piling out of a truck. "There's still considerable danger, though, that they might spread. It's been very dry lately and the wind is picking up."

The scene shifted to a studio desk, where a man in a good suit, evidently the US anchor, was looking anxiously at the camera. "Still no figures," he asked, "on the number of dead and injured?"

"Still nothing official." Now the screen showed a thin young man holding a microphone. His short-sleeved khaki shirt was badly rumpled and his hair hung limp across his forehead; deep stress lines showed at the corners of his eyes and mouth. Behind him smoke rose above a scene of general destruction.

"But," he said, "I'd say it's got to be in the hundreds at least, even leaving aside the passengers and crew of the aircraft. This is a holiday here in Australia, so a lot of people were home."

Back to the anchor desk, where the suit said, "This just in: the aircraft has been identified as a Japan Air Lines Boeing 747, inbound from Tokyo. No further details at this time. We'll be right back."

The camera pulled back, as a different voiceover said, "This has been a special news bulletin, brought to you as part of our ongoing coverage of the HUE crisis. And now these messages from our local affiliates."

The picture dissolved into a view of a 777 under attack, with a garish red-lettered legend TERROR IN THE SKIES. So they were still using that same stock photo, not that there were all that many available with the various governments sitting on most of them. Another fuzzy gun-camera shot, but you could clearly see the white forms of half a dozen angels crawling over the rear fuselage and the wing roots, with bright spots where their torches were cutting into the shiny metal. That particular plane had survived, thanks to a king-hell pilot and the nick-of-time arrival of the fighters, but it was still a stomach-churning picture.

I went ahead and ate my dinner and watched as more reports came in. They showed the wreckage of the JAL plane, or the biggest recognizable pieces; you could just make out that distinctive humped shape of the 747's upper forward section, lying amid the blackened ruins of several small houses.

There were no details on the attack, or how the angels had gotten past the escort. The Australians, from all I'd heard, had a first-class air security force, with their own specially-designed planes. Maybe they'd gotten careless; somebody said they'd had very few attacks in the last year.

And then again maybe it was nobody's fault; maybe the angels had just been unusually lucky. Or unusually smart.

After an hour or so the suits ran out of new information and started repeating themselves. When they showed that damn photo again I grabbed the remote and switched channels at random.

A muscular man with his shirt off stared earnestly out at me and assured me that a revolutionary new exercise system would make me look just like him. I punched more buttons and finally found a panel discussion in progress on one of the allegedly educational channels. A liverish-looking woman with a bad hairdo was saying, "So the human race has finally made contact with an alien species, and what do we do? Kill them, or try to. It's so typical."

Beside her a willowy grey-haired man nodded slowly. "Yes. Typical, even predictable." He fluttered an elegant long-fingered hand. "The compulsion to destroy whatever we don't understand."

The camera switched to a bespectacled man at a lectern. "And to those who would ask, 'What about the attacks?'" he asked.

The woman shook her head impatiently. "'Attacks'? I don't think we know enough about their motives to use that sort of judgmental language. 'Contacts' would be a better term. But," she went on, "if the governments of the world would give up this insane campaign to kill them off, and put the same effort and resources into trying to communicate with them, perhaps we could find out where they come from and what they want—"

"What they *want?*" I said aloud. "You useless cow, don't you watch the fucking news? Take a look at what they just did in Australia. That's what they *want.*"

I gulped the rest of the beer and crumpled the can in my hand and threw it at the screen. It fell short and hit the floor, just as the willowy man said, "And anyway, what about the attacks by the United States on other countries and their people?"

I found the remote and hit the power button and watched the screen go black. Talking back to the people on TV now? Not a good sign. Definitely need to get out more. Take up karaoke, maybe, or enroll in a square-dance class, or join a BDSM club.

There was a taste in my mouth like old pennies. I got up and headed toward the kitchen again to get another beer, but then I changed my mind and went into the bedroom and got the bottle of Scotch from the bedside table instead. Better go easy on the beer. When you spend half your waking life in the cockpit of a Pitts you have to watch your calories.

Next morning I assigned Lewis to my flight, switching Hardin to Alfa flight, which was short with Carmody away. Hardin wasn't happy about it but I told him the arrangement was temporary. I had a fairly good idea what was going to happen when Carmody got back.

For the rest of the week Lewis flew on my wing. There was no action, only routine patrols, but even that was enough to show that he hadn't just been on a hot streak that first day. God, he could fly. Even without the aerobatics, even with the most ordinary moves, you could see it: that intangible whatever-it-is that only a very few pilots have, that invests every movement of the aircraft with a special grace.

"I swear," Larabee said, "he looks good just sitting on the apron with the engine off. Can he shoot too?"

"Going by his scores from training school," I told her, "yes. Second in his class in marksmanship."

She'd brought up an important point. The one big shortcoming of the light gun is that you can only use it for a maximum of two seconds at a shot before it overheats; in fact there's an automatic cutoff to keep excited pilots from burning out the taxpayers' property. So you can't just spray a general area; you've got to use it more like a rifle than a machine gun. Which is why angel kills are so uncommon, and why a sharpshooter like Carmody was a top ace while someone like Orozco, who could outfly him forty ways but couldn't shoot worth a damn, never scored.

"All that and a tight little butt too," Larabee said. "If he were a woman I'd marry him."

Carmody was back the following Monday. I spent most of the morning in the office with him, going over various adminstrative details. Finally he said, "So. This new man, Lewis. Any good?"

I told him. He whistled. "Really? I was going to take him up for a little tryout, but I guess there's no point. If he can stay with you, then he can sure as hell stay with me." He snorted. "Hell, if he can stay with you, I probably can't stay with *him.*"

That was a stunner; I almost felt like looking around for a ventriloquist. But then Carmody had been surprising me all morning. I'd been ready for him to be an even bigger pain in the ass than usual, but instead he seemed more human, less full of himself. Maybe getting what he was after had mellowed him a bit.

He leaned back in his chair and played a couple of
arpeggios on the desk with his fingertips. "Well," he said, "I
think we'd better put him in my flight, where I can keep an eye
on him and teach him the ropes. I know you'll be glad to get
Hardin back."

Stealing the hot new jock for his flight, just as I'd
expected. That was more like the Carmody we all knew. It was a
relief, really. When the Carmodys of the world quit acting like
assholes it makes me nervous; you have to have some constants
in life, so you don't lose your bearings.

And so Lewis became Carmody's wingman, and for the next few
weeks they flew together, with Orozco and Robinson on their
flank; and Lewis quit being the new guy and became just another
name on the roster board. Everybody settled down again into the
old routine, one day pretty much like another, not much
excitement except now and then when the wind got crazy. A
Pitts isn't an easy plane to land anyway—we used to say that
there were two kinds of Pitts pilots, those who had groundlooped
and those who were about to—and in a gusting crosswind it can
be almost unbearably fascinating. You'd never have guessed it,
though, watching Lewis come in with the wind blasting across
the runway; he made it look not just easy but inevitable.

We did get one more angel attack, right after the first of
the month, but it didn't amount to much. They materialized out
over the Mesa area, eight or so of them, converging on a little
Fokker 70 regional flight coming in from Albuquerque.

Delta flight was flying escort. Tsosie got an angel almost
immediately and the others scattered and then started to vanish.
They hadn't had a real shot at the Fokker anyway; they'd
spawned too far astern of their target. The whole thing was over
in hardly any time.

"They weren't very good," Tsosie said at the debriefing.
"They didn't really seem to know what they were doing. The
only smart thing they did was disappear when we came at them."

Carmody looked at me. "Hm. The last ones were like that
too, weren't they?" And then quickly, "Well, maybe not *this*

bad." After all, that had been the engagement that made him a big hero; mustn't imply that it had been a turkey shoot.

He laughed suddenly. "You suppose they've made Phoenix their training ground? Where they send their new guys to get some experience? Boy, did they ever pick the wrong place."

A couple of weeks later the angels showed up again.

Bravo flight caught the first contact. It was just before noon and we were escorting a Southwest 737 coming in from Tulsa. Off to the west Alfa flight was flying cover for a Fedex cargo plane taking off from the south runway. That was a situation nobody liked, when there were two planes to cover at the same time, and the controllers tried to avoid it but now and then it happened.

Phoenix is a little over eleven hundred feet above sea level, so by the time we picked up the 737 at five thousand he was already into his approach, wheels and flaps coming down as we fanned out behind him and a little above, Hardin and me to port and Sheridan and Foley to starboard. I glanced down to check airspeed—just under 150 knots, he was coming in a little hot but they all do that now, trying to reduce the danger period— and that was when the angels hit us.

Hardin's voice sounded in the earphones: "Hueys, eleven o'clock low!" I'd already seen them, though, spawning just astern of the 737's port wing, and Christ but there were more of them than I'd ever seen at one time, the air was full of white wings and not all of them going for the 737 either, several were coming straight toward *us.*

I pushed the Pitts's nose down and thumbed the safety cover off the firing button on top of the joystick and laid the gunsight's center pip on an angel coming at me head-on. The light beam flashed red on the middle of its body and I flinched instinctively as I flew through the explosion, but as usual there was no turbulence or heat or debris, or any other sign that anything had ever been there.

The flash had momentarily blinded me, though, and I leveled off to let my vision clear. I hit the com button to switch frequencies. "Alfa One," I called. "Alfa One, major attack. Can you assist?"

"Affirmative," Carmody came back immediately. "On our way, Bravo One."

By now I could see again. What I could see was almost enough to make me wish I couldn't. The angels were swarming over the 737, torches already glowing. Off to my right Sheridan was rolling frantically, trying to shake off an angel, while Foley hung on astern, his light gun intermittently flashing as he tried to pick the angel off.

I pulled the Pitts around and bore down on the 737, laying the sights on an angel doing something right above the main passenger cabin. I didn't hit it but I must have come uncomfortably close; it gave a sudden jump and flew upward, away from the 737. I watched the green LED below the gunsight, waiting for it to tell me that the light gun was ready to use again, but then Hardin yelled, "Bravo One, check six!"

I jerked around and looked back just in time to see a big white shape closing in fast from astern. I said, "Shit!" and flipped the Pitts onto its back and hauled back on the stick. At the bottom of the inverted loop I eased off on the stick and let the Pitts straighten out into a forty-five-degree zoom that I was pretty sure no angel could follow; they maneuvered like bats out of hell but they didn't have much of a climb.

I looked back but I didn't see the angel, or Hardin either. What I did see was a long dark gash across the skin of the Pitts's fuselage, just ahead of the vertical fin. My stomach did a slow roll; I hadn't realized the bastard was that close. A wonder it hadn't cut a control cable, but everything seemed to be working.

But the evasive maneuver had taken me away from the main fight. I said into the mike, "Bravo two, you are released for independent action." Right now protecting the 737 took priority over covering my butt.

And it was in serious need of protection. Climbing back up to rejoin the action, I could see what was going on: the jetliner pilot had panicked and was trying to abort the landing and run out. Which wasn't necessarily a bad move—he had more than enough power to outrun any angel ever seen—but he was trying to climb, too, instead of holding altitude till he got some speed up, and that was killing him. Or was going to kill him, along with a bunch of other people, if we didn't do something fast, because by now the angels were all over him.

I saw Hardin come in over the 737's port wing and a moment later there was a big yellow flash right over the wing root as an angel exploded. Another Pitts was moving up from astern—Sheridan or Foley, I couldn't tell which—and I was almost within range too, but we weren't going to be enough.

And then, by God, just like the good guys in an old movie, Carmody's flight arrived. All of a sudden there were black-and-white shapes streaking in head-on over the 737 and light guns flashing and two angels blew almost simultaneously.

The others rose up off the 737 like vultures flapping up from a carcass. Now was the time for them to do their vanishing act; but this bunch hadn't read the script or they'd said the hell with it. They went for the fighters.

I blew an angel off Robinson's five o'clock and came around to take a long shot at another one as it danced away from Orozco's fire. While the light gun cooled and recharged I made a fake pass at a couple that were closing in on Hardin, breaking up their attack and letting him climb clear. By now there was a full-scale furball going on, biplanes and angels whirling this way and that, light guns and torches flashing. It must have been a stirring sight for anyone watching from the ground. Close up, it was merely terrifying.

A white shape appeared in the mirror and I yanked the Pitts up in a tight Immelmann. As I rolled upright I heard Carmody's voice in the headset: "Alfa Two, clear me."

I looked around to see what was going on, but that angel was still after me and I had to do some tricky maneuvering to get rid of it. In the middle of a hard flick roll, though, I heard Carmody again, much louder and sharper: "Alfa Two, I say again, clear me!"

The angel dropped away at last and I leveled out just as Carmody's voice rose in a near-scream: *"Alfa Two, for God's sake get him off me!"*

Escaping the angel had left me well above everybody else, and the view through the cockpit-floor windows was too blurry to see anything. But I leaned far over to my left and stuck my head over the coaming and banked the Pitts a little to port and then I saw what was going on.

A big angel, maybe the biggest I'd ever seen, was right over Carmody's tail and moving in. Carmody wasn't taking any evasive action, and after a moment I saw why: his rear control surfaces were in blackened tatters. It was surprising he could even fly straight.

Lewis was sitting just astern, his nose not more than fifty feet behind Carmody's tail. He didn't seem to be doing anything else.

I cursed and whipped the Pitts over and down, leveling off a hundred yards or so behind the two biplanes and cramming on full throttle to overtake them. I couldn't see the angel; I could only see a little of Carmody's plane, because Lewis was in the way.

"Alfa Two," I called, "break left."

And, when he didn't: "Lewis, get the fuck out of the way!"

He didn't move. I hadn't really thought he would.

I said some more bad words and pulled up, over Lewis's plane, and rolled the Pitts onto her back. I caught a brief glimpse of Lewis sitting absolutely straight and still at the stick, his face hidden by his helmet's visor. I didn't really look at him, though; I was locked in on what was happening in front of him.

The angel was on top of Carmody's plane now. Its wings hid the cockpit area.

I pulled back on the stick, still flying inverted, to bring the gunsight to bear on the angel. It was an easy shot, even from that angle. I thumbed the trigger button, knowing it was too late.

The angel flashed and vanished. I rolled up and swung out to port, looking down. I could see into Carmody's cockpit now. Or what had been Carmody's cockpit. What was left in it now couldn't really be called Carmody any more.

The other angels were starting to wink out now. Off in the middle distance the 737 was climbing away, apparently undamaged.

Carmody's plane continued to fly straight and level for another minute or two. Then its starboard wingtips dropped and it fell away in a long spiral dive. I thought at first it was going to hit the university campus area but instead it smashed into the dry bed of the Salt River.

After a little while I shook myself like a wet dog and spoke into the mike again. "This is Bravo One," I said. "All pilots return to base. I say again: everybody go home."

Lewis was already standing beside his plane, taking off his helmet, when I came up behind him. He must have heard my boots on the concrete; he turned around to face me before I spoke.

"System malfunction, Lewis?" I asked. I didn't raise my voice. "Trouble with the gun and the radio?"

He swallowed hard; you could see his Adam's apple bobbing. He opened his mouth but nothing came out. He swallowed again and then, in a kind of dry croak, he said, "No, sir."

"Everything working properly?"

He nodded. His face was the color of cigarette paper.

"Thank you. That's what I needed to know."

I paused a moment, fighting for control. "Lewis," I said, still keeping my voice low, maybe not entirely steady. "Lewis, there'll be a formal inquiry into what happened up there and why. So you don't have to tell me anything. In fact I'm officially advising you not to."

He didn't respond. I said, "And besides, just between us and strictly off the record, I already know the story and you know I know it. "

I wouldn't have thought he could go any paler, but he did. His lips worked soundlessly. "I," he finally got out. "I."

I said very quietly, "Couldn't do it, could you?"

The tears started coming then, trickling down on either side of his nose. "An angel," he said, nearly whispering. "An *angel*. I couldn't, I, how, how can anybody—"

He ran dry again. I said, "I know, Lewis. Trust me, you're not the first."

I turned and walked away, leaving him standing there alone. Maybe I should have said something to try to make him feel better, but I didn't really give a damn.

Off to the east you could just barely make out the smoke from Carmody's plane, already thinning and drifting away in the desert wind.

Unusually long incubation period on this one; I got the idea clear back in the summer of '96, filed it away, and didn't even try to do anything with it for over seven years. Then all of a sudden one day it had *to be written. Don't ask me.*

Written January 2002
First published April 2005

Not Fade Away

It was around the middle of June that I saw him again, and realized at last that it was really true. Like everybody else on Corregidor, I'd heard the reports—first the rumors, which I ignored because you could hear all sorts of tales on the Rock; then the initial reports on the radio, which most of us put down as Japanese propaganda, and finally the official word from General Wainwright's headquarters.

But it didn't really register, somehow. I guess there was a tendency to denial, about that and a lot of other things, at that time. Even after the fall of Corregidor, as we sat around the old Spanish prison in Manila waiting for them to decide what to do with us, there were people who still refused to believe MacArthur had been captured. It was just a Jap trick, they'd tell you, the General was already in Australia getting ready to lead a huge force back to the Philippines and rescue us. . . .

I wasn't one of the holdouts, but I have to admit it didn't fully sink in, wasn't quite real to me, until I saw him coming in the gate flanked by half a dozen Japanese guards.

That was a couple of weeks after they took us out of Bilibid Prison and moved us north to a former Philippine Army camp near the little town of Tarlac. They hauled us in trucks; nothing like the infamous forced march from Bataan, which had happened before Corregidor fell, and in fact we hadn't even heard about it yet. Anyway, they treated the senior officers a little better than the juniors and the enlisted men. We were of course worthless *gaijin* prisoners, permanently dishonored by having surrendered, but the Japanese obsession with hierarchy did get us a few privileges. You could still get slapped around by any Japanese private who didn't think you'd saluted him smartly enough, but serious beatings were fairly rare.

I got off even easier, in that respect, than the others; the guards would yell at me but rarely laid a hand on me, once they got a look at the freshly-healed stump of my right arm.

"It's got nothing to do with sympathy or consideration, you know," Carl Norton told me. He was a Marine major who had been stationed in China until just before the outbreak of war, and had had a good deal of contact with the Japanese officers there. "It's just another of their quirks. Most Japs are uncomfortable about physical contact with anybody who's, uh, damaged, you know? They figure your luck must be bad, and it could be catching."

They might have had something there. After all, I'd lost my arm and my command a mere three days into the war, when a stick of Jap bombs blew my submarine to scrap metal at the Cavite dock. I wouldn't have wanted to get too near me either.

When we got to Tarlac we found other prisoners had gotten there before us, officers captured in the fall of Bataan. They'd been through the Death March, and then the filthy hell at Camp O'Donnell, not far from Tarlac, where disease and thirst and hunger had decimated their already pathetic ranks. We were appalled at their appearance; we'd thought we'd had it pretty rough, but obviously we had no idea. And these were senior officers like us; what it was like for the enlisted men, I didn't even want to imagine.

So Tarlac must have looked pretty good to them; and it wasn't all that bad, really, by the standards of Japanese prison camps—not, God knows, that that's saying much. The food was monotonous and tasteless and not very nutritious and there was never enough of it, but they didn't actually starve us, and the living quarters weren't too squalid. We actually had bunks to sleep on, and blankets; at Bilibid most people had had to settle for the concrete floor.

The original commandant was a colonel named Ito, and he seemed a decent sort, but a few days after we arrived he suddenly left. His replacement was another colonel named Sakamoto, a heavy-set son of a bitch with a permanent scowl. Sakamoto made it clear right away that he intended to run a tight ship and didn't give a damn for his prisoners' exalted rank. But at least he wasn't a brutal sadist or a screaming nutcase like some of the commandants you heard about.

The real hardship for most of the prisoners at Tarlac was mental. This was a camp for colonels and generals, after all, with a handful of lower ranks—as a mere Navy commander, I was pretty close to the bottom of the totem pole—and promotion had been slow in the peacetime years. So what you had was mostly a bunch of middle-aged and even elderly men; many of them had served in the last war, in France. The physical privations were rough enough on them, but the humiliation—having to salute and bow to teen-aged Japanese privates, getting slapped like unruly children for trivial offenses—was far worse.

And then there was the shame of defeat. Especially this particular defeat. "They got their asses handed to them," Carl Norton said, "by a bunch of people they'd always looked down on as ridiculous little monkeys who couldn't do anything right. That's what's really eating them."

"But not you?" I asked him, grinning. We were good friends; we'd known each other since Corregidor.

"Not me," Carl said. "I saw the little bastards in action in China, remember? I knew the minute the war started we were in deep shit."

There was a lot of arguing among the Army officers, too, about the reasons for the defeat, a lot of recrimination and blame-swapping, some of it pretty bitter. All that frustration and anger had to find some sort of outlet, after all . . . and anyway, there really wasn't much else to do. The senior officers didn't have to pull labor details, and the supply of reading matter or writing materials was nearly nonexistent, so squabbling like a bunch of old ladies was just about all there was left. That or simply sitting around staring silently off into nowhere.

General Wainwright arrived a few days after the rest of us, in a car from Manila. As senior American officer he might have been expected to do something about the state of morale, but his own obviously wasn't so great either. He looked and moved like a man in tremendous pain, even though they hadn't harmed him; and it wasn't hard to understand why. He'd been the one to surrender—not just Corregidor, but all the American forces in the Philippines. That was one of the things people talked and argued about, though not within his hearing.

Anyway, that was what things were like at Tarlac when they brought MacArthur in.

He wasn't wearing his trademark cap; I guess he'd lost it when Bulkeley's PT boat was sunk. He was bareheaded and his uniform was a stained and rumpled ruin, and he wasn't wearing his stars—none of the prisoners were allowed to wear rank insignia—but it didn't matter; he'd have been recognizable in a jockstrap. He still carried himself tall and straight—he towered over the Japanese guards like an Oregon cedar—and he still moved with that long-legged stride, so that they had to hustle to keep formation around him.

But God, he looked old . . . he wasn't a young man, of course, but he looked ten years older than when I'd seen him last.

"He looks like hell," Carl Norton said. We were standing maybe twenty or thirty yards away from the gate; we'd just happened to be walking across the compound when the motor convoy drove up in front of the gate. No one in the camp, even General Wainwright, had been told MacArthur was coming. Maybe the commandant didn't want us holding some kind of parade or ceremony to welcome him. More likely it just didn't occur to the Japs to tell us, any more than you'd bother telling the stray mutts in the pound that you're bringing the big dog in.

"Still got that presence, though," Carl mused.

"It's about all he's got left," I said.

"Yeah. Poor devil."

We watched as they escorted him toward the headquarters building. Colonel Sakamoto had come out onto the porch and was waiting. A Japanese lieutenant came up and saluted and handed Sakamoto some papers. Then he shouted a command and the guard detail stamped to a halt.

The commandant stood staring at MacArthur. I couldn't see MacArthur's face from where I was standing, but I was pretty sure he was staring back.

And then, after what seemed like a long time, MacArthur saluted. It was an absolutely West-Point-correct salute, but it was as if he had enormous weights lashed to his arm.

Colonel Sakamoto didn't return the salute; they never did. He just turned and walked back into the building, gesturing for MacArthur to follow. The lieutenant screamed at the soldiers again and they about-faced and headed back toward the gate.

Carl Norton let his breath out in a long ragged sigh. "Jesus," he said.

And after a minute: "I never liked him, you know. I always figured him for a showoff and a glory hound. I still think he handled the defense of the Philippines like somebody trying to stick his dick in his ear. But you can't help feeling for a man who's been knocked down that hard."

We still didn't know, though, just how hard this particular man had been knocked down. We found out a couple of days later, when Sergeant Watanabe, the chief interpreter, told us MacArthur's wife and son had been lost when the PT boat was sunk.

"There's no question about it," Watanabe said. "The bodies were found, washed up on the beach, the next day. The torpedo boat was literally blown out of the water, you know, by the destroyer's guns. The only survivors were the General himself and an ordinary sailor who died of his wounds on the way back to Manila."

He spoke in a clear, flawless English with only the faintest touch of an accent; four years at Princeton had left their mark, and not just on his language skills. He wasn't happy about the war and he'd tell you privately that it was going to end catastrophically for Japan.

"I know Americans," he would say. "You seem so easygoing, but under the surface you are a violent and vengeful people. You also think life is like your Western movies, in which the hero never draws first. An attack like the one at Pearl Harbor was the surest possible way to enrage the American people beyond all reason. You will not stop now until you have had your vengeance, no matter what it takes."

Now Watanabe said, "It was a strange business in Colonel Sakamoto's office. General MacArthur stood there looking straight ahead, without expression, while the commandant spoke and I translated. He only spoke in reply to direct questions, and when he did speak his voice was hoarse and indistinct, as if it hurt him to talk."

He raised an eyebrow. "How has he been behaving, since his arrival?"

We both shook our heads. "We haven't seen him," I said, "except at a distance. The generals don't mix much with us lower orders."

Which was true, not that we'd have told Watanabe if we had known anything. The Japs made a point of not recognizing distinctions in rank among the prisoners, but even so, the generals had their own barracks, and had their meals together and so on.

And MacArthur had stayed out of sight; as far as I knew he hadn't left the barracks except when he had to. We'd seen him at the morning roll-call formations, when we all had to bow in unison to the Emperor, who was represented by a white post at the end of the parade ground. Really, I'm not making this up; you should have seen us, over a hundred middle-aged-to-elderly men lined up in ranks, bowing respectfully to a wooden post. Carl kept saying he was going to sneak out some night and piss on it, but he wasn't suicidal enough to do it.

We'd seen MacArthur at mealtime, and a couple of times on the way to the latrine. But we hadn't been close to him, and it wouldn't have mattered if we had; there was a wall around him that was almost visible. It wasn't just the traditional isolation of the man at the top; MacArthur seemed to be on another planet. One of the outer ones, cold and dark and with crushing gravity.

"They say he doesn't talk to anyone," Carl reported, later that evening. He was friendly with a couple of artillery colonels, and they in turn knew some of the generals, and so from time to time he heard things. "They say he just sits around, or lies on his bunk looking at the ceiling."

MacArthur not talking? There was a thought to shake your faith in the immutable laws of the universe.

"Some people are worried he might kill himself," Carl said.

"It's possible." On Corregidor it was common knowledge that MacArthur had said openly that he intended to shoot his family and then himself if capture was imminent. He probably meant it, too. "In some ways," I said, "he thinks a lot like our beloved captors."

"Yeah," Carl said. "He'd have made a great samurai. Ironic as hell, huh?"

But then the following day, as we were walking across the parade ground, there he was, striding briskly toward us. He was wearing an old-fashioned campaign hat someone had given him—you didn't go bareheaded in the Philippine sun if you could help it—and the brim shadowed his eyes, but there was something different about the set of his jaw and the way he held his head; or rather something more like the MacArthur I remembered. We stopped and came to something resembling attention, while Carl snapped off a salute. The stump of my right arm came up reflexively before I could stop it.

MacArthur ground to a stop in front of us and returned Carl's salute. I suppose I looked embarrassed, because he turned to face me, still holding the salute, and said, "That's all right, Commander. It's fitting that I salute *you,* in view of the sacrifice you have made for our country."

Then, lowering his hand, he added in a lower voice, "I too have lost my right arm. . . ."

I couldn't think of a damn thing to say.

After a second he said, "Well, Commander, I haven't seen you since Corregidor." His voice had changed again; now it rang with a kind of strained heartiness. "How's the arm? Healing well?"

"Yes, sir. Seems to be."

"Good, good." He nodded energetically. "And Major Norton, you're looking well. I want you to know," he said, "how much I appreciated the Marines' contribution to the defense of these islands."

I still couldn't see his eyes clearly in the shadow of the hat's brim, but there was something truly terrible in the lines around his mouth. It was as if the skin of his face had been stretched too tight.

Carl mumbled an indistinct thanks. MacArthur said, "Well, gentlemen, I'm afraid I haven't time to stop and talk. But don't hesitate to come to me if there's any way I can be of help. We all have to help one another get through this time of trial."

He turned, or rather did a parade-ground about-face, and strode away. We watched as he marched across the parade ground, somehow giving the impression of being followed by at least a division.

Carl said, "What the hell . . . ?"

"Don't ask me," I said. "I'm in shock too."

"Well," Carl said, "at least he's got the line of bullshit back. Wonder what the story is?"

I said, "I doubt if we'll ever know."

But in fact we did find out the following day, by way of one of Carl's artillery colonel buddies. "It was Bluemel," he told us, and right away things started to make more sense.

General Bluemel was a monumentally tough old infantryman who had commanded a Philippine Army division in the Bataan campaign, and from all accounts he was absolutely fearless. His own subordinates had been terrified of him; there were rumors that he had personally shot men trying to retreat. "Son of a bitch should have been a Marine," Carl Norton often said, bestowing his highest accolade.

"I wasn't there," the colonel said, "but what I heard was that Bluemel just walked up to him in the barracks, while he was sitting on his bunk staring at the wall, and laid into him. Chewed him out like an awkward recruit, right there in front of the other generals. They couldn't hear all of it, but everybody clearly heard the phrase 'sitting on your ass feeling sorry for yourself.'"

"No," I said, and Carl said, "You're kidding."

The colonel shook his head, grinning. "I tell you, Bluemel's something else. On Bataan he was up front with a rifle leading counterattacks like some young lieutenant. His men held their positions when everybody else was breaking and running, just because they were more afraid of him than the Japs."

"So what did he say to MacArthur?" Carl prompted.

"From what I heard, he told him to pull himself together and start exercising some leadership. Said, 'You're not the first general to lose a campaign, or even the first man to lose his family.' Asked him if he thought his son would want to know his father had turned out to be a quitter."

It was like hearing that someone had gone up and kicked God in the ass. No, that would have been more believable; God, they tell us, forgives, which MacArthur never did.

"Bluemel told him he had a responsibility to the men in this camp," the colonel went on. "And that it was time he started fulfilling it. Then he turned and walked away, without even giving MacArthur a chance to reply."

"And?" I asked.

"And MacArthur just went on sitting there, still without speaking, the rest of the evening. But then the next morning he was up before anybody else, and he was—" The colonel spread his hands. "As you've seen. He's been like that ever since. I'm not sure whether I want to thank Bluemel or kill him."

In the days ahead there were times when I felt the same way. MacArthur was back in full force-of-nature style. He reorganized the mess and somehow persuaded Colonel Sakamoto to improve the food allowance. He instituted a series of classes in which officers lectured the rest of us on their various subjects of knowledge, from military history to Shakespeare. Christ, he even started group singing sessions in the evenings!

None of which went over all that well with the men whose morale it was supposed to restore. For one thing, they were veteran professional soldiers; they didn't appreciate being hustled like a lot of homesick Boy Scouts. For another, a considerable number of them—probably over half the officers in camp—blamed MacArthur for the military debacle that had put them behind barbed wire to begin with.

Still, they went along, if only from boredom and because resistance would have taken too much energy. And the additional food, and the other small concessions MacArthur managed to get from Sakamoto, did a lot to improve his popularity.

Watanabe asked us a couple of times whether we knew anything about the sudden change in MacArthur's behavior. I wouldn't quite say he tried to pump us, but he was pretty persistent. Needless to say we didn't admit to knowing a thing.

"Very strange," Watanabe said. "His earlier despondency, I can understand. After all, to become a prisoner is bad enough, but to be captured while trying to flee—the humiliation must be all but unbearable." He shook his head. "The fortunes of war, as they say. If that destroyer hadn't happened to be where it was that night, if General MacArthur had made it to Australia, he would be a great national hero now."

"After getting whipped the way he did?" Carl Norton snorted. "I don't think so."

"Oh, but you forget your country's admiration for brave losers. The Alamo, Custer's last stand and all that. It is one of the aspects of your culture," Watanabe said, "that we Japanese find most baffling."

"Something phony about that son of a bitch," Carl said after Watanabe was gone. "Somebody that smart, that well educated, and he's just a buck-ass sergeant at a prison camp? Bullshit. I'd bet my rapidly diminishing ass he's with Jap intelligence. All these senior officers here, they're a gold mine of information on the U.S. military. A man like Watanabe, with his good-guy act, could pick up all sorts of valuable information."

"Or he's playing some kind of private game," I said.

"Could be," Carl said. "In my experience most people are."

A week or so later the camp had a visitor.

He didn't arrive with any sort of fanfare; he just rode up in an unmarked car, unaccompanied except for the driver. I happened to be passing nearby as he got out of the car, and I got a pretty good look at him. He got a look at me, too, and his face went dark and he started to open his mouth, no doubt to yell at me for not saluting him; but then he saw the stump of my arm. While he was registering that I threw him a quick bow—I had a feeling this was somebody I better not piss off—and when I straightened up he was standing there staring at me, the way you'd look at something really disgusting you'd just stepped in.

He wasn't much to look at; he was short and squat even by Japanese standards, with a bristling black beard and mustache and thick glasses—none of which hid nearly enough of his face; he really was an ugly little bastard. He wore an ordinary field uniform, badly rumpled and a little too big for him; his collar bore the three stars and three red stripes of a colonel.

He stood for a moment giving me that hating glare, and then suddenly he turned and headed toward the headquarters building, walking very fast, with an odd, almost loping gait. And I hauled ass away from there before he could change his mind; I didn't know who the hell he was, but he had *bad news* written all over him.

Sergeant Watanabe was standing near the fence, watching the visitor as he stalked across the HQ porch and disappeared inside. "You are a lucky man," he said to me. "I thought for a minute you were in big trouble. You don't want to attract Colonel Tsuji's attention."

"Tsuji?" The name was a new one on me.

"You don't know, do you? You should. All of you should know about Colonel Tsuji." There was no one anywhere near us, but Watanabe's voice was very low. "Because he wants you all dead."

"I thought that was what you all wanted." I held up my stump. "You sure try hard enough."

"It's not a joke." Watanabe looked serious, even scared. "When Bataan fell, he tried to have the prisoners executed, and in some cases he succeeded. General Homma gave orders that the prisoners should be treated humanely, but Colonel Tsuji countermanded them."

"What the hell?" I said. "Since when do colonels countermand orders from generals?"

"There is a great deal General Homma does not know about what goes on in his command. Perhaps he chooses not to know."

Watanabe grimaced. "I'm afraid our army isn't quite like yours. Your officers form cliques to advance your careers. Ours form secret societies for the purpose of changing the nation's destiny, and terrorize and even assassinate those who stand in their way. Colonel Tsuji," he said, "is the leader of one of the most radical groups. Even his nominal superiors are wary of crossing him. In Malaya he once stormed into a general's bedroom and harangued him for not being aggressive enough."

Watanabe certainly seemed to know a lot, for a mere sergeant. Carl Norton's theory was beginning to look more credible. I said, "And he got away with it?"

"Colonel Tsuji gets away with things. Don't misunderstand, he's a brilliant officer—they call him the God of Operations; in his way he really is a genius—but he's also quite mad."

He looked off toward HQ again. "I don't know why he's here today, but it worries me. I think he was responsible for having Colonel Ito replaced, because he was too soft on you prisoners."

"Sakamoto belongs to Tsuji's secret society?"

"I don't believe so. But I'm afraid he's under their influence."

"But what's this about executing prisoners? I mean, why?"

"If all the prisoners are executed," Watanabe said, "then there will be no turning back for Japan. There will be no more possibility of a negotiated peace, as some still hope for. It will be all or nothing."

"He wants to kill us," I said incredulously, "just to burn the bridges?"

"Yes. And also," Watanabe said, "because he hates white people."

Tsuji left the same day, and despite Watanabe's fears, there were no immediate changes in our lives. MacArthur continued to organize new projects to improve our lives if it killed us.

Then one morning, as Carl Norton and I were standing in the shade of our barracks talking about this and that, MacArthur appeared in front of us. "Good morning, gentlemen," he said. "Would you come for a little walk with me?"

There was another man with him, an Army Air Corps lieutenant colonel named Fannon who had been on the staff at Clark airfield. He was close to my age, maybe a little older. That was all I knew about him, except that he was one of the more devoted MacArthur loyalists.

We fell in with them as MacArthur led the way out across the compound. "Look casual," he said, "as if we were merely out for a walk. We don't want to look conspiratorial."

That wasn't altogether realistic, since we were now well into the hot season; strolling casually under the Philippine sun was not something many people cared to do. But it was still early and the sun wasn't high yet, so I didn't say anything.

MacArthur clasped his hands behind his back. "Robert E. Lee often said that duty is the sublimest word in the language. And no one can deny that every man in this camp, during the recent campaign, did his duty with exemplary devotion."

He glanced in the direction of the generals' barracks, where General Wainwright was standing in the doorway. "Perhaps some of us . . . had different concepts of where our duty lay," he said, "but that is neither here nor there. Gentlemen, we all know the duty of a soldier who has been captured."

I realized suddenly where this was going. Oh, I thought, shit.

"Of course," he continued, "this camp poses special problems. Many of the officers here are, to put it baldly, too advanced in years for feats of derring-do. Others, especially the survivors of Bataan and Camp O'Donnell, are badly weakened in health. Still, I confess I am disappointed that there has not been a single escape—nor even an attempt—from this camp."

He looked at Fannon. "Until now. Colonel Fannon proposes to change that. Don't you, Colonel?"

"With your permission, sir." Fannon looked at Carl and me. "I don't know if you've noticed, but every afternoon about the same time, there's a Filipino who rides in on a carabao cart bringing fresh produce for the Japs' mess. The guards never search it, coming or going, and he parks it around back of the kitchen where it isn't clearly visible from any of the guard posts."

"And you're figuring to hide in the back of the cart," Carl said, "and hitch a ride out of here? Okay, what then?"

Fannon shrugged. "I know my way around the Philippines pretty well. I've dealt with Filipinos, too, and I know how to handle them. I'm confident I can find people to help me work my way down to Mindanao, and from there maybe I can find someone with a boat who'll take me to New Guinea or Australia. I'll have to play it by ear, but I'm not worried about it."

"The ability to improvise is the hallmark of a good soldier," MacArthur said approvingly. "However, I've got one problem with your plan. I don't like the idea of your going alone. You should have someone with you, for help and support."

I said, "General—"

"No, Commander." MacArthur almost managed a smile. "I'm sure you're not afraid to go, and I'm sure you'd try your best, but—well, please don't take offense, but taking you along might pose problems, surely you can see that?"

Actually I'd been about to say it was a damn fool idea, or words to that effect, but if MacArthur chose to believe I was a hero I wouldn't disillusion him.

"I'm afraid," he added, "that I'm exploiting your misfortune, and for that I beg your forgiveness. You see, your presence will keep our captors from suspecting anything, should they notice us talking together. A group that includes a one-armed man, they will think, cannot be up to anything very serious."

He turned to Carl. "Major Norton, on the other hand, strikes me as the ideal candidate. Possibly the youngest man in camp, almost certainly the fittest. What do you say, Major?"

Carl said, "Sir, are you ordering me to escape with Fannon?"

MacArthur paused in mid-stride. "You're refusing?"

"I won't refuse if it's a direct order," Carl said. "If it's my call, though, then with respect, I think not."

MacArthur was looking seriously pissed. He never did like it when people didn't want to go along with his ideas, and it was obvious that this one meant a lot to him. For a minute I thought he was going to lay into Carl.

But all he said was, "If that's your choice, Major, then I won't make it an order. I must say I'm disappointed," he said very stiffly. "I thought the Marine Corps produced a special breed of men. Apparently I was misinformed."

"What the hell?" I said to Carl after MacArthur and Fannon were gone. "You've been talking about escaping ever since we got here. I'd have thought you'd jump at the chance."

"I'm still planning to do it," Carl said. "In fact I ought to do it right now, tonight, before that fool Fannon makes it harder. That's what's going to happen, you know. Even if they don't catch him, and ten gets you one they will, the shit's going to come down big time."

"You don't think his plan will work?"

"Oh, he can get out that way, sure. Anybody could get out of this camp right now. I don't know why he's making such a fancy-ass production of it."

That was true enough. The security at Tarlac was ridiculous; the guard force was inadequate and the physical setup was laughable. The fence around the compound consisted of half a dozen strands of ordinary farm-and-ranch barbed wire that wouldn't have stopped a determined range cow.

"The real problem," Carl said, "is going to be surviving in the mountains and the jungle, and finding friendly locals who won't turn you in for Jap money. And Fannon hasn't got a clue how to do any of that, hasn't even thought it out. If MacArthur had asked me to go alone, all right, but no way in hell am I going to hook up with that asshole. If the Japs didn't kill him I probably would."

He made a face. "But it's going to be a bitch around this place after he makes his try. You'll see. Even Ito warned us we'd all be penalized if anybody tried to escape. God knows what Sakamoto's liable to do."

I don't know if MacArthur made any further efforts to find someone to escape with Fallon, but if he did he wasn't successful, because when Fallon went out the following day he went alone. Just as he'd said, he went out in the back of the carabao cart, and sure enough, the guards didn't look.

He wasn't alone when they brought him back, though, two days later, right after roll call. He was surrounded by guards, stumbling along being half-carried by a couple of them, while the others encouraged him in various ways, mostly involving their rifle butts and bayonets. His head hung limp on his chest; his eyes appeared to be swollen shut. His feet were bare and bleeding, and his clothes were so ragged he was for all practical purposes naked.

Everyone gathered up near the gate to watch, and for once the guards didn't break it up; probably Sakamoto wanted us to get a good look. There was a certain amount of angry muttering, though not as much as you might think. Life had been very hard in the last couple of days; Sakamoto had handed out mass punishments like Captain Bligh, cutting off the extra food supplies MacArthur had arranged, outlawing any sort of group gathering—even religious services—and conducting a surprise midnight shakedown in which a couple of bad-tempered lieutenants confiscated most of the pitifully few personal possessions we'd been able to hang onto. The guards had turned mean, too, slapping and punching for any reason or none—one of them gave General Wainwright a black eye for not saluting quickly enough; I even got kicked a couple of times myself.

And Colonel Tsuji had been to see Sakamoto again, the next day after the escape. Nobody else knew who he was, though, and I kept my information to myself. I got enough criticism as it was, for being too friendly with Watanabe.

Anyway, a lot of people were pretty annoyed with Fannon, for bringing all this down on us with his half-assed little glory play, and maybe they felt he deserved whatever he got. But you couldn't help feeling sorry for the poor silly son of a bitch, seeing what they'd done to him and wondering what more they were going to do.

We learned the answer soon enough. That afternoon they called a second roll call formation, and after we had been counted and bowed to His Imperial Japanese Post, Sakamoto came out on the porch of the headquarters building and delivered a speech. Watanabe stood nearby and shouted the translation:

"Colonel Sakamoto says you were all warned against attempting to escape. He says he attempted to treat you well and deal justly with you. Now you have all had to suffer because of this one stupid man. This is how it is. Any time one of you does wrong, everyone will pay. This was the first time, so the punishments have been very light. Next time he will not be so lenient.

"Now he wants you to see what awaits those who try to escape."

He turned and said something in Japanese and a lieutenant shouted an order. A moment later a pair of guards came out the door of HQ with Fannon between them. This time there was no question about it; they were carrying him, dead limp, between them. His bare feet dragged helplessly in the dust.

Sakamoto began talking again; Watanabe resumed his translation:

"You think this was done to him by our soldiers when he was captured. In fact this is essentially how he looked when he was found, wandering in circles in the forest. Colonel Sakamoto says this just goes to show that you white men don't belong in this part of the world."

Sakamoto's voice rose higher; he seemed to be working himself up to something. "Now," Watanabe said, "this man is going to pay the penalty for what he did. The same thing will happen to anyone else who tries to escape, or anyone who helps him. The Colonel says you should all be glad this man was captured. Otherwise some of you would have to be punished in his stead."

And while that was sinking in, Watanabe added, "He says that is all. You are dismissed."

Sakamoto turned and stomped back into HQ. While we stood there, too shocked to move, the two guards began dragging Fannon toward the gate. A truck had driven up in front of the compound, with half a dozen armed soldiers in the back.

Carl Norton said softly, "Oh, my God."

The two guards loaded Fannon into the truck, with some help from the soldiers already on board, and then climbed up to join them. The truck pulled away in a cloud of dust and a clatter of badly-shifted gears.

Somebody nearby said, "They wouldn't."

Somebody else said, "Yes they would. They're going to."

And a little while later, from somewhere down the road and out of sight, the sound of a volley of rifle fire drifted to us on the afternoon breeze.

"I hope everyone understands," Watanabe said to me next day. "I hope everyone realizes that Colonel Sakamoto is serious. He is under great pressure, you know. Colonel Tsuji already tried to persuade him to execute the senior generals, on no grounds at all, and then in reprisal for Colonel Fannon's escape. If there is any further pretext—"

He shuddered visibly. For once I didn't doubt his sincerity; he looked genuinely worried. "I think something terrible is going to happen. I hope I'm wrong."

That was the following morning after they shot Fannon. When I got back to the barracks Carl Norton was sitting on his bunk looking through his gear. It wasn't much; like everybody else, he'd lost most of his belongings in the shakedown.

He made a little gesture with one hand, beckoning me closer. I went over and sat down on the bunk beside him and he said in a low voice, "I'm going out tonight."

And, when I started to speak, "Keep it down, okay? I don't think anybody here would rat me out, but the way things are going you never know."

I said, "You can't be serious. Now of all times—"

"Now's the best time. They won't expect anybody to try, this soon after what happened to Fallon. Besides, it's the last night of the dark moon. I've been keeping track."

He looked at the little pile of odds and ends at his feet and sighed. "God damn it, they even took that old beer bottle I found, that I was going to use for a canteen. I had more stuff than this back when I was a kid riding freights during the Depression."

"But you saw what happened to Fallon—"

"Fallon was a silly jackass who didn't know shit. I can take care of myself in the jungle," Carl said. "That's one thing I know how to do. Hell, that's how I got my start in the Corps, back when I was an enlisted man, chasing around Nicaragua with a crazy bastard named Lewis Puller."

"How are you planning to get out? They're strengthening the fence, you know, and posting extra guards."

"No sweat. There's a drainage ditch out back of this barracks, runs past the cook shack, goes right under the fence. They've stuck in some bamboo stakes to try and block it, but nothing I can't get through."

"You do know," I said, "what this is going to mean for the rest of us. If you make it."

"Yeah. I know." He looked at me and shrugged. "What can I say? I'm sorry."

I said, "Does MacArthur know?"

"Oh, sure. I already talked to him about it. He actually apologized for what he said before. Said if I made it he'd see to it I got a medal, after the war. Like I give a shit for that."

"Carl," I said, "there's something you need to know."

I told him what Watanabe had said about Sakamoto and Tsuji. At the end he blew out his breath in an almost-whistle. "Damn. I don't know, then . . . well," he said, "only one thing to do. Take it to the man, see what he says."

MacArthur listened quietly to the whole thing, not interrupting. At the end he nodded. "Thank you, Commander. You did right to come to me with this information. Please let me know if you learn anything more."

Carl said, "General, what about tonight? Do I go or not?"

"Well, of course. Why—oh." MacArthur actually smiled. "You think Colonel Sakamoto might retaliate against me. I am moved by your concern."

He reached out and put a hand on Carl's shoulder. "Don't worry about me, Major. They're not going to do anything to me. Nothing I can't handle, anyway."

Watching his face as he said it, it hit me what he was really saying. I could almost hear it, clear as if I were reading his mind: *Nothing they haven't already done.* And I knew then that it was useless to say any more. Watanabe was right; it was going to happen. If ever a man's fate was written on his face, MacArthur was wearing his. I wondered why I hadn't noticed before.

Carl went out that night, some time after midnight—I didn't know the exact time; they'd taken my watch in the shakedown—and I stood in the deep shadow of the barracks and watched him go. He moved quickly and silently across the open space and vanished into the ditch.

I couldn't see him any longer, but I continued to watch, trying to estimate his progress, picture it in my mind. By now he should be passing the kitchen . . . only a little farther to the fence. . . .

Then I saw the guard.

He wasn't moving in any purposeful way; he was just ambling along in the starlight, a skinny little man with a long rifle slung over his back. He went up to the edge of the ditch, looked quickly around, and began undoing his fly. A moment later I heard the sound of trickling liquid.

I choked down a hysterical urge to cackle, picturing Carl lying in the ditch not daring to move, maybe getting pissed on. But then there was a startled grunt and the guard took a jerky step backwards. *"Nan desu ka?"* I heard, and he started to unsling his rifle, while my heart slid down into my stomach and stopped.

And there, by God, was MacArthur! To this day I don't know where he came from; lurking somewhere in the shadows, I guess, like me, watching to see if Carl made it.

He came up behind the guard, moving incredibly fast for a man his age, and piled into him with a shoulder block. For a moment the two dark shapes merged in the dim light, and then MacArthur stepped back and I saw that he had the rifle.

He didn't try to fire it; he just held it by the barrel and forestock with both hands and swung it like a baseball bat at the guard's head. The guard got an arm up in time to take part of the impact—I was certain I heard bone snap—but it still knocked him off his feet. It must have stunned him; he lay on the ground for several seconds before he began to scream.

By the time the other guards got there MacArthur had thrown the rifle away. That was probably the only thing that kept them from killing him on the spot, but it didn't stop the other things they did. Or so I heard; by then I was back inside, in my bunk, trying to look as if I were sleeping, wondering if I ever would again.

And Carl was long gone. They never caught him; he made it to the hills, hooked up with some friendly Filipinos, got a ride south aboard a fishing boat, and eventually became one of the most famous guerrilla leaders on Mindanao—but of course I didn't know anything about that till long after the war.

* * *

They did it the following Monday morning. They marched us out onto the parade ground and had us stand in a kind of big hollow square, facing the center, so we could all see.

When they brought MacArthur out he had his hands tied behind his back. He was blindfolded, too; the soldiers on either side of him were holding his upper arms and steering him. Watanabe walked beside them. A young lieutenant I'd never seen before led the way. He was carrying a long sword.

Somebody—I think it was General Bluemel—called sharply, "Atten-*shun!"*

Standing on the HQ porch, Colonel Sakamoto looked around angrily as a hundred and some-odd scarecrows snapped to a ragged attention. But he didn't say anything.

The guards led MacArthur to the middle of the square. The lieutenant said something, not loudly, and Watanabe translated, though we couldn't hear the words. MacArthur nodded and started to kneel. He lost his balance and the guards caught him and helped him down, very gently and solicitously.

Everything got very quiet.

MacArthur bowed his head. "Ready when you are, Lieutenant." he said. He didn't raise his voice; he might have been requesting a subordinate to hand him a map. His voice carried in the silence, though, like an organ chord.

The lieutenant took a step forward, raising his sword. He brought it down slowly, turning it to touch MacArthur's neck with the back of the blade. Then he swung it up again. The steel caught the sun for an instant before it flashed down.

I confess I closed my eyes then; but I heard the sound, and that was enough. And when I opened my eyes again, what they saw was still something no man should ever have to see.

"Such a tragic thing," Watanabe said. "Such a waste."

We were standing near the gate, almost exactly where Carl and I had been standing that morning when they brought MacArthur in. It was late afternoon, almost time for dinner. You'd think no one would have had any appetite after what we'd seen that morning. You'd think that if you'd never been a prisoner of the Japanese.

"Just a little longer," Watanabe said, "and none of this would have happened. They're going to close this camp down, you see. All the senior officers are going to be moved to a camp on the island of Taiwan, which you call Formosa."

He looked off across the now-empty parade ground. They'd spread earth over the stained spot, but you could still see where it had happened.

"And General MacArthur—there were plans for him, because of his high rank. He was to be confined on the mainland of Japan, in a special facility which was being prepared for him. In my own hometown, as it happens." Sakamoto looked wistful. "So much better than this place . . . a beautiful city, I think you'd like it. I don't suppose you heard of it."

He cocked his head to one side, seeming to think of something. "Although—you know, when I was at Princeton, there was a silly little ragtime song the boys used to sing around the piano—"

And he began singing, in a high uneven tenor, the ridiculous words contrasting strangely with the deep sadness on his face:

> *"Nagasaki, where the fellows chew tobacky,*
> *And the women wicky-wacky-woo!"*

My final contribution to Harry Turtledove's Alternate Generals *series; and by that time I was pretty tired of the whole thing. Yet the story came out far better than I had expected. One never knows, does one?—as Lightning Hopkins used to say.*

Most of the background is historically authentic; the camp at Tarlac, for senior US prisoners, existed and, going by survivors' accounts, was pretty much as described. Most of the prisoners are fictitious, but the redoubtable Bluemel was a very real and heroic figure.

Colonel Sakamoto is an invented figure but Colonel Tsuji was all too real, and was indeed responsible for many atrocities. (Yet somehow he was never tried as a war criminal.) He eventually disappeared in Southeast Asia, under circumstances that look suspiciously as if he was working for the CIA.

Written January 2003
First published April 2005

Acts

Well, well. I tell you, this is really something. This is just amazing.

Yes, I've known your parents a long, long time. All five of them, ever since we were not much more than hatchlings. In fact we used to get mistaken for brood sibs, we spent so much time together. It's true we've been a little out of touch lately, but oh, the memories. The stories I could tell you.

And now here's their youngest, coming around wanting to interview me for a big entertainment magazine yet. Who would believe it?

Of course another thing that is to me incredible is that anybody would want to hear about me and my business. The glamorous life of a performers' agent? It is to exfoliate already.

And Hnb'hnb'hnb knows it's not like I'm some big success. I swear if I was a yingslaagl people would stop gn'rking . . . but okay, I see, you're not just interviewing me, right? This is something, you're asking different people in the business? Like a survey?

All right, I can see that. In fact I could maybe give you a few tips, before you leave, who you should make sure and talk to. And who not, if you know what I'm saying. Like a certain client-stealing party right here in this building, two floors down, his eyestalks should only drop off. Or another certain individual whom I will not name, over at Galactic Artists and Performers. A real bloodsucker—and I know he says he can't help it, it's a dietary requirement of his species, but I still say *feh*.

But listen. Now I think of it, this is a good thing. This is a chance, I can maybe say some things that need saying. Maybe this is an opportunity to educate people a little about what it means to be an agent. I'm sorry, but believe me, they have no idea.

They think it's so easy. They look at somebody like me and they're thinking, what a racket. Just look at this bum, sitting on his tail crest, you should pardon the language, in a fancy office, making such a good thing for himself off other people's work. Maybe makes a few calls, sends out a few messages, does lunch with some big shots, for this he takes twenty percent of the poor struggling entertainer's pay?

Sure, right. It should only be so simple.

Leave aside for the moment all you really have to do, which believe me is plenty, you wouldn't believe the hours I put in sometimes . . . do you have any idea, my dear youngster, what an agent has to *know* these days? The sheer amount of *information* he has to carry around in his head—or heads, as the case may be, hey, I've been accused of many things but nobody can call me a bigot—just to function at all in this business?

All these different worlds, all these different races, they've all got their tastes and their customs and they all assume theirs is the only possible way and surely everybody else knows about it so of course they wouldn't bother to *tell* you anything— and so you have to learn it all. Have to know it all from memory, there's no time to be pulling up files and studying background when you're negotiating with some promoter on the other side of the galaxy who needs an act yesterday if not sooner. Which by the way I hate, retro-relative time shunts are more work to set up than you'd believe and when you mention the extra charges they go h'nogth on you. But I digress.

I was going to say, you have to know all this stuff, easily as much as any cultural scientist, just to operate. Operate shmoperate, to stay out of *trouble*, which believe you me there is plenty of just waiting for you to make one little mistake.

And I mean big trouble. Not just the ordinary stuff, like the fact that on Z'arss any kind of music in three-four time is considered pornography, or that doing impressions on Uuu will get you two hundred to life for personality theft. I'm talking nova-grade catastrophe.

Like this certain former colleague whom I used to see at the agents' conventions, nice enough young fellow if maybe a bit on the smart-alecky side, who made the mistake of booking a Xee wizard for a big simultanous-live-and-vid appearance on Kabongo. He was really excited about that, because the Xee home world was still a recent discovery and this was going to be the first offworld performance by one of their wizards, which nobody really knew anything about except that they were supposed to be extremely hot stuff. So my colleague figured he'd pulled off a real coup in signing this one up, and for a time there, up until show time, he got pretty hard to take.

Hah. And again hah. Ever seen a Xee wizard work? No, of course you haven't, ever since what happened on Kabongo they're banned from performing offworld and you better be glad of it or you might be permanently blind and deaf and paralyzed like all those poor devils on Kabongo. I understand the insurance lawyers are still appealing the judgment, but that's not much help to Mr. Smart Guy. Who had broken one of the most basic rules: *never book an act you haven't personally seen.*

Or take what happened to a very dear friend of mine only last year. One day he gets a call from Keshtak 37, over in the next arm, wanting a whole lineup of acts, price no object. Seemed the Emperor of the Oomaumau had passed away, and they wanted only the best for his funeral festivities, which would go on for weeks because the Oomaumau believe in giving a ruler a first-class sendoff.

So my friend is naturally very pleased to get to handle something that big, and as soon as the contract is signed he starts calling around, seeing who's available. But then he happens to do a bit of research, to see what kind of acts the Oomaumau might like, and finds out something extremely disturbing. The Oomaumau, it develops, have another unusual mortuary custom: the performers at the royal funeral are given the honor of accompanying the Emperor to the Hereafter, so his spirit shouldn't get bored.

Yes, that's right. Well, not strictly speaking; they just bury them alive beneath the royal mausoleum.

My friend is not really to blame for not knowing about this, which is not well known outside learned sociological circles because the last time an Emperor died on Keshtak 37 was well before the memory of any living person on this world. Long-lived race, the Oomaumau, especially the royal family . . . but ignorance, as they say, is no excuse before the law, and the contract had already been signed.

And the Oomaumau were not about to let my friend out of it. Though he tried hard enough, went so far as to travel personally to Keshtak 37 to plead for a release. He was so desperate he even got an audience with their spiritual leader, the Papa Oomaumau, at the great temple of the goddess L'vira. No go. A contract is a contract and if he reneges, they tell him, he will find himself up to his nictitating membranes in litigation with the Emperor's attorneys.

Yes, that was what my friend asked. Turns out it's not at all unusual for dead people to file lawsuits on Keshtak 37. Don't ask me.

My friend doesn't know what to do, but then while he's there he picks up another bit of information. The only entertainers who don't get interred with His Imperial Awesomeness are the ones who perform so badly that they are deemed unworthy of the honor. Yes. On Keshtak 37, when you stink at the Palace, you *don't* die at the Palace.

So my friend rushes back here and starts calling in all the lousiest acts he can find. Which takes very little searching, because every agent knows plenty of hopeless no-talent losers; they come around begging you to represent them, and they're so persistent and so pathetic you take their names and information down just to get rid of them and then they call you every few days for the rest of your life wanting to know when you're going to get them some work.

In almost no time my friend has assembled a collection of the worst stinkeroos in this part of the galaxy. Tone-deaf musicians, stumblebum dancers, comics unfunny enough to induce suicidal depression, he's got them all. He said he had to open the office windows to air the place out after they all left.

No, he didn't tell them. He felt bad about that, but it really wouldn't have done to let them in on what was going on. Entertainers and artists, you see, are very touchy people that way, and the bad ones most of all. The worse they are, the greater they believe they are and the harder they believe it. If he'd told them the truth, they'd have been furious and chances are they'd have walked out on him.

So off they went to Keshtak 37, and—ah, yes, I'm seeing this look on your face, you're way ahead of me, aren't you?

That's right. The thrill of finally getting a professional gig, and a prestigious offworld one at that, got them so worked up they barely needed a ship to get to Keshtak 37; they could have gone into warp by themselves. And by the time they went on at the Imperial Palace, they were so inspired that they performed, all of them, better than they'd ever done in their lives.

Or ever would again, in what little was left of them . . . my friend was very upset. Not that anybody would miss that particular bunch, but the Oomaumau buried their paychecks with them and he never did collect his cut.

But listen, don't misunderstand, I'm not disrespecting my colleagues. It's not like I've never made any mistakes myself. How I only wish. . . .

Let me tell you about the comic.

Or rather tell you what happened, I can't really tell you about *him*. Can't do justice to his talent with a simple description, you'd have had to see him in action to fully comprehend just how great he was. And yes, great I said and great I meant. All these people like to think of themselves as "artists" but in his case it was the simple truth. A genuine comic genius is what he was, and he could just maybe have been the greatest ever, if only—but I'm getting ahead of myself.

I found him working open mike night at a cheap club down in the Ginzorninplad district. He'd just gotten into town, worked his way here from his home world aboard a worn-out old tub of a bulk freighter, and he didn't have much more than the clothes on his back. I watched his act and then I caught him backstage and signed him up, just like that. And said some very sincere prayers to Hnb'hnb'hnb for granting me the privilege.

I got him a few local gigs and he did just fine, even got some good ink from the critics. But you know this town; an outsider has a tough time getting accepted. Especially an outsider from, and I don't mean this in any derogatory way, a *different*-looking race. I hate to say that but it's true.

So when this opening turned up for a long offworld tour, I advised him to go for it. Oh, it wasn't much of a booking—the world was a pretty backward sort of place, off in a distant arm of the galaxy where hardly anybody ever went even to visit, and the pay was worse than lousy.

But I didn't really have anything else for him at the moment; things were slow, all the best clubs were booked up solid. And I figured this was a chance for him to get some experience, develop his material and practice his technique out in the sticks, without having to worry about bombing because even if he did have a bad night nobody who mattered would ever hear about it. Meanwhile I could work on lining up something better for him.

Well, what can I say? It seemed like a good idea at the time, I should hit myself repeatedly with the nearest blunt object.

Don't get me wrong, it's not that he went into the sandbox or anything like that. On the contrary, they loved his act—or at least they loved *him*; right away, almost as soon as he arrived, they started making a big fuss over him. In no time at all he was playing to packed houses.

You understand, he was sending back regular reports, keeping me up on what was going on, and every time I heard from him he sounded more amazed. People followed him around on the street, came up to him wanting to meet him and trying to touch him, and before long he even had his own fan club. In fact there were about a dozen of them who took to traveling around with him, seeing to his needs, just like he's a big superstar.

But what was really strange was the way the audiences reacted to his act. *Nobody ever laughed.* He'd do his funniest routines, stuff that would make a Rhrr laugh, and they'd just sit there staring at him with these very serious faces and nod and look at each other and nod some more, like he'd just said something wise and profound.

He tried everything. He even tried dumping his own material, since they didn't seem to get it, and doing corny old gags about farmers and animal herders and fishermen, thinking maybe they just weren't ready for sophisticated modern humor. Didn't make a bit of difference. They still came to see him, more and more all the time, but they still didn't laugh.

And this was starting to make him crazy, as you can imagine. He got so desperate he started doing magic tricks. Now I mean that's pretty bad, when a talented performer has to reach that low. What next, I thought, he's going to take up juggling? But these hicks absolutely ate it up. They liked the tricks even better than the comic routines; the crowds started getting really huge.

Finally the time came for his debut at the big city—well, the biggest in that part of that particular world, it wouldn't have made a slum neighborhood here—and off he went, hoping the city audiences would be a little more hip.

He made something of an entrance, too; his twelve roadies did a really great job of getting the word out, making sure there was a big crowd to welcome him when he arrived in town. By the time he did his first show, the turnout was so big they had to hold it outdoors on a mountainside, where he gave possibly his greatest performance ever. Still no yocks, but he thought he saw a few of them smiling a little toward the end.

So things were looking up; and so my boy didn't think anything of it, a few nights later, when a bunch of people showed up, right after dinner, and wanted him to come with them. Some kind of fan thing, he thought, and he said sure, and went along without argument, though some of his entourage tried to talk him out of it.

And when they got where they were going, he still didn't tumble to what was happening. Not even when they started bringing up the lumber and nails. In fact he gave them a hand. He figured they were getting ready to build a stage for him. There were some cops standing around but he assumed they were just security.

By the time he found out different it was too late.

If I told you what they did to him you would not sleep tonight and you would have dreams for years, just as I did when I heard about it. So I think I better not go into the details. Enough to say it was a terrible, terrible thing and I've never heard of anything quite like it, even on the most barbaric worlds.

The shock and the pain were so great that it was three planetary rotations before he could pull himself together enough to activate his recovery circuits and get out of there. He came back here and told me what had happened—I had naturally been worried sick—and then, despite all my pleas and reassurances, he got on the next available ship back to his home world, and as far as I know he never got on stage again. I understand he went into the family construction business. Such a waste, and I can't help feeling responsible.

But there was one thing I want to tell you about, because it illustrates just what kind of a person he was. Right after he got his body systems working again, he was just about to send the emergency beam-up signal when he thought of something he wanted to do. And as bad as he wanted out of that place—and who can blame him?—and as stiff and sore as he was, he stayed around long enough to put in a final appearance to his original fan club, and do a little farewell routine just for them. Now is that class or what?

You can see why it broke my heart—no, both of them—to see him go.

Well. So much for my little reminiscences. I'm sure you've got a whole list of questions.

So ask.

"Acts" is in one respect unique: with this one exception, I haven't done aliens (unless you count the "angels" of "Angel

Kills" and I deliberately left it unclear just what they are) or anything to do with other planets, space travel, that sort of thing. Even though I have been called a science fiction writer, very little of my work has involved any of the usual gags and gimmicks of traditional science fiction—except for time travel— and, frankly, I've never been much on reading about that stuff.

So when Mike Resnick asked me for a story from the viewpoint of an alien, I knew immediately it would have to be something completely ridiculous; and so "Acts" came to be.

When I turned it in Resnick said, "Funny, you don't look Jewish."

Written February 2005
First published December 2005

Amba

The client looked at his watch and then at Logan, raising an eyebrow. Logan nodded and spread his hands palm-down in what he hoped was a reassuring gesture. The client shook his head and went back to staring at the clearing below. His face was not happy.

Rather than let his own expression show Logan turned his head and looked toward the other end of the blind, where Yura, the mixed-blood tracker, sat crosslegged with his old bolt-action Mosin rifle across his lap. Yura gave Logan a ragged steel-capped grin and after a moment Logan grinned back.

When he could trust his face again he turned back to look out the blind window. The sun was high now; yellow light angled down through the trees and dappled the ground. The early morning wind had died down and there was no sound except for the snuffling and shuffling of the half-grown pig tethered on the far side of the clearing.

The client was doing something with his camera. It was quite an expensive-looking camera; Logan didn't recognize the make. Now he was checking his damned watch again. Expensive watch, too. Definitely an upscale client. His name was Steen and he was an asshole.

Actually, Logan told himself without much conviction, Steen wasn't too bad, certainly not as bad as some of the other clients they'd had. He had a superior attitude, but then most of them did. But he was impatient, and that made him a real pain in the ass to have around, especially on a blind sit. All right, it was a little cramped inside the camouflaged tree blind, and you had to keep as still as possible; but all that had been explained to him in advance and if he had a problem with any of it he should have stayed back in Novosibirsk watching wildlife documentaries on television.

They'd been sitting there all morning, now, and maybe Steen thought that was too long. But hell, that was no time at all when you were waiting for a tiger, even on a baited site within the regular territory of a known individual.

Steen's shoulders lifted and fell in what was probably a silent sigh. At least he knew how to be quiet, you had to give him that much. Not like that silly son of a bitch last year, down in the Bikin valley, who made enough noise to scare off everything between Khabarovsk and Vladivostok and then demanded a refund because he hadn't gotten to—

Logan felt a sudden touch on his shoulder. He looked around and saw Yura crouching beside him, holding up a hand. The lips moved beneath the gray-streaked mustache, forming a silent word: "*Amba.*"

Logan looked out the blind window, following Yura's pointing finger, but he saw nothing. Heard nothing, either, nothing at all now; the pig had stopped rooting around and was standing absolutely still, facing in the same direction Yura was pointing.

Steen was peering out the window too, wide-eyed and clutching his camera. He glanced at Logan, who nodded.

And then there it was, padding out into the sunlit clearing in all its great burnt-orange magnificence.

Out of the corner of his eye Logan saw Steen clap a hand over his mouth, no doubt to stifle a gasp. He didn't blame him; a male Amur tiger, walking free and untamed on his home turf, was a sight to take the breath of any man. As many times as he'd been through this, his own throat still went thick with awe for the first seconds.

The pig took an altogether different view. It began squealing and lunging desperately against its tether, its little terrified eyes fixed on the tiger, which had stopped now to look it over.

The client had his camera up to his face now, pressing the button repeatedly, his face flushed with excitement. Logan wondered if he realized just how lucky he was. This was one hell of a big tiger, the biggest in fact that Logan had ever seen outside a zoo. He guessed it would go as much as seven or eight hundred pounds and pretty close to a dozen feet from nose to tip of tail, though it was hard to be sure about that last now the tail was rhythmically slashing from side to side as the tiger studied the pig.

If Steen was any good at all with that camera he ought to be getting some fine pictures. A bar of sunlight was falling on the tiger's back, raising glowing highlights on the heavy fur that was browner and more subdued than the flame-orange of a Bengal, the stripes less prominent, somehow making the beast look even bigger.

The tiger took a couple of hesitant, almost mincing steps, the enormous paws making no sound on the leaf mold. It might be the biggest cat in the world but it was still a cat and it knew something wasn't quite right about this. It couldn't smell the three men hidden nearby, thanks to the mysterious herbal mixture with which Yura had dusted the blind, but it knew that pigs didn't normally show up out in the middle of the woods, tethered to trees.

On the other hand it was hungry.

It paused, the tail moving faster, and crouched slightly. The massive shoulder muscles bunched and bulged as it readied itself to jump—

Steen sneezed.

It wasn't all that much of a sneeze, really not much more than a snort, and Steen managed to muffle most of it with his hand. But it was more than enough. The tiger spun around, ears coming up, and looked toward the direction of the sound—for an instant Logan had the feeling that the great terrible eyes were looking straight into his—and then it was streaking across the clearing like a brush fire, heading back the way it had come. A moment later it was gone.

Behind him Logan heard Yura mutter, "*Govno.*"

"I'm sorry," Steen said stupidly. "I don't know why—"

"Sure." Logan shrugged. He heaved himself up off the little bench and half-stood, half-crouched in the low-roofed space. "Well, at least you got some pictures, didn't you?"

"I think so." Steen did something to his camera and a little square lit up on the back, showing a tiny colored picture. "Yes." He looked up at Logan, who was moving toward the curtained doorway at the rear of the blind. "Are we leaving now? Can't we wait, see if it comes back?"

"He won't," Logan said. "His kind got hunted almost to extinction, not all that long ago. He knows there are humans around. He's not going to risk it just for a pork dinner. Hell, you saw him. He hasn't been starving."

"Another one, perhaps—"

"No. Tigers are loners and they demand a hell of a lot of territory. A big male like that, he'll have easily fifty, a hundred square miles staked out. Maybe more."

They were speaking English; for some reason it was what Steen seemed to prefer, though his Russian was as good as Logan's.

"Now understand," Logan went on, "you've paid for a day's trip. If you want to stay and watch, you might get to see something else. Wolves for sure, soon as they hear that pig squealing. Maybe even a bear, though that's not likely. But you already saw a couple of bears, day before yesterday, and you said you'd seen wolves before."

"Yes. They are very common around Novosibirsk." Steen sighed. "I suppose you're right. May as well go back."

"All right, then." Logan started down the ladder and paused. The pig was still screaming. "Yura," he said tiredly in Russian, "for God's sake shoot the damned pig."

A little while later they were walking down a narrow trail through the woods, back the way they had come early that morning. Logan brought up the rear, with Steen in front of him and Yura leading the way, the old Mosin cradled in his arms. Steen said, "I suppose he's got the safety on?"

Yura grunted. "Is not safe," he said in thickly accented but clear English, not looking around. "Is gun."

The back of Steen's neck flushed slightly. "Sorry." he said, "Really, I'm glad one of us is armed. With that animal out there somewhere."

Logan suppressed a snort. In fact he was far from sure that Yura would shoot a tiger, even an attacking one. To the Udege and the other Tungus tribes, *Amba* was a powerful and sacred spirit, almost a god, to be revered and under no circumstances to be harmed.

On the other hand Yura was half Russian—unless you believed his story about his grandfather having been a Krim Tatar political prisoner who escaped from a gulag and took refuge in a remote Nanai village—and there was never any telling which side would prove dominant. Logan had always suspected it would come down to whether the tiger was attacking Yura or someone else.

The gun was mainly for another sort of protection. This was a region where people got up to things: dealers in drugs and stolen goods, animal poachers, army deserters, Chinese and Korean illegals and the people who transported them. You never knew what you might run into out in the back country; tigers were the least of the dangers.

The trail climbed up the side of a low but steep ridge covered with dense second-growth forest. The day was chilly, even with the sun up, and there were still a few small remnant patches of snow here and there under the trees, but even so Logan had to unzip his jacket halfway up the climb and he could feel the sweat starting under his shirt. At the top he called a rest break and he and Steen sat down on a log. Yura went over and leaned against a tree and took out his belt knife and began cleaning the blade on some leaves; despite Logan's order he'd cut the pig's throat rather than waste a valuable cartridge.

Steen looked at Logan. "You're American," he said, not making it a question. "If I may ask, how is it you come to be in this country?"

"I used to be in charge of security for a joint Russian-American pipeline company, up in Siberia."

"This was back before the warmup began?"

No, just before it got bad enough for people to finally admit it was happening. "Yes," Logan said.

"And you haven't been home since?"

"Home," Logan said, his voice coming out a little harsher than he intended, "for me, is a place called Galveston, Texas. It's been under water for a couple of years now."

"Ah." Steen nodded. "I know how it is. Like you, I have nothing to go back to."

No shit, Logan thought, with a name like Steen. Dutch, or maybe Belgian; and what with the flooding, and the cold that had turned all of northwest Europe into an icebox after the melting polar ice deflected the Gulf Stream, the Low Countries weren't doing so well these days.

Steen would be one of the ones who'd gotten out in time, and who'd had the smarts and the resources and the luck—it would have taken all three—to get in on the Siberian boom as it was starting, before the stream of Western refugees became a flood and the Russians started slamming doors. And he must have been very successful at whatever he did; look at him now, already able to take himself a rich man's holiday in the Far East. Not to mention having the connections to get the required permits for this little adventure.

Logan stood up. "Come on," he said. "We need to get going."

The trail dropped down the other side of the ridge, wound along beside a little stream, and came out on an old and disused logging road, its rutted surface already overgrown with weeds and brush. A relic from the bad old days, when outlaw logging outfits ran wild in the country south of the Amur and east of the Ussuri, clearcutting vast areas of supposedly protected forest with no more than token interference from the paid-off authorities, shipping the lumber out to the ever-hungry Chinese and Japanese markets.

It had been a hell of a thing; and yet, in the end, it hadn't made any real difference. The old taiga forest, that had survived so much for so many thousands of years, hadn't been able to handle the rising temperatures; the warmup had killed it off even faster and more comprehensively than the clearcutters had done.

But by then the markets had collapsed, along with the economies of the market countries; and the loggers had moved north to Siberia with its vast forests and its ravenous demand for lumber for the mushrooming new towns. Left alone, the clearcut areas had begun to cover themselves again, beginning with dense ground-hugging brush and then ambitious young saplings.

Which, to the deer population, had meant a jackpot of fresh, easily accessible browse; and pretty soon the deer were multiplying all over the place, to the delight of the tigers and bears and wolves that had been having a pretty thin time of it over the last couple of decades.

On the road there was enough room for Logan and Steen to walk side by side, though Yura continued to stride on ahead. Steen was quiet for a long time, and Logan had begun to hope he was going to stay that way; but then finally he spoke again:

"It was not much."

Startled, Logan said, "What?"

"It was not much," Steen repeated. "You must admit it was not much. A minute only. Not even a minute."

Logan got it then. Christ, he thought, he's been working himself up to this for better than three miles.

He said carefully, "Mr. Steen, you contracted with us to take you around this area and give you a chance to see and photograph wildlife. You'll recall the contract doesn't guarantee that you'll see a tiger. Only that we'll make our best effort to show you one. Which we did, and this morning you did see one."

Steen's face had taken on a stubborn, sullen look. "Legally you are correct," he said. "But still it doesn't seem right. For all I am paying you, it was not much."

"Mr. Steen," Logan said patiently, "you don't seem to know how lucky you've been. Some of our clients spend as much as a week, sitting in a blind every day, before they see a tiger. Some never do."

Steen was shaking his head. "Look," Logan said, "if you think you didn't see enough this morning, if you'd like to try again, we can set you up for another try. Add it onto your original package, shouldn't cost you too much more."

Steen stared at Logan. "I will think about it," he said finally. "Perhaps. Still I don't think I should have to pay more, but perhaps. I will come to the office in the morning and let you know."

"Fine," Logan said. "I'm sure we can work out something reasonable."

Thinking: you son of a bitch. You smug rich son of a bitch with your God-damned fancy camera that someone needs to shove up your ass and your God-damned fancy watch after it. But he shoved his hands into his jacket pockets and kept walking, holding it in. The customer is always right.

A couple of hours later they came out onto a broad clear area at the top of a hill, where a short stocky man stood beside a big Mi-2 helicopter. He had a Kalashnikov rifle slung over his back.

"Logan," he called, and raised a hand. "*Zdrast'ye.*"

"Misha," Logan said. "Anything happening?"

"Nothing here. Just waiting for you, freezing my ass. Where is all this great warming I hear about?"

"Bullshit. Ten years ago, this time of year, you really would have been freezing your ass out here. You'd have been up to it in snow."

"Don't mind me, I'm just bitching," Misha said in English, and then, switching back to Russian, "How did it go? Did he get his tiger?"

Logan nodded, watching Steen climbing aboard the helicopter. Yura was standing nearby, having a lengthy pee against a tree. "So soon?" Misha said. "*Bozhe moi,* that was quick."

"Too quick." Steen was inside now and Logan didn't think he could hear them but he didn't really care any more. He told Misha what had happened. "Don't laugh," he added quickly, seeing Steen watching them out a cabin window. "He's not very happy just now. Doesn't feel he got his money's worth."

"*Shto za chort?* What did he expect, tigers in a chorus line singing show tunes?" He glanced around. "What happened to the pig?"

"I had Yura kill it. Too much trouble dragging it all the way back here, and I couldn't very well leave the poor bastard tied there waiting for the wolves."

"Too bad. We could have taken it to Katya's, got her to roast it for us.*"

He unslung the Kalashnikov and handed it to Logan. "Take charge of this thing, please, and I'll see if I can get this old Mil to carry us home one more time."

"So," Misha said, "you think it was the same one? The big one, from last fall?"

"I think so," Logan said, pouring himself another drink. "Of course there's no way to know for sure, but the location's right and I can't imagine two males that big working that near to each other's territory."

It was late evening and they were sitting at a table in Katya's place in Khabarovsk. The room was crowded and noisy and the air was dense with tobacco smoke but they had a place back in a corner away from the worst of it. There was a liter of vodka on the table between them. Or rather there was a bottle that had once contained a liter of vodka, its contents now substantially reduced.

"In fact," Logan went on, "it's hard for me to imagine two males that big, period. If it's not the same one, if they're all getting that big, then I'm going to start charging more for screwing around with them."

Misha said, "This is good for us, you know. If we know we can find a big fine-looking cat like that, we'll get some business."

He scowled suddenly. "If some bastard doesn't shoot him. A skin that big would bring real money."

"The market's just about dried up," Logan said. "The Chinese have too many problems of their own to have much interest in pretty furs—drought and dust storms, half the country trying to turn into Mongolia—and the rich old men who thought extract of tiger dick would help them get it up again are too busy trying to hang onto what they've got. Or get out."

"All this is true." Misha nodded, his eyes slightly owlish; he had had quite a few by now. "But you know there are still those who have what it takes to get what they want. There always will be, in China or Russia or anywhere else." He grinned crookedly. "And a good thing for us, *da?*"

Logan took a drink and made a grimace of agreement. Misha was right; their most lucrative line of business depended on certain people being able to get what they wanted. Between the restrictions on aviation—Russia might be one of the few countries actually benefiting from atmospheric warming, but enough was enough—and those on travel within what was supposed to be a protected wilderness area, it was theoretically all but impossible to charter a private flight into the Sikhote-Alin country. There were, however, certain obviously necessary exceptions.

Logan said, "Come now, Misha. You know perfectly well all our clients are fully accredited scientific persons on essential scientific missions. It says so in their papers."

"*Konyeshno.* I had forgotten. Ah, Russia, Russia." Misha drained his own glass and poured himself another one. "All those years we were poor, so we became corrupt. Now we are the richest country in the world, but the corruption remains. What is that English idiom? 'Force of hobbit.'"

"Habit."

"Oh, yes. Why do I always—"

He stopped, looking up at the man who was walking toward their table. "*Govno.* Look who comes."

Yevgeny Lavrushin, tall and skinny and beaky of nose, worked his way through the crowd, the tails of his long leather coat flapping about his denim-clad legs. He stopped beside their table and stuck out a hand toward Logan. "Say hey," he said. "Logan, my man. What's happening?"

He spoke English with a curious mixed accent, more Brooklyn than Russian. He had driven a cab in New York for a dozen years before the United States, in its rising mood of xenophobia, decided to terminate nearly all green cards. Now he lived here in Khabarovsk and ran a small fleet of trucks, doing just enough legitimate hauling to cover for his real enterprises. He was reputed to have mafia connections but probably nothing very heavy.

Logan ignored the hand. "Yevgeny," he said in no particular tone. "Something on your mind?"

"What the hell," Yevgeny said. "You gonna ask me to sit down?"

"No," Logan said. "What did you want?"

Yevgeny glanced theatrically around and then leaned forward and put his hands on the table. "Got a business proposition for you," he said in a lowered voice. "Serious money—"

"No," Logan said again, and then, more sharply as Yevgeny started to speak, "No, God damn it. *Nyet.* Whatever it is, we're not interested."

"Besides," Misha said in Russian, "since when do your usual customers travel by air? Did they get tired of being crammed like herring into the backs of your trucks?"

Yevgeny's coat collar jerked upward on his neck. "Christ, don't talk that shit. . . ." He glanced around again. "Look, it's not Chinks, okay? Well, yeah, in a way it is, but—"

"Yevgeny," Logan said, "it's been a hell of a long day. Go away."

"Hey, I can dig it. I'm gone." He started to move away and then turned back, to lean over the table again. "One other thing. You guys know where there's some big tigers, right? If you ever need to make some quick money, I know where you can get a hell of a good price for a clean skin—"

Logan started to stand up. "Okay, okay." Yevgeny held up both hands and began backing away. "Be cool, man. If you change your mind, you know where to find me."

"Yeah," Logan muttered as he disappeared into the crowd. "Just start turning over rocks . . . hand me the bottle, Misha, I need another one now."

"Wonder what he wanted," Misha mused. "As far as I know his main business is running Chinese illegals. You suppose he's branched out into drugs or something?"

"Doesn't matter." Logan finished pouring and looked around for the cap to the vodka bottle. "I don't even want to know . . . well, this has to be my last one. Have to deal with Steen tomorrow," he said, screwing the cap down tightly, "and I definitely don't want to do that with a hangover."

But Steen didn't show up the following morning.

"He hasn't been here," Lida Shaposhnikova told Logan when he came in. "I came in early, about eight-thirty, so I could have his account ready, and he never showed up."

Logan checked his watch. "It's not even ten yet. He probably slept late or something. We'll wait."

The office occupied the front room of a rundown little frame house on the outskirts of Khabarovsk, not far from the airport. The office staff consisted entirely of Lida. The back rooms were mostly full of outdoor gear and supplies—camping kit, camouflage fabric for blinds, night-vision equipment and so on—and various mysterious components with which Misha somehow managed to keep the old helicopter flying. The kitchen was still a kitchen. Logan went back and poured himself a cup of coffee and took it to his desk and sat down to wait, while Lida returned to whatever she was doing on her computer.

But a couple of hours later, with noon approaching and still no sign of Steen, Logan said, "Maybe you should give him a call. Ask him when he's planning to come."

He got up and walked out onto the front porch for a bit of fresh air. When he went back inside Lida said, "I phoned his hotel. He checked out this morning at nine."

"Shit. You better call—"

"I already did." Lida leaned back in her chair and looked at him with dark oblong eyes, a legacy from her Korean grandmother. "He left on the morning flight to Novosibirsk."

"Son of a bitch," Logan said in English.

"So it would seem," Lida said in the same language.

"Well." Logan rubbed his chin. "Well, go ahead and figure up his bill and charge him. You've already got his credit card number, from when he paid his deposit."

Lida nodded and turned to the computer. A few minutes later she muttered something under her breath and began tapping keys rapidly, as the front door opened and Misha came in.

"*Sukin syn,*" he said when Logan told him what was going on. "He's run out on us?"

"It's all right," Logan said. He nodded toward the front desk, where Lida was now talking to someone on the phone. "We'll just charge it to his credit—"

"No we won't." Lida put down the phone and turned around. "The credit card's no good. He's canceled it."

"He can do that?" Misha said. "Just like that?"

"He did it yesterday," Lida said. "He paid his bill at the hotel with a check."

Everyone said bad words in several languages. Misha said, "He can't get away with that, can he?"

"Legally, no. In the real world—" Logan shrugged heavily. "He's got to be connected. You know how hard it is to do anything to someone who's connected. We can try, but I don't think much of our chances."

"At the very best," Lida said, "it's going to take a long time. Which we don't have." She waved a hand at the computer. "I've been looking at the numbers. They're not good."

"Got some more costs coming up, too," Misha put in. "We're overdue on our fuel bill at the airport, and the inspector wants to know why he hasn't gotten his annual present yet. I was just coming to tell you."

"Hell." Logan felt like kicking something. Or someone. "I was counting on that money to get us off the hook. Well, I'll just have to get busy and find us another job."

There was a short silence. Logan and Misha looked at each other.

Misha said, "We could—"

"No we couldn't," Logan said.

But of course they were going to.

* * *

Yevgeny said, "Like I tried to tell you before, it's not Chinks. I mean, it's *Chinamen,* but it's not your regular coolies coming north looking for work and a square meal. These are high-class Chinamen, you know? Some kind of suits. The kind you don't just cram into the back of a truck behind a load of potatoes."

"Sounds political," Logan said. "No way in hell, if it is."

"No, no, nothing like that. This is—" Yevgeny hunched his bony shoulders. "I'll be straight with you guys, I don't really know *what* the fuck it's all about, but it can't be political. The people who want it done, that's just not their thing."

Which meant mafia, which meant Yevgeny was blowing a certain amount of smoke, because in Russia nowadays the concepts of mafia and political were not separable. This was starting to feel even worse.

Misha said, "I'll tell you right now, I'm not flying into Chinese airspace. Money's no good to a man with a heat-seeking missile up his ass."

"That's okay. See, there's this island in the river—"

"The Ussuri?" Logan said skeptically. The Ussuri islands were military and heavily fortified; there had been some border incidents with the Chinese.

"No, man, the Amur. Way to hell west of here, I'll show you on the map, they gave me the coordinates and everything. It's just a little island, not much more than a big sandbar. On the Russian side of the channel, but nobody gives a shit either way, there's nothing much around there, not even any real roads."

His fingers made diagrams on the table top. "You guys set down there, there'll be a boat from the Chinese side. Five Chinamen get out, you pick them up and you're outta there. You drop them off at this point on the main highway, out in the middle of nowhere. There'll be some people waiting."

"Sounds like they've got this all worked out," Logan said. "So why do they need us? I'd expect people like that to have their own aircraft."

"They did. They had this chopper lined up for the job, only the pilot made some kind of mistake on the way here and spread himself all over this field near Blagoveshchensk. So they got hold of me and asked could I line up somebody local."

"Yevgeny," Logan said, "if this goes wrong you better hope I don't make it back, because I'm going to be looking for you."

"If this goes wrong, you won't be the only one. These people," Yevgeny said very seriously, "they're not people you want to fuck with. Know what I'm saying?"

Lida said, "I wish I knew what you're getting mixed up in. Or perhaps I don't. It doesn't matter. You're not going to tell me, are you?"

"Mhmph," Logan replied, or sounds to that effect. His face was partly buried in his pillow. He was about half asleep and trying to do something about the other half if only Lida would quit talking.

"I talk with Katya, you know," she went on. "We've known each other for years. She's seen you with Yevgeny Lavrushin."

Logan rolled onto his back, looking up into the darkness of the bedroom. "It's nothing. Just a quick little flying job."

"Of course. A quick little flying job for which you will be paid enough to get the company out of debt. You can't help being a fool," she said, "but I wish you wouldn't take me for one."

She moved closer and put out a hand to stroke his chest. "Look at us. You need me more than you love me. I love you more than I need you. Somehow it works out," she said. "I'm not complaining. Only don't lie to me."

There was nothing to say to that.

"So," she said, "at least tell me when this is to happen."

"Tomorrow night. Wha," he said as her hand moved lower.

"Then I'd better get some use out of you," she said, "before you get yourself killed or imprisoned."

"Lida," he protested, "I'm really tired."

She slid a long smooth leg over him and moved it slowly up and down his body. "No you're not. Maybe you think you are, but you're not. Not yet. See there," she said, rising up, straddling him, fitting herself to him, "you're not tired at all."

Logan's watch said it was almost one in the morning. He shivered slightly as a chilly breeze came in off the river.

Not too many years ago, at this time of year, the river would have carried big floes of ice from the spring thaw; but now there was only the smooth dark water sliding past in the dim light of a low crescent moon, and, away beyond that, a dark smudge that was the distant China shore.

The island was about half a mile long and maybe fifty or sixty feet across. As Yevgeny had said, it wasn't much more than a big sandbar. The upstream end was littered with brush and washed-up dead trees but the other end was clear and open and flat in the middle, with plenty of room for the Mil.

He dropped his hand to the butt of the Kalashnikov and hcftcd it slightly, easing the pressure of the sling against his shoulder. Beside him Misha squatted on the sand, his face grotesquely masked by bulky night goggles. "Nothing yet," Misha said.

"It's not quite time."

"I know. I just don't like this waiting."

Logan knew what was eating Misha. He hadn't wanted to shut down the Mil's engines; he'd wanted to be ready to take off fast if anything went wrong. But it wouldn't have done any good; as Logan had already pointed out, with those twin Isotov turbines idling they'd never hear a border patrol unit approaching until it was too late to run for it, and after all where would they run to?

Somewhere on the Russian side of the river a wolf howled, and was joined by others. Standing in the shadows nearby, Yura said something in a language that wasn't Russian, and chuckled softly.

"Wolves all over the place these days," Misha said. "More than I've ever seen before. I wonder what they're eating. I know, the deer population is up, but I wouldn't think that would be enough."

"It's been enough for the tigers," Logan pointed out.

"True . . . speaking of tigers," Misha said, "I've been thinking. Maybe we ought to start giving that big male some special attention, you know? Take a pig or a sheep or something down there every now and then, get him used to visiting that clearing. A tiger that size, he's money in the bank for us if we can count on him showing up for the clients."

"Hm. Not a bad idea."

"Have Yura put out some of his secret tiger bait powder." Misha dropped his voice. "You think that stuff really works?"

"Who knows?" Logan wished Misha would shut up but he realized he was talking from nerves. "Could be."

"Those tribesmen know things," Misha said. "Once I saw—"

He stopped. "Something happening over there." He reached up and made a small adjustment to the night goggles. "Can't really see anything," Misha added. "Something that could be a vehicle, with some people moving around. Can't even be sure how many."

A small red light flashed briefly on the far shore, twice. Logan took the little flashlight from his jacket pocket and pointed it and flicked the switch three times in quick succession.

Misha said, "*Shto za chort?* Oh, all right, they're carrying something down to the river. Maybe a boat."

Logan wished he'd brought a pair of goggles for himself. Or a night scope. He listened but there was no sound but the night breeze and the barely audible sussurus of the current along the sandy shore. Even the wolves had gone quiet.

"Right, it's a boat," Misha said. "Coming this way."

Logan slipped the Kalashnikov's sling off his shoulder, hearing a soft *flunk* as Yura slid a round into the chamber of his rifle.

Misha stood up and slipped off the goggles. "I better go get the Mil warmed up."

A few minutes later Logan saw it, a low black shape moving toward the island. There was still no sound. Electric motor, he guessed. As it neared the bank he saw that two men stood in the bow holding some sort of guns. He reached for the Kalashnikov's safety lever but then they both slung their guns across their backs and jumped out into the shallows and began pulling the big inflatable up onto the sand.

Several dark figures stood up in the boat and began moving rather awkwardly toward the bow, where the two men gave them a hand climbing down. When the fifth one was ashore the two gunmen pushed the boat back free of the shore and climbed back aboard while the passengers walked slowly across the sand to where Logan stood.

The first one stopped in front of Logan. He was tall and thin and bespectacled, wearing a light-colored topcoat hanging open over a dark suit. In his left hand he carried a medium-sized travel bag.

"Good evening," he said in accented Russian. "I am Doctor Fong—"

"I don't want to know who you are," Logan told him. "I don't want to know anything I don't need to know. You're in charge of this group?"

"I suppose. In a sense—"

"Good. Get your people on board." Logan jerked the Kalashnikov's muzzle in the direction of the helicopter, which was already emitting a high whistling whine, the long rotor blades starting to swing.

The tall man nodded and turned and looked back at the boat and said something in Chinese. The boat began to move backward. The tall man spoke again and the others moved quickly to follow him toward the Mil, lugging their bags and bundles.

"Let's go," Logan told Yura. "*Davai poshli.*"

Off down the river the wolves were howling again.

The road was a dark streak in the moonlight, running roughly east-west, across open plain and through dense patches of forest. There was no traffic in sight, nor had Logan expected any. This had been one of the last stretches of the Trans-Siberian Highway to be completed, but the pavement was already deteriorating, having been badly done to begin with and rarely maintained since; very few people cared to drive its ruinously potholed surface at night.

"Should be right along here," Logan said, studying the map Yevgeny had given them. "That's the third bridge after the village, isn't it?"

Beside him, Misha glanced out the side window at the ground flickering past beneath. "I think so."

"Better get lower, then."

Misha nodded and eased down on the collective. As the Mil settled gently toward the road Logan felt around the darkened cockpit and found the bag with the night goggles. The next part should be straightforward but with people like this you couldn't assume anything.

Misha leveled off a little above treetop level. "If there's one thing I hate worse than flying at night," he grumbled, "it's flying low at night . . . isn't that something up ahead?"

Logan started to put on the night goggles. As he was slipping them over his head a set of headlights flashed twice down on the highway, maybe a quarter of a mile away.

"That should be them," he told Misha. "Make a low pass, though, and let's have a look."

Misha brought the helicopter down even closer to the road, slowing to the speed of a cautiously-driven car, while Logan wrestled the window open and stuck his head out. The slipstream caught the bulky goggles and tried to jerk his head around, but he fought the pressure and a few seconds later he saw the car, parked in the middle of the road, facing east. He caught a glimpse of dark upright shapes standing nearby, and then it all disappeared from view as the Mil fluttered on up the road.

"Well?" Misha said.

Logan started to tell him it was all right, to come around and go back and land; but then something broke surface in his mind and he said, "No, wait. Circle around and come back up the road the same way. Take it slow so I can get a better look."

Misha kicked gently at the pedals and eased the cyclic over, feeding in power and climbing slightly to clear a stand of trees. "*Shto eto?*"

"I'm not sure yet." Something hadn't looked right, something about the scene down on the road that didn't add up, but Logan couldn't get a handle on it yet. Maybe it was just his imagination.

They swung around in a big circle and came clattering back up the road. Again the double headlight flash, this time slower and longer. "Slow, now," Logan said, pulling the goggles down again and leaning out the window. "All right . . . that's it, go on."

He pulled off the goggles and closed his eyes, trying to project the scene like a photograph inside his head: the dark shape of a medium-sized car in the middle of the road, flanked by a couple of human figures. Another man—or woman—standing over by the right side of the road.

"Shit," Logan said, and opened his eyes and turned around and looked back between the seats. "Hey. You. Doctor Fong."

"Yes?" The tall Chinese leaned forward. "Something is wrong?"

"These people you're meeting," Logan said. "They know how many of you there are?"

"Oh, yes." Reddish light from the instrument panel glinted off glasses lenses as Fong nodded vigorously. "They know our names and . . . everything, really. This is certain."

"What's happening?" Misha wanted to know.

"Three men in sight, back there," Logan said, turning back around. "At least one more in the car, operating the headlights. Five men expected."

"So?"

"So that's not a very big car to hold nine men. You could do it, but it would be a circus act. Which raises some questions."

"Huh." Misha digested this. "What do you think?"

"I think we better find out more." He thought for a moment. "All right, here's how we'll do it. Set her down right up here, past that rise, just long enough for me to get out. Then circle around a little bit, like you're confused, you know? Make some noise to cover me while I move in and have a look."

He tapped the comm unit in the pocket on his left jacket sleeve. "I'll give you a call if it's all right to land. If I send just a single long beep, come in as if you're going to land and then hit the landing lights."

"Got it," Misha said. "Taking Yura?"

"Of course. Right, then." Logan undid the seat harness and levered himself out of the right seat. As he clambered back into the passenger compartment Doctor Fong said, "Please, what is the matter?"

"I don't know yet." Logan worked his way between the close-spaced seats to the rear of the cabin, where Yura sat next to the door. "Don't worry," he said over his shoulder, hoping Fong couldn't see him getting out the Kalashnikov. "It's probably nothing."

Misha brought the Mil down and held it in a low hover, its wheels a few feet above the pavement, long enough for Logan and Yura to jump out. As Logan's boots hit the cracked asphalt he flexed his knees to absorb the impact and almost immediately heard the rotor pitch change as Misha pulled up on the collective to lift out of there.

Yura came up beside him and Logan made a quick hand signal. Yura nodded and ran soundlessly across the road and disappeared into the shadows beneath the trees on the right side. Logan walked back along the road until he reached the top of the little rise and then moved off the pavement to the left.

The cover was poor on that side, the trees thin and scattered, with patches of brush that made it hard to move quietly. Logan guessed it was about a mile back to where the car was parked. Moving slowly and carefully, holding the Kalashnikov high across his chest, he worked his way along parallel to the road. The night goggles were pushed up on his forehead; they were too clumsy for this sort of thing and anyway he could see all right now. The moon was higher and the clouds had blown away, and his eyes had adjusted to the weak light.

The Mil came back overhead, turbines blaring and rotor blades clop-clopping, heading back down the road. It swung suddenly off to one side, turned back and crossed the road, did a brief high hover above the trees, and then began zigzagging irregularly along above the highway. Logan grinned to himself;

whoever was waiting down the road must be getting pretty baffled by now. Not to mention pissed off.

He thought he must be getting close, and he was about to move over by the road to check; but then here came the Mil again, coming back up the road maybe twenty feet up, and suddenly there was a bright light shining through the trees, closer than he'd expected, as the car headlights flashed again.

He stopped and stood very still. As the sound of the helicopter faded on up the road behind him, he heard a man's voice say quite distinctly, "*Ah, yob tvoiu mat'.*"

He waited until the Mil began to circle back, so its noise would cover any sounds that he made. A few quick steps and he stood beside the road, pressed up against an inadequate pine. He slipped the night goggles down over his eyes and leaned cautiously out, feeling his sphincter pucker.

There they were, just as he remembered: the two men standing on either side of the car, and another one over by the far side of the road. All three of them, he saw now, were holding weapons: some sort of rifles or carbines, he couldn't make out any details.

He pushed the goggles back up, slung the Kalashnikov over his shoulder, and took the comm unit from his pocket and switched it on and pressed a single key. He held it down for a count of five, switched the unit off, slipped it back into his pocket, and unslung the Kalashnikov again.

The Mil came racketing up the road once more, slowing down as the headlights flashed again. Logan stepped out from behind the tree and began moving quickly along next to the road, not trying to be stealthy; by now these bastards wouldn't be paying attention to anything but the helicopter with the impossible pilot.

It was moving now at bicycle speed and then even slower. When it was no more than twenty feet in front of the parked car it stopped in a low hover. Logan stopped too, and pushed the Kalashnikov's fire selector to full automatic as Misha hit the landing lights.

The sudden glare threw the scene into harsh contrast, like a black-and-white photograph. One of the men beside the car threw a forearm over his face. Someone cursed.

Logan raised the Kalashnikov and took a deep breath. "Everyone stand still!" he shouted over the rotor noise. "Put down the weapons!"

For a second he thought it was going to work. The men on the road froze in place, like so many window dummies. Logan had just enough time to wonder what the hell he was going to do with them, and then it all came apart.

The man over on the far side of the road started to turn, very fast, the gun in his hands coming up and around. There was a deafening *blang* and he jerked slightly, dropped his rifle, and fell to the pavement.

While the sound of Yura's rifle was still rattling off through the trees the two men by the car made their play, moving simultaneously and with purposeful speed. The nearer one took a long step to one side and whirled around, dropping into a crouch, while the other dived to the ground and started to roll toward the cover of the car.

Logan got the farther one in mid-roll and then swung the Kalashnikov toward the remaining one. A red eye winked at him and something popped through the bushes, not very close; the gunman had to be shooting blind, his eyes still trying to catch up to the sudden changes in the light. Backlit by the landing lights, he was an easy-meat target; Logan cut him down with a three-shot burst to the chest.

The car door opened and someone stepped out. Yura's old rifle boomed again from the trees across the road. Four down.

Logan walked slowly toward the car, the Kalashnikov ready. A man lay beside the open door, a machine pistol in one hand. Logan looked in and checked the interior of the car.

He took the comm unit out and flicked it on again. "All right, Misha," he said. "You can set her down now."

He walked over to the body of the last man he had killed and studied the weapon that lay beside the body. A Dragunov sniper rifle, fitted with what looked like a night scope. Definitely some professional talent, whoever they were.

He went back and sat down on the hood of the car, for want of any better place, while Misha set the helicopter down. He noticed with disgust that his hands were starting to tremble slightly.

Yura came up, his rifle over his shoulder and what looked like a Kalashnikov in one hand. "Sorry I was so slow on that last one," he said. He raised the Kalashnikov and gestured with his free hand at the body on the far side of the road. "This is what he had."

"Then for God's sake get rid of it." Remembering, Logan cleared the chamber of his own rifle and slung it over his back. For the first time in a long time he wished he hadn't quit smoking.

The Mil's rotor blades were slowing, the turbine whine dropping to idle. A couple of minutes later Misha came walking toward the car. "*Bozhe moi,*" he said, staring. "What—?"

"Reception committee," Logan said. "Had a nice little ambush set up. At least that's how it looks."

Misha was looking around dazedly. "You're sure?"

"About the ambush, not entirely. It's possible they were going to let the passengers disembark and wait for us to leave before killing them. Hell," Logan said, "just look at the kind of firepower they were carrying. I don't think it was because they were afraid of wolves."

Yura was going over the car. "Couple of shovels in the trunk," he reported. "Some wire, some tape."

"See?" Logan turned his head and spat; his mouth felt very dry. "They weren't planning on taking anyone anywhere. Not any farther than a short walk in the woods."

The Chinese men were getting out of the helicopter now, stopping in front of the nose and staring at the car and the bodies. Misha cursed. "I told them to stay inside—"

"It's all right," Logan said. "Doesn't matter now."

Doctor Fong appeared, walking toward them. He didn't look happy, Logan thought, but he didn't look all that surprised either.

Logan said, "I don't suppose you have any idea what this was all about?"

Fong stopped beside the car and looked around. "Perhaps," he said. "I—let me think."

"Don't think too long," Logan said. "We've got to get out of here."

"Yes." He looked at Logan. "Do you speak English?"

"After a fashion."

"Aha." Fong's mouth quirked in a brief half-smile. "An American. Good. My English is much better than my Russian."

He pushed his glasses up on his nose with the tip of a slender finger. They weren't slipping; Logan guessed it was a nervous habit. He made a gesture that took in the car and the bodies. "Can we perhaps move away from . . . ?"

"Sure." Logan slid off the car and walked with Fong over to the side of the road. "I just need to know," he said, "what kind of trouble this is about. If you guys are anything political—"

"Oh, no." Fong stopped and turned to face him. "No, we're not, as you put it, political at all. Merely a group of harmless scientists."

"Some pretty heavy people trying to stop you," Logan said. "Someone must not think you're so harmless."

"Yes, well. . . ." Fong looked off into the darkness under the trees and then back at Logan. "You saved our lives just now," he said in a different tone. "This is a debt we can hardly repay, but there's something I can give you in return. Some information."

"Scientific information?"

"Yes." If Fong noticed the sarcasm he didn't show it. He pushed his glasses up again. "It's the warming."

It took a moment for Logan to realize what he was talking about. The adrenalin edge had worn off; he felt tired and old.

"It's still getting warmer," Fong said. "I'm sure you already knew that, it's hardly a secret. But—" He paused, his forehead wrinkling. "The curve," he said. "I couldn't remember the word . . . the curve is different from what has been thought."

His forefinger drew an upward-sweeping curve in the air. "The warming is about to accelerate. It's going to start getting warmer at an increasing rate, and—I'm not sure how to say this—the rate of increase will itself increase."

"It's going to get warmer faster?"

Fong nodded. "Oh, you won't notice any real change for some time to come. Perhaps as much as two to five years, no one really knows as yet . . . but then," the fingertip began to rise more steeply, "the change will be very rapid indeed."

"You mean—"

"Wait, that's not all. The other part," Fong said, "is that it's likely to go on longer than anyone thought. The assumption has been that the process has all but run its course, that a ceiling will soon be reached. It's not clear, now, just where the ceiling is. Or even if there is one, in any practical sense."

Logan's ears registered the words but his fatigue-dulled brain was having trouble keeping up. "It's going to keep getting warmer," he said, "it's going to do it faster and faster, and it's going to get a hell of a lot warmer than it is now. That's what you're saying?"

"Even so."

"But that's going to mean . . . Christ." Logan shook his head, starting to see it. "Christ," he said again helplessly, stupidly. "Oh, Christ."

"You might well call on him, if you believe in him," Fong said. "If I believed in any gods I would call on them too. Things are going to be very, very bad."

"As if they weren't bad enough already."

"Yes indeed. I don't know how long you've been in this part of the world, but I'm sure you've heard at least some of the news from other regions."

"Pretty bad in China, I hear."

"You have no idea. Believe me, it is much, much worse than anything you can have heard. The government keeps very strict control over the flow of information. Even inside China, it's not always possible to know what's happening in the next province."

Fong put out a hand and touched the rough bark of the nearest pine. "You live in one of the few remaining places that have been relatively unharmed by the global catastrophe. A quiet, pleasant backwater of a large country grown suddenly prosperous—but all that is about to end."

He gave a soft short laugh with absolutely no amusement in it. "You think the Russian Federation has a problem with desperate Chinese coming across the border *now?* Just wait, my friend. Already the level of desperation in my country is almost at the critical point. When people realize that things are getting even worse, they will begin to move and it will take more than border posts and patrols, and even rivers, to stop them."

Logan started to speak but his throat didn't seem to be working so well.

"Your American journalists and historians," Fong added, "used to write about the Chinese military using 'human wave' attacks. This frontier is going to see a human tsunami."

Logan said, "You're talking war, aren't you?

"Of one kind or another." Fong fingered his glasses. "I really am not qualified to speculate in that area. All I'm telling you is that this is about to become a very bad place to live."

"Thanks for the warning."

"As I say, you saved our lives. In my case, you probably saved me from worse." Fong turned and looked back at the scene in the middle of the road, where the other Chinese were still milling around the car and the bodies. "I suspect they meant to question me. That would not have been pleasant."

Logan said, "So what was all this about? Since when is the mafia interested in a bunch of physicists or climatologists or whatever you are?"

"What?" Fong looked startled. He pushed his glasses up again and then he smiled. "Oh, I see. You misunderstand. None of us is that sort of scientist. No, our field is chemistry. Pharmaceutical chemistry," he said. "Which *is* of interest to . . . certain parties."

Logan nodded. It didn't take a genius to figure that one out.

"The information I just gave you," Fong went on, "has nothing to do with my own work. I got it from my elder brother, who was one of the team that made the breakthrough. He told me all about it, showed me the figures—it's not really difficult, anyone with a background in the physical sciences could understand it—just before they took him away."

"Took him away? What for? Oh," Logan said. "This is something the Chinese government wants to keep the lid on."

"That is a way to put it."

"And that's why you decided to get the hell out?"

"Not really. We've been working on this for some time. We had already made contact with the, ah, relevant persons. But I admit the news acted as a powerful incentive."

"And this business here tonight?"

Fong shrugged. "The so-called Russian mafia is no more than a loose confederacy of factions and local organizations. I would assume someone got wind of the plan and, for whatever reason, decided to stop us. Possibly rivals of the ones who were going to employ us. But that's only a guess."

He made a face. "I am not happy about being involved with people like this, but I would have done anything to get out of China. And I can't imagine myself as an underpaid illegal laborer on some construction project along the Lena or the Yenesei."

Logan nodded again. "Okay, well, we'd better get moving. What do you guys want to do? We can't very well take you back to Khabarovsk with us, but—"

"Oh, we'll be all right. The car appears to be undamaged—that really was remarkable shooting—and one of my colleagues is a very expert driver. We have contacts we can call on," Fong said, "telephone numbers, a safe address in Belogorsk."

Logan noticed that a couple of the Chinese men were examining the dead men's weapons, handling them in quite a knowledgeable way. Some scientists. He wondered what the rest of the story was. Never know, of course. What the hell.

"So you may as well be going." Fong put out a hand. "Thank you again."

Logan took it. "Don't mention it," he said. "A satisfied customer is our best advertisement."

"So," Misha said, "you think it's true?"

"Right now," Logan said, "I don't know what the hell I think about anything."

By now they were about three quarters of the way back to Khabarovsk. The moon was well up in the sky and the Trans-Siberian Highway was clearly visible below the Mil's nose. Perfect conditions for IFR navigation: I Follow Roads. Back in the cabin Yura was sound asleep.

"He could have been making the whole thing up," Misha said. "But why?"

"People don't necessarily need a reason to lie. But," Logan said, "considering the situation, I don't know why he'd want to waste time standing around feeding me a line."

"Those people," Misha said, centuries of prejudice in his voice. "Who can tell?"

"Well, if Fong was right, there's going to be a hell of a lot of 'those people' coming north in another couple of years—maybe sooner—and then it's going to get nasty around here. Even if Fong's story was ninety percent bullshit," Logan said, "we're still looking at big trouble. Those poor bastards have got to be pretty close to the edge already, from all I've heard. If things get even a little bit worse—" He turned and looked at Misha. "I think we don't want to be here when it happens."

Misha sighed heavily. "All right. I see what you mean."

In the distance the lights of Khabarovsk had begun to appear. Logan looked at the fuel gauges. They'd cut it a little close tonight; they wouldn't be running on fumes by the time they got home but they'd certainly be into the reserve.

Misha said, "Where are you going to go, then?"

"Hell, I don't know." Logan rubbed his eyes, wishing they'd brought along a thermos of coffee. "Back up north, maybe."

"Ever think of going back to America?"

"Not really. Actually I'm not even sure they'd let me back in. I've lived outside the country almost twenty years now, and anything over five automatically gets you on the National Security Risk list. Anyway," Logan said, "things have gone to hell in the States, and not just from the weather and the flooding. It's been crazy back there for a long time. Even before I left." Like that proposal to change the name of the country to the Christian Republic of America. It hadn't passed, despite the President's support, but who wanted to live in a country where almost half the population thought it would be a good idea?

Misha said, "Canada, then?"

"Canada's harder than this country to get into, these days. Especially for people from the States. Alaska, now," Logan said thoughtfully, "that might be a possibility. They say the secessionists are paying good money for mercenaries. But I'm getting a little old for that."

"You weren't too old tonight." He could just make out the pale flash of Misha's grin in the darkness. "Man, I'd forgotten how good you are."

"Bullshit. No, I think it's Siberia again, if I decide to pull out. I know some people from the old days, we've kept in touch. You want to come along? Always work for a good pilot."

"Maybe. I'll think about it. We had some pretty good times in Siberia in the old days, didn't we? And now it wouldn't be so damned cold."

Khabarovsk was coming into view now, a sprawl of yellow lights stretching north from the river. Moonlight glinted softly off the surface of the Amur, limning the cluster of islands at the confluence with the Ussuri.

"Going to take Lida with you?" Misha asked.

"I don't know." Logan hadn't thought about it. "Maybe. If she wants to come. Why not?"

He sat upright in his seat and stretched as best he could in the confined space. "You understand," he said, "I haven't made up my mind yet. I'm not going to do anything until I've had time to think this over."

He stared ahead at the lights of Khabarovsk. "Right now I've got more urgent matters to take care of. Starting with a long private talk with Yevgeny."

* * *

But next day everything got crazy and there was no time to think about Yevgeny or the Chinese or anything else. A perfectly legitimate scientific expedition, some sort of geological survey team, called up from Komsomolsk in urgent need of transportation services, their pilot having gotten drunk and disappeared for parts unknown with their aircraft.

And so for the next couple of weeks life was almost unbearably hectic, though profitable. Logan was too preoccupied to pay much attention to anything but the most immediate concerns; he barely listened when Yura came in to say that he was taking off for a few days to check out something he'd heard about.

But at last the job was finished and life began to return to a less lunatic pace; and it was then, just as Logan was starting to think once again about old and new business, that Yura showed up at the office saying he'd found something Logan ought to see.

"You come," he said. "I have to show you."

There was something in his face that forestalled arguments or objections. Logan said, "Will we need the Mil?"

Yura nodded. Logan said, "All right. Let's go find Misha."

"Well," Misha said in a strangled voice, "now we know what the wolves have been eating."

Logan didn't reply. He was having too much trouble holding the contents of his stomach down.

"Bears too," Yura said, and pointed at the nearest body with the toe of his boot. "See? Teeth marks too big for wolves."

There were, Logan guessed, between fifteen and twenty bodies lying about the clearing. It was difficult to be sure because some had been dragged over into the edge of the forest and most had been at least partly dismembered.

"Tigers, some places," Yura added. "Not this one, though."

"How many?" Logan managed to get out. "Places, I mean."

"Don't know. Eleven so far, that I found. Probably more. I quit looking." Yura's face wrinkled into a grimace of disgust. "Some places, lots worse than this. Been there too long, you know? Gone rotten, bad smell—"

"Yes, yes," Logan said hastily, feeling his insides lurch again. "I'll take your word for it."

The smell was bad enough here, though the bodies didn't appear to be badly decomposed yet. At least it was still too early in the year for the insects to be out in strength. In a few more weeks—he pushed the picture out of his mind. Or tried to.

"And these places," Misha said, "they're just scattered around the area?"

Yura nodded. "Mostly just off old logging roads, like here. Always about the same number of Chinese."

Logan wondered how he could tell. The bodies he could see were just barely recognizable as human.

"They came up the logging road," Yura said, pointing. "One truck, not very big, don't know what kind. Stopped by those trees and everyone got out. They all walked down the trail to right over there. Chinese all lined up, facing that way, and knelt down. Four men stood a little way behind them and shot them in the back. Kalashnikovs." He held up a discolored cartridge case. "Probably shooting full automatic. Some of the Chinese tried to run. One almost made it to the woods before they got him."

Misha was looking skeptical; probably he wondered if Yura could really tell all that just by looking at the sign on the ground. Logan didn't. He'd seen Yura at work enough times in the past.

"Did it the same way every place," Yura added.

"Same truck too?"

"Couldn't tell for sure. A couple of places, I think so."

"Poor bastards," Misha said. "Packed in the back of a truck, getting slammed around on a dirt road, probably half starved—they'd be dizzy and weak, confused, easy to push around. Tell them to line up and kneel down, they wouldn't give you any trouble."

"One place," Yura said, "looked like some of the Chinese tried to fight back. Didn't do them any good."

"Your people," Logan said, "they knew about this?"

"Someone knew something. Stories going around, that's how I heard. Not many villages left around here," Yura said. "Most of the people moved out back when they started the logging. Or the loggers drove them out."

"Any idea how long it's been going on?"

"From what I heard, from the way the bodies looked at a couple of places," Yura said, "maybe a year."

Logan and Misha looked at each other.

"I think," Logan said, "there's someone we should go see."

"Chinks?" Yevgeny Lavrushin said incredulously. "This is about fucking *Chinks?*"

He rubbed the back of his hand against the raw spot on his face, where Yura had peeled the duct tape off his mouth. He did it clumsily; his wrists were still taped together.

Beside him in the back seat of the car, Logan said, "Not entirely. We were already planning to have a talk with you."

"Hey," Yevgeny said, "I don't blame you guys for being pissed off, I'd be pissed off too. I swear I didn't know it was going to get fucked up like that."

His voice was higher than usual and his words came out very fast. There was a rank smell of fear-sweat coming off him, so strong Logan was tempted to open a window despite the chill of the early-morning air.

"There's a *lot* of people pissed off about what happened," he said. "Some pretty *heavy* people. If they thought I had anything to do with what went down that night, I wouldn't be alive right now talking to you guys. Trust me."

"Trust you?" Misha said over his shoulder. "The way those Chinese did?"

"Oh, shit. What's the big deal? Look," Yevgeny said, "you gotta understand how it works. Used to be you could bring in as many Chinks as you could haul and nobody cared, it's a big country and the big shots were glad of the cheap labor and the cops were cool as long as they got their cut."

Misha swerved the old Toyota to miss a pothole. Yevgeny lost his balance and toppled against Yura, who cursed and shoved him away. "God *damn,*" Yevgeny cried. "Come on, you guys, can't you at least take this tape off?"

"No," Logan said. "You were saying?"

"Huh? Oh, right. See, everything's tightened up now. You can still bring in a few now and then, like those suits you guys picked up. But if I started running Chinks in any kind of numbers," Yevgeny said, "enough to make a profit, man, the shit would come down on me like you wouldn't believe. A bunch of them get caught, they talk, it's my ass."

"So you take their money," Logan said, "and you load them into the truck and take them out into the woods and shoot them."

"For Chrissake," Yevgeny said. His voice had taken on an aggrieved, impatient note; his facial expression was that of a man trying to explain something so obvious that it shouldn't need explaining. "They're *Chinks!*"

"They're human beings," Misha said.

"The fuck they are. A Chink ain't a man. Anyway," Yevgeny said, looking at Logan, "like you never killed anybody? I heard what you did up in Yakutsk—"

His voice died away. "Sorry," he said almost in a whisper.

Logan looked out the windows. "Almost to the airport," he said. "Now you're not going to give us any trouble, are you, Yevgeny? You're going to go along with us without any noise or fuss, right? Yura, show him."

Yura reached out with one hand and turned Yevgeny's head to face him. With the other hand he held up his big belt knife, grinning.

"Okay, okay. Sure." Yevgeny's face was paler than ever. "No problem . . . hey, where are we going?"

"You'll see," Logan told him. "It's a surprise."

* * *

Going up the logging road, watching Yevgeny lurching along ahead of him, Logan considered that maybe they should have let him put on a jacket or something. He'd come to the door of his apartment, in answer to their knock, wearing only a grubby sweat suit that he'd evidently been sleeping in; and they'd let him put on his shoes, but by the time anyone thought about a coat they'd already taped his wrists and it was too difficult to get one onto him.

Now he was shivering in the cold breeze that blew across the ridge; and Logan didn't really care about that, but he was getting tired of listening to Yevgeny complaining about it. Well, it wouldn't be much longer.

Up ahead, Misha turned off the overgrown road and up the trail toward the crest of the ridge. "That way," Logan said to Yevgeny.

"Shit," Yevgeny whined. "What's all this about? I'm telling you guys, if you found some stiffs or something out here, it's got nothing to with me. I never operated anywhere near here. I never even *been* anywhere near here."

"Shut up," Logan said, prodding him with the muzzle of the Kalashnikov. "Just follow Misha and shut up."

It was a long slow climb up the ridge and then down the other side. Yevgeny was incredibly clumsy on the trail; he stumbled frequently and fell down several times. At least he had stopped talking, except for occasional curses.

When they finally reached the little clearing he leaned against a tree and groaned. "Jesus," he said. "You guys do this all the time? What are you, crazy?"

Logan looked at him and past him, studying the tree. It wasn't the one he'd had in mind, but it would do just fine. He turned and nodded to the others.

"So," Yevgeny said, "are you gonna tell me now—hey, what the fuuuu—"

His voice rose in a yelp as Logan and Yura moved up alongside him and grabbed him from either side, slamming him back hard against the trunk of the tree. Misha moved in quickly with the roll of duct tape.

"Hey. Hey, what, why—" Yevgeny was fairly gobbling with terror now. "Come on, now—"

"*Harasho,*" Misha said, stepping back. "Look at that. Neat, huh?"

Logan walked around the tree, examining the bonds. "Outstanding," he said. "Very professional job."

Misha held up the rest of the roll of tape. "Want me to tape his mouth again?"

Yevgeny was now making a dolorous wordless sound, a kind of drawn-out moan. Logan started to tell Misha to go ahead and gag him, but then he changed his mind and shook his head.

Yura had already disappeared up the narrow game trail on the far side of the clearing. Now he came back, carrying a small cloth bag from which he sprinkled a thick greenish-brown powder along the ground. When he reached the tree where Yevgeny hung in his tape bonds he pulled the mouth of the bag wide open and threw the rest of the contents over Yevgeny's face and body.

"Now you smell good," he told Yevgeny.

Yevgeny had begun to blubber, "Oh God, oh Jesus," first in English and then in Russian, again and again. Logan didn't think he was praying, but who knew?

"All right," Logan said, "let's go."

They made better time going back over the ridge, without Yevgeny to slow them down. They were halfway down the other side when they heard it: a deep, coughing, basso roar, coming from somewhere behind them.

They stopped and looked at each other. Yura said, "*Amba* sounds hungry."

They moved on down the trail, hurrying a little now. Just as they reached the logging road they heard the roar again, and then a high piercing scream that went on and on.

"Amba" is of course a Hemingway hommage, based on the brilliant story "One Trip Across" which later evolved into the disastrously flawed novel To Have And Have Not.

One reviewer referred to my "Bogartian" protagonist, which confused me for a moment until I realized he was probably thinking of the movie version of the novel. (Which bore almost no relationship to the book, William Faulkner having had the good sense to discard the hopelessly chaotic text.) But then reviewers sometimes have very strange ideas; a couple of them referred to the story as being set in Siberia!

Sometimes I despair. . . .

Written April 2006
First published July 2006

Going To See The Beast

It was along about nine in the morning when Boss Lady called me in to tell me we were going to go see the Antichrist tomorrow.

"Make sure your best suit is clean and pressed," she said, "and tell Joe Bob to wash and wax the car."

"The big car?" I said. She's got like half a dozen of them. "The limo?"

"Of course," she said. She said it with that kind of a sharp voice that she gets when she thinks somebody is being dumb, which with her is most of the time. "See to it his uniform is presentable, too. I couldn't believe those boots, last time."

We were in her office up on the second floor of the big house. She was setting at her desk with her back to the window. I think she does that so the light will hurt your eyes when she's talking to you. She had on a white silk shirt. She won't wear no other kind of a shirt but silk. Even with the light behind her you could see she wasn't wearing no brazeer.

She give me this little bitty smile, without showing no teeth. It made her look exactly like her picture in the newspapers that she used to write for. There was a big framed copy of that picture on the wall by her desk, next to the one of her with the President.

"I bet you never guessed," she said, "back a couple of years ago, that you would some day be meeting the Supreme Ruler of the World."

"No, ma'am," I said, "I sure never."

I still remember the day it all started. Me and my cousin Joe Bob was just walking down the street in Fort Worth when all of a sudden there was all these people flying up through the air. Just sailing straight up towards the sky, easy as you please, and ever single one of them buck bare ass naked. It was the prettiest sight I ever saw. Well, except for the men and some of the real old ones.

You could hear this music, too. Wasn't very good music, you couldn't boogie to it, mostly sounded like a bunch of horns blowing, but it was plenty loud. It kept playing while the people flew on up into the sky and then you couldn't see them no more and then it stopped.

Well, I don't mind telling you I just stood there on the sidewalk with my mouth hanging open through the whole thing and then some. I didn't know what to think. Then it hit me.

"Joe Bob," I said, "we been *left behind!*"

Joe Bob didn't say nothing. I don't think he heard me. He was walking around picking up and sniffing the underpants some of the ladies had left on the sidewalk when they flew away.

Me, I was just so shook I had to go over and set down on the hood of this Cadillac that was parked close by. I put my face in my hands for a minute, thinking Lord God, what's going to happen to me now?

I mean I knew what was going on. Mama always took me to church with her and I had heard the preacher talk about the Rapture and the End Times and all that stuff. And I *believed* it, you understand, he was reading it out of the Good Book so it had to be so. But I never thought I'd live to see it *personal.*

I set there a long time, feeling awful and even crying a little, wishing I'd lived a better life and not done all that drinking and card playing and looking at them magazines with the nasty pictures. Then I could have flew away too and be in Heaven now instead of being left behind where all kind of bad stuff was sure to happen.

But after a while it come to me that I didn't really feel no different from how I did before. Everything around me looked the same, too, except for the little piles of clothes laying around where the people used to be. I got to thinking maybe this might not be so bad after all.

I got up and had a look at that Cadillac I had been setting on. I seen now that the door was open and there was what looked like a pretty good suit laying on the street beside it. I picked up the pants—took me a minute before I could make myself do that—and went through the pockets and sure enough, there was the keys.

"Hey, Joe Bob," I said. "Let's go for a ride."

Joe Bob looked around and let out one of them yeehaw yells. "All *right!*" he hollered.

He came around and got in. "I bet we can get ourselves plenty of women with this baby," he said.

I thought about that. Joe Bob ain't too smart but sometimes he has some good ideas. After all, I thought, any women left now would just naturally have to be sinners, wouldn't they?

It was about a week later when we met Boss Lady.

We was setting on the hood of the Cadillac down by the rodeo grounds, drinking Coors and shooting at the cans with the new Glock pistol that I had just got in trade for some jewelry we found next to a lady's clothes that first day. Actually I was the one doing the shooting, doing some fancy tricks while Joe Bob finished up the last of the Coors.

Then we both noticed this nice black BMW car that had drove up. Setting behind the wheel looking at us was this blond headed lady who I felt sure I had seen before only I couldn't remember where.

I was a little embarrassed because we both had our shirts off, it being a hot day and all, but then I remembered the Rapture was over so there wasn't no sense in being ashamed in front of somebody else who had been left behind. So I just looked back at her and when she rolled down her window I said, "Hi."

She said, "You're pretty good with that thing."

I saw she was talking about the Glock pistol. "Yes ma'am," I said, "I guess I am."

I looked closer at her. "Ain't I seen you on TV or somewheres?"

"It's possible," she said. "Do you read the newspapers?"

"Sure," I said. "Well, sometimes." To tell the truth mostly I just looked at the sports but sometimes when I had to wait a long time at the unemployment office or the rehab I would look through the papers that people had left laying around.

Then I remembered. "That's where I seen you before," I said. "You write all that stuff about the liberals and all."

She didn't really smile but she looked pleased. But she said, "I did. That's all over now. A lot of things are changing."

I said, "I never knowed you lived in Texas."

"I don't. Or I didn't. As I say, changes." She was looking me over and not bothering to be sneaky about it. "What's your name?"

"Bobby Joe," I said. "This here's my cousin Joe Bob."

She give Joe Bob the same kind of look-over. "Can you drive, Joe Bob?" she asked him.

"Sure," he said. He wasn't really paying attention because he was busy opening the last can of Coors. Joe Bob is a good old boy but he can't pee and blink at the same time.

I said, "I tell you what, ma'am, Joe Bob can drive anything with wheels. He's drove all kind of cars and trucks." I didn't mention that a whole lot of them belonged to other people. "He even raced stock cars once," I said. "Met Dale Earnhart his own self."

She went "Hmm," and looked us over some more. "Well, gentlemen," she said, her voice getting kind of funny on that last word, "I'm in urgent need of a couple of employees right now. Specifically a chauffeur and a bodyguard."

Joe Bob said, "You talking about a job?"

"We're not really looking for work right now," I told her.

"Listen," she said, "I don't know what kind of games you've been playing to support yourselves—probably living off the taxpayers' money on some socialist welfare program—but I can tell you that's something else that's over and done now. Along with soft-headed judges and lazy cops and the other people who have been letting your kind get away with your parasitic lifestyle."

Joe Bob said, "Hey," but she kept on talking. "For your information, within a few months anyone who can't show means of support is going to be taking up residence in a labor camp. You'd better take my offer," she said. "You'll never get a better one. And you really won't like it on a chain gang."

I said, "How much did you say you were paying?"

So that was how me and Joe Bob came to work for Boss Lady. She said later on she didn't expect we'd last more than a couple of weeks, she just hired us till she could get somebody steadier, but the way things turned out she was so happy with us she kept us on permanent.

It was a pretty good job, too, most of the time. Joe Bob drove her around places and I set next to her and guarded her body though to tell you the truth I never seen why she needed anybody to. Didn't nobody ever try to hurt her or nothing. And after the Antichrist appointed her to be the Minister of Truth she could of had all the guards she wanted if she'd of asked him. I think she just wanted her own private bodyguard for the style of it.

Of course there was other parts to the job too, that she hadn't said nothing about at the start. First time she ever called me up to her room and I found her standing there in nothing but them black stockings and them skimpy little drawers, I like to shit.

I got the idea pretty quick, though. It was the hardest I had worked in a long time but it was kind of fun sometimes. I got to say, though, she did have some strange ideas.

Standing there in front of her now, I wondered what was on the program tonight. Maybe she would call Joe Bob in instead. I just hoped she wouldn't want both of us. She didn't do that very often but I really hated it when she did. Joe Bob hated it even worse because she always made him be the one on the bottom.

But she must of guessed what I was thinking because she said, "No, Bobby Joe, there won't be any extra activities tonight." She smiled that little smile again. "We all have to be at our best tomorrow, don't we?"

I kept my face as straight as I could. I didn't want her to see I was kind of relieved. A lot of people probably would of thought I was crazy but if you want to know the truth Boss Lady ain't as great as you might think. For one thing she's awful stringy and she ain't got hardly any ass or titties. And I know she looks real fine in the pictures and on TV but if you seen her up close like I have, with all that makeup off, you probably wouldn't even recognize her. On her neck and around her eyes it looks like an old saddle that got left out in the sun too long.

"All right, ma'am," I said, trying to look disappointed. "I'll go tell Joe Bob."

"Do that." She give me this kind of a look. "It's all right, Bobby Joe," she said. "We'll make it up afterwards."

That's what I was afraid of. Every time she meets with the Antichrist she comes home all hot and horny and that's when me and Joe Bob really earn our pay. The last couple of times I got to wondering if that chain gang would really of been that bad.

So next day we drove into town to the Palace and Boss Lady and I went in, while Joe Bob turned the car over to the parking attendants and went to wait with the other hired help. A man in a uniform led us down a bunch of hallways to this big room with a long wooden table and showed Boss Lady where to set, even though she already knew from being here so many times. I went over and stood behind her like I was supposed to, in this position like what they called Parade Rest when I was in the Corps. There wasn't no reason for me to be there since there was regular Palace guards standing around the room and anyway they had took my gun away back at the gate. But like I say I think it was just her way of putting on the dog.

Next to Boss Lady set Brother Apollyon, the High Priest, looking around from under his big old hairy eyebrows and grinning that goofy-ass grin of his. I always thought he looked weird even back when he had his TV preacher show that Mama used to watch and send money to. Now, with that red robe and that tall pointy hat shaped like a dick, he just looked like something that got loose from a nut house.

On the other side of the table was the Minister of Peace—the Pale Horse's Ass, Boss Lady called him behind his back—scratching his forehead, which was all red and spotty because he had had some kind of allergy reaction when he got the tattoo. You couldn't hardly make out the three sixes. The chair next to him was empty and I was starting to wonder about that but then the door opened again and Miz Babylon came in.

Miz Babylon—that's what I always call her, I know that ain't her right title but I just feel like she ought to get some respect—was wearing her full dress uniform today, with the little bobtail skirt and the boots and the fish net stockings and the red and gold jacket hanging open so her titties were showing. Boss Lady told me once she hadn't wanted to dress that way but the Antichrist told her if she was going to be the Whore of Babylon she was damn well going to look like it. Boss Lady was jealous of her because she had wanted to be the Whore of Babylon her own self but the Antichrist never even asked her.

I thought she looked real pretty, myself, and I don't even usually go for colored ladies. She was kind of on the skinny side but it looked better on her than it did on Boss Lady and she had a nice tight looking little ass. I saw Brother Apollyon checking it out as she went by, too.

And it looked like that was it for this meeting. The other places around the table didn't have no name plates or water glasses or nothing in front of them. So it wasn't going to be a big meeting today.

All of a sudden the big doors opened at the end of the room and a couple of Palace guards came stomping in and stood at attention on either side of the doorway. There was a big honk of trumpets from the loudspeakers overhead and a voice hollered, *"All hail, the Antichrist!"*

I come to attention quick, while everybody around the table got up and stood—Brother Apollyon took his time about it, but he stood up too—and then there he was, coming through the big doors with that quick little walk of his, smiling at everybody and sort of bobbing his head. "Sit down, sit down," he said as he come up to the head of the table and set down in the big chair with the 666 on the back. "Make yourselves comfortable, ladies and gentlemen. This isn't going to take long. Just an informal meeting to discuss a few little problems that have come up."

They all set back down and I went back to Parade Rest. He looked at the Minister of Peace. "Rash still bothering you? You know, I'm real sorry about that. But everybody has to have the Mark. Can't make any exceptions. It's in the Prophecy."

He turned and give Boss Lady a long look. "My," he said. He had that funny grin on that always makes me think of one of them big monkeys in the zoo. "You're looking good today, Little Orphan Annie."

I seen the back of her neck go red when he said that. It really pisses her off when he calls her that. But of course she can't say nothing, seeing who he is. Her voice was pretty choked, though, when she said, "Thank you, Mr. Antichrist."

He looked at Miz Babylon. "And you too, of course." He kind of snickered. "Good enough to eat."

She blushed some—I never knew before that colored people can do that—but she didn't say nothing. I guess she knew that everybody there had heard the stories about how she got her job. Boss Lady claimed to have done a three-way with them once but I never was sure whether to believe it.

The Antichrist was looking sad now. "Course," he said, "there's somebody who isn't here. Still doesn't feel right without him. I guess the shock of the Rupture was just too much for that bad heart of his."

"It was ordained," Brother Apollyon said in his funny soft voice. "What is to be will be."

"You got that right, podner." The Antichrist shook his head. "Boy, I tell you, I don't mind admitting it was a shock to me too. I hadn't really expected the Rupture would happen in my lifetime but I always figured if it did I'd be one of the ones—

" He jerked his thumb upwards toward the ceiling. "I mean after all I did for the church people and all."

He leaned back in his chair and spread his hands out on the table. "But you know, seeing how things turned out, I can't complain, can I? Oh, I know there's gonna be trouble one of these days, bottomless pit and all that, but that's a long time to come and I didn't get where I am today by worrying about the future."

He looked at the Minister of Peace. "So," he said, "first thing I wanted to ask you, how's the nucular warhead supply holding up? We gotta have been going through those things like doodoo through a duck, now we've got this new front in Indonesia."

The Minister of Peace took off his glasses and wiped them and put them back on. "Well, Mr. Antichrist," he said, "here's the situation on that—"

I quit listening along about then. It wasn't anything interesting, just a bunch of numbers and names of places I mostly never heard of. Instead I watched Miz Babylon's titties. The little ends always stood up and got hard when they started talking about dropping nucular bombs on people. I seen Brother Apollyon looking at them too. His fingers were kind of twitching in his lap.

They talked for a pretty long time. Finally the Antichrist said, "All right, I guess that covers it. Well, then." He turned in his seat to face Boss Lady. "How are we doing on the information control front? Everybody falling into line?"

Boss Lady nodded. "The media never give us any trouble, of course. Still having some problems on the internet, sometimes it's hard to track down these unauthorized—"

The Antichrist was holding up his hand. "Wait, wait. Hang on there, honey. All this talking is dry work." He reached out and tapped on this silver button thing in front of him. "Let's take a little refreshment break."

This colored guy in a fancy uniform come in and everybody give him their orders. Boss Lady said she'd have a glass of white wine. Miz Babylon said she'd have the same. The

Minister of Peace asked for a gin tonic. Brother Apollyon wrinkled up his nose and said nothing alcoholic for him, thanks, he'd have a Coke.

"Yeah," the Antichrist said, "I'm pretty fond of Coke myself." He grinned at everybody and they all kept their faces straight like they didn't know what he was talking about. Even from where I stood I could see the little bits of white powder on his nose.

"Well," he said to the waiter, "you know my usual. Just sparkling mineral water." He gave the waiter a big wink. I wondered why he wanted to go through all that silliness. Shit, he's the Supreme Ruler of the World, he can do any damn thing he wants to, can't nobody say nothing less they're good and tired of living.

While they were waiting for their drinks him and Boss Lady talked a little bit about the movie she was going to make about him and how he got to be the Antichrist. *Triumph of the Right* was the name of it. It didn't sound like the kind of movie I'd want to see but I did like the idea of being around movie stars. There was sure plenty of big ones left, too. The Rapture hadn't got hardly any of them.

The colored guy came back carrying a silver tray balanced all neat and smooth in one hand, moving with that easy way colored guys can do, and set out the drinks. When he was gone the Antichrist said, "Now something else that's been bothering me." He picked up his glass and took a sip and set it back down on the table in front of him. "I'm disappointed in the level of cooperation we've been getting on the Mark program. Still got a lot of folks out there without the Mark."

"That's true," Boss Lady said. "And even worse, I'm hearing stories about people faking it, making phony tattoos with ink that they can wash off afterwards."

"There's a lot of resistance," Miz Babylon said. "It's not just the Christian Underground. Some people just don't like the way it looks. The ones that already have tattoos are the worst, too. They can't stand the thought of having one just like everybody else's."

I noticed Brother Apollyon was shifting around in his chair. He wasn't looking at Miz Babylon's boobies no more. He was staring straight at the Antichrist. The look on his face was weird even for him.

"It's all so inefficient," the Minister of Peace said. "I wish we could drop this whole six-sixty-six business and go over to bar codes. Or better yet, embedded chips—"

Brother Apollyon picked up his Coke. It looked like his hand shook or something. Anyway he spilled some of it on the table and on his red robe. "Oh," he said. "I'm sorry—"

He reached over to his left to grab a napkin. The Antichrist didn't even look at him. "Yes," he said to the Minister of Peace, "that would be nice. The chips especially. Normally I'd say that might be the nuculus of a good idea."

I guess I was the only one that seen it, and I nearly missed it. Old Brother Apollyon had damn fast hands for a man his age. I've seen top card sharps and pickpockets that weren't any slicker.

"But we can't do it," the Antichrist was saying. "It wouldn't be allowed."

There wasn't no mistake about it, though. I couldn't actually see what it was he dropped into the Antichrist's drink, but I seen him do it.

"It's in the Prophecy," the Antichrist said. "'And he causeth all to receive his mark,' something like that. Anyway it doesn't say a thing about bar codes or embedded chips."

He shook his head and reached for his drink.

That was when I lost it. I let out a big yell and run around past Boss Lady's chair and jumped up on top of the table and made a wild dive, knocking the glass out of the Antichrist's hand. "No," I hollered. "Don't drink that!"

Well, naturally in about half a second I was flat on my ass on the floor with half a dozen Palace guards pointing guns in my face. I figured I was dead. If they didn't kill me Boss Lady would.

But the Antichrist said, "Wait," and everybody held still. "Let him up," he told them, and when I was on my feet he said, "What's this all about?"

I started to speak but before I could say anything there was this real high giggle, like a girl. Everybody turned and looked at Brother Apollyon.

He had his hands up to his cheeks. His face was the flat-ass craziest I ever seen on a human.

"The pellet with the poison," he said in this creepy whispery voice, "is in the Palace that's in Dallas."

The Antichrist's mouth was hanging open. He wasn't the only one.

"It was supposed to be me, you know," Brother Apollyon said. His eyes were all walled back like a spooked horse. "It was revealed to me long ago, in a vision. All I had to do was wait and do as Satan commanded, and one day I would be the Antichrist, the Great Beast that hath power over the kings of this world—"

He stuck out his hand, pointing at the Antichrist. "You robbed me," he screamed. "After all I did for you, you robbed me of that which was to be mine!"

"Barking mad," the Minister of Peace said. His voice was a little shaky.

"Out of his damn mind," Miz Babylon said. "Crazy as a two-dick dog."

By now the Palace guards had Brother Apollyon by the arms and were pushing him down on the floor and slapping the cuffs on him. They weren't being none too gentle about it. He didn't hardly seem to notice, though. He was carrying on now in what sounded like some foreign language or maybe that Unknown Tongue that they used to speak in Mama's church.

The Antichrist was still setting there, not moving. He had finally shut his mouth but his face was white as a Zig-Zag paper.

"I could have been," he said. His face worked some. "I could have been *killed,*" he finally got out.

"Be sure and collect a sample of that drink," the officer in charge of the guards was saying. "It'll have to be analyzed."

The Antichrist was looking at me now. "You saved my life," he said. His voice was like somebody with a bad sore throat. "You saved my life," he said again, a little clearer. "Son, what's your name?"

* * *

And so that's how I got to be a big hero and got my picture in the papers and my face on TV and Boss Lady is even fixing it up for some people to make a movie about me.

Looks like the best thing that ever happened to me was getting left behind.

This was something I wrote when we were starting the new magazine Helix. *At the time I wasn't sure whether our business model was going to work and, therefore, whether we'd be able to pay contributors more than token amounts. So I figured I'd write one myself, and take no pay for it, just so the money wouldn't have to be divided as many ways.*

I was (eagerly) anticipating a tsunami of hate mail, but do you know, there wasn't a single angry message, nor, as far as I ever knew, any public denunciation of this scurrilous attack on a group of fine and dedicated Americans. Life is so disappointing at times.

Written February 2006
First published January 2007

The Contractors

We were six miles above the North Atlantic when my wrist watch began flashing, a soft pulsing green glow like a mutant firefly. I picked up the earphones from my lap and held one up to my left ear, and a familiar voice said, "Now."

I waited a second but that was all. I thumbed the little button to make the watch stop blinking. A quarter to midnight, it said. Chicago time; I hadn't reset it yet. Three hours later here? Or four? I wasn't sure what zone we were in.

That time, anyway. I laid the earphones on top of the laptop on the seat beside me and unlatched the seat belt and got to my feet, glancing around at the darkened cabin. Up toward the front a couple of lights were showing, and the glow of somebody's laptop screen; over on the far side a woman was trying to quiet a fretful baby. Most of the passengers, though, seemed to be sleeping. Or trying to; now and then you could hear bodies shifting restlessly, and an occasional muffled grunt.

I started down the aisle toward the rear of the cabin, taking the plastic pen from my shirt pocket and holding it down by my side. The lights were on back in the galley but no signs of movement.

I could see my man, though, sitting by the window, two rows ahead of the rear bulkhead. The seat next to him was empty, as were the seats behind him. It was too dark to see him very clearly, but I'd already had a good look at him back while we were boarding: a skinny, swarthy young man with a thin scrubby beard—or maybe just badly in need of a shave—in a surprisingly decent dark suit without a tie. Now I saw he'd added a yarmulke-like skullcap to his ensemble.

He didn't look up as I approached; I saw now that his eyes were closed. He was rocking slowly to and fro in his seat; he wasn't making any sound but his lips seemed to be moving.

It would have been easier if he'd been on the aisle, but those coach-class seats aren't all that wide. I didn't even have to lean over to reach him. His eyes snapped wide and white when the pen touched the side of his neck and the spring-loaded needle drove home, and his mouth opened, but nothing came out. A little book fell from his hands and slid off his lap to the floor as he sagged back in his seat.

I closed his eyes with my fingertips and moved on down the aisle, not looking back or around; if anybody had seen anything, it was too late to do anything about it now. There were no sounds of surprise or alarm behind me, though. As I came up to the restroom door I saw one of the flight attendants, a slightly chubby redhead, asleep on one of the galley seats.

The restroom was unoccupied. I latched myself in and got a paper towel from the dispenser and wiped the trick pen, being very careful of the needle point, before stuffing it down into the trash disposal. The odds of anybody finding it, let alone checking it for prints, probably approached zero, but why take the chance?

I stood there for a minute exchanging red-eyed stares with my reflection in the mirror above the sink. The sight was less than impressive: lined jowly face, gray hair in need of a trim, overnight whiskers starting to show. I wouldn't have bought a used roller skate from me.

Nobody was looking at me as I started back up the aisle, or at the body by the window. Everything was still dark and quiet; even the crying baby had settled down, leaving no sound but the great soft sigh of engines and slipstream as the big 747 bored on through the night sky.

I dropped into my seat, buckling up automatically, and sat back and closed my eyes for a moment, letting my pulse slow down a little. Then I reached over and lifted the laptop out of its case and set it on my knees. I stuck the button phones into my ears, took a deep breath, and opened the lid; and there was Himself waiting for me.

And he was doing the whole bit, too: the horns, the pointy goatee, even the reddish skin. Everything but the pitchfork and the flames. I suppose I winced; he laughed.

Grinding my teeth, I reached for the keyboard and typed:

Do you HAVE to do that?

"Sorry," he said, grinning. The screen flickered briefly and he reappeared in his more usual form, minus the horns and the rest of the comic-book look. He'd kept the mustache, though. It made him look a little like Harry Reems.

"Cheap and obvious, I know," he said. "What can I say? For a professional tempter, I'm no good at resisting temptation."

I typed:

It's done.

"Yes," he said. "You did that well. Not that I ever doubted you would."

I think we cut it a little close.

"I'm afraid so. He was definitely getting ready. My fault," Himself admitted. "I was momentarily distracted . . . at any rate," he said, "you were quick enough. Well done. A very clean bit of work, Major Hackett."

I didn't bother telling him not to call me that. We'd been there before; he was just trying to jerk my chain. I typed:

I don't think anybody saw anything.

"No. You might have noticed that the seats in the immediate area were unoccupied. This," he said, "was not coincidence."

I should have known. I started to ask how he'd managed it and then decided I didn't want to know.

He said, "I wish you'd relax. You need to get some rest. Things are going to get very stressful in a few hours."

If not sooner.

"Oh, I wouldn't worry about that. Who's going to pay any attention to an unimportant passenger on an overnight flight, apparently asleep in the cheap seats? No," he said, "you'll see. No one will notice anything until shortly before arrival at Heathrow, when they hand out the immigration cards, and find that Mr. Wazir doesn't respond to their efforts to wake him. After a certain amount of consternation and confusion, the young Scottish doctor up in business class will no doubt be summoned."

His teeth flashed. "And almost immediately will discover that the deceased is wearing a belt of Semtex explosive around his waist; and then for a time things are going to become intense."

No shit.

"Well, it shouldn't be too bad for you. After all, there's no reason anyone should suspect the truth. We've used that formula before," he said. "Even a full autopsy won't show anything but heart failure, no doubt brought on by extreme emotional stress. I tell you, that dear old woman at Johns Hopkins is worth every dollar I pay her . . . so no one will be thinking in terms of, ah, foul play. They'll be looking for possible accomplices—and," he added, hoisting an eyebrow, "you really don't fit the profile, do you? So lighten up."

Sorry. I just killed a man.

"Thereby saving several hundred lives."

And your concern for humanity is well
known.

"Touché." He laughed. "But as I already explained, up
on the first class deck are a couple of aging gentlemen who in
their dissolute younger days once recorded a song expressing
sympathy for me. One feels a certain obligation."

He raised a hand and wiggled it at me. "'Bye, now,
Major Hackett. Try to get some sleep. It's going to be a long
day."

It was that. And it got a lot longer before it got any shorter.

Not that anybody leaned on me, individually. Himself
had been right about that; middle-aged security consultants from
Albuquerque clearly weren't high on the list of potential
terrorists. Early on they pulled a lot of passengers out of the
waiting area—people with non-European-sounding names, or
passports from Middle Eastern countries, or maybe just a
vaguely Levantine appearance—and took them away for special
attention; but the rest of us white-bread types mostly got to wait.
Especially if we'd been in coach; naturally the first-class
passengers were long gone before they even let us off the plane.

(At least there was one bright spot: the news people had
of course shown up in battalion force, but the big story was the
presence of celebrities on board, so only the rich and famous had
to slog through the mikes-and-cameras jungle.)

It was the middle of the afternoon when they finally got
around to me. A pleasant, ruddy-faced Scotland Yard inspector,
about my age and size but wearing a much better suit, asked me
a few questions about my background. Private security
consultant, eh? And retired military? Hm, then I must be quite an
observant chap. So had I noticed anything unusual during the
flight? Any other passengers behaving oddly or suspiciously?
Anyone talking with Mr. Wazir? No? Hm, well, too much to
hope for, eh? Now where would I be staying in London? And for

how long? Yes, well, officially he must warn me that I might be called upon for further questioning, but between us he didn't really think it likely. Sorry about the delay; he hoped I had a pleasant stay.

And that was that. Only of course it wasn't; there were still my possessions to be tracked down and reclaimed, all baggage having been taken away for examination. The young Sikh who brought mine, after another interminable wait, was interested in the laptop; he wanted one, he said, was this a good make? I told him only if he was prepared to make a pact with diabolical powers. When I left he was still chuckling.

The light was starting to fade by the time the cab finally dropped me off in front of the old red-brick building just off King's Road. I knew I should go get something to eat, but I just wasn't up to it. I went on up the steps and unlocked the front door and took the slow German-made elevator up to the fourth floor, feeling the fatigue come down on me like a heavy gray blanket.

The flat was looking good, with none of the musty smell of long disuse; the cleaning people must have been in recently. I dumped the bag and the laptop on the couch and went into the kitchen, wondering if there was anything to eat. I hadn't used the place since last winter, but I seemed to remember leaving a few odds and ends on the shelves.

I found some cans—sorry, *tins*—of soup, and a still-sealed box of some sort of biscuits. Good enough; my stomach was in no state for anything more serious anyway. A few minutes later I had myself a saucepan of cockaleekie heating on the stove. While it warmed I looked around the kitchen, experiencing the usual dislocation at the familiar-yet-alien appliances and switches and plugs. At least the strangeness had a friendly feel, as if things were trying to look right but just couldn't get the hang of it.

The contents of the saucepan began to bubble and I turned off the heat and carried the pot into the front room, not bothering with a bowl. And sat at the table having my cockaleekie—cockaleekie! The names these people hang on perfectly good food!—and watching the street get dark beyond the big front windows.

Halfway through the meal my wrist watch began flashing. I looked at it for a couple of seconds and then pushed the button to turn it off.

A few minutes later it started flashing again.

I stood up and undid the watch and went back into the kitchen and put it in the refrigerator. Then I went back and finished my cockaleekie; and then I got up and stumbled into the bedroom.

While I was taking off my shoes the bedside lamp began flashing on and off. I said a couple of bad words and bent down and yanked the plug out of the wall socket. I wasn't sure that would work—you never know, with Himself—but it did.

I finished undressing and got into bed. Whatever Himself wanted now, it could wait till morning. Or maybe it couldn't, but I didn't care. For the rest of this night, I was no longer a working number.

And, he should pardon the expression, to hell with Himself.

Next morning when I got up the hallway light was flashing. I flipped it a one-finger salute and went into the kitchen and located a jar of instant coffee. While I was waiting for the water to boil the oven light began going off and on.

I said aloud, "All *right,* just hang on, will you?"

The flashing stopped. A few minutes later, carrying my cup of alleged coffee carefully in both hands, I went into the front room and sat down on the couch. The muck was too hot to drink but I held it up to my face and took a couple of tokes of steam before setting it down on the coffee table and turning to unzip the laptop case.

Himself was right there when the screen came on. He didn't look happy. "Good morning," he said in a voice that could have eaten the armor plate off an M-1 tank. "I trust you had a pleasant night's sleep?"

"Sorry," I said to the face on the screen. At least now we had some privacy, so I could dispense with the typing and just talk normally. If "normally" applied to a conversation like this.

"But I wouldn't have been any use to you last night," I said. "Wouldn't have mattered if you'd been trying to tell me the building was on fire, I couldn't have handled it."

"Yes, of course." He sighed. "It's just that something has come up, requiring my full attention in another part of the world. And contrary to the claims of certain employees of the Opposition, I can't be everywhere at once."

He sounded bitter, as he always did when he talked about the limitations he had to operate under. You'd think he'd have gotten used to it, in a million years or however long it's been. It certainly was a complicated business, from what he'd told me; I'd been amazed at the number of things he couldn't do—not just wasn't allowed to do, by the rules of the treaty or covenant or whatever had been laid on him, but literally *couldn't* do. Couldn't, for one thing, personally kill or even physically injure a living human; couldn't do personal appearances on Earth, except under very special arrangements—which, according to him, didn't include any nonsense with pentagrams; you really didn't want to get him started on pentagrams—and all sorts of other things you'd never suspect.

And this, of course, was why he had to contract out so many of his operations, even simple jobs like last night's. As one of the better-paid contractors, I could hardly complain; but I could see how he might feel a certain resentment.

"And so," he said, "I'm not going to have time to brief you personally on this mission. Unfortunately, because there are certain unusual aspects, but it can't be helped. Instead I've arranged a meeting, where you'll learn the details and meet the people you'll be working with. I suggest you freshen up and get dressed; you're to be there at eleven-thirty this morning."

"Okay," I said. "Where do I go?"

He told me.

I said, "You're kidding."

* * *

John Wesley's statue stands in a kind of little garden in back of St. Paul's Cathedral. The church grounds were lively with tourists and school groups, but back here there was nobody around but John and me. He didn't look happy to see me; I was pretty sure he didn't approve of me. But then from all accounts there was a lot he didn't approve of.

It was a mild sort of day, for London in mid-April, but there was enough bite in the wind to make me wish I'd worn a topcoat. It wasn't raining but the gray sky beyond the great dome of St. Paul's looked as if that could change at any time. I turned my back to the breeze and stared back at John Wesley; and a few minutes later a woman's voice behind me said, "Major Hackett?"

She was standing a few feet away, giving me a cautiously inquiring look: a small, compact young woman with dark Mediterranean features and thick curly black hair. Her hands were shoved into the pockets of a long black leather coat that hung open to reveal an attractively packed black knit dress. All in all she was a considerable improvement on John Wesley.

I confessed to being me. She stepped forward and put out a hand. "Leila Aziz."

Which answered a minor question and raised at least one very big one, but this was no time to go there. I gave her back her hand and she said, "Come with me, please."

She led the way over toward the church, where a man was standing beside an open doorway at a spot where I was almost certain there hadn't been a door before. He was a tall, broad-shouldered young guy—or maybe not; he had one of those pale smooth long faces that don't show the years—in a neat white warmup suit, and he was looking at us with an expression that made John Wesley look like a Miss America emcee.

But he said, "Come in, then," and motioned toward the door. Which turned out to open onto a flight of steps that spiraled steeply downward into a brightly-lit well, terminating in a long narrow corridor. "All the way to the end," he called from behind us. "Last room. I'll be right with you."

We walked down the corridor, past an open door through which I got a glimpse of a couple of white-clad figures working on a mainframe, to a low-ceilinged room, maybe thirty feet square. The only furnishings were a big metal desk and some folding chairs, and, sitting on the desk, a computer with a large flat-screen monitor.

I said, "Do you have any idea what this is all about?"

Leila shook her head. "I was told where to meet you, and then him. That's all."

The tall guy came hustling in as we were sitting down. He was holding a CD disk. "My name is Michael," he said. "I've been assigned to work with you."

He didn't look happy about it. He might have been saying, "I've been told I need root canal work."

"As you've no doubt guessed," he went on. "I represent what your master would call 'the Opposition'—"

"Not my master," I interrupted. "Preferred client, maybe."

"Whatever." He made an impatient gesture. "You must find it strange that we should be working together. However, it's not as unprecedented as you might think. From time to time it happens that, um, interests converge. Certain temporary common-cause arrangements are made."

He inserted the disk in the computer and picked up a wireless mouse. "I understand you haven't been briefed—"

He clicked a button and the big screen lit up with a large color photo of a heavy-set, dark-skinned man, maybe about my age, wearing white robes and a turban. It was an outdoor shot, taken on a street somewhere; in the background a couple of blurry figures were holding up a large banner in Arabic script.

"This," Michael said, "is Abdelkader Sayid. Perhaps you've heard of him."

I'd heard the name but I didn't recall any details. "Some kind of militant mullah, isn't he?"

"Yes. He preaches at a mosque here in London." Michael's mouth twisted. "Preaches hate, rage, violence . . . but of course he's not unique in that, is he? One of the great curses of today's world," he said, "and not confined to Abdelkader's sect, either."

He clicked the mouse again and the photo changed to a closeup of the same man, staring straight into the camera. The eyes were profoundly disturbing; they had that burning intensity, that absolute psycho certainty, that you see only in the face of the man who *knows* he's right and it's his sacred duty to straighten you out or kill you. And yet there was a certain hypnotic, irresistible-force quality, too; it was easy to believe that he'd be good at getting people to listen to him.

"What makes Abdelkader special," Michael said, "is that he doesn't just preach the jihad, he actively supports it. And not just by the usual fund-raising activities."

The picture changed again; now it showed a good-sized building, obviously a mosque—it had the dome and the minaret—but of modern design. "His mosque," Michael said, "is in effect a recruiting office and primary training center for some of the most dangerous, irreconcilable groups in the European terrorist underground. He's very effective indeed; the jihadist Pied Piper, one journalist called him. Very powerful speaker, very charismatic personality. Amazingly good at persuading otherwise intelligent, educated people—especially young men—to give up everything, even their lives, for the holy war he preaches."

Leila said, "The authorities can't do anything?"

"They've tried. This country has laws, too, specifically meant to stop that sort of thing. But Abdelkader has been very careful. He never says anything directly illegal in public, and he doesn't keep incriminating materials at the mosque or his home."

Michael clicked again and the screen went dark. "And now your employer, your *client* if you will, wants Abdelkader removed. You'll have to ask him why," he said. "All I know is that he applied a short time ago—he's required to file notice, you see, before taking action against any member of the clergy—and on consideration it was decided that the project was not only permissible but desirable. Even worthy of a certain degree of cooperation and support."

"OK," I said, "everybody agrees this bastard needs to go. But why does your boss need our help to take him out? Good old-fashioned lightning strike, or whatever the current technique—"

I'd thought Michael's expression was unfriendly. I hadn't seen anything yet. He clamped his mouth shut; you could see the little muscles working along his jaw. "Even if that were an option," he said at last, in a very tight dusty voice, "it wouldn't solve the problem. Abdelkader's death just now would make him an even bigger hero. People would be inspired to join the jihad to honor his memory. Recruiting might actually increase."

"OK, I can see that," I said. "So what's the plan?"

"There is no plan. The goal is for Abdelkader to be eliminated, image and all. Not merely removed, but thoroughly disgraced and discredited. The plan," Michael said, "is for you to develop and carry out."

He touched the eject button and took the disk from the computer and put it in a plastic case. "This contains the full file on Abdelkader—personal background, known habits and behavior patterns, structure of his organization, layout of the mosque and so on. If there's anything else you need to know, you'll find a number for contacting this office."

He held out the disk. I nodded in Leila's direction; she took it and slipped it into her big leather purse.

"Understand this," Michael said. "Our participation will be limited strictly to intelligence, logistic support, that sort of thing. We will not actively participate in any act of violence."

I said, "This is really getting your ass, isn't it? Having to work with us?"

He winced and closed his eyes. "My personal feelings," he said, "if any, are immaterial. I do as I am told."

He waved a hand. "I take it you can find your way out?"

We did. The door opened as we reached the top of the stairs. Outside, I turned to close it, but there was no door there, only the unbroken gray wall of St. Paul's.

"That," Leila said some time later, "was a very strange business."

We were sitting at a corner table in an undistinguished pub in Blackfriars, having an undistinguished late lunch. It was about half past one and the noon crowd had mostly gone back to work; a few customers still sat at the bar but nobody within earshot.

I said, "Strange, all right. I guess it was even stranger for you."

She gave me a funny look. "Why?" Then her eyebrows went up. "Oh, I see. You mean because I—look, Major Hackett—"

"Please. My name's Gordon Hackett. That 'Major' thing was a long time ago." I sat back and reached for my beer. "It's just something Himself does to annoy me."

"'Himself'?" Her eyes lit up. "Is that what you call him? I love it . . . look, Mr. Hackett—Gordon?—don't assume too much about me." Her English was more American than British, but she had, I noticed now, just the tiniest touch of another accent, too faint to identify. "My family left Beirut the same year I was born. I grew up in Brussels," she said, "and I wasn't brought up in any religion at all. My parents were very upper-middle-class, very modern, very secular."

I started to speak but she raised a finger. "Please, I want to tell you this . . . my brother," she said, "was like the rest of us at first. Then in his late teens he began hanging out with some young men from an extremist group. Pretty soon he began going to services at a jihadist mosque, attending classes and meetings and so on. My father was annoyed, but he didn't take it seriously, none of us did. Just a phase, we thought.

"You understand, I was away at school—University of Chicago—for much of this time. When I came home in the summer I hardly knew him. He'd shaved his head, he never smiled—" She looked down at her plate. "He slapped me," she said in a barely audible voice, "and called me a whore, because I didn't cover my head."

I kept quiet. After a minute she looked up. "Later that year," she said, "after I'd gone back to the university, he left without a word to anyone. A few months later he blew himself to bits on a street corner in Tel Aviv."

She made a bitter little snorting sound. "He didn't even succeed in killing anyone but himself. Evidently the bomb went off prematurely."

I couldn't think of a damn thing to say.

"And so," she said, "I said some things about being willing to sell my soul if I could get revenge. And was contacted, in time, by—Himself."

"Who told you that, contrary to general belief, he wasn't in the market for souls," I said. "But that he had plenty of openings for certain types of contract work."

"Exactly. The same for you?"

I nodded and sipped at my Foster's. One of the better side effects of the Australian invasion has been that you can finally get a decent cold beer at most London pubs.

Leila said, "You lost someone too? The Trade Center?"

"The Pentagon." The one nobody ever talks about. "I didn't lose anyone in particular, though," I said. "See, I was supposed to be on board that plane. Only I overslept and missed it."

"Oh." Her eyebrows shot up. "You think if you'd been on board—but you couldn't have stopped it," she said. "Not by yourself. And no one would have helped you."

"No. In fact there's a good chance the other passengers would have stopped me. They'd all had it drilled into their heads: do what they say and nobody gets hurt. But," I said, "guilt isn't exactly the most logical of human feelings."

I finished my beer and set the glass down. "Well, if we're both done, I guess it's time to get to work. First off I think we both need to spend some time studying the contents of that disk. Which means we need another copy, so let's drop by my flat and I'll burn one."

"Yes." She reached for her purse and paused. "Gordon, you seem like a nice man, but—well, on some of these operations, in the past, I've worked with men who seemed to expect certain things that weren't in my job description. If you follow me."

"I imagine I do." I stood up. "Don't worry about it. I think I can hold my rampaging libido in check."

She was looking embarrassed. "It's just that these awkward situations always seem to start with the words 'Let's drop by my flat.'"

"I can well imagine," I said. "And now we've got that out of the way, let's see if we can get a cab. Looks like it's started raining."

I spent the rest of the day and the evening going over the material on Abdelkader. Leila phoned once, around six or so; she'd been doing the same thing and a couple of questions had occurred to her. I thought about asking her to dinner but decided against it. Instead I went down to the neighborhood pub and insulted my heart with the steak and kidney pie.

Walking back to my building in the rain, I saw how the job could be done. It wouldn't be all that difficult, if certain things could be managed. At the flat I thought it over some more, had another look at the contents of the CD, and phoned Michael. He didn't sound happy to hear from me, but there was a note of reluctant relief in his voice when I told him I had a plan.

"More pictures of Abdelkader?" he said when I made my request. "Surely you've got enough. We collected—"

"Wait up." I told him the kind of pictures I needed.

That set him off big time. He didn't actually yell at me but he came close. I must be joking. What in the world would I want with something like that?

"Are you sure you want to know?" I asked.

No, he didn't. In any case it was out of the question. He couldn't believe I'd ask such a thing. Even if it were possible—

"Come on," I said. "You're the ones with all the special powers, right? All-Seeing Eye and all that? Surely you can get a few candid-camera shots for me."

There was a long silence. I was beginning to wonder if he'd simply thrown the phone down and walked off, but then his voice came back on again, surprisingly quiet and calm now. "I'll have to take it up with Higher Authority." You could hear the caps. "I'll get back to you."

* * *

Leila came by next morning and I laid the plan out for her. When I was done she sat back on the couch and looked thoughtful. "Hm. You think we can do it?"

"I don't see why not. If I can get everything I need. Can *you* do it? Your part of the setup, I mean."

"Oh, yes. In fact I'll go and start work on it right away."

She started to get up. I said, "You don't have to leave yet. There's not that big a hurry."

She smiled. "No, I really need to—"

The laptop's incoming-message buzzer went off. I said, "Excuse me," and went over and sat down on the couch next to her and flipped up the screen. Sure enough, Michael had come through. I hadn't expected to hear from him so soon. Higher Authority must have told him to move his ass.

There was no text message, only an enclosed zip file full of jaypeg images. I opened it and had a look. Beside me Leila made a strange muffled sound. "What in the world?" she said.

"Just some stuff I needed. You know, for the job."

"Ah. Of course." She scooted closer and leaned forward for a better look. "Oh, dear. He's . . . not in such good shape, is he?"

"Looks like he's got a nice place, though," I said, trying not to be distracted by the soft pressure of her hip against mine. "The faithful must be supporting him well."

"And he certainly needs it. Well." She stood up. "As I say, I'd better get to work. After seeing what someone else is going to have to work with, I can't complain about my part of the job."

Christiaan Goosen said, "Gordon, my friend. A pleasure to see you again." He grinned up at me. "Come in and let's see what you've brought me."

He spun his wheelchair around and I followed him down the hallway of his Golders Green home. It wasn't easy keeping up; he still used an old-fashioned hand-powered chair but he was damn fast with it. He'd had enough practice; he'd been in it, or one like it, since the Gestapo got through with him in '45. "Slow down," I said. "Damn it, you cheap old Dutch bastard, when are you going to get an electric? Don't tell me the pornography business doesn't pay enough."

He gave a scornful snort. "What for? My arms still work." He rolled through a doorway into a big room lined with computer hardware and file cabinets and turned to face me. "Here." He held out a brown-spotted hand. "Let's see what you've got."

I handed him the CD disk I'd burned back at the flat. He popped it into the nearest computer and studied the photos for a few minutes. "All right," he said. "Sure, I can do what you want. How soon do you need it?"

"As soon as possible. But it's not a rush job," I said. "Take as long as you need to do it right. There's no actual deadline."

"Good. What level of quality are we talking about?"

"In terms of pictoral quality, not very high. If it's too professional-looking it won't be credible. But," I said, "if you mean the shop job, I need your very best. They'll have to pass extremely close scrutiny by experts."

"Not to worry. When I get done even the—your employer won't be able to tell what's been done." He looked around at me with bright white-browed blue eyes. "Speaking of whom, give him my regards and tell him when he gets the time I'd like another chess match. Last time he almost beat me."

Back at the flat I phoned Leila and asked if she'd like to go to dinner. There was a pretty long silence and then she said, "I think we'd better not. Don't misunderstand," she added quickly. "It's a very attractive offer. But this wouldn't be a good time to get off on a tangent, would it?"

"Okay. Looks like it's going to be a pretty lousy night for going out anyway." I looked out the window at the gray rain slanting across Draycott Place. "Come by tomorrow," I said. "Say about half past one. There's somebody we both need to see."

* * *

The sign over the door said NIGEL'S ANTIQUE MILITARY TOYS. The display window was filled with lead soldiers in hand-painted 19th-century uniforms, knights in armor, horses pulling old-fashioned cannon and the like. "Wow," Leila said.

The interior of the shop was packed with glassed-in display cases containing more miniature armies. Wooden and cast-metal airplanes dangled on wires from the ceiling. Behind the counter Nigel St. John, three hundred pounds of ex-Royal Marine Commando dressed in a purple silk caftan with matching eye liner, sat meticulously cleaning dust from a Dinky Toys armored car with a soft brush. "Gordon!" he cried delightedly as we entered. "Just a sec, I'll be right with you."

He set the little car down carefully on the counter and came around to meet us, Birkenstocks slapping softly on the gleaming parquet floor. "And this is of course Ms. Aziz?" He grabbed Leila's hand with both of his, making it disappear completely. "So pleased to meet you. Watch out for this old beast." He rolled his eyes at me. "He's a flaming hetero, you know."

He rubbed a palm over his shaven scalp and sighed. "Well, I suppose you want to get right down to business, in your usual crass way. Just a moment, then—"

He went to the front door and locked it. Then he led the way to the back of the shop, through a bead-curtained doorway and into a cluttered storeroom. Pushing back the ornate fringed rug, he hooked his fingers through a ring set in the floor and with no apparent effort hoisted a large block of concrete, revealing a deep recess from which he lifted a long metal box.

"You understand," he said as he carried the box over to a nearby desk, "I don't have anything on the premises beyond your common or garden-variety hardware." He set the box down and opened the lid. "Which nowadays, in London, generally means former-Iron-Curtain ironmongery."

He reached into the box and took out a lumpy object wrapped in soft black cloth. "For example," he said, unwrapping it, "the seven point six-two Tokarev. Practically the default weapon among our local street yobs, I'm afraid."

He handed it over: a hefty, slabsided semi-automatic, roughly finished, vaguely similar in shape to the old GI .45. "Typical Russian effort," Nigel said. "They're all over Europe, now, since the collapse of the jolly old Evil Empire. The police aren't keen, because that little high-speed bullet will go through a protective vest like shite through a duck. Pardon the language, Ms. Aziz."

"Have you got anything smaller?" I asked.

"For Milady here? Yes, of course." He rummaged in the box again and came up with a seriously ugly pistol. "Here we are. Makarov, almost as popular as the Tok. Fires the short nine-mil round, not terribly noisy yet adequate stopping power."

"See how it fits your hand," I told Leila.

I wasn't expecting much—I was ready to grab it away from her, in fact, if she did anything silly with it—but to my surprise she took it from him with a quick sure motion and swung around to point it at the doorway in a very professional two-hand grip. "Not bad," she said thoughtfully. "Good balance."

She looked at me. "Himself saw to it that I learned certain skills. In the Chicago area it wasn't hard to find instruction."

"Now if you want something more discreet," Nigel said, "what about a genuine original silenced Sten? Second World War vintage, but clean. I don't have it here, but—"

"No, that's all right. We'll take these," I said. "And a clip's worth of ammo for each." If we needed more than that the mission would be hopelessly blown anyway.

On the way back through the showroom Nigel said, "You really must come again when you've got time to chat. I don't often get such interesting visitors."

"You're pretty interesting yourself," Leila told him.

Nigel laughed. "What you're thinking," he said, "is how did a nice girl like me get into a business like this? Some tragic story, perhaps?"

He raised his hands palm-up. "I'm sorry, but the truth is quite simple and sordid. For what your employer pays me, I would agree to dance the gazotsky each day at high noon in front of the Imperial War Museum, clad only in an organdy athletic supporter and playing 'Blue Bonnets Over the Border' on a Bolivian nose flute."

He unlocked the door. "Have a lovely day."

"And now," Leila said, after I had stashed the guns away in the hidden space behind the mantlepiece, "what happens next?"

"We wait. If you've got anything you want to do this weekend, go ahead. I'll call you when I hear from Christiaan."

"All right. Meanwhile," she said, "aren't you going to ask me out to dinner again?"

"Should I?" I said.

"Oh, yes," she said. "I think you definitely should."

"Would you like to have dinner with me?" I said.

"I thought you'd never ask," she said.

"This is a nice restaurant," she said, a few hours later. "Never been here before. I'll have to make a note."

She reached for the wine bottle, which by now was going on empty; we were just about finished with dinner. She'd made a solid contribution to the reduction of the bottle's contents, too. I was glad she liked it; from the price it must have been made from unicorn's blood.

She looked up and saw me watching her. "What?" she said.

"Nothing. It just seems a little strange. Sorry."

Her forehead wrinkled slightly. "But I don't—oh, you mean that I'm drinking wine? I told you," she said, "I'm strictly secular. I don't believe in any of that."

"Even though you're personally employed," I said, "by one of the most important figures in at least three major religions."

She laughed. "You're right, of course. I'm being completely irrational. It's just that somehow I don't think of . . .

them in any religious context. More like a couple of warring alien entities, like in some science fiction story."

She made a face. "And that, of course, is even more illogical. But then the whole thing is illogical," she said. "Even within its own terms. Look at what we're doing and who we're doing it for. Why should he be involved in any of this? Especially on the side of, as you'd say, the good guys?"

"You don't know?" I said. "Himself is an art lover. All the arts, any kind—painting, sculpture, music, you name it. Not just the highbrow kind, either, he's a big Tom Waits fan for example."

"Which naturally puts him on the the other side," Leila said, nodding slowly, "from people who don't believe in any of those things. All right, that makes sense. I had no idea."

"I remember once," I said, "I happened to mention the Taliban, and he said, 'I'll always wish I'd done something about them before they did it.' I thought he meant nine-eleven. Turned out he was talking about the Buddhas of Bamiyan."

I surveyed the table. "We seem to be finished, don't we? So," I said, "what now? Do I take you home, or do we go somewhere for drinks, or what?"

She set her glass down and gave me a long cool look. The tip of her tongue appeared for just an instant between her lips.

"I don't really want anything more to drink," she said. "But I'd very much like to go back to your flat and go to bed with you."

When I got my voice back I said, "I thought you didn't want to get off on a tangent."

"That was then. We both had things to do. Now—" She shrugged. "You said if there was anything I wanted to do I should go ahead and do it. Well, this is what I want to do. Don't you?"

There were any number of possible clever responses but I wasn't in the mood for Noel Coward dialogue. "Yes," I said. "I'm just starting to realize how much."

* * *

I woke up with the sun high outside the windows. I lay there for a moment, no doubt wearing a very goofy smile, and then sat up and swung my feet to the floor. While I was sitting there experiencing a great reluctance to stand up, the bathroom door opened and Leila came up the hall, dabbing at her neck with a towel. She was wearing a cheerful expression and nothing else.

"Hi," she said. "How are you feeling?"

"Ask me after I'm awake." I watched her walk across the room toward the chair where she'd hung her underwear, enjoying the slight jiggle of breasts and bottom—she was a trifle full-bodied for the modern style, which suited me just fine—and the warm sheen of her skin. I said, "Is it hot in here or is it just you?"

She shot me a grin and bent down to step into her panties. That was worth watching too. I fell back across the bed. "Damn, woman," I said, "you're *dangerous,* you know that? I think you killed me. Have you no mercy on your elders?"

"Aww. Poor old man." She settled the panties over her hips and reached for her bra. "You didn't seem all that old last night. I was impressed."

"I was a bit surprised myself. It's been a long time."

"For me too. Well," she said, "since doing it *with* someone, if you know what I'm saying."

She paused, holding her bra not yet hooked. "Gordon—I don't want to seem pushy, but would you like me to move in here with you till the mission's over? It would simplify things, wouldn't it?"

I thought about it. Just from a logistical and operational angle, it made sense. And it would be a pleasant change from Lonely, Bored, and Horny, Attorneys-at-Law. "Sure," I said. "Why not?"

"Then I'll go pack a few things," she said, "and come back here."

When she was gone I got up and walked into the living room and turned on the laptop. There was one message:

I tried to reach you last night but you were otherwise engaged.

Looks as if you've got everything under control. Carry on.

I'll be in touch before long. Oh, and congratulations.

Monday Christiaan called to tell me the pictures were ready. Well, it had been a damn good couple of days while it lasted.

He had everything ready for me when I showed up: a big envelope full of prints and a carton of CD disks. I opened the envelope and looked through the prints. My stomach did a slow roll. "Christiaan, this is beyond a doubt the most disgusting thing I've ever seen."

"Understand," he said, "no young boys were harmed in order to make these. The source material was hacked from the private collection of a Bengali stockbroker who lives in Marylebone, and whom I'm going to do something about one of these days." He tapped the box. "The disks, are you sure that's enough? I could quickly make more copies."

"No, that's all right. The disks are just for backup and effect anyway. This stuff is going to be all over the Internet and that's what matters."

"I could take care of that for you," he offered.

"Thanks," I said, "but no need. There's somebody who'll just love to do it."

"Leila," I said as I came in the door of the flat, "have you got that note ready?"

"Sure." She held up a yellow legal-pad sheet covered with Arabic script. "I was just looking it over, in fact."

"Good." I sat down on the couch, dumping the box and the envelope on the coffee table. "What's it say?"

"Roughly, '*Death to the false teacher, the evil deceiver and perverter of Muslim youth.*' Signed, the Brotherhood of Islamic Purity."

"Perfect." I looked around. "Where did I put that phone—"

While I was looking for the cell phone she bent down and opened the envelope. I started to warn her but it was too late. She dropped the pictures and ran for the bathroom, holding her hands to her mouth. I heard retching sounds and then running water.

After a few minutes she reappeared, her face very pale. "Gordon, that's *vile.*"

"It's supposed to be," I said. "That's the idea, remember?"

She dropped into the nearest chair. "Who are you calling?" she asked.

"Michael. I've got to have his help distributing this stuff," I said. "It's got to be absolutely untraceable—there are going to be some extremely sharp people trying to track where it came from—and his lot are the only ones who can guarantee that."

"He's not going to like this," she said.

"Oh," I said, "once I've explained the situation, I'm sure he'll be a regular angel."

Michael said, "No. *No.* I can't believe you're even asking. And did you have to show me that—" He shuddered.

"Oh, come on," I said. "Like you haven't seen worse?"

We were standing in back of St. Paul's. This time he hadn't invited me in.

"Michael," I said, "let's cut the bullshit. We both know what's going on. The good guys, as usual, are willing for the bad guys to do what needs to be done, because that way you can go on telling yourselves how good you are. Just as long as you don't get *your* hands wet."

He flinched. I said, "I'm not asking you to kill anybody—"

"No," he said. "Just distribute child pornography."

"If you want to think of it that way. Or you can come down off your holy cloud and get real. Look," I said, "do you think I like this any better than you do? But it's the best possible way to get the results we're after, and I'm willing to swallow my precious scruples for that and you can damn well swallow yours too. Check with your Higher Authority if you want, but we both know damn well what the answer's going to be."

He took a long slow ragged breath. "Is there anything else?"

"As a matter of fact, yes. Neither of us has any experience driving English style, so we're going to need transportation to and from. I take it that's not a problem?"

"No. When do you plan to . . . do it?"

"Tomorrow night. I'll get back to you with the time. Oh, and one other thing," I said. "A thunderstorm would be very helpful. A big noisy one, a real blaster. See if you can get that laid on for tomorrow evening, won't you? There's a good chap."

Late Tuesday afternoon I stripped the guns down and checked the actions and added a few drops of lubricant here and there. It was all completely unnecessary—Nigel would no more have sold a dirty gun than he'd have pissed on Judy Garland's grave—but it helped pass the time.

I was wondering about the weather; for most of the day the sky had been clear except for a few patches of cloud, and the TV forecast hadn't said anything beyond the standard "chance of rain." I needn't have worried; Higher Authority came through in plenty of time. By the time I got the guns back together the sky had clouded over with big heavy masses of cumulo-nimbus and you could hear an occasional low rumble not far away.

We had an early dinner, frozen stuff from Waitrose; Leila had confessed to total incompetence in the kitchen and I wasn't much better, but that's why Michael's boss gave us microwaves. We didn't talk much.

After dinner Leila went into the bedroom and came out a little later wearing a long shapeless black dress, her head covered by a black *hijab* scarf. "Don't laugh," she said. Her face was as stormy as the sky outside. "Don't you dare laugh, and don't make any jokes. There's nothing funny about it."

I handed her the Makarov and she made it disappear somewhere in the folds of her outfit. "Ready?" I said, and she nodded. "All right, then." I stood up and slipped the Tokarev into the waistband of my pants and zipped my black windbreaker halfway up to cover it. I picked up the backpack off the couch and hooked it over my shoulders and got out my cell phone and keyed it.

Michael answered immediately. "Time," I said, and stuck the phone in my pocket and jerked my head toward the door. "Let's go."

The rain was fairly bucketing down as we came out the front door of the building. A black cab sat at the curb. Its lights flashed, twice. "Run," I said, and we sprinted across the sidewalk.

Michael was sitting behind the wheel. He was wearing a tweed jacket and a cap instead of his usual white getup. He didn't look around, let alone make any move to help, as I wrenched the door open and we tumbled into the back seat. He put the cab in gear and pulled away from the curb without a word, while we tried to wipe the rain from our faces. Should have brought an umbrella, I thought, but some things are just too ridiculous.

The storm was really hitting its stride as we rolled through the dark streets, great white forks of lightning stabbing down toward the city and thunder blamming and slamming away like a bombing strike. I started to tell Michael to convey my thanks, but he didn't seem to be in a mood for conversation.

Abdelkader's mosque was located on a crooked one-way street in a north London neighborhood. His home was just down the street, but according to Michael's information he'd be working late tonight in his office in the rear of the mosque. There would be a single bodyguard; otherwise, at this hour and in this weather, there shouldn't be anyone else around.

Michael stopped the cab in front of the darkened mosque and waited while we jumped out and ran for it. I headed around the corner of the building at a dead run, Leila splashing along behind me. By now we were both drenched to the marrow; lucky if we didn't catch pneumonia, but the storm made unbeatable cover.

A paved walkway ran along the side of the mosque, toward the rear, where lights shone through a couple of windows next to a small door. I flattened my back against the wall beside the door and nodded to Leila.

She went over and began to pound. I could barely hear her knocking over the boom of the thunder and the pounding of the rain, but no doubt it sounded louder inside. In less than a minute the door opened.

Leila began screaming in Arabic, a high penetrating wail that cut through the racket of the storm like a runaway chainsaw. She had her headscarf pulled over the bottom part of her face to form a veil, but it didn't muffle her a bit. She waved her hands frantically, pointing back up toward the street, the way we'd just come. I couldn't understand a word but the meaning was obvious: come quick, hurry, look—

And a moment later there he was, a husky young man in a camo jacket and a fancy skullcap. He stood there, peering the way she was pointing and trying to shield his eyes from the rain, while I came up behind him. The Tokarev made a solid thunk against the side of his head and I caught him as he went down.

Leila took his feet and we dragged him inside and shut the door. I checked for a pulse and found one—I don't know why, I didn't give a damn one way or another—but he was going to be out of the picture a lot longer than we needed.

To the left of the entrance was another door, with a sign in Arabic. The handle turned readily in my left hand. The room beyond was brightly lit and I blinked involuntarily as I stepped through, holding the Tokarev ready, into Abdelkader's office.

It was a good-sized place, bigger than it had looked in the pictures, the walls paneled in some sort of dark wood and hung with prayer rugs and banners with calligraphic inscriptions stitched in gold. At the far end, behind a massive wooden desk, sat a man in a white robe and turban. I didn't have any trouble recognizing him; I'd been looking at that face for over a week.

He looked up; his eyes went wide. He said something in Arabic, first in a puzzled voice and then an angry shout. He started to get to his feet, still yelling. Maybe he was calling for the guard; maybe he was telling me to get the fuck out. I didn't really care. His time was up.

I held the Tokarev out in front of me and sighted. I was just taking up the slack when there was a loud bang and a tiny dark spot appeared on the front of the white robe, a couple of inches below where I'd been aiming.

Abdelkader stopped shouting. He stopped moving, and then, after a second or so, he stopped being alive. You could see it happen; there is nothing quite like that sudden total slackness. A moment later he slid down behind the desk out of sight.

Beside me Leila said something I didn't understand. Then, in English, "I'm sorry, Gordon. I couldn't—"

"That's all right." I gave her a quick touch on the shoulder. "I should have asked if you wanted to do it. All right, let's finish up."

I stuck the Tok back in my belt while Leila stepped behind me and unzipped the backpack and got out the box of CD disks. I went over and switched on the computer on Abdelkader's desk—good computer, latest model Dell; whatever else the deceased had had against Western civilization, he'd certainly been up on the technology—and put a disk in. The drive hummed and then the screen displayed the first of Christiaan's doctored photos, depicting Abdelkader apparently sodomizing a dark-haired, scared-looking teenage boy.

I set the box of disks beside the computer. Leila had already opened the envelope and scattered the prints artistically about the desk and floor. She leaned over the desk and dropped a couple on Abdelkader's body and then dug out her hand-written note. She started to put it on the desk but I said, "Wait." I'd just spotted a big curved Middle Eastern dagger in a fancy sheath on the wall.

Leila saw where I was looking. "Oh, yes," she said, and went to get it, while I used the sleeve of my soggy windbreaker to wipe everything I'd touched.

The guard was still limp on the floor of the entrance hall. Leila held the note up to the office door and I drove the dagger through to pin it in place.

Outside it was still raining as hard as ever. As we reached the street I took out the cell phone to call Michael, but before I could key it the black cab appeared at the curb. Not showed up, *appeared,* just like that, without even any beam-me-up-Scotty shimmering. This time the back door swung open for us. "Go," I said as we piled inside, but Michael was already going, snaking down that crooked street and around the next corner like a Grand Prix driver going for the money lap.

I took Leila's pistol and cleared it and dropped it into the backpack along with mine. "You can dispose of these, can't you?" I said to Michael. "Beat them into pruning hooks or whatever."

Then I got out the cell phone again and made a call to Scotland Yard.

"Outstanding," Himself said. "Absolutely brilliant. I couldn't be more pleased."

We were sitting on the couch in my flat. Or rather Leila and I were; Himself, of course, was looking out at us from the laptop screen. Behind him the TV was showing a BBC newscast. The sound was off but it didn't matter; they weren't saying anything they hadn't already said at least half a dozen times this morning. Right now the screen showed a picture of Abdelkader's mosque.

"I was a bit unhappy last night," he said, "when you left the bodyguard alive. If he'd regained consciousness before the police arrived, he might have ruined things. But no harm done."

He smiled at me. "And I'm definitely going to have to give your friend Christiaan a bonus. All those people viewing those forged photos," he said, "they'll never know they're looking at the work of an authentic genius."

Leila said, "Not everyone is going to be convinced, you know. A lot of people are simply going to refuse to believe it." Her mouth quirked ruefully. "I'm afraid we're very good at denial."

"Like everyone else in the world," Himself said. "And in fact those things are being said even now. Al-Jazeera has already run several statements by various prominent persons, denouncing the whole thing as the work of the CIA, the Israelis, or both."

He made a dismissive gesture. "It doesn't matter. I've gotten what I was after."

I said, "Just what *were* you after, if you don't mind my asking? I never did get your angle on this business."

"Oh, that's simple enough. In that same neighborhood," Himself said, "less than a kilometer from the mosque, lives a Syrian family with a sixteen-year-old son. The parents are neither religious nor political, but the boy has been showing signs of interest—attending services now and then, talking with some of Abdelkader's younger followers—"

He looked at Leila. "I'm afraid you'd recognize the pattern all too well."

"Yes," she said. "Oh, yes."

"And," he said, "it couldn't be allowed to go on. Because that boy has a musical talent such as I haven't seen since the young Mozart—even now, he can do things with a violin to make your heart stop—and it would have been an unspeakable tragedy to let those lunatics destroy him."

"Do you think it worked?" Leila said.

"No doubt about it. Already young Jamal is in a state of shock at the news," he said. "A few reinforcing images planted in his mind as he sleeps, and he will never again feel anything but revulsion at the thought of Abdelkader and all he stood for."

I said, "I'm a son of a bitch."

"I won't argue the point. But in this case you did a truly worthy thing. And now," Himself said, "I have pressing business to attend to, so I'll leave you to yourselves. I'll be in touch, though. Quite soon."

The screen went dark. I flipped the laptop shut and turned to face Leila. "Well," I said, "what do you want to do now?"

"What now?" Her voice and face had gone bleak. "Now," she said, "we say goodbye."

I opened my mouth to protest but she raised a hand. "No, please. The longer we're together, the harder it's going to be to end it. Even one more day together—let alone another night—"

She shook her head. "Reality time," she said. "It's over."

"It doesn't have to be." I looked at her, wanting badly to reach out to her but knowing she'd pull away. "As far as I'm concerned it doesn't ever have to be."

"A pretty thing to say. Maybe you even mean it. But it wouldn't work," she said. "It couldn't. This has been an unusual assignment for me, you know. Most of the time I have to operate in communities where you would never blend in—where you'd probably be killed—and anyway I couldn't do my job with you along. And you've got your own work to do, too."

"We could ask Himself to release us from our contracts."

"And we could ask the sun to rise in the west. Don't talk nonsense," she said angrily. "You know better."

She was right, of course. For all the witty urbane persona, Himself was still who he was, and his contracts had extremely serious penalty clauses. People didn't make deals with him and then back out when they realized they'd made a mistake. If they could, where would he be?

She stood up. "I've already packed my things. Please, Gordon," she said, "if you care for me at all, don't try to stop me."

I watched as she went into the bedroom and came back carrying her bag and her coat. I got up and followed her to the door. She turned and looked up at me and I raised a hand toward her face, but she said, "No, please. If you touch me I may not be able to do this at all. Goodbye, Gordon," she said. "Take care of yourself."

"Goodbye, Leila," I said.

After the door closed behind her I stood there for a few minutes tasting those last two words in my mouth, knowing at last what the trapped wolf tastes when he chews off his own leg.

That afternoon I took a cab out to Heathrow and sat for a couple of hours waiting for my plane, watching all the people who knew where they were going.

I'd thought for several years that I ought to do a story set in London, and I finally did it. Even included our old flat on

Draycott Place, just for sentiment. I miss London. Don't suppose I'll ever see the old town again. . . .

This was an important story in my life, in ways I never expected when I wrote it. I was really surprised when it started coming back; I'd just assumed it would be an easy sell, but even editors with whom I'd had long and agreeable relationships were sending it back with little round marks where they'd been touching it with eleven-foot poles. One well-known editor took something like twenty minutes to reject it.

I finally realized what was going on; people were simply scared. It was a risky time to publish anything that might offend the more intense devotees of any religion, and one in particular; it was a time when there were riots and death threats over a few cartoons.

It wasn't just that, though; for some time it had been increasingly clear that the major genre magazines were becoming very nervous about what they published. The writers and the fans talked about it a lot; it had become a truism that "the Dangerous Visions days are over."

One night, after the third or fourth bounce, I went to bed with a bottle of whiskey, of a cheap Canadian blend that I cannot recommend. (This was in the days when I did that on a nightly basis; before it was discovered that my liver had its own area code, and I had to quit.) And at some point between intoxication and oblivion an idea came to me.

Next day I shared it with some friends, merely for laughs—a comic example of the kind of silly ideas you can get when you're drunk—but to my amazement they thought it was quite a good one: start our own magazine, with the purpose of publishing stories that nobody else wanted to touch. And, some time later, Helix came into being.

And Helix has been very important in my life. In fact it's one of the most important things I've ever done, as a writer. So this story carries some extra significance.

Afterword

There.

Copyright and Credits

All Stories Copyright © by William Sanders

Printed in the United States
129211LV00001BA/2/P